Daranna Gidel

Ceremony *of* Innocence

A DUTTON BOOK

DUTTON
Published by the Penguin Group
Penguin Books USA, Inc., 375 Hudson Street,
New York, New York 10014, U.S.A.
Penguin Books Ltd, 27 Wrights Lane, London W8 5TZ, England
Penguin Books Australia Ltd, Ringwood, Victoria, Australia
Penguin Books Canada Ltd, 2801 John Street,
Markham, Ontario, Canada L3R 1B4
Penguin Books (N.Z.) Ltd, 182-190 Wairau Road, Auckland 10, New Zealand

Penguin Books Ltd, Registered Offices:
Harmondsworth, Middlesex, England

First published by Dutton, an imprint of New American Library,
a division of Penguin Books USA Inc.
Distributed in Canada by McClelland & Stewart Inc.

First Printing, August, 1991
10 9 8 7 6 5 4 3 2 1

REGISTERED TRADEMARK

LIBRARY OF CONGRESS CATALOGING-IN-PUBLICATION DATA

Gidel, Daranna.
    Ceremony of innocence / Daranna Gidel.
       p.   cm.
    ISBN 0-525-93348-4
    I. Title.
    PS3557.I25C47   1991
    813'.54—dc20   91-16569
                                                                         CIP

Printed in the United States of America
Set in Baskerville
Designed by Eve L. Kirch

PUBLISHER'S NOTE
This is a work of fiction. Names, characters, places, and incidents either are the
products of the author's imagination or are used fictitiously, and any resemblance
to actual persons, living or dead, events, or locales is entirely coincidental.

To my father,
Darwin Gidel,
and
in loving memory
of my mother,
Beverly Pell Gidel

PART I

The Souls of Children

1

Lucy

Every child is a victim.

Each tiny soul inherits more than mingled blood and essence.
Each is also a legatee of chance, an innocent receptor, subject to
the whims and circumstances of its parents' ongoing lives.

Lucy Clare arrived in the world with her father's fair skin and
her mother's dark hair and the weight of hopeless poverty that
the two had shaped together. She was born into a family where
she was just another burden, and into a rigid town where she was
irredeemably second-class.

Of course, Lucy was not aware of her grim beginnings. Like
all small children, she believed her narrow orbit to be the universe, and she was perfectly happy in the Trailer Village on the
outskirts of Walea, Texas. She shined her daddy's boots each
morning and helped her older sister, Suki, with the inside work
and tended to the chickens in the pen out back, and after the
chores were finished she roamed the surrounding countryside
with Tippy, her imaginary friend. Together they caught polliwogs
that turned magically into frogs, charted the movements of mysteriously shaped clouds, and watched for the sleek, deadly rattlesnakes that sometimes sunned themselves on her favorite rocks
by the creek.

Lucy grew into a sensitive and impressionable child, nourished by a life so rich in fantasy that her mother's weary disinterest and her father's rages and silences barely touched her at all.
She was protected, safe within the prism of her own illusions.

There was a new baby sister when Lucy was five, and the birth
resulted in a reprieve of sorts. Lucy was held back from starting
school because she was needed to watch the infant while her
mother kept up with the washing and ironing that formed a large
part of their livelihood. Lucy didn't mind. She and Tippy took

3

baby Anita outside with them for tea parties and grasshopper catching and treasure hunts, and the idea of school seemed very far away.

When her turn finally did come to be bound over to the town of Walea in the guise of kindergarten enrollment, Lucy was anxious. But she was excited as well. Suki rode the school bus each day to Ira C. Eaker Elementary and reported the most wonderful adventures. Part of Lucy had been longing to follow Suki onto that bus and another part wanted to stay home with her baby and her mama and keep life just as it was.

Eaker was a sprawling collection of long buildings and open playing fields that had sprung up in the fifties in answer to the baby boom that peopled the northeast quadrant of Walea. The town fathers were quick to point out that it was a fine school even though it wasn't in one of the better sections of the community. And most residents of the area were firmly convinced that an education in even the least impressive of their town's schools was superior to an education anywhere else in the world. Walea's schools didn't teach just reading and writing, they molded character and shaped future generations.

Walea, Texas, pronounced *Wah*-lee-ah by the locals, was a town with pride. The citizens took pride in everything they had, pointing not only to their schools but also to their Pee Wee football field with the fully electronic scoreboard and to their members-only golf and country club. And they took just as much pride in what they didn't have. There were no pinkos in Walea and no protesters spouting un-American ideas, and no good-for-nothings cluttering up the streets. Walea was a modest, godly place where decent people could lead decent lives—a haven from the turmoil that the sixties were bringing to other parts of the country.

The town did have a few sources of blight: for instance, Bob the Bum. Bob wore gloves winter and summer and argued with his reflection in store windows, but Waleans had too much pride to allow him to become an eyesore. He was clothed, bathed, and fed by members of the Walea Ladies' Club, who had a column in their budget journal labeled simply "Bob."

And all these riches did not even begin to tap the town's greatest source of pride, the wellspring that nourished the very heart and soul of the community—its churches. Walea boasted one hundred and eighty-seven Christian houses of worship—more per capita than any other town in East Texas and just short of holding the record for the entire state. This was a shortcoming which caused no elevated blood pressure or pulpit pounding (like the

regional football standings) because everyone in town knew they
could beat the record anytime they decided to lower their standards for the official count and include the Christian Science
storefront near the highway and the Catholics' little cement block
building up by the migrant camps and the hallelujah houses across
the river.

But it was a matter of principle.

Everyone knew that the Christian Scientists were all nutty old
ladies and the Catholic idolaters were mostly "wetbacks" and the
hallelujah houses only served that area of the community tradi-
tionally referred to as Nigger Town. How could they be fairly
included in an honest listing of churches? Walea's town fathers
would not stoop to such underhanded tactics to inflate their
count.

This was the arena that Lucy was thrust into when she was
herded through the green double doors to join the student body
of Eaker Elementary.

Her first few days were pleasant enough. The restlessness she
felt at being confined was balanced by the wonder of jars of white
paste with little brushes stuck in the lids, and stacks of stiff colored paper and scissors sized for small hands, and brightly colored paints and boxes of fat crayons and books full of incredible
pictures.

She felt awkward and shy in the company of other children,
but some of them seemed just as shy, and this gave her the confidence to communicate. She began hesitantly sorting through the
biters and criers and bullies in search of kindred souls.

The kindergarten and first-grade children at Eaker were
housed together in a side wing of the school that had a special
bathroom with six miniature sinks where even the smallest child
could reach the faucets.

"Cleanliness is next to godliness," Mrs. Lomer announced on
the first day of class as she marched her charges in to see the
amazing little sinks. The teacher demonstrated the use of the towel
holder with its long loop of white cloth.

"The whole class will wash up on arrival," Mrs. Lomer instructed as she used a child's hand to show them the proper
method for wetting the grainy pink soap from the dispenser and
working it into knuckles and around fingernails, "and after all
recesses and before lunch. Anyone wishing to relieve themselves
in the facilities"—she waved toward the two beige metal stalls
across the room—"will do so during cleanliness periods only."

"Now, class," she said as they were preparing to leave, "y'all will notice there are only two commodes to six sinks. That is to ensure the swift completion of necessary duties. No dawdling with your britches down." She looked up and down the line of children. "Is that clear?"

Lucy's mind wandered now and then during school, but she still managed to follow most of the rules. She recapped the paste immediately, she used the sides of the crayons and not the tips, she seldom chewed on her eraser, and she tried to "use the facilities" quickly.

By the second week of class, however, she was telling Tippy that maybe school wasn't so terrific. Mrs. Lomer scolded her when she colored ducks purple and flowers black. The playground teacher yelled at her when she took off her shoes during recess. And the other kids made fun of her whenever she talked to Tippy.

She'd been trying to follow the rules, but nothing was working quite right and she was thinking that maybe she was as dumb as Suki said. Silently she tore at her cuticles and picked the scabs from her body faster than they could form and felt sick to her stomach when it was time for the bus each morning.

By the third Wednesday of school she knew she would never be as happy at Eaker as her sister, but she was still hoping to fit in somehow. In that spirit, she was patiently waiting her turn in the sink line after last recess while the children ahead of her pounded the soap dispensers and splattered water.

Suddenly the urge to use the toilet hit.

Lucy checked the stalls. Both doors were locked, but this didn't necessarily mean they were occupied. The latches tended to stick, so children often crawled in and out underneath the doors, leaving the locks perpetually in place.

Lucy bent and peered under the first door. Clytie Burright stuck her tongue out and said, "It's mine. I got here first."

Lucy ducked to check the other stall. A classmate of hers named Joe Ed was sitting quietly on the stool. When he saw Lucy, he brightened and began to visit.

Lucy liked Joe Ed. He didn't bite or spit and he was always willing to share the scarce red crayons. She couldn't understand why the other kids were so cruel to him about his lisp. It made her feel extra friendly toward him, like she could make up for the meanness of the others. So when Joe Ed started to visit, Lucy stayed there on her knees with her head stuck halfway under the door and kept him company.

Suddenly there was a shrill cry. Lucy's heart leapt and she banged the back of her head on the bottom of the door. Steel fingers closed around her arm and she was jerked to her feet and shaken like a puppet.

"What are you doing!" Mrs. Lomer demanded. Her face was red and her eyes were wide and angry.

Before Lucy could summon the courage to answer, Joe Ed cracked the door open and peeked out.

Mrs. Lomer's free hand—the one that wasn't hurting Lucy's arm—shot out and yanked the door open, exposing poor Joe Ed. He stood frozen in terror with his pants and underwear pooled around his ankles. Lucy glimpsed his white face and shriveled genitals and bare goose-pimpled legs before Mrs. Lomer screamed and slammed the door.

"Peeping at a naked boy! May God have mercy, Lucy Clare!"

Mrs. Lomer drew in a deep, fighting breath and marched for the door, dragging a terrified Lucy along like a rag doll. They went straight to the principal's office, where Lucy heard Mrs. Lomer relate the tale of her filthy, sinful peeping. The principal, Mr. Perkins, turned bright red and then nodded knowingly when Mrs. Lomer whispered, "She's part of that white trash from out at the Trailer Village."

Lucy was left alone in the office while the two adults went to arrange her punishment.

Mr. Perkins came for her. His jaw was set and there were beads of sweat showing on the bald part of his head. He didn't say a word. He took Lucy's arm, the same arm that was still aching and imprinted with Mrs. Lomer's finger marks, and he marched her down the hall and into the school's combination lunchroom-auditorium. The faces of her classmates, and of the children from the other two kindergarten classes and the first grade, swam before her eyes. She blinked hard against the tears that threatened.

Mr. Perkins did not hesitate. He led Lucy to the front of the gathering and ordered her to bend over a chair. He pulled her dress up so that everyone could see the graying cotton panties her mother had patched and repatched. Lucy squeezed her eyes shut against the burning humiliation and poured her soul into wishing herself either dead or invisible.

The paddling—seven strokes—seemed to take an eternity. And the hurt only started with her stinging bottom. The hurt spread through her entire body and bounced around in her stomach and screamed out loud in her brain.

She walked all the way home, unable to face her sister or anyone else on the bus. Her mother was busy ironing when she crept into the trailer.

"Watch the baby awhile," Wanda said without looking up from her work.

Lucy went straight to the bedroom and lifted Anita out of her crib and onto the bed. She held the baby close and sobbed quietly into the soft folds of Anita's fragile neck.

Over dinner that night Wanda said, "The school called. Lucy was in trouble today."

Lucy swallowed clumsily and stared down at the chicken fry with cream gravy that was congealing on her plate.

"That so, Lucy?" her father asked.

Lucy nodded.

"Everybody was callin' her a pre-vert!" Suki blurted out. "I don't want her goin' to my school anymore."

"Hush, Sherry Kay," Lydell ordered.

"Principal said she was peepin' at a naked boy," Wanda said flatly. "Starin' right at his thing like a New York whore."

Shame sucked the strength and spirit from Lucy like a hot, bitter wind. She felt degraded and worthless and she wished God would just send down the lightning because she couldn't face her family another minute. Stinging tears welled in her eyes and dripped down into her mashed potatoes.

"Come on, Luce," Lydell said gently. "You and me need ta get some air and talk this out a bit."

Lucy followed her father out into the yard and haltingly told him the story. When she was finished, Lydell looked at the bruises on her arm and her bottom.

He sat quietly beside her on the grass for a moment, staring off into the distance with a fierce concentration that frightened Lucy a little. Everything in her chest hurt while she waited for him to speak. She tried not to breathe. She tried to make her heart calmer.

A jay scolded loudly from the top of a telephone pole and Lydell's gaze fixed absently on the bird. "If I was any kinda daddy I'd pack you up and move you outta this town."

Lucy studied him intently, trying to determine whether he was mad at her or not. He didn't look mad. He looked like he was about to cry. "I'm sorry I'm so bad, Daddy," she whispered.

"Oh, baby . . ." Lydell grabbed her, hugging her so tight she thought her bones might snap. And to her complete surprise, he did cry. Great wrenching sobs shook his body.

Lucy's guilt increased a hundredfold. Her daddy loved her too much to be mad at her, but what she'd done was so terrible that it was making him cry. His sobbing wound down and then quieted. He released her and Lucy slipped off his lap to sit beside him.

He coughed self-consciously and scrubbed his face with his hands. "There's bad people in this town, Luce. They'll wave their Bibles and spout Christian talk and stomp right on your face while they're doin' it."

He drew in a deep breath. "I never let your mama drag you girls off to no church ... thought I could protect you. But this whole town's so rotten with Christian hate that there just ain't no way to keep clear of it. So you listen good, Luce. Don't never trust nobody in this town. You gotta always keep an eye out for trouble. And ya gotta grow a thick skin so they can't hurt you inside. Know what I mean?"

Lucy listened gravely and nodded to please him, though she didn't exactly know what he meant. She had only three things figured out. One: Looking at a boy's peepee was about the most horrible thing a girl could do. Two: It made no difference that she hadn't set out to look at Joe Ed's naked parts—the fact that she had seen them even by accident was shameful enough to make everyone mad at her. And three: Apparently it was the person who did the looking that was the sinner, because nothing had happened to Joe Ed at all. Or maybe it was just always the girl who was the sinner, because whenever she heard talk of sinning, there was always a female at the heart of the blame.

"You hold your head up, Lucy girl. Hold it up and look this town right back in the eye no matter what." Lydell threw a fake punch at her nose. "There's a whole wide world out there waitin', where this town and what it sets store by don't mean diddly-squat ... and when you get growed ... hell, when you get growed I'm hopin' you got the strength to leave here for good."

Late that night her father woke her from a troubled sleep. In her dreams she was stricken blind as punishment for seeing a small wrinkled penis and her skirt was torn off so that everyone could see her ragged underwear.

"Nightmares?" he asked in a whisper.

Lucy nodded.

He put his finger to his lips and motioned her to follow him. "Shhhh, we don't wanna wake nobody."

She crawled out of the bed she shared with Suki and tiptoed past the crib and into the hall. She mimicked her father's exaggerated efforts at silence as he led her through the creaky trailer and out into the liquid warmth of the September night. Together they lay on their backs in the grass and looked up at the starry sky.

"Did you know there's other places up there? Whole other worlds where little girls and their fathers could be staring right out into space at us and seeing nothing but tiny dots of light where we are."

Lucy considered this. She squeezed her eyes shut and tried to send silent messages to those little girls out in space the same way she sometimes sent messages to Tippy.

"I used to look at the stars a lot when I was a kid," her father said wistfully.

"In Nebraska?"

"In Nebraska."

"Why don't we live in Nebraska?"

" 'Cause I aint' got no more folks there and 'cause this is your mama's home and she don't want to leave it."

"Even to go to Nebraska?"

"Specially to go to Nebraska. That's a promise I made her when we married . . . that I'd make her home mine."

"Was I here then?"

"No." He laughed. "Your mama wasn't much more than a child herself then. A shy little slip of a thing with big eyes and . . ." He shook his head. "That was a long time ago."

"Were the stars in Nebraska as good as our stars?"

He sighed. "They were better. I could look up and see a sky full of animals and hunters and gods and goddesses."

"But we got 'em here too, Daddy! And not just in the stars. I can see them in the clouds during daytime."

He chuckled softly. "I bet you can, Lucy. I bet you can." Lydell pulled his lanky form up off the grass and stood. "Stand up," he said. "I'll show you something I learned when I was about your age."

Lucy jumped to her feet.

"Take a deep breath," he said, and she inhaled the fragrance of pine and oak and clean earth and drying grass.

"No. You gotta throw your head back and look up and suck in as much as you can." He spread his arms out as though to embrace the endless shimmering canopy overhead, and he filled his lungs with a great rush of air. Lucy followed suit, flinging out her arms and lifting her face to the sky like the priestess of some ancient night ritual.

The moment stretched on and on, and finally Lydell turned to her and grinned. "Now we're filled with stardust," he said. "And there's always more . . . anytime you need it."

From that night on Lucy had a special connection to her father. He helped her care for the baby birds and wounded raccoons and stray puppies she was forever finding. He took her with him whenever he went to play dominoes or pitch horseshoes or fish for mudcats in the river. He showed her his medals from the Korean War and he spent long hours teaching her to shoot into the exact middle of a beer can. Sometimes he had spells and silences when Lucy didn't exist for him. But she held fast to the bond, imagining that she carried his quiet love with her all the time like a magic shield.

Unfortunately, her peers were not as understanding or sympathetic as her father. She was stared at and teased and generally snubbed at school, even by her own sister. And she was convinced that there was something dirty and shameful about her now—she could feel it inside every time the other children giggled and pointed.

"Spook," they began to call her as she burrowed inward, becoming a silent, self-contained child whose inner realm was far more beautiful and nurturing than anything the real world had offered her.

Lucy was promoted to first grade and then to second. The kindergarten incident faded in the collective memory of the school. Still, Lucy remained "Spook," the girl who seldom spoke. The girl who sat alone in the lunchroom.

Meanwhile, Anita went from baby to toddler to Lucy's special pet. Her mother had two miscarriages and then a hysterectomy, and, upon recovery, seemed happier and more energetic than she had in years. Wanda took in additional washing and mending to make the payments on her hospital bill, and she convinced Flora Anderson to give Suki baton-twirling lessons in exchange for the weekly laundering of Flora's husband's mailman shirts.

Lucy watched her mother spend backbreaking days toiling over other people's dirty laundry and tending Anita during the baby's frequent sickly spells. Whatever time Wanda could spare went to Suki—or Sherry Kay, as she'd been officially named—who was the firstborn and an uncommonly pretty child. Suki's ginger-red hair and bright eyes and quick smile made Wanda behave like a lovestruck fool at times, insisting that her eldest daughter was a prize, a reward for hard work and unswerving faith. Lucy often heard her mother tell people that little Sherry Kay should have been born to some fine, wealthy family, and Wanda pampered her and catered to her as though she were visiting royalty.

As for Lucy, Wanda could not seem to summon the energy or

the incentive to involve herself with her strange, secretive mid-dlechild. She loved the girl, but it was the sort of love one might feel for a wild fawn. There were no solid connections, no dreams invested, no hopes for the future.

When Lydell began to take a special interest in Lucy, Wanda was relieved of whatever guilt she'd felt over the situation. Lydell had total responsibility for Lucy from that time forward. That, coupled with her liberation from fertility, seemed to renew Wanda's optimism and convince her that the Clare family was going to do just fine now.

The good Christian community of Walea grew and prospered, spreading out toward the empty Trailer Village and adding to the Clare family's possibilities. A second and then a third indoor movie theater was built, and there was even a rumor that a McDonald's was going in on the empty stretch of Main Street between the high school and the downtown. And not three miles down the road from the Clares', the Royal Home Trailer factory sprung up, with employment opportunities in all departments. At Wanda's urging, Lydell quit his job as high-school janitor and went to work on the line assembling Royal Homes "Fit for Kings and Their Queens."

The pay increase made life more comfortable for them all. The faltering black-and-white television was traded in for a larger color set. The old black telephone was replaced with an aqua Princess model, complete with light-up dial. And there was money for fancy twirling costumes for Suki and store-bought pies and cookies, and tickets to the discount Sunday matinee movies once or twice a month.

And there were the magazine subscriptions. A salesman caught Wanda at a weak moment, and suddenly the trailer was buried under a monthly avalanche. *Home Handyman* and *Scientific Gazette* arrived for Lydell, *Ladies' Home Journal* for Wanda, and *Life, Look,* and the *Saturday Evening Post* for everyone.

Lucy passed through these years like a sleepwalker. She did just enough at school to pass and she did just enough at home to keep Wanda satisfied. She loved her family, especially her father and her little sister, but it was far more comfortable to savor that love and hold it inside than it was to confront the everyday reality of Wanda's and Suki's indifference and Lydell's growing despair and Anita's restless hungers.

She continued to ramble through the countryside, frequently carrying a borrowed book from the tiny school library or the latest issue of a sleek magazine full of rich people in New York and artists in Paris and hippies in San Francisco and war in some faraway place she couldn't pronounce.

Like a prisoner marking time toward parole, she put in her hours at school, but she didn't let it touch her. Daydreams carried her through, insulating her against the snide remarks of her classmates and giving her a world so rich and full that she sometimes pitied them for being outsiders. This dreamstate even carried her through Lydell's downward spiral, cushioning the grief, keeping him whole and close in her fantasies.

Everything began to fall apart about the time she turned eleven. And though the deterioration happened over a period of time, she wasn't aware of it, or at least she wasn't letting it touch her, until that summer.

That was the summer that building began on the tire plant out near the highway, and overnight the Trailer Village filled up with young men who came from other towns to weld and hammer and rivet on the plant. It was the first time the Clares had ever had neighbors.

The Trailer Village had been the brainstorm of a farmer who believed all he needed to do was dig a septic tank and string a few electric wires and dump some gravel on the back end of a pasture that fronted the county road, and he'd have a money-making concern. He put up a wooden sign with a tepee and a campfire pictured on it and he lowered the rent six times before he attracted a customer.

The farmer, who was now the Clares' cranky landlord, had neglected to take a number of things into consideration. His land was in an outlying area of town that was too close to the migrant camps to ever be considered desirable. And he had major competition in the form of the Cozy Court Mobile Home Park with its picket fences and clubhouse and central location. Any folks too poor to afford the Cozy Court usually had a relative with a back forty where a trailer could be set up for free.

So the Clares had been the only permanent residents of the Trailer Village. The other trailers and campers and tents that came to rest in the Trailer Village were usually occupied by drifters or vacationers or others on their way somewhere else. None of them ever stayed long enough to be called neighbors.

Now, twenty identical trailers filled the area and there was music and the sound of traffic all night long. Beer cans and liquor bottles sprouted like ragweed, and alcohol-fueled parties spilled into the night, with the merrymakers often passing out near the Clares' front door.

Lucy ignored her mother's warning to "stay away from them trashy men" and openly watched the activity. The hard-drinking men in the company trailers did not frighten her. After all, her own beloved daddy was rarely sober when he was home.

She didn't understand what had happened to her father. The tighter she tried to hold on to him, the more she felt him slipping away. And no one else would help. Anita was too little and Suki was too busy being embarrassed by him and Wanda couldn't seem to do anything but nag at him.

Now there was little left of the man who'd taught her how to fill herself with stardust. Lydell started drinking on his way home from work and didn't stop until he'd passed out for the night. Lucy had gradually assumed all responsibility for him. She comforted and reassured him when he thought he was back in Korea or when he imagined people after him. She coaxed him into eating. She made certain he found his way to bed each night and was dressed and pointed toward work each morning.

Maybe it was school being out and the overload of free time. Maybe it was the heat. Maybe it was the doctor's warning that Lydell was killing himself. Lucy didn't know why everything felt so drastically different in those first weeks of summer, but it did. There was a pain inside her, swelling up sometimes so that she had to double over and breathe deeply. And there was loneliness. Big empty places that she didn't know how to fill.

When she tried to will herself away into other worlds, she usually found only a wall to stare at. The magic was gone, even from her dreams, and the summer hung around her, weighing her down, sucking the energy from her.

"What's wrong with you?" her mother demanded over and over, but there was nothing Lucy could put into words. She shrugged listlessly and downed the spoonfuls of Geritol her mother forced on her.

The only relief was the constant movement and excitement of her boisterous neighbors. For hours each day she lay in the shade between a discarded refrigerator and a solar-powered gizmo that her father had built but never made work, and she watched. The easy camaraderie and raucous good humor of the workers fascinated her. They were so different from the people she'd grown up around.

When some of the men began to wave and wander over to say hello, she welcomed their attention. Her favorite was Billy, a short, stocky, freckle-faced twenty-year-old from Nacogdoches. Billy always stopped to say hi or tell her a silly joke. One day he brought her a strange-looking horse that he'd welded together on the job from bolts and nuts and scrap metal. It wasn't long before Billy rekindled her dead daydreams.

At first she imagined him only as her savior—someone brave and strong who would thunder in on his white horse when she needed him. Then, gradually, he transformed into someone more exciting than just a savior. He became the prince who would look beneath the patched jeans and the silence and discover that she was really a beautiful princess.

She was out alone on a late-June afternoon, dreaming up just such a scenario, when suddenly her prince appeared in the flesh. She gaped like a fool as he stepped into her favorite clearing by the creek.

"Hi, kid," he said brightly, as if his appearance in one of her secret places was nothing out of the ordinary.

"Hi," she said timidly. It was one thing seeing Billy on the edge of her own front yard, and a different thing altogether having him materialize in the quiet of her special hideaway.

"I like this place," he announced, and took a seat on the same flat rock that the rattlesnakes favored.

"You do?"

"Yeah. I seen you come here before." He nodded and looked around as though appraising the value of the secluded clearing.

Lucy swallowed nervously. Billy was a lot more appealing in her dreams than he was sitting here in her spot.

"You mean you like to walk out this way too?"

"I like to follow you out this way." He grinned a mischievous little-boy grin.

Lucy tried to grin back, but the corners of her mouth wouldn't hold a curve.

"Well," she said, taking a step backward. "Reckon it's gettin' close to suppertime. My mama'll skin me if I'm late."

Billy stood up. "It ain't that late. What'sa matter ... ain't we friends anymore?"

"Sure ... it's just ..." Lucy shrugged.

"Ya know ..." Billy said, moving closer to her, "you gonna be real pretty when you grow up. Know that?"

"Nah." Lucy shook her head and backed sideways a few paces. "My sister's the one who's gonna grow up pretty. My mama says I'm gonna grow up to be a hard worker and a good Christian."

Billy threw back his head and laughed.

"Well, your mama ain't took notice a them long coltish legs a yours and that way you got with your eyes. You're gonna be a fine looker, all right."

"No," she protested. "Suki's the pretty one. She's got that pretty red hair and . . . and—"

Billy reached out and picked up one of Lucy's braids.

"Your hair ain't bad," he said, rubbing his thumb back and forth across the ragged plaits. "It's just messy. Anyways, I ain't never been partial ta sorrels . . . whether they was gals or horses. And besides bein' a sorrel, that sister a yours is too short . . . kinda like a li'l ole chunky pony. I like my gals tall and leggy like racehorses."

He dropped her braid and Lucy stumbled backward—right into a big tree. Quick as a cat, Billy trapped her, leaning forward to press her against the rough trunk with his thick body.

"Don't be scared," he said. "I like you a lot. You got the makin's of a thoroughbred if I ever seen one."

Lucy's heart raced and her eyes darted from side to side in search of escape. She didn't want to hurt Billy's feelings or offend him, but she didn't like this one bit.

He clamped onto her shoulder with one hand and leaned back to stare at her. His eyes went up and down her body. Up and down. She could feel his eyes touching her, slithering across her skin like a leech looking for a place to take hold.

"See, I got ta make friends with you now, Lucy, so's you're already mine when you start turnin' into that fancy racehorse. That's the only way I can be sure you ain't had no other men sniffin' around you. See?"

Lucy nodded eagerly. She was certain that if she just kept being nice to him, Billy would release her and let her go home.

He dug his fingers deeper into her shoulder and pushed her hard against the tree, using his free hand to rub her all over. He rubbed at the zipper of her jeans so hard that the skin underneath grew raw. Then he clumsily unbuttoned her plaid shirt, tearing two of the buttons off in the process, and yanked it wide open and down off her shoulders.

"You barely got titties a'tall!" he said. His face held the delight of a child who's just torn open a present.

Lucy's stomach ached and she felt sick and shaky all over. She hated Billy now. His hands felt dirty against her skin and she gagged when his lips brushed her neck. And she was going to be in bad trouble when her mama saw that torn shirt.

She didn't know what Billy was doing or why. She just assumed it was a grown-up version of throwing girls down on the playground and torturing them by pulling their dresses up and shoving grass down their panties. The bullies at school reveled in that kind of prank.

"Please," she sobbed. She hated to cry, but she was real close now. "My mama's gonna be so mad about my shirt."

"I'm sorry," he said. He used his free hand to pull out a five-dollar bill and stuff it into a side pocket on her jeans. "You buy ya a new one, okay? Special from me."

The hand on her shoulder loosened slightly and she tried to jerk free and run, but he caught her and smacked her back against the tree so hard she saw stars.

"Don't you be a bad girl, now. Don't make me whip you."

"I won't," she whispered.

He smiled. "Now, I got somethin' I wanna show you. Somethin' just for you."

He pinned her against the tree and tore at his brass Peterbilt Truck buckle and the copper snap on his jeans. His movements grew jerky and frantic as he struggled to accomplish a one-handed unzipping of his pants.

Oh, no, Lucy thought. Not again. He was getting out his thing and she would see it and she would be punished and humiliated just like in kindergarten and everybody would be mad and it would all be her fault and her poor drunken daddy would sob and drink even worse.

Anger kindled inside her. There was no way she was going to go through all that again. She didn't care what his excuse was for getting it out and she didn't care if she hurt his feelings or offended him or had to suspend her good manners.

She turned her head and bit down hard on one of his fingers. He yowled and jerked his hand away. She ducked free. He grabbed the flopping tail of her shirt but it was already hanging half off her and she twisted and shrugged right out of it and ran like she'd never run in her life.

2

Lucy didn't tell anyone about Billy. She managed to sneak a clean shirt off the clothesline and sit down to a big helping of pinto beans and cornbread without anyone suspecting a thing. She gave the five dollars to her mother, saying she'd found it near the road. No one noticed her moodiness or lack of appetite. She felt safe. The terrible secret was buried inside her and no one would ever find out how close she had come to being branded a shameful sinner once again.

Lucy spent the rest of the summer as a prisoner in her own yard, afraid to venture out alone, even after the tire plant was completed and Billy and the rest of the men left town for other work. She stopped wearing shorts or sleeveless tops for fear some man like Billy might look at her bare skin in that slithery way. And when the first promise of swelling brought tenderness to her bony chest, she was afraid that Billy's cold, reptilian fingers had triggered some awful malady.

"It's only your titties," Suki diagnosed matter-of-factly during a shared bath to conserve hot water. "They're sore 'cause they're fixin' ta grow. Mine did the same thing."

Lucy hunched her shoulders forward anxiously to protect this new vulnerability from view. Before Billy, the countryside had been hers. Now, even in the calm of the familiar fields and trees, she was wary. There was something worse than just snakes out there.

The sticky blood that appeared in her panties one morning was something else she connected with Billy. Something else to be feared and hidden. Her mother reinforced those fears with an explanation of menstruation that included cautions against a spot of blood seeping through her clothing or a sanitary pad bulging beneath her clothing—both of which would reveal the secret of

18

her humiliating condition to men. Wanda also lectured Lucy about disposal, demonstrating the proper way to roll up the pad and wind it around with toilet paper and spray it with air freshener and drop it in a paper bag and bury it in the trash so that even a town garbage man would never guess what it really was.

A week after this upheaval came the talk about sex. Lucy had packed her father's lunch pail and waved him off to work. She was in the middle of cleaning up the breakfast dishes when suddenly her mother motioned her into the back of the trailer. It was only nine o'clock but the still August air was already hot and sticky, and the sheets felt damp when she sat on the edge of her unmade bed.

"What's wrong, Mama?" she asked weakly as Wanda settled onto the bed beside her. She could think of nothing she'd done lately to warrant a private scolding from her mother.

"What's wrong is . . . you've got the female curse now. Your life ain't ever gonna be the same."

Lucy listened to a dark tale of male animal instincts that brought Billy's greedy hands and slithering eyes back as sharply as if the incident had taken place days instead of months ago. The tale explained Billy's intentions. And she almost wondered if her mother didn't know about Billy—her cautions about what could happen with a man so closely paralleled Lucy's ugliest memories of the encounter. The shocking climax of Wanda's talk was that a man's "thing" could change and grow into a hard weapon with the power to stab and hurt and tear and make a girl unclean forever. This could happen at any time, without warning, so the best policy was to stay completely away from males as much as possible.

By the time Wanda was finished and Lucy returned to the dirty breakfast dishes, her knees were shaking so badly she could barely stand at the sink. Suki snickered and made fun of her and later demanded an exact retelling.

"Yeah, it's the same stuff she told me," Suki reported, "only she also told me about chickens. You know the way the roosters run after the hens and jump on 'em from behind and hold them down and peck their heads while the hens screech and scream?"

Lucy nodded. She'd been around chickens all her life, and of course she knew.

"Well, that's sex. Chicken sex. And Mama says men are just like roosters, only sneakier."

Lucy digested this disgusting bit of news. She was torn between anger at her sister for having kept all this secret and curiosity as to what else Suki might know.

"But what about when people get married?" Lucy wondered. "Mama didn't say nothin' about that."

"Oh, it's different then," Suki assured her with all the wisdom of her fourteen years. "That's romance . . . like in those books at the drugstore . . . and that's a whole different thing than this stuff."

Lucy breathed in a sigh of relief. She was glad to know that her mama and daddy hadn't been forced to behave like chickens in order to have their babies. And she was glad to know that marriage held the promise of something gentler than the picture her mama had painted.

"There's nothin' to be scared of, dummy." Suki was smug in her role as teacher. "You just have to be smarter than boys . . . and quicker, so's you don't end up like some poor ole screechin' hen. See, it's like a war. The boys are the enemy, and you just gotta survive till you find romance and get married and the war's over."

Suki elbowed her and grinned slyly. "When you get to be my age you'll learn that it's easy to handle boys. You can tame 'em down and teach 'em tricks easy as puppies."

Romance. The word developed mystical significance for Lucy. What was it and where was it and how did a person know when she'd found it? Did it happen to plain girls or shy girls or girls who didn't want to treat boys like puppies? Did it happen with boys who sat just rows away in school and had burping contests in the cafeteria?

When Lucy started sixth grade and went to a new school full of unfamiliar children, she looked around and wondered if this was the beginning of real life. Would she find friendship and romance in this new setting?

Barnett Fussell Middle School for the sixth and seventh grades was larger than Eaker and incorporated students from the entire northwest quadrant of town. Lucy was swallowed into the melting pot of Fussell along with scores of other twelve-year-olds. Everyone her age was new to the school. Everyone was starting from scratch. It was the equivalent of going West. New reputations were forged, new cliques were formed, and the adolescent social structure had to be created anew like a phoenix rising from the ashes of early childhood.

The upheaval fit in perfectly with Lucy's changing perspectives. She no longer had the desire or the strength to be a self-sustaining loner. Puberty was stirring up a whole new set of needs and fears inside her. She wanted friends. She wanted to belong to something larger and more exciting than her family. The hunger for acceptance built inside her until she was convinced that every original thought, every part of her character that rendered her slightly different from the town norm, was a fault to be excised at all cost.

She had spent her childhood living by her father's standards, but now she saw that her mother had been the one who was right all along. Happiness was rewarded to those who were accepted. Contentment lay in learning to live by the patterns and rules that served the rest of the community so well. Suki was the proof. For a brief period Lucy hung suspended, malleable and trusting and desperately wanting to belong. She would have gladly changed anything about herself for a favored place in the adolescent social order.

But her poverty was against her, and her address at the Trailer Village was against her, and her lack of a church affiliation was against her. She was the daughter of a woman who washed other people's clothes and an eccentric drunk who worked in the most menial positions at the trailer factory. She had few social skills and she lacked the personality and looks that had enabled Suki to rise above her origins. Even the fact that she was trying so hard was a mark against her. In the end the one chance she did have came about as a mistake.

Fussell had a bona fide art program with a full-time teacher. Classes were offered twice a week to all students, and extracurricular projects were available to those who qualified. Lucy had always liked to draw (or doodle, as Wanda called it), and she had often carried a pad and pencil with her to sketch birds and strange insects and newly opened flowers. In Fussell's art class she found materials and mediums she hadn't known existed—charcoal, pastels, acrylics, and dry brush pencils—and the possibilities consumed her.

The art teacher, Ms. Conroy, recognized Lucy's fledgling talent immediately and enlisted her to design and paint the sets for the school play. In this elevated position, Lucy was working on the stage when the cast was issued their invitations to Clytie Burright's dress-rehearsal party. Mrs. Burright's maid, Thelma, brought the invitations to the auditorium and handed one to every student onstage, including Lucy.

Wanda was ecstatic. Suki was envious. It was well known that Dr. Burright's house boasted a Texas-shaped swimming pool and that Clytie had a canopy bed and a lighted Hollywood-style dressing table in her room.

Lucy arrived at the Burrights' wearing a new dress her mother

had made and sporting a stiff hairdo Suki had spent hours on.
Her old leather shoes had been spit-shined by Anita so that Lucy
could see herself in them.

"What was that again ... Lucy Clare?" Mrs. Burright asked
after Thelma had shown Lucy into the hall. "I surely don't recall
that name from the cast list, dear."

Lucy swallowed hard and explained that she wasn't a member
of the cast. She was painting the sets.

Sissy Lee Burright rose to the occasion like a true Southern
hostess and assured Lucy that anyone as vital as the set designer
was of course welcome. But Lucy knew that the invitation had
been a mistake. And though she worked at mingling and remembered to keep her knees together (Wanda's parting advice) and
let the boys win the games (Suki's offering), the knotty, sick feeling in her stomach wouldn't let go. She didn't belong. They hadn't
really wanted her.

When the buffet was set up out by the pool, Lucy tried to
soothe her nerves with eating, but the food made her feel worse.
There was no place to sit because the places were always saved
for someone else and there was no conversation she could take
part in because everyone was talking about posh Bible camps and
shopping trips to Neiman-Marcus and tennis lessons at the country club. The knot in her stomach tightened.

She sealed her fate forever by throwing up lime Jell-O cake
and miniature cocktail wieners in barbecue sauce and Big Red
soda all over Mrs. Burright's cream-colored rug and Becky Jo
Fimple's candy-pink shoes and Kay Kay Harrison's sundress.

The disaster (as she would forever think of it) was devastating
to Lucy. She refused to go to school, unable to face anyone who
had been a witness. But even at home she found no peace. Both
Wanda and Suki berated her continuously for her stupidity and
accused her of shaming and embarrassing them all. Lydell was
too drunk to come to her aid, so it seemed the only friend she
had in the world was little Anita. Like a faithful dog the girl crept
around after Lucy, offering sympathy with her eyes or reaching
out to hold hands.

Lucy clung to her little sister's love, but it wasn't enough. She
felt ill and used up and worthless. With all the raging intensity
of her twelve-year-old emotions, she believed her life to be over,
destroyed completely and irrevocably. The despondency fed on
itself and grew, weighing her down till she felt too weak to even
think.

It was Ms. Conroy who saved her. The art teacher pulled up

in her funny little Volkswagen on Saturday morning. She didn't ask why Lucy had been absent for the whole week or say much of anything. She just gathered Lucy up and carried her off to the empty school and put her to work finishing up the play's sets.

Ms. Conroy worked right beside Lucy. Her long straight hair was pulled back into a loose braid and silver peace signs dangled from her pierced ears. She wore a baggy T-shirt with a faded zodiac symbol printed on the front, and old jeans that were patched at the knees and trimmed with embroidered flowers.

There was no conversation, nothing except "try the green" or "what about the wider brush" or other basic communications relating to the task at hand. At first Lucy was nervous and vaguely angry, but gradually she relaxed, losing herself in the motion and color.

"Wow," Ms. Conroy sighed. She sagged against a backdrop and wiped her forehead with the back of her paint-stained hand. "I can't believe how late it got. It's four o'clock!"

Lucy dropped her brush and looked around as though suddenly coming awake. "Four o'clock?"

Ms. Conroy put down her brush and rag and stepped back to look at their accomplishments. She studied the work for a long time, then smiled. "This is what it's all about, Lucy. What you have inside you . . . what you can create or give. That's what teaching is about . . . and painting . . . and everything else that's worthwhile in the world." Her expression changed and her eyes narrowed. "I know what you're thinking: What does she know? She's a teacher. She's old. She couldn't possibly understand. So I'm not going to drop a lot of heavy stuff on you. But I have one piece of very serious advice: Fuck them all."

Lucy was stunned. The F word! The word no decent female was supposed to say out loud and no man was supposed to say in the presence of decent females. The F word. Right out loud. And from a teacher.

"Well"—Ms. Conroy turned away from her and briskly began the process of cleaning brushes and capping paints—"all I can think about right now is food. How does pizza sound?"

That was the beginning. From that day forward Lucy became a militant individualist, scornful of the Fussell social set and disdainful of her sister Suki's preoccupations and contemptuous of the entire town of Walea. She poured everything positive into worshiping Junelle Conroy. She signed up for every art project, volunteered for art-room cleanup after school, and coaxed the teacher into sending her on personal errands.

Ms. Conroy was different from everyone else in Walea. Lucy could remember her first class with the teacher. How unsettled she'd been by Ms. Conroy's straight swinging hair and weird jewelry and long flowered skirt. She could remember being shocked when the boys whispered that the new teacher had no bra on under her embroidered cotton blouse. Lucy had stared and stared, trying to see for herself whether it was true. And the things the teacher said! Though she'd been raised in Dallas, Ms. Conroy had gone to California for college. Someplace where they had protest marches and sit-ins. The comments she made during art were often cause for outrage.

Now Lucy took great pride in Ms. Conroy's strangeness. The unconventional clothing, the straight hair, the unshaven legs—all took on significance. They were symbols of daring, of an intellectual, artistic, enlightened otherworld that existed above the realm of Walea. Lucy was sometimes caught off-balance by Ms. Conroy's passionate ideas on civil rights or commune living or feminism. They were so far away from what she'd been raised to think. But she always came around to Ms. Conroy's way of seeing things. This violent reshaping of attitude and restructuring of expectation was difficult, but she was at a point where she was willing to shed the cocoon of her parents' beliefs so the transformation brought ecstasy rather than pain.

Everything seemed like a miracle to Lucy—the greatest miracle being that a woman like Ms. Conroy had come to a town like Walea in the first place.

"Why did you come here?" Lucy finally asked when they were alone working on a mural for the PTA's jubilee.

Ms. Conroy cocked her head sideways and thought about it a moment as though weighing the amount of honesty she could afford to share. Afternoon sunlight streamed through the banks of art-room windows, burnishing her dark blond hair and gleaming on the twisted-snake earrings that rested lightly against the line of her jaw. Lucy drank in every detail greedily, memorizing each gesture and expression. She wanted to absorb the woman. She wanted to become Junelle Conroy.

"Sometimes a person gets caught up, Lucy," Ms. Conroy began hesitantly. "And you can either run away or run straight into the middle." She shrugged, and the red-eyed silver snakes danced with her movements. "I ran to Walea."

Lucy could not have loved anyone more than she loved Junelle Conroy at that moment. Everything seemed so perfect and pure that she closed her eyes and wished for time to stop, to leave her suspended there, warmed by the gift of intimacy. Ms. Conroy was more than teacher and mentor now. Ms. Conroy had become her friend.

But, not only did that treasured moment pass too quickly, the entire school year ran through her fingers like sand. She tried to hold on and stretch out every day, keeping her time with Ms. Conroy sharp and clear in her mind so that she could savor and relive each exchange during the hours they weren't together. She drew no boundaries between her obsession with art and her love for her teacher. They were intertwined and symbiotic. When she thought of a design to try or a particular scene she wanted to attempt, or even an interesting use of color, it was linked with Ms. Conroy. What would Ms. Conroy think? Would Ms. Conroy like this? How would Ms. Conroy do it?

For her thirteenth birthday her mother made her a tunnel-of-fudge cake (Suki's favorite) and gave her a pink blouse with a big bow that tied tight to her throat and a white Leatherette Bible with her name on the cover in gold letters. Her father gave her candy from the trailer factory's snack machine. Anita and Suki made her elaborate cards decorated with hearts, and Suki presented her with a half-empty bottle of pink-pearl nail polish.

But only Ms. Conroy's gift mattered. The teacher gave her a camera. A real camera.

"It's beat-up and used," Ms. Conroy said, "but it's a Rolleiflex—just what an artist needs. You can set up things and get the picture just right . . . then you can take all the time in the world painting it."

Lucy held the camera carefully and flipped up the top and looked down into the square lens the way Ms. Conroy showed her. She was close to tears over the fact that the woman had remembered her birthday at all. And a camera! The magnitude of the gift, the seriousness of it, was awesome.

"This isn't like a little Instamatic," Ms. Conroy explained. "It uses different-size film and you get a nice big square negative. Maybe later . . . in high school or in college . . . you'll get to take a photography class, and this size film is really easy to work with."

High school? College? Ms. Conroy had so much faith in her abilities. More than anyone else. More than Lucy herself. Lydell had always said that a high-school education was absolutely necessary in today's world, but even he had never suggested that one of his girls might go to college.

The camera came with a roll of film and Lucy insisted on taking pictures of Ms. Conroy. Then they recruited a school janitor to take a shot of the two of them together.

It took the money Lucy had saved for six months to get the

film developed. But the pictures were worth every cent. She gave Ms. Conroy the one with them together and she taped the rest on the wall beside her bed. The negatives were stored carefully in a special box in case she should ever need more prints.

The end of school would have been a disaster for Lucy if it hadn't been for Ms. Conroy's plan to give free summer art classes to the children in the "outlying areas." When she asked if Lucy might be interested in assisting her, Lucy felt as relieved and grateful as if she'd been given a stay of execution.

Wanda simply nodded when Lucy explained the project and her intention to volunteer. What her mother didn't know wouldn't hurt her. And Lucy was careful to keep the definition of "outlying areas" vague. It would only cause trouble if Wanda knew that meant Colored Town and the migrant camps. Or Negro Town, as Lucy had started saying. She still felt funny saying "black" the way Ms. Conroy did.

Their first art session was scheduled for the Wednesday after school closed. Ms. Conroy had arranged to use the activity room in one of the colored churches as the program's home base.

Lucy was surprised to see how normal the church looked. She had always heard stories about voodoo and snake-kissing and all sorts of carryings-on that passed for Christian worship across the river. But the white clapboard building with its Spartan interior and lines of wooden pews could have passed for a "regular" church anywhere in Walea. And the minister, Reverend Luke, radiated the same gentle assurance and command as any white minister she'd ever met.

Lucy was very nervous at the beginning. She would have died if Ms. Conroy found out . . . but she had never really known a colored person. That is, unless she counted the maid who had given her the invitation and opened the door for her at the Bur-rights' party. All she had was thirteen years of hearing stories and jokes about colored people. Black, she reminded herself. Ms. Conroy insisted on her using "black," even though many of the people across the river were still referring to themselves as col-oreds.

The children filed into the room silently. They seemed to be as nervous about Lucy as she was about them. But once the paints and the crayons and the glue and the scissors were passed out, and Reverend Luke made a few jokes and announced that there would be cookies after class, the children relaxed. And Lucy was struck with the evidence of their sameness. There were shy kids and clownish kids and bullies and smooth talkers just like in any white class. There were kids dressed in brand-new clothes and kids like Lucy who were dressed in hand-me-downs.

They held the art sessions every weekday, sometimes bumping across rutted dirt roads to a spot in the migrant camps or heading out to a rural church that invited them—but most often crossing the river straight to Reverend Luke's. The group there swelled from fifteen to fifty and had to be split up, so that Lucy was in charge of her own class. She delighted in being the teacher, in having the power to give. She taught the children how to see the patterns and colors around them, just as Ms. Conroy had taught her, and she began to dream of a career in teaching.

By the third week Lucy no longer thought of the kids as colored or black. She didn't think of them as anything but kids. She had crossed more than just the bridge into Colored Town.

Through a long liquid June and a blistering July and into a suffocating August Lucy bounced around in the "Yellow Bug" with Ms. Conroy. She was absolutely happy. Her gawky, awkward body no longer bothered her. Her poverty was of no consequence. The prospect of returning to school was undaunting. Ms. Conroy had cast a magic spell over her life.

But the magic spell was fragile, and shattered with the delivery of one piece of mail—Ms. Conroy's termination notice.

The notice arrived just weeks before the new term. Ms. Conroy had not been well-received by the community. Her hiring had been accomplished long-distance, based on sterling academic credentials and the fact that a long-dead second cousin of hers had owned a popular sporting-goods store in Walea at one time. The school officials realized their mistake as soon as they saw her, but they'd decided to try her for a probationary period, allowing her latitude because "artistic types couldn't be expected to behave the same as normal folks" and because they had no ready substitute.

There was no explanation for the sudden termination, just a curt advisement that the Fussell art program had been canceled for the coming year and her services would not be needed.

Lucy was terror-stricken.

"You won't go, will you? You won't move away?"

Ms. Conroy, pale and obviously shaken, mumbled something about calling Luke. Lucy clutched at the thought immediately.

"That's it! Reverend Luke will help get you another job. You could teach art in one of the schools across the bridge."

Ms. Conroy smiled strangely and shook her head. "They don't have art in the schools across the bridge, Lucy. I'll have to think of something else to do if I want to stay. Private art lessons. Free-lance illustration maybe." Her voice faded uncertainly.

Lucy did not question Ms. Conroy's desire to stay in Walea. She didn't question Ms. Conroy's apparent willingness to give up her chosen profession. She didn't wonder why a twenty-five-year-old woman with no ties would choose to stay in a town that had blacklisted her. In the insular manner of youth, not one question occurred to her. Ms. Conroy was staying. That was all that mattered. Ms. Conroy would not abandon her. And so she was totally unsuspecting, totally unprepared for the events that set disaster in motion.

Ms. Conroy was subdued and distracted after the letter, but she insisted on finishing out the summer art program. There were only three days left, all to be spent at Reverend Luke's.

They crossed the bridge and conducted the morning session as usual. Lucy took the children outside for an exercise break in the graveled parking area behind the church, as usual, and Ms. Conroy stayed inside to visit with Reverend Luke and set up for the next projects, as usual.

Lucy shaded her eyes with her hand and watched the children play. Some were engaged in tag, some in jumping rope. Two of the boys started to fight. Lucy called out for them to stop, and started toward them.

Then the car came. Black with dark windows. It raced from around the church and fishtailed through the gravel parking lot, scattering children like quail before it slowed. "Nigger lovers!" came the hollow chorus from inside the car as a white arm appeared and a rock sailed through the air toward the church. The rock missed the window it had been aimed at, thunked harmlessly against a shutter, and fell to the ground as the car sped away.

Lucy's heart lurched frantically but her feet were wooden. She couldn't move. The children were gone. They'd vanished into the trees and were running for home. Or so she hoped.

The church stood before her silently. The sun beat down on the empty parking lot and on the rock gleaming whitely where it had fallen. Slowly she edged toward it. The rock wasn't white at all, but light gray. And smooth. A river rock.

She began to shiver. She wanted to scream for Ms. Conroy and Reverend Luke, but her throat wouldn't work. She wanted to run for them, but her knees were suddenly too weak to support her weight.

The back door was closest. She willed her trembling legs into motion and carried the plain, smooth rock through the back door and the kitchen and the hallway. She heard a noise from the reverend's office, a muted voice, and the promise of comfort sent a rush of energy through her and made her burst through the door. And stop.

The drapes were pulled and the office was in shadow. A fan burred softly on the desk. Ms. Conroy's eyes were wet with tears. Her blouse was open. Reverend Luke's hand was dark against the pale swell of her naked breast.

"Lucy!" Ms. Conroy cried.

The rock fell from Lucy's hand.

"Dear God . . ." the reverend moaned.

Lucy turned and ran. She raced blindly out the door and across the gravel and cut through fields to the main road. She was nearly to the bridge before Ms. Conroy's Volkswagen came skidding up beside her.

"Get in," Ms. Conroy ordered flatly.

They rode in silence till they were through Walea and close to the Trailer Village turnoff. Then Ms. Conroy pulled over beneath a stand of trees. She scrubbed at her face with her hands before turning red-rimmed eyes toward Lucy.

"I'm sorry you found out this way," she said quietly. "We should have told you before."

The words buzzed and echoed in Lucy's mind, tumbling into incoherence. Ms. Conroy's mouth kept moving, but the words made no sense.

"We wanted you to . . ."

We. We. We. Why did Ms. Conroy keep saying "we"? Just like she and Reverend Luke were a couple. Like it was real. Like it was right for a white woman to be with a black man. Like it was right for unmarried people to be doing things like that.

"Talk to me, Lucy. Don't shut me out."

The dashboard swam in front of Lucy's eyes.

"And tell me what happened. Where did all the children go? Why were—?"

"What do you care where the children went! You never cared about the kids! You never cared about anything but him!"

Ms. Conroy drew in a deep breath and let it out slowly. "Yes, the program made it easy for us to see each other. It's hard to be together in this town. But that doesn't mean I don't care about the kids or the program."

"How long have you . . . have you known him? Longer than me?"

"What difference does that make."

Lucy held her lips together as tightly as possible to keep them from trembling. She stared hard at a spot in the distance behind Ms. Conroy's head.

"He's the reason you're staying in town. It's because of him, right? You woulda never stayed because of me, would you?"

"Lucy, Lucy, Lucy. You're my dear friend. You're like a little sister to me. But I'm in love with Luke. I want to marry him. I want to have children with him. That's one of the strongest bonds there is in life. You can't expect me to—"

Lucy threw open the door and leapt from the car.

"You're dirty!" she screamed. "You were doin' dirty things with a nigger!"

Ms. Conroy reeled as though she'd been struck. Her eyes widened and her mouth opened to an O.

Lucy took a few mechanical steps backward. Her shoulders began to shake and tears streamed from her eyes. "Dirty," she cried. "A dirty liar. And a sneak. All the things you told me never to be."

Slowly Ms. Conroy got out of the car, but she made no move toward Lucy. She just stood there, looking at Lucy across the Volkswagen's weathered yellow roof.

"Please . . ." There was pain in her voice and her eyes. "Give yourself some time to think, and when you're calmer—"

Lucy whirled and ran.

"Be careful," Ms. Conroy called across the widening space between them. "This isn't a game."

For three days Lucy stayed in bed. She refused meals and buried her head beneath her pillow every time Wanda came at her with hand outstretched to check for fever or Suki peeked in to ask if she was well enough to take over the dishes. Lydell and Anita took turns staring down at her in silent confusion.

"I'm sick! Leave me alone," she yelled at them, and they backed away in confusion, leaving her alone with the monstrous emotions spinning and twisting so rapidly inside her that she really did feel sick.

She hated Ms. Conroy. She hated Reverend Luke. She hated her family and she hated the town and most of all she hated herself. But mixed in with the rage were questions. Was Ms. Conroy a sinner? Was she unclean and destroyed? She'd fallen prey not just to a man, but a black man. Could God or Walea ever forgive her? Could Lucy somehow save her?

That stupid Reverend Luke. It was all his doing. He had sweet-talked poor Ms. Conroy into ruination. Of course no one would ever blame him because he was a man. Because things were always the girl's fault. She could just hear what people would say—that Ms. Conroy shouldn't have gone shashayin' around a black man. That any white woman who did that deserved what she got.

But then, what if it was romance? Real romance. Was that possible between black and white? The longer Lucy considered it, the more she realized that Reverend Luke was a good deal more suited to Ms. Conroy than Heiny Hutzell or Newt Falhaber or any of the other bachelors that had tried to catch the teacher's attention. So maybe romance had struck them. Like a lightning bolt from the sky. And they would get married and have a little house and then Ms. Conroy would settle in Walea forever and everything would stay the same.

Only how could they get married in Walea? She could just imagine the uproar if Ms. Junelle Conroy, formerly of Dallas, and Reverend Luther Byers of the Heavenly Tabernacle announced their engagement in the Sunday paper just like any regular couple. What a storm that would cause.

Lucy remembered the black car and the white arm and the rock and the shouted "Nigger lover!" that came from inside that car. She'd thought at the time that people were angry about white girls teaching art in a black church. Could it be that they were angry about more than that? Could it be that others knew about Ms. Conroy and Reverend Luke?

She shivered in spite of the stifling heat in the trailer, and a gnawing emptiness developed in the center of her belly. What if something bad happened to Ms. Conroy? "Be careful," Ms. Conroy had said. Had she meant be careful about the secret? Had she thought Lucy would tell?

Quietly Lucy slipped out of bed so as not to wake Suki or Anita. The night was moonless black outside the window.

If only Ms. Conroy had trusted her. If only she hadn't said "we" with Reverend Luke being the other half of that "we." The big "we." The secret "we." Excluding Lucy completely.

Lucy was up when the rest of the household awakened. Suki resumed her taunting and Wanda heaved a sigh of relief. Anita brightened and Lydell relaxed back into his old patterns. They thought Lucy was finally well and everything was normal again.

Lucy humored them, but she didn't feel normal. Something restless and wild was gnawing at her.

All morning she roamed the trailer, pausing only to stare into the face of the roaring, leaking dinosaur of an air conditioner that her mother had rescued from someone's trash the week before. It was perched in the living-room window, held up by the back of a chair inside and a network of boards outside.

Ms. Conroy had been right. She'd calmed a lot with all her thinking. And now she was developing a big empty spot right about the center of her belly. She felt terrible and she knew that only seeing Ms. Conroy could fix it.

She tried the teacher's number all morning and even resorted to trying Reverend Luke's home phone and church office. There was no answer anywhere.

"When you going to town today?" she asked her mother.

The question seemed to fluster Wanda a little.

"Heavens! Ain't you heard the radio? Storm warnings for this afternoon. Could even churn up a tornado. I ain't budgin'.'"

Lucy looked out the window at the line of gray clouds hanging in the distance. She tried Ms. Conroy's number again and then paced back and forth in front of the spitting, roaring air conditioner.

"What're you so antsy about?" Wanda asked. She pulled a wad of damp starched shirts from the refrigerator and eyed Lucy as she arranged the first shirt on her ironing board.

"I wanna go see Miz Conroy." Lucy hugged herself to ward off the shivers and moved back away from the air conditioner, where the blast of cold air couldn't reach her.

"Miz Conroy, Miz Conroy. I'm so sick a hearin' about Miz Conroy. I ain't never heard of a teacher spendin' so much time with students."

"Miz Conroy's not just my teacher, Mama. She's my friend."

"Well, that ain't natural! There's something wrong with a grown woman pickin' a thirteen-year-old for a friend."

"She's not a normal woman, Mama," Suki remarked from behind the pages of the magazine she was engrossed in. "Miz Conroy's a hippie. A *real* hippie. Like those ones out in California doing free love and devil worship and marijuana and all."

"I'll slap you alongside the head if you keep talkin' like that in my home," Wanda threatened.

Lucy drew in a deep breath. Her mother was obviously in a bad mood about something, and it wouldn't do to start too big a fuss.

"Miz Conroy isn't like that at all," she whispered to Suki. "You're just jealous 'cause she's not your friend."

"Hah! What've I got to be jealous of? I got plenty a friends."

Lucy plopped down on the lumpy couch beside her sister.

"Looka this, Luce." Suki held the open magazine over so Lucy could see the pages. "Says here that this little girl could be one a the richest women in the world when she grows up. Imagine bein' that lucky."

The picture was a black-and-white family portrait, a mother, father, and daughter all dressed up and stiffly posed. The mother was beautiful but sad-looking. The girl was about Anita's age or a little younger, and in spite of her frilly dress and ribbons, she had the same thin, frail look as Anita. And the same eyes. Wounded eyes. Angry eyes. Eyes that were too careful for such a young face. They made Lucy uneasy and she jumped from the couch and began her restless pacing again.

Both Ms. Conroy and her own father, back when he used to talk about things, said being rich was no better than being a criminal anyway.

"If they were any kind of decent people they'd use their money to buy shoes for children in migrant camps and food for people over in . . ." Lucy struggled to come up with the name. ". . . Biafra and places."

"Yeah, and a car and a stereo record player for poor Suki Clare out in Walea, Texas," Suki said.

"And a new washer-dryer and that nice orange-brown shag carpeting for me," Wanda chimed in.

"Why don't you write to 'em about that?" Suki said with the most irritating wide-eyed sweetness.

Lucy sighed and made a show of ignoring them.

"That storm's a million miles away, Mama. How 'bout if Suki drove me into town?"

"Suki ain't got no driver's license!"

"She drives all the time anyway," Lucy protested. "You're always lettin' her drive."

"That's for errands and such." Wanda stabbed at a shirt collar with the point of her iron. "That's different. Besides . . . Suki's gotta practice."

"Oh, Mama!" Suki slapped the magazine against the couch. "I already practiced this morning."

"That pageant ain't but two months away, girl, and there's all them new routines to learn and that flamin'-baton trick to get right."

"Oh, Mama," Suki moaned.

"Don't use that high-school sass-mouth on me, Sherry Kay Clare!" Wanda's face turned red and she looked as close to exploding as Lucy had ever seen her. "Who gets you to them contests? Who makes them fancy costumes?"

"Okay, Mama. Okay." Suki stood and dropped the magazine on the faded floral slipcover. "I'll go out and practice."

Something was very wrong. Lucy shifted nervously, uncertain as to whether Wanda might attack her next.

"Lucy," Wanda snapped, "you run out and shake your daddy and tell him to check the tires on the roof. They need to be tied down real tight if this storm's comin' on like the radio says."

Lucy turned toward the door.

"And then you round up your little sissy and keep her busy, hear?"

"But, Mama, Nita's fine. She's playing dolls underneath the trailer in her regular spot. She don't need me to—"

"Hush! You do as I say, hear? You do as I say and forget goin' into town. Forget that no-count hippie teacher and think about your own family for a change."

Lucy stared at her mother in disbelief, then turned and pushed through the door out into the stifling heat. Her father was slumped over asleep in his favorite place—a row of movie seats that he'd salvaged when the downtown theater was remodeled. He'd positioned them beneath the big oak tree and he kept his beer cooler on the seat to his right and his gun on the seat to his left. Every so often he'd call Lucy to set up some cans for him to fire at across the yard.

"Daddy," she said, gently shaking Lydell's shoulder.

He roused, sitting up straight and rubbing his eyes.

"Mama says to check the tires on the roof, 'cause a storm's comin'."

"Uh-huh," he said. "Get right to it." He reached into the cooler for another beer.

Lucy was aware of her mother watching her through the window. She walked over and bent down to check Anita. The girl was intent on arranging her filthy dolls for a tea party.

"How you doin', sissy?" Lucy asked.

Anita looked up and her face registered pleasure. "Lucy . . . you wanna come to my tea party? You wanna be the white rabbit again?"

"How come I'm always the white rabbit?"

"Because the dolls can't pretend," Anita said solemnly.

"You're right, they can't, can they? Well, I'll be the white rabbit again for you tomorrow. Today I've got to do something."

Disappointment flickered briefly but was quickly eclipsed by blankness. Anita's shell had two sides—blankness and anger.

"Tomorrow," Lucy promised again. "For as long as you

want . . ." But the child had already turned back to her tattered dolls and her vision of afternoon elegance.

Lucy straightened. Her mother was still at the window. Something strange was going on. Something was not right. Storms had never made Wanda so evil-tempered or nervous before.

Lucy squinted off into the distance again. That storm wouldn't hit till late, and if somebody gave her a ride she could be to town and back in an hour.

"Don't you even think about it, Lucy!" her mother shrilled from the doorway. "Lydell! You keep that girl in this yard. She ain't ta go to town today."

Lucy looked back and forth from her father's hazy, puzzled expression to her mother's wild-eyed, panicky face in the doorway. And suddenly she knew that her mother was afraid. And it had nothing to do with the storm.

Lucy turned and ran. She cut through pastures just in case her mother decided to hop in the pickup and chase her. Then she swung west to connect with the old highway. Ordinarily she would never have considered hitching a ride anywhere, but today she was desperate. Fortunately an old man with a pickup load of watermelons stopped as soon as she put her thumb out.

Ms. Conroy's car was not in the driveway, and the lawn in front of her rented duplex was chewed up like somebody had driven circles on it. Lucy looked up and down the street. It was quiet and normal-looking. She eased up the concrete steps to the small front porch. The clay pots that usually lined the porch were all smashed and there was dirt and broken pieces of geranium scattered all over.

Lucy knocked and knocked and knocked. The woman from the other side of the duplex stuck her head out her front door.

"I'd stay away from there if I was you," she warned. She shook her head so hard that a pink roller came loose and dangled beside her ear. "There's been trouble over there, ya know. Best stay clear."

Lucy watched the woman retreat back inside. She looked up and down the street once more and then ran around and through the side gate to Ms. Conroy's yard. It was a tiny patch full of all sorts of strange-smelling things that Ms. Conroy grew to use in cooking recipes. The plants were all trampled and the small concrete-slab patio was littered with the broken and bent parts to a chaise lounge and several webbed fold-up chairs.

"Ms. Conroy!" Lucy called over and over.

She ran toward the sliding glass patio doors and stopped. They were covered with huge spray-painted words: "NIGGER LOVER."

Lucy tore at the doors. They were unlocked.

The house was dim and silent.

She stood in the middle of the living room for long minutes, absorbing the shock of the wreckage. The floor was littered with broken lamps and shredded artwork and shards of crockery and glass. The phone had been ripped from the wall. The couch that had come with the rental was untouched, but the chair Ms. Conroy had brought with her was slashed and ripped apart.

"Ms. Conroy?"

Inside she was begging: "Please be all right. Please be safe."

She picked her way through the litter to check the other rooms, but each was empty and ransacked. She didn't let herself think until she saw the closet in Ms. Conroy's bedroom. The familiar tapestry suitcases were gone and there was nothing hanging on the rod.

Frantically Lucy ripped open the dresser drawers and the drawer in the bedside table. All were empty. Only Ms. Conroy's antique shawl had been left behind. It lay forgotten, a silken puddle in the corner of the closet.

Lucy held the shawl to her face and breathed in the familiar scent, a mix of wildflower soap and herbal shampoo and the musk of Ms. Conroy herself. She hugged the wad of fabric tightly to her chest and sagged down weakly onto the edge of the bed. Ms. Conroy was all right. She had packed her clothes and gone, hadn't she? She wouldn't have packed if she'd been hurt at all. She was hiding somewhere . . . but she was safe. She had to be safe.

Lucy's certainty grew and energized her. She searched the house for clues—notes, addresses, a phone book—anything that might help her find Ms. Conroy. There was nothing. The teacher had obviously taken more than her clothes.

Lucy folded the shawl carefully and went back out through the patio doors. She peered up and down the street before stepping out of the side gate, though she didn't know who or what to be on the lookout for.

"Hello," she called, rapping on the neighbor woman's door. There was no answer, but Lucy knew the woman was there, probably listening just inside.

"Hello . . . do you know where Miz Conroy went? Did you see her when she left?"

"Go home," a disembodied voice ordered. "She's gone back to where she belongs."

Lucy stood on the porch clutching the shawl for several minutes. Then the thought struck her. Maybe Ms. Conroy had gone to Reverend Luke's.

Her hitchhiking luck was not so good going toward the bridge. It was close to six by the time she made it to the river and joined the streams of maids and gardeners and cooks and janitors and baby nurses heading home across the bridge from their jobs in Walea proper. The sky had turned leaden, with a sickly yellow cast, and the air was so hot and still and moist that Lucy felt close to drowning every time she took a deep breath. The storm would break soon.

She got a lot of sideways looks as she crossed the bridge and headed down to the Heavenly Tabernacle. "Where's that li'l whitey goin'?" she heard someone say. But no one challenged her openly or tried to stop her.

Her hopes sank when she saw the reverend's house. Even from the end of the lane she could tell that the front door was hanging off the hinges and all the windows were shattered.

"Reverend?" she called through the yawning doorway, but there was no answer. She steeled herself and took a quick, disheartening look inside. The place was empty and the destruction was much more complete than it had been at Ms. Conroy's. Walls were punched through and sinks were torn from their moorings.

She left quickly and hurried down through the trees to the church. The sky was now a heavy pewter, roiling and churning and reflecting eerie silver-gray light. Little pockets of wind sprang up. They tugged at her clothes and hair and danced through the limber cedar branches around her. The first sharp crack of thunder sounded, signaling the rain and sending shivers down her spine even before the cool drops spattered on her arms and face.

The outside of the church appeared untouched, and the sight of it raised Lucy's dwindling hopes. Maybe Ms. Conroy was inside. She imagined the two of them safely huddled in the back of Reverend Luke's office or beneath the cross in the main prayer hall.

"Ms. Conroy!" Lucy cried, pounding on the solidly locked front doors. "Reverend Luke!"

Deep rumbling began and built into a firecracker explosion of thunder. The drops of rain fused into solid liquid sheets driven before shifting gusts of wind. Lucy clutched the shawl tight to her chest and ran around the building. The back entrance was open.

She stood in the dark hallway a moment, listening and praying silently. But the only sound she heard was the water that dripped from her hair and clothing into a puddle at her feet.

"Reverend Luke," she whispered as she tiptoed through every room and peeked into every closet. When she had made the circuit, she felt her way back down the dark hallway to his office, where she had started.

The heavy drapes were open but the storm had hit full fury and the room was shrouded in a dusky half-light. She stood inside the door, overwhelmed by the emptiness pressing in from all sides. This was where she had seen that dark hand against the pale breast. This was where it had all started.

She buried her face in the shawl and inhaled Ms. Conroy's scent and wished that she could start over again . . . right here . . . right back at that moment.

The wind rattled the windows in their frames and whipped the rain against the glass in deafening bursts, and the entire building shuddered and creaked. Lucy crept across the room to turn on the desk lamp. The switch made a hollow clicking noise, but there was no light. The lines were already down somewhere.

With her back against the desk, she slid down to a sitting position on the worn carpet. She squeezed her eyes shut and pressed her hands over her ears and screamed.

And screamed.

And screamed.

3

Juliana

Far, far away, in a completely different world, lived another child who also believed her sphere to be the universe. Chance had entrusted this soul to the Van Lydens of New York City, a bloodline descending from one of the great robber barons and possessing the history of a Rockefeller or a Vanderbilt.

Juliana Van Lyden was born to a level of grandeur that few ever taste, but luxury is wasted on the very young. The trappings of her privileged life meant nothing to Juliana. Not the fact that she lived in the last of Manhattan's great privately owned mansions—a dinosaur of a house that was both a tribute to the acquisitive frenzy of the founding Van Lyden and to the unrestrained materialism of a bygone era. Not the fact that her baby clothes were designed in Europe. And certainly not the fact that she would be one of the richest girls in the world someday.

All that mattered to her was the circle of adults who frowned down at her. The grandfather who'd wanted a male heir. The father who'd expected a dimpled, fun-loving imp rather than this plain, solemn child. And the mother, the quiet young mother, who was trying so hard to distance herself from the pull of tiny fingers and hungry eyes.

Juliana played with her extravagant toys, learning quickly that she could pull the bellcord and have a servant bring tea to her dolls. She obeyed her nurse and accepted the comfort of the woman's soft bosom when she scraped her knees or woke with nightmares. She learned to pay attention when her grandfather lectured her about their great family, and to feel very big when he told her how the family's future depended on her.

And perhaps, if she'd been an easy-natured child, she might have skimmed along on this bright-surfaced life. She might have learned to be content with the magnificence and the self-importance and the surrogate affection.

But she was not a child of ease. From the beginning she was weighted with insecurities and possessed of a fierce intensity that magnified every emotion. And from the beginning, from the first moment that her eyes found theirs, she worshiped her parents.

Aubrey Van Lyden was her sun, golden fair and beaming with energy, quick to anger and enthusiasm and possessed of a scathing wit. Yvonne Van Lyden was her moon, silvery, distant, and beautiful, with an air of mystery that made the princesses in fairy tales pale by comparison. Like the gods of Greek mythology, they hovered over Juliana's life, beautiful faces over a crib, pleasing fragrances wafting through rooms, melodious voices in the darkness. But like the gods, they floated beyond her reach.

She was obsessed with them. She was forever searching for them through the big house, crawling, then toddling, then running ahead of her elderly nurse in hopes of finding them.

Juliana's nurse, Gittie, had been through this before with little ones who were overly infatuated with their parents. She had attended children since her teens, and she knew that some were slow to learn the rules that went with their privileged lives. But after forty years as a nurse she'd never seen a child quite so fixated or tenacious as this one.

The sight of her mother or father could send Juliana into uncontrollable fits, crying and clinging and even tearing at their clothes with the effort to hold on to them. And as she grew, the behavior grew worse rather than better. Her parents were bewildered and her grandfather was horrified. Finally Grandfather Edward Van Lyden ordered Gittie to punish every outburst with days or even weeks of nursery seclusion, and he instructed his son and daughter-in-law to be completely unavailable to the child after particularly bad displays.

By the time Juliana was four years old, her grandfather's method had broken her of the childish notion that her parents belonged to her. She was still battered inside by crashing waves of feeling and she still wanted her parents as much as ever, but she kept it hidden. She'd learned the rules. She'd learned to be good.

And this goodness was rewarded. Not with ice-cream cones or more life-size stuffed animals, but with the most valuable prize of all—her parents' attentions.

Her father took her to his basement shooting range and let her watch him shoot the pictures of snarling animals and mean-faced men. He invited her to the screening room to watch movies about bullfighting, and he showed her pictures of mountains and told her about a monster named Big Foot that lived there.

Her mother took her to the library to cut pictures from fashion magazines or to the garden to gather flowers, or sometimes, if Juliana was very lucky, up to her mother's private suite, where she could lounge on the drifts of ruffled bed pillows or try on jewelry or brush her mother's glistening dark hair.

She cherished her time with each of them equally, even though she had more fun with her mother, and the periods between the random invitations seemed endlessly long. She spent the empty days or weeks in a state of suspension, always listening and hopeful, always ready to drop what she was doing and run if they called.

When she was five her father decided to take her down to his gym with him one morning a week.

"Look at her," he said to Yvonne, "she gets no exercise."

A whole morning every week! Juliana was ecstatic.

He came for her at nine o'clock and led her down, down into the subbasement of Great House. She had never been down there with the boilers and storage rooms and she had never seen the huge mirrored gym with all its strange-looking equipment.

"This is my private place," her father said with a teasing gleam in his eye. "And everything that happens here is secret. Like being in a club. Do you want to be in my club?"

She nodded. She would have done anything to be in his club. Anything to see herself shine in his eyes.

He disappeared into the bath–dressing area and came out in one of the stretchy bikinis he favored for swimming. Then he told her to strip and he produced a miniature of the same bathing suit for her. When it was on he tucked all her hair up under a small baseball cap and turned her to face the mirror.

"You're ready for action," he said. "No one would ever guess you're a girl!"

Juliana stared at the reflection of her boyish self beside the muscular maleness of her father. Her limbs were like sticks compared to his. Her chest and shoulders narrow. And her own triangle of fabric was flat where his bulged.

A strange gust of emotions rocked her. She wanted to stare at her father in his bikini, but at the same time she was disturbed by the sight of him so bare beneath the harsh fluorescent lights. The differences between them were overwhelming ... almost threatening. And there was a deep ache inside her because she wanted so badly to puff out her chest and be as good as a boy— be all the things a boy stood for—but the scrawny body confronting her in the mirror made her feel more hollow and inadequate than ever before.

The rest of the morning slid into a miserable blur. She couldn't do the simplest exercise or lift the smallest weight without "No! No! Not that way!" or "Can't you follow instructions at all?" or "Don't you know your right from your left?"

The disappointment grew in her father's eyes and she knew that she was losing the chance she'd been given.

"I suppose you take after your mother," he said with a final dismissive shrug that told her there would be no more mornings in the gym for her.

"You look sick," Gittie declared when she was delivered back upstairs to the nursery.

The nurse insisted she lie down awhile, further confirming her weakness. Her father shook his head and walked out without a word.

It was then that Juliana's universe shifted. She continued to idolize her father, but she was left with that disturbing mirrored portrait of vibrant man and pathetic counterfeit boy, and the sense of failure that went with it. The sound of his voice filled her with anxiety as often as delight, and the slightest hint of expectation from him brought on attacks of painful clumsiness and reticence. From that day forward it was her mother's company she craved.

By the age of six Juliana was at once spoiled and deprived, childish and mature. She'd grown acutely perceptive and was attuned to every nuance of her mercurial parents' moods. She knew the undercurrents of trouble. She knew them as a six-year-old knows things—not with sets of facts like her humorless tutor drummed into her, but instinctually, with her stomach and her heart and the skin on the back of her neck.

She knew that her mother wanted to please her father but couldn't, and that her father displeased her grandfather on purpose. She knew that the adults' feelings for each other were as changeable as their feelings toward her. And she knew that her family was somehow vulnerable in spite of their big houses and the long line of ancestral portraits staring down from the walls.

She'd grown into a careful, watchful child with eyes that looked closer to thirty than to six, and she kept herself small and quiet in her parents' lives. She kept all the bad thoughts and the wildness locked away.

Within the walls and gardens of Great House Juliana could go for days without bothering her parents at all. She could hide in her secret places and play her games and tiptoe past the rooms they occupied without disturbing them or making them call for the nurse to come get her. And when she needed her mother, she could move softly, ever so softly, across the carpets and shining floors . . . she could be invisible in the big rooms full of big furniture . . . and she could creep up beside her mother's chair and sit on the floor while her mother read or listened to music. She could watch her mother breathe. She could fill herself with the scent of her mother's perfume and the whisper of her mother's silk clothing. And, if she was very lucky, her mother's trailing hand might absently reach her, resting lightly on the top of her head or stroking her hair, and Juliana could close her eyes and absorb the magic of her mother's touch.

She never wanted to creep in beside her father, which was just as well, because the same technique wouldn't have worked with him anyway. He always noticed her in a room immediately. "What's Jinxie up to?" he would call merrily, and then, regardless of her answer, he'd follow it up with, "Well, then, run along and play now. That's a good girl."

Though he would have hated to hear it, her father was just like her grandfather. Neither wanted her around unless she'd been specifically invited. Neither wanted to be with her except on his own terms. She might be included in something they had chosen to do, but they never let her have a choice or bothered themselves with her interests.

That was the way her grandfather arranged the playdate. He didn't ask her what she wanted or offer her a choice. Without any discussion he announced that he was hosting all his friends with granddaughters, and inviting them to bring the girls and their nursemaids along to meet Juliana. He hinted that the future could hold more of these playdates.

She was wildly excited that Saturday, darting back and forth between nursery and playroom as she waited for the girls to arrive. All six came. Daphne, Olivia, and Whitney first, followed by Kathryn, Caroline, and Alexandra.

They were all two to three years older than she and very proper in their velvet dresses when they said hello, but as soon as the nurses went down to the kitchen for tea, the atmosphere changed.

"Give me that!"

"No! I saw it first!"

They fought viciously over Juliana's toys, ignoring her completely. When the novelty of destruction and battle wore off, they settled down to cruelty.

"What babyish toys!"

"And what a stupid, boring room!"

"Don't you have a stereo in here?"

"My nurse says you don't go anywhere. They keep you hidden away in this house. What are you, some kind of freak or something?"

They all dissolved into fits of giggling.

Juliana swallowed hard and lifted her chin. "I go out with my grandfather."

"Oh, wow! She goes out with her grandfather!"

"I went on a cruise once with my grandfather," Olivia put in shyly.

"Shut up, Gabby. No one wants to hear about your cruise with your grandfather."

"We have a secret club." Daphne narrowed her eyes at Juliana. "But I don't know if we want any babyish freaks in it."

Juliana stared right back at her even though she felt very small and uncertain. There it was. Another secret club. She hadn't been admitted to her father's club, but maybe she could make it into this one.

"I'm not a freak. And I'm six. I'm no baby."

"Just forget her, Daffy," Whitney said, sounding bored with the whole thing.

"Yeah, forget her," Kathryn and Caroline chimed in. "Let's sneak around the house like you said we would, Daffy."

"Hold it. I'm the president and I say we have to find out if she's a freak or not."

Daffy advanced and Juliana retreated until she was backed into the wall.

Whitney walked to the window and stared out as though she'd lost interest. The others giggled hysterically.

"The only way to see if she's a freak is to take off her clothes," Daffy said.

An expectant hush settled over the room.

Juliana tried to distance herself. She tried not to feel the rough hands and the shoving as Daffy stripped her. She squeezed her eyes shut against the staring. Goose bumps rose on her arms and legs, and her cheeks burned.

"Guess she's not a freak after all," Daffy said. "Maybe they don't let her out of the house because she's like her mother."

The giggling erupted again.

"My stepmother says Mrs. Van Lyden isn't a real lady," Gabby said with wide eyes.

"See there. Even Gabby knows about your mother."

Juliana felt the tears start. She didn't think of herself as crying. The tears were just there.

"Your mother's from some Indian reservation out where people have dirty feet and don't use napkins." Daffy pushed her face close. "She's nobody. That's what your mother is . . . nobody!"

Juliana hit that leering face as hard as she could. She flew into it. And they fell and rolled together on the floor and Daffy started screaming and Juliana kept hitting her.

"Oh, my God!" . . . "What in heaven's name . . . ?" . . . "Jesus, Mary, and Joseph!"

The nurses swarmed in around them. Gittie yanked Juliana to her feet and dragged her out of the playroom and into the nursery.

"Get your clothes on and wait here," Gittie ordered.

The nurse's chest was heaving and her face was almost purple and her eyes were murderous. Juliana had never seen her that way.

It seemed like hours before the door opened and her parents and grandfather came in. Her mother stayed by the door and her father stationed himself next to the window. The center belonged to her grandfather.

"Is it true that Gittie caught you buck naked, attacking the Buchanan girl with your fists?"

Her grandfather filled the room. His fierce eyes bored into her and she cringed beneath the scorching weight of his anger.

"Answer me!" he thundered.

She stared at the floor and whispered, "Yes."

The storm that broke around her was frightening but easy to close herself to, just like the storms that rattled her windows. Only a few words registered. One was "shame." Because her grandfather kept using that word over and over again, saying how she'd shamed him.

Finally, after her grandfather was worn completely down, her father straightened from where he'd been leaning against the window frame. He cocked his head, studying her with a quizzical, almost approving look.

"Why'd you jump her, Jinxie? What set you off like that?"

Juliana looked up at her father and grandfather, but she couldn't meet her mother's eyes.

"They took off my clothes to see if I could be in the club," she said, "but then . . ." She sobbed once and swallowed hard to keep from crying. "Then they were saying things about Mama."

Complete silence. The adults seemed to freeze before her. Then, wordlessly, they slipped from the room.

The subject wasn't mentioned again, but her grandfather was suddenly very attentive to her, coming for her more often in his car and including her in more of his outings.

She was seldom allowed beyond the tall iron gates of Great House except in her grandfather's long silver car with the extra-thick glass and the big, silent men who rode in front and jumped out at every stop to shield her. Sometimes they pressed in so close to her that she thought she might be squashed. The men wore guns underneath their jackets, just like television characters.

Didn't those other girls have the same kind of men and the same rules from their grandfathers? Didn't they know that little girls from big houses couldn't go to parks or department stores or skating rinks or shows because there were bad men who would steal them from those kinds of places? Hadn't their grandfathers told them about the bad men?

She felt very big thinking that she knew something so important, something that those other girls were completely ignorant of. She might be younger than they, but her grandfather had told her all about the bad men. And about diseases too. Terrible diseases that children could catch from strange people.

The leaves were turning and the maids had put warm comforters on all the beds when her grandfather announced that their next day together would be a surprise trip. When he came for her he usually took her to Mignon, the smaller version of Great House that he lived in, and they would have lunch and look at the latest pieces in his art collection. Occasionally he took her driving and they lunched out. Either way, the outings were more duty than enjoyment. Surprises were different, though. Each of the surprise trips he'd taken her on had been wonderful and strange.

She let Gittie dress her in a scratchy dress and itchy tights without any complaint at all because she was so excited about the surprise. They went downstairs and Gittie took off her shoes and lowered her bulk onto a chaise in the solarium to rest. In just minutes she was snoring and Juliana tiptoed away.

It was hours and hours before her grandfather was expected. Hours and hours to wait. She kicked off her shoes and crawled into her special place beneath the desk in the library. The desk was very big and had a solid wood front that hid her. Sometimes she played tent or cave or house in it and sometimes she just curled up with a pillow and enjoyed the feeling of security and the smell of polished wood and leather bookbindings. She was so cozy and so busy guessing about the surprise that she didn't hear her name called at first.

"Juliana! Juliana, where are you?"

She knew it was Mrs. Greevy, the housekeeper, because Mrs. Greevy was the only one who pronounced her name Jul-*yah*-na like her grandfather did. The others called her a blend of things that sounded more like Juli-anna.

Huddling in her spot, she debated whether to answer or not.

"Juliana!" The irritated voice came closer and then faded as the woman passed the open library door. "Where are you, girl! Your parents want you at breakfast."

Her parents wanted her! She was so thrilled that she almost jumped right out from her hiding place. Bumping her head on the wood brought her back to her senses, and she waited till the voice was far away. It would be a disaster if anyone ever saw her emerging from her special place, or even from the library. She would never be able to hide there again if that happened.

She crept out of the library and into the glass-walled solarium, past Gittie and the plant jungle and into a hall. She hesitated at the ballroom, considering whether to go the long way and give herself an excuse to slide across the polished floor. Sometimes, when her parents were both out and no one was looking, she pretended she was a famous ice skater. With the chandeliers blazing on their highest setting, she would glide and spin, imagining herself as graceful as Sonja Henie in the old movies Gittie loved.

Quickly Juliana decided against the ballroom and zigzagged through the sculpture hall instead. The marble faces stared down at her blankly.

"Not now," she called to them as she raced by.

She usually stopped to chat with her favorites or bring them tea. On holidays, either real or invented, she would entertain them. She brought piles of shawls and hats down to dress them up, and she arranged her dolls to keep them company. They'd had some grand parties together and she'd promised them another soon. But not today. Not now. Without slowing her stride, she burst through the heavy gilt doors into the morning room.

Her parents were both seated.

Her father occupied the head of the table, a spot that was his only so long as her grandfather wasn't present. This morning Aubrey was dressed for riding in a jacket and open-necked shirt. His straight blond hair was combed damply back and his skin had a sun-kissed glow from recent days on the polo field.

Her mother sat on his left side, radiant in the palest silk. She was dressed well enough for a luncheon or theater engagement, but this was the way she always dressed. From the sleek Dutch-boy cut of her dark hair to the handmade perfection of her shoes, she always looked to Juliana like one of the fashion-magazine covers, regardless of the time of day.

Both adults were startled when Juliana burst into the room. Aubrey laid down the *Times* section he was reading and Yvonne put her teacup back in its saucer, and together they stared at their daughter for long silent moments.

"You wanted me?" the child asked timidly. She knew she'd made a big mistake by letting her excitement spill out.

"Yes," Yvonne said softly. "But you're—"

"Look at you!" Aubrey cut in. "You look as though you've just come in out of the bush . . . And where are your shoes?"

Juliana stared down at her feet and wiggled her toes inside her white tights. By damn! She had left her shoes in the library. If they were found there by a servant, her hiding place would be blown for sure.

"Come here, dear," Yvonne said.

Slowly Juliana padded around the table.

"Let's smooth you out a little, shall we?" Her mother's slender fingers with their perfectly shaped nails and heavy weight of jewels combed through Juliana's tangled hair. "There, now," she said, resecuring the headband and straightening the lace collar of Juliana's dress. "I think you're presentable."

Juliana could smell her perfume and see the faint smudge of eye shadow above her mother's dark almond-shaped eyes. She was the most beautiful woman in the entire world.

Yvonne looked toward Aubrey for approval, but he only snorted through his nose and picked up the newspaper again. "This was your idea," he said in a tone that separated him from whatever happened.

Yvonne's expression was wounded for an instant, but she quickly composed herself and focused on Juliana. "How would you like to join us for breakfast a few mornings a week?" she asked. "I think six is old enough to understand manners and polite table behavior, don't you?"

Juliana nodded eagerly, causing tendrils of hair to fall down over her eyes again. She hated her hair. It was flyaway fine and stuck out all over. And it was neither the streaky gold of her father's hair nor the gleaming black of her mother's, but a nondescript shade of light brown.

Yvonne patiently smoothed the escaping hair back under the headband and nodded toward the empty place set directly across the table at Aubrey's right. Juliana slipped around the table and into her seat as unobtrusively as possible. She'd already had oatmeal at her small table in the nursery, but she didn't say that.

"Grandfather says I have very good manners at lunch now," she whispered to her mother as she carefully unfolded her napkin.

Yvonne made a slight motion with her hand and suddenly there was a parade of servants streaming through the door with fresh-squeezed juice and fragrant breads and small silver bowls of preserves. This was followed by Virginia ham and shirred eggs and pancakes and two kinds of melon—far more food than they could ever hope to eat. But Juliana knew that the remainder would go back to the kitchen and appear on the servants' breakfast table.

"What is this country coming to!" Aubrey slammed the paper down, spilling his juice. Two servants jumped in to clean up the mess, but he ignored them and continued his tirade. "Protests, peace marches, mewling politicians ... Do you realize we have less than four hundred thousand fighting men left in Vietnam? And all because the cowards in this country have managed to capture the media."

Yvonne bowed her head and nibbled gracefully on a slice of dry toast.

"By God, Frank Fielding may be a maniac, but I still say he's the one with the right idea. Get in there and get our hands dirty. Show what Americans are made of."

"Bree ..." Yvonne warned. She glanced at her husband and then across at Juliana.

Juliana was listening intently while pretending interest in her food. Frank Fielding was a taboo subject. He was the man who had married Aunt Grace and taken her away and caused her to be disinherited. This was all before Juliana's birth, and she had never seen her lost aunt or the terrible Frank or her boy cousin, but any mention of them fascinated her just the same.

"I know, I know," Aubrey said, "my father would be incensed if he heard me say such a thing ... but by damn, Frank's got a uniform and a gun and he's out there doing something. Frank Fielding is showing the whole world what a real man's made of, and I think this family ought to give him some credit."

"Bree, please!" Yvonne glanced at Juliana as if telegraphing a warning to her husband.

"I won't tell Grandfather," Juliana promised quickly.

Aubrey chuckled. "You're a little trooper, aren't you, Jinxie?"

"This isn't a game," Yvonne said. "Frank Fielding has caused much grief in this family, Juliana. And I don't want you to think that we take it lightly."

"Yes, Mama."

They ate in silence for several minutes and Aubrey again picked up his newspaper. "Here's a fellow caught a thousand-sixty-one-pound mako shark off New Zealand. What do you think of that, Jinxie? How would you like your papa to take you fishing for something big like that one of these days?"

"Oh, yes, Papa ... but I think I'd rather do the elephant rides or the tiger hunt or the whale spotting first."

Aubrey frowned. "You've got quite a list there, young lady."

"You've made a lot of promises," Yvonne reminded him with the barest hint of sarcasm.

"Well, then. We'll just have to do all those things, won't we? One of these days we'll just strike right out. Never mind what your grandfather says ... we'll just strike out on our own, won't we?"

Juliana nodded.

"Besides"—Aubrey winked at his daughter and beamed one of his mischievous looks at her—"your grandfather is already so furious with your mother that we couldn't make him much madder if we tried."

Yvonne didn't redden like Aubrey when she was angry or embarrassed, but Juliana didn't need to see a flush to tell when her mother was upset.

"I wish you wouldn't keep bringing that up," Yvonne said in as harsh a tone as she ever used with her husband. "It was a mistake. I didn't know I was signing a magazine release. I thought I was giving the photographer permission to use the portrait in his show. That's all. Just his show. Can't everyone accept that? Do you think I wanted our picture on newsstands?"

Yvonne's voice shook and the tremor carried like a shock wave through Juliana's system. It was rare to see her mother so openly upset.

Though she hadn't been privy to the heated discussions and no one had bothered to fill her in, Juliana's radar had picked up the ongoing story. Her mother had hired a photographer to make a portrait of them as a surprise for her grandfather's birthday. Edward had been pleased ... until the picture turned up in a magazine. Edward Van Lyden detested the media and had an old-world view of publicity as distasteful, but it was more than that:

ever since Juliana's birth he had fiercely shielded his granddaughter from the public eye, and now she was suddenly exposed to all.

Edward was beside himself. He saw Yvonne's error as a complete betrayal, and all the years that his daughter-in-law had bowed to his wishes and catered to his eccentricities and worked so hard to fit in and be an old-line blue-blood New Yorker instead of an oil-rich half-blood Indian from Oklahoma—all those years suddenly counted for nothing.

"Well"—Aubrey's mouth and eyes sharpened with the sarcastic amusement that was so characteristic of him—"I think you deserve a rousing cheer for shaking Edward up, my sweet, but your method certainly makes it all the more impossible to get Jinxie out. Father's convinced that picture went straight onto every criminal's bulletin board."

He grinned playfully at Juliana. "Most-wanted kid in America, huh Jinxie?"

Juliana looked back and forth between her parents in an effort to follow their moods. Were they fighting or was everything fine now? Did they hate her? Were they sorry they'd invited her for breakfast?

Her father's grin faded when she didn't respond to his teasing. He sighed, shook his head, and resumed reading the paper. The table was cleared and a silver coffee service appeared on the sideboard.

"Bree . . ." Yvonne said hesitantly.

"Yes," Aubrey answered, but he kept his eyes on the newspaper.

"About this weekend. Since the Marburys' dinner dance is Saturday night, I thought—"

"Dinner dance? You can't be serious?"

Yvonne stared down into her coffee cup.

Aubrey smiled and laid the paper aside. "I've made other plans, anyway. I'm taking a group of fellows up to Elysia for a little fishing and some card playing. You're included too, of course, if you'd care to tag along."

"But the Marburys . . ." Yvonne said quietly. "We've had that invitation such a long time. We replied months ago."

Aubrey knit his brows and studied his wife. "Why would you want to go?" he asked. "It will be the same old dull business and you'll come away from it feeling that all the women have snubbed you. I thought we'd agreed we wouldn't do these sorts of things anymore."

Yvonne sat very still.

"Didn't we? Didn't we agree we were through with all that?"

"Yes," Yvonne whispered. "But I didn't take that to mean we would never go out together again. I didn't take that to mean I would be abandoned—"

Aubrey cleared his throat and glanced around at the servants to remind her that they were not alone, and once again Juliana felt her mother's embarrassment.

"Just send the Marburys an apology and a barrel of truffles or whatever." Aubrey smiled sympathetically. "And you really are invited to the country if you'd like to come along. I'm sure the boys would be amused by your poker strategies."

Before Yvonne could answer, the butler stepped quietly through the side doors.

"Mr. Van Lyden is here for Miss Juliana," he announced.

"Thank you, Westlake," Yvonne said. "She's ready."

Juliana slipped carefully from her chair. Her parents seemed so intent on each other that she was afraid to interrupt with good-byes. She quietly followed Westlake from the room.

"Have a lovely day," her mother called absently as the heavy door closed.

Juliana hesitated. The two big stone-faced men that her grand-father had sent in to fetch her filled the hallway and took up all the air. She hated having them come for her, but ever since the infamous magazine picture had appeared, her grandfather re-fused to come inside Great House to get her. He waited in the car when he picked her up. This was part of Yvonne's punish-ment.

"Good morning, Da Da," Juliana said as she kissed his smooth-shaven cheek. There was a tiny yellow rosebud in his lapel and she could smell the delicate sweetness of it.

He accepted the kiss and they settled silently into their usual places on either end of the long leather seat.

Edward Van Lyden was a member of a unique American ar-istocracy. He dressed impeccably, had regal manners and bearing, shunned publicity, and lived on a fortune that he hadn't earned and couldn't understand without an army of advisers. Most of his energy was devoted to his exclusive men's club and the proper spending of money—which in Edward's case was the ruthless building of an important art collection that would bear his name. His father before him had lived a similar life. But in the murky Van Lyden past were unscrupulous, hard-living men—men who had made the fortune and built the houses and hadn't had the time or inclination to behave as highborn gentlemen. And as for the Van Lyden family's future ... Edward's kind appeared doomed to extinction.

To Juliana, Edward was a puzzle. She couldn't read him like she read her parents, and her stomach hurt sometimes from trying to figure out what he wanted from her. She knew he wished she was a boy, yet he scolded her if she was rambunctious, ordering her to "behave like a well-bred lady." She knew he wanted her to be silent unless spoken to, but if she made herself too small and quiet, like with her parents, he accused her of being timid and said he wanted to see some spirit. Above all he wanted her to be smart, but she wasn't quite sure what to be smart about.

The car hummed through the streets of Manhattan and down into a long tunnel. Juliana wanted badly to ask where they were going.

"There's a special auction next week," Edward said. "Would you like to go with me?"

"Yes, please," Juliana replied, though in truth she found the auctions confusing and dull and had no interest in his obsessive pursuit of art.

"Very well, I'll arrange it. And perhaps we'll lunch out together afterward. Would you like that?"

No, she wouldn't. She hated sitting in quiet rooms surrounded by empty tables and hovering waiters, and she hated having to work so hard on manners and being still and figuring out what her grandfather wanted, all at the same time. Maybe it would be all right if they'd get to eat in the main part of the restaurant, where she could watch all the people. But that wasn't safe. Her grandfather always arranged private rooms to protect her from the bad men and the germs and the reporters.

"Yes, I'd like to have lunch with you, Da Da."

"Good. That's settled. Now, I suppose you're wondering what the surprise is today." He cleared his throat and fixed his pale blue eyes on her. "It is very special. An experience I remember fondly from my own childhood."

Juliana waited for more, but instead he changed the subject. "You may now tell me what you're learning from that tutor of yours."

Sometime later they arrived at a very large building with a big empty parking lot. She went inside with Edward and the two bodyguards and the driver.

Her eyes adjusted from the bright sunshine and she gasped at the cavernous interior that opened up before her. She'd never seen anything like this yawning space filled with dusty light and zoo smells. The ceiling was as tall as the sky and the floor was a huge oval studded with an odd assortment of poles and wires and curbed rings.

It looked like pictures she'd seen of . . .

She looked up at her grandfather, questioning whether to believe her eyes or not. His expression was merry, but he didn't speak. Instead he motioned the bodyguards forward and they led the way down steps, past rows and rows of empty seats, to the very center front.

As soon as they were seated, the arena darkened. Then suddenly there was an explosion of spotlights and music, and it was exactly what she'd thought it was! The circus!

She sat amidst the thousands of empty seats and feasted on the glitter and the beautiful performers and the animals and the silly clowns, and for a while the magic took her. For that brief window of time she was outside Juliana. She was not the hungry child or the nervous child or the silent, wary child. She was not the sole heir to the Van Lyden fortune. She was free.

4

Ellis

Somewhere between the worlds of Lucy Clare and Juliana Van Lyden lived another child of chance, a boy named Ellis Fielding. At nine years old, Ellis was a calm child, with an insatiable appetite for learning and an inborn sense of the possible and the impossible.

That was why he was hiding quietly in the bushes while two bullies gleefully shredded his book *The Modern Ant Farm*. He knew he couldn't possibly rescue the book from those boys, and he knew that trying would only earn him a mudball in the face.

Ellis was a natural for bullying. He was twig-skinny, with wide eyes peering from behind corrective glasses that wouldn't stay on his nose. His mother made him wear clothes she ordered from stores in New York City, making him the laughingstock of Fort Bragg, North Carolina, in his coordinated outfits. And instead of Fred the barber, his mother took him to a lady stylist who insisted on a perfect part that required tons of sweet-smelling goo to stay in place each day.

Grace Fielding was a devoted mother but she didn't understand the social dynamics of elementary school. She'd never attended a public school herself and she couldn't see how unacceptable Ellis was to his peers. But even if she had understood, the problems might not have been solved by regular clothes and regular hair. The fact was that Ellis didn't fit in with the other boys. While they played war, he flew kites. While they picked fights, he collected ants for his ant farm. While they tried to outbrag each other over their fathers' latest military exploits, he looked at slides under his new microscope.

Ellis knew that he didn't fit in and he'd always pretended that it didn't matter. He'd pretended that he didn't notice being the last choice for teams during gym class and the one who was excluded from recess play. He'd pretended that he wanted to be left alone. And eventually that pretending had come true. He preferred keeping to himself.

He could run up and down the creek being a cowboy on a white horse or he could sprawl on the fragrant needles beneath a stand of pine and let an exciting book take him away or he could concoct weird science projects. And if he ever ran out of inspiration, Grace was never too busy to make up songs on the piano with him or shape wet clay or set up her easel so he could paint.

Sometimes his father tried to do things with him too—things like teaching him the best volleyball serve or swimming laps against the clock or rocketing a football into his stomach so he'd learn to play tough—but Ellis dreaded those activities. The sessions always ended with his father disgusted at him because whenever he tried to perform for his father he suddenly became clumsy and stupid. And then his father would drag him home, muttering and cursing about how his own son had been turned into a "wet-nosed candy-assed mama's boy."

Ellis had memories of his father smiling affectionately and swinging him up to ride on sturdy shoulders above the crowd and calling him Bird, which was short for Bird Colonel. He had memories of his father laughing with his mother, too. But those memories had no connection to his father today.

This father was grouchy and hair-triggered. He stormed in the door each night with his jaw set and his eyes searching for trouble. During dinner, when his father recounted his day, it was one story after another about the stupidity of his superiors and the idiocy of his inferiors. Ellis had learned to sit quietly through dinners, trying to be as inconspicuous as possible, but his mother foolishly tried to respond to his father's diatribes.

She would say things like "Aren't you being awfully hard on him?" or "What if you just had a talk with him?" or, worst of all, "Maybe you'd be happier doing something else, Frank." His father usually exploded by dessert, but if he did make it all the way through the whole dinner, that just meant the explosion would occur after Ellis went to bed. Sometimes Ellis lay awake and listened to the nighttime fireworks.

The first spark might be as small as his mother commenting on the landlord's refusal to fix the toilet again. That could set his father off cursing the landlord and calling his mother a nag, and his mother would cry and say that a husband was supposed to be concerned about problems like the toilet and if they didn't live in such a shabby rental there wouldn't be so many problems. Then the explosion happened.

Ellis was both frightened and awed by the power of his father's explosions. They were fueled by a force that was as pure and uncontrollable as the hurricanes that struck the Carolina coast. If Ellis was in the room, he crept away when the storm struck. If he was in bed, he usually covered his head with his pillow. He still heard things, though. Things about how the Van Lydens were spleenless no-accounts with contaminated blood. Blood so tainted that it had destroyed the strong Fielding genes and spawned a weak sissy boy after generations of proud military men.

He'd heard his father call his mother ugly names and he'd heard his father accuse his mother of stalling his career by not being a good military wife. He'd heard his mother scream about how much she hated North Carolina and Fort Bragg and he'd heard her sobbing about how she never wanted to be a military wife.

The fights had seemed to be escalating in intensity. Then, just the night before, Frank had come home late after Ellis was already in bed. Ellis heard him stumbling around and slurring his words. He heard the plate of reheated dinner shatter against the kitchen wall.

"What was that for?" his mother cried.

"That was for all the pig swill you've ever fed me."

"So my cooking's suddenly not good enough?"

"It's never been good enough. I should have known when you couldn't make a damn hamburger in college that spoiled rich bitches never learn to cook."

"How would you know what good food is? Your ignorant mother raised you on brown sugar and lard."

"Don't you bring my mother into this!"

"Oh, yes, your dear sainted mother who abandoned you because she couldn't stand that stone-faced arrogant father of yours."

"You castrating bitch!"

There were low noises. Scufflings and bangings. Then silence. Then his mother's crying.

"You push me too far, Grace. Why do you push me so far?"

"You can eat in the officers' club from now on! I'm not feeding you."

"I can't go in there." His father's voice broke into horrible drunken sobs. "Everybody would . . . Everybody knows."

"Knows what? Frank! What's wrong?"

"I've been passed over. No promotion. Know what that means? It means I'm finished. Washed up. Once they pass you over, that's it."

"Oh, Frank ... Frank ... Frank. Come here. You're not finished. What do you need this life for? Forget it. Forget your father's dreams. You can be anything. You can go into forestry like you always wanted to."

Frank's hoarse sobs continued and Ellis knew that his mother was holding his father the same way she held him.

"Come on. Let's get you to bed. We'll talk about this tomorrow when you feel better. This might be the best thing for us, Frank. It could be a whole new start."

Ellis had never heard a fight end like that, with his mother consoling and hopeful and his father doing the crying. And there'd been an odd finality to it, as if it were the grand climax toward which all the smaller conflicts had been leading.

Maybe there wouldn't be any more fights. Maybe his parents would go back to the way things used to be. A whole new start— wasn't that what his mother had said?

That's what Ellis was thinking about as he crawled out from under the bushes and started home. The mini-terrorists were gone. The tattered remnants of his book were gone too. He would have to tell his mother, and she would pay the library. She never got mad at him about things like that, though. In fact she rarely ever got mad at him for anything. All her anger was saved for his father.

But maybe that was over now. Maybe their house would be happy again with this new start.

Ellis didn't have long to wonder. The shouting hit him as soon as he opened the back door. He stood for a moment, bleakly considering whether to head to his room or stay outside. What was going on, anyway? His father was never home in the middle of the afternoon. Was this what the new start meant—that they could fight in the middle of the day too? He sighed and tiptoed through the kitchen toward his room.

It took several minutes for the ominously different tone of this fight to register with him. His mother was the one who was out of control and shouting wildly. His father's voice was loud but strangely cool. If there was any emotion in it at all, it was pleasure, gloating almost, as if he'd won some monumental victory over her.

"This is not a discussion, Grace. This is an advisement. I am leaving in three weeks. I suggest you plan accordingly."

"Why? Tell me why! You didn't have to do it. No one asked you to do it. Just because you didn't get the promotion this time, that doesn't—"

"Enough! I am a fighting man. From a long proud line of fighting men. I have sworn to protect and preserve this great country and keep it safe. This war needs men like me. Men with guts. That's what's wrong with it. That's why it's going sour—too many sniveling spoiled kids and not enough real fighting men."

"So you're abandoning us! You're leaving us to run off and play war. Who's going to take care of us?" Grace's voice rose hysterically. "What are we going to do?"

"That's your problem, isn't it?"

The front door slammed and Ellis knew his father was gone. His mother's grief-stricken wails sent shivers up his spine. He learned later that his father had volunteered to go to Vietnam.

Ellis knew that he should feel sad about his father's leaving, but he didn't. He shook his father's hand and said good-bye with a great sense of relief. There would be peace and safety in his home now. His father's terrible rages would devastate some other part of the world. Not for a moment was Ellis worried for his father's safety, for to him Frank was too fearsome and invincible to be touched by a mere war.

After his father had been gone a few weeks, his mother announced that she refused to spend her time alone anywhere near a military base. She intended to find them a new home away from Fort Bragg. And she intended to use her forbidden trust fund so that she could buy instead of rent. The move and the tapping of the long-ignored trust were acts of rebellion that Ellis understood. And although she had waited till Frank was safely overseas before revealing her intentions, the fact that she had the courage to propose such a plan at all was astonishing.

Ellis was ecstatic over the thought of a new environment. He was adept at ignoring the bullies and braggarts and miniature sergeants who hounded him, but the prospect of complete freedom was sweet indeed. He began to hope for a more ordinary life, a life filled with kids and parents like he saw on television.

His days shimmered with excitement. And in the middle of all the excitement, something amazing happened. They received an invitation from New York. His Grandfather Van Lyden wanted them to come visit while Frank was gone. Ellis had never met his grandfather or his Uncle Aubrey or Aunt Yvonne or little cousin, Juliana. For a long time he hadn't even known they existed. But after the fighting started between his parents, his mother had started telling him secrets. And some of the secrets were about her family and the big houses they lived in and how she'd run away and married Frank Fielding because she didn't want to live with them in New York.

He was angry and disappointed when his mother declined the invitation. She used the excuse that they were moving immediately and didn't have the time for a trip, but he could tell she was afraid to go.

Ellis forgot his disappointment once they were settled into the Fayetteville house. He had a big room and a terrific yard and a great new school. His mother enrolled in classes too at the state university and in the evenings they did their homework together. On weekends they ate pizza and listened to the stereo or took in a movie or attended the occasional concert that the town offered. Ellis developed a passion for music that his mother actively encouraged. His biggest trauma came when he realized she wouldn't let him take violin and piano lessons simultaneously.

They received no more invitations from New York. But every few weeks a letter would come from his father. The letters were full of battles and heroics and the philosophy of war, but somehow, when his mother read them aloud, she endowed them with an affectionate tone.

Ellis gradually lost all recollection of the reality of his father. By the end of a year's passing the strong uniformed presence in the picture on the mantel became a fantasy figure for Ellis. His father was a hero. His father was everything Ellis wished him to be. His mother joined in this fantasy and encouraged it, and together they missed a father and husband who existed only in their imaginations.

Ellis was ten and a half years old when his father wrote and invited them to join him in Hawaii. Ellis was so excited that he couldn't eat or sleep or do his homework. His mother's sudden nervousness meant nothing to him. He was going to a fairy-tale place of palm trees and hula dancing to see the father he'd created in his dreams, and he attached no significance to the shadow of terror that crept into his mother's eyes.

She drank three gin and tonics as soon as their flight was airborne.

"Are you sure he's going to be there?" Ellis asked again and again as they flew over the sparkling ocean.

"Yes. He arrived last night on a military transport," she explained the first few times. Then, as the question grew tiresome for her, she simply answered, "Yes."

"Will he still know us?" "Will he recognize us?" "Will he have his medals on?" "Will he stay with us in the hotel?" "Will he go swimming with me?"

"Yes." "Yes." "Yes." "Yes." "Yes."

Ellis stepped out of the aircraft into diamond-bright sunshine. He shaded his eyes with his hand and squinted. A man in a uniform waved to him stiffly. He sprinted down the portable stairs with his mother calling, "Wait!" behind him. He raced across the tarmac, ignoring the Hawaiian ladies with the flower leis, and he didn't stop until he stood directly in front of his father.

Frank was taller and leaner and harder than the picture on the mantel. And his eyes had developed a flinty look that wasn't present in the old photograph.

"Stand tall, son," Frank said with a solemn salute. He was rigid and so imposing that Ellis was filled with awe.

His mother arrived breathlessly.

"Frank . . ." she said. Her voice had hairline cracks in it.

She took a small step closer, as though she might attempt to hug him, but then she stopped herself. Her shoulders sagged and she focused on her purse and the tickets and the wad of tissue in her hand.

Frank pivoted on his heel briskly. "First things first," he said. "It's baggage detail for this platoon."

Their hotel was luxurious and boasted a huge pool and a magnificent view of the ocean. Ellis had trouble keeping his mouth closed and his neck from swiveling wildly as he followed his parents to their room. At the door Frank handed Ellis the key and insisted he do the honors.

While Ellis was fumbling with the lock, Frank grabbed Grace and tried to pick her up. The attempt was a clumsy failure and both adults looked uncomfortable.

"What are you doing, Frank?" Grace asked nervously.

"Carrying you across the threshold . . . what else?"

"You didn't do that for our wedding night."

"I'm doing it now."

He made another try and this time swept her off her feet. She didn't protest, but she still didn't look happy. He took a step and she clung to his neck reluctantly.

Ellis swung the door open wide and hurried inside. His parents' performance in the hall made him uneasy and he felt a twinge of jealousy.

"To the victor go the spoils!" his father shouted, and charged wildly into the room. He crashed into a chair and both adults landed in a pile on the thick carpeting.

Ellis was surprised by the display and worried about his mother's reaction, but she laughed as she picked herself up, shaking her head in an exasperated, indulgent way that reassured Ellis even though it shut him out. This was adult play. These were games he was unfamiliar with and it was obvious that he wasn't included.

He consoled himself by wandering through the three-room suite, but he could not help but be aware of his parents' conversation. It was light and careful at first. Then it began to edge into dangerous territory. He had shut away the bad memories so effectively that he had no sense of the deteriorating scene as familiar; instead he was gripped with an eerie feeling of déjà vu.

"Frank, we need to talk ... privately," he heard his mother whisper. He knew she was referring to his presence.

There was pleading and desperation in that whisper.

His father responded by launching himself from the couch and calling, "Anybody hungry?" in Ellis' direction.

Ellis started to say yes. He was hungry all the time since a recent growth spurt had stretched him upward.

"No. We had dinner on the plane," his mother said quickly.

She caught his eye and he could tell that she wanted him to agree. He could tell that she wanted him to cooperate with her and be on her side like always, but his father's larger-than-life presence was all that mattered.

"All right, then, how about we all go downstairs for one of those pussy drinks with the fruit salad in it?"

"Yeah, yeah! Pussy drinks!" Ellis shouted. He raced across the room and recklessly jumped onto a chair, astonishing both himself and his parents.

"I won't have that kind of language," Grace said, leveling the accusation at Frank rather than her son.

"Shape up, soldier," his father ordered sharply. "And get your shoes off the furniture."

"This is serious, Frank. We have to talk alone." His mother wasn't bothering to whisper now.

"Grace ..." Frank said as though he was running out of patience. He grinned at Ellis. "We can't ignore the boy or leave him shut up in his room on his first night of R-and-R, can we?"

His mother sighed and gathered her purse, but there were tight frown lines around her eyes. His father winked at him, then opened the door and ushered them out in a sweeping gesture.

Ellis was fascinated by the giant lighted aquariums in the bar. He sucked on the speared fruit from the drink his father had called a screwless driver and pressed his face to the side of the aquarium flanking their table. The fish skittered away from him.

His parents engaged in careful dull talk awhile, and then his mother mentioned Fayetteville.

"I don't recall wanting to live in Fayetteville," Frank said. His brows nearly touched and his eyes burned. "And I sure as hell didn't buy a house there. Or anywhere else."

"Oh, but you're going to like it, Frank. I know you're—"

"I don't want to hear this shit, Grace. By the time I get home I want this Fayetteville nonsense over and done. I want the house sold and all that dirty Van Lyden money back in its hole and you back in the town where I left you."

He chugged down his drink and waved to the waitress.

"Bring me two more, honey. On the double, huh?"

His silence engulfed them, and only after he'd finished both new drinks and ordered another did he speak again.

"This war's out of control," he said. "And those fairy-ass politicians in Washington know it but they aren't doing a damn thing. Not a damn thing." He fixed Ellis with a fierce look, then sighed and tipped up his glass. "Never thought I'd hear myself say it, but I'm glad my son isn't serving in this mess."

Ellis was transfixed. He wanted to ask his father a hundred questions about the war and about being a hero and about what a fairy-ass was.

"Did you—?" he started to say, but his mother glared at him sharply and cut him off with, "We're in Hawaii and we haven't even seen the beach yet!"

The moon was huge and white hanging over the ocean and there were so many stars that it didn't seem like nighttime at all. Ellis took off his shoes and dug his toes into the clean, sugary sand. He wished he could scream and shout and race up and down the beach, but he was afraid to disturb his parents' quiet mood. He trailed along silently, contenting himself with kicking little plumes of sand and making tracks and patterns in the smooth, pale surface.

When they arrived back at the suite his mother insisted that Ellis bathe and go straight to bed. He mumbled a halfhearted complaint that dissolved mid-grumble under the force of a hard look from his father's flinty eyes. He got the bath over as quickly as possible and was grateful that his mother didn't come in to wash his ears or anything. He certainly didn't want his father to think he was still a helpless baby.

After he had crawled between the crisp sheets, his father came
in and perched on the edge of the bed.

"That's a good soldier," Frank said, reaching up to ruffle Ellis'
damp hair. "Now, tell me . . . what sports are you in at this new
school? What are you good at?"

"I'm not in any sports," Ellis admitted reluctantly. "I play kick-
ball in gym a lot . . . but I guess that's not a real sport."

"Why aren't you in any sports?" his father demanded.
"Couldn't you make the cut for any teams?"

"There aren't any teams. My school doesn't believe in having
teams and stuff, you know?"

"What kind of a school is that?"

Ellis shrugged. He loved his school, but he wasn't about to try
to defend anything against the force of his father's disapproval.
"I don't know," he said vaguely. "Mom put me in it."

Frank's face registered momentary disgust. Then he smiled
and ruffled Ellis' hair again. "You're a Fielding," he said. "You
have to be good at something. Tell me what it is." He winked.
"You're looking sharp now that you're rid of those damn glasses.
Maybe you're a ladies' man, huh?"

"I'm good at science and music," Ellis told him proudly.

Frank gave a sarcastic laugh. "Science and music, huh?" He
stood and stared down at Ellis a moment. "I won't let you down,
soldier," he said. "I'll make you a man. I promise." His voice was
startlingly full of emotion. He wheeled and left the room with his
back ramrod straight.

Ellis lay in the dark puzzling over his father's intense declaration and listening to the cadence of his parents' voices through
the closed door. Frank talked about the psychology of gooks and
dinks for a while, which was meaningless to Ellis, as he had no
idea what a gook or a dink was. His mother was trying to change
the subject and talk about her classes and the degree she wanted,
but his father kept pulling away from what she was saying. Without realizing he was tired, he drifted into dreamsleep.

"Please, Frank! I told you. I need some time to sort out my
feelings. It's been over a year since we've been together, and so
many things have changed! You can't just expect—"

At first Ellis thought the loud voice was part of his dream. But
the words didn't fit his dream and the voice was his mother's.

"Expect! I don't seem to be able to *expect* much from you, do
I? I can't expect you to stay in the home I made for you. I can't
expect you to raise my son to be a man. Now I can't even expect
you to behave like a normal, warm-blooded woman.

"What do you think I dream about in that stinking jungle . . . polite little conversations? Mealymouth nicy-nice bullshit? Hell, if you were a real wife you'd want what I want too. After all this time apart—"

"All this time apart! Whose fault was that, Frank? You're the one who had to volunteer in the first place. And this isn't your first break, is it? You could have seen us months ago, but no, you went to Bangkok instead!"

"You don't know what you want, do you, Grace? You're still the spoiled little trust-fund bitch who thinks she's better than everyone else."

"Frank, don't. You're hurting my wrist!"

"You're my wife, Grace. My wife! I think you've forgotten that while I've been gone. I think you need to be reminded."

"Please . . . Frank . . ."

"What? Speak up if you have something to say, wife."

"No. No, don't. Frank!"

"Don't ever push me away like that, *wife.*"

Ellis sat up in his bed and rubbed his eyes. He could hear his mother sobbing quietly now.

"It's that father of yours, isn't it? Edward's behind all this. As soon as he found out I was gone, he started poisoning your mind, didn't he? He's the one who talked you into using that fucking trust fund, isn't he? Tell me!"

"Please, Frank! Don't do that . . . Please! Just let me answer you! My father did ask to see us, but I didn't go . . . I didn't even speak to him . . . I promise, I—"

"I can't trust you anymore, can I, Gracie?" Frank's voice was falsely sweet now, and more frightening than when he was shouting.

"Grace's forgotten how to obey her husband, hasn't she? Grace's forgotten about her duties. Has Grace been fucking around too? Has Grace been riding cocks while her husband is off defending his country?"

"Oh, God, Frank . . ." Her words dissolved into sobbing. "How can you say that . . . how can you—?"

"I'm no fool! I don't have the money or the ass-licking skills of a Van Lyden, but I sure as hell know what's what in the world. And I know what lonely women go back to college for."

"No, Frank. Please . . . not like this . . . please. We need to talk. I've been . . . I've been thinking about us a lot. I've been thinking about how much we've both changed, and—"

"You're mine, Grace." The statement sounded like a threat.

"Stop it! You've had too much to drink. Maybe tomorrow we can . . . What? What are you—?"

"What's mine is mine. Nothing changes that. I've been waking up in the jungle with hard-ons over you."

"Don't! I'm begging you . . ."

Ellis climbed out of bed and padded silently to his door. A faint bar of light shone beneath it, but he couldn't see under it. He pressed his ear to the smooth wood and waited, wondering what to do—what his mother would want him to do.

He heard them moving, heard them banging into things. Was this another game they were playing? Was his mother really mad, or would she laugh soon?

"Scream and you'll wake up your little sissy boy," he heard his father say. Then there were no more sounds.

Ellis waited forever inside his room. The fantasy was shattered. Once again his father was the terrible giant that brought the storms and fear into his life.

Finally he could stand it no longer. He inched the door open a crack. The living room was empty. With a pounding heart he tiptoed out across the carpeting. The room was a mess and he stubbed his toe on an overturned table.

A faint noise came to him from the master bedroom. The door was ajar and a light was on inside. He eased carefully toward it. He was afraid of being punished by his father, but he was more afraid for his mother.

Ellis stood trembling before the door for several minutes before he gathered the courage to look. Quietly, with his heart in his throat, he stepped forward and peeked in. What he saw made his mouth go dry and his stomach twist.

His mother lay spread-eagle on the bed, naked except for a few shreds of torn underwear. Panty hose bound her wrists to the headboard posts and her ankles to the footboard. His father labored on top of her, bare skin gleaming with sweat. Steadily, brutally, his father's body slammed into his helpless mother.

In stunned disbelief Ellis pushed open the door and took a step inside. His movements made little sound against the rhythm of Frank's grunting. He stared at his father's body, at the sway of the hairy sweating scrotum and the clenched muscles in the lean buttocks. He stared at the thick base of the frighteningly large penis, visible each time Frank rose up to slam into his mother again.

His mother moaned softly like a wounded animal. She turned her head. Tears streamed from the corners of her eyes, but she couldn't cry out because a sock was stuffed into her mouth. When she saw Ellis standing in the doorway her eyes widened in terror.

His father's movements quickened into a frenzy and his grunting mixed with words. "Thawin' out? . . . Huh, bitch? You wanted it . . . wanted a cock, huh? Here it is. Take it, bitch! Take it!"

His mother continued to stare at Ellis in wild-eyed panic. He was certain she was sending him a message. He took another step forward and she shook her head ever so slightly. She pleaded desperately with her eyes and shook her head again. He suddenly knew that she wanted him to go. He retreated as quietly as he'd entered, pulling the door back to its original position. He stumbled to the bathroom and threw up until he thought his stomach would turn inside out.

He crawled back into his bed, shaking and weak, covered with a clammy sweat. He hated his father. He wished his father would return to the war and never come back. When he finally slept, he dreamed of battlefields littered with bleeding, torn corpses. He woke to lie in the dark, crying softly and shaking. Every corpse in his dream had his father's face.

5

"Ellis ... dear ... you've got a fever." He awoke to the touch of his mother's cool hand against his forehead.

Night memories flooded his senses and brought the burning sting of tears to his eyes. But he blinked away the tears quickly. His mother looked so normal, sitting on his bed in the gentle morning light with her hair tied back in a bright scarf.

He reached out to touch her, and the softness of her cotton sweater soothed him. The ugliness couldn't have been real. The bedroom scene must have been part of his horrible dreams.

"Frank," his mother called, "Ellis is pale and feverish. I think he's coming down with something."

His father appeared in the doorway, fully dressed and frowning. He scrutinized Ellis with unsympathetic eyes.

"So what about breakfast?" he asked.

"Why don't you go on ahead, Frank. Buy the paper and relax a little. I'll order from room service and then I'll call the desk about someone to come in and stay with Ellis ... so you and I can still have the day out together."

"Okay, okay," his father grumbled. He crossed the floor to ruffle Ellis' hair. "Get tough, soldier," he ordered, and frowned sternly.

His mother smiled with a brightness that seemed oddly off-key. And she winced as Frank reached out to pinch her cheek. The pinch left a momentary red mark.

"Feeling better this morning, aren't you?" Frank said. "See, I knew what you needed, didn't I?"

The suggestive tone made Ellis' skin crawl.

His mother smiled again. Her bottom lip quivered slightly.

"A-okay, then." Frank stiffened and moved toward the door.

Ellis watched his father leave the room and then shifted his puzzled gaze to his mother. She was sitting still as a statue, but her expression was alert and listening.

Ellis started to speak, but she put a finger to her lips. The solid thunk of the outer door echoed in the stillness.

"He's gone," she said with a rush of air that meant she'd been holding her breath.

She jumped up and threw the sheet off Ellis. "Get up and get dressed. Fast!"

She rushed out the door and he heard her talking on the phone in the living room. She was saying something about a flight.

Ellis slowly pulled on his pants. Something strange was going on, and he didn't like it. He was both irritated and afraid.

"Ellis! I said hurry!" his mother hissed from the doorway.

She seldom spoke to him so harshly, and it took him by surprise. Tears burned in his eyes and he blinked furiously, stopping all efforts to button his shirt. "But I really don't feel very good," he complained.

"Oh, Ellie, Ellie . . ." His mother rushed to him and hugged him tightly. "I'm sorry . . . how can I expect you to understand what's happening?"

She knelt, holding him at arm's length to make eye contact. His tears were under control now.

"I need your help, honey. I need you to be very grown-up right now." She paused and stroked his cheek with her fingertips. "Your father is . . . he isn't himself right now. He's . . ." She drew in a deep breath. "We can't stay here with him while he's like this. We . . ." She looked down and reddened slightly, as though ashamed. "We're running away, Ellis," she whispered.

This was something he could understand and agree with. "Good," he said firmly. He pulled away from her and quickly fastened his shirt. "Do we take our stuff?"

"Yes," she answered with a funny little smile. "We never even had to unpack, did we?"

His mother was edgy and pale going through the hotel lobby, and she looked like she might be sick during their taxi ride. Ellis held her hand. He felt very big and very brave in the face of her fear. She didn't improve until their plane had lifted off the runway; then she heaved a great cleansing sigh, let her head fall back limply against the headrest, and closed her eyes. Lines of tears streamed from the outer corners of her eyes.

"We made it, Mom. He can't catch us up here in the air."

His mother looked at him and started to laugh, but the tears didn't stop. If anything, they flowed more freely. Ellis searched her face with mounting concern.

She breathed deeply, smiled, and wiped her tears with the back of her hand. "It's hot in here. Why don't you fix the air vents?"

Ellis concentrated on the controls while his mother shrugged out of her cotton cardigan. When he had the air adjusted, he settled back and turned to grin at his mother. But his lips froze and a giant vise clamped down on his chest.

Her bare arms were covered with ugly bruises. Raw skin circled her wrists.

"Ellis?" She looked down at her arms, suddenly realizing what he was seeing.

He tore his gaze from the marks but couldn't meet her eyes.

"Oh, honey, I'm sorry," she said gently. "I didn't think . . ."

She began pulling the cardigan back on.

"It wasn't all a bad dream, was it?" Something was wrong with his throat and his voice sounded like he'd swallowed a frog.

"Yes," she said firmly. "That's exactly what it was—a bad dream. And now it's over, and we're going to forget about it."

He sat for a moment with his head down. Then he pulled a magazine from his seat pocket. "Feel the air now, Mom?" he asked, trying to sound very casual and very grown-up. "I turned it as high as it would go." He shrugged. "But it's still pretty warm in here. I think you'd probably feel better if you took that sweater off."

She looked up at him, her eyes so filled with love and gratitude that he felt his cheeks burn from embarrassment. He ducked his head, and when he glanced back up again there were more tears wetting her cheeks, but she was smiling.

Hours later they landed to change planes and his mother went straight to a pay phone. She gave him money and sent him to the gift shop so he wouldn't overhear the conversation, but as soon as she was finished she came and put her arm around him.

"I called your Grandfather Van Lyden," she said. "He's taking care of everything."

The Fayetteville house was stuffy and silent when they walked in the door.

"Let's open some windows, dear," his mother said. But she didn't help. She walked straight to the mantel, picked up his father's picture, and left the room with it. He never saw the picture again.

Nothing was the same from then on. There were new locks

and an alarm system and men from New York who lived in their spare room and escorted them everywhere. And there were endless trips to offices and several long sessions with a judge.

Finally his mother told him that it was over. She took him out for pizza without their armed escorts and she said, "We don't have to be afraid anymore. As of today your father no longer has a legal right to either of us."

"Does he know that?" Ellis asked.

"Yes. And he's far away from here, so you don't have to worry."

"Will we ever see him again?"

His mother fidgeted with her napkin a moment. "Why? Don't you think we can be happy on our own?"

"No! I mean yes! I don't want to see him anymore ever."

He'd thought she would be pleased by such a firm declaration of his being on her side, but she looked suddenly sad. "I loved your father very much when I married him . . ." Her voice broke and she struggled to continue. "How has it come to this? Whatever happened to us?"

She covered her face with her hands for what seemed a long time. Ellis waited. His mother's sadness made him hate his father all the more.

"Don't feel so bad . . . please, Mom. He never loved us anyway," Ellis said.

"Don't say that! Don't ever say that, because it's not true!"

Ellis was startled and a little hurt by her anger. He set his jaw to keep from crying.

"Your father wasn't always like he is now." She drew in a ragged breath. "When we met in college, he was studying forestry and he was set against a military career." She shook her head. "Then, right after we were married, his brother died." Bitter sarcasm crept into her voice. "And suddenly it was up to your father to carry on the Fielding tradition."

"You mean he wanted to be a forest ranger?" Ellis was amazed.

"Yes. He was crazy for the mountains. He was going to protect forests and I was going to grow vegetables and milk goats and weave my own cloth. We both wanted to escape our families and our pasts." She shook our head. "Sounds pretty silly now, I guess." She reached across the table to take his hand. "You're my best friend. My very best friend. And now we're a team. Just you and me. That's all that's important."

The pizza arrived steaming at their table and his mother busied herself with serving him a slice. They both burned their mouths on their first bites, and Ellis dissolved into laughter. His mother smiled with him.

"I'm sorry," she said, turning suddenly sober again. "You've been exposed to so many terrible things."

He shrugged and stared down at the pizza.

She reached out to touch his arm. "Nothing bad is ever going to happen again," she declared.

The next day a big black car pulled up into their driveway. Ellis ran to the window and leaned halfway out to stare. He'd never seen such a long car. The driver got out, and his clothing scared Ellis for a moment. The outfit looked like a military uniform. But then Ellis saw his mother running down the walk toward the car, so he knew everything was all right.

"I've brought some gifts for you, miss," the driver said.

"Oh . . ." Grace stopped. "You mean my father isn't . . . ?" She gestured toward the dark glass. "He didn't come?"

"No, miss." The driver handed Grace an envelope.

Ellis ran downstairs and out the door. The driver was lifting a candy-apple-red bicycle from the trunk. When he saw Ellis he smiled and said, "From your grandfather."

Ellis looked at his mother. She had a funny expression. "Go ahead," she said. "It's yours."

The bike had mirror chrome and a red finish deep enough to get lost in. Behind the seat was a miniature license plate with "ELLIS" in reflective letters. Ellis was dazzled. All this from a grandfather he'd never seen.

The driver handed over the bike and pulled out a large box.

"This is for you, miss," he said. "Should I carry it in?"

Ellis lost track of what his mother and the driver were doing. The gleaming bicycle grew, filling time and space. Carefully he toed the kickstand up and climbed onto the triangular seat.

Later, after the limousine and driver were gone, he parked the bike safely on the porch and went inside. The huge box lay open and empty on the floor. The letter lay next to it.

Dear daughter,
    Now that you are free, you must make the decision about how you want to live. I have forgiven the past.
    The bicycle is a gift for my grandson. I am sending the fur to replace those that you gave away during your protest phase. If your moral outrage still exceeds your need to be warm and

attractive, then by all means call the furrier and have it picked up.

    You know where I am.

Your father,
Edward Van Lyden

Ellis dropped the letter back to the floor and listened intently. He heard no movement or sound downstairs, so he went up to his mother's bedroom to look for her. The door was open. She was lying on her bed, holding the dark fur like a giant teddy bear, and crying softly.

He rushed to the side of the bed. "What's wrong? Why are you sad?"

She shook her head but wouldn't answer.

After a while he left her there and went back down to his bike. His mother appeared at dinnertime as though nothing had happened, and Ellis was afraid to ask about her crying. He was also afraid to ask when they were going to see his grandfather.

His mother was hesitant at first about letting Ellis venture off alone on his new bike, but he knew that he was big enough to keep from getting lost and he itched to explore on it.

"I'm eleven now, Mom. I'm not a baby anymore."

She sighed and gave him permission, but she stood at the door to watch him leave, with one hand pressed to her chest and the other covering her mouth.

The freedom was exhilarating. Ellis pedaled fast, enjoying the way he could create a wind hard enough to sting his eyes. He drank in the smell of morning air and the sight of a raccoon leading her babies across the road. But he didn't forget to keep track of the time, arriving home exactly when he promised, and he could tell by his mother's expression that he'd earned his wings.

One day he packed his lunch and his bird guide and his binoculars and asked to go out for the whole afternoon. His mother paused and frowned a little, but finally nodded. "Back by four!" she called as he bounded down the front steps. "Remember to look at your watch!"

He pedaled along the small road that snaked past his house, enjoying the warm morning sun and lazily planning which of the side roads he would cut off onto. He wasn't conscious of the car at all in the beginning. Then, when its existence registered, it was only as a safety concern—don't veer out in front of the car. He didn't think about why it was trailing so slowly behind him. He was too intent on his own pursuits.

The car finally passed him and disappeared around a bend in the road, leaving him completely to the warbling chorus of birds and the breeze stirring the trees. A beetle trundled down the road in front of him. He slowed and studied the creature, considering capture but deciding against it.

He picked up speed, pedaling hard around the hairpin curve and letting loose with a loud siren sound that startled a wave of birds into flight. He clamped his mouth shut when he saw the car again, embarrassed that his siren might have been heard. The car was parked on the right-hand shoulder, just on the other side of the blind curve.

He ducked his head and pedaled casually, charting his course around the obstruction. Just as he came alongside the vehicle, the driver's door snapped open. Ellis braked hard. His tires slid out from under him on the loose gravel of the shoulder and he went down hard on his hip.

A man's hands were on him instantly, pulling the bike off and helping him to stand.

"You all right, son? Nothing broken, I hope."

He heard the familiar voice and looked up into the flinty eyes and he nearly fainted. It was his father.

"Say, there, son. Your mother told me I'd find you out here. She thought you and me ought to have a visit."

It seemed very odd to Ellis that his mother wanted him to visit with his father. It seemed very odd that his father was here at all. Hadn't his grandfather fixed it so that Frank couldn't come near them? Hadn't Ellis' mother promised that he didn't have to see his father again?

He tried to make some sense of it, but Frank's shocking appearance and biting grip on his upper arm made Ellis' thoughts go around and around in confused circles.

"Get in the car, soldier," his father ordered, pushing him in through the open driver's door as he spoke.

As soon as he was inside, Frank slid in behind the wheel and started the car.

"But . . ." Ellis began feebly. "But, where—?"

Frank jammed the car into gear and roared away from the shoulder.

"My bike!" Ellis yelled, jumping and twisting in the seat to watch a cloud of grit envelop his treasured bicycle.

"Sit down," Frank ordered sharply.

"But my bike. Somebody will take my bike—"

"Forget it."

"No! No! I gotta go back! Lemme out!" Ellis cried. He clawed at the passenger door, but the handle was gone. He frantically worked at the window, but it wouldn't open. He pounded his fists against the door in desperation and sobbed.

"Shut up! Just shut up, sissy boy!"

Frank's voice stopped him cold. Absolute terror and bleak despair filled him as he turned to face his father. The veins stood out like cords on Frank's neck and flecks of spittle flew from his mouth. His hard-chipped eyes were wild.

"I've come to make a man out of you, boy. A man! Not some violin-playing candy-ass. No, sir." He snorted laughter. "No, sir. You're still mine, by God!"

Frank's voice faded into muttering and Ellis sagged down into the seat. He felt numb now. He watched the blur of landscape speeding by without actually seeing anything. A dull pulsing began in his brain, like the metronome on top of his piano, and he turned inward, focusing on his own rhythm and shutting out the rest of the world.

6

Juliana

Juliana controlled her urge to dart around the slow-moving body-guards and run across the tarmac to the waiting helicopter. Instead she plodded dutifully along with them until she reached the droning machine with the Vanden corporate logo. She turned to wave to her grandfather and Aunt Grace inside the limousine, then clambered aboard. Her mother and Gittie climbed in behind her.

It was June and Juliana was ten and her family was going to the country for the summer just as they always had. And Juliana fluttered inside with excitement because summer was the best time, the absolute best part of the entire year. Only this time her excitement was tainted somewhat by her father's absence and her mother's darkly fragile mood.

The past four years had been filled with trouble. It had started with Aunt Grace's arrival. A hysterical Aunt Grace. A wailing, screaming Aunt Grace who brought private detectives and frantic telephone calls. The house had been full of whispers and exchanged glances and discussions that Juliana wasn't allowed to hear, but of course she knew everything that went on. Aunt Grace had gotten rid of the terrible husband and started speaking to the family again, but then she'd suddenly lost her son. The cousin Juliana had never met was gone. The bad men had stolen him.

When Aunt Grace moved in, the delicate balance of their lives changed. Aunt Grace's presence overwhelmed Great House. The woman was either emotionally distraught and needing everyone's attention or she was frenetically reorganizing and revising the household, which, she reminded everyone, was as much hers as her brother Aubrey's. The discord was further fueled by Edward. With the black-sheep daughter's return to the fold and the campaign to find the missing boy, all of Edward's attention was focused on Great House. He became a daily presence at the head of the table.

Even to Juliana the house didn't seem quite so big anymore. There were loud voices and tensions and annoying disturbances everywhere. Her father stomped from room to room, saying he couldn't find any peace, and she knew exactly what he meant. But even so, she didn't understand why her father started leaving them. Why he stayed gone for evenings at first and then for whole nights and then for days at a time. Why he didn't care about her mother's pleading or her own tears.

Sometimes it seemed as though he was actually relieved when he was pushed far enough to walk out. When he could throw down his napkin or slam his hand against a wall and shout, "That's it! I don't have to live this way!" He'd shut them off then. Everyone. And he'd appear eager and almost cheery as he called for a car. As though he were embarking on some grand adventure rather than walking out on his family.

And each time the door closed behind him, Juliana asked herself how he could leave her and her mother behind. Didn't he miss them? Didn't he love them anymore?

She hated Aunt Grace, blaming her and her stupid missing son for everything. Not just the tensions and the arguments and her father's absences, but also her mother's obvious suffering. Whenever Aubrey was gone, her mother wandered about the house in a state of nervous distraction, wavering between sharp-tongued crossness and complete despondency.

But even as she silently cursed her aunt, Juliana had the gnawing deep-down fear that Aunt Grace wasn't the real thing wrong.

What was wrong was her.

She was the underlying cause of all the trouble. It was because of her inadequacies that Edward had become obsessed with the loss of the phantom boy cousin. If she were everything her grandfather wanted, Edward wouldn't have allowed Great House to become a war zone in the effort to recover a grandson he'd never known and sworn never to acknowledge.

And if her grandfather were pleased with her, he wouldn't be so dissatisfied and antagonistic toward her father. Or so callous toward her mother. And if she were not so disappointing, her father wouldn't want to leave, no matter how mad he got. And if she were more lovable, she would be able to comfort her lonely mother whenever her father did leave.

She was the reason that her family didn't sail along happily like the families on the television shows Gittie let her watch. She knew from watching those shows that she had exceptionally beautiful parents and she lived in a grander house than most. She was the imperfection in the midst of it all. She was the girl-child no one had wanted. The child who wasn't clever enough or pretty enough or agile enough or endearing enough for the life she had been born to.

And now it was her fault that her father wasn't there with them in the helicopter. For the first time ever, he wasn't there to tease her and hold her on his lap in the front seat so she could see the pilot and the breathtaking view through the curved glass bubble. He wasn't there to make her mother smile.

It had to be her fault because there was no one else to blame. Neither Aunt Grace nor her grandfather was accompanying them to the country. It had to be her fault, because her father still loved her mother. And he still loved Elysia as much as ever, still insisted that his soul lived in the sprawling, turreted country house—on the estate where he'd spent every summer of his life. Until this summer.

The engine noise intensified and the helicopter lifted off. Yvonne squeezed her eyes shut and gripped an armrest with pale fingers. Gittie shifted and snorted on her way to sleep. The thrill of lift-off erased Juliana's darker thoughts and rekindled her spirits. She pressed her face against the small side glass. They tilted and roared away from the heliport and the island of Manhattan. Cars turned into ants. Trees became a green blur.

This was what God saw when he looked down—which explained why all the messages from God were garbled. God was confused when he looked down at the tiny muddled world. As confused as the adults who lived there.

She watched the city thin out and turn into zillions of miles of wilderness, and her mind skipped wildly about while her body tingled with anticipation. Soon the helicopter would land on the wide lawn in front of Elysia's main house, and she could jump out and run all over the huge estate without bodyguards or her parents or even Gittie. She was safe there, in the heart of a thick forest protected by distant electric fences and shadowy men with leashed dogs.

And that wasn't all. At Elysia she had a friend.

His name was Sparky and he was the son of the gatekeeper who had been hired four years ago and lived in the cottage beside the entryway to Elysia. He was two years older than Juliana but so small that there had never seemed a difference in age. And he had always been uncoordinated the same way she was, forever swinging on branches that broke and tripping over rocks that weren't there and losing his share of the games Juliana challenged him to.

Sparky's real name was Keith, but the McCanns were crazy for nicknames. Mr. and Mrs. McCann both went by nicknames, and they called Juliana "Jinx" the way her father did. They had nicknames for the rest of the Van Lyden family too, though they were always formal when face-to-face.

Behind his back Aubrey was slyly referred to as "Quickdraw" for his shooting prowess and Yvonne was labeled "The Princess." This did not refer to Yvonne's elegance but rather to the fact that she was part Cherokee Indian. Juliana knew that her mother's coolness toward the McCanns resulted from this reference to her Indian blood and the heritage Yvonne wanted to forget.

As soon as they arrived, Juliana greeted the staff with her mother and then ran upstairs to say hello to her room. She had been there just minutes, watching Gittie supervise the unpacking, when a staccato tapping on the glass signaled Sparky's presence in the tree outside the window. Gittie frowned but excused her to race outside. When she reached the tree he was gone, so she ran to their usual meeting spot just inside the dense woods that bordered the old croquet lawn.

She was stricken when she saw him. He'd grown taller than she, his shoulders had broadened, and impending masculinity had begun to define his features. He had betrayed her. He'd grown beyond their genderless union.

But slowly, hopefully, came the realization that his sandy blond hair still hung the same way across his eyes, and his feet and hands were still too big for his body. And before she could speak, he waved hello and fell backward over a tree root. He was the same old Sparky. The same Sparky who had cut each of their fingers with his pocketknife so they could become blood brothers. The same Sparky who had shared the purest and happiest part of her life.

"Come on," he called breathlessly, "there's new baby ducks at the pond and monster tadpoles in the ditch."

But instead of charging toward the pond with him as she would have in previous years, Juliana hesitated. The difference in Sparky had thrown her off-balance and opened her to other worries. She glanced back toward the house, where her mother sat alone, and she felt herself pulled in both directions at once. Should she run off to have fun or should she go back to her mother?

The lure of baby ducks and Sparky and the woods won out. And Juliana rushed headlong into the glorious afternoon.

Weeks passed. Yvonne drifted around the house or lay beside

the pool on a chaise, but she didn't swim or ride or shoot skeet or take the rowboat out on the lake as she had always done when Aubrey was with them. Juliana frequently felt torn between roaming with Sparky and staying close to her mother.

She wanted to cheer her mother and ease the troubled silence. She wanted to fill the void her father's absence created. But when she did spend time in the house, she felt awkward. What did she have to offer? The days of slipping quietly into rooms to sit on the floor beside her mother's chair were over, yet she lacked the poise or self-confidence to walk boldly in, take a seat, and cheer her mother with conversation. So all she could do was lurk on the edges, trailing Yvonne from room to room and hoping her presence was somehow comforting.

Then one hot night, two months into the summer, her mother suddenly surprised her with a picnic dinner. Juliana felt as if she'd fallen into the rabbit hole when her mother called her out onto the terrace. The table was gaily decorated and her mother was renewed.

Yvonne's eyes glowed and her mouth held the suggestion of a smile. Her hair, grown out over the years to please Aubrey, was loose instead of confined in its usual updo. And to Juliana's amazement, she had on one of Aubrey's old hunting shirts. This was an Yvonne that Juliana seldom saw, a casual, carefree woman who bore no resemblance to the elegant mistress of Great House.

Juliana was dumbfounded at first. She sat where she was told to sit and made puppet responses. Then Yvonne leaned across the table toward her and clinked her goblet of wine against Juliana's ginger ale and said, "To a new beginning," and Juliana fell into those glowing dark eyes in a giddy, dizzying spin.

She was transformed by her own reflection in those eyes and suddenly she overflowed with confidence and wit. She mimicked her grandfather's legendary rambling toasts and poked fun at the newest bodyguards he'd hired and told silly stories about Elysia's aging staff. And her mother laughed. Her mother liked her. She sailed completely out of herself, flying on the intimacy, and believing that somehow, some way, she had finally become worthy of it.

After dinner they spread a blanket on the damp grass of a wide lawn. Gittie sent the butler out with an old astronomy book and a flashlight, and mother and daughter lay on their stomachs with heads almost touching and studied drawings of constellations.

"I see it! I see Orion!" Juliana cried.

But her mother had stretched out lazily on her back and closed her eyes.

"Don't go to sleep, Mama. Please ... we don't have to look at stars. We can tell funny stories again."

Yvonne opened her eyes and leaned her head back, exposing her slender neck. She stared into the sky and frowned slightly. "I used to look at stars when I was your age," she said. "I suppose they were the very same ones. It seems strange ... that was so long ago and so far away."

"Did you look at the constellations?" Juliana asked.

"No," Yvonne sighed, "I thought they were just stars. But I did like to wish on them. I used to say that little rhyme about the first star of the night and make secret wishes."

"Did Grandma sit out with you like this?" Juliana asked hopefully. She had an image of belonging to an unbroken chain of mothers and daughters sitting under the stars together—a chain that stretched back into the exotic past of her mother's ancestors.

"No. My mother wasn't the type for stargazing. She didn't like anything that was impractical or out of reach."

Juliana thought about that awhile, wondering if that was why her grandmother hadn't ever wanted to visit them in New York when she was alive. Maybe they'd been out of reach too.

"When I grow up—" she started to say, but Yvonne was reading her diamond-faced watch with the flashlight's weak beam.

Before Juliana could think of a way to hold her, Yvonne stood. The quarter-moon was at her back, casting her in silhouette.

"You never told me what you wished on stars for," Juliana said with a mixture of hope and desperation.

The lure didn't work. Instead of sitting back down, Yvonne began to tug at the corner of the blanket and pull it out from under the girl. Reluctantly Juliana stood and helped her shake and fold it.

"I wished for all kinds of things," Yvonne said. "Ice cream. Puppies. A date for the school dance." She laughed, and suddenly she was made of moonlight. Even her laughter was silver.

"What else?" Juliana asked eagerly.

Yvonne hugged the folded blanket to her chest and stared over Juliana's head toward the velvety darkness of the trees. Her mouth curved into one of her mysterious barely-there smiles.

"I wished for a man like your father."

Languidly she brushed the fingertips of one hand across her cheek and down her neck. "By tomorrow night he'll be here," she said, more to herself than to Juliana.

"Who?" Juliana asked.

"Your father, of course." Yvonne's eyes flickered over her impatiently. "That's why we're celebrating. We won't be alone anymore."

"Oh . . . right," Juliana said.

But she hadn't known he was coming and she hadn't known that what they were doing was celebrating, and she wanted to say that they hadn't been alone, they had had each other. As she walked back to the house beside her mother, her emotions were so jumbled that she had to remind herself to be glad her father was coming.

The next morning the house buzzed with expectation over Aubrey's arrival. He hadn't given a time, so everyone rose early just in case he came in the morning. His favorite foods were prepared. The billiard room was opened and his horse and saddle were readied at the stable.

Juliana let Gittie coax her into a sundress and then wandered through the house restlessly. She hadn't been surprised when her father said that his soul lived here. She was convinced that the house was filled with ghosts and other supernatural things and she could easily imagine a human soul lurking somewhere on the premises. Everywhere she turned in the musty, shadowed rooms, there was some dead creature watching her.

The walls of the house were filled with the mounted heads from four generations of hunting. There was every size and shape imaginable. Immense elephant heads, sleek wolverine heads, ferocious tiger heads. And beneath each trophy was a plaque giving the date and location of the kill in addition to the killer's name. Aubrey was almost as fond of pointing out the animals that had been taken illegally as he was of pointing out the plaques with his own name engraved.

Juliana liked only a few of Elysia's rooms. Her own bedroom was good in that it didn't have any mounted heads or footstools made of body parts. Then there was her mother's room, with its pale lemon-silk walls and delicate furniture, the sun porch with its scattering of plants and rattan chairs, and the long echoing room that faced the pool. The servants called this the hunt room because it was originally built to serve formal hunt breakfasts.

In spite of its name, the hunt room was one of the few communal rooms that held no mounted trophies. There simply wasn't a place to hang them. Three of the walls were entirely comprised of horizontal beams and wide expanses of glass punctuated by large French doors. The fourth wall and the arched and beamed ceiling were decorated with intricate gilded murals in which elegantly dressed men and women rode sleek thoroughbreds through forests and over fences in pursuit of an elusive fox.

Juliana had spent endless hours searching through the mural for that fox. She liked to think that the fox had escaped the painting completely and was forever out of reach.

By midmorning the temperature had climbed to eighty-five and she was tired of sitting inside in her dress, so she called Sparky and changed into her bathing suit. The buzz of a helicopter sounded just as she stepped out of the hunt room's French doors onto the terrace. Sparky was already in the pool. She called to him and the lifeguard frowned down from his perch as the boy lunged from the water and raced across the terraces to join her.

They watched the helicopter settle on the grass.

Aubrey smiled and waved at her through the glass bubble. He had another man with him and the two were slow about getting out. Juliana waited impatiently, poking and pinching Sparky with an overflow of high spirits. Her usual caution around adults had been eroded by the evening with her mother and the excitement of her father's arrival.

Aubrey gave Juliana the customary hug and greeted Sparky with polite reserve. Then he fell in beside his guest and the two of them picked up an apparently ongoing conversation about hunting. Juliana tagged along quietly for several minutes, then grew bored. She signaled Sparky with an elbow in the ribs and together they loped out ahead of the men.

"Gotcha!" Juliana cried, sprinting past Sparky and swatting his bottom for good measure.

Sparky responded with a burst of speed and a shoulder tackle. They laughed and rolled on the manicured lawn, then separated, still laughing, to rub at their grass stains.

When Juliana looked up, the two men were frozen in place, staring silently down at the children as if brought to a standstill by the behavior they'd witnessed. Disapproval, disgust, annoyance—she read it all in varying degrees. But there was more. There was something very strange in her father's gaze.

Quickly Juliana nudged Sparky and jumped to her feet.

"We're swimming now, Papa!" she called as she led the run back toward the pool.

Later, when they'd finished swimming, she discovered that the adults had retired to the dining room for a formal lunch, so she talked the cook into packing a food basket for Sparky and her.

They hiked to their favored picnic spot, a shaded outcropping of rock with a sweeping view of the countryside, and they ate the delicious meal. It was a hot, lazy day. She knew she ought to go back because her father had just arrived and because there was a guest and because her presence would be expected. But she was afraid to go back. A nameless apprehension held her, and she didn't want to leave her special spot or her special friend. She wanted the afternoon to go on forever.

Silence settled between the children, but it was not a disturbing silence. It was familiar and comforting.

They watched a party of ants discover the cupcake wrappers; then they stretched out on the grass. Juliana lay on her back with her hands behind her head. Towering walls of clouds were suspended above her in the sky, and she imagined them falling and crushing her.

Sparky began idly speculating about hidden caves or sacred Indian burial sites on the grounds of Elysia, but she didn't respond. Suddenly she felt older than Sparky, and the daydreams she had always shared with him seemed foolish.

A noise, not unlike a fly's buzzing, sounded off in the distance. It grew closer and louder. Someone was out riding on the three-wheeler that was kept to check fences. Without intending to, Juliana fell asleep.

When she woke, her father was standing over them.

"Papa," she said, pulling herself out of a fuzzy dream state.

Sparky also struggled to sit up, shaking off his drowsiness.

"I thought I'd find you here," Aubrey said. His strange stare dissolved into a smile. "I came to get Sparky." He moved forward casually and bent to poke at their picnic remains. Then he straightened and fastened one of his electric smiles directly on the boy. Sparky appeared confused and self-conscious.

"I hadn't realized how fast you were growing," Aubrey said. "You're big enough to help around here." He turned and started off down the trail. "Come along, now," he ordered. "I brought the three-wheeler up as far as the meadow."

Sparky got to his feet slowly and dusted off his jeans. He shot Juliana a puzzled look, then shrugged and followed Aubrey into the trees. She didn't see him the rest of the day.

That evening, after dinner, Gittie took Juliana upstairs.

"What about our game?" Juliana asked. "You promised to play cribbage with me before I had to go to bed."

Gittie shook her head sadly as she moved a collection of dolls and settled her bulk into the upholstered window seat. "Come here," she said, patting the cushion beside her. "Come sit with Gittie."

Hesitantly Juliana obeyed.

"You're a big girl now." Gittie encircled Juliana's shoulders with a thick arm and pulled her close. "You're ten years old."

Juliana waited.

"And your friend Sparky . . . he's almost a teenager. And, well, boys and girls do not play together when they get so big."

Juliana tilted her head back to look into Gittie's face.

"Your parents do not want you to play with Sparky anymore."

"Anymore tonight?" Juliana asked blankly.

"Anymore never."

"Never?"

Gittie sighed. "Never," she repeated softly.

Juliana allowed herself to be enfolded against Gittie's ample bosom, but she refused to cry. She blinked hard against her burning eyes and the rage that roared inside her. Only later, when it was dark and Gittie was snoring in the adjoining room, did she let the tears come. Her entire body shook with all the grief and anger.

The next morning she ignored Gittie's pleas and ran down to her mother's bedroom. Both her parents were asleep in the sea of pale ruffles that engulfed her mother's bed. The sheets were tangled and covered their bare skin haphazardly.

Juliana was startled and vaguely disturbed by the sight. Rarely had she been aware of her parents sleeping in the same bed together. She'd been accustomed to the idea that they had separate rooms and separate beds. She stared at them together. One of her father's arms trailed across her mother's naked back.

Yvonne raised her head and frowned at her daughter in a sleepy, unfocused way. Carefully she eased herself away from Aubrey and out of the twisted bedclothes, then padded across the room to grab her robe.

Juliana opened her mouth to speak, but her mother put a finger to her lips and motioned her into the adjoining bathroom.

"What's wrong, Juliana? Where's Gittie?"

"You didn't really mean that I can't play with Sparky anymore," the child whispered fiercely. "You didn't really mean that, did you, Mama?"

Yvonne swept her hair back out of her face with a weary sigh. "It's your father's decision," she said, "but it does make sense, don't you agree?"

"No! No, Mama, it's not—"

"Shhhhhh," Yvonne hissed sharply. "You'll wake your father. Do you want to bother him on the first morning he's here?"

Juliana shook her head no and stared down at the intricately tiled floor.

Yvonne sighed again and stroked the child's cheek lightly. "Being the Van Lyden heiress isn't easy, is it?" She put her arm around Juliana's shoulders to guide the child out of the bathroom and quietly to the bedroom door. Before closing it and sending her daughter away, Yvonne bent toward her. Juliana was enveloped in her mother's perfume and pinned like a butterfly beneath the sudden sharpness in her mother's dark eyes. "Everything has a price, Juliana. Everything."

In confusion and despair, Juliana ran from the house. She was winded and weak-kneed by the time she reached the gatekeeper's cottage.

Mrs. McCann opened the door before Juliana had a chance to knock. "What is it?" the woman asked curtly.

Juliana was taken aback. Always before Colleen McCann had treated her in a friendly, deferential manner.

"I, uh . . . I need to see Sparky."

"Sparky has chores to do this morning and Mr. Van Lyden is taking him down to the lake to check for algae later. Besides"— Mrs. McCann's eyes narrowed—"you fixed Sparky's wagon already, didn't you, now? I warned him not to play with a girl. I warned him girls was trouble . . . but no!"

Juliana felt her face flush. She whirled and raced away into the woods alone.

The summer turned bleak and cruel after that. She saw Sparky only in passing, and when she did, he ducked his head and avoided her eyes. Her only friendship had been destroyed. And the destruction carved a piece from her childhood and left a black emptiness in its wake.

A week before they were slated to return to the city house, she ran into Sparky alone in the woods.

"I just wanted to say good-bye," he said, making her realize that he'd planned the meeting. His eyes held a weight of sorrow.

"Thanks," she said, overwhelmed by emotions she couldn't express. "Maybe next year . . . maybe they'll change their minds."

"Sure," he said. He tried to smile. One corner of his mouth quivered, tearing at her heart.

"Someday—" she said, but before she could say more he turned and ran.

Juliana raced back to her house and burst in on a luncheon

that included her parents and two Englishmen who'd arrived the day before to see her father. All the caution, all the self-control, evaporated in the heat of her pain and anger. "Sparky is still my friend!" she shouted at her father. "And you're stupid if you think you can keep me from seeing him!"

Yvonne set her fork down stiffly and turned toward Aubrey with a helpless, almost fearful expression. Aubrey's face reddened and the muscles on the sides of his jaw bulged. "I will not respond to a display of this sort," he said through clenched teeth.

Frustration and helplessness churned inside her. She wanted to smash all the crystal and china to the floor. She wanted to shout ugly things. But the violent intensity of this new range of emotions overwhelmed her so completely that all she could do was burst into loud, strangled sobs.

Aubrey stood and threw his damask napkin on the table beside his plate. "Why is this child here?" he demanded. "Where is her nurse?"

The maid who'd been serving shrank back against the wall.

There was a charged moment of silence; then Aubrey composed himself and turned to his English guests. "I'll call for the helicopter," he said. "We can leave this afternoon."

"Oh, no!" Yvonne stood so quickly that she knocked over a glass. Red wine splashed onto her linen dress and pale pink pearls.

Juliana gasped and fought to bring her sobs under control.

"Bree ... please," Yvonne pleaded. She reached for his arm, but he brushed her hand away.

He picked up his napkin and handed it to her. "I know that you weren't raised to appreciate fine jewelry, my sweet, but those pearls are a hundred years old. I'm afraid that a wine bath might not be the healthiest thing for them."

The wound registered in her eyes. She took the napkin from him and blotted furiously at her dress and the necklace, ducking her head as though absorbed in the task. Juliana could see that she was close to tears.

Aubrey gestured to his guests, and all three men left the room. Yvonne raised her eyes to watch. Then she threw down the napkin and tore the long single-strand necklace off over her head. She dropped it on the table carelessly and stalked out without a backward glance at her daughter.

Three hours later Aubrey and his friends were gone. Yvonne locked herself into her lemon-silk room and refused to answer either the maid's or Juliana's calls at the door.

The next morning the entire household was surprised by the

arrival of Edward Van Lyden's limousine. The elder Van Lyden seldom visited Elysia. He had a profound dislike of flying and was bored by the long car ride that was the alternative, so he rarely appeared. Juliana knew immediately that her grandfather was there because of her.

The servants darted around nervously until Edward announced that he wasn't staying. He had come to get his granddaughter.

Without protest Juliana let Gittie button her into a dress with a scratchy French-lace collar. She wiggled into white tights and put her feet into the hated white balletlike slippers that came untied and flew off her feet if she ran. She knew that her grandfather had to be deadly serious to have driven all the way up to get her. Her stomach and knees felt like gelatin.

She paused on her way downstairs to tap on her mother's door. "Mama," she called softly. "Grandfather's come to take me back with him." She waited, straining to hear the slightest sound or response. But there was only silence. "I'll see you at home, Mama," she said. Then she pressed her face close to the smooth, deeply carved wood of the door and whispered, "Please come soon."

Juliana huddled in the limousine, feeling very small and alone in the chill of her grandfather's anger. She waited for him to speak, but he seemed preoccupied with the scenery outside his window. They passed the McCanns' cottage and Juliana stole a wistful look backward.

"Your father called me last night," her grandfather said.

Juliana hung her head and waited.

"Look at me."

She looked up into her grandfather's face. Sunlight filtered through the dark glass windows and she was suddenly aware of the encroaching gray in his bushy eyebrows. He looked older and his grooming was not as flawless as usual. But he was still the formidable Van Lyden patriarch.

"You are not just any child, Juliana. You are all that stands between a great family and oblivion."

He took her small hand and gripped it between his larger ones. His skin was soft but cold. The contact made her flinch.

"You cannot afford to be ordinary. Not now. Not ever. Ordinary people are weak and undisciplined and insignificant. You must be strong. You carry the weight of generations of Van Lydens on your shoulders. You are my primary heir. You know what that means ... one day everything will be yours. You'll become one of the most important women in the world." He squeezed her hand tighter. "But before that happens, you must learn to be invincible. You must become immune to all that is beneath you."

Her hand ached from his grip.

"Do you understand me?"

She nodded to please him, but in truth she didn't quite understand the part about being invincible and immune.

"I knew you would. You are exceptionally bright for your age. Brighter than your father ever was. I think you knew from the beginning that you had no business tearing through the woods with that common child . . . but you're young. You're still young. Others should have taken control of the situation."

He relaxed his grip on her hand and she quickly tucked it safely into her lap.

"And as for your outburst, your shameful display of temper and bad manners . . . I cannot believe that my granddaughter would stoop to such behavior over a petty grievance."

She hung her head even lower and felt a sudden terror that her grandfather might excommunicate her the way he had Aunt Grace for so many years.

He cleared his throat. Reluctantly she raised her head to meet his gaze.

"I can only conclude that Aubrey was greatly exaggerating your disruption of his luncheon." He measured her with his eyes. "Is that the case?"

Relief coursed through her and she nodded immediately. Yes! Yes! She hadn't really been bad. She hadn't really called her father stupid or humiliated him in front of those men. She knew how her grandfather's revisions worked and she knew that revision meant complete forgiveness because once her grandfather revised something the truth was erased completely.

"Good. I suspected as much." Edward smiled. "Then we can put all that unpleasantness behind us, can't we? And this will just be a day for an outing. How would you like that?"

She nodded again eagerly.

"Very well, then. Since we're up this way, I know of a treasure we can examine, a hammered-silver clock reputed to be just like the one in your mother's bedroom."

"But why do you need another one?" she asked timidly. "Can't you just put the one from Mama's room into your collection?"

He frowned and stuck out his chin. "That clock was purchased in 1879 by one of your ancestors. I did not find it or acquire it myself. What victory would there be in simply taking it from your mother's room?"

"Victory?"

Edward straightened the already perfect Windsor knot of his tie and turned his head to stare out the window.

"Each of us must create his own victories, Juliana."

There was a stretch of silence, and then her grandfather started talking about where they'd eat and whether she'd sleep at Great House that night or at Mignon with him.

"But what about Gittie?" she asked in a sudden panic. She had not spent a night of her life without the comfort of Gittie close by.

Her grandfather sighed deeply. "You may as well wean yourself from Gittie as of now. I've dismissed her and she'll be gone as soon as I find a suitable replacement."

"Gittie ... gone?" Juliana stared at him blankly. He might as well have said that he was dismissing the earth beneath her feet.

"Yes. The woman is clearly no longer able to provide the firm hand that a child of your age and stature requires. She's being retired."

"She'll still live in Great House, though, won't she?" Juliana's voice was so small that she could barely hear it herself. "I'll still see her, won't I?"

"Now, that wouldn't be very practical, would it? The house would be overflowing if we let the help retire there."

The car and her grandfather's face receded. He spoke again, but it was an echo from far away. Down and down she fell, down into the dark and poisonous place that had threatened so often. Down where no one could reach her.

7

Lucy

Lucy stared down into her father's grave. The plain unfinished coffin stared back at her in accusing silence. "It ain't so great, Lucy. It ain't so great."

Those had been her father's last words, and now she was wondering what he had meant. Had he been referring to something immediate, like the care at the Walea Community Hospital, or had he been commenting on life? Or death? Or maybe both?

Her thoughts were cut short by the Reverend Skidmore, who took his place at one end of the grave and began shaking his fists and waving his arms and begging God to forgive Lydell Clare's sinning ways and give him a chance in heaven.

In spite of the emotional distance she'd established, Lucy cringed. Her father would have hated the service. He'd always said preachers were just common salesmen, the same as the hawkers at Howard's A-1 Car Emporium. Only with preachers, the product they were selling was nothing more than tall tales and chicken spit. During his last weeks of life he had made his view clear to the various ministers who prowled the hospital's halls.

"I'm in the salvage-and-repair business," a Baptist preacher had told Lydell one afternoon while Lucy was sitting beside his hospital bed.

"Well, my soul ain't ready for no junkyard," Lydell had retorted weakly. "So get your two-faced butt outta my room."

That was the reason her mama had had so much trouble finding someone to do the graveside service. Only Reverend Skidmore, the new evangelist who'd pitched his tent on the edge of town, would agree to give Lydell Clare his send-off.

The reverend finally stopped and everyone watched in silence as Lucy's mama bent to scoop up a handful of dirt. The heavy East Texas soil struck the wood with a thud that echoed through

91

Lucy's entire body. Her sisters dutifully followed suit. First Suki and then Anita cast in their handfuls of dirt. But Lucy couldn't bring herself to do it. Instead, she threw in the wilted bunch of marigolds she'd picked that morning.

The little circle of people around the grave faded back and Wanda motioned for the three girls to follow her. "Let's get a move on," she said. "We don't want folks beatin' us there. Wouldn't look right. No, sir. Wouldn't look right for the grievin' family to traipse in with the callers."

Wanda was exhibiting too much energy and enthusiasm. Lucy blotted her own tears and wished her mother would cry too.

"Not one store-bought flower." Wanda shook her head. "Your daddy threw away his life, girls. He wasn't worth one store-bought flower to nobody."

"Why didn't we buy him some flowers, Mama?" Anita asked in a small, quavery voice.

"What with?" Wanda demanded angrily. "I had to go into hock for what we did get. You know how much all this is costin' us?"

A silence fell over them. Wanda's bitter anger hung in the still, hot air.

The pickup cab was crowded, but they had on their good dresses, so no one could ride in the back. Lucy couldn't stop crying. She wished she had just turned six instead of sixteen so she could open up and make noise and kick and scream instead of sitting quietly while her eyes ran like faucets and her insides twisted.

Wanda drove like a maniac so they could be first to the Holy Redemption tent. Reverend Skidmore had graciously allowed them to use it after Wanda pointed out that their tiny trailer house wasn't big enough for company.

"Fetch the boxes from the back," Wanda ordered as she skidded to a stop on the newly spread gravel between the tent and the Skidmores' fancy new Expando double-wide mobile home. "And no smoking here, Sherry Kay!"

Suki scowled. She was one month away from eighteen and didn't like taking orders. But she didn't start trouble. She put out her cigarette and fell in beside Lucy to take one of the three boxes. It was almost noon and the temperature had climbed to the high eighties. The sweat beaded on Lucy's skin beneath the dime-store hose and the mended nylon slip and the ill-fitting polyester dress. She looked across at Suki and saw that her sister's carefully pressed suit was already limp and developing stains underneath the arms.

The door to the Skidmores' Expando home opened and Charity Skidmore stepped out onto her scrolled-wrought-iron porch and called to them. "You poor thangs! Y'all shouldn't be workin' at a time like this." She looked back over her shoulder into the mobile home. "Buddy boy! Pull your boots on, Buddy, and come help the bereaved."

Charity hurried down the steps and minced across the gravel in spike heels. She gave Wanda a stiff hug with almost no body contact. "You poor thang," she declared, drawing out "thang" into three syllables.

"Thank you, Miz Skidmore. We 'preciate all that ya'll are doin' . . ."

"Nonsense. We're just doin' like good Christian folk should."

Charity led the way toward the tent. "Now, did you bring the paper plates and the cups and napkins?"

Wanda nodded. "And the plastic forks and spoons."

"Fine. And the bread . . . the bread was on ya'll's list."

Wanda nodded again. "I got a loaf and buns for barbecue."

"We're all set, then. The other mourners brought by pies and Jell-O salads before the service. And several of the ladies you wash for got together and pitched in on a nice baked ham."

A look of surprised satisfaction crossed Wanda's face. "A ham, you say? That must have set 'em back a piece."

There was the loud crunch of running feet on the gravel behind them, and suddenly a very large, very self-conscious-looking boy was beside Lucy.

"There you are!" Charity turned to smile at the girls. "This is my boy, DuWayne Junior. Buddy." She shot an adoring look at her son. "He's just home from college. Now he's out here to make hisself useful, so I want you girls to put him to work."

Without a word Buddy reached out and took Anita's box from her. "Put those others right on top," he mumbled, and Suki gave him hers with a dainty, brave smile.

Lucy ignored him and marched toward the tent.

"Buddy's been out here all morning fixin' it up for you," Charity announced as they stepped underneath the pitched canvas.

The tent had two sides rolled down and two sides open. The chairs had been folded and stacked in the corner except for a scattering left around the perimeter. On one side stood a long table covered with white butcher paper and laden with food. The ham had the central position of honor. Next to it was a covered roaster full of chipped-meat barbecue.

Wanda crossed to the food table and inspected the ham. Then

she opened the lid on the roaster and sniffed disdainfully. The barbecue had been sent by Lydell's bosses at the trailer factory, but it was the same canned stuff that was sold at the rodeo each year. And it didn't compare to a fine baked ham.

Flanking the ham and barbecue was a green Jell-O mold studded with chunks of pineapple and tiny marshmallows, and a red Jell-O mold laden with fruit cocktail. The pies had been arranged on a smaller side table.

Lucy stood woodenly as Wanda and Charity bustled about laying out bread and paper goods. Charity's makeup and hair were perfect and her dress was a summery lilac print with puffed sleeves. Beside her Wanda looked pathetic and worn. The borrowed black dress hung limply from Wanda's bony shoulders and her eyes were shadowed and etched with deep lines.

The two women reached out to smooth the paper table cover and their hands lay side by side for a moment. Wanda's coarse, reddened hands with the ragged nails met Charity's smooth white hands with the oval pink-lacquered nails, and Lucy had to turn away. The sight only added to the ache inside her.

She wandered aimlessly around the tent, stumbling a little in her scuffed handed-down heels. Suki had cornered Buddy. Anita sat alone in the shadows against one side.

Lucy unfolded a chair and carried it over to sit by Anita. The eleven-year-old's gaze was fixed and trancelike. Gently Lucy stroked her little sister's long silky hair.

After several minutes the girl turned to look at Lucy. Her eyes were red and swollen and her heart-shaped face was pale. "What are we gonna do now?" she whispered. "What are we gonna do without a daddy?"

Lucy could not have spoken even if she'd had an answer. Anita's words burned through her eyes and her throat and her chest, and all she could do was hold her sister close and cry with her. The fact was that they hadn't had a real daddy for ages.

Tires crunched on gravel and car doors slammed, announcing the arrival of the first guests.

Wanda hurried over to her daughters. "Quit the sniffling, now," she ordered in a fierce whisper. "It's our duty to visit with all these folks who're kindly payin' your father last respects . . . so don't go all teary, now, hear?"

The gathering under the tent took shape quickly. Lucy watched the collection of decaying men with tobacco-stained fingers who professed to have known Lydell. Their wives gossiped and laughed and eagerly heaped their plates with food. No one had bothered to wear a tie except Reverend Skidmore.

Over and over Lucy listened to declarations of friendship and descriptions of where this or that fellow's work station in the trailer factory had been in relation to Lydell's. She endured the clumsy condolences from the men and the clucking and questioning from the women. Where had all these people been when her father was alive?

The strain of being polite was wearing Lucy's nerves to fine threads and she was having trouble following conversations, when suddenly she caught a name. Shenandoah Circle. "Shenandoah Circle?" she asked like a sleepwalker who has just been awakened.

A threesome of women parted and swept her into their group eagerly.

"Why, yes, sweetie," a large woman replied. "That's my street. Now how're you li'l gals holdin' up through all this?"

"You live on Shenandoah?"

"Sure nuf. For seventeen years. But we're thinkin' a sellin' now that my husband's—"

"I had a friend who lived on that street."

"Do tell? Well, my husband always says there ain't a body on that street that I don't—"

"She's gone now. Her name was Conroy. Miz Junelle Conroy. She was my teacher."

The smile melted from the woman's face.

"Why, Patsy! wasn't that—?" one of her companions began, but the words died beneath an intimidating glare from the big woman.

"Don't believe I know of no one by that name, sweetie."

"Please, you know something, don't you? It's been three years now, and I still don't—"

The woman called Patsy gripped Lucy's forearm with a wide work-strengthened hand. "Forget it, hon." Her voice was hard but her eyes were kind. "Some things are best forgot."

"Then you know what happened?" Lucy asked anxiously. "Did you see her leave? Did you—?"

"I don't recollect nothin'," the woman said firmly. "And that's the way I aim to keep it." She turned and walked away from Lucy, and her companions scurried after her.

Lucy wanted to run after them. She wanted to chase the woman down and beg and plead and threaten—whatever it took to learn the truth. But she knew it would do no good. Lucy had already tried everything.

She had ridden out the storm inside the church and emerged the next morning to find chaos. A tornado had touched down in Walea, cutting a wide swath of destruction, killing five people and injuring many more. All telephone and electric service was out. The National Guard and the Red Cross were arriving as Lucy picked her way along the rubble-filled streets.

She went straight to the sheriff's office to tell them about the terrible things that had happened at Ms. Conroy and Reverend Luke's houses. She believed that a squad of uniformed men would immediately investigate and find the criminals and, most important, find Ms. Conroy and save her from whatever was happening. But no one would even listen to her story. The place was swamped with pleas for help and reports of missing children. The officers were all out on duty, and the people manning the desk were elderly volunteers in a state of confused panic.

Lucy was pushed back and forth, out of the way of hurrying, desperate people. She had never felt so helpless. Finally she collapsed against a wall in a fit of hysterical sobbing.

She couldn't remember how she ended up at the hospital. The doctors there insisted she'd had a breakdown. Looking back, she saw just how ridiculous that diagnosis had been. How was a thirteen-year-old supposed to react when she was frightened and distraught and exhausted?

"Lucy's always been wild," she'd heard her mother tell the doctor. "A big imaginer ... if you know what I mean. An overacting type."

"Ah," the doctor had responded knowingly.

They kept her in the children's ward of the hospital for three days. Just down the hall they also had her daddy. Lydell had hurt his back in a fall when he had tried to do a belated check of the tires on the trailer's roof. Wanda and Suki had had to drag him to the storm cellar. Miraculously, the trailer itself had sustained only minor damage.

By the time Lucy was able to go back to Ms. Conroy's duplex, the mess had been cleaned up and a new tenant had been installed. There was no proof left that anything bad had happened at all. She had the crazy feeling that maybe she had imagined it. Maybe she'd been caught in the storm and swept into a nightmare like Dorothy in Oz.

But at Reverend Luke's the boarded windows and door gave mute testimony to the truth. There were hand-lettered "KEEP AWAY" signs. When she saw them, Lucy felt they'd been posted just for her.

For months she badgered the police and the school officials and asked everyone she could think of if they knew what had happened or where Ms. Conroy had gone. But no one cared. The night had swallowed up Ms. Conroy and Reverend Luke, and the mystery of their disappearance was as tightly sealed as a bank vault.

In three years Lucy had not spent a day without wondering and worrying, and hoping that Ms. Conroy was doing fine somewhere.

There was more than the loss and the uncertainty to torture her. There were agonizing questions: Had it been her fault somehow? Had her fight with Ms. Conroy triggered something awful? Worse, had she unknowingly given away Ms. Conroy's and Reverend Luke's secret, causing terrible things to happen to them?

"Geeminy, kid ... you look like you seen a ghost!" Suki declared as she planted herself next to Lucy. She held out a loaded paper plate. "Wanna bite?" Suki grinned. "Got plenty here."

Lucy shook her head.

"I wish I could be like that," Suki moaned. "Just wastin' away with no appetite whenever I was sad." She took a big bite of a bun dripping barbecue.

Lucy sighed and rubbed her scratchy eyes with the heels of her palms. Mechanically she reached to tighten the large barrette that held her thick hair firmly against the back of her neck.

"Wonder how much longer folks are gonna stay," she said listlessly.

Suki screwed her mouth sideways. "They won't leave till the food runs out."

"You girls oughta be tryin' ta make the reverend's boy feel more at home," Wanda scolded as she moved in to join her daughters. "Appears like he don't know a soul, and he looks real lost and left out."

"This isn't a party, Mama," Lucy said. "It's not like we—"

"I'm talkin' good manners, Miss Lucy Smart Britches. I'm talkin' Christian decency." Wanda used her fingers to sample a bite of sliced ham from Suki's plate. "Not a canned ham. Nosiree. My ladies sent a nice big fresh ham."

"It's a good ham, Mama," Suki agreed.

"You ate yet?" Wanda asked Lucy.

"No, Mama. I don't feel like eatin' anything."

"I'll swear! You and Nita ..." She carefully wiped her fingers and mouth on a paper napkin. "You wanna be finicky, that's fine by me ... but you two best be rememberin' that there ain't no supper at home. If you turn up your noses at all this good food, I don't wanna hear no bellyachin' about how hungry y'all are tonight. Understand? This family's gotta learn to make do with less now that we don't have your daddy's paycheck no more."

"Yes, Mama."

Wanda studied Lucy as though just seeing her daughter. "Those hands a yours . . ." she muttered, grabbing one of Lucy's hands in a pincerlike vise and pulling it up for inspection. "How could you come to your daddy's funeral with your hands looking like this?"

Lucy looked down at her hands. They were stained. She rarely had the heart for painting anymore, but this morning she hadn't been able to sleep so she'd gone out and dabbled at a sunrise. It had turned out poorly, as she had known it would.

"It's just a little paint, Mama. Suki was using the nail brush this morning, so I couldn't get them all the way clean."

"Paint," Wanda said, flinging Lucy's hand away from her in disgust. "How many dollars have we been wastin' on that worthless hobby a yours?" She drew in a deep, determined breath. "This family's gonna learn to make do on less, all right. A lot less."

"Less," Suki said sarcastically. "We didn't have nothin' before. How we gonna live on *less* than nothin'?"

Wanda ignored the question and stared off across the tent. She wasn't old in years, but a life of backbreaking work had hardened her and drained her of whatever softness and beauty she had once possessed. "We're gonna get Nita some kinda job," she said. "She's good with her hands. Maybe she could take in mending or sewing." Wanda turned to study Lucy again. "And you're gonna have to start earning your keep, girl. No more a this part-time work. You're sixteen now, so you need to be bringin' in adult wages."

"But, Mama, soon as school starts back up, I can't—"

"No more school, missy. Sixteen's legal quittin' age. I figure you done learned more now than you're ever gonna need."

"No, Mama!" All the blood in Lucy's body raced for her stomach, and her face and hands went cold. "I can't quit school. A person is nothin' nowadays if they don't graduate from high school. Daddy used to say so all the time."

"Your daddy's not here anymore, child," Wanda said softly. "And it's plain where his thinkin' got him . . . and us."

Lucy opened her mouth to protest again, but Wanda held up her hand. "This ain't the place for decidin'. We'll sit down and get it settled tomorrow. Tomorrow's Sunday. Thank the Lord we have a day of rest to put our house in order 'fore we go ta work."

"Thank the Lord for a day to sleep late," Suki said around a bite of Jell-O.

"No more a that! Uh-uh." Wanda shook her head righteously. "Now that your daddy's gone, this family's gonna get back on the right path. Church every Sunday mornin', rain or shine."

"Oh, Mama!" Suki lowered her plate as though she'd suddenly lost her appetite. "You gotta be kiddin'!"

Wanda leaned close. "Look at this bunch a no-accounts," she whispered. "Your daddy mighta been satisfied fittin' in with this sorta folk, but I ain't." She looked at Suki and her eyes glittered with something fierce and almost frightening. "And I ain't about to let my Suki baby marry one a their trashy sons. No, sir. This family's gonna show we're made a finer stuff. And we're gonna start by bein' just as God-fearin' and churchgoin' and respectable as the ladies I wash for."

"We don't even have a church," Suki protested. "We'd look like fools if we just showed up at a church we've never set foot in."

"I was raised in Church of Christ, so I'd say I got a right to go there," Wanda declared stubbornly.

"You're crazy, Mama. I ain't . . . I mean, I'm not settin' foot in no Church a Christ and having the whole congregation stare and point and talk about me and my dead daddy." Suki glared at Wanda. "Besides, I'll be leavin' soon anyway, so there's no point my startin' with a church." She cast a scornful glance around her. "And you sure don't have to worry about me marryin' none a this."

"You're makin' frown lines," Wanda cautioned.

Suki instantly relaxed her face and smoothed the skin between her carefully tweezed eyebrows with her fingertips. "I'll be glad when I'm outta here," she said. Her face was perfectly composed but her voice was venomous.

"You ain't goin' nowhere, girl. That crazy notion shoulda never been started in your head, 'cause it's gonna lead you to heartbreak. Just listen ta your mama. Things are gonna be fine for you now right here in Walea. Just you wait and see. There's nothin' to hold us back anymore. You're gonna marry up and be a real lady in this town."

"Lower your voice, Mama," Suki hissed.

Lucy wanted to jump in and demand to know if her mama meant that their daddy was the something that had been holding them back and keeping things from being fine for them. But Lucy had been functioning as the family peacekeeper for several years and she knew it was up to her to pour water on the fire, and not gasoline.

"You know, Mama," Lucy remarked quickly, "you seem to be gettin' on real well with the Reverend and Miz Charity."

"That's right, Lucy," Wanda agreed impatiently. "They've been real Christian to me."

"Well, he has regular Sunday services under the tent now—"

"Yeah!" Suki cut in. "If we gotta go to church, let's come to the tent, Mama. The whole congregation's new here, so we wouldn't stick out like sore thumbs. And there's lots of important folks crossin' over to Reverend Skidmore."

"Is that right?" Wanda asked thoughtfully.

Suki was watching Buddy Skidmore cross the tent behind her mother's back. Wanda closed her eyes and rubbed her hand across her forehead a moment, and Suki winked at Lucy and grinned.

"I reckon you're right, Suki. That's a good idea you got there." She looked around quickly. "I believe I'll just go tell the reverend right this minute that he's got four new souls comin' under his wing."

Wanda hurried off, and both girls gave involuntary sighs.

"You're always the thinker, aren't ya, Lucy?" Suki shook her head and chuckled. "Too bad you can't come with me when I leave. We'd make a helluva team."

Lucy flinched at the word "hell" spoken beneath the reverend's tent. "You're really goin', huh?"

"You bet I'm going! This is my chance to make it big."

"Mama's going to take it hard when you go."

"She'll get over it. She's got you and Nita to fuss over." Suki finished the last bite of her barbecue sandwich and dabbed at her mouth with a napkin. "Besides, Mama's the one who's always pushed me to get out there and try harder. Well, I did. And I won me a real chance to be something in the world. And I think it's damn selfish of her to be tryin' to ruin it for me now." Suki handed Lucy her limp plate full of melting Jell-O. "Toss this for me, will ya, sweetie? I need to find the little girls' room and fix my face."

Lucy watched her sister walk away. Lydell used to make fun of Suki's constant need to "fix her face." It had come on her suddenly—right after she had been promoted to head clerk in the cosmetics section at the five-and-dime and a visiting makeup salesman had told her that sophisticated ladies did not allow their freckles to show.

"There's not a thing wrong with your face," Lydell used to insist, "except it's covered with this mess a stuff . . ." and he'd touch his index finger to his tongue and chase Suki around with her squealing like a pig stuck under a gate, and Lucy and Anita doubled over with laughter.

That was all over now. There would be no more of Lydell's teasing or his rambling talks or his offbeat projects. The lump swelled in Lucy's throat again and her eyes burned with the effort to blink back the tears. Quickly she found a trash barrel to toss Suki's plate into and then escaped outside to sit on a patch of dry grass in back of the tent. She pressed her fists to her mouth and wept silently.

"I know how bad you're feelin'."

Startled, Lucy looked up through blurry eyes to find Buddy Skidmore standing over her with a look of embarrassed compassion. She sniffed and wiped at her eyes with her palms, trying to suppress the involuntary sobs that tore at her chest.

"I felt just like that when my grandpa died last year," Buddy said. He squatted down on the grass beside her and offered her a drink of iced tea from a soggy waxed cup.

Lucy accepted the drink and glared up at him. "He was nothin' but a drunk anyway. Doctor said it's a miracle he lived as long as he did." She wasn't used to talking to boys and it made her defensive and wary.

"Mind if I sit here with ya?" he asked as he eased himself down onto the grass.

His bulk made her very nervous. She had never been close to anyone with such wide shoulders and thick arms.

"You're Lucy, huh?"

She nodded.

"And the little one's Anita?"

She nodded again.

"And the redhead's Suki? Is that a nickname or what?"

Lucy relaxed. Now she knew what Buddy Skidmore wanted from her. She reached for another drink of his tea. "Her real name's Sherry Kay." She eyed him curiously. "How come we never saw you around town before?"

He grinned a little. "Just got here. I'm in college, ya know. Sophomore next year. This is my summer break. That's the only time I live with my folks."

"Oh. So where'd you go to high school?"

" 'Round Amarillo. That's where my folks moved from."

"And you made it into college."

"Yeah. I'm on a football scholarship."

"Suki's got her a scholarship too. Won it at the Texas Twirlers for Jesus Pageant. Actually, she won her choice of cash or a scholarship . . . but she's gonna take the scholarship."

"What kinda scholarship?"

"To a school in Dallas for executive secretaries. She's gonna get Finished Up there . . . besides learning typing and all. It's guaranteed."

Buddy nodded as though he knew all about such places. "She's gonna stay around for the summer, though, ain't she?" he asked hopefully. "I mean . . ." He cleared his throat and tore at the grass with his thick squared-off fingers. "Bein' that I just got here and I don't know my way around yet, I was thinkin' maybe she could sorta interduce me to the place."

"I don't know," Lucy said, remembering how Suki's eyes had followed Buddy across the tent. "She's already got more boys lined up than you can shake a stick at. And besides, it don't take much to find your own way around here."

"Oh." Buddy sagged a little. "I was hopin' I might take her ta supper or somethin'. Kinda to console her, ya know?"

Lucy suddenly felt very sad again. Her daddy was gone, but not many folks cared about his passing. Life was ready to charge on ahead without him.

"Who knows," she said wearily. "We're comin' to your daddy's service tomorrow morning, so maybe you can ask her yourself then."

Buddy grinned and reached out to tap Lucy's cheek with a huge fist. "You're a pal," he said. "I knew the minute I saw you that you'd be a pal."

Lucy watched him brush grass from his backside as he walked away. She felt a little sorry for him, but then, she usually felt sorry for all the boys who swarmed around Suki like blowflies after rot. None of them meant a thing to her sister. Suki was hungry for city men with fancy manners and pretty faces like those who populated her favorite television soap operas. She toyed with the boyish hearts of Walea only for sport.

"He's just another dumb redneck," Suki would say of each boy she dated. "You just hide and watch, little sister. Sherry Kay's gonna find her a real catch one a these days."

Lucy knew that big, bashful Buddy Skidmore was not the catch Suki was looking for. Poor old Buddy would be just another statistic in Suki's ruthless forward march. Their daddy had always said that Suki . . .

The raw lump filled Lucy's throat again. Daddy. Daddy. Daddy. What a waste. What a terrible waste his life had been. Lucy closed her eyes and tried to imagine him smiling his quirky smile and poking fun the way he loved to in his rare sober moments. But the only picture she could fix in her mind was of Lydell's waxen, still face just before the mortician closed the coffin. Even in death he had looked slightly drunk.

Urgently Lucy blocked the vision and groped for something good to cling to. The stardust night drifted into her memory. She held on to that keepsake stubbornly, determined to remember her daddy as something more than a worthless drunk with occasional flashes of personality.

She didn't want the good parts to dim and fade away. She didn't ever want to forget that it was her daddy who had taught her to laugh and to dream. It was her daddy who had been her friend. And even at the end, a part of her had never quit hoping that he'd stop drinking and get well and be her friend again.

She'd never stop loving him ... even though he was gone. Just like Ms. Conroy. Gone from her life forever but never from her thoughts.

She buried her face in her hands and let the grief take her.

8

Ellis

Ellis shifted from foot to foot, adjusting the weight of his back-pack and waiting for his father to make a move. They were standing in a grove of trees beside a narrow two-lane road. The pickup truck they'd hitched a ride in was long out of sight and Ellis didn't know if they were waiting for another ride or settling in to make camp for the night. Frank was staring off into some inner distance.

"You ever learn about mountain men in those candy-ass schools of yours?" Frank asked. "Jim Bridger ... Liver-Eating Johnson ... Jed Smith?"

Ellis nodded.

"What?" Frank demanded. "I can't hear you."

"Yes, I've read a little about—"

"What!"

"Yes, *sir.* I have read about them."

Frank relaxed. "They were the finest men this country's ever produced. The finest. Tough, self-reliant, fearless. . . . If we had men like that in Vietnam—or in the White House, for that matter—the whole country wouldn't be fucked up like it is now." Frank tilted his head back and took a deep breath. "Smell that? That's purity. That's freedom."

Ellis shifted again. He wanted to sit down but he knew Frank would take that as a sign of weakness.

"Are we going to McLeod?" he asked.

Frank's head snapped around and he eyed Ellis suspiciously. "What do you know about McLeod?"

"Nothing ... sir. The man in the truck just said we were nearing McLeod and I saw a sign—."

Without warning Frank struck off through the trees. Ellis sprinted to catch up.

104

"Pace yourself, son," Frank ordered. "You're still soft as a girl."

"Yes, sir." Ellis fell back and worked at even pacing.

He didn't know where his father was leading him, but Frank had seemed to be full of purpose from the beginning. The glove compartment of the car had held maps with carefully marked routes that Ellis caught glimpses of. The trunk had held dehydrated food and streamlined backpacks and the finest down-filled sleeping bags and hiking boots and heavy clothes.

Where were they going? And why had Frank abandoned their car in favor of hitchhiking? And why did they have to walk now? Was this his father's idea of a father-son camping trip? Was this supposed to be fun?

He had tried to keep track of their journey, but he had lost the thread somewhere. Frank was tireless and had driven while Ellis slept, so he often missed the state-line signs, and as they progressed, the city names on the highway mileage markers became unfamiliar and yielded no clues.

He had no idea how much distance they'd covered before or after they'd left the car. And he wasn't even certain of how many days had passed. The time had been distorted by fear of the menacing father who had taken control of his life and by wounded anger toward the mother who had allowed it to happen.

"Your mama wanted me to take you, sissy. She forced me into it. And now she's glad to be rid of you ... glad she's free to do all that important stuff she's always wanting to do."

"But can't I just talk to her?" Ellis had pleaded over and over. "Can't we just go to a phone somewhere and call her? She might be really anxious to have me back now."

But Frank always laughed and made nasty comments about how busy she was with all her boyfriends. Ellis didn't believe that part. When had she ever had a boyfriend before? He wondered if his mother knew how miserable he was. Did she know Frank was making him walk till his calves knotted, and making him chop firewood with a hatchet even after his hands were blistered and raw? Did she know that he had to carry a heavy backpack and eat disgusting dried food out of foil packets for every meal? Did she know that he was lonely and sometimes very afraid? How could she have agreed to this?

The terrain steepened and Ellis struggled to keep moving forward. His thigh muscles burned deeply, and he couldn't get enough air in his lungs. He fell further and further behind Frank. Just when he thought he couldn't take another step, he broke through the trees and saw that his father had stopped ahead.

Frank was gazing outward. He stood on a large flat rock with one foot resting on a slightly higher rock. The land fell away beneath him, separating into stands of trees and strips of meadow that were slashed by gaping, jagged rock and twisting ribbons of water. An uneven mountain range loomed in the postcard distance.

The vista was dazzling. Ellis forgot his exhaustion and stepped forward with a feeling of awe and reverence. They stood in separate silence for a time before Frank spoke.

"Do you know what destiny means, son?"

Ellis shrugged. "Sort of."

Frank snapped his head around to frown down at Ellis. "What?"

Ellis straightened. "Yes, sir. I think I know . . . sir."

Frank turned back to the magnificent sweep before them. "Good," he said. "A man should have a sense of his destiny. It's so easy to get lost."

"You never get lost," Ellis said. "Mama said you hid all over the jungles in Vietnam and you never got lost."

"Oh, she did, did she?" Frank stepped down from the ledge and shrugged out of his bulky pack. "Well, she's wrong. I was lost over there. As lost as I've ever been."

He moved back to the shelter of trees and chose a spot where he could sit down and lean back against a fallen log. Ellis followed suit, gratefully pulling off his own pack and sinking down to the cushion of pine needles.

"Women don't understand a lot of things about men, son. That's a fact. It's always been that way and I don't care how many girls go to college and get jobs, it's always going to be that way." He opened his pack and began sorting through the foil packets of food.

"Where are we, Dad?"

"You're on your way to becoming a man, Ellis. And that's how I want you to think of me—man to man." He handed two foil packets to Ellis. "Call me 'sir' for now."

"Yes, sir. But where are we?"

Frank glanced around and breathed a deep sigh of satisfaction. "You've heard of no-man's-land, haven't you?"

"Yes, sir."

"This is it. No man owns this land. It's completely untamed. Its spirit is untouched. Names here are irrelevant because naming land is only for humans to control and claim it."

"But how do we know where we've been or where we're going?"

"We can go any direction. We can go where there's food or water. We can go where there's a good place to camp. It doesn't matter where we've been because we have no need to go back."

Ellis stared down at his packaged lunch in an effort to hide his confusion. He tore open the foil and concentrated on chewing a strip of dried apple.

"Tonight we'll hunt and build a fire and have a real meal," Frank said.

"You mean shoot something and eat it?" Ellis stared at his father in disbelief.

"Yes." Frank shook his head in unveiled disgust. "Of course I mean shoot something and eat it. I suppose you think meat grows on supermarket shelves in plastic wrappings."

Ellis swallowed hard.

"Get used to it, sissy boy. We're just like cougars or bears now. We're going to live off the land the way the good Lord and Mother Nature intended." He took a drink from his canteen, then softened. "Here," he said, handing the canteen across to Ellis.

Ellis drank, but it didn't help the queasiness in his stomach.

"Don't worry," Frank said. "You'll get used to it." He settled back against the log and smiled at some distant thought. "I remember when my grandfather, Colonel Ellis Fielding—your great-grandfather—first took me out. I must have been about seven, because it was the first summer after his retirement." He smiled again at the memory. "He took me to Sawtooth ... not so far from here ... and he handed me a fishing rod and said, 'Catch us some dinner, Frankie.'

"Well, I scampered right on down to that stream and dropped my line in and pulled out a nice rainbow, and he came over and took it off my hook and dropped it in a basket, and I caught another and another until he had about seven in the basket.

"He told me that was enough, and I was feeling pretty pleased with myself. Then he handed me a knife and told me those fish weren't dinner yet. He said to take them down close to the water and slice their bellies open and pull out their innards and rinse them clean while he got a fire going."

Frank chuckled. "Hell, I'd never killed anything, much less cleaned it. And I didn't know I was supposed to knock them in the head first to be sure they were dead."

He chuckled again and filled his mouth with dried beef. The chewing didn't stop him from talking.

"I'll tell you, that fish flipped and flopped, and I sliced and hacked, and guts and blood flew every which way. Once I finally got the job done, I leaned right over and tossed my own guts.

"The old colonel . . . he didn't say anything. He just kept build-ing that fire like nothing unusual was happening. So after I fin-ished puking, I went on and attacked the rest of those fish the same way, and by the time we sat down to dinner, I looked like I'd been involved in a massacre."

Frank sighed gently. "But I learned, son. And so will you. You can't live out here long and stay a sissy. No, sir. This land will make you a man or kill you. And you'll learn what the colonel taught me: hunting an animal and killing it, smelling that fresh blood and knowing you've won the ultimate contest . . ." He paused a moment, his expression aglow with remembered plea-sures. "It's better than taking a woman, son. And you can't get much better than that."

He laughed and stood up. "Now, that's something you wouldn't have learned in that fancy school of yours!"

Ellis tried to smile. Something cold and heavy was taking root in his belly and sucking the energy from his entire body.

"On your feet, soldier," Frank ordered cheerfully. "We've got some miles to cover."

Ellis heard the same order every morning for weeks. "On your feet, soldier—we've got some miles to cover."

If nothing had a name and there was no place special they needed to go and they were on their own schedule, then why was his father in such a hurry?

Why, when Ellis stopped to look at something interesting, did his father react with so much impatience? "That might be pentste-mon, but hell's bells, boy, we don't have time for flowers." Or: "That's a kingfisher. Come on, they're not worth a damn to eat."

But he didn't dare question his father out loud. Frank's moods were as mercurial as March weather, and Ellis had learned that questions were often all that was needed to trigger a storm. Si-lence seemed to be the best policy with Frank, so Ellis developed the ability to keep silent as quickly as he developed strong leg muscles and the stamina to keep up with his father's pace.

For over a month Ellis trudged dutifully behind his father. And layer by layer he grew a hard, impenetrable exterior—an invisible shield that kept disturbances out and kept his emotions hidden safely inside. Frank's hostility and disapproval could no longer pierce through to hurt him. The sight and smell of an animal's death and the whispered "you're mine" as Frank squeezed the trigger no longer touched him. But he still woke each morning with an ache that was part yearning for his mother and his comfortable, secure world and part dread of what the new day would bring. And the only thing that kept him going was the knowledge that their camping trip had to have an end.

Finally, after they had caught and smoked a beautiful salmon and Frank was in a particularly good mood, Ellis gathered his courage and asked, "When are we going home?"

Frank exploded. "Home! You mean back to that whining blue-blood mother of yours? You mean back to your rich relatives who don't know how to wipe their own asses? Back to where there's air that rots your lungs and pissant rules and a lot of ball-less politicians who want to fuck up the world?"

Frank paced back and forth in front of Ellis. His face was red and the veins at his temples throbbed and his chin jutted out at a sharp angle. *"This* is your home, boy. The best home there is! And thank God there aren't many shitheads in this world who are smart enough to figure that out, or this place'd be fucked up by people too."

Ellis' shield cracked and shattered and he sagged down against a rock, fighting back tears. It was so clear now. His father had not been given visiting rights or permission for the trip. This was no regular father-son outing. Frank had stalked him and whispered "you're mine" and swooped down and taken him.

He decided right then to run away. How far could they really be from cities or farms or at least a ranger station? His father liked to think they were in the middle of an immense wilderness, but how big a chunk of wilderness could be left right in the middle of the United States? Surely a few days' walking would find a road or some other pointer toward civilization.

He lay still that night until he heard Frank's soft snoring begin. Then he eased out of his sleeping bag and crept into the dark forest. The day had been cloudy and the night was a black hole without moonlight or starlight. He tripped and stumbled, unable to see well enough but afraid to stop. At dawn he crawled beneath a rock overhang to rest and think. He realized that he had been foolish not to wait for a clear night, but that regret was eclipsed by the heady sense of freedom that coursed through his veins like a drug. The fact that he had succeeded in spite of the darkness made him feel strong and invincible.

He decided to travel east and launched himself on a path directly into the blinding glare of the sunrise. His stomach growled and he thought of the wild berries he would find along the way and the pink-flowered plant that would yield roots to eat. He had been afraid to try sneaking food from Frank's pack for the trip, but he wasn't worried. The forest was full of food.

By dusk his hunger was sharp and constant and he was desperate for a drink of water. Where were the cool, trickling streams that his father seemed to find so easily? Where were the tangles of wild raspberries and the carpets of tart strawberries that Frank always led them to?

He huddled in the hollow of a dead tree and listened to the stirring of the night animals. Owls hooted in the rustling canopy over his head, and the howls of wolves sounded in the distance. He wondered if he would ever see his mother again.

At some point he drifted off into exhausted sleep, only to wake in panic at the piercing scream of a cougar. The night was an alien force around him. He had always felt so safe with his father. Not once in their days of hiking deeper and deeper into the wilderness had he feared anything but Frank Fielding himself.

His every waking moment had been governed by Frank's cloudy, searching eyes and rigidly set spine. And his sleep had been threaded with Frank's chilling smile as he spotted prey and swung a rifle from his pack, sighting and shooting with the deadly precision of a natural predator. Ellis had believed that all the danger and treachery existing in the wild, beautiful land they traveled lay within the reach of Frank Fielding's shadow.

Now, as he pressed his back against the rotting bark of his shelter, clutching a stick as a weapon and peering out into the menacing darkness, Ellis realized that he had been naive and foolish. In running from Frank he had simply exchanged one danger for another. The forest held no lovable bears or nurturing wolves or other protections for lost children. He was alone. And he was ill-equipped to take care of himself.

Sunrise freed him from the terror of night and he pulled himself up and forced his leaden feet to carry him forward. The thick fragrance of pine and spruce and fir burned his parched nasal membranes and he could no longer summon enough saliva to swallow.

The trees gave way to sage-covered rocky outcroppings. Then the ground sloped downward and he stumbled into a narrow meadow, startling several grazing deer and causing a flash of color as bluebirds and redstarts and jays rose and circled around him. He waded through the grass, crushing bright petals of Indian paintbrush beneath the tread of his heavy boots.

It was all so beautiful, but as deadly as his father. He knew that he could collapse in that meadow and die, and the animals would feast on his flesh and the plants would suck the glut of minerals from the earth around his rotting body, and his death would have no more significance than that of a worm shriveling to a husk on some crowded city's hot pavement. The phrase "survival of the fittest" suddenly took on substance and meaning. It was no longer a worn cliché from nature shows and science texts. The grim reality of it gripped him, etching itself permanently into his perceptions.

He pushed the building terror away and tried to imagine what his father would do. Frank had told him a story about a hero who was sent home from the jungles of Vietnam and went straight into the mountains in the state of Washington. With nothing but the clothes on his back, the man had managed not only to survive but the last time anyone made contact with him he was thriving.

Ellis felt disgust with himself. The weather was mild. He had on comfortable clothing and sturdy hiking boots. Yet he wasn't able to provide himself with the most basic of needs. All this time he had followed Frank to water and food, but now that the responsibility was his own, he was lost.

Water. That was the most important thing. The birds, the deer, the flowers—they all needed water to survive. But where was it? How could he learn their secrets?

He walked the perimeter of the meadow, searching for clues. At the opposite side he found a trail leading through a grove of quaking aspen and on into the beginning of more coniferous forest. The discovery filled him with hope and renewed determination, and he struck out in a purposeful, measured gait.

He realized that he'd been traveling blindly before, letting his thoughts meander and his senses idle, just as though he were still following Frank's lead. Now he strained to catch every tiny sound and stray scent, every subtle variation of his surroundings.

In spite of this awakened alertness, he traveled all day without finding water or food. His tongue became a thick lump in his mouth and his eyelids rasped across his eyes when he tried to blink. He lost track of where he was going.

Lodgepole pines surrounded him. They pressed in on him like the bars of an endless cage. The thin straight shafts of their trunks pointed upward like hundreds of arrows telling him the way was up. He leaned back, trying to see how high they went.

Suddenly he was on his back on the ground. The tops of the pines swayed gently as though bending to look down at him from their great height. They looked sad. His eyes lost focus and his heavy eyelids fell. Rest. He just needed rest.

Sometime later he dreamed that his mother had come to give him water. Her hair was down and loose and she was smiling and crooning as she lifted his head and held the cool liquid to his lips. He gulped greedily and choked and shuddered.

Cold water ran down his neck and soaked his shirt, shocking him into gasping consciousness. He opened his eyes and met his father's hard, unflinching stare.

"Don't drink too much at once," Frank ordered.

He pulled the canteen away and lowered Ellis' head to the ground. Then he leaned back on his haunches and studied his son for a long deadly moment.

"We'll camp here tonight," he announced. "You aren't fit to go much of anyplace."

When Ellis woke again, his father was holding a tin cup of steaming liquid out to him. Frank helped him pull up into a sitting position and then placed the cup in his hands.

"Take it slow, but drink all of it."

Ellis leaned against a tree and sipped at the broth. His father had cleared a space and made a fire while he slept. The boiled carcass of a squirrel rested in liquid in the center of their one frying pan and he knew that the animal had just been sacrificed to provide the life-giving broth. He thanked the squirrel silently and felt a great welling-up of acceptance. Survival of the fittest. The law of nature. One life supporting another in a great unending chain.

This was the natural order. There was no way to change it or run away. And just like a hatchling eagle or a mewling bear cub, his existence depended on the dedication and resourcefulness of his parent and keeper. Without Frank he was dead.

When Ellis finished the broth, Frank took the cup and refilled it with the remainder of the liquid. He walked back from the fire and squatted, facing Ellis and fixing him with a dispassionate half-lidded stare as he handed back the full cup.

"Next time I'll leave you out there to die," he said.

And Ellis had no doubt that his father meant it.

9

Lucy

Lucy's life changed immediately after her father's death. The luxury of a gradual ascent to awareness and maturity was no longer hers. She was yanked through the entrance to adulthood and the door was slammed permanently behind her.

Two weeks after the funeral she began work at the trailer factory. Wanda engineered the job by greatly exaggerating Lucy's skills to a washing customer who happened to be married to the factory's office manager. Lucy was offered a beginning wage to type and file. Since full-time positions were scarce for sixteen-year-olds, she accepted without complaint or comment. Her mother had been right. They could not survive without another full salary coming in.

By day she struggled to hide her inexperience and learn as she worked. By night she struggled to keep the unraveling threads of her family together.

She became the enforcer, insisting that half of Suki's dime-store paycheck be contributed each week regardless of Suki's whining about how she couldn't save for her own future, and making certain that Anita addressed and rubber-banded the weekly stacks of "Swapper/Shopper News" that were her responsibility. And when Wanda and Suki began one of their screaming fights or Wanda and Anita butted heads, she mediated, cushioning them from each other.

The fantasies that had always insulated her were not strong enough to soften the new truths she faced. Even the loss of Ms. Conroy had been something she could swaddle with hope. She could picture her teacher leading a glamorous life and she could imagine Ms. Conroy sending for her someday.

Her life held no scraps of hope to cling to or embroider on now. She wouldn't finish high school. She would never go to college or become a teacher. She would never get enough money to move her mama out of the old trailer or lighten the backbreaking work load. And she would never see her father again.

Whenever she had the energy left at the end of the day to stare at the dark ceiling and consider it all, she could feel the bitterness creeping up. She thought about the story of the young Lydell, fresh from the Korean War and touring around by bus to visit service buddies and see the country whose uniform he had been wearing. He had stopped in Walea and bought a hamburger at a place that had recently hired a slender brunette named Wanda Kunkel.

The story had sounded so romantic to Lucy when she was young. She and Suki had loved to stare at the pictures of their father with his shy grin and his uniform, self-consciously posing beside a vivid, lush version of their mother. Wanda's heritage was a crazy quilt of Irish, Mexican, French, and Creek Indian, and to Lucy the nineteen-year-old Wanda had been beautiful.

She viewed those same pictures with sadness now. How different would her father's life have been if he had passed right on through Walea? If he had resisted the temptations of a hungry-eyed girl and pursued his own dreams? Or if he had found a more forgiving place to settle and a gentler woman to love? The questions had begun to haunt Lucy even before her father's death. She had done more than her share of bedside duty during the weeks Lydell lay in the hospital with his damaged liver, choking and sputtering, and she had often spent the endless hours wondering over the twists and turns of her father's history.

She had always thought of it like that—her father's history, her father's bad luck. As though her mother had been a brick wall that her father accidentally collided with. And she blamed Wanda for trapping Lydell and dragging him into poverty with her, for failing to keep Lydell happy and sober and productive, for not loving him enough to save him.

But as the summer wore on and the weight of Lydell's death settled on them like the heat, Lucy began to see her mother differently. There were no secrets anymore. They were all wage earners now, so Wanda kept nothing hidden. She discussed everything with them and then quietly solved the problems herself while the girls argued and worried over a course of action. She negotiated a payment schedule for the mountain of medical bills that Lydell's dying had incurred. She traded Lydell's shotgun and shells to the landlord for back rent due on the trailer. She gave Lydell's hunting dogs to the mortician for the balance due on the coffin. And, to Lucy's amazement, she even talked the ruthless Howard of Howard's A-1 Used Cars into a swap. She'd learned that Howard had a girl taking baton lessons, so she convinced Howard to give her clear title to their truck in exchange for the battery-operated, light-up twirling costumes that Suki had worn to fame.

Through the years the incoming money had seldom equaled the bills due, and Lucy slowly realized that it was her mother who had kept the electricity flowing and the truck running and food on the table. And it was her mother who had magically conjured up the extra resources for occasional gifts and entertainment for each of them. While her father daydreamed and joked and tinkered, Wanda had kept the family afloat.

Her father was not the suffering hero to her anymore, and her mother was not the brick wall. They were both victims of something big and evil. And Lucy felt herself being sucked into the same treacherous whirlpool.

The hot, dreary summer wore on, stretching them all to breaking points. Wanda began having faint spells that she insisted were only due to the heat. The spitting air conditioner gave out. The television set developed an unpleasant roll to the picture. The telephone was disconnected. Lucy caught Anita smoking.

Only on Sundays was there any relief. Then they went to tent service and stayed afterward to visit and drink cold lemonade and listen to Brother Dean Ed and Sister Dora Mae pick their guitars and sing Christian songs. Lucy always took an old quilt so she could lie on the grass at the tree line, just far enough away to feel separate from the adults on their folding chairs at the mouth of the tent and the young people playing on the lawn. She liked to lie there and watch Buddy Skidmore show off with the other boys. They'd lob the ball in lazy arcs at first and then the play would become more intense and they would take off their shirts and let the sun beat down on their sweat-glistened backs. Suki always sat across the way with two other girls her age, chanting and cheering, and the boys rolled their shirts into balls and threw them to the girls like damp offerings.

Lucy looked forward all week to Sunday. To emptying herself of worries and stretching out on the quilt, her body easing into languor in the afternoon heat. The adult voices and the music fading into a background roar. There were no daydreams in her life anymore. This was as close as she got. Lying in the shade, her mind drunk on sunshine and idleness, her senses alive. The smell of grass and dust, the taste of cold lemonade, the occasional breeze playing on her skin, and the curious sensations brought on by watching the dance of sweaty male flesh. This was a dream-state created by an absence of thought, a loss of memory, a denial of both fantasy and emotion.

Today was Friday. Sunday was not coming around fast enough this week. Lucy kicked at flattened Budweiser cans in the road as she walked home from work, and she thought about the other kids her age in Walea who were getting ready for the new school year to begin. They were worrying about new clothes and sharpened pencils and teachers who were known for surprise tests or extra homework or frequent detention punishments. They were planning who to sit by in the lunchroom and who to support for homecoming queen.

Wearily she dragged heavy feet toward the concrete blocks that served as steps. The long-ago storm that had carried away Ms. Conroy had also carried off their little front porch, and it had never been replaced. It probably never would be.

She paused to check her flowers. The marigolds in the discarded bathtub were dying. Even with her best efforts, something was wrong.

It occurred to her that maybe no one was home. The truck wasn't in the yard and the trailer was closed up in spite of the stifling heat. Lucy reminded herself to check the cost of a new screen door to replace the one that had been torn off by the high wind of the previous week. An involuntary sigh escaped her. The temperature was unbearable, tonight was her night to cook, and both Anita and Wanda would be tired and irritable. Friday night meant finishing up the rush laundry orders for Saturday delivery. And it meant finishing up the "Swapper/Shoppers" because Saturday was the day they went out as well. Suki would of course be cheery and not needing any help or consolation. But then, Suki would be home only long enough to change her clothes and redo her makeup before speeding off beside Buddy Skidmore or some other boy.

Buddy. Lucy brightened at the thought of him. He had promised to bring by a watermelon. Maybe it would be tonight. Maybe he would stay and they would all sit in the yard and spit seeds on the ground while Buddy told them one of his funny slow stories.

Reluctantly Lucy stepped onto the concrete blocks and opened the trailer door. The metal knob was hot against her palm. There were sounds from inside. Someone was home.

"Why is the door . . . ?" she started to ask, but before she could finish the question, she realized that she heard sobbing. "What is it? What's wrong?" Lucy's heart hammered as she rushed inside.

Wanda never cried. She had broken down only once during Lydell's prolonged illness, yet here she was on the couch with her face buried in her hands and her shoulders shaking with emotion.

At the sound of Lucy's voice, Anita came running from the bedroom. Tears streamed down her cheeks and her expression was wild and disoriented. "Suki's gone," Anita cried. "She's gone!"

Wanda dropped her hands and lifted her head. She didn't exactly look at Lucy. She just turned her face in Lucy's direction. Her eyes were red and brimming with tears and her expression was strange.

Lucy's pulse slowed and she took a deep breath and sat down on a dinette chair. "Suki left to go to that school, didn't she, Mama?" The oscillating fan on the Formica table stirred the dead air around her.

One of Wanda's hands drifted uselessly across the chenille bedspread that covered the tattered couch, then stopped to tear absently at the shreds of floral upholstery where the bedspread didn't quite cover the arm. The blankness in her eyes was scary.

"Mama!" Lucy shouted. "Tell me what happened."

Wanda's head snapped and she glared at Lucy. "What do you think happened!" Spittle flew from her mouth, and her face contorted into a seething mask of rage. "She ran out on us! She left us!"

"And Mama was gonna kill her with a gun!" Anita sobbed.

The hard angles of Wanda's face dissolved into shame and new tears sprouted from the corners of her eyes and flowed down to drip from her chin.

Lucy looked from her mother to her sister and back again.

"She came home early from work," Wanda said. She blotted her face with a handkerchief, but the stream of tears cut a new course. "She'd talked to that school on the pay phone at the dime store."

Wanda's bottom lip quivered and Lucy had to look away.

"Did you know she'd already signed the papers for that school, Lucy? Did you know she's been lyin' ta me all along? She signed 'em and sent 'em the day she turned eighteen! Didn't ask my permission or give one thought to me . . . her own mother."

"I didn't know, Mama. But I'm not surprised. Eighteen is legal, you know."

Wanda bolted from the sagging couch, nearly knocking it off the brick that propped up the legless corner. She raised her arms and looked up as though summoning divine help. "Does eighteen mean a mother ain't no good anymore? Does eighteen mean a child forgets all the love and care and raisin' she's had?"

Lucy looked nervously toward Anita, whose face was pale and drawn. "So exactly what happened?" she asked, unable to keep the accusation out of her voice.

"The school had got her a job." Wanda sniffed and dropped back down onto the couch. The tears were in remission and her tone was resigned. "Startin' Monday." She swallowed hard. "I told her she wasn't goin' and she put up a fight and then just threw some stuff in a box and stomped out."

Lucy realized with sudden alarm that the missing pickup and the missing Suki must be together. "Did she take the truck?"

"Said she'd leave it at the bus station," Wanda said.

"That's just about right!" Lucy jumped up and started to pace.

It wasn't enough that her sister had walked out without saying good-bye. It wasn't enough that her sister hadn't trusted her enough to share her plans. Now Suki had fixed it so Lucy would have to walk five miles to the bus station. And she'd have to do it that night or they wouldn't have the truck in time to deliver laundry and the "Swapper/Shopper" the next morning.

"She wouldn'ta left like that," Anita whispered. "But Mama went back to her bedroom and got that old gun a Daddy's and told Suki to get out now 'stead a Monday. Mama told Suki she'd just as soon shoot her as watch her go."

Wanda folded inward, shrinking and aging before Lucy's eyes. She huddled on the couch, hugging herself and rocking slightly, and a low keening moan escaped from her.

The eerie sound made the hairs on the back of Lucy's neck stand up, and the anger that had erupted inside her died as quickly as it had flared. She turned, anxiously scanning the trailer until she spotted the pistol lying on the floor beside the gas heater. She picked it up, handling it just the way Lydell had taught her when she was seven years old and they'd whiled away Sunday afternoons putting holes in cans.

The moaning continued, eroding the fine edge of calm that separated Lucy from a mass of exposed nerves. Her hands shook slightly as she broke open the gun. The round brass ends of bullets stared at her from the cylinder like dull eyes of death. Wanda had loaded the gun before waving it at her daughter.

The next thing she knew, Lucy was out in the yard sitting on Lydell's decaying row of theater seats. He never had fixed them up to sell for valuable antiques as he'd planned. They were still propped up in the yard, where the sun and the wind and the rain were finishing what fifty years of moviegoers hadn't been able to accomplish.

Lucy leaned her head back and stared up at the sky. The sun glared from the west—a malevolent red eye peeping over the horizon—yet she could see the moon already. It looked fragile, almost transparent.

Anita crept out silently and sat on the mat of weeds at Lucy's feet. Automatically Lucy reached out to smooth her sister's hair, just as she had been doing since before Anita really even had any hair.

"What are you smilin' about, Luce?"

"Was I smiling?" Lucy looked down into Anita's sad heart-shaped face and felt a wave of tenderness. "I was thinking about what a bald baby you were," she teased gently.

Anita grinned and then swatted Lucy's leg. "Get outta here." But the playfulness drained from her as quickly as it had risen, and she stared at the gun lying in Lucy's lap. "Why'd Mama do that?"

"You know, Nita, how sometimes when somebody hurts you, you want to hurt them back? Well, that's all Mama was doing. Suki hurt her bad and she was trying to do something big enough to hurt Suki back." Lucy felt like a fraud as she spoke. Her words sounded so wise and calm, but she didn't feel that way at all.

"Think she woulda really shot Suki?"

"No. 'Course not. Mama loves Suki a bunch . . . why would she want to shoot her?" But Lucy wasn't so sure at all, not at all.

Just then Buddy's black dualie pickup roared into the yard. He looked to be in a terrible state as he slammed his way out the door, banging his elbow and knocking his rifle and ropes off the gun rack. "Is it true?!" he demanded, advancing on the sisters like an enraged football player after a stolen ball. "There's people sayin' Suki got on the evenin' bus to Dallas. Is that true?!"

"Yeah, it's true," Lucy said flatly.

Buddy's anger dissipated in a long helpless sigh. "Shit," he said, sinking down onto a stack of old tires.

No one spoke for a long while. The sun eased on down and the night chorus of cicadas and crickets and coyotes and bullfrogs began to tune up, making the human silence insignificant.

"Guess that's ya'll's truck parked at the bus station, then, ain't it?" Buddy asked. His voice hung somewhere between bravery and despair.

"Guess so," Lucy agreed.

"Guess I oughta give ya a ride in ta fetch it, then." Buddy stood and pulled at his starched Wranglers to straighten the knife creases. "We was s'posed ta have a date," he said sadly. "I was

takin' her ta the movies and then . . ." His voice trailed off and
he shook his head.

"I wouldn't mind seein' a movie," Lucy said.

"Well, c'mon, then."

"Tell Mama for me, will ya, Nita?" Lucy called as she hurried
to the hulking black truck. She felt bad about leaving Wanda and
Anita when they were upset, but she'd learned that opportunities
were scarce as hen's teeth and she needed an uplift right then.

She climbed up into the cab and smiled at Buddy. "Thanks,"
she said. "You saved me a long walk."

"Sure," he said mechanically. "Anytime."

Lucy looked back as Buddy roared out of the yard. Anita was
still standing in the same place. Lucy waved. Anita turned and
ran into the trailer without waving back.

"It was nothing, Anita," Lucy assured her sister the next day
as they delivered the "Swapper/Shoppers."

Anita's sullen glare showed no improvement. Obviously she
didn't believe it was nothing.

And she was right. Buddy showed up every night after that for
Lucy's company and consolation. Lucy didn't know what to make
of the situation. It wasn't "nothing," but it didn't feel much like
"something" either.

Lucy had never been around boys much before. She didn't
know what to expect from a boy and she didn't know if Buddy's
invitations constituted dating or not. She just followed Buddy's
lead, agreeing to whatever entertainment he'd planned, whether
it was a movie or spotlight shooting at snapping turtles in a pond.
She answered his questions about Suki and endured his long
gloomy silences and listened to his football stories and she remained cheerful and compliant no matter what.

Sometimes he would take her out into the country to drink
beer. This worried Lucy whenever it happened. The only drinker
she'd ever been around was her father, and alcohol had poisoned
him to death. She hated to think that Buddy was destined for the
same fate. And she was also afraid of what would happen if Buddy's father found out. Reverend Skidmore's most frequent sermons were against "the demon corrupters of our moral fiber."
That included alcohol, drugs, and ungodly women.

But even when Buddy asked if she was ready for a "six-pack"
night, Lucy was afraid to speak up and say no. She was certain
that Buddy would stop seeing her at the first unpleasantry or sign
of disagreement.

Three weeks flew by and Buddy left for his sophomore year

in college. His departure threw Lucy into what her mother called a "state." She wasn't exactly depressed, but she was down and she was easily irritated and she had a hard time thinking a positive thought about anything.

When she read Suki's letters—addressed to Anita and Lucy only—detailing the wonders of Dallas and the excitement of training for a "real career," she wanted to scream and throw things. When she read Buddy's brief notes about the dorms or the parties or his football buddies, she went into black moods.

Work was becoming easier. She'd mastered the filing and doubled her typing speed. Her pay had been increased by a nickel an hour. And she'd developed confidence in her abilities. When an office contest was announced, she accepted the challenge with excitement. The woman who had the highest grammar and spelling score would win a special position and a substantial raise and would thereafter be responsible for proofreading all work. Lucy checked out grammar books from the Walea library and stayed up late for weeks before the test, poring over the material and testing and retesting herself. She was determined to win.

The results came back and a coworker was named the winner.

The office manager took Lucy aside. "You had the best score, Lucy. But we couldn't give it to someone so new ... and so young. You understand, don't you? It would have caused hard feelings."

That night Lucy began reading the classifieds. She was restless and unhappy and she knew that whatever it was that she wanted, she would never find it at the trailer factory.

Money pressures bit down even harder on them with the loss of Suki's weekly contribution. The washing machine's motor went out and Wanda had to do the wash by hand. The television did its final roll and the refrigerator developed a strange chirping noise that signaled the permanent thawing of the freezer compartment.

The blow that finally broke Wanda came when two of the truck's tires self-destructed within days of each other. Lucy found her tough, iron-willed mother sitting in the bathroom on Saturday morning, staring at the wall.

"You know, your daddy never believed in insurance," she said hollowly without acknowledging Lucy's presence. " 'Why scrimp when you're alive so's you can pay into a policy that allows folks to have a good time after you're gone?' he always said. Your daddy never believed in a lot of things ... including himself. But he always believed in me."

"C'mon, Mama," Lucy coaxed. "Why don't you take a little

nap?" She started to offer Wanda some iced tea, but remembered that they didn't have ice anymore.

"I'm beat, Lucy. Beat."

"Stop it, Mama. Everything's going to be fine again. You just rest a little and I'm going to take care of things."

She talked her mother into bed, leaving Anita to sit with her. Then she searched the trailer. There were Lydell's two war medals and some diamond-chip earrings that had belonged to his mother. There was a good Buck knife. There was a silver tray Suki had won in a twirling pageant. There was the pistol Wanda had waved at Suki. And there were her own treasures: the birthstone baby ring Lydell had bought for her when she was born, the camera Ms. Conroy had given her for her birthday, and the antique shawl she'd found in Ms. Conroy's empty closet.

She gathered everything on the Formica table. She stared at the assortment, refusing to allow herself one regret, one sentimental thought. Did all this equal two tires and a washing machine? There was only one way to find out.

She loaded everything into grocery bags and walked out to the two-lane to hitch a ride into town.

When she returned later that afternoon, Lucy was the owner of two retread tires, a rebuilt washing machine, and a stray black kitten with three white paws. She'd sold or traded everything except Ms. Conroy's shawl. No one at any of her stops had been interested in the delicate silk-fringed antique, so she carefully folded it and put it back in her drawer.

Her holding action worked, and both Wanda and Anita were ecstatic. Anita named the kitten Socks. Wanda declared the washing machine to be the best she'd ever had.

Lucy's pleasure in her own success faded quickly. She needed more. She wanted more. She was determined to make a better life for them all.

Finding another job proved more difficult than Lucy had imagined. With her long working hours she had little time to devote to job interviews, and in spite of her acquired secretarial proficiency, her age was still against her.

The low point came for her during Christmas. She missed a good job opportunity because the company had a high-school-diploma requirement. Her long-awaited Christmas bonus turned out to be a ten-dollar bill. And they received a card from Suki saying she wouldn't be home for the holiday because she'd met the man of her dreams and was going to Illinois with him over her Christmas break to meet his parents.

The only thing that kept Lucy going was the promise of seeing Buddy again. Each Sunday after church, Charity Skidmore talked about Buddy coming home for Christmas, and Lucy's excitement grew by weekly increments. The Sunday before Buddy's expected arrival, Lucy asked Charity to please tell Buddy to just come on out, since there was no way for him to call on the phone first.

Charity's eyes narrowed at the request, but she smiled sweetly and promised she'd deliver the message.

Buddy did not come by. Lucy was disappointed, but she poured her energy into anticipating the Christmas Eve service. Buddy would be there and they would be able to talk, maybe even go out for a Coke afterward, and they could make plans for the remaining week of his vacation. She'd saved to buy him a small Christmas gift—a fancy shift knob for his pickup—and she couldn't wait to surprise him with it.

She carefully pressed her best dress and bought a new pair of panty hose at the dime store. She rummaged through the box of castoffs Suki had left and found some old lipstick and powder blush to experiment with. And she twisted her long thick hair up in an effort to look more sophisticated.

She walked into the crowded tent between her mother and sister and immediately began standing on tiptoe to find Buddy.

"Why, there y'all are. I know Buddy will want to say hi to y'all." Charity Skidmore bustled over to them like a party hostess and ushered them off to the side.

"Buddy, yoo-hoo, Buddy darlin' . . . I've got some folks who want to say hi to you."

Buddy appeared from around a knot of people and his face lit up in a wide grin. "Hey! How y'all doin'!"

Trailing behind him was a wide-hipped blond in an outfit that was color-coordinated from her shoes to the bow in her hair. The girl caught up with him and moved in possessively beside him.

"Mind your manners, now!" Charity ordered. "Introduce your friend."

"Oh, sure. Ah . . . this here's LaDonna Newberry. LaDonna, that there's Anita and Lucy and Wanda Clare." He glanced around casually. "Suki ain't with y'all, huh?"

Lucy shook her head.

"LaDonna's daddy is the new podiatrist," Charity explained, "and the whole Newberry family has joined our flock."

"That's real nice," Wanda said.

"Yeah, Mama thought I oughta show LaDonna around a little while I'm home," Buddy said.

LaDonna blushed slightly and Charity shot her son an exasperated look.

"Well, we have to find seats," Lucy said. "Come on, now, Mama. You know how you like a good seat for Christmas sermon."

Wanda and Anita looked at each other and then at her, but she marched off ahead before they could say anything to embarrass her. She found them seats right up front, but she didn't hear a word of Reverend Skidmore's Christmas goodwill sermon. She was too busy thinking of all the reasons she hated Buddy.

Buddy Skidmore was not the only boy in the world, just as Royal Home trailers wasn't the only place to work. She didn't need him or his meddling mother. She would show everyone that she could do just fine without Buddy Skidmore. Just fine.

10

Dating. How simple Suki had always made that seem. Yet, for Lucy, dating proved to be nearly as demoralizing as her search for another job.

Who should she date? Her crushes and fantasies had never included boys she knew. Her dreams had been of nameless, faceless strangers who swept her away in a white heat. Of consuming passions and grand sacrifices. She'd dreamed of the kind of romance that haunted the songs on the radio and burned in the movies and lingered for years in books. Not the kind that could be had with boys who threw spitballs and engaged in burping contests.

She worried over it for a while and then realized that dating could be separate from romance. She didn't have to find romance to date. That was the way Suki had kept it and that was the way she would keep it too. Dating was simply for fun. Buddy had spoiled her with movies and bowling and miniature golf, and all she wanted from dating was to replace the anticipation and the lightness that he'd taught her to enjoy.

But then how was she to date? What magic signal had Suki broadcast that made men ask her out? Lucy studied the people at work for clues. Gradually she became aware of undercurrents of behavior that she'd never paid attention to before. She wished Suki was around for advice. But since she wasn't, Lucy did the next best thing: she pawed around in Suki's stored box of possessions again.

This time her search yielded a black eye pencil to go along with the lipstick and blush she'd found before. She drew heavy lines around her eyes and giggled at herself in the mirror. The black pencil made her look faintly raccoonlike, but at least the raccoon was older than sixteen.

It took three weeks of wearing makeup to work and endless trips out to the drinking fountain near the assembly line and endless laughing at stupid jokes before she was asked on her first official date. She was ecstatic.

Ben Bill Robertson seemed just fine when he smiled in the trailer-factory coffee room, but he carried a hemorrhoid pillow and a Coke bottle half-full of tobacco spit into the movie theater. He punched her arm during the funny scenes and made loud wisecracks that had people turning around and glaring.

By the time he drove her home that night, Lucy was wavering between pity and revulsion. She never wanted to speak to Ben Bill again, but she didn't want to hurt his feelings. Dating was more complicated than she had expected.

She barely had enough warning before his kiss to squeeze her eyes shut and clench her teeth together. He smelled like dirty laundry and tasted of tobacco juice. The ordeal was mercifully short and she said good night and hurried into the trailer with a churning stomach and an urgent need to brush her teeth. It was nothing like the first kisses in the books she read.

"You're turning into Suki," Anita accused, which was ridiculous, because Suki would never have given the time of day to anyone like Ben Bill Robertson.

To Lucy's great relief, Ben Bill did not ask her out again. She filed her date with him as a learning experience. It taught her to decline gracefully until someone a little more promising came along.

That someone turned out to be Gary Hunsacker, a tall, clean-looking young man who worked in quality control and wore a tie to work every day with his monogrammed factory shirt. He came by the office daily to pass out Juicy Fruit gum to the women and joke.

Lucy was thrilled when Gary suggested they "get together." He asked her not to say anything to the other women because he hated being the object of office gossip. And the fact that their date was a secret made it all the more exciting to Lucy.

They had dinner out on the edge of town at the Fina truck stop. Lucy picked at her roast beef and listened to charming stories about his childhood and impressive stories about his years in junior college. He was older than she'd thought, but age didn't seem to matter much anymore. Quitting high school and working had slipped her into another category where age lost its significance.

She couldn't finish her dinner. He had wonderful brown eyes

and a soft way of smiling and a voice that sounded like a movie star's. When he leaned close and looked straight into her eyes, Lucy's heart dipped clear down into her stomach. This was more exciting than she'd imagined possible.

After dinner they drove for a while in his car and listened to tapes. He had an eight-track with two speakers mounted in the front and two in the back, and the sound enfolded Lucy. The night and the music cradled her, shutting out everything else.

"Beer stop," Gary announced as he whipped the car into a Git Kwick parking lot. "How many you want?"

"One's fine," Lucy said, hoping to sound breezy.

"One six-pack?"

"No ... uh ... just one." Buddy had broken her of worrying about boys drinking beer, but she was still afraid of drinking it herself. "You know ... one can."

Oh, God, she knew she sounded like a clumsy idiot and she wanted Gary to like her so much. She wanted something good to happen. She wanted her life to open up and expand. She wanted more of the heady rush she'd felt when he leaned across the table and swallowed her with his eyes.

Gary grinned and shook his head, then went into the store.

She watched him go. He looked so good in his pressed jeans and crisp snap shirt. How did she look? She reached up to feel her new hairstyle. It was copied from a popular country singer and had required nearly a full can of hair spray, but she could already feel escaping strands. She tried to tilt the rearview mirror down for a look, but the lacy garter and the rabbit's foot and the plastic Jesus and the tree-shaped air freshener vibrated with her touch and she was afraid to displace them.

Gary was still busy in the store. Lucy fidgeted in the car and idly popped open the glove compartment. A tiny light winked on, casting a jaundiced glow over the contents as she peered inside. Jammed into the small rectangular space was a bottle of Brut cologne, a double pack of Juicy Fruit gum, a concentrated squirt breath freshener, a packet of premoistened towelets, a box labeled "French-tickler Rainbow Condoms," and a pressurized can of contraceptive foam.

Lucy slammed the lid shut and sat up straight, praying Gary hadn't seen her. She had never seen a box of condoms but she knew what they were. Condoms were rubbers. One time during her freshman year a boy named Bubba Jeeters had inflated some rubbers with helium and let them go in the high-school cafeteria during lunch. But Gary was not Bubba Jeeters and this was not a high-school prank. A dull sickness spread through Lucy like black oil on a pond. She doubted that Gary used his rainbow-colored French ticklers as balloons.

Gary slid into the car and tossed two six-packs into the back. "Did ya miss me?" he teased and reached over to give her knee a squeeze.

Lucy smiled weakly. "You know," she said, "I'm feeling real tired tonight. Maybe I better take a rain check ... wait for a time when I'm better company."

"Sweet thing ... you're dandy company! Just dandy. Now, let's find us a place for a private party."

"Gary ..." she began hesitantly, but he turned and winked, smiling at her in a way that made her ache inside, and she was afraid to say what she had intended.

He made her feel so good, like she'd been reborn into someone special. She didn't want to throw that away. Maybe Gary would be different toward her. Maybe he used those things in his glove compartment with other girls who didn't matter to him.

Expertly Gary steered the car off the two-lane and onto a dirt road that led into a stand of pines. He shut off the engine and headlights, and the night closed over them like a vampire's cloak. Lucy shivered and swallowed hard against the sudden lump in her throat.

Gary fished two beers from the back and handed her one. He plugged in a soft, romantic tape and eased across the seat to put his arm around her shoulder. Playfully he guzzled beer and sang along with the music.

She took tiny sips of the beer and tried to pretend that his hand wasn't dangling down off her shoulder just millimeters from her right breast.

Gary downed two beers, one right after the other, and tossed the cans out the window. The action tarnished him a little for Lucy. She despised people who littered.

"Not much of a drinker, are ya?"

Lucy shook her head.

"Ya know, you got pretty eyes. I noticed that when you first came to work at Royal Home."

Lucy was glad it was dark so he couldn't see the blush that burned her face. She stared down at her beer can and tried to think of something to say.

In one fluid motion he took Lucy's beer from her hand, tossed it out the window, and kissed her. The kiss was soft and short and not at all disgusting like Ben Bill's kiss had been. She didn't mind this kiss at all.

When it was over she tried to smile at him but found the eye contact too embarrassing, so she cleared her throat and fiddled with the hem of her dress.

"Come on ... loosen up, darlin'!" Gary popped open another beer and insisted she take a drink. "That's a baby ... come on. Just a little more. Just so's you relax a little."

She drank more to please him. Fuzzy edges spread around her thoughts and she couldn't seem to blink her eyes enough.

"That's my girl." Gently he pushed her so that her back was against the passenger door. Then he kissed her hard and long. The armrest cut into her backbone and her neck was at an uncomfortable angle. She tried to ease herself down to adjust her position, and he took that as a good sign.

"Oh, yeah," he breathed. "Now we're relaxed."

He came at her from every direction. His mouth smashed against hers and his tongue worked to open her teeth. One hand ground against her breast roughly and the other weaseled up under the back of her blouse toward her bra catch.

She batted at his hands and squirmed to free herself. When he finally pulled back, she sat up and gasped for air. "I like you, Gary," she began in a shaky voice. "But I ..."

"I like you too," he said with fervent sincerity. "I haven't been able to think about anything but you since that first day I saw you sitting behind the typewriter."

Lucy was stunned. She stared at him in openmouthed wonder.

"You've been driving me crazy with those sideways looks of yours. Really crazy. I was hopin' you'd notice me."

"Oh, I did notice you," she assured him. "I always thought you were so nice. I mean, the way you always gave us all gum and told jokes ..."

"Oh, Lucy darlin' ... You know what that means. That means we were meant to be together like this."

She started to say "It does?" but before she could speak he had launched himself at her again. His wet mouth covered hers and he pressed his upper body hard against her, pinning her against the door, while one hand wormed its way up under her skirt.

Without losing mouth contact, he pulled her down so she was lying on her back in the seat with her knees jammed sideways into the steering wheel. She shook her head and pushed against him with her hands, but the protests only added fuel to his fire. He jerked at her knees and tried to move them and force them apart.

Tears leaked from the corners of Lucy's eyes. She couldn't let him do it, but she didn't know how to say no without making him mad or making him hate her.

The long-suppressed memory of her encounter with Billy flashed into her mind. She had liked Billy, and the same thing had happened. All he had wanted from her was sex. Sex! The thought of what could have happened with Billy turned her cold. She had almost had sex forced on her before she even knew what it was.

Now, here was this man poking and grinding and prodding at her. He didn't want to know what she thought about or how she lived. He didn't want romance or sweetness or even friendship. All he cared about was sex. Using her body to make himself happy.

Lucy threw herself forward, pushing Gary off with a force that surprised her as much as him. He bumped his head on the rear-view mirror and scowled at her as he rubbed the spot. "What's wrong with you?" he demanded.

Lucy scooted away from him. She buttoned the top two buttons on her blouse and straightened her skirt, pulling her outward self together as she struggled to assemble her inner strength. "I want to go home now, Gary."

She drew herself up and sat facing stiffly forward, but as close to her door as she could get.

"You bitch!" he exploded. "You cock-teasing bitch!"

She shrank against her door, disheartened and frightened by his outburst.

He slid behind the steering wheel and ground the motor viciously. The car roared into life and he slammed the gearshift lever into reverse.

"You're nothin' but a white-trash cunt. A white-trash cunt!"

The ride home was terrifying. Gary squealed around corners and ran stop signs. When they reached the Trailer Village he slammed on the brakes without turning into her yard. "Get out!" he ordered.

Lucy put her hand on the door handle and turned to look at him. She wanted to say something, but wasn't sure what. Something about wishing things could have been different between them.

Gary glared at her. He didn't look so good anymore. His eyes were narrowed and cruel, and his mouth was twisted into an ugly sneer. "I'll fix you, bitch." His voice was menacing. "I'll show you your place."

Lucy dreaded going to work the following Monday morning. She huddled behind her typewriter, refusing to go out to the coffee room or the drinking fountain or anyplace else she might run into him. Every time someone opened the door, she jumped. But it was never Gary. He was obviously avoiding the office as carefully as she was avoiding his turf.

By Tuesday she felt fairly relaxed. As she walked along the road to work she wondered over what had happened. Had it all been her fault? Did she send out the wrong kind of signals to men?

Or was it that boys were entirely different from girls? Maybe boys didn't have the same kinds of needs and insecurities. Maybe boys were so driven by animal lust that they didn't have room for any other kinds of feelings.

When she walked through the door of the office she saw a scattering of women who had arrived before her huddled together. They looked up nervously and hurried to their stations and ducked their heads without saying good morning.

Lucy swallowed hard against the tightness in her throat and went straight to her desk. She felt like she was back in kindergarten with the kids staring at her because she was bad. She set her sack lunch on her desk and pulled off her jacket clumsily. What was wrong with everyone?

"Lucy," the office manager called. "I'd like to see you in my office."

She stepped inside.

"Close the door please," he said.

He pulled a straight-backed chair from against the wall and motioned her into it. He circled back around his desk but remained standing.

"We had an anonymous report that you smoke marijuana in the bathroom on your breaks. This morning we searched your desk and found this."

He pulled a plastic bag from his top drawer. The contents looked like lawn clippings.

"That's not mine," Lucy said.

He acted as though he hadn't heard her. "I'm not calling the police, Lucy. And you have my promise that word will not go beyond this office. I'll even furnish you a decent work reference . . ." He tugged at his shirt collar. "But I hope this serves as a lesson to you. You're a good girl, with a decent hardworking mother and a lot to be thankful for. But you have to curb this evil habit or . . ."

He shook his head as though the consequences were too awful to contemplate.

"That's not mine," Lucy said again. "I don't know where—"

"Please." He sounded angry now. "Don't compound the crime by lying to me. Just get your things and go."

The walk home from the factory took forever. She was angry at the unfairness of the situation and humiliated at being fired. There was no doubt in her mind who had engineered the anonymous tip and the marijuana in her desk.

When she reached the Trailer Village sign she wiped her eyes and straightened herself. Her mother was in the yard hanging clothes on the line.

"What're you doin' home, girl?" Wanda asked with alarm. "You sick?"

"No, Mama. I've got to find another job."

"What! What are you tellin' me?"

"Don't worry, Mama. We'll make it. I'll find something better and everything will be just fine."

She took the truck and went straight to the library for a book on résumés. One of her last job interviews had asked her for a résumé, and she was determined to find out what it was and how to get one.

Using the book as her guide, she composed a brief résumé. The facts looked pathetic on paper, so she stretched and embellished and added a little to her age. The librarian let her use the library typewriter and then she fed coins into the copying machine to make a stack. Through it all she refused to acknowledge the little nagging voice at the back of her mind that said what she was doing was dishonest.

That afternoon she dressed in the best of her four outfits and began answering classifieds with a vengeance. She refused to sink into despair. She wouldn't listen when Wanda moaned about the bills or discussed the shame and degradation of having to ask for public assistance.

Five days later she was behind a desk in a huge law office, replacing a girl who had suddenly eloped. She had no idea how to do the work they'd hired her for. But she wasn't worried. Her time at the trailer factory had given her faith in her ability to learn. And her experience with Gary had made her feel stronger and wiser. This was her lucky break and she was determined to make the most of it.

Not only was the salary better in her new job, but the working conditions were more dignified and the work itself was challenging. Lucy began to think of herself and her contribution as important. She was not just a clumsy high-school dropout anymore. She was someone with value.

As the months passed, Lucy tried harder and harder to mold herself after the other women in the office. There was a paralegal in particular who impressed her, and Lucy adopted the woman's patterns of movement and speech. She copied the woman's discreet makeup and simple hairstyles.

By the time she heard from Buddy again she'd celebrated her seventeenth birthday and was secure in the niche she'd carved for herself. Her days were filled with work and her evenings were taken by the high-school-equivalency course she'd enrolled in. On the weekends she immersed herself in homework and reading and chores around the trailer.

She was cautious about men now, agreeing to go for coffee after an evening class occasionally but refusing any invitation that smacked of a real date. Her only weakness had been for the shy young mechanic who replaced the pickup's brakes and then asked her to the Pack-a-Pup for a hot dog. The next evening he drove clear out to the Trailer Village to ask how the brakes were behaving.

In spite of his continually dirty hands, Rusty had turned out to be the most polite male she'd ever known. He called her "ma'am" and held doors for her and took her arm on stairs as though she were made of china. He hardly ever tried to kiss her. And when he did, it was always chaste.

But Rusty was hopelessly dull. His span of interest stopped after cars and sports and he had no plans for himself beyond his next paycheck. Whenever they went to a movie he fell asleep.

She felt she ought to be grateful for Rusty, but whenever they sat together out under the stars he weighed her down just by being there beside her. And he made her feel guiltier and guiltier because he had started talking about a future when she knew all along they had no future.

A moment of weakness and a hot dog at the Pack-a-Pup had turned into a miserable situation in which she had to hurt someone or sacrifice herself. By the end of June, when Buddy came by, she had broken with Rusty and was thinking that life was a whole lot simpler without any males involved in it at all.

Then Buddy drove into the yard, calling, "Hiya, Lucy," as though no time had passed, and she was seized with a flash of extrasensory inevitability.

"When are y'all ever gonna get that phone back on?" he asked.

Lucy shrugged and continued with her project. She was filling some of the old tires with soil and planting tomatoes.

Buddy sat down and pulled a weed to chew. "You still workin' out to the trailer factory?"

"No. I'm downtown now. With a big legal firm."

"Oh. Well . . . that sounds pretty good."

Lucy concentrated on scooping manure and dirt into a tire, and Buddy scuffed his toe into the dirt like a shy two-year-old.

"I had a good year playin' ball," he said.

She smiled.

"Might be you even saw my name in the papers a few times."

"No. But then, I don't look at sports."

"Yeah . . . well . . ." He shrugged as though it didn't matter.

"You're lookin' real good, Lucy."

The compliment surprised her and she rocked back on her heels and squinted up at him. "Thanks, Buddy. You look good yourself." She picked up a spindly tomato plant and dug a hole for it with her hand spade. "You know," she offered casually, "Suki's not coming home this summer. She's got a good job in Dallas, so she's staying and taking extra classes."

Buddy sighed and scrubbed his hand across the back of his neck. "I don't care about Suki no more," he said.

"You don't?"

"Nah."

Lucy nodded. Buddy was making her feel very funny. She walked over to the hose and drank from it.

Buddy stood as though ready to leave. "Ya know, I just stopped by 'cause . . . well, you're an old friend and all." He grinned wryly and pulled his baseball cap from his head. "But I don't know. Seein' ya has kinda made me realize that I missed ya." He tortured the cap with his blunt fingers.

Lucy met his eyes and waited. She wasn't sure what she wanted him to say.

"Well, anyway . . . what say we go out for a bite or something tonight? How 'bout it?"

Lucy dropped the hose and walked back over to her tomatoes. She considered telling him that she already had a date. She considered telling him to go to hell. "All right," she said.

They went to the Girlie Pancake House for strawberry waffles and they talked about Buddy's plans for a professional football career and Lucy's renewed hopes of someday going to college. Buddy told her all about his team initiation after he'd played his first varsity game. How they'd rubbed some kind of hot liniment on his private parts and locked him outside of the dorm naked.

Lucy laughed so hard that tears streamed from her eyes. She tried to remember if Buddy had been this funny before, and she didn't think that he had. The realization that he was trying extra hard to be entertaining touched and flattered her.

When they drove back into her yard that night they were still talking and laughing and Lucy didn't hesitate to say yes to his invitation for a picnic after church the next day.

He kissed her good night lightly and his lips felt pleasantly warm and soft on hers.

"So it's Buddy Skidmore again, is it?" Wanda asked when she waltzed gaily into the trailer.

Lucy laughed and Anita looked up from her magazine to scowl.

"Well, you could do a lot worse," Wanda sniffed.

Lucy knew what her mother really meant—that she was damn lucky to have a chance with Buddy Skidmore at all.

That night she lay in bed next to Anita and stared at the yellowed pictures of Ms. Conroy that were still tacked to the wall. Even Ms. Conroy had been vulnerable. Even Ms. Conroy had not been able to take care of herself.

She thought about her childhood in Walea and she thought about her prospects for the future and she felt a moment of pure panic. What had ever made her think that typing and filing in some fancy office protected her? What had ever made her think that she could take care of herself and her family and stay free of the endless drudgery that had trapped her mother? What had ever made her think that she could shut off her yearning for the larger world that Buddy represented? And what had made her think she'd become immune to the strength and excitement he generated?

She felt like a drowning swimmer, and the only life raft in sight was Buddy Skidmore.

From that weekend on, Lucy spent each Friday and Saturday night with Buddy. On Sundays they went to church together and on Sunday afternoons they picnicked or swam at the lake. Sometimes he came by work to take her to lunch and sometimes he turned up after class to take her out for a quick soda.

June and July slipped by in a whirl of activity. With August she began thinking about his leaving. Would she still be as important to him after he left Walea and went back to college to be a football star? Would he want to date other girls?

By the end of August she was obsessed. She was terrified of losing him and desperate for some sign of commitment on his part. On their last Saturday night together he drove to a ridge overlooking Gum Springs and cut the engine. The Texas night stretched out around them warm and languid and heavy with fragrance.

"I wish I could just go away to college with you," Lucy said wistfully.

"Yeah. That'd be something."

"We could study together."

"And you'd get to watch me play ball. Maybe you'd even bring me some luck."

"I'd like that."

"Ya know, my folks are plannin' on drivin' over to some of the home games. How 'bout if I asked them to bring you along to one?"

"Sure." Lucy turned to face him in the seat. "Are you going to miss me, Buddy?"

" 'Course," he said. He tilted the steering wheel out of the way and pulled her toward him for a kiss. " 'Course I'm gonna miss you. Are you gonna miss me?"

"Yes," she said simply,

The fact was, she couldn't imagine continuing in Walea without him. Buddy gave resonance to her life. He gave her life possibility. He gave her hope.

Buddy kissed her hard, and his breath accelerated. His hand moved to her breast and he kneaded roughly through the layers of cloth separating their flesh. He always began at the beginning, even though they'd progressed to what she thought of as halfway. It was like a board game with squares marked "Soft Kisses," "Deep Kisses," "Touching Through Clothing," "Undoing Blouse Buttons," and so on. Buddy always started exactly at "Go."

His demands had been so gradual that she'd never felt pressured or threatened. He'd spent weeks just moving through the kissing squares. Then, by tiny increments, he had touched and rubbed and nuzzled his way through various operations until they now ended each session with his hand slid up under her bra. The process was never verbal. If she pushed his hand away he stopped. If she didn't respond at all, he went forward. Afterward neither of them referred to what had happened. It was the dark, unmentionable side of their relationship. And there was no touching or kissing at all in daylight.

Sometimes Lucy looked at Buddy's guileless square-chinned face shining in church or beaming at her as they downed Pack-a-Pup specials for lunch and she hated the thought of that dark side. Not that Buddy wasn't a good kisser. He was. At least, from what experience she'd had, he was good. He had never made her sick like Ben Bill, or afraid like Gary, or bored like Rusty.

And not that there wasn't something exciting and compelling in those mysterious forbidden acts they performed.

And not that she didn't want, not that she didn't *need*, the heady rush that came with being the center of Buddy's universe for the span of each Braille-like session.

But it was confusing. Everything was so clean and nice when they were together in the daytime. Neatly pressed clothes, and ladies first through doors, and polite table manners. She could sit beside him in the cab of his pickup and feel proud and possessive and content and know that God and everyone else who saw them was smiling favorably. But when they were together late at night in the same pickup it was all sweat and wrinkles and chafed skin and hoping that God and everyone else in town never ever found out what she let Buddy do in the darkness. And the darkness was vaguely connected to the long-ago horror of Billy's slithery hands and being spanked and shunned at school.

Buddy fumbled at the tiny buttons on her blouse and she mechanically reached to help. She pulled the blouse free of her waistband and let it hang open, feeling as self-conscious as ever over the fact that her bra was old and stretched-out and one breast didn't fill its cup as well as the other. Thankfully, Buddy seldom looked at her. He kept his eyes closed.

They assumed their standard position, with Lucy's back leaned up against the passenger side and the driver's door open so that Buddy's long legs had room to stretch as he sprawled across the seat. She wished he would kiss her some more, but they were past the kissing parts and he never backtracked.

She twined her fingers in his fine hair and thought about him leaving for college. Would he forget her as soon as he left? Did she matter at all to him? Buddy loomed so large in her life that he blocked the sky. If he disappeared forever, there would be a great black hole, a sucking emptiness waiting to swallow her.

She broke the rule of silence to whisper, "Do you love me?"

" 'Course I do," he answered hoarsely.

"I'm afraid."

"Aw, Luce," he muttered impatiently, "there ain't no spooks out here."

"That's not what I mean."

He pulled back and stared up at the quarter-moon. "What's eatin' you tonight?"

"I just . . ." she began, but she knew better than to try explaining it to him. Instead she eased out of her panty hose and stashed them carefully in the glove compartment. Buddy glanced sideways at her but made no comment. Her heart raced from fear, but she was determined now. She slid down, letting her skirt work its way up as she moved.

His fingers inched toward her thighs. She lay still and unre-
sisting. Gingerly he rested his square hand on her pubic bone.
His eyes were on the distant moon and his Adam's apple was
working furiously in his throat. The hand was hot and heavy
against her. It was a question mark.

Yes! she wanted to shout. Yes! Do it! Do it so I won't have to
worry about yes or no anymore. Do it so I'll be more important
to you than anyone else. Do it so I'll belong to you and I won't
ever lose you and I won't have to become my mother.

Finally he jerked his hot hand away and began tearing at his
belt and zipper.

Lucy closed her eyes and let her head fall back against the
padded armrest. She didn't want to know what was happening.
In particular she didn't want to have anything to do with his
penis.

Buddy was banging around awkwardly in the confines of the
cab. She kept her eyes squeezed tightly shut and focused on how
much she loved him and how much she needed him and how
beautiful it would be to cook him dinner each night and sign her
name "Mrs. DuWayne Skidmore, Jr."

The weight of his body settled against her. She held her breath.
He'd pushed his jeans down about halfway and the crumpled
denim bit into the skin on her shins. There was no sound or
movement. He was waiting again, double-checking.

She shifted, opening her legs slightly. It wasn't so much a signal as it was a way to escape the discomfort of his stiff jeans. But
the movement activated him. Something poked at the entrance
to her vagina. It was bigger than his finger.

Panic flurried and she couldn't breathe right. The jabbing
stopped, but the thing remained against her.

"What about . . ."—she had to swallow before she could force
the words out—"you know . . . birth control?"

"Oh," he said with obvious relief. "Yeah. Don't worry. I know
how to take care of that."

What else was there to say? All the forces in the universe
seemed to be pushing her toward this. So why not do it now when
it meant something? Why not do it now when she needed to show
Buddy that they were meant to be together? God wouldn't mind.
She was sure of it. God understood how the world really worked.

She encouraged Buddy with a little subtle body language, and
the jabbing began again. Then came a hard insistent push and
Buddy grunted and there was a burning followed by a dull rasping sort of pain. She tensed and waited for something worse, but
that was all, and it quickly faded to minor discomfort.

Buddy gave her a brief afterthought of a kiss. Her long hair was bunched up between her ear and the seat, and he buried his face there and snuffled softly.

She shifted. There were pressure points everywhere—misplaced elbows and gearshift and knees and door handle—she couldn't escape the discomfort.

"Oooo . . . Oooooo."

Alarmed, Lucy's eyes flew open against her will.

Buddy had flung his head back and raised up on his hands. His face was contorted and sweat stood out on his forehead. "I'm gonna mess!" he cried. "I'm gonna mess!"

He jerked back, pulling his penis out, and his entire body convulsed and shook. Jets of warm liquid squirted against her leg. When the shuddering was over, he sagged down and rested his head on her partially clothed breast.

They lay there together quietly. The cooling semen oozed down the side of her leg.

"Oh, Lucy," he said ardently. "I'm gonna miss you so much at school."

Gently she ruffled his hair with her fingers and caressed his faintly stubbled cheek. She'd given him the ultimate gift. When he went away to college now, his soul would be bound to hers. He couldn't possibly forget her.

She felt uncomfortable and a little bruised and desparately in need of a bath, but very wise and mature. This was all there was. She'd traveled through that dark, whispered life center with its fabled vortex of sin and shame and passionate ecstasy. She'd given herself to the sticky baptism, and nothing terrible had happened. There'd been no damning bolts of lightning or fits of chicken-ugliness. Of course there'd been no princes or romance or starry moments either. But then, everything was a trade-off. Everything was a compromise. And this fitted with the pattern of truth she'd been learning—that the gateways to adulthood could not be entered until all myths and illusions were dead.

11

Ellis

Ellis pulled down the hides hanging on the open side of their shelter. He rolled them tightly, tied the bundles with rawhide cord, and lashed them to the bottom of his pack. That was it. He was ready to go.

On the other side of the dying fire Frank cursed softly and struggled with the arrangement of his own pack, but Ellis knew better than to offer help. He turned away from his father and ducked out of the three-sided shelter to savor the morning. He straightened and looked around. The light was changing from mauve to gold with the sunrise. Pockets of snow gleamed from rock crevices, picking up the changing colors and reflecting them. Above him wispy streaks of clouds were pink against an orange sky.

He inhaled the sharp clean air, fastened the front of his heavy coyote-fur coat, and crossed the clearing to lean back against a larch. Birds rioted and scolded over his head and the faraway call of a wolf drifted on the still air.

Spring was barely a whispered promise, but the long hard winter had created an eagerness that made whispers enough. Every living thing in the forest was stirring with hope, responding to the lure of that promise, ready to put the winter behind and believe that the last killing storm was over.

Ellis had always responded to spring with joy and relief, but this spring was pulling at him in a different way. It burned in his veins and the pit of his stomach, igniting a restlessness in him that surpassed even Frank's. The restlessness churned and bubbled, tugging at his thoughts and tingling in his fingertips so that he felt always on the verge of something.

This was the sixth shelter they'd built for protection during the deep winter months, when death hovered over the mountains.

Now they were moving on, abandoning this crude home just as they'd abandoned the others. Ellis surveyed the rough log-and-brush structure and wondered how long it would take for the forest to reclaim it—for the vines and the rot and the gnawing animals and burrowing insects to reduce it to nothing. A year maybe, and then there would be no sign of his passing.

Frank ducked out of the shelter, shouldering his pack and scowling. "Cut the daydreaming and get your ass in gear!"

Ellis pushed off from his tree. He was able to look his father straight in the eye now, which put him somewhere over six feet. His shoulders were broad and his entire body was corded with wiry muscle. Though the fact was unspoken, his pack had been gradually expanded until he carried more weight than Frank.

Ellis had no way of keeping track of exact months or days. Time had fallen into seasons for him. But he knew he had to be close to seventeen, and he knew that the fine hairs on his face and the change in his voice were all part of becoming a man. And he wondered sometimes whether Frank had made him a man or whether it had happened in spite of Frank.

He took one last look around their winter home and pulled on his heavy pack, shifting it to find just the right balance.

"We'll head down past the moose yard," Frank said. He took a few steps and made a face. "These damn sissy slippers . . . I can't wait to do some trading . . . find a decent pair of boots . . . maybe even luck onto a good pair of camo pants."

Ellis looked down at his own moccasins. He couldn't imagine walking in heavy boots again. And he couldn't understand preferring cotton duck to the buckskins they wore now. But he realized that his father's preferences were not governed by comfort. Frank had always thought the buckskins looked a little too much like Hollywood Indian clothes, and more important, he had always resented the way in which Ellis learned how to make them.

A flood of memory washed through Ellis and he was back . . . back with Badger. Aside from Frank, Badger was the only human being Ellis had seen in the six years he'd lived in the mountains.

How dumbstruck he'd been when they stumbled across Badger's cabin. A dumbstruck kid. Lucky Badger hadn't killed him. How old had he been then? Three falls ago. Fourteen probably.

What did it matter? Who in the world cared how old he was or how old he had been when he stepped into the clearing and discovered the neat little log house? He had stood there in plain sight . . . gaping . . . while an apparition flew at him with a shotgun.

"You will not take me alive!" the man yelled.

He had long gray-black braids and creased earthen skin. The clearing rang with his battle cry as Frank stepped in beside Ellis.

"Send the whole army! I'll take you all with me!"

Frank raised his hands high in the air and smiled. "Say, buddy," he said calmly, "look us over. Do we look like any kind of law?"

Frank, usually so quick to anger, sounded amused by the encounter. He convinced the man that they weren't government agents bent on arresting him or running him off the land, and he tapped into some long-dormant vein of charm that melted Badger's paranoia and had the man begging them to stay for a visit.

Ellis had been fascinated with Badger. The man was just as isolated from civilization as Frank and Ellis were, yet he led a completely different life. His cozy cabin was stocked with cleverly fashioned utensils and handmade furniture. He had animals that he fed and called by name. And he hunted with a bow and arrows that he'd fashioned himself.

Nothing Badger did was insignificant enough to escape Ellis' attention, and nothing Frank did could distract the boy from the object of his admiration. Ellis spent every waking moment with Badger. He learned how to weave baskets of bark strips and make a sleeping cot of rawhide and supple tree limbs. He studied Badger's bow-and-arrow technique and worked to copy it. He spent an entire morning crouching beside Badger to marvel at a beaver dam that was at least eight feet high and ten feet thick. And at night he lay beside the fire and listened raptly to Badger's stories of wolverines with the souls of tigers and eagles that soared with the spirits of the dead.

After a week at the cabin Frank's initial amusement soured. He made fun of Badger's stories and belittled Ellis for being so enthralled with them. He asked barbed questions about Badger's history and political opinions, and labeled the man un-American and cowardly. He ridiculed Ellis for the "sissy" skills he was learning.

It was no surprise when Frank abruptly announced that they were moving on. Ellis had been expecting and dreading the news.

"I'd like to stay a while longer," Ellis told his father quietly. "You said you were ready for a trading trip ... I thought you could go on and I'd stay here while you were gone."

"Since when do you make my plans, boy? Get your gear and get ready to move now!"

Ellis held his ground. "You're going trading anyway. It makes sense for me to stay here while you're gone. That way you won't have to worry about me."

Frank was so unbalanced by his son's sudden show of determination that his rage lacked substance. In the end he stomped off in a fury. "You don't have to tell me to leave!" he shouted. "I can't wait to get away from here. Anything's better than watching you lap up the shit that little dog-faced bastard is dishing out."

Frank was gone for two months, much longer than past trading expeditions. Whenever Frank had gone away before, Ellis had been left alone to stare at the dwindling food supply and huddle small against the night and ask himself what he would do if his father never came back. But the time with Badger made Frank's extended absence seem like a gift. So much so that when the tiny voice in the back of Ellis' mind began whispering, "What if he doesn't come back?", the boy had been filled with a shameful hope.

During the blissful days with Badger, Ellis' skills were enlarged and fine-tuned. With Badger's patient guidance he learned the art of brain-tanning and smoke-finishing hides—techniques that were incomparably superior to the crude sun-dried method Frank used—and he eagerly absorbed the fine points of belly hide versus back, and doe versus buck, and hair-on versus hair-off. Even the time of year affected the quality of a skin, and Ellis was amazed to learn the differences between fall, winter, and spring hides.

Badger led him from tanning to making rawhide laces and gut thread and whittled-bone needles. Then, step by step, he showed Ellis how to construct shirts and pants and moccasins, and heavy fur coats and hats, and pouches and parfleches and medicine bundles to store the healing herbs that they gathered.

The intensity of Ellis' desire to learn seemed to please Badger, and several times the man chuckled and said that Ellis reminded him of himself. Ellis couldn't explain his need. The lesson from his disastrous escape attempt had burned deeply, and he was determined to master survival skills. But there was more. He yearned to prove himself to his father, to show that he could measure up to the man he so hated and admired.

And he needed to learn to be different from his father—to prove to himself that he wasn't destined to become Frank.

Frank was the giant creature in a black-and-white monster movie, trampling indiscriminately across the land and taking what he wanted with malice and muscle and gunfire. Ellis wanted to become part of the natural order. He wanted harmony. He wanted to join the ebb and flow of life around him, surviving with grace and wit and courage rather than mindless brutality.

Under Badger's tutelage he refined and rounded out the

knowledge he'd been gleaning on his own. From Frank he knew how to gather dew for drinking and he had a rudimentary knowledge of where creeks or streams were likely to be found. Now, from Badger he learned to listen for water—for the calls of birds going to water and the whispered passing of deer on their way for a drink. And he learned to close his eyes and detect the subtle scents that might lead him to water or a host of other things.

He learned to take cues from the forest's other inhabitants. For instance, bear could be followed to water as well as to berries and honey and good salmon fishing, so he learned to identify bear trails and bear spoor and the established "bear trees" with their clawed bark and oozing pitch and clinging patches of matted hair. With practice he could even spot the scooped-out bear-resting places among the creek bank's willows and alders.

From Badger he learned the feel and scent and leaf patterns of edible plants that his father didn't know existed. And he added to the food possibilities with a menu of grubs and insects that Badger taught him to find and toast as emergency sustenance.

Fishing bored Frank. Though trout and salmon were often the most easily obtainable and easily preserved foods, he disliked waiting for bites and hated what he called the "impersonal nature" of killing a fish. So fishing had always had a great attraction for Ellis. Frank often mocked the boy, but Ellis had persisted in learning to hand-fish in the icy streams or spear salmon with a sharpened stick or stand patiently over a line and hook whenever they had those items. Now Badger taught him the tricks of bow fishing and showed him how to fashion woven traps for use when other methods weren't suitable.

Finally Badger gave him the ultimate gift of power and independence by teaching him the art of the bow. Ellis was a natural marksman, Badger said in the first week they were together. He told Frank that Ellis had the eye.

Frank promptly ridiculed his son for being good at such a worthless pursuit. The bow was a cowardly weapon, he declared. Not much better than a musical instrument. Only real men had the guts to use the deadly power of a firearm.

Thus Ellis' passion for the bow was cemented. Using it divorced him completely from his father's way of claiming an animal's life, and bow hunting fit into the natural order that Ellis had come to revere.

Badger reinforced this by teaching him how to make his own arrows. The ritual of choosing the birch and shaping and measuring each arrow lent his hunting a reverence. He was putting as much effort into survival as any other animal who lived there. And there was spiritual grace in the flight of a well-aimed, carefully crafted arrow, connecting his soul to the animal whose life would sustain his own.

Frank reappeared at Badger's cabin suddenly. He roared in, boisterously displaying new sleeping bags and a heavy flannel shirt and a precious stash of dried fruit and nuts. He raved about what good trading he'd encountered, but was vague as usual about details. Badger greeted the tales with silence and narrowed eyes. Ellis tried to join in his father's celebratory mood, but Frank's arrival made him feel heavy and sad.

After Frank was settled in and quiet, Ellis displayed the best of the buckskin garments he'd made. It was a shirt the color of cream, with long sleeves and lacing at the neck.

Frank snorted. "Looks like something a hippie would wear to burn his draft card in."

Ellis stiffened and glanced at Badger. The older man's eyes were sad but his facial expression was carefully neutral.

"It's my first try, sir," Ellis told Frank carefully. "I'll get better and then we won't ever have to worry when our clothes wear out." He offered a corner of the shirt's long squared-off tail for Frank's inspection. "Feel it. It's soft . . . and it has a nice smoky smell."

Frank gave another sarcastic snort and ignored Ellis' offer. Instead he reached into his pack and pulled out two boxes. "I've got a surprise for you," he said, brushing away any other subject. "Shells. So you can learn to kill like a man. Just like I always promised." He slapped a box of shells into Ellis' hand. "I always keep my promises, right?"

Ellis nodded. He looked down at the Remington box and then up at his father. "I don't want to learn to shoot," he said.

Frank's eyes darkened, and Badger shuffled sideways and disappeared into his cabin.

"You know how hard those shells were to get?" Frank demanded.

"Yes . . . so why waste them teaching me to shoot? I've been practicing on the bow while you were gone and I learned to make traps and snares and fishnets. I don't need to use a gun."

Ellis bent to pick up a slender shaft from a jumble of peeled branches and curls of bark. He held it up for Frank to see. "Badger even showed me how to make my own arrows." He dropped the shaft back into the unfinished pile. "I can do everything I need to do with the bow now. Why learn to shoot?"

"Christ Almighty!" Frank exploded into movement. He took

several menacing steps toward Ellis before wheeling away to stomp back and forth in an enraged variation on his customary pacing. "You've been listening to that mewling little bum too long!"

Ellis waited, forcing himself to stand quietly in the face of Frank's anger. He was determined not to cower or flinch.

Frank wheeled again and pushed his face close to his son's to stare at him in the fiercely challenging way Ellis thought of as eye-wrestling.

Ellis held as long as he could—longer than he ever had before—but in the end he had to back down and turn away.

Frank grinned and cuffed Ellis' arm. "Still no match for your old man, huh, kid?" Frank threw his head back and laughed.

Ellis remembered that moment as clearly as if it had happened yesterday instead of three falls ago. And he remembered how his father's laughter made him feel an inexplicable pity.

His expression must have reflected this strange twist of emotion, because Frank's laughter had stopped and there had been a flash of uncertainty in his eyes before he turned abruptly away to sling the thirty-thirty's strap over his shoulder. "Get your gear," he'd ordered. "We're moving on."

"But—"

"No buts."

Ellis had known that he could push his father no further. "Badger!" he called toward the cabin. "We're leaving."

Badger came outside and silently watched Ellis sort through his belongings and assemble his pack. "Take these," Badger insisted, adding a bundle of his finest arrows and a rolled hide to Ellis' stack.

Ellis didn't trust himself to speak.

"Why don't you let me clean you up before we go, old man?" Frank asked gruffly. "I could cut your hair with a knife same as I do mine."

"No," Badger said. "Then it would be too short to tie back and it would blow in my eyes as yours does."

Frank frowned but kept his temper. "Well, then. Thanks for your hospitality and for your patience with this boy of mine."

"Come back soon," Badger said as they walked away from the clearing. "You will always have a home with me."

Ellis turned from his father and ran back across the clearing to throw his arms around Badger in a clumsy hug. Before Badger could recover from the surprise, Ellis wheeled and ran to rejoin Frank.

"Jesus Christ," Frank muttered. "He probably thinks you're a faggot now." He turned his head to glance at Ellis in disgust. "And there's no telling what bugs you caught just by touching the filthy little son of a bitch."

Ellis thought of Badger often after that, but Frank would not hear of returning to the cabin. So Badger became a memory . . . like his mother . . . like that other life he'd led so long ago. And the memories helped him divide time in his mind. It was much more reliable than figuring out what month or year it might have been or how old he'd been at a given point. Instead he thought in broader terms. The Other Life. This Life. With His Mother. Without His Mother. Before Badger. After Badger.

Before Badger, Frank had been responsible for feeding them and keeping them in clothes. After Badger, Ellis provided much of the food and he made every item of clothing they needed. Before Badger, Ellis had still been very afraid of Frank. After Badger, the fear lost its edge and faded slowly into guarded wariness.

Badger was in the past. Ellis' boyhood was in the past. What lay ahead in the future?

"God, what a bitch of a winter that was." Frank tilted his head back and drew in a forceful breath. "I'm hungry for a real hunt. I want to see something strong and proud in my sights instead of all these starved winter-poor bastards we've been eating." He patted the rifle hanging from his shoulder. "I've got five rounds left. I can't wait to smell the gunpowder."

Ellis fell in behind Frank silently. He didn't understand his father's obsession with guns. The twenty-two was long gone, but Frank had stubbornly held on to the thirty-thirty through the years despite the fact that he rarely had shells for it.

Frank picked up speed, giving Ellis an opportunity to stretch his legs. He realized then that he had to hold his pace back to stay in place behind Frank. When had that happened? he wondered. When had he become faster than his father? Or when had Frank begun to slow down? Had it all slipped by him while he was daydreaming?

He had the feeling lately that all of life was slipping by him. That he was trapped in a calm pool, just out of reach of the singing current in midstream.

Since his time with Badger, the days had been fluid, sliding into one another and creating endless, unbroken blocks of time that Ellis floated through. He had spent most of that time perfecting the skills Badger had taught him, ignoring Frank's irritation and derisive comments, enduring Frank's moody silences and sudden fits of ebullience.

Now, after walking for hours, pacing himself to stay behind his father on the steep mountain trail, Ellis tilted his face up to the pale early sunshine and felt at peace. The restlessness was at bay, sated by the breaking of their long winter camp. His muscles ached pleasantly with the stretching demands of this first long trek of the season. He was home. And home was good.

The gnawing pain he'd carried inside those first hard years, the need to hear his mother's voice or feel her cool touch, the yearning for shared laughter and affection—all that had slipped into his subconscious. It still mingled with his dreams at times, but it had no place in reality. Reality was the mountain and the forest and the thin sweet air. Reality was the delicate pink of a salmon's flesh and the breathtaking speed of an eagle dropping from the sky to kill. Reality was this silent migration to spring hunting territory—hours of walking punctuated by an occasional pause to sip water or chew on venison jerky.

The afternoon shadows were lengthening when they broke through the tree line and Frank stopped. "We'll camp here," he said, shrugging out of his pack and immediately settling into a relaxed state.

Ellis tested the mingled scents on the air and listened.

Frank began to talk about good wars versus bad wars. Ellis knew the discourse by heart. Frank was afraid that there weren't enough honorable men left in the world and that it had become impossible to have a good war.

As Frank rambled, Ellis surveyed the area. To their back was a stand of spruce. In front was a rocky clearing, and then the willows and cottonwoods that marked the edge of a clear running stream. Some twenty or thirty feet upstream he could see a tumble of boulders and then a series of rock shelves cutting into the mountainside like the ruins of a giant's staircase.

"This doesn't feel right," Ellis said, cutting into his father's monologue. He'd made no move to take off his pack or untie the quiver of arrows he wore at his waist.

"Bullshit," Frank said. "This is so perfect we might just spend a week here."

Ellis knew that Frank had no intention of staying anywhere a week. They would push on day by day until they'd shaken the staleness of the winter's confinement. But he also knew that the declaration meant that Frank would sleep here tonight no matter what.

Ellis slipped out of the pack, untying his bow and shouldering it. "We passed a bear tree a short ways back," he said. "And I think I smell bear."

"Oh, you do, huh?" Frank pulled a weed to chew. "Is that supposed to be some kind of ESP crap, or did you just turn into a bloodhound before my very eyes?"

Ellis moved in a widening circle, one hand on his bow and the other resting lightly on the hilt of the broad-bladed knife he wore on his hip. He bent to examine the ground in several places and then rose to test the air and listen.

"At ease, boy. There's no trail. There's no tracks. There's no bear shit. There's no nothin'." Frank tossed the weed aside and pulled off his heavy boots. "So will you cut the great-white-warrior act and go catch us some dinner?"

Ellis looked down at his father. There was no point in arguing. He pulled his spool of line from his pack and headed warily to the stream for trout.

As soon as he reached the water he was screened from Frank by the graceful river trees. The slender willow branches and the dancing cottonwood leaves furred the breeze with their rustling. They joined with the rushing snow-fed stream to wrap him in a lulling blanket of sound. Still, he couldn't relax.

He stood a moment, staring down into the water, considering whether to bait a hook or use his bow. The water was too fast here. He glanced up and down the stream for a natural pool. The breeze stirred around him erratically—sighing and singing and shouting. Shouting?

He focused his attention, concentrated on his sense of hearing. There it was again. A shout. His father's shout.

He raced back through the trees toward Frank in time to hear the shout turn into a scream. His long legs broke into a leaping run even before his searching eyes found the scream's source.

He stopped when he saw the bear cubs. They were huddled together at the edge of the trees, near where he'd left his father. Frank was nowhere in sight. The scream pierced the crisp air again and he snapped around to follow it.

There, balancing on the tumble of boulders, was a female grizzly. She was standing to full height, trying to reach into a narrow space between two of the rock steps. A bare foot appeared, futilely kicking at her massive head.

Ellis ripped his knife from its sheath and ran forward several feet. Then he stopped. His mind raced. Attacking the bear with nothing but a nine-inch knife would not save Frank.

The bear dropped down onto all fours. The wind was with Ellis and she hadn't scented or seen him yet. She clambered around the uneven rocks beside the steps with an awkward grace, her heavy coat shaking loosely and the fatty hump on her back jostling as she moved. There was a quiet, determined precision to her movements, and Ellis saw that she intended to get on top of the step that shielded Frank and try to reach him from above.

He touched the quiver. It was filled with the light, slender arrows he made for fishing. They would cause no more than bee stings in the bear's thick hide.

The rifle.

He dropped his bow and sprinted toward his father's pack. The cubs scampered further into the trees as he skidded in to grab the gun. It was unloaded. He ripped open the pack and emptied it onto the ground. Five shells. There were supposed to be five shells, but he saw only three.

He fumbled with the loading, glancing up to check on the bear's progress. She was leaning over now, fishing between the rocks with a powerful razor-clawed paw. He heard his father scream again, and the sound sent an icy chill through his blood.

The cubs had edged back and were watching him. They peered from around a tree like Disney characters, their shiny black eyes full of curiosity. They had nothing to worry about. Their mother was taking care of the danger.

Ellis grabbed his tattered trap-camouflage netting. In one motion he rose, leaping forward and throwing the flimsy net over both cubs. They rolled, flailing at the netting and squealing in terror. In moments their sharp little claws had ripped it to shreds and they were up and running.

Ellis scooped up a handful of rocks and followed them, peppering them from behind and causing more squealing. He knew the female was on her way to the rescue by now. When he ran out of rocks, he shouted and waved the rifle to keep them going.

He guessed at the female's rate and angle of travel. She would come from behind and to the left, and she would be on him shortly. He ran. She had his scent by now. He leapt over rocks and gnarled roots. Branches slapped his face. Ahead, he saw a wide meadow. If she caught up with him in the open, he wouldn't have a chance.

Instinct took over. He slung the rifle strap across his shoulder and leapt into the lower branches of a sturdy pine at the edge of the meadow.

Before he'd climbed five feet, she was on him. She reared up to her full height and raked the tree in silent anger. Her lips pulled back from her large yellow teeth and her nose twitched and her hooded black eyes fixed on him in single-minded rage.

Ellis continued upward until he could see out over the meadow. The cubs were slowing down and glancing back over their shoulders, trusting in the appearance of their invincible mother. Ellis steadied himself in the crook of a limb and raised the rifle. His hands shook. He'd had limited, halfhearted shooting lessons and he had no confidence in his aim.

The cubs were furry dots in the sight, but he knew they were well within range. They had forgotten their fears and were ambling along now, swatting at the tender new grass.

He held his breath and squeezed off a shot. The cubs started and looked around, but that was all. The female at the base of the tree was certainly not impressed.

He cursed himself for the stupidity of his plan. He'd thought he could scare the cubs with the gunshot and send them running and squealing again, with their mother following on their heels.

He watched the cubs roll and tumble sideways, stopping as they hit a large outcropping of rock. If he could hit the rock the bullet might make a sharp-enough noise to set them off. He aimed and shot. Nothing. There was one shell left. One chance.

He didn't know Frank's condition. He didn't know how long the female might keep her vigil at the base of the tree. Long enough for his father to bleed to death? Long enough for Frank to assume it was safe and drag himself out to look for Ellis?

He imagined his father stumbling upon them and the female catching him and tearing him apart before Ellis' eyes. How stupid he'd been not to use the shells to kill her. Now he had one left. He knew that he couldn't kill a seven-hundred-pound grizzly with one poorly aimed shell from a thirty-thirty. And he would only be creating worse trouble by wounding her. His father was right. He was a fool. And now they were both going to pay for his foolishness.

He looked at the cubs. They were on top of a flat rock now, playing a king-of-the-mountain game.

Ellis took a deep breath. He willed himself to be steady. He aimed beneath their paws and tried to empty his mind just as he did when sighting his bow. Slowly he squeezed the trigger.

The shot rang in his ears. He could barely hear the cubs squealing as they dived off the rock and streaked across the meadow in the opposite direction. The huge female let loose of the tree, dropped to all fours, and launched into a powerful, lumbering run after her babies.

Ellis watched her cross the meadow and disappear into the

thick trees behind the cubs. He prayed that they would keep going. By the time he climbed down and jumped to the ground, his knees were trembling. The air was thick with the scent of pine pitch and bear and his own fear.

"Dad!" he yelled. "I'm coming. I'm coming."

Ellis was still yelling when he reached the rock steps. He saw the blood dripping down from one ledge to the next, and he stopped. His heart leapt crazily in his chest and a dark tide of fear surged through him. He dropped the gun and scrambled up the rocks.

"Will you quit all the hollering and get me out of here," Frank whispered weakly.

Tears of relief sprang to Ellis' eyes as he reached into the narrow space to grip Frank's hand.

"She got me good, didn't she?" Frank said, lifting his head feebly in an effort to look at his leg. His face was drained of color and his eyes were two staring dark holes.

Quickly Ellis scanned for injuries. Frank had small wounds on one of his hands and assorted scrapes and scratches, but the majority of the damage was confined to one leg. It lay in a pool of blood with the skin flayed open and shreds of tissue hanging off in grotesque strings.

"Stay right here," Ellis said.

"Don't worry," Frank chuckled weakly.

Ellis raced back to where the packs lay and shoved their gear together. Not only did Frank need attention fast but also the bear could decide to return at any moment. This was her territory. Ellis had felt it from the first.

He struggled beneath the weight of both packs but made it back to his father in a matter of minutes. Frank gritted his teeth and moaned when Ellis eased him out of his hiding place onto the rock shelf below. Beads of sweat stood out on Frank's brow, and when Ellis began to bind the injured leg with strips of hide, Frank slipped into unconsciousness.

Ellis didn't hesitate. He left Frank to find two strong, straight limbs to cut and clean. When he had them he used rawhide strips to lace hide between them.

He half-carried, half-dragged his father to the contraption, a travois. He tied Frank onto it, then lashed one of the packs across Frank's chest. He shouldered his own pack and picked up the ends of the long poles. It didn't glide along over the ground like those in the movies, but dragged behind him like a load of rocks.

Ellis breathed deeply, set his jaw, and began the grueling task of pulling Frank downstream. Later he would worry about a more efficient method. A leather harness maybe, or even just a strap to pull against his chest so that all the effort was not in his arms.

It was long past dark when Frank finally came to full consciousness. Ellis had set up camp in a rocky crevice with sheer stone walls at their back and along two sides. In front of them he'd built a roaring fire. He was not certain that the angry grizzly had lost interest in them, and he was taking no chances.

"Where are we?" Frank asked. He propped himself up on his elbows and looked around.

"How do you feel?" Ellis asked.

"I feel like hell. How else would I feel?"

"Ready for some broth? I've been stewing this rabbit for nearly an hour."

"Sure. Bring it on."

Ellis refilled the tin cup twice for his father and then Frank sank back down.

"Look in my pack. There should be some pills. Penicillin. I've been carrying them around for years and I think this is as good a time to take 'em as any."

Ellis found the bottle of tablets, handed one to Frank, and helped him take a swallow of water from the canteen.

"So where's the hide?" Frank asked when he was finished. "I'm gonna carry a piece of that bitch around with me for the rest of my life."

"There is no hide," Ellis said.

"What do you mean? Didn't you skin her out?"

"I didn't kill her."

"Hell, I heard three shots! If nothing else, she should've bled to death after a while."

Ellis stared into the fire.

"Forget it, son. I'm talking out of turn. I've never downed a grizzly myself . . . and I hear they're like killing a damn tank. There's no shame at all in facing one of those monsters with a thirty-thirty and not claiming a kill." Frank closed his eyes a moment. "Never came so close to the end," he said softly. "Even in Nam." He chuckled and shifted his body, wincing as his leg moved. "That old she-bear has a story to tell her grandchildren. How she got the best of two strong men. She'll be laughing at us for the rest of her life." He chuckled again. "Damn, she caught me with my boots off and my pants down."

Ellis threw another piece of wood on the fire and watched a ribbon of sparks dance upward into the night.

"You know, I'm the one who named you Ellis," Frank said after a long silence. "Named you after my grandfather—the strongest, bravest man who ever lived." He cleared his throat. "For a long time I was sorry I'd given you that good strong name. Thought you'd never live up to it."

Ellis continued to stare into the fire.

"Now it looks like you've damn near grown into it."

Ellis watched the flames for several minutes. Then he turned to his father. "I didn't try to kill her," he said quietly. "I never shot at her once."

"What? But I heard—"

"I was trying to scare the cubs so she'd run."

"You didn't even try to hit her?"

"No."

Frank had a strange expression on his face. "Will you explain to me why you didn't try to take her?"

Ellis raised his eyes to meet his father's. "This is her territory . . . we were the trespassers. We were the ones in the wrong. And if I killed her, I'd have been condemning the cubs too. Scarce as grizzlies are, that didn't make sense."

Frank opened his mouth to speak, then shut it. He rubbed his bearded chin and then examined the small wounds on his hand. "You've got guts, Ellis Fielding. Your reasoning isn't always what it ought to be . . . but I have to admit, you've got guts."

12

Ellis worked hard at caring for his father. He moved their camp to a more comfortable location, transporting a grumbling, cursing Frank with the travois, and he tended Frank's leg wounds daily and took great pains to keep him warm and well-fed.

Frank grew increasingly angry and resentful over his own helplessness. And he turned those feelings on Ellis, berating and belittling and nagging in fits and starts like a frustrated dog lunging and growling at the end of a chain.

Through all this Ellis was coping with problems of his own. The restlessness was back, and it had nothing to do with being fresh from winter confinement or setting up a stationary camp so soon. It was about something else entirely.

He had had episodes of this malady before. They had come with increasing frequency and greater pitch through the years, surfacing and resurfacing like a parasite growing inside his brain. Now he was in the throes of it again and it was more intense than ever. It burrowed through his bones as relentlessly as a wood grub. It sizzled in his blood and throbbed in his testicles and sent jolts of electricity through his stomach.

Always before he'd been able to shake it off at will, but now it was unshakable. He sighted his bow on sleek speckled trout while his thoughts jittered and danced in strange directions. He carved toothbrushes from cottonwood and wove snare netting from balls of rawhide cord and laced together the leather pouches that he would fill with dried fruit over the course of the summer, but the satisfaction didn't come anymore. The simple tasks did not soothe him. There was no relief from the feverish churning and tugging that possessed him.

He had dreams of metamorphosing into some nightmarish creature, and he woke with each dawn feeling more vulnerable

155

and less tolerant of his father. As his patience eroded, he fantasized about bandaging Frank's mouth every time he changed the
dressings on the wounded leg. And little by little Frank's barbs
hooked under his skin until he was bleeding in dozens of invisible
places.

Ellis was cleaning up after lunch when Frank reared back to
study him and pick his teeth. "I think you like being a nursemaid," he said.

Ellis ignored him and left the circle of their camp to bring in
an armload of firewood.

"Say something," Frank ordered. "Tell me what eagles dream
or some of that other fairy bullshit that goes on in your head."

Ellis squatted to pile the wood next to the fire. He glanced up
at the sun to gauge the time of day.

"You give me the creeps," Frank said. "The way you move
around . . . and all this instinct stuff. Hell, you aren't normal anymore. You're half-animal. You're some kind of freak."

Ellis spun on his heel to face his father. Everything that had
been simmering inside him suddenly hit the boiling point. "Isn't
that what you wanted?" he demanded. He was as close to shouting
as he'd been in years. "To make me into a freak so I couldn't live
with normal people . . . so I'd have to stay with you?"

Victory flickered in Frank's eyes and curled one corner of his
mouth. Then he screwed his face into a pouting parody. "Isn't
that what you wanted?" he mimicked in a spoiled child's voice.
"Jesus. You'll never be anything but a whiny, tit-sucking baby."
He shifted his injured leg and drew his shoulders up and fixed
Ellis with his most intimidating, dissecting glare. "What I wanted
was to make a weak sissy-boy into a man . . . the kind of man who
could lead and fight. The kind of man who could save this country and make it great again."

Ellis laughed. Sarcasm rolled from him in waves, and it felt
good. "You thought you could teach me how to save the country,
huh? How? By taking me away from it?"

"Taking you away!" Frank shouted. "All I ever took you away
from was a spineless, tight-assed family and a castrating bitch of
a mother and a crooked fucked-up system that said I wasn't fit to
raise you because I didn't have as much money as they did. But I
never took you away from this country." He shook his head. "No,
sir. This is America's heart right here. I didn't take you from it—
I brought you to it." He swept his arms out, and his voice deepened with reverence. "This is where honor is born. This is where
patriotism begins."

Ellis wanted to plunge something into his father's belly and twist it. He wanted to grab Frank's shoulders and shake him till his neck snapped. He had never felt so close to violence.

"Oh, no . . ." Ellis shook his head and willed his hands to be still. "Don't try to camouflage it with honor and patriotism. You're a thief and a liar. You stole me! Just like I was a . . . a set of hubcaps. You never cared what I thought or how I felt. And I think you did it because you were afraid."

"Afraid! Are you calling me a coward?" Frank's eyes glittered and the muscles and veins stood out on his neck.

Ellis met Frank's eyes and saw his own rage reflected in them. "You didn't come way out here just because of me. And you didn't do it just to hide from Mom. You came here to hide from yourself. You were turning into a monster and you couldn't face that or stop it, so you ran away from it."

There was a moment of stunned silence.

"I . . . I . . ." Frank swallowed hard. His shoulders sagged and he suddenly looked older. "I wanted to be with my son. I . . ." He blinked rapidly and cleared his throat. "I wasn't making a difference anywhere. . . . Not in Nam. Not at home. And I thought I could make a difference with you."

Ellis drew in a deep breath and blew it out through his mouth. He was so close to the kill. For the first time he had his father belly-up and vulnerable. But he couldn't do it. He saw the naked emotion in his father's eyes and all the anger inside him melted into unbidden compassion. "Damn!" He slammed the palm of his hand against a tree.

"You think I'm a fuckup, don't you?" Frank asked woodenly. "You think everything I've ever done has been wrong."

Ellis was startled. He had never dared criticize his father and he hadn't considered Frank sensitive enough to be aware of unspoken attitudes.

But Frank didn't wait for a reply. "I've always known. I've never been good enough for anyone. I disappointed my father . . . I made major, for Chrissakes! I volunteered for Nam duty. What more did he want? Then your mother started looking at me like . . . like she'd finally realized what a mistake she'd made. Then . . ." His voice broke. ". . . my own son. When I saw that look in my own son's eyes . . ."

"I never said you were all wrong," Ellis insisted. "I never thought you were a fuckup. We're just different, that's all. Very, very different. And I've always wished you could accept that and stop trying to make me into you."

Frank's mouth turned down in a puzzled frown. "I was just—"

"You say you've been trying to make me into a man. I say you've been trying to make me into you . . . or into what you wished you were. But that's not possible because we're different. You fight for survival. You wrestle for everything—whether you have to or not. You see all of life as a victory or a defeat. I don't. And I don't need conquests to feel alive."

Ellis rested his forehead in his hand a moment. He had never been so open with his father, and he felt like the blood was spilling out of his veins with the effort.

"I used to hate you because you made me feel that Mom and I were worthless . . . that we didn't measure up. You made me feel like I was a hopeless misfit. I used to hate you—but wish I could change for you, at the same time. I think I stopped hating you when I started to like myself—when I realized that I would never be you, but that being me was good enough." Ellis sighed. "All I want now, what I've wanted for years, is for you to see the differences between us and accept me anyway."

Frank snorted softly. "Hell," he said. "You might think we're different, but you're as stubborn and tough as me. That's for sure."

"Maybe so." Ellis rose and picked up his bow. He suddenly needed air and distance. "Guess I'll get the jump on dinner. Maybe hunt around for some fresh greens."

"You'll be gone awhile then, huh?"

"Yeah."

"But not for good?"

Ellis stopped and turned back to stare at his father in dismay. "No. What makes you ask that?"

Frank frowned so hard that his whole face became a series of furrows. He squinted and fixed his eyes on some point far to the right. "You're pulling away. You're itchy to try your own wings."

"Maybe I am," Ellis admitted slowly. He was talking more to himself than to Frank.

"I've known it would come." Frank met Ellis' eyes again. "You remind me of myself about the time I stood up against my father and refused to go to West Point. Damn, it felt good to make a stand on something . . . to finally be my own man. Even if it did get me kicked out of the house. I loved making my own way and I loved that pissant college I went to and I loved the idea that I was going to decide my own future. That was when I met your mother. And I loved her the same way. Married her without ever introducing her to my family."

Frank smiled ruefully. "The crazy thing was that after all the dust settled and I started to get serious about life, I found out that my father had the right answers all along. That he knew where I belonged better than I did."

"I'm not leaving," Ellis reassured him. "You said it yourself— I'm a freak now. I can't leave the mountains. Where else would I fit in? Who would want me?" He shouldered his bow and tied his quiver at his waist. "And as long as I'm staying, I might as well stick with you. Otherwise I'd start talking to myself."

Was Frank right? he wondered as he broke into a lope through the trees. Was it itchiness that was eating him from the inside? It felt good to stretch out his legs and cover ground. To give himself to the rhythmic actions of heart and lungs and muscles. The physical exertion was soothing. But he longed for a destination— something to run to, something to charge him with anticipation and excitement.

The thick canopy of the forest pressed down on him, and he suddenly felt claustrophobic. He needed light. He needed air. Without breaking stride, he swerved, heading uphill. Gradually the trees thinned and boulders cropped up like overgrown toadstools. He slowed a little to leap and sidestep. The ground became rockier and steepened, forcing him into a climb. Pebbles bit through his moccasins into the callused soles of his feet and fell clattering behind him. Jagged edges of broken stone scraped his rough hands.

He climbed until the sun was a low orange disk on the western horizon. Then he sank wearily to a ledge and allowed himself to look down. This was where the big birds nested—the eagles and hawks of his fantasies. This was where he dreamed of living, with the world spreading out distant and surreal at his feet and the sky touching his head.

Was this what he wanted?

Want. Such a simple word. What did he want? Was it ripe berries in summer and the firm sweet flesh of salmon and the truest birch for his arrows and a good cache of food for the winter? Or did he want crazy things like his father said? Did he want to be transformed into a great bird or lifted into the sky to live with the gods of Badger's legends?

What did he want? What did he hunger for? What would quiet the roaring and fill the hollow spaces inside him?

He closed his eyes and listened to the wind play in the rocks. It whistled and hummed. Like music. He thought of his violin and the clear strains of a Brahms concerto. But the memory was somehow intertwined with the sound of his mother's voice and he had to shut it off abruptly to protect himself from the pain.

He stood and stretched his muscles. It was turning cold, and unless he started down now, the dark would catch him. He laced his fingers and raised his arms above his head, turning as he stretched. A trail of matted twigs and grass caught his eye. It began on a narrow ledge to his right and trickled down into a crevice below. The wind picked up sections of it and raised them, tossing fragments into space each time. Ellis was certain it was part of a bird's nest, and he eased over to peer down at it.

The bodies of three downy hatchlings lay in a limp pile at the bottom. More remnants of nest were scattered around and over them. Ellis scanned the rocks and then the sky, but there was no evidence of what had happened and no sign of a frantic parent.

He edged closer to the crevice. A thin shelf of rock disintegrated beneath his foot, and he pulled back just in time. It tumbled downward, smashing into bits against larger rocks. He took a deep breath to steady himself and climbed up to approach the crevice from another angle.

Two of the hatchlings were cold and stiff. The third had a faint heartbeat. He put it gently under his shirt next to his belly and tucked the front of the shirt into his pants to form a pouch. Then he started down.

Frank had dragged himself closer to the fire and was adding wood when Ellis burst into the clearing. Frank was visibly relieved at the sight of him. "Got a bobcat in your pants?" he teased as Ellis rushed toward the fire, shucking his bow and tearing at his clothes.

"No." Ellis' voice echoed his excitement. "Got a bird in my shirt."

"Guess that's almost as bad," Frank said, peering curiously at the creature Ellis pulled from under his shirt. "Is it alive?"

Ellis pressed his ear to the bird's chest. "Still ticking," he said. "He's a tough little guy."

"So is that all you brought for dinner?"

Ellis ignored the sarcastic question and studied the hatchling carefully in the firelight. "He's some type of eagle or hawk. The nest was too far gone for any clues, and he's so young that I can't tell by looking at him. I wish I knew more about birds."

"So I take it you're going to keep the little shitball."

Ellis nodded. His thoughts were on building a warm substitute nest by the fire. How was he going to force food down an unconscious bird?

"What did I tell you?" Frank muttered. "You like being a nursemaid. You should have been born a girl."

Ellis ignored his father. He sat down near the fire, cradling the bird in his lap. He picked up a canteen and dripped water off the ends of his fingers onto the bird's face. Nothing happened for a moment. Then the reptilian eyelids slid up and the scrawny neck stretched out weakly. The mouth opened wide and Ellis gently dripped water into it. He knew it wasn't natural for a nestling to take water, but he was more worried about dehydration than about the bird's natural pattern.

The baby flopped and squirmed in his hand. Ellis let go of him and the bird settled into his lap as though right at home. The eyelids sank to halfway, then slowly closed.

"He's going to be a noisy little fucker if you get him well," Frank grumbled.

Ellis smiled down at the miracle of the sleeping bird in his lap.

"Can you manage dinner now"—Frank raised his voice to a feminine pitch—"while the baby is sleeping?"

"I'm not moving," Ellis said. "There's jerky in my pack."

"We should roast the damn bird," Frank complained as he fished for the jerky. "Not that we'd get much." He peered across at the feathered lump in Ellis' lap and shook his head. "I've raised an idiot," he said. But the words were almost affectionate.

The bird thrived, filling their camp with its raucous squawking. It bonded to Ellis almost instantly, causing Frank to heap on insults about Ellis' ability to communicate with a bird brain. All of Frank's comments were tinged with jealousy. The bird did not react to him at all. Just the sight of Ellis could send it into a begging frenzy and the comfort of Ellis' warm body could lull it to sleep instantly.

Frank's leg improved to the point that he could use the wooden crutches Ellis had fashioned for him. And the sturdy little bird grew. His down changed to ratty adolescent feathering and his strength and coordination developed day by day.

Frank christened the bird Noisy, and in spite of his complaining, he took turns chopping and mixing food to poke into Noisy's endlessly gaping maw. He cursed the bird flamboyantly but gave Ellis hours of unsolicited advice as Ellis designed and constructed a perch-and-tether arrangement to replace Noisy's makeshift nest.

By the time the high-country warm weather had settled in to stay, Frank was navigating with a cane and Noisy was developing

brown wing and back feathers and an underside of buff white
mottled with black—the coloring of a young female goshawk.

They finally broke camp in midsummer. Frank still walked
with a severe limp and had to stop and rest every few miles, but
he was anxious to be on the move again.

Ellis was by turns edgy and lethargic. His mind wandered. He
dredged his memory for connections from the past. Classmates,
teachers, any face he could conjure up. He wondered where they
were now and what they were doing, and he wondered what they
would think of him. How would he appear to them? As he trailed
his struggling father, he sometimes fantasized about meeting
strangers and having conversations.

He was frightened at the thought of a real encounter. His social skills had been weak even when he was "normal." How could
he possibly function now that he'd become a freak? How could
he ever find acceptance? How could he ever leave the mountains?
He expected that he would end up like Badger—hungry for companionship but living out his days in lonely silence.

"I could never take you out on a trading trip," Frank had often
told him. "You're too wild and weird. You'd scare people to
death."

Ellis fantasized about things being different. About walking
down out of the mountains and having people smile at him. About
having girls smile at him. Soft, good-smelling girls with long hair
and long legs.

On hot sleepless nights his dreams were filled with women.
Not girls his own age, but real grown-up women. Women in short
skirts and bathing suits. Women with flirty eyes. Women who
kissed him softly and invited him to touch their warm, bare skin.

Frank's leg strengthened and his limp was reduced to a slight
hesitation in his stride. His stamina was returning as well, and
they began to cover more territory. With the return of self-
sufficiency Frank's need to goad and bait faded. He began to treat
Ellis with a grudging respect.

Ellis, however, continued his downward spiral. He felt increasingly alone and bereft. Even the mountains turned—becoming a
prison instead of a paradise. There were days when he wanted to
curl up in a fetal position beneath a rock and there were days
when he wanted to shout and break things. Except for Noisy, he
could find no pleasure in his daily life.

Late into the summer they found a hot spring and camped
near it. After tethering Noisy, Ellis abandoned his clothes and slid
into the chin-deep water. He leaned back into the water and

closed his eyes. The spring jetted up from below him, mixing with the icy current of the stream to create ribbons of hot and cold that played up and down his body. Darting schools of fingerling trout nibbled at his skin when he let his arms drift out into the cooler water.

Frank eased into the water across from him and began to talk. "You're going to be saddled with that damn bird till the day it dies, Ellis. How are you going to take care of it in the winter?"

"Saddled? . . . What?"

Frank sighed. "I said, you're going to have to do something with that damn bird before winter."

"Oh . . . yeah."

"What is wrong with you these days? I swear if we weren't out in the middle of nowhere, I'd suspect you were on dope."

Ellis pushed his wet hair back out of his eyes. It was darker now than it had been when he was younger. Would his mother be disappointed? She'd liked it blond. Van Lyden hair, she'd called it. Did he still look like a Van Lyden? he wondered. Did he still have connections to people other than Frank?

"She'll hunt on her own by this winter," Ellis said.

"Hah! She hasn't even learned how to fly yet."

"She will. And then I'll teach her to hunt."

Frank grew quiet. "Funny . . ." he said in a soft voice. "You're nearly a grown man now, and yet this is the first pet I can recall you having."

"Noisy's not a pet," Ellis said. "She'll have a life of her own. As soon as I can teach her to hunt, I'll set her free."

"Uh-huh . . . that's what I thought you might be planning." Frank hesitated a moment. "When she's gone, maybe we should try to find you a good dog. A dog can be a lot of company. Wouldn't mind having a dog around myself."

"Sure," Ellis said. He closed his eyes and let himself go limp. The fingers of water caressed his body. The current pushed him from beneath until he was nearly floating on his back. His thoughts drifted and eddied with the water, back to a drive-in movie in the summer dusk, peeking through the fence to watch a woman with platinum hair soundlessly unbutton her blouse and reveal huge red-nippled breasts.

Frank suddenly exploded into hoots of laughter, evaporating Ellis' daydream.

"All this time, I've been thinking you need a pet!" Frank snorted. He pointed toward Ellis' crotch and laughed so hard that he tipped forward and choked on a mouthful of water.

Ellis knew his penis was betraying his thoughts. He leapt from the stream and ran toward camp with his face burning and one hand shielding his embarrassment. He was dressed and swathed in an angry calm by the time Frank pulled himself out of the water and came up the hill in pursuit.

"Hell, that's nothing to be ashamed of," Frank said clumsily. "It's the most normal thing in the world."

Ellis turned away from him and stroked Noisy's soft breast. She made a show of aiming her sharp curved beak at his hand, striking him so lightly that the gesture was one of affection rather than hostility.

"It's me who's been the fool," Frank said, and the novelty of those words amazed Ellis. "I shoulda remembered what it was like to be young and horny. Hell, you're seventeen! I should have seen to it that you had a girl by now."

Frank said it as though a girl was something to be picked off a tree or captured in a good snare. As though a girl could be hunted and taken like an animal.

Horny. He'd heard the term only a few times in his life. The horrible, long-suppressed vision of his father on top of his mother suddenly loomed like a monster in his mind. "I'm horny," he'd heard Frank say to his mother just before he brutalized her.

Was *that* what it was all about? Did his penis lurch and his thoughts wander and his dreams fill with perfume and naked flesh in pursuit of *that*? Had he been so long with Frank that he was turning into his father in every way?

Ellis kept to himself for days after that, taking Noisy on long walks so he could launch her from high places and run to catch her as she sailed down. She was becoming stronger every day and he knew she would take off and fly soon.

Ellis was relieved when Frank announced a trading trip. He was disgusted by the snide little sexual comments Frank now managed to work into every conversation.

"Try to find me some real fishing line," Ellis said as his father was leaving.

"Sure," Frank said, and winked. "I always try to bring you a little surprise, don't I?"

Ellis filled his days with swimming and fishing and experimenting with ways to teach Noisy to hunt. He wished he knew something about falconry, thinking, as he often had over the years, that he needed a library to go to for answers. After numerous failures he tied together a crude bundle of feathers and rabbit meat that was close to the size of a small bird. He held it out for

Noisy and let her tear off one small chunk of the meat. Then he
perched her on a stump, showed her the meat again, and pitched
it into the air. It was a laborious process and Ellis' arm grew stiff
from the throwing. She was interested in the meat, but obviously
waiting for him to hand-feed it to her.

Every day he worked with the bird. Finally, just when he
thought she would never grasp the idea of catching anything in
midair, she sailed out impatiently to strike the lure just as it left
his hand. After practicing that maneuver repeatedly, Ellis tethered Noisy to his wrist, padding himself heavily with layers of
leather so her sharp claws did no damage. He packed jerky for
himself and several of the meat-and-feather lures for her, then
walked for three hours, until he came to a rocky sage-covered
ridge. He climbed to the top, ignoring Noisy's protests and nervous shifting. She didn't like riding on his arm while he climbed.

"Look," he said, holding out his arm and moving it so she had
a view in all directions. The land fell away below them, and in
the distance he could see the sunlight striking silver and knew
the reflection came from the steam near their camp.

"This is your home. High places like this. You don't belong
on the ground with me."

He untied her tether and showed her the first lure. She lunged
at it greedily, but he pulled it back and then heaved it out into
the open air. Ellis could tell she was watching it. Her sharp ancient eyes locked on the falling object and held fast till it disappeared from sight below.

Ellis sat down with a dispirited sigh and ate a piece of jerky.
The bird hopped from rock to rock around him, obviously uncomfortable in the surroundings. When he took another piece of
jerky from his pouch, she settled on his shoulder and tried to
grab it from him.

"No!" Ellis jumped up. "No! No! No!"

He pulled out another of the smelly lures and held it out for
her to see. "You're a hawk. A hawk!"

He coaxed her onto his wrist, holding the meat just out of her
reach. Then he threw the meat high and wide. It sailed out in a
long slow arc and the bird's head jerked around to follow it.

"Go," Ellis whispered. He held his arm out as far as possible
and shook it a little to urge her on.

Suddenly, as though she'd been doing it all her life, Noisy
launched herself into the air. She soared out on powerful wings,
paused, and then dropped into a dive that took Ellis' breath away.
When she was almost to the tree line she hit the lure, catching it

in her steel grip, and then she turned and flew effortlessly back to the ridge. She perched on a rock and tore into her catch as though nothing unusual had happened.

Ellis grinned to himself all the way back down to camp. That night he dreamed that he and the hawk were soaring above the wilderness and hunting together. The land spiraled away beneath him and the wind sang in his ears. Suddenly she dived and he knew that her fierce eyes were locked on quarry, though they were so high up that he couldn't see anything himself. He followed her. Like a vengeful goddess she was plummeting toward some hapless inhabitant of earth. It was Frank.

Ellis sat up abruptly. His heart was pounding and he was covered with a thin film of sweat. The familiar sounds and smells of night surrounded him, as soothing as his mother's touch. He sat up to stir the embers of the fire and then lay back to sleep till morning.

Frank had been gone nearly three weeks and Ellis was growing worried. His ears were tuned for the sound of Frank's return, and he was already asking himself if he could follow a track that was nearly a month old.

It was dusk. Ellis had just started a cooking fire and was putting away the flint and steel when Frank's distant "Hello, coming in!" sounded. The shadows lengthened and the light turned from copper to rose to violet as Ellis listened to his father's approach. He would have sworn he heard two humans approaching. Two sets of feet. Two moving bodies disturbing brush and leaves.

When Frank stepped into camp he was not alone.

Ellis stood and stared behind his father with a mixture of curiosity and alarm. It was a girl. Ellis took a step closer, and the girl shrank back.

There was a rope tied to Frank's waist. He grinned widely and jerked on the rope. The girl lurched forward. The other end of the rope was fastened to her waist. Her hands were bound together with cord, and a strip of cloth was tied over her mouth.

"Told you I'd bring you a surprise," Frank said. He untied the rope from his waist and handed the end to Ellis.

Ellis stared at the girl. She had on jeans and a grimy sweatshirt. Her light brown hair was parted in the center and drawn into two loose, disheveled braids. Her eyes were wide pools of shock.

He looked at his father and felt an anger so vast that it swallowed him whole. "What have you done?" he asked. The words sounded hollow.

"Just what I said . . . brought you a surprise. She's a little skinny, but she's strong and young. Better tie her to something. She's bad about taking off."

Ellis looked down at the end of the rope dangling limply from his hand and then back up into the girl's face.

Frank gave an exasperated sigh and stomped over to take the rope from Ellis. He pushed the girl down into a sitting position against a young lodgepole and wrapped the rope around her waist and the tree. "You can take off the gag if you want. I just got tired of hearing her whine."

Frank busied himself with threading trout on sticks for cooking, and Ellis knelt before her and gently untied the cloth around her mouth. "Can you hear me?" he whispered. He felt like he was talking to a creature as unlike himself as Noisy. And he was startled when she responded with a nod.

"Are you thirsty?"

Another nod.

He held up his water bag so she could drink.

"She's probably hungry," Frank said, without taking his attention from his roasting dinner. "I didn't feed her today."

Quickly Ellis set two more trout up to cook. When they were done, he carried the stick over to her and she grabbed for it greedily. She clutched one of the hot fish between her bound hands and tore at it with her teeth.

"I can't let you loose," Ellis told her softly as she ate. "If you ran away, you could get lost or hurt." He gestured toward the trees. "You could die out there."

He left her to her fish and went back to sit across from Frank. "Where'd you find her?"

"Near a highway," Frank said between bites of fish.

Ellis raked his hair back from his forehead with one hand and shook his head in agitated disbelief. "We have to take her somewhere now . . . help her find her way home."

"Like hell." Frank reached for another sizzling trout. "I took her. She's mine. And I'm giving her to you."

Ellis searched for something to say, something to make the nightmare rational. "It's against the law," he said lamely.

"What law?" Frank bellowed. "We can make any law we want out here."

"That's not true. There's already a law here. A natural law."

Frank laughed. "You bet there is. And that law says you can have whatever you can kill or catch."

"No. The law out here gives permission to take what's needed for survival. There's a difference."

"You've got your asshole where your mouth oughta be," Frank said. "Why don't you go back to thinking about tree spirits and hawk magic and let me worry about the real stuff."

"We can't keep her," Ellis insisted quietly.

"Shit!" Frank jumped up and threw his half-eaten fish into the fire. "You're ruining my dinner!" He stomped over to his pack and pulled out a bottle of whiskey. "Another surprise," he said, and tilted the bottle up for a long drink. He held it out and shrugged when Ellis refused.

"I couldn't take her back if I wanted to," Frank said, settling back down near the fire. "There was some trouble when I got her, and it's going to be a while before they stop looking for me." He held the bottle up so that the fire reflected off it. "Pretty sight, huh?"

Ellis stared down into the fire with clenched fists.

Frank raised one hand in a conciliatory gesture. "All right. We have permission to take what we need for survival. Well, I took a mate. That's a natural-enough thing. A mate for my son." He tipped the bottle up for a drink. "I took her just like I've taken shells and boots and fishing line and food."

Ellis looked at his father and struggled with what he'd just heard. "Took? But I thought . . . you said you were trading . . ."

"What the hell did I have to trade that anybody wanted? The first time I went down, I traded off that other gun. But after that . . . Shit. You think people place a lot of value on tanned hides and smoked fish?"

Ellis bent forward and cradled his head in his hands.

"More, please," he heard a small voice say. He turned to look at the girl.

"Can I have more fish?" she asked.

There was plenty of trout. Ellis had planned on smoking some after dinner, so he had caught nearly two dozen. He put three more on to cook and began walking aimlessly in a circle around the camp. He hadn't felt so lost or helpless since his escape attempt. How could he convince his father to change his mind? How could he stop this ugly nightmare and return things to the way they were? That was the worst part. Even if Frank released the girl immediately, Ellis would never be able to forget what his father had done. Nothing could ever go back to the way it had been. Nothing would ever be the same between them.

Frank lounged contentedly by the fire, taking long noisy drinks from the bottle of amber liquid. "C'mon, boy. Your daddy's rounded you up your first taste a whiskey an' your first woman.

Loosen up and get started here." The words slurred faintly and his eyes were developing a hypnotic glaze.

"You can have it," Ellis snapped. At any other time he would have been curious about the taste of whiskey. But not now.

Frank pulled himself to his feet and moved toward the girl.

She cowered back against the tree as he unwound the rope at her waist.

"She's still hungry. I'm going to feed her some more fish," Ellis said, as though he could control the situation by being calm and practical.

"She can eat later." Frank jerked her to her feet. "You want her tied or untied?"

"I don't want her at all," Ellis said.

"Whatsamatter?" Frank chuckled suggestively. "Shy? Can't get it up maybe?" He dragged the girl away from the firelight to the shadows edging the camp. "Come on over to this romantic spot, son." Frank pushed the girl's hands upward and around the back of her head until her tied wrists were hooked behind her neck.

She grunted and kicked out wildly, but nothing connected.

Frank's lips peeled back into a tight smile and his eyes glittered with excitement. He hooked a foot behind her leg and shoved, and she fell backward, hitting the ground with a solid thunk that left her breathless and still for several minutes.

"There are different kinds of women," Frank said, "but almost all of them need to be reminded of their purpose in life once in a while." He unzipped her jeans and yanked them down to her knees.

Ellis watched his father in frozen horror. The figures before him blurred and distorted in the flickering firelight, reforming into old pictures. His father naked and grunting. His mother bruised and gagged, with silent tears streaming from her eyes.

"Get over here and rub your dick against this little beaver. That'll make it come to attention."

The girl started to move again. She bucked and kicked her feet and thrashed her head back and forth.

Frank leaned forward and slapped her as casually as if he were swatting at a mosquito. The crack of his hand against her cheek snapped Ellis back to the present.

The girl lay still now. Her eyes were closed and she might have been unconscious except for the soft whimpers that escaped with her breathing.

"Come on and get it before it gets cold," Frank called out. He chuckled at his own cleverness and then belched loudly.

"Leave her alone," Ellis said.

Frank's eyes darkened. "I went through hell to find a girl for you. And I kept my hands off her so she'd be yours first."

"I won't be like you," Ellis said. "No matter how many years we're together and how hard you try to force me, I won't be you."

"Like me?" Spittle sprayed from Frank's mouth. "I'm a man, goddammit! And whether you like it or not, that's what I've made you into. So get over here and put some spine into that cock of yours and do what a man's supposed to do."

Frank stared at Ellis with a murderous glare that made his skin crawl and his belly twist. But it wasn't fear that he felt. It was revulsion. It was the sickening weight of betrayal and the agonizing knowledge that he was the same flesh and blood as the monster before him.

Frank straightened and moved toward his son. Ellis braced himself. But the blow never came. Frank passed him and bent to pick up the quart of whiskey he'd left by the fire. He drank from it and carried it back to stand over the girl. She had not moved.

"What a skinny, pathetic cunt," Frank said.

She opened her eyes and jerked her head up. Cords stood out on her neck and her eyes bulged. "Just do it!" she screamed at Frank. "Get it over with!"

Frank blinked and grinned. "Still a little spunk left, huh?" He took another drink from the bottle, then screwed the cap on and carefully set it down on the ground. "You heard the little lady," he said to Ellis as he stooped to pull one of the pant legs free from her ankles.

The girl sighed and spread her legs. Then she squeezed her eyes shut and went limp again.

"Guess if you aren't man enough to do the honors, I'm going to have to."

He knelt between the girl's sprawled legs and fumbled with the front of his pants.

"No," Ellis whispered. He took several steps toward Frank. "Leave her alone."

Frank looked up at Ellis with a smirk that was equal parts dare and ridicule. He finished opening his pants, and the hard length of his penis sprang into view. It was the color of a purple bruise in the firelight. He paused for a moment, displaying his erection.

"No!" Ellis shouted.

The word made Frank laugh. He focused on the girl, and his eyes glittered with the ravenous, cold joy of a buzzard about to dip his beak into the dark liquid of the dying. He drew in a deep breath and launched himself forward.

Moments stretched, and the only sound was a rushing pulse in Ellis' ears. Frank fell toward the girl in slow motion. The firelight flickered eerily. Ellis floated. Close. Closer. The liquor bottle was in his hand. He swung it out and down. There was a hollow wet sound as the heavy glass connected with the back of Frank's head.

Then there was nothing.

13

Juliana

Juliana paced pack and forth in the shady gazebo. The row of dolls stared up at her. She'd never had anything but tutors, but playing school was one of her favorite games.

"Now, class," she began, "today's lesson is history."

She'd taught history several times that week and she could tell that the class was bored. Something big was needed to get their attention back. She waved her hands to cancel what she'd said and then assumed her sternest professorial posture.

"I've decided on a special lesson today. Sex." She smiled. "I see that all of you are interested."

Juliana had been thinking a lot about sex since Charlotte sat her down and explained the blood in her panties and the mechanics of human reproduction. Charlotte was the governess who'd replaced dear old Gittie. She'd been a hospital nurse before she became a governess, so her explanations were filled with technical terms that Juliana had to look up to understand.

Imitating Charlotte, she taught her class the details of penis, vagina, and sperm. Then she told them about menstruating and how her period had started and how she had hair growing in new places.

Suzy, the blond girl with the blue eyes and china face that Aunt Grace had sent from England, raised her hand. She wanted to know when sex happened and whether people knew it was happening.

These were very good questions, but then, Suzy had always been a bright and outspoken student.

"Sex happens three ways," Juliana explained. "When people are married they go to bed together sometimes and it happens in the night while they're asleep. My parents sleep in different bedrooms, so that's why I don't have any baby brothers or sisters."

172

She surveyed the garden to make certain she was still alone. The pink granite walkways and the curving, patterned flowerbeds spread out empty in the sunlight. There were no sounds except for the buzz and honk of Manhattan traffic beyond the wall, no gardeners lurking about or servants taking their lunch break beneath the trees.

"The next way sex happens is because of men. A man's penis can go wild if he sees dirty pictures or bad movies."

She glanced around again, then pulled the pictures out of their hiding place. They were black-and-white postcards showing naked Oriental ladies. One woman was lying on her back with her legs spread apart. One was sitting in a chair with her legs open. The last was twisted so that her rear end was to the camera. Each of the women was holding her lips open and each had a blank face with dead, flat eyes.

The pictures had been inside a drawer in the toolhouse, where the gardeners kept all their equipment. When she found them she had been horrified and quickly stuffed them back in the drawer. But she couldn't get them off her mind. She had often sneaked looks at them, and finally had stolen them.

"If men see pictures like this or if men even read a book with a nasty part in it, they can go crazy. That's when they rape women or try to do sex right in the middle of the day or something.

"And the third way sex happens is because of glands and drugs while people are teenagers. This is something we don't have to worry about, class, because we run an all girls' school here.

"Now, any other questions?"

She hoped there weren't any, because she didn't know much more herself. She'd gleaned what knowledge she had from Charlotte's technical talk and the few television shows she was allowed to watch and the movies Charlotte ordered for the screening room and the books Charlotte stocked on the shelf. Charlotte was a governess who ruled with an iron hand.

Before any of her pupils could ask a question, Juliana heard the big iron gates swinging open. She tucked her pictures away and abandoned her students to run down the walk. The guard at the gate waved at her and grinned as an unfamiliar car entered.

"It's Mr. Aubrey!" the guard called.

Juliana dropped her stately teaching demeanor and ran.

Her father stepped out like a conquering general, dressed in a dashing mix of safari and combat clothes. "Jinxie! You little devil!"

She stopped several feet from him and waited hopefully. He

swept her up into a hug and she pressed her face against his neck. His skin smelled like sunshine. The hug was over too quickly, but he allowed her to hold his hand on the way into the house.

"Bring me something cool to drink," he said to the maid who came fluttering nervously to the door to welcome him.

He led Juliana through the breakfast room with its brilliant stained glass, through the velvet and gilt of the tea room, and into the smoking room with its heavy walnut walls and carved walnut ceiling and dark paintings in lunettes above the doorways.

This was the only room in the house without brocade or velvet or fabric of any kind. The couches and wing chairs were covered with Italian glove leather in a shade her father called oxblood. And instead of curtains the windows were fitted with ornately filigreed folding wooden screens. There was a fifteenth-century Persian hunting rug that felt coarse beneath her bare feet, as opposed to the soft, thick carpets she was used to.

Aubrey seated himself in a wing chair beside the huge onyx fireplace and motioned Juliana into the chair opposite. It was four months since he had last been home.

"And how are you doing with your studies?" he asked. His blue eyes were startlingly pale in his weathered face. His skin was ruddy from a recent sunburn.

"Fine. The tutors say I'm way ahead of my age."

"You're bigger."

"Yes. I'm twelve now."

"Oh! that's right—I missed your birthday party!"

"We didn't really have a party. Grandfather's been sick with gout, and Mama ... Mama's been staying upstairs, and Aunt Grace went back to France ... so I had cake with Charlotte and the servants."

"Hmmm. Well, then, I suppose you're due a celebration, aren't you? I'll call some friends and borrow your grandfather's body-guards and we'll go out for a big party. How's that sound?"

"Could we really do that?" she asked cautiously.

"Yes," he said firmly. "Your grandfather cannot stop us from having a party." He sounded more definite, more sure of his position with Edward than she'd ever heard him sound before. "Now, where's your mother?"

"Probably in her room. We didn't know you were coming."

"Neither did I, Jinx. Nothing like a surprise, is there?"

"Tell me about where you were, Papa."

"Oh ... you'd have loved this one. I was on the grizzly project. We tranquilized and tagged in some pretty rugged areas."

"For conservation?"

"You bet! What would the world be without grizzlies? I'd hate to think that future generations would never have the opportunity to hunt the great bears."

"I hope you'll be home for a while now, Papa. It's so much more fun when you're home."

"Well, we'll see what we can do about that."

He pulled off his battered panama and Juliana was surprised to see that his hair had thinned.

"Are you going to be bald, Papa?"

He frowned and jammed the hat back onto his head. "That's not something a child should say to a man."

"Yes, Papa." She studied him while a maid delivered his drink. "You won't go away again soon, will you?"

"I can't say right now, Jinx." He turned and stared off through the prisms of beveled glass that fractured the view to the garden. His expression was closed and distant.

"Please, please stay. It's so lonely around here. Or take me and Mama with you, please."

He sighed. She was used to the sounds and texture of his disappointment and she knew that she had failed by asking.

"You sound like your mother," he said. He softened then and grinned. "Someday I will take you. Your grandfather won't like it, but I'll take you anyway. And you can learn to shoot something besides skeet and trap."

This promise was made of air. Like so many others he'd made. And instead of responding, she quietly studied his face, wondering if he himself believed the promises.

"Well. Well, then." He jumped from his chair to escape her gaze and crossed to the fireplace, where he examined the decorative logs and the same bronze poker that had always been there. "You do know why I'm home so suddenly, don't you?" he asked finally.

She shook her head.

"My God! I can't believe you weren't told. Your cousin has been found. He turned up some place in Idaho."

"My cousin? I thought he was dead."

"No. No one ever said he was dead. We had just given up hope of ever seeing him again." Aubrey leaned against the carved mirror darkness of the ebony and drew in a deep breath. "It's quite amazing. He's apparently been living in the mountains all this time like some sort of noble savage. And Frank Fielding was the culprit after all. Frank took the boy and kept him up there all these years." He stared off a moment, as though indulging in some fantasy. "Anyway, your Aunt Grace is on her way to claim him now, and she intends to bring him straight to Great House."

"And that's why you came back early?"

"Yes. Isn't it exciting? You'll have a pal now—just the way Sparky used to be."

Juliana stared down at her hands. Sparky's name caused a flicker of pain in her chest. The McCanns had left Elysia right after that terrible summer and she had never seen Sparky again. She was offended by her father's suggestion that this unknown cousin would fill Sparky's place.

"He's a lot older than me, and I don't want to be friends with any noble savages."

"Hah! You've got a little savage blood in your own veins. Your mother's mother, Wenona, was more wild and dangerous than anyone I've ever come across."

"Because she was a Cherokee Indian, you mean?"

Aubrey laughed. "Among other things. Anyway, I expect you to be friendly and welcoming to your cousin. He's been through enough without his family turning against him."

He slid his hands into his pockets and strolled toward the window as though dismissing her.

"Well, go on, then. Go tell your mother I'm home."

Juliana didn't race through the house any longer. She didn't skate in the ballroom or hide beneath desks in the library. She was above all that. But this was a special occasion, so she took the curving grand staircase in a leaping run.

She didn't stop running until she reached her mother's door. There she stopped. She hesitated to knock on that solidly locked door. She pressed her ear and her cheek and the palms of her hands to the smooth surface. No sounds penetrated the thick wood, but then, she hadn't expected any. Yvonne kept herself wrapped in a cloak of silence. It defined and protected her as effectively as a nun's habit. And when Yvonne took to her rooms, the silence of her seclusion seeped through the door to blanket the entire upstairs, making everyone whisper as though they had entered a church.

It wasn't sound that Juliana sought. Instead, she kept hoping for signals, vibrations, clues to the mysteries her mother kept locked so tightly inside.

She took a deep breath and knocked. "Mama," she called gently. "Mama, can you hear me?"

Nothing.

"Mama. Mama, please!"

Still nothing.

Then faintly, "Juliana? Is that you?" Her mother sounded as though her daughter's presence at her door was inconceivable.

"Hurry, Mama! Hurry downstairs. Papa's come home!"

The door opened and Juliana's senses filled with the exotic presence of her mother. Yvonne had let her hair grow out completely in an attempt to please her husband, and now it hung loose, framing her face and covering her shoulders and breasts with long straight lengths like the fringes of a Gypsy shawl. She was wearing a milk-white dressing gown, and when she moved, the satin whispered and Juliana caught the heady scent of gardenias.

Gardenias. White flowers. Her mother was obsessed with white. Most of Yvonne's clothes were a shade of white. The rooms she locked herself into had French-cream patterned carpets of knotted silk and curtains of Chinese-ivory shantung. The bed coverings and linens and the fabric on the chairs and chaises were all pristinely pale.

The walls and woodwork were painted a shade called eggshell, and indeed the whole room reminded Juliana of the inside of an egg. It made her think of the rhyme about the woman who was kept in a shell—only her mother wasn't living inside a pumpkin, she was living in an egg.

"Aubrey is home?" Yvonne seemed vague and distracted.

"Just now. To surprise us. He wants to see you right away." Juliana didn't say that he'd really come home because of the cousin. She wanted to protect her mother. She wanted her mother to be happy.

Yvonne combed a dark curtain of hair back away from her face with slender fingers. "He's here now?"

"He's in the smoking room. Come on!"

Juliana studied her mother intently. If only her own bland skin were the same maple-gold as her mother's. If only her nondescript brown eyes were as mysteriously dark as her mother's. If only her flyaway cardboard-colored hair were as sleek and black as—

"Oh, Lord. I look terrible." Yvonne suddenly came alive, touching her fingertips to her cheeks and tugging at the sash on her gown.

"No! You look beautiful, Mama. You always look beautiful."

Juliana studied her mother's eyes. What had her Aunt Grace

meant when she said Yvonne's eyes looked haunted? Had she meant sad? That's the way they looked to Juliana—sad and romantic and full of mystery.

Her mother brushed past her suddenly, as if she'd forgotten her daughter was there. Juliana turned to follow in her gardenia-scented wake, but then stopped. Yvonne had left the door to her rooms open. It had been over a year since Juliana had been inside. Cautiously she stepped in and surveyed the sitting room. It looked just as she remembered. She tiptoed across the snowy expanse of rug toward the bedroom.

Her mother's most private space was even more wonderful than she remembered it. The dresser tops were covered with porcelain jars and crystal falcons and sterling brushes. Diamond earrings and pearl necklaces and jade bracelets littered the ornate dressing table.

She was afraid to touch anything. She ran her gaze lovingly around the cluttered room, memorizing every detail. The bed was a tangle of white silk and damask and piles of handworked pillows. There were papers strewn about one side.

Juliana moved closer. They were letters. Old letters from her father. She was seized with a curiosity so strong it eclipsed all else. These letters held the answers. She was certain.

She perched gingerly on the edge of the bed, carefully avoiding the jumble of pill bottles and whiskey decanters on the side table. Her hands trembled and butterflies careened in her stomach. She picked up one on top. It looked very old.

> Dearest Vonnie,
>   Why were you so upset at the airport? I told you before you came that my father wouldn't like you and that you'd be uncomfortable in Great House, so why had you expected it to be otherwise? And as to the other—what good is more discussion? I love you as much as I can love any woman. I can't be more honest than that.
>   When I met you in Paris I was stunned. This was not something I'd been looking for or expecting. And I ask myself even now if it's something I want or if I shouldn't forget you and find a simpler arrangement. I think about your happiness too, and what's best for you. I know that I should leave you alone, let you remain safe in Oklahoma with your own people. You'll eventually find a man there who adores you as you should be adored—

"Juliana!"
Her mother's voice sliced through the silence and she dropped

the letter and jerked upright. Yvonne stood framed in the doorway like a dark, angry angel. "You were reading my letters?"

Juliana couldn't speak. She was overcome with remorse.

"What are you, a little spy? A sneaking little spy looking for evidence to use against me?"

Juliana broke down completely. "No, Mama! No! I'm sorry. I was just ... I wanted ... wanted to ..." But she couldn't put it into words. She couldn't say that she was desperately searching for the key to her mother's affection. Even if she had understood that herself, she could never have admitted it aloud.

Yvonne moved toward her slowly. She reached out and cupped Juliana's face in her hands, tilting it up. "Shhh," she whispered. "You're a big girl now. You should know that crying is useless." The dark, dark eyes focused on Juliana's face intently, searching briefly. The ghost of a smile tugged at the corners of the perfect mouth. "What can I expect—you're not mine, are you? I let them have you a long time ago."

"Oh, Mama," Juliana cried, flinging herself against her mother's body and twining her arms around the slender waist, "I'm yours, I'm all yours. I'd do anything for you!"

Yvonne stood stiff and unyielding in the arms of the clinging child. Then, little by little, her resistance melted. She touched Juliana's hair, let out a deep sigh, and folded her into an embrace.

Juliana pressed her face against her mother's breast, and the satin and the gardenias and the warm softness of Yvonne's body consumed her. She wanted the moment to stretch on forever. She wished that her flesh would weld to her mother's so the embrace could never be broken.

But Yvonne pulled back. With her arm around Juliana she examined herself in the cheval mirror. "I should dress before I see him," she said softly. "Something special. What do you think?"

"You look good to me in everything, Mama."

Yvonne smiled gently. "Would you please go tell him that I'll be down in ten minutes?"

Juliana wanted to stay, but it was no use. Her mother was already dismissing her.

"And tell Mrs. Greevy to plan a welcome-home dinner." Yvonne's voice became distracted, dreamy. "On the covered terrace, I think. Yes. With the French café table and candles and a good wine ..."

Juliana went back downstairs very slowly. Her feet were heavy. Her hand trailed beside her, bumping against the deeply carved balusters of the staircase. The French café table was a little table for two. Juliana was not included. Her mother didn't want her there. And the welcome home was a joke anyway, because her father didn't want to be home. He hadn't come to see her—he'd come to witness the return of the savage cousin.

Juliana went first to give Mrs. Greevy the dinner instructions.

"And what about you?" the housekeeper asked sympathetically. "Would you like to send out for pizza maybe?"

"No. I'm not hungry."

"It's hours till dinner, girl."

"I said I'm not hungry."

Juliana returned to the smoking room and soon after, Yvonne stepped into the filtered light of the room like an apparition. Her hair hung in loose braids and her feet were bare. She wore a soft buckskin dress the color of a dove's breast. For a heartbeat she stood here, hesitant, looking self-conscious and vulnerable and hopeful.

Juliana gaped. Her mother had always hated the mixed blood in her background and avoided all things Indian even when they were in fashion. Now here she was, an illustration straight out of Juliana's old *Hiawatha* book.

Yvonne moved forward a few steps toward Aubrey, who turned from the window at her approach. The light touched her hair and eyes and bathed her skin in gold. It shone across the beadwork of her dress, brightening the jewel tones and heightening the intricate patterns.

"I was reading your old letters," Yvonne said, "and I remembered how much you loved my grandmother's dress."

"You are beautiful," Aubrey breathed. He sounded almost reverent, and Juliana tore her eyes from her mother to study this strange reaction from him.

He was perfectly still and his eyes were burning with the vision of Yvonne in the dress.

Juliana backed toward the wall, feeling suddenly more awkward and unwanted than she had in a long time.

Their eyes locked. Their hands touched. They turned in one graceful motion and left the room together. Without a word to her. Without so much as a backward glance.

Juliana picked up a thirteenth-century Chinese bowl from its recessed niche in the wall. The porcelain was smooth and aloof. Only the unglazed rim felt vulnerable. She ran a finger around the rough, dull whiteness of the rim, then held it up to look for her reflection in the ivory glaze. There was nothing there.

She didn't throw the bowl or purposely smash it. She simply

let go. Her hands pulled away from it and she watched it drop to the floor in slow motion, cracking and splintering and flattening into white fragments against the emerald, crimson, and blue of the woven rug.

No one came. The house absorbed the sound, reducing the destruction of the ancient bowl to nothing. Quickly she kicked the pieces under the couch and fled.

The days following her father's arrival were filled with activity. There was a steady parade of guests playing Ping-Pong and pool, and the projection-room shelves suddenly sported new-release movies. Yvonne joined them downstairs every morning with a childlike eagerness, and the only time she went back to her room was to change clothes or freshen up.

Adding to the furor was the unfolding drama of the lost cousin's reappearance. Each new bulletin sent the entire household into a buzz of conjecture. Grace had rushed to Idaho and found trouble with the police and wild, conflicting stories. There was something about a kidnapped girl and about Frank dying and about Ellis not being able to remember exactly how anything happened. It sounded as though Ellis Fielding had come down out of the hills without his sanity.

Juliana listened and watched with mounting trepidation. Her father's excitement grew daily and he was incited to a near-rage over the news that the boy was to be secluded and under a doctor's care from the moment he arrived in New York until he was judged strong enough to face the world again. This unseen, barely known cousin had already captured more of her father's attention than she ever had.

And her mother ... Her mother had been transformed. Yvonne's dark eyes glowed and her lips seemed perpetually on the verge of a smile. The miracle Juliana had been hoping for all through the grim months had taken place. Her mother was happy. But that happiness had been created by Aubrey's return and the drama over the lost cousin. It had nothing to do with Juliana. She was invisible in the huge, preoccupied household. Even her grandfather—who called daily from his sickbed to agonize over whether this barbarian was actually his long-lost grandson—even he was not interested in Juliana. She would race to the phone before Aubrey could pick it up, and she should say, "Hello, Da Da. How are you feeling?" and her grandfather would dismiss her impatiently with "Not now, child. Not now. I have important matters to discuss with your father."

Her belated birthday party seemed like nothing more than an

afterthought in the face of all the lost-cousin mania. No one asked her what kind of party she wanted. No one even talked about it except Charlotte.

Charlotte kept insisting that she should ask to invite some girls, but she knew which girls Charlotte had in mind. Daphne Buchanan, Whitney Chandler, and Olivia Gabby Gravesend. The governess was always talking about them and their horse-show trophies and their charity fashion shows and their parties, information she got from the network of governesses and servants that linked all the prominent old families of New York. And whenever a publication mentioned one of the girls, Charlotte clipped it out and saved it.

"You'll be one of the golden girls, too, someday," she'd always say. "Your rightful place is with them."

"But I don't like those girls," Juliana had finally told her. "They were mean to me and they said bad things about my mother."

"Ah, but that was years ago, wasn't it? People change, you know. You'd get along just fine now, I bet."

"Maybe," Juliana conceded, but she had no intention of asking that they be invited to her birthday party.

As the nature of the party became clear, Juliana was glad she hadn't been asked to invite anyone. Her father booked the upstairs of an old New York steakhouse that boasted stuffed antelope heads and worn wooden floors, and he nudged and winked over the fact that her grandfather's gout was still giving him enough trouble to prevent his censoring attendance.

The guests were a crazy quilt of Aubrey's longtime hunting partners and short-term business acquaintances, with a sprinkling of professional athletes he currently admired. They jammed into the restaurant's upstairs and the waiters kept them occupied with a continuous supply of food and drink. Two large tables were filled with elegantly wrapped presents.

Juliana took her status as guest of honor very seriously. She sat quietly in her thronelike chair, watching over the crowd of merrymakers as they became increasingly loud and boisterous. She didn't want anyone to be sorry that they'd come to a kid's party.

The cake was rolled out at midnight. Juliana thought it exquisite—a creation from a storybook. But when the woman jumped out of the middle, smashing all the pink-frosting flowers and shouting "Happy Birthday!", Juliana was crushed. The woman danced around in her skimpy outfit, smearing frosting on the laughing men, and when the music ended she plopped down into Aubrey's lap.

Juliana looked to her mother, but Yvonne's face had turned to stone. She wished she could go home and be alone in one of her secret places. She wished she were anywhere but here watching the frosting lady paw at her father. Why did the men think it was so funny?

She turned her head away from the scene and surveyed the gooey pink mound that had been her cake. "My cake," she whispered in despair.

A sharp-eyed waiter bent over her. "Don't worry," he said in heavily accented English. "Another is to eat. Very pretty too." He winked at her and gave her a pat before rushing off toward the kitchen, and the unexpected kindness caused a lump in her throat. She wanted to go home.

All evening she had tried to pay attention to the conversations raging around and over her. Once the frosting lady was gone and the real cake was served, the talk resumed. But now she could no longer pretend interest. The hunting and fishing stories were all sounding the same and she was sick of the speculation revolving around the imminent arrival of her cousin.

Stifling a yawn, she slipped from her chair and moved to her mother's side. She laid her head on the smooth silk-covered line of Yvonne's shoulder and breathed in the faint scent of gardenias surviving the room's smoky air. "Can we go home now, Mama?" she asked softly.

Yvonne took her arm and pulled her around so they were facing each other. The hard look in her mother's eyes was frightening. "No. You wanted your father to give you a birthday party, and here it is. So no complaining."

"I'm not complaining! I'm just tired, and . . . this wasn't exactly the kind of party I wanted."

"Well, it's the only kind of party your father gives. And it's a good lesson for you."

Juliana returned to her seat and fell asleep just before everyone realized that the gifts hadn't been opened. She didn't see the men descend on all her gaily wrapped presents and tear them open. She didn't see the free-for-all that left the floor littered with ribbons and torn paper and broken toys.

She was awakened by the rasping of a rough tongue over her cheek. Fighting free of a dream, she jerked her head from the table and met a pair of slitted golden eyes. The sandpaper tongue attacked again, this time cleaning the frosting from her fingers.

"See, I told you she wouldn't be afraid of it. Not my Jinx. Nothing scares her."

The voice was her father's and it was full of whiskey-sodden pride. "Looka that, they're already friends."

The lanky cat gave an unconcerned yawn and stretched out across the table. Still slightly dazed, Juliana opened the card hanging from the orange bow around the animal's neck. "To Juliana," it said. "From the Hole-in-the-Wall Gang." She knew vaguely who the "gang" was, knew that they were a group her father hunted with every year. "P.S.," the note continued in smaller letters, "she's been declawed and almost house-trained."

"Pick a name for her!" someone shouted.

"Yeah!" a chorus insisted.

"Is she a baby?" Juliana asked.

"She's a cub," her father explained. He reached out to reverently stroke the animal's back. "A mountain-lion cub. One of North America's finest animals."

"And she's mine?" Juliana whispered. A mountain lion when she'd never been allowed so much as a parakeet?

She didn't wait for confirmation. She threw herself forward, burying her face in the animal's thick tawny hide and hugging it until her arms ached.

Yvonne frowned, but Juliana ignored the disapproval. She held on tight to the animal all the way home in the limousine and dragged it up the stairs to sleep with her beneath the pink satin coverlet of her antique canopy bed.

"Kitty," she whispered. "Your name is Kitty. And you're mine. All mine."

14

"By damn! This is exciting, isn't it?"

Juliana watched her father pace restlessly back and forth in front of the living room's mammoth marble fireplace. The pillars on either end were sculpted into female figures in flowing robes. Juliana had always thought of them as the Roman ladies and marveled at their implied strength, but now they looked as if they were supplicating themselves before Aubrey's enthusiasm instead of bowing beneath the weight of the huge mantel they supported.

"Will you stop that pacing!" her grandfather insisted impatiently. "You should have learned some restraint by your age." He shifted slightly in his chair, as though his back ached, and then he turned his fierce bushy-browed gaze toward Yvonne. "Do something!" he ordered. "Calm him down."

"I have no control over him," Yvonne said simply.

"Good Christ, Aubrey. You're pacing like a man who's becoming a father again."

"Not Bree," Yvonne said. "He didn't pace at all when Juliana was born."

Edward frowned. His eyes skated up and down Aubrey as though just seeing him. "Look at you. You had more decorum when you were fifteen than you do now."

Aubrey was wearing the same open-necked cotton pullover and tan jodhpurs and high boots that he had worn to exercise his polo ponies that afternoon. He smelled faintly of leather and horses and sunshine.

Juliana squirmed in her spot on the brocade-covered love seat, imprisoned in a stiff dress that cinched her waist and pinched her neck. She wondered if Charlotte had fed Kitty on time and she wished she could run and check. But she knew better than to ask.

"I can't believe you are all so obsessed with niceties," Aubrey said. "This isn't a tea-party guest we're receiving."

Edward grumbled and frowned again.

"Don't you people understand the significance of this?" Aubrey asked with a sweeping gesture that could have meant anything. He resumed his pacing. "What an opportunity! A savage! A wild creature! A cunning predator"—he stopped pacing—"who is also a human being." He turned to face them like an actor punctuating a dramatic scene. "And not just any human being! No. A human whose veins run with Van Lyden blood. A creature whose genes are imprinted with the heritage of—"

"Here, here, Aubrey." Edward held up his hand and signaled for a drink. "I'm afraid your frontiersman fantasies are getting the best of you. This boy is an unfortunate child who was torn from his mother by a demented man and warped beyond imagining. He is a burden and an embarrassment." Edward accepted the drink from the maid, sipped from it, and frowned. "This is not an opportunity, Aubrey. It is a tragedy." He sipped again. "It would have been kinder for all concerned if one of the police bullets had gone through his head."

Juliana's eyes widened at the idea of bullets through her cousin's head, and she wondered if that would contribute to her father's excitement. Everything to do with guns and shooting excited her father.

"Please, everyone," Yvonne pleaded elegantly. "Grace asked that we all welcome her son back into the family. This gathering tonight is very important to her."

"As it should be to all of us," Aubrey added. "This young man could change history."

"And remember ... don't ask him any questions about his years away," Yvonne said. "Grace says that his partial memory loss is very traumatic for him."

Edward snorted sarcastically and muttered again.

"Maybe it's not memory loss at all," Aubrey suggested. "Maybe he takes after his grandfather and remembers only what he wants to."

"Would you two please stop!" Yvonne sounded like a teacher with unruly pupils. "Grace has had enough pain, don't you think?"

"You're right, Yvonne," Edward agreed. "My daughter has suffered enough. Ever since the day she first brought home that blackguard she married. . . . I told her then, I told her—"

"You told her nothing." Aubrey did not look at Edward as he spoke. "You turned her out and refused to speak to her. I don't remember any of us advising Grace against that marriage until after it was a fact. You, Father, were too angry to deal with her, while I myself was quite taken with the man. And I must admit that I still feel a good deal of admiration for Frank, even if he did go round the bend."

Edward puffed up and reddened, but before he had a chance to speak, there was a tap at the door.

"Excuse me," Westlake interrupted politely. "Miss Grace and her son are here."

"Send them in," Edward said formally, and Yvonne and Juliana rose from their chairs.

Aunt Grace entered the room looking radiantly happy. Her hands fluttered in the air and then twisted together as though they had a life of their own. Her eyes sparkled enough to cancel out the dark shadows beneath them. She wore an outfit suitable for church or high tea.

Behind her trailed the notorious cousin.

At first he was just a tall skinny shadow in the doorway; then Aunt Grace grabbed his hand and pulled him with her into the room. Juliana gaped. He looked so completely wrong in his suit and tie and fresh haircut, like Kitty forced into a doll's dress.

He was tall and lanky, with that awkward still-growing appearance, but he wasn't clumsy at all. He moved with a sureness and an energy that fascinated Juliana. And as he moved, his eyes took in everything. They were spooky eyes, she thought. X-ray-vision eyes. They slid over the elaborate inlays of white mahogany and rosewood and satinwood in the marquetry walls. They swept over the Saint-Gaudens fireplace and the ornate vaulted ceiling and the inlaid marble floor and the beveled glass windows and the stained-glass fanlights, and Juliana suspected that he hadn't missed one detail of the room. Or one potential escape route.

"Grace," Yvonne said warmly, and held out her arms to hug her sister-in-law. From there Aunt Grace made the circle, bending to kiss Edward's cheek and then bending again to hug Juliana.

The cousin stood on the edge, as alert and still as a wild thing testing for danger. A wild thing that might bolt and leap over the furniture and smash through a window at any moment. Juliana half-wished that he would go berserk. She suppressed a smile as she imagined the commotion that would cause.

"Come, darling," Grace coaxed. "Here's your grandfather." She pulled the boy over to stand in front of Edward.

"Hello, young man," Edward said in a politely measured tone.

The boy stared at him.

"And here's your Aunt Yvonne . . ."

Grace pulled him around and Yvonne said, "Hello, Ellis," and Juliana felt something happen. Something that stirred in the boy's eyes and echoed in her mother's. Something that darted through her like tiny sharp-toothed fish.

She stared hard at them. Their masks were instantly back in place, but she could sense the changes in them. The boy's wary watchfulness softened with confusion, and the polite concern in her mother's gaze deepened into startled warmth.

"Hello," Ellis said, and Juliana wanted to leap up and insert herself between them.

Aubrey stepped in then, trapping the boy with a vigorous handshake. "Welcome home, Ellis. We're here this evening to give our support and encouragement . . . to show we're behind you all the way! Welcome back to the family, son." With that he added a hearty slap on the back.

The boy flinched but kept himself separate, enduring Aubrey's assault with narrowed eyes.

Grace bit her lip. Yvonne's eyebrows drew together.

Aubrey finally wound down, backed up a step, and cleared his throat self-consciously. Juliana had never seen her father so animated by anything to do with the family.

"And Juliana . . ." Aunt Grace said, pushing the boy toward her. "Darling, this is your little cousin, Juliana."

"Jinx," her father insisted. "Ellis can call her Jinx, just like I do."

No one else but Sparky had ever called her Jinx. The name had been private. Something special that linked her with her father. But now her father was giving it away like it was nothing.

The boy stared down at her for several moments and she saw curiosity in his guarded look. "Jinx," he said finally, and she wanted to leap at him and punch his spooky eyes.

She glared up at him. "You aren't so wild," she said. "I think you're just crazy."

It slipped out from under all her practiced manners and her efforts to be good.

"Juliana!" everyone gasped in horror.

Just then a loud thunk sounded—like a body being hurled against the closed side door.

"Dear me!" the butler exclaimed as he put down his coffee tray and hurried across the room. He cracked open the door to peek out, and Kitty launched her powerful body through the opening, flinging the heavy door and the butler aside as she charged. In three weeks she had grown tremendously and changed from a cuddly toy to a gangly, mischievous bundle of energy.

The boy crouched and pivoted in one flashing movement so that he was facing the advancing cat. To Juliana's horror, a knife suddenly glinted in his hand.

"No!" She threw herself at the boy, using her own body to protect the cat.

She heard screams and a chair toppling and her dress tearing and the whoosh of expelled air as she plowed into Ellis' midsection. Her chest burned. Then she was falling. The last thing that registered was the hollow thud of her head striking a table.

It seemed like only moments later that she was swimming upward through thick, muffling layers of darkness.

"Poor baby ... poor, poor baby," she heard a female voice crooning softly. She resisted the urge to open her eyes and sit up. Any movement on her part might stop the flow of love and concern. She lay very still, absorbing Yvonne's whispered crooning, drinking in the light touch of the fingers stroking her hand.

"We ought to have called an ambulance," she heard her mother say. But the voice came from across the room.

"Mama?" She opened her eyes in confusion.

Somehow she'd been spirited into bed. And it wasn't her mother leaning over her—it was Charlotte. Her mother and father and grandfather were huddled together near her curved window seat, having what appeared to be an argument.

"There you are!" Charlotte exclaimed, and reached out to smooth the hair back from her forehead. As soon as the words were out, the others rushed over and peered down at Juliana.

"Don't move," ordered her grandfather. "The doctor will be here momentarily."

Charlotte got up and retreated.

"Was I asleep?" Juliana asked. "How did I get upstairs?"

"You hit your head," her grandfather explained gruffly. "You've been unconscious for"—he checked his watch—"seven minutes."

The idea of being unconscious appealed to Juliana and she considered it a moment. Then she saw her ruined dress on the floor, and the scene with Ellis and Kitty flooded back to her.

"It wasn't my fault," she said, struggling to sit up.

"Shhh. Be still." Her mother bent to touch her forehead. Juliana inhaled the fragrance of gardenias and sank back to enjoy her mother's presence.

"Of course it wasn't your fault," her grandfather said. "Allowing an unbalanced boy like that to carry a knife," he grumbled, "sheer idiocy!"

"Is Kitty all right?"

"Yes," her father said, exchanging looks with Edward.

"What'd you do with *him*?" Juliana asked, hoping to hear that Ellis had been punished soundly. "Did the police take him to jail?"

"Certainly not!" her father answered. "This is private family business. The boy's your cousin, Jinx!"

"Aunt Grace is taking him to a special place where there are doctors to help him," her mother said. "He was very upset by what happened. He didn't mean to hurt you. He was confused and thought he was protecting you."

Yvonne seated herself on the bed and took Juliana's hand. The joining of fingers and press of warm palms sent an intense rush of feeling through her. She floated upward into her mother's compassionate gaze, shutting out the droning voices of her father and grandfather. Nothing mattered but this sudden connection, this passage to her mother's heart.

Yvonne turned to look at Aubrey, and the spell was broken.

"And so . . . we all agree that the cat must go."

The words sank in to her slowly. They were talking about Kitty. She looked at up her father and then back to her mother in disbelief.

Yvonne nodded. "Wild animals do not belong in the house."

"She's not wild!" Juliana protested frantically.

"Mrs. Greevy says she's been doing quite a number on the furniture," her father said.

"That's not the problem," her grandfather said. "The problem is that the animal could be dangerous to you, Juliana."

"You can't teach a wild creature to forget its natural ways," her mother said gently.

"Yes you can," Juliana insisted. "She's very smart. She can learn anything. And besides, they're taming Ellis, aren't they, and he's wilder than Kitty ever was."

"Ellis is a human, Juliana. That's a ridiculous comparison."

The doctor arrived then and Juliana submitted to his pokings and proddings in mute misery. If she lost Kitty it would all be Ellis' fault. Why were they being so unfair? The boy was a maniac! He had pulled a knife in her family's house just like some hoodlum off the street. Like one of the bad men that her grandfather was so worried about. They should be chaining him up instead of sending Kitty away. They should be planning a terrible punishment for him.

When the doctor pulled back the covers and examined her chest, Juliana was amazed. There, skittering slantwise across her ribs, was an angry red gash. The maniac had actually cut her! How could they possibly defend him when he'd done this to her?

"I'm going to stitch it and try to minimize the scar," the doctor said. He motioned to his nurse to begin preparations.

"Will you hold my hand, Mama?" Juliana asked.

Yvonne reached out and took Juliana's hand, pressing it firmly between both of hers. She forced a reassuring smile, but her face was drawn with worry.

Juliana gritted her teeth against the stabbing pain of the needle. A special place. They were taking Ellis to a special place . . . hah! She knew what that meant—a place for crazies. She hoped it was an asylum full of bloodthirsty lunatics. She hoped they chained him to the wall and brought him wormy food and make him go to the bathroom in his pants. And most of all she hoped that he would never, ever, ever set foot in her house again.

The doctor finished with his work and announced that Juliana was to spend the next five days in bed because of a slight concussion. She complained a little because she knew it was expected, but in fact she was deeply pleased by the orders. Nothing like this had ever happened to her, and it felt good to be the focus of so much activity and concern.

Her term in bed proved to be the most glorious five days of her life. The maids brought her cookies and cocoa constantly. Mrs. Greevy brought her magazines and Charlotte had a new game or book for her every day. But the best times—the times she would remember forever—were the times she spent with her parents. Yvonne came for an hour every morning and Aubrey came for an hour every afternoon.

In the afternoons Aubrey taught her to play blackjack and five-card draw and seven-card no-peek. He filled the bed with blue and red clay chips and showed her how to bet millions while keeping a straight face. She laughed with him and enjoyed his company, even when he lost and erupted into cussing and throwing cards on the floor.

Her father's visits were fun, but her mother's visits fed her soul. Yvonne spent the hour sitting beside her on the bed and telling stories. They were light stories about growing up in Oklahoma or about meeting Aubrey, and they never answered the hundreds of questions Juliana wanted to ask on each subject, but none of that mattered. The important thing was that her mother was giving an entire hour of herself.

Juliana soaked in every word and touch and gesture of her

mother's, tucking them away like treasures to be guarded. As her convalescence drew to an end, she wished that she could always be sick, binding her mother to her for one hour a day forever.

On the afternoon of the fifth day, Yvonne perched on the edge of Juliana's satin-covered bed. Her black hair hung down her back in a single thick braid. She had on slacks and there was a wind-blown look about her that puzzled Juliana. It wasn't like her mother to appear so disheveled.

"Just think, tonight you'll be at the dinner table with us." Yvonne smiled. "You're anxious to be up, aren't you?"

Juliana nodded obediently.

"I know that all this time in bed has been awful for you, but the doctor says you're fine now ... and I hope that means you're feeling well enough to be on your very best behavior."

"Why?" Juliana pulled herself up straighter against the pile of pillows. "Are we having company?"

"No. Not company. Family." Yvonne fixed Juliana with a firm look. "Your grandfather is coming, and Grace and Ellis will be at the table as well. They moved into the third-floor guest suite last night, so this will be a reunion of sorts. A chance for us all to start again."

Juliana was stunned by the news. "Ellis isn't still—"

"Everything has been going very smoothly with Ellis," Yvonne warned, "and you must be extra careful not to make any mistakes and upset him."

Not make any mistakes and upset him! She was the one with the stitches and the mild concussion and the lost pet, and she was supposed to be careful not to upset him?

"You must not mention anything about the incident with the cat ... except of course as an apology. But keep that vague. Just say you're sorry about everything."

"An apology?" Juliana asked in disbelief. "You mean you want me to make it sound like his stabbing me was all my fault?"

" 'Stabbed' is a bit of an exaggeration, don't you think?" Yvonne's voice was devoid of sympathy. "Fault is not important. It's keeping peace in the family that's important. Now, please, Juliana ... you must promise to put aside this childishness and behave perfectly or we will have to exclude you from family gatherings until Ellis is stronger."

All the warmth and contentment of the past five days evaporated and she saw her mother slipping from her again. But this time it wasn't one of Yvonne's inner mysteries that was pulling her away. It wasn't a retreat to silence or a sudden melancholy or Yvonne's natural elusiveness. This time there was something sinister—something dark and looming that sent a chill through Juliana in spite of her warm comforter and the cozy nest of her sickbed.

"All right, Mama." Juliana pulled the covers up to her chin. "I promise. I'll be very, very good. No matter what happens. I'll do whatever you want."

Yvonne studied her a moment, as though gauging her sincerity. "Fine," she said. She reached out to smooth her daughter's forehead before leaving, but there was no connection. The brush of fingertips felt icy and distant against Juliana's skin.

Like a prisoner being readied for execution, Juliana mutely cooperated as Charlotte bathed her and dressed her for dinner. The stitches pulled and itched inside her clothing, but she didn't complain. A careful stillness gripped her as she went down to join her family.

Everyone was seated when she entered the dining room. Her father and grandfather were at opposite ends of the table. Her mother and Aunt Grace were seated on one side, and the empty place that had been left for her was next to Ellis on the other side. She ducked her head and went quietly to her chair.

The chandeliers blazed, bouncing light off the huge beveled mirror and the opalescent glass fanlights and the polished silver serving pieces and the gleaming cherrywood furniture. She felt exposed in the flood of brilliance. Trapped. Everyone stared at her. Their eyes speared her.

She blinked and focused on the china service plate in front of her. It too was bright, reflecting a blurry monster face that moved when she moved. Her head began to throb dully.

"This child's not well enough to be up," she heard her grandfather protest. "Look at her!"

"She's fine, Edward," Yvonne said. "The doctor wants her up and about. She's just weak from so much time in bed."

Edward grumbled something under his breath.

"We're all very glad to see you up, Juliana," Grace said, "Aren't we, Ellis."

Ellis stared down at his plate. He tugged at his collar and tie and shrugged inside his jacket as though trying to escape. "Yes," he said. "And I'm sorry about . . . about . . . ." His voice trailed off.

Yvonne cleared her throat and caught Juliana's eye with a clear warning.

"I'm sorry too," Juliana whispered.

"Splendid!" Aubrey said. "Now that that's out of the way, we can get on with it."

Everyone was dressed more formally than usual for a family

dinner. Grace had on a deep green chiffon dress and pearl ear-rings. Edward was wearing a dinner jacket, and even Aubrey had donned a suit. They were all awesomely elegant. Except for Ellis, of course, whose clothing was askew and whose haircut was ridic-ulous. And except for her mother, who went beyond elegance.

Her mother was glowing tonight, radiating something deeper and richer than the surface shine of her upswept hair and her iridescent silk and her diamond eardrops. There was a light in her eyes and an upward tilt to her chin and a softness at the corners of her mouth.

Suddenly Juliana realized that Ellis was studying her mother too. His gray eyes were locked on her mother in a way that made her want to stab his hand with her fork.

Yvonne glanced toward their side of the table. Juliana smiled hopefully. But it was Ellis that the warm gaze lingered over. It was Ellis who brought the ghost of a smile to her mother's lips.

And suddenly Juliana was filled with little fish again. Thou-sands of them this time. Tiny darting monster fish with needle teeth and poison spines.

She forced herself to eat, but the food was tasteless. Beside her Ellis rattled his soup spoon and plowed through his salad. No one seemed to notice except her grandfather. She saw him raise an eyebrow and frown. But he didn't scold Ellis as he'd scolded her when she was younger.

Juliana tuned back into the conversation when Aunt Grace said, "I've decided to take Ellis to live in Europe," taking everyone by surprise.

Juliana looked down and mashed her lips together to keep from showing her delight at this news.

"Now, that's an idiotic idea!" Aubrey said finally. "He needs to be acclimated to his home before you drag him off to stuff him with foreign culture."

Grace sat up very straight. She held her fork and knife tightly but made no pretense at eating. "Dr. Sun believes that travel could be very beneficial."

"Dr. Sun believes whatever you pay her to believe," Aubrey said. He waved his salad plate away and leaned forward. "I'm telling you, Grace, you don't know what Ellis needs. All you're thinking of is yourself."

"Aubrey!" Edward cautioned sharply.

Aubrey sank back into his chair with a ferocious scowl, and Edward turned to Grace. "Did you have specific plans in mind, Grace?"

"Yes." Grace sighed in relief. "Hopefully we'll leave by spring."

She smiled tenderly at her son. "He's missed so much of life. In Europe he would have education and a break from this city and all the nosiness and publicity and—"

"What do you expect?" Aubrey asked. He was sarcastic now. "You started the publicity. You talked to the press when you arrived, and now you've launched into changing Ellis' identity without any discretion at all."

Juliana put her fork down and listened intently. Something was going on that she didn't know about.

Grace flushed a deep red and her bottom lip trembled. "The Van Lyden name is as much mine as yours, Bree. And I can give it to my son if I choose. You keep forgetting that I was raised with the name and in this house just like you were."

"Enough!" Edward glared at his son and then at his daughter. "This squabbling must stop or I'll banish you both from the table as I did when you were children!"

A charged silence descended and hovered over the magnificent beef Wellington. Juliana cut into her meat mechanically and wondered about what she'd heard. Her aunt had long ago changed from Fielding to Van Lyden. Was she now trying to make Ellis a Van Lyden as well? Surely her grandfather wouldn't allow that.

After several minutes Edward turned to Yvonne and smiled approvingly. "I understand you took Ellis out today."

Yvonne gave her father-in-law a sideways look and a smile. "Yes. We had a lovely time." Yvonne's look slid over briefly to include Ellis. "We found sneakers for him and took a walk through the park to break them in."

Juliana nearly choked. Her mother had taken Ellis out shopping? Her mother had gone with Ellis to Central Park? Those were things Juliana had always wanted but never been allowed to do, and the unfairness churned and twisted inside her, providing more food for the ugly little fish.

"And how is the gala coming?" Edward asked. "Any disasters to report?"

"The gala has a life of its own," Yvonne said. "The menus and entertainment are decided, and the invitations have all gone out, so there's not much left for me to do."

"Have you found a gown yet?" Grace asked.

"No. I liked one designer's sketches well enough, but I'm holding out for something special."

"Why don't you check the bridal shops?" Aubrey suggested. He frequently teased his wife about her penchant for white, but his current mood gave the teasing a cruel edge.

There was forced laughter. Juliana glanced at Ellis. She wanted to send arrows of hatred straight into him, but he didn't look up or notice her attention. He was different now than he'd been at that first disastrous encounter. Less threatened maybe. He was still as tightly wound and ill-at-ease, but she no longer had the sense that he might go wild and escape at any moment. And his eyes had changed. He was watching them all from some distant shuttered place now, someplace where they couldn't reach him. A spark of curiosity flared inside her, but it was quickly snapped up by the deadly little fish's jaws.

"I was wondering if you might have the time to help me choose my gown?" Grace asked. She looked hopefully at Yvonne.

Yvonne hesitated a fraction, as though puzzled or surprised. "Certainly. I'm flattered that you ask."

"Oh, no ..." The sarcasm in Aubrey's voice was ugly now. "Next thing you know, Grace will be dyeing her hair black and showing up in white dresses."

"Men are so lucky," Grace said, ignoring the comment. "You don't have to give a thought to what you'll wear to the gala."

"That's not true," Aubrey protested in a lighter tone. "There is more to ordering a tux than women know. Just wait till Ellis goes in for his fittings." He winked at Ellis. "He'll tell you it's no small chore."

"You're having a tux made for Ellis?" Edward stopped a fork-ful of beef midway to his mouth. "Surely you aren't suggesting that Ellis should attend the gala?"

Juliana smiled inwardly. Her grandfather would never allow him to go to the gala.

"The doctor said a public appearance would be good for him, isn't that right, Grace?" Aubrey downed his remaining wine in one gulp and signaled for a refill. "You haven't been keeping up, Father."

Grace glanced around nervously. "Yes, well ... it depends on how Ellis feels. The doctor said that it should be up to him, and that if he attends, one of the family ought to stay with him all evening in case he becomes nervous or upset or ..." Her voice trailed off.

Ellis continued eating in a slow mechanical fashion. Juliana wondered if he disliked the way everyone was talking about him. Like he wasn't there. Or like his feelings weren't important. They did that to her sometimes too, and it bothered her—not as much as when they ignored her, but still, it did bother her.

"No decisions have to be made yet," Yvonne said in her quiet, peacemaking voice. She focused directly on the boy. "But I think

Ellis would do very well at the party. I'd be delighted to have him as my escort for the evening."

The tops of Ellis' ears turned bright red and he stopped chewing and swallowed hard.

Inside Juliana the needle-toothed fish swelled into monstrous red-eyed sharks.

"Nonsense, Yvonne." Edward scowled down at his plate. "You are the hostess. You can't be saddled with extra baggage." He speared the last bite on his plate and chewed it vigorously, transferring his scowl from the plate to the occupants of the table. "Each of us has a hosting responsibility at the gala, and I won't hear of anyone dividing the time between guests and baby-sitting duty."

Yvonne's mouth hardened into an angry line. Juliana held her breath. Ellis chugged the water from his goblet and plunked the fragile crystal back down onto the table with a thud.

Suddenly Juliana had a flash of startling clarity. The sharks deflated back into little fish, then the little fish retreated into hiding, and she was suffused with a perfect dispassionate calm. Her mother had been right to accuse her of childishness. She had been childish. And she saw now that she couldn't afford to be a child any longer. The stakes were much too high. She had to gather her wits and fight like an adult.

"I could take care of Ellis at the gala," she announced.

Everyone looked at her. Varying degrees of surprise and skepticism showed on their faces. Her grandfather rubbed his mouth with his hand to hide a smile, but the twinkle in his eyes gave it away. His amusement was encouraging.

Yvonne sighed. "We've always said you wouldn't be allowed to go till you were sixteen . . ."

Edward drew in a deep breath and blew it out. His bushy eyebrows knit together and the corners of his mouth turned down. Silence blanketed the room.

He cleared his throat. "It's a possibility," he said.

And Juliana knew she had won her first battle.

15

Ellis

Ellis walked silently beside her. Careless drifts of gold and russet leaves swirled and scattered in the breeze, and he thought about the snow that would blanket the mountains by now, and the snow that would eventually cover this path in Central Park, and the snowshoes he'd made just last winter, and animal tracks in the snow, and other snow-related thoughts.

With her he could let his mind wander. He could put down his guard and be himself.

"Fall is my favorite time," she said.

He felt no obligation to respond. The mountains had done that to him—eliminated the need to fill silences with the sound of his voice or to connect with people through unnecessary strings of words. His mother and his uncle and the psychiatrists pressured him constantly about what they termed his "unwillingness to communicate." But with her it was okay. With her he knew that he could talk or not talk. She'd never pressured him. She'd never demanded anything of him.

He glanced over at her. She was almost too beautiful. Certainly too beautiful to be anyone's aunt. Or mother. Or even wife. Too beautiful to be walking along beside him as though they belonged together. As though she was comfortable with him, whoever he was or whatever he'd done.

He felt guilty about that. Guilty that he hadn't told her the truth. What would she think if she learned she was walking beside a murderer? Would it drive her away? Would it destroy their closeness?

He was afraid to find out the answer, yet he knew he had to tell her. There was too much trust between them to allow such a horrible secret.

"Let's go this way," she said, touching his arm lightly as she struck out onto a smaller forking path.

Her touch burned through his sleeve, making him angry at himself. How had this happened? What strange combination of elements or chemicals had forged their friendship? What had he seen that very first time he looked into Yvonne Van Lyden's eyes? He didn't know any more now than he'd known then. It was a mystery to him, and their long walks and hours of shared time had only complicated that mystery.

The problem was that he was losing the sense of her as his aunt or, more specifically, as his uncle's wife.

He was feeling things about her that he shouldn't. Like when she touched his arm or when she looked sideways at him with one of those half-smiles. And he cursed himself for it and worried that he was doomed to be as sexually twisted as his father.

"We should have brought a picnic," she said. "Or maybe some fruit and cookies."

His anger at himself transferred to her and he took the offer of cookies as an insult. As proof that he was no more than a child to her. "Why don't you bring Jinx out here?" he said. "Did you see her today? Watching us leave. She's the one who needs your walks and your fruit and cookies."

Yvonne stopped. Her lips compressed into a hard line. Then she sighed and softened as if she couldn't be angry with him. "You'll have to speak to your grandfather about that. He's the one who decides what is safe for Juliana to do."

"But she's your daughter, isn't she? She belongs to you."

Yvonne bent to pick up a huge crimson maple leaf. She turned the brilliant leaf over and over in her slender hands. The diamonds on her fingers winked in the light. Then she smiled with maddening vagueness, making him feel light-years away from whatever she was seeing. "She doesn't belong to me any more than the jewels in the Van Lyden vault do." She dropped the leaf and pulled the cashmere sweater tighter around her shoulders in a hugging movement. "Is your mother having another of her meetings with the attorneys today?" she asked.

He nodded.

"Have they included you in any of the discussions?"

"They don't care what I think," he said. "My mother wants to reshape my life. And she believes changing my name to Van Lyden will somehow erase my father and the past five years."

"And what do you think?"

Ellis raked his fingers through his hair, combing it back off his forehead like he used to when it was long and tied back with a ragged buckskin strip. The strangeness of his short haircut was just another of the unfamiliar pieces in the puzzle that his life had become. "I'm tired of being treated like I have no opinions and will follow along with anything. As to changing my name— it won't make the magic difference my mother thinks it will, and it won't wipe my memory clean, and it won't make me fit better in a tuxedo."

"You don't want the name change, then?"

"No ... I guess I can't say that. Of all the things my mother's done, that's the one I can agree with. I hate using the name Field-ing. I hate any connection to it."

"Then it makes sense to use Van Lyden, doesn't it?" She stared off into the distance and he could feel her sadness stronger than ever.

"I remember when I became a Van Lyden. I thought ..." She shook her head and smiled as though belittling whatever she'd been about to say. "But then, you aren't really becoming a Van Lyden. You were born to be one. It's only a quirk of the legal system that you didn't start with the name."

Ellis studied his moving feet for several minutes. The sneakers Yvonne had bought him were still ridiculously white against the stones and earth and dying leaves. But they felt good. Almost as good as moccasins. He glanced over at her, absorbing the details of her profile furtively. She was pensive. The corners of her mouth had a slight downturn and there were vertical lines between her eyebrows.

"I wonder what time it is," she said.

He checked the sun. "It's nearly two."

"How do you do that?" She laughed. "Bree says you're always right, too."

"It's not that hard. Except when the buildings get in the way."

"Could you teach me?"

"Sure."

He moved around behind her and bent close to her shoulder so their eyes were at the same level. The scent of gardenias and the scent of her skin and the just-washed fragrance of her hair whispered to him.

"Just think about it," he said, using his outstretched arm to indicate quadrants of sky. "Straight that way is sunrise, and the opposite is sunset. This time of year the sun rises just before seven and sets just before seven ... so you figure east is seven and west is seven and the sky is an arc divided into the twelve hours in between. Twelve is about there. Not really midpoint like peo-ple assume."

He moved away from her.

"So that's the way you knew the time all those years in the mountains."

He laughed. "There weren't any appointments to keep up there. I didn't really care about the time. I just grew to know the sun."

"Well ..." She seemed momentarily flustered. "You're riding with Bree again this afternoon, aren't you?"

The mention of Aubrey brought instant guilt. Not only was he having inappropriate thoughts about his uncle's wife, he was compounding the crime by trying to hide from the man.

Aubrey wanted to be uncle and surrogate father and friend to him, but all the boyish confidences and masculine ribbing only made Ellis uncomfortable. He felt no affection for Aubrey, and the previous day's experience with his uncle had pushed the discomfort toward distrust.

They'd set out for a day of riding, supposedly in Central Park, but Aubrey had driven them forty minutes north of Manhattan to a place he referred to as his secret hideaway. "This is just between us," Aubrey had said with an exaggerated wink.

They'd left the city skyline behind and headed north into the lush New York countryside, finally turning off the Saw Mill Parkway to wind down narrow roads past elegant country homes set back among the trees. White fences and jumping rings abounded.

Aubrey's hideaway was set even further back than the rest. When his uncle stopped to undo the padlock on the white wooden gate across the entrance, Ellis could see no sign of a building through the trees. Aubrey's place was conspicuously private.

Ellis was surprised by the layout. There was a rambling modern house and a terraced pool in addition to the stables and horse-related areas.

"Does anyone live here?" Ellis asked as Aubrey raced the Porsche up to the front door.

"I do!" Aubrey said gaily. "Our secret," he added quickly. "This is my getaway. You know how it is," he said, oozing camaraderie in the security of his smooth blond, wealthy, muscular tanness. "When the family and the city get to be too much, I just buzz up here and unwind."

Ellis was gripped with an aversion so strong that he had to fight his facial muscles for control. He stepped out of the car and looked around to cover whatever distaste might have seeped into his expression. Aubrey eased out of the car and sauntered around to stand beside him. Ellis focused his attention on the horses in the pasture.

"Men are not naturally domestic," Aubrey said in a wise and confidential tone. "A man needs diversions in order to bear all the domesticity that's expected of him."

A rangy sorrel raised its head from grazing and whinnied so hard that Ellis could see his belly shake across the distance that separated them. The horse was looking at the stable, and Ellis could see a figure in the doorway there. "Someone's at the barn," he said, but Aubrey was already waving for the person to come down.

"That's my stableboy," he said. He waved his arms again and called, "Come on, Sparky! Come meet my nephew!" Aubrey turned to Ellis. "So, this is just between us, right, mountain man?" He winked and threw an arm across Ellis' shoulders. "I knew it the minute I saw you go for that cat's throat with the knife ... I knew we were just alike."

Yvonne spoke, jarring Ellis back to the present with a question about whether he needed to get back to meet his uncle.

"Not yet," he lied, vowing that this would be his last lie to her and hating himself for not having had the nerve to refuse Aubrey's invitation for another ride.

"Let's rest for a bit, then, shall we?" she said.

They sat on a flat outcropping of rock surrounded by thick trees. The city seemed distant and there wasn't another person in sight. It made him homesick for the mountains.

"So," Yvonne said brightly, "ready for the gala?"

This was the other Yvonne, suddenly glossy and cheerful, fabricated of something she imagined was required. This was the Van Lyden hostess.

"Don't ..." he said, intending to tell her that she didn't need to be something different for him. But he couldn't finish. Her questioning glance was too quick, too fragile. "Don't ask," he finished lamely. "My dancing teacher says I may be impossible."

Yvonne laughed. "You've got your tux?"

"Yes. And the wooden shoes that go with it." He noticed that the tips of skyscrapers were visible to the west. Seeing them above the treetops destroyed the illusion of nature for him. "It doesn't make sense to me that humans invented hard-soled shoes when they could have stuck with moccasins." He glanced over at Yvonne. "Did you ever wear moccasins as a kid? I mean ... being part Indian and ..."

Yvonne's face stiffened and the brightness disintegrated just as surely as if Aubrey had launched one of his well-aimed barbs. Something had offended or wounded her.

Ellis stared down at his hands, hating himself for whatever he'd said and hating himself for not knowing what it was that he'd said. He would never learn the subtleties of civilized life. He belonged in the woods, where he couldn't cause hurt or shame.

"Please . . ." Yvonne said, and he reluctantly met her eyes. "I'm sorry. I'm so used to being on the defensive. There's been no one to talk to the way we talk." She drew in a deep breath and watched a pair of squirrels chase each other. "When I gave birth to a daughter, I imagined her growing into my dearest friend," she said wistfully. "I was so foolish then . . . so naive about how my life would be." She stopped herself.

Vulnerability welled up in her dark eyes, stirring a fierce protectiveness in him. "You can talk to me anytime," he said.

"I know. Do you understand what a gift that is?" She sighed and slipped into light, self-directed sarcasm.

"My mother's family was Cherokee. They lived in Anadarko, Oklahoma—the Indian Capital of the World they called it—and all their friends were Indian and they spent their time going to powwows and sings and clinging to the past. They lived in a decaying old wooden house with asphalt sheets nailed over the wood siding. Like asphalt roof shingles, only in bigger pieces. And the ones on my grandparents' house were dark rust and black in this geometric design, so that from a distance it looked like the house was made of brick. 'Nigger brick,' my father called it, and whenever he got mad at me, he'd say that bad girls ended up married to bums and living in nigger-brick shacks."

She glanced over at him coolly. "I guess I showed him, didn't I?"

Ellis kept silent.

"Anyway . . ." She picked at a patch of flaking rock with her perfectly manicured fingers, cracked a nail, and absently tore it the rest of the way off. "The kids in school used to call me a dirty half-breed before my dad's well came in, and I grew up with this image of my grandparents as lazy paupers and my mother as tainted, and all of that was bound up with being Indian and living in a nigger-brick shack. My mixed blood was something to escape. My family was something to escape. The whole damn state of Oklahoma was something to escape."

She smiled ruefully. "I wouldn't have been caught dead with moccasins. Or braids. Or anything else that spelled Indian."

"And your father . . . ?"

"Fair-skinned. Blue-eyed. Your basic redneck who struck it lucky with oil." She laughed. "A carefree man who usually meant well." She stared into herself awhile, then drew a deep breath. "I never appreciated him or my mother while they were alive. All I could see was that they were both ignorant and old-fashioned and embarrassing to be seen with.

"I used my high-school-graduation money to run away to France. And I met Aubrey . . . and thought he'd protect me from all the shame and all the separateness I'd felt as a child. I thought I could be reborn as a Van Lyden and become the person I'd always dreamed of being."

He waited.

"I guess I should have joined a religious cult or the Foreign Legion!" She laughed. "So . . . that's why I reacted when you asked about wearing moccasins. I was afraid you were belittling me."

"No one could ever belittle you," Ellis protested. "You're the most elegant . . . most beautiful . . ."

Yvonne chuckled. "The blue bloods in this city might argue that."

"Who?" he demanded. "Just tell me who and I'll—"

"Oh, Ellis . . ." She smiled gently. "You're so much better than the rest of us. So generous and unspoiled. So shiny with principles. I'm afraid those aren't survival skills in this world."

"No!" He was suddenly so agitated that he couldn't sort out his thoughts. "You're wrong about me, just like you're wrong about yourself. I'm not better than anyone! I don't have principles. I'm not what you think."

Her face grew very still and her dark eyes burned into him. "I'm listening," she said.

The park and the sky and the intruding skyscrapers faded from focus, and those eyes, so dark that pupil and iris melded into one, seemed to see right through to the fear and self-loathing that formed his core.

"I'm a murderer." His throat closed on each word and he had to force the sounds out. "I killed my father."

He held his breath, waiting for the outburst of horror and rejection. But she barely blinked.

She already knew about Noisy and Badger, and he'd shared other memories with her—of sharp-scented pine and dusky sage and biting high country winds and sweet smoked salmon. But even with her he'd barely been able to talk about Frank. Not even small things. Now, here he was poised at the brink of his own private hell and pulling her down with him.

He took a deep breath. "It was night. I was alone by the fire. Suddenly there was my father, dragging a girl into camp.

"I couldn't believe it. Even after the cruelty I'd seen him capable of, I couldn't believe what he was doing. It was unreal. This terrified girl with her wrists tied and my father laughing and eating and drinking and telling me she was a present. It was a nightmare, and I just wanted to wake up.

"Then he got mad. He said if I didn't want her he'd take over. And he threw her down and ... and I remembered something terrible I'd seen him do to my mother before their divorce. And I hit him. I hit him with a whiskey bottle. More than once ... but I don't remember that. The girl told me afterward. She said she had to yell to get me to stop hitting him.

" 'He's dead!' she kept screaming. 'He's dead! Get him off me.'

"I pulled her free of him and untied her. I don't remember what I felt. Maybe nothing. If it hadn't been for her, I would probably still be sitting there staring at his bloody head, his empty eyes.

" 'We have to bury him.' She pulled her clothes back together and looked around the camp. 'Do you have anything to dig with?' She was so calm and controlled, and I was like a little kid—just waiting for someone to tell me what to do.

"It took us almost till dawn to get him buried. The ground was rocky and packed there. We collapsed afterward and slept till the afternoon. Noisy woke us up wanting food.

"She told me she was hungry too, so I took my bow down to the stream for trout just like nothing in the world had changed. I felt very strange. Like I was watching myself.

"After we ate, I took her to the hot spring. We were both still splattered with dried blood and filthy from the burial. She stripped off her clothes like it was the most natural thing in the world and just stepped down into the water and closed her eyes.

"I couldn't stop looking at her. The water was so clear ... I could see all of her. I started to think about her body ... what it would feel like to touch her bare skin ... and all of a sudden I was sick. I jumped out of the water and ran, and then I started throwing up. My insides felt like they were tearing loose and coming out. When it was over I curled up on the ground in the puke and wished I could die right there.

"I was a murderer. A murderer! I'd just killed my own father, yet I could fish and eat and get excited looking at a naked girl. I knew I deserved to die and I knew that death would come for me if I waited long enough, so I just closed my eyes and lay there. I wanted everything to be over with. I wanted to be dead.

"But Thea found me. She kept touching me and poking me

and saying things like 'Wow, what a bad trip,' and all of a sudden
I started to laugh. I laughed and laughed while she took me back
down to the water. And all the time I was laughing, I kept thinking that I was scaring a lot of animals. That I might be scaring
Noisy. That I was even scaring myself.

"She splashed water in my face and I choked on it. And I
stopped laughing. She washed me off, but I didn't look at her. I
didn't look directly at anything. I was watching it all from someplace else.

"Days passed ... or maybe longer ... I'm not sure. Thea led
me around and pointed me at things and told me to get food. It's
all a little hazy to me.

"Then one morning she went crazy and started screaming, 'Get
me out of here, you fucking zombie! Get me out of here!' She
slapped me and threw things at me. Then she sort of folded up
and started to sob, 'I wanna go home ... I wanna go home ...'
over and over. And everything snapped into place for me.

"There were debts to be paid. I had to take care of her and
get her out of the mountains somehow. I had to undo what had
been done. That was why I was alive.

"We started that day. She couldn't remember anything about
the direction she'd come from, and I didn't know which way to
take her. Frank had always been careful not to let me know anything about where we were in relation to the rest of the world.

"All I could think about was that Badger would help. But I
wasn't even sure of the way to find him. I kept wishing Noisy
could talk. She flew free over us every day, but she couldn't tell
me what was up ahead.

"We'd traveled about a week and I'd recognized the landmarks
that put us close to Badger's, when suddenly Thea collapsed. The
going had been slow to begin with. She couldn't carry much
weight, and she tired easily, even when I kept the pace down and
let her rest every so often. Then one morning she just couldn't
get up. 'I've had it. I'm so bummed out. I feel like I'm gonna die.'

"Her skin was burning hot but she kept having spells of shiv-
ering. And she did look like she was going to die. She looked
terrible.

"I made broth but I couldn't get her to take much. I bathed
her with cool water when she was hot and wrapped her up and
held her when she was cold. That was the longest day of my life.
I thought I would lose her if I left her or slept or even relaxed
for a few minutes. I felt like my heartbeat and my breathing and
my strength were all that was keeping her alive.

"The next morning she was worse and I knew I had to get her to Badger's or lose her. I left the gear and carried her. We reached Badger's at sunset. He didn't ask any questions. He just took over. I was so tired I barely remember all the mixing and chanting and potions he used. Who knows what worked? All that's important is that she woke up the next morning and said, 'I could eat a horse. Got any horses around?'

"By evening she was sitting up beside the fire and laughing and eating a huge meal as if she'd never been sick at all. We had fixed Noisy a perch and settled in for the evening, and it felt good and right . . . like we were a family. And I told her that maybe she shouldn't go back down. Maybe we should all winter in Badger's cabin together.

"She laughed as though I'd made a joke, but she was happy there. I could tell she was happy. And she liked Badger. She kept encouraging him to tell stories.

"She was careful, though, about what she said to him. Nothing about who she was or how she'd come to be with me. And she kept sending me looks, warnings about keeping quiet, keeping the terrible secret.

"I didn't need warnings. The enormity of what I'd done kept me quiet. I could barely meet Badger's eyes. I felt guilty. Dishonest. Unworthy of his friendship.

"She did tell Badger that she was lost and I was taking her out. He drew me a map on a piece of buckskin. Instead of roads, it had crude drawings of meadows and streams and split trees and odd-shaped rock formations.

" 'That's the closest place to take her,' he said, drawing an X near the edge of his map. 'Be very careful.'

" 'I'll come back,' I told him.

"We left the next morning but traveled only as far as the gear I'd abandoned when I took her to the cabin. I wanted to give her a chance to get her strength back before asking her to put in a full day walking.

"We made camp and ate smoked salmon. Suddenly I felt very self-conscious about being alone with her in the night.

" 'So, did I blab all my secrets while I was out of it?' she asked.

" 'You talked some, but I couldn't make much sense of it.'

"She was very thin, but she looked almost pretty in the firelight. 'You took good care of me. Better care than anybody's taken since I was a little girl . . . since my mother. I didn't know a man could be so gentle.' She laughed. 'But you're not a man. You're just a kid. How old are you, anyway?'

" 'I'm around seventeen.'

" 'Yeah. Well, I'm twenty. But compared to you I'm a hundred and ten. How long you been playing Tarzan, anyway?'

"Everything she said—her words and her way of putting sentences together—all sounded so strange to me. I was used to listening to Frank. Sometimes I had to stop and think to be sure of what she meant.

" 'I've been here since I was twelve.'

" 'What a fucking drag. You ever get newspapers or anything?'

" 'No.' I was amazed by her language. I'd been raised to think there were certain words that females never used.

" 'Oh, wow. Let's see. Five years. You know about Bobby Kennedy getting shot?'

" 'You mean John Kennedy.'

" 'No, his brother Bobby Kennedy. He was going to run for president, and some camel jockey shot him in Los Angeles. Martin Luther King got killed around then too. And Jackie . . . you know . . . JFK's widow? She got married to this rich Greek guy. It was kinda sad . . . like she didn't care anymore. Then Ted Kennedy was fooling around on his wife and ended up in this car accident where the girl he was with died. That was the end of the Kennedys, ya know? Pouf. Let's see . . . what else? Oh, there was Woodstock, this really beautiful rock concert where everybody kind of ran around doing free love and dope while all this far-out music played. I didn't get to go, but I watched a lot of stuff about it. And some guys walked around on the moon finally. I watched that on TV too. And Vietnam's about over. Or maybe it's over already. I been kinda out of touch myself lately. They're ending the draft too. Or that's what they say, anyway. Marty, the guy I was with, thought it was just a trick to catch a lot of people who've been hiding. Flush 'em out, ya know. Like you. You could be drafted as soon as you turn eighteen . . . if they could find you up here. Not that you're up here because of that . . . but you could be, ya know? That's about it, I guess. Too much, huh? Five years gone, and that's about all you missed. 'Course, you missed a lot of far-out music . . . movies too. Like *Easy Rider* . . . wow. That was too freaking much. But when you come back, you can always listen to an oldie station on the radio to catch up. And just watch television. Television will make it like you were never gone—old movies, reruns . . . they show it all.'

"I felt like I was listening to a foreigner talk about events in some far-off place. I couldn't relate anything she said to the life I'd led with my mother. We had seldom watched television, rarely went to movies, and listened to the radio only when we were driving. Our life had been wrapped up in art and music and school and each other. I kept asking myself: had I been odd even then? Had I been destined to be a freak from the beginning?

"I was convinced that Thea represented the real world. Had it changed that much in five years? Or had I been sheltered from that real world even while living in the middle of it?

" 'You're very cute, ya know. Kinda like the guy in this mountain-man movie I just saw' Thea reached out and touched my cheek. 'Only you're a lot younger.'

"She looked at me in this strange new way and my breath caught. She was suddenly the most beautiful girl I'd ever seen.

" 'Since you were twelve, huh? And no girls? No visitors or native squaws or anything?'

"I must have shaken my head, but I don't remember. I was entranced. I wanted to look at her face forever.

"She held out her hand and pulled me up to stand close to her. Her eyes held me. I was lost in her eyes.

"She took off her blouse and guided my hand onto her breast. That moment was . . . I can't really describe it. Even now. It was like an awakening. Like learning that there was a range of colors and scents and textures that I hadn't known existed.

"She tugged off my shift and ran her fingers over my chest, and then she put her arms around my neck and kissed me. And I was lost. Everything melted into sensations. She kissed and touched me everywhere, softer and lighter than a spring breeze. Then she guided my hands across her body, showing me how to touch. I was afraid I might hurt her at first. She felt so fragile and small beneath my hands, as though the slightest pressure might break something.

"She lay down by the fire. Her skin was pink and gold and her eyes were burning and she held out her arms to me. And I knew that nothing I'd ever imagined or dreamed could compare to the sight of her lying there naked with her arms out to me—eyes full of me. Me! She wanted me!

"When it was over, we lay there together for a long time. I didn't ever want to let her go. But she pulled away finally and propped herself up on her elbow. She looked down into my face, and her eyes were very old. 'That was real,' she said. 'But you haven't missed much, 'cause most of the time it's not real. Not for girls anyway. Most of the time it's just part of the act.' She laughed. 'You are so far-out innocent. And so sweet. I can't remember the last time I fucked a guy and didn't have to do any lying or faking to get through it.'

"I didn't understand a word she was saying. All I could do was look at her. I was feeling so many things—gratitude, infatuation, wonder—and the intensity of it all had me stunned.

"She met my gaze for a moment, then shook her head and frowned. 'Come on, Tarzan ... it was no big deal. I'm just your average lay.' She sat up and rubbed her arms so I added wood to the fire. 'Don't you get bored out here?' She looked around at the darkness and shivered, even though the fire was now roaring. 'Don't you get lonely?'

" 'No. Not exactly. I have—' But something stabbed into my chest and I couldn't breathe for a minute because whatever I'd had was gone.

" 'Yeah.' She looked at Noisy on her perch. 'I guess ya got animals and stuff. I mean, that is a pretty cool bird.'

"I had encouraged Noisy to fend for herself while Thea was sick. She had hunted on her own a little, but still wanted her food from me. I thought it was just a matter of time and she'd take off.

" 'She'll be gone soon.'

" 'Why?'

" 'She can hunt on her own now. She doesn't need me.'

" 'How sad.'

" 'Not really. She doesn't belong down here.'

" 'What about you? Do you belong down here?' She looked around and shivered again 'I sure don't. It's pretty creepy if you ask me.'

" 'It's my home.'

" 'No it isn't. You didn't come here till you were what? Eleven ... twelve? Before that you were a regular kid, right?'

"I answered yes but I pictured myself hiding under the bushes from the other boys, and I wondered again. Had I ever been 'regular'?

" 'Well, you're free now, so why don't you do gown to civilization and try it out? What have you got to lose? If it doesn't work, you could always split and run back up here.' She smiled dreamily. 'That's far-out, ya know. Havin' a whole other world to run to whenever life gets to be a bummer.' She leaned back and stretched. 'God, what I'd give for a joint right now.'

"She kept talking but I couldn't listen for a while. All I could think about was what she'd said. 'You used to be a regular kid, right? Why don't you go down? What have you got to lose? You could always split ...'

"I'd been so afraid of leaving the mountains. Afraid that I wouldn't fit into the world anymore. And I'd thought of leaving as an absolute thing—that if I left I'd be giving up the safety of the mountains forever. But what Thea said was right. The mountains would always be there ... and I could go back whenever I needed to. I felt like I'd had a revelation.

" 'You got any family down there? Anybody who cares about you?'

"I nodded. 'But I don't know how they'll feel about me now. I'm not the same as I was.'

" 'Yeah. I know whatcha mean. My old man ...' She sounded even more sarcastic than she usually did. 'Harry Baldwin of Baldwin's Home Bookkeeping Service. He probably hasn't looked up from his papers long enough to notice that I been gone for three years. And if he did see me—see me the way I am now—he'd probably have the cops haul me off.'

" 'Why did you leave?'

" 'Oh, you know. The standard stuff. He didn't like my boyfriends. Came down on me for doing dope. Treated me like a prisoner. I just split one night. Ran off to San Francisco with a guy.' She shrugged. 'It was a great trip at first. Then the guy left me and ... you know. I knocked around. Panhandled. Joined a Jesus group for a while, but that was a real downer—worse than life at home with my old man. And the jerk who ran it was this nut who wanted to say his bedtime prayers while one of the flock gave him a blow-job. I split from there the first chance I got.

" 'Then I got hooked up with Marty. The one I was with when your father did his bit.' She shook her head. 'Marty got me into so much trouble. Every time we were out of dope, he'd steal something. And he'd hit me if I said anything. Made me wish I was living back in Sacramento. He was so crazy. The reason we were in Idaho was 'cause he heard about some commune up here where everybody was a draft dodger and you could have all the dope you wanted if you just worked in the garden every day. Some story, huh? I mean, Marty just wasn't all there, ya know?'

" 'Did Frank ... did my father ... hurt Marty when he took you?'

" 'I hope so.' She chuckled. 'Man, I'll never forget Marty's face. There we were just walking along in the middle of fuckin' nowhere, hitchin' 'cause our car quit us, and p.o.'d as hell 'cause we hadn't had any dope for a week—and out jumps your old man like some kinda freaked-out Davy Crockett.' She chuckled again. 'I thought Marty was gonna lose it. Then, when he saw that all your old man wanted was me, he got real cool. He said, "Sure, take her, man. She's yours."

" 'Your dad had that big gun, so I wasn't about to make trouble. I let him put the rope on me. Everything would have been peaceful except a car came along and Marty started screaming and your dad hit him and the people from the car jumped out and chased us. Your dad probably did me a favor by getting me away from that creep.' She started to cry, and I sat there feeling clumsy and useless. Then something connected and I started to cry too.

"The next morning I felt better . . . cleaner . . . than I had since Frank's death. I got us packed up and moving again. The aspens were going yellow and the night temperatures were growing colder. I knew I had to get her out of the a mountains before the first snow. She wasn't strong enough for a mountain winter.

"Those weeks of traveling together were good. She made me laugh. She showed me how to be light and silly and to do things just for the fun of it. And every day she taught me something new about pleasure and giving. Without realizing it, I slipped into a fantasy. I believed that we'd go on like that forever.

"When we finally topped a hill and saw a town below us, I wanted to turn around and run back the other way. She was so excited, though. She jumped up and down and hugged me. 'We made it! We made it!' But I looked down at that town, so small and narrow in the little valley below us, and it filled me with dread.

"It was nearly evening, so we agreed to camp on the hillside and go down into town the next morning. That whole night was torture for me. I felt this terrible mixture of fear and anticipation. And for the first time I couldn't respond when she touched me.

" 'It's all right,' she said. 'It happens to guys all the time. We can just hold each other till we fall asleep.'

"But there was no sleep for either of us. She was full of plans and I was full of terror.

" 'Did you see that little truck stop on the edge of town? I'll go there and find a good ride. Someone heading south or west. I don't know. I might even go check out my dad in Sacramento. Tell him he can stop wondering if I'm dead or not. It's a good time to go. I'm off the shit and as clean as I'll ever be right now.'

"I didn't know what she meant by being clean and I didn't care. All I could think about was how thoroughly she was shutting me out. None of her plans included me at all. 'So what do I do? Just wave good-bye while you drive off in some truck? How do I see you again? How do I—?'

" 'Hey, you won't want to see me again, Tarzan. There's too many other Janes out there.'

" 'Don't talk like that, Thea. We could travel together. I could meet your father and than take you to meet my mother.'

"She laughed out loud then, making me feel small and foolish. Making me angry. 'Trust me, Ellis. We are not a compatible unit, ya know?'

" 'What are you telling me? That none of this meant anything? That everything—'

" 'Don't,' she said. 'Don't say a lot of shit. Because that's all it is. Sure we had a good time up here in Bambi-land, but the only part of it that was real was the sex. Don't you understand that? Once we got into making it together—worrying about money and dope and where to live and who blows their nose too loud and who left the milk out of the fridge—there'd be nothing left. Even the sex would go sour. Because that's the way it works in the real world.'

"Suddenly I felt lost and afraid. 'What should I do when I get down there?' I asked. 'Go to the police station and ask them to help me find my mother?'

" 'No! No way. That's one place we both need to stay away from. They'd hassle us no end. They'd dig up the old drug charge on me and probably slap you with a murder rap. I mean, you think they're gonna take your word about what happened to your old man?' Her eyes got narrow and cold. 'And if you do decide to spill your guts about this whole scene, just leave my name out of it because I was never here. Understand?'

"I did understand, and it hurt. 'I didn't mean that I would tell them everything. I just thought I'd ask them for help getting home.'

" 'Are you for real?' She snorted and shook her head. 'You think they'd smile nice and give you a hand? They'd take one look at you and hit you with every unsolved crime they had.'

"I thought about that awhile, wondering if I looked that terrible to everyone or just to her, wondering if I wanted to chance it and find out. 'Could I catch the first ride with you? Just to get me going. I mean . . . I've never hitchhiked before.' I didn't have a plan. I just wanted to stay with her as long as possible.

"She laughed. 'Sure. Why not? But what about the bird?'

"I hadn't thought about Noisy. What would I do about her? She seemed fully capable of surviving on her own now, but she was still bonded to me. I could see her flying behind a truck down the highway, trying to keep me in sight.

"It was dawn so fast. The night seemed to speed past me. I had a solution for the problem with Noisy, but I had no idea what I was going to do about me.

"We ate jerky and dried fruit for breakfast. Then I found some tall dry grass and tied several strands of it together to form a long leash. I waited till we were ready to start down; then I used the grass to tether Noisy.

"Thea watched me. 'What are you doing?'

" 'She's used to being tethered. She'll sit here quietly till she gets hungry. Then she'll start hopping around and pulling on it. When she pulls hard enough, it'll break and she'll be free.'

" 'And by that time we'll be gone.'

" 'Right.'

"I stroked the hawk's breast and she rubbed her head against my hand. I knew I had to leave her. I'd known all along that the time would come. But that didn't make it hurt any less.

"I led the way down to the truck stop. We didn't talk. My hands were shaking and I could feel Thea's tension. When we reached the edge of the graveled parking area she stepped up beside me and took my arm. 'I hope I'm not on some kind of wanted poster or something. I let Marty bully me into some pretty stupid things there at the end.'

" 'We don't have to go inside,' I said. The truth was that I didn't want to go inside either. It had been so long since I'd faced people. I didn't know if I could take a roomful right away.

"I had a feeling of being watched as we walked up, but the sun was glinting on the windows and I couldn't see anyone.

" 'I want to use the bathroom before we catch a ride,' Thea said. 'God, it feels like ages since I sat on a real john.'

"She was walking very close to me. I could smell the acid of her nervousness mixing with my fear. No one came in or out of the building. Except for the few vehicles in the parking lot, the place could have been deserted. We headed around the side, and I stood like a guard at the door while she went into the ladies' room.

" 'I'm going to wash up too,' she called through the door. 'There's real soap in here!'

"I tried to gauge my own reactions. How did I feel—seeing the building and the cars and trucks, smelling gasoline and old tires, listening to the gurgling of plumbing fixtures? Was there going to be a transition, a period when everything seemed odd—or would I slip right back into civilization as though I'd never left it?

"Suddenly there was noise and confusion. Cars raced toward me, sliding to a stop in the gravel. They were police cars. My first instinct was to protect Thea. I ran from the door and out into the open, thinking I would lead them away from her. Men jumped out of the cars and I heard the thunk of doors slamming and the click of rifles being readied.

" 'Halt!' a voice blared through a bullhorn. 'Stop right there or we'll shoot.'

"I stopped and turned around. There were three cars and ten men—some in uniform and some not. All had guns. I thought about the thirty-thirty I'd buried on the mountain with my father. What would they do if I was carrying a gun?

" 'Put your hands in the air!' the bullhorn ordered.

"I raised my arms high above my head and waited. The men fidgeted and I could tell they weren't ready to put down their guns. They reminded me of my father at the end of a heated hunt with the game finally cornered.

"I was so afraid for Thea ... afraid that if she came out at that moment they would all turn and shoot her. But gradually they relaxed. The ones who'd been sighting their rifles across the hoods of the cars straightened. I could see the fingers easing off the triggers. That was when I heard the familiar cry. I squinted up into the sky and saw Noisy circling overhead. She had broken free much sooner than I'd expected, and she'd found me easily, standing in the middle of an open space with my hands in the air.

"The men were easing toward me in a cautious semicircle. I doubted that Noisy would come down with so many other people around me, but I wasn't sure of anything at that point. And I was worried about what the men might do if she did decide to come down. I thought if I warned them ...

" 'The hawk. She's—'

"But Noisy swooped down then and the men panicked. One of them screamed something and they all started firing."

Ellis buried his face in his hands. He was trembling. When he looked up, Yvonne's eyes were filled with tears.

"You know most of the rest," he said. He had to clear his throat several times as he spoke. "I guess it was a miracle that I didn't get shot too. They beat me and yelled and cursed. I think they were really frustrated at not being able to kill me. And it made them even more furious when I wouldn't talk. They never did find Thea. I guess she ducked out during the shooting and found the ride she was looking for."

"They thought you were Frank, didn't they?" Yvonne asked. "When the authorities explained it to Grace, they said that the area had been on the alert for some crazed mountain man who'd kidnapped a girl, and that it had been a case of mistaken identity. That was Frank they were looking for, wasn't it?"

Ellis nodded. "The truck-stop owner saw us walk up and called the police. He was certain that I was the homicidal mountain man dragging the kidnapped girl in."

Yvonne shook her head. "Your father reached out to hurt you even from the grave."

Ellis stood and studied Yvonne's face. Was it possible that she could still accept him after hearing that whole story? After knowing the depth of his guilt? "So ... if you want me to go to the police now and turn myself in for Frank's—"

"No!" Yvonne stood as though to block him with her own body. "Absolutely not! How can you imagine I'd want you to do something like that? You've suffered enough. I'm sure you'd be found innocent, but why put yourself through an ordeal like that? What purpose would it serve? The whole thing would turn into a media circus that would haunt you for the rest of your life. And it would kill your mother. You have to consider her too."

"Then what should I do?"

"Only you can answer that, Ellis." She reached out to touch his hand, but then drew back as though changing her mind. "The choice is really very simple. You learn how to live with things and make a life for yourself . . . or you give up. It's the same for all of us. And ultimately"—her dark eyes grew darker, as though she were seeing her own nightmare—"we all face the choice alone."

16

The morning of the Van Lyden gala found the household in a flurry of last-minute details. Ellis had spent the previous days with the various deliverymen and cleaning crews coming and going through the house, but his grandfather had caught him and now he was expressly forbidden to help. He drifted about aimlessly, finally settling for an afternoon movie with Juliana.

"It's another Disney," she told him when he asked if he could join her. "They save all the sexy stuff for themselves."

Ellis grinned. "You're only twelve. What do you know about sexy stuff?"

"Plenty. And I'm almost thirteen."

"I didn't know anything when I was twelve," he admitted.

"That's because girls mature faster than boys. And besides, you were a real creepy little kid."

"Oh, I was, was I? Where'd you hear that?"

"I didn't have to hear anything. Aunt Grace showed me pictures of you."

Juliana was as keyed-up as he was. Ellis could hear the tension singing just beneath the sass. The funny thing was that he liked her best when she was on edge. That was when the spirited irreverence surfaced. That was when she stopped being so obsessed with pleasing her parents.

The film started and he studied her in the projection room's dim light. She was a puzzle to him—one moment as knowing and self-possessed as a woman and the next all gawky uncertainty. Once moment a mess of falling hair and flying shirttails and the next a perfect lady in a fancy dress. She changed so often it made him dizzy. And she changed not just with her own moods but in response to the moods of others.

The picture was an old one about two dogs and a cat traveling across Canada in search of their family. The wilderness shots made him homesick and sad. He closed his eyes to picture himself back in the mountains, only to be confronted with images of Noisy's bloody body lying in the gravel at his feet and his father's empty eyes staring at him in accusing silence. He thought of Thea. Thea had saved him. Thea had rescued him from himself and from the grip his solitary life had on him. If it hadn't been for Thea . . .

He stood and tried to creep quietly from the room.

"Don't tell me you're bored already," Juliana said before he could reach the door.

"I've already seen this one."

"Who hasn't?" She peered through the darkness at him. "All right . . . I'll see you upstairs, then. And remember. I'm in charge of you tonight, and you better not get me in trouble."

"I'll remember," Ellis assured her. "Don't worry. I won't even step on your toes while we're dancing."

He went into the kitchen for a snack and then wandered into the ballroom to watch the orchestra set up. The stringing of wires and tuning of instruments threatened to go on forever. He went up the back servants' stairs to the second-floor library and discovered Yvonne curled up in a chair, writing in a small book. She closed it quickly and smiled. "Uh-oh, I can tell you have something on your mind." She swung around in the chair gracefully and rested one foot on the floor. "You're not bowing out at this late hour, are you?"

"No, nothing like that. I keep thinking about Thea. You know, the girl from the mountain."

"Yes . . . ?"

"I keep wondering how she's doing."

Yvonne nodded. "You know, I think she was probably very wise in saying you two should go your separate ways. Wise . . . and brave."

"Maybe. I just hope she's all right. I . . ." Ellis stared down at his hands a moment. There were times when he still felt as clumsy as a lion cub tripping over its paws. "This family is very rich, right?"

Yvonne hesitated. "Yes."

"Does that mean I have money that I could do something with?"

"I suppose so. Why?"

"I'd like to send something to Thea. Anonymously or whatever. Something to help her get back on her feet."

Yvonne smiled gently. "I think that could be arranged. The first step of course would be locating her." She opened her book again. Ellis could see that it was some sort of journal. "Didn't you say something about her father?"

Yvonne jotted all the information down. "FIND THEA!" she wrote in large flourishing letters at the bottom, saying the words aloud as she wrote them. "Don't worry. I'm sure something can be done." She stood and tucked the book under her arm. "Now . . . I have to get busy. Only three hours left, and my fairy godmother hasn't even arrived yet."

Three hours seemed like forever to Ellis. He wandered through the house restlessly, eyeing each door and window as a potential avenue of escape. Only when it was near time for Aubrey's valet to put him into his tux did he finally go up to his room and take his shower.

The hot water beat against his skin, soothing him temporarily. This was a luxury he hadn't had in the mountains. He thought then of the other things he'd missed. Drinks with ice in them and clean white sheets and fresh fruit whenever he wanted it, not to mention the larger losses—books and music and companionship. He reminded himself of how much life here had to offer, how many reasons for not sneaking out of Great House that very minute and running back to the mountains.

How bad could the gala be, anyway? How many mistakes could he make in one night?

He wiped the steamy bathroom mirror and stared at himself. He'd gone so many years without a mirror that his own reflection had become foreign to him. In his mind's eye he still had the perplexed round face and sandy hair and owlish glasses he'd had at twelve, and what he saw now—the angular cheeks and jaw, the brownish hair, the thin lines of scars at temple and chin— registered as a disguise beneath which lay the old and true Ellis Fielding Van Lyden.

Aubrey's valet arrived and the tux was assembled. They finished as Juliana walked in. She circled Ellis with a critical, measuring gaze.

"Well?" Ellis asked her.

"Someone will probably try to order a drink from you," she said dryly.

"Well, you sure look good," Ellis said, amazed at her transformation.

Her shiny gold-brown hair was twisted up and decorated with baby roses. A rustling pale green gown softened her gangly form.

She lifted her chin, her eyes glowing with his compliment, and Ellis caught a glimpse of the striking woman she would soon be.

"Hah," she said, pretending his opinion was worthless. "Come on. Grandfather sent me up for you. I think he wants to inspect you now so he still has time to change his mind about you coming." She glanced at him suspiciously. "You aren't feeling wild or crazy or anything tonight, are you?"

"No."

"And you don't have any knives or tomahawks or spears hidden underneath your jacket?"

"No."

"Okay, just stick close to me and try not to say anything too stupid if somebody talks to us."

"I'll try." He looked down at her and smiled. "And thanks."

"You know it, buster. You're going to owe me for this one."

The crack made him grin again, which was exactly why he was thanking her. She had put him at ease and he felt secure knowing that she would be beside him for the evening.

Edward appraised them as they came down the grand staircase past the cascades of fresh flowers. Ellis braced himself for criticism.

"I believe you just might favor your great-grandfather," Edward said with a note of surprise in his voice.

Juliana's mouth dropped open. She stared at Edward with wounded eyes, then shot Ellis a poisoned look. Edward hurried off to solve some last minute problem, but the poison remained, glittering in her narrowed eyes.

Her fierce jealousy wasn't new to Ellis, but he still felt just as helpless when confronted with it. There seemed to be no way to convince her that he wasn't her rival. That he wasn't any threat to her. How could he be? He would forever be the interloper, the outsider. Frank Fielding's blood ran in his veins and stained his soul, and no amount of wishing or name-changing could erase that simple truth. Was Juliana too young to understand, or was she already infected by the same competitive nature that made both Edward and Aubrey look at everything in life as either victory or defeat?

The answer was beyond Ellis, as was the means of forging a lasting peace between them. All his efforts seemed to fall flat. He was the enemy, and she guarded herself against him with a ferocious tenacity, ready to defend her perimeters at the slightest incursion. Perversely, the strength of her stand against him caused

Ellis to admire her even more. She had such substance, such intensity. Hate, love, loyalty, jealousy—she conceived each in its most powerful form.

If only that terrible beginning with the cougar hadn't happened. If only he hadn't been so jumpy and frightened and confused. If only he'd been warned that she had a mountain lion as a house pet. But "if only" couldn't change the fact that he'd been the cause of grief and pain for her.

"There you two are!" Yvonne called from across the room. She moved sensuously toward them in a floor-length dress that managed to be outrageously revealing and primly Victorian at the same time. It was an off-white with the same subtle luminescence as the nacre in the miles of pearls she wore on her neck and wrists—so many strands that there was an illusion of elegant bondage. Ellis was transfixed.

Yvonne's skin shone through the sheer insets in the high, fitted bodice and long narrow sleeves, and somehow the rich color of it beneath that flimsy fabric was more enticing than if her arms and neckline had been completely bare. A fall of pearls swayed languorously at her ears and brushed her neck as she moved. Her black hair was swept up and crowned with a magnificently intricate tiara of amber diamonds and dangling pearl drops and large pale yellow diamonds cut in faceted triangles and set into a central star shape.

Ellis' throat and chest and groin tightened at the blinding sight of her and he could feel the blood rushing into all the wrong parts of his body.

"Don't you both look gorgeous!" Yvonne cried in an uncharacteristically effusive show. She tortured Ellis with one of her breath-stopping sideways looks and then winked at Juliana. "You'll have to protect this dashing young man from all the ladies, Juliana."

"Oh, Mama." Juliana rolled her eyes in embarrassment.

"I'm serious," Yvonne insisted. "Ellis will make hearts flutter tonight."

"Mama! How can you say that? Most of the ladies coming tonight are old and married!"

Yvonne smiled her mysterious half-smile. "Of course, dear. How foolish of me." She touched Juliana's cheek with her fingertips, a gesture that would have placated her daughter if it weren't for the fact that she touched Ellis' cheek with her other hand at the same time.

Juliana flashed Ellis a blistering look.

"Save a dance for me, Ellis," Yvonne said gaily as she started away.

"Do I get a dance with Papa?" Juliana asked.

Yvonne hesitated. "You can ask him. But you know how many friends he's invited ... people from all over the world. He might not have time to dance."

Aubrey came down the stairs at that moment. He had four men with him and he was the center of an animated discussion. His expertly fitted tux lent elegance to his athletic body, and his face glowed with vitality and good health. He stopped upon seeing Yvonne and his eyebrows shot up in surprise. Ellis could feel the sudden change in Yvonne. She lifted her chin and stood very still, as though awaiting a verdict.

"Gentlemen!" Aubrey held out his hands. "As I'm sure you all know, this stunning creature before you is my wife!" He hurried down the last few stairs and made a show of kissing Yvonne's hand.

Juliana tugged on Ellis' sleeve and pulled him back toward the wall.

"You know our houseguests, don't you, my dear?"

Yvonne inclined her head and greeted each one of the men by name. They were all somewhere in their thirties or early forties, with the same nonchalant, overindulged air that frequently surrounded Aubrey. And they were clearly impressed with Yvonne's décolleté.

"Yvonne is far too exciting to be anyone's wife," commented one of the men. He bowed with a great flourish. "Do you have a scarf I could carry into battle, my queen?"

Yvonne laughed and placed her hand lightly on his lowered head. "I dub thee Sir—"

"Fool!" Aubrey shouted good-naturedly. He put his arm around Yvonne's shoulders possessively. "Be good sports and run along," he ordered. "I'll be with you in a moment."

The men hooted and winked like boisterous schoolboys. "I smell Scotch," one of them announced as they drifted toward the ballroom.

Aubrey nuzzled Yvonne's neck. "You are spectacular tonight," he said in a throaty whisper. "And very daring. Has my father seen the dress yet?"

"No. I just came down." Yvonne's eyes were heavy with the pleasure of his lips against her neck. She swayed slightly, then roused herself and regained her regal bearing. With a playful smile she turned Aubrey so that Juliana and Ellis were in his line of sight.

"Oh, hello," Aubrey said. "I'd almost forgotten about you two. Big night, huh? You don't mind if I kiss this devastating woman, do you?" But instead of kissing Yvonne, he moved away from her a fraction and studied Ellis. "Well, well," he said, nodding in approval. "What a difference a tux makes. I'll have to introduce you around later. You can talk hunting with the boys."

"Will you dance with me, Papa?" Juliana asked breathlessly.

Yvonne's perfect eyebrows formed a worried line.

"You know the rules, Jinx," Aubrey said sternly. "None of us are here tonight to baby-sit you, so if you can't entertain yourself, you'll be sent upstairs."

Juliana shrank into herself like a balloon losing helium. Aubrey seemed not to notice. He gave Yvonne one more measuring look, then strode off across the floor. "The host comes," he called toward the ballroom.

Before anyone could speak, Edward appeared from the direction of the gallery and bore down on them. His eyebrows also shot up on sight of Yvonne, but instead of surprise his face registered horrified shock. He stopped several paces from her. "Was there a costume theme that I was unaware of?" he asked.

Yvonne's cheeks colored slightly.

"Or have the dictates of good taste changed without my knowledge?"

"I'm sorry you don't like it, Edward."

"Of course I like it," Edward said. "What male wouldn't? It would be delightful on Alexander the Great's favorite concubine."

Yvonne stiffened and raised her chin.

"I must say the jewels suit you," he conceded gruffly. "It's about time some of them saw the outside of a vault again."

Yvonne didn't acknowledge the compliment, but Ellis could feel her relaxing a fraction.

Edward pulled out an engraved gold pocket watch and clicked it open. "You have a good fifteen minutes before the receiving line forms. I'm certain you can find a more suitable gown in that length of time."

Yvonne drew in a sharp breath and her mouth hardened into a line. Her usual vague pliancy was suddenly transformed into something solid and unyielding that echoed in every line of her body. "I do not intend to change."

Edward was taken aback, but recovered quickly. "Are you ill?"

"No." Her voice was tight. "I've decided that pleasing my husband is more important to me than conforming to your dictates of good taste."

"Yvonne—" Edward began.

"No!" Her eyes flashed and her voice fell to a heated whisper. "I am suffocating in good taste! Good taste hasn't made me acceptable to your social *Who's Who.* Good taste doesn't keep me warm or make me laugh. Good taste doesn't bring my husband home to my bed at night!"

"But, my dear, I thought it was so important to you to prove that—"

She laughed and shook her head. "Life isn't just, is it, Edward? You couldn't raise a perfect son. And now you don't have a perfect daughter-in-law anymore either."

She whirled and left Edward to stare after her with his mouth slightly ajar. Ellis watched her go. The dress had a plunging back held together with strands of pearls that crisscrossed her tawny skin. The bottom of the long slender skirt flared out into the suggestion of a train and made her appear to glide rather than walk as she left them.

Ellis glanced over at Juliana. She too was watching her mother's retreat. Her eyes were wide with disbelief.

The crowd began to take shape. Ellis felt lost in the swirl of color and perfume and jewelry. There were people everywhere. People staring at him. People leaning to whisper to their companions as soon as the recognition dawned. He could feel their eyes on him.

His mother sought him out periodically to whisper, "How are you doing, dear?" with little nervous smiles.

"Fine," he answered mechanically each time.

Luckily his grandfather had forbidden her to hover over Ellis, or her nervousness would have destroyed what composure he had.

He followed Juliana around like an obedient dog—nodding in response to her endless introductions, smiling whenever she nudged him. But he couldn't distinguish one face or voice from another. They all looked and sounded uniformly cultured, and they all treated him like a circus exhibit or an anthropological discovery.

Yvonne floated by them. In her wake Ellis heard snippets of conversation. "Can you believe it!" "Did you see!" "My God, she had on the Kushan Star!" "The what?" "That yellow-diamond center in the tiara. It hasn't been seen in public for twenty years!" "My dear ... I never got as far as the tiara—I was paralyzed by that ghastly gown!" "What can you expect? With her background ..."

Ellis glanced over to see if Juliana had heard. Her face was unreadable, but she was very still.

"Want to try dancing now?" he asked her. "I've got the fox-trot whipped."

"Okay." She walked stiffly beside him to the ballroom.

They had made it through three endless dances when Yvonne cut in. Her eyes were alight and her cheeks carried a high flush. "My turn," she said brightly.

Juliana retreated, casting a sulky look back at them.

Yvonne raised her arms and Ellis assumed the dance position, trying to stay as far away from her as his arm length would allow.

"How the hours fly when having fun," Yvonne teased. "You *are* having fun, I trust?"

"The hours aren't flying."

"Now, now. It could be worse." Her body moved effortlessly to the music. "I've diverted most of the interest that would have otherwise been focused on you. Instead of 'here comes the jungle boy' they're preoccupied with 'there goes the slut.' "

Ellis grinned down at her. She was about five-foot-seven and far more comfortable to dance with than Juliana had been.

"You think it's funny, do you? Well, just wait till they all realize the slut and the jungle boy are dancing together."

"That's not why . . . I mean . . . I'm not smiling at that. I just realized I like dancing."

They moved in lazy circles around the room. His mother waved at him from a table and he waved back.

"Has Aubrey introduced you to any of his friends yet?"

"No," he said, wishing he could add that he didn't want to meet them.

"He has so many friends. And does so many interesting things . . ." Her smile and her eyes were unreadable. "Someday you'll be married. I wonder if you'll leave your wife alone all the time while you run off with the boys." She laughed at his discomfort and then cocked her head and let her gaze drift.

"Maybe I should try riding again. I didn't like it before, but maybe I will now. Aubrey used to want me to ride with him."

The idea brightened her. "You've enjoyed learning to ride, haven't you?"

"Yes," he said carefully, hoping to avoid the question of whether he'd enjoyed being with his uncle. "I love the horses. Just being around them and taking care of them. . . . Sparky showed me how to clean their hooves and—"

"Sparky?" Her brows knit in a delicate frown.

He knew he had made a slip. The blood rushed to his face and even his earlobes burned. He hated dishonesty, and if there was anyone in the world he did not want to lie to, it was Yvonne, but he had promised to keep the secret of Aubrey's hideaway.

"Yeah ... he's just a kid who takes care of the horses at this place we ride."

"This place? I thought you always went straight to the park."

Ellis groaned inwardly. Everything he said seemed to be dragging him deeper, and Aubrey had been so adamant about keeping all this from Yvonne. "The secret's for her own good," Aubrey had insisted.

"Yeah, well, we do go to the park ... mostly. But this time we went somewhere else. I don't know where exactly. Somebody's house, I think. That's where this kid was."

"Really?" Yvonne's eyes were strange. "Somebody's house ..." She stopped dancing so abruptly that he nearly stepped on her. "Please," she said, "don't mention the name Sparky to Juliana. She used to have a friend with that nickname, and it could upset her."

Ellis nodded. Just what he needed—another secret to keep.

Then she was gone. Without a good-bye. He stood alone on the dance floor, bewildered and a little hurt, until the flow of circling couples forced him to move out of the way.

Juliana was nowhere in sight. He left the ballroom and began a halfhearted search through the house. He saw Aubrey step out of the solarium leading a boisterous group. Reluctantly Ellis started toward them, thinking he'd better tell his uncle about letting Sparky's name slip. But before Ellis could attract his attention, Yvonne appeared from the dining room and spotted Aubrey herself.

"There she is!" "There's that ravishing morsel!" "What a lucky fellow you are, Aubrey."

Yvonne was cool to the reception, but Aubrey basked in the envy of the group and beamed at his wife.

"Don't know why you want to be running off to the arctic for so long when you have such a pretty lady at home."

Ellis saw her back stiffen. He saw the stillness settle over her.

"The arctic?" Her voice was deathly careful.

"For the polar-bear project!" "Aubrey just closed the deal with Daines there from Canada."

She looked at her husband.

"Wait'll you hear, Vonnie. An outpost on Ellesmere Island! Do you know what that means?"

Daines grabbed Yvonne's hand and shook it vigorously. "It's not every woman who'd sacrifice months of time with her husband to benefit polar bears. Let's give her a cheer, eh, boys?"

The group launched into hurrahs.

Yvonne turned and walked away. She moved like a sleepwalker. Aubrey watched her for a moment with a look of dismay, then shrugged and rolled his eyes to the accompaniment of laughter and back-slapping.

A wave of disgust swept over Ellis and he turned to hurry after Yvonne. She was heading toward the servants' stairs. Should he call out? Should he rush after her? He was torn between feeling and reason for an instant, then took the stairs two at a time. The hall was empty. The door to her suite was ajar. He knocked softly and then stepped into her sitting room. "Yvonne?"

No answer.

He crossed to her bedroom door and tapped again. It swung open. She was standing in front of a large oval mirror. Staring into it. The emptiness in her eyes sent a chill through him. "Yvonne . . . are you all right?"

When she spoke, it was as if she were talking to the mirror, and her voice was eerily distant. "Nothing is different . . . nothing will ever change. All the promises were lies. The arctic . . . Sparky . . . lies on lies on lies. A life of lies."

She reached up and slowly unpinned the elaborate headpiece from her hair. When the tiara was free, she stared at it as she had at the mirror. Then she dropped it. She unwound the miles of pearls and pulled the rings from her fingers. All the jewels dropped to the carpet. "It's finished," she said.

"Yvonne . . ." He gripped her shoulders and turned her toward him.

"Ellis?" She seemed vaguely puzzled at seeing him there. She studied his face as though looking for something, then brushed the tear from his cheek with her fingertips. "Oh, Ellis, Ellis . . ." she sighed.

"I'll take care of you," he said. "You don't need him."

She was focused now. The sleepwalker awakened. But her movements were still oddly languid. She ran her fingers over the planes of his face as if seeing him through her sense of touch.

"I love you," he said. "I—"

But she covered his mouth with her hand.

There was a flash of something in her expression. Gratitude? Compassion? Acceptance? It vanished too quickly for him to pin it down.

Her eyes held him. He felt himself falling into her eyes. Falling so fast that he couldn't breathe and couldn't hear anything but the rushing air and the pulsing of his own veins.

There was something changing in her. It washed over him. Hot and tender and fragile. And he opened himself to it ... gave himself to the falling.

His shirt opened beneath her fingers. She leaned into him and her lips brushed the hollow of his throat, her breath fluttered over his skin. Her palm rested on his chest, cool and dry against his burning skin.

She sighed, and he bent to kiss her. Gently, fearfully, he touched his lips to hers. The contact trembled through him, weakening and igniting and terrifying in one reverent instant. She curled an arm around his neck and pulled his mouth down hard and pressed the length of her body into his.

Movement blurred. He lost the order of things. The smooth skin of her back. Her dress falling. Taut nipples beneath a lace bra.

He picked her up. A chair toppled. She wrapped her legs around him and they kissed until his knees grew weak. Long, slow kisses that spun in his groin and his heart.

Then they were together, one solitary being ... circling, floating, rocking ... caught by tides as strong as moon and sea. And they came as one, unleashing a crashing torrent that left him shaking and disoriented in its wake.

Reluctantly he separated from her. The reality of having her was already fading and he wanted to crawl back into her eyes again.

She curled into him, small and vulnerable, burying her head in his shoulder as though hiding. He could feel the wetness of tears.

"Are you ... ? Was it ... ?"

"Shhh," she whispered.

He held her like a child, cradling her gently and stroking her back till he could feel her calm. She sighed, first in pleasure and then in resignation, before she sat up and reached for a dressing gown. "You have to get back downstairs," she said, "before someone comes looking for you."

She helped him with the tux. There was an urgency about her now that hurt him and made him want to be stubborn. What if he refused to leave? What if he insisted on having it out with Aubrey that very night?

But he let her hurry him to the door. "What about you?" he asked. "You'll be down for supper, won't you?"

She made a vague gesture. Her eyes were faraway and closed to him. He caught her by the shoulders roughly. "Look at me!"

But it was no use. She was startled, then sympathetic, but she remained separate.

She took his hand and raised it to her lips. "My sweet Ellis," she murmured. "My sweet, sweet Ellis."

He left her there at her bedroom door and stalked through her sitting room. Rational or not, he was feeling the churning torment of rejection. How could she pull back so far from him right after making love the way they had? Did she regret her decision? Was that dark gaze turned inward to Aubrey, accepting him back into her heart even now, before Ellis was washed from her body?

He straightened his jacket, checked the studs in his shirt, and combed his hair back with his fingers as he stepped out into the hall, coming face-to-face with Juliana.

"What are you doing in my mother's room!" she hissed. She pushed past him, trying for the doorknob, but he grabbed her waist and spun her back away from it.

"Your mother isn't feeling well, Jinx. She wants to rest awhile."

Her eyes flared with hurt and jealousy and worry and indecision. She was so unlike her mother, Ellis thought. So buffeted by her own intensities. He felt a rush of sympathy for her. Which she immediately detected and hated him all the more for.

The ballroom had been filled with tables, and people were already searching out their place cards. Ellis followed Juliana to his seat and tried to still the turmoil inside him. The sparkling setting, the lavish meal, the roomful of chattering, puppet people—nothing mattered. All he could think about was Yvonne.

"It looks like Mama's not coming down," Juliana said. "I guess she's had enough of you."

The meal dragged on and on. Through Edward's speech about how it was the seventy-ninth annual Van Lyden gala and the endless rounds of food and the famous singer who got up to do a number with the orchestra, Ellis felt a mounting restlessness. It grew until he could barely stay still in his chair, and as it grew, it transformed into a sense of dread. Every sinew in his body sang with the tension of it.

Suddenly he had to move. He leapt up, tipping his chair and startling even himself. Juliana scowled. He mumbled "bathroom" and hurried toward the door.

But the quiet hallway didn't soothe him. The sensations mounted and sharpened. Danger! That's what he was feeling. He could smell its heavy scent and taste it at the back of his throat. Danger. Just as clear as bear sign or the faint rumble before an avalanche of snow. Danger. Yvonne!

He took the curving grand staircase at a leaping run.

"What's wrong with you?" he heard Juliana call from behind him. "Are you flipping out?"

He was at the top when the noise sounded. A familiar noise. It exploded through his heart and lungs and sent him bursting into Yvonne's suite. Through the pale sitting room, white on white on white. Into the bedroom. More white . . . and red. Dark, dark red.

She was on the floor in her white satin dressing gown. Twisted sideways. The robe hanging open. Tawny legs exposed. Arms extended. One hand clinging to a gun.

Part of her head was gone.

Ellis fell to his knees beside her. The carpet was soaked beneath him. He felt frantically for a pulse in her neck. "Be alive. Please!" He touched her face. "Yvonne," he whispered. "Yvonne."

She was sleeping. He mustn't wake her.

Where had a gun come from? Did Yvonne know she was sleeping with a gun?

There was a chilling shriek behind him and then another. It was puzzling. He turned to see what was wrong. It was his cousin. Juliana ran forward and threw herself on Yvonne. Terrible sounds filled the room. Anguished, tormented sounds that tore at his insides and squeezed the air from his lungs.

He had to get away. To escape the sounds and the pain and the suffocation. He had to get back to the mountains.

He moved slowly, methodically. Out of the white rooms and toward the stairs, ripping off the black tie and opening the shirt collar as he went. Servants passed him, running the other direction. More screams. People swarmed into the hall below him.

"She's dead!" someone at the top of the stairs cried.

None of it mattered. He was on his way home.

When he reached the last step, the crowd parted. People streamed past him up the stairs. The screaming and shouting hurt his ears.

To the mountains. Back to the mountains. Out the huge double doors. Into the night. The cold air struck him and he stopped.

He looked down at himself. Black and white and red. So much red. He staggered forward a step and sank to his knees.

    Yvonne . . .

    Yvonne!

    He threw back his head and howled her name into the empty darkness.

PART II

Blood Tides

17

Lucy

Lucy Clare became Mrs. Buddy Skidmore two weeks after her eighteenth birthday. It was an afternoon ceremony held at Reverend Skidmore's newly opened Temple of Light Tabernacle, with a reception to follow in the basement. The bride wore a white ruffled gown that Charity Skidmore had found in Dallas, and a veil borrowed from her sister Suki. The groom wore a rented powder-blue tuxedo that Charity had also arranged.

Reverend Skidmore believed in strictly traditional wedding ceremonies and had been disturbed by the fact that Lucy had no male relative to give her away. At Charity's urging, Lucy timidly asked the attorney she'd been assigned to at the law office if he would do the honors. Preston J. Tully was amused by the request but good-naturedly consented. He was the youngest member of the firm and the only bachelor—a constant source of kidding from his colleagues—and the day after Lucy's request he brought "It's a girl!" cigars to the office and started a round of bantering about his newly acquired daughter. Strangely, Mr. Tully began to hover over her after that, as if her welfare truly had become a concern to him.

Suki and Anita stood up as attendants in candy-pink organdy dresses that Wanda hunched over her sewing machine for a month to make. The bride's only contribution to any of the decisions surrounding the wedding was a refusal to designate either sister as maid of honor. Lucy insisted that her sisters share equal status. For their walk down the aisle the girls were partnered by two of Buddy's football teammates from college.

As a special addition to the ceremony Reverend Skidmore delivered an original talk entitled "God Loves a Good Wife." As with all his compositions, the text was typed by a faithful parishioner and copies were handed out for the assemblage to take home and keep. Charity presented a hand-calligraphied, gilt-framed version to Lucy as a keepsake.

The ceremony went according to Charity's detailed plans. Everyone stood or sat in preassigned places. There was no fumbling for lost rings or untimely giggling or stammering over vows. Even the guests behaved correctly, filing out pew by pew behind the bride as if they'd been included in Charity's exhaustive rehearsals.

It was a big crowd. Because of Reverend Skidmore's rising popularity, the nuptials registered on the Walea social scale. Most of the invitations had been sent to the reverend's flock and a sampling of influential Waleans who Charity wished were members of the congregation. Lucy's only additions to the guest list were the people from the law firm where she worked and the washing clients of Wanda's who had sent the ham to her father's funeral.

The basement reception turned into a lively party. Reverend Skidmore had adopted the "no-dancing" policy of many of the area's other churches, and of course there was no alcohol allowed, but there was a rousing country band and mountains of food.

Lucy drifted through the merrymaking in a state of amazed shock. Was she really married now? Was she a part of all this? Had the entire town of Walea opened its arms to her as soon as she was pronounced a Skidmore? Reason told her that acceptance could not possibly come with such sudden ease. Yet she was being kissed and hugged and cried over and wished well by an endless flow of people like the Burrights and the Fimples and the Harrisons—people who had snubbed her entire family before.

"Some bash, Luce," Suki commented sarcastically when the two sisters finally had a chance to speak at the reception. "It's a regular Walea *Who's Who.*"

This was only the second time that Suki had been home since her sudden departure for secretarial school the summer after Lydell's death. On her first visit she hadn't seemed very different to Lucy. Now Lucy had to look hard to find remnants of the sister she'd grown up with.

Suki had either finished secretarial school or quit—depending on which version she was telling—and had gone to work for a prestigious company as an executive secretary. The position sounded to Lucy like a glamorized version of her own job at the downtown Walea law firm. The boyfriend Suki had been in love with had faded into history, but she hinted about being more than just a secretary to one of her company's attractive young executives.

The change in Suki's appearance was startling. She had cut her long red hair to a length that just barely brushed her shoulders. She worked for hours every morning, blow-drying it so that the natural waves would disappear and it would fall into a perfectly smooth line, with the ends turned under slightly. She had also frosted it, adding what she called "strawberry highlights."

"See, it's the natural look," Suki explained while she and Lucy were dressing for the wedding together. "All this teased and sprayed hair around here is so out of style! You could never go to the 'in' places in Dallas with hair like that."

But Wanda and the Skidmores all considered Suki's hair and long fluorescent-orange nails and huge geometric earrings as tainted rather than fashionable. And Suki, who had been expecting to play the successful sophisticate returning to her roots, was clearly disappointed over her reception. "I'm so glad I left here," she inserted at every opportunity. Especially when Wanda was present.

Suki and Wanda were both set in the bitterness and resentment of the past. Wanda could not let go of the fact that her most cherished child had abandoned her. Suki could not forget that her own mother had wanted to deny her the good life, and had been willing to shoot her to keep her from it.

The two were by turns cutting or cool toward each other, causing Anita to cry and Lucy to perform contortionist feats in order to preserve peace in the small trailer during the hectic days preceding the wedding. As much as she missed her sister, Lucy was relieved that the wedding visit would be short.

"I never thought I'd have a wedding like this," Lucy said as she and Suki watched a group of women admire the four-tiered cake.

"Yeah, funny, isn't it?" Suki said. "I mean, who would have thought?" She raised her perfectly tweezed eyebrows and her tanned shoulders in a dainty shrug. "And to Buddy Skidmore, of all people! I mean, isn't it strange how life works? Seems like just one little minute ago Buddy Skidmore was madly in love with me."

"It's been more than one minute," Lucy commented.

"Oh, well . . ." Suki tossed it off with a wave of her well-manicured hands. For the ceremony she had changed her orange polish to fuchsia and adorned her fingers with several large rings that she referred to as cocktail jewelry.

"I hope you catch my bouquet," Lucy said. She wanted Suki to be happy, and of course happiness consisted of finding a husband regardless of which town or life style her sister had chosen. Suki rolled her eyes skyward as though the idea were silly, but later, when the bouquet was thrown, Suki knocked all other contenders aside and captured the prize in a move that Buddy swore was worthy of professional football.

"Too bad there's no dancing," Suki whispered later. "I'd like an excuse to rub up against that boss of yours."

"Mr. Tully?" Lucy asked in disbelief.

"You bet. He's a cutie. Don't know how you keep your mind on your carriage return when he's around."

Lucy frowned later when she saw Suki sidling up to Preston Tully with all charms in high gear. Lucy had never thought of Mr. Tully that way. She realized he was attractive, but he was one of the bosses, an intelligent mature man—not one of Suki's "cuties." And she was embarrassed by her sister's flirting and making a pest of herself, and convinced that poor Mr. Tully was undoubtedly annoyed but trying hard to be polite for Lucy's sake.

Later, at cake-cutting time, Lucy saw Suki and Mr. Tully slipping out the back way together. She gritted her teeth and had to force her hands to be steady as she lowered the knife.

It was close to suppertime when Lucy finally went into the Tabernacle's bathroom and changed out of her wedding gown. She hung the gown carefully and draped Suki's veil on a separate hanger. Her sister never had said what she was doing in possession of a white silk-net veil. "I've got a veil I'll loan you," Suki had written in a letter, "but only if you promise to be careful with it." Lucy had been afraid to ask any questions.

The dress she changed into had been a present from her fellow workers at the law firm. Instead of buying her shower gifts, the women had all taken her shopping on their lunch hour and bought her what they all called a "going-away dress." The term struck Lucy as funny, since she was only going from the church to the Skidmores' mobile home.

Of course, it wasn't the Skidmores' mobile home anymore. As of the "I do" it had become Lucy and Buddy's new home.

The town's love of Reverend Skidmore and his stern fundamental Christianity had gone deep into people's pocketbooks, and as a result, the Skidmores had been able not only to retire the Holy Redemption tent in favor of the new concrete-block temple but also to build a brand-new house. They'd moved into the house early, before it was completely finished, so the newlyweds could have the Expando double-wide as their home.

Anita came into the bathroom as Lucy was zipping up her new going-away dress.

"Like it?" Lucy asked. She was acutely aware of Anita's mood.

"It's okay." Anita folded her arms self-consciously and huddled close to the wall.

At thirteen she was all arms and legs and frowns. Her hair was between Lucy's dark chestnut and Suki's bright red. Her skin was the compromise between Lucy's delicate fairness and Suki's freckles. Her height was that midpoint between Lucy's five-foot-eight and Suki's five-four. And she hated everything about herself—firmly believing that she was the leftover, the worst of everything. No amount of Lucy's reassurance could convince her otherwise.

Lucy reached into her tote bag and pulled out a small gift-wrapped box. "This is for you . . . for being my bridesmaid, and also . . . just because."

Anita stared at the box a moment. Finally she opened it. She looked down at the heart-shaped gold locket lying against the black jeweler's velvet.

Lucy waited. She had gone into debt to buy the necklace, but she had wanted to give Anita something special. "They engraved an A on it for you," she said.

Anita nodded and closed the box. She looked up at Lucy with tears in her eyes. "I never thought you'd leave us too."

"Oh, Nita . . ." Lucy gathered the girl into her arms. "I'm not leaving you. We'll see each other every day and you can come stay with me whenever you want."

Anita pulled back stiffly. "It won't be the same. It'll never be the same." She turned and ran from the bathroom with the box clutched to her chest.

Lucy could feel her little sister's pain and fear, but she had no doubt that things would be fine once Anita calmed down. In fact, things would be better. Lucy intended to make a real difference in her mother's and sister's lives as soon as she was financially able.

When Lucy stepped out of the bathroom to take Buddy's arm for the run to the car, the first person she saw was her mother. Wanda was standing with a group of women. Her workworn hands were carefully hidden in the flowing sleeves of the dress Charity Skidmore had lent her. Her back was straight and her shoulders squared. The self-consciousness and trepidation that had gripped her on their way to the church that morning were no longer in evidence.

As soon as she saw Lucy, Wanda's face lit with pride. It was the same pride that had danced in her eyes whenever Suki won a baton competition, and it was a look that Lucy had yearned for but never earned till now.

"What's wrong?" Buddy asked, and Lucy realized that she was crying.

"Mama!" she called, but it was too late. The rice was flying and Buddy was pulling her toward the car.

They rode together in silence awhile. Lucy stole a glance across the car at him and felt a little thrill. He had changed into slacks and a starched white shirt and he looked very handsome. And he was her husband.

"I hope everything comes off the car," Buddy said finally.

The car was new. At his father's urging he'd traded in his bachelor pickup truck for a sedate Chevrolet sedan. "A married man's car," his father had called it. The vehicle was now covered with "JUST MARRIED" slogans in different shades of paint.

"I'm sure they used water-based," Lucy said. She felt very odd. Like something monumental had happened in her life but no one realized it except her.

They drove around aimlessly for close to an hour. Charity had instructed them to do that so Buddy's rowdy football friends wouldn't know they were going to the mobile home for their wedding night and harass them with pranks.

"Wonder what the guys are doing tonight," Buddy said wistfully. "Maybe they'll figure out where we are anyways, huh. . . . Maybe they'll cover the place with toilet paper or shove a billy goat in the door or drag us out and ride us around in wheelbarrows like they did Myron Bevins when he got hitched last year."

"Maybe," Lucy said.

When they arrived at the mobile home Buddy went straight around to the trunk to get the cooler full of beer that he'd hidden there. "Damn, I been needin' one of these babies," he said as he carried the heavy cooler up the steps.

Lucy hurried around him to open the door. She stood on the porch and watched through the open door as Buddy put the six-packs into the refrigerator.

"Boy, I'm glad I didn't stash it in here this morning," he said. "My mother's been over and left us supper. She'da hit the roof at the sighta beer in her refrigerator." He turned and looked at Lucy. "Hey, what's wrong? Ain't ya comin' in?"

"Well," Lucy said shyly, "I thought you were supposed to . . . you know . . . carry me or something."

"Oh, yeah!" Buddy rushed back out and swept her clumsily but enthusiastically into his arms. He was so strong. She felt like Scarlett in *Gone with the Wind.*

He negotiated the narrow front door sideways, walked to the middle of the living room with her, and then set her down gingerly on the couch. "There," he said. "It's official!" He crossed back over to the refrigerator and began pulling out beer and food.

Lucy listened to tops popping and plastic wrap tearing and jars opening as she wandered from room to room in the mobile home. She had never lived anywhere but the tiny trailer out at the Trailer Village. She felt like she had fallen through the looking-glass into *Better Homes and Gardens.*

Everything was perfect. Charity had generously left most of the furniture and accessories in place, explaining that each item had been shopped for and carefully chosen for the exact spot it occupied, so it belonged where it was. And Lucy wholeheartedly agreed. How on earth would she have ever been able to duplicate Charity's precise color coordination and eye for detail if she'd had to redecorate the mobile home herself?

Not to mention the money question. There would be no money for niceties until Buddy got on his feet as an insurance salesman. Her salary at the law firm had to stretch far enough to cover their expenses and help Wanda and Anita as well.

Buddy was very sweet about her family obligations. Not only did he understand her need to help financially, he'd also promised to pitch in himself with "the sorta chores they gotta have a man do." Lucy was touched and proud at his plans to change the oil and ream out the plumbing and fix whatever needed to be mended around the Clare place. She didn't tell him that in her family those had never been a man's chores.

"I'm starved, Luce. Why don't you go ahead and dish this stuff up for us?"

With a sense of awe Lucy took her place in the gleaming kitchen and served the food Charity had left on the matching dishes.

"My mother makes the best damn potato salad," Buddy said around a huge mouthful.

Lucy smiled and watched him devour the food. It occurred to her suddenly that she would be responsible for feeding him from now on. The thought was staggering.

He finished off a can of Budweiser, tossed it toward the sink, and burped loudly. "Not bad manners"—he grinned—"just good beer!"

She ate a small plate of food and then washed the dishes while he worried over how to conceal his beer in the event of a visit from his parents. "Ya know, we might have to get one of those itty-bitty refrigerators and hide it somewheres just for beer." He scratched his head. "I'd hate ta have ta keep it out in the trunk all the time."

"We'll work it out," Lucy assured him. She put the dishes away carefully, conscious of keeping everything just the way Charity had left it.

"Boy, there sure was a pile a presents at the church," Buddy said. "Guess my folks will bring 'em home, huh?"

"I'm sure they will."

"Well, it's Saturday night," he said brightly. "Wanna go to a movie or somethin'?"

"No. I'd feel funny . . . I mean . . . if we saw somebody we know . . ."

"Yeah. S'pose so." Buddy shoved his hands into his pockets. "Wish we had a *TV Guide.* Maybe I oughta run out and get one."

"Let's not watch television," Lucy suggested timidly. "Let's just kind of lie around together." She glanced in the direction of the bedroom.

"You mean, startin' now?"

"Well, we could take showers and get comfortable and then just kind of lie on that big bed and talk. We've never been on a real bed together."

"But it's still light out, Lucy. We can't do that kinda stuff yet."

They ended up watching television for several hours. Lucy was feeling celebratory, so she had two beers instead of her customary one. Buddy finished a six-pack.

Lucy had stifled several yawns by the time Buddy announced, "Time to hit the hay. You go on in and get yourself ready," he said. "I'll be along in a minute."

She showered with perfumed soap, unpinned her long hair, and put on the new smocked and ruffled and ribboned nightgown that Charity had presented her as a gift. When she peeked out the bathroom door she saw that Buddy was still in the living room.

Nervously she tiptoed into the bedroom and sat down on the king-size bed's flower-sprigged quilted spread. As with everything else in the house, the bedroom was the ultimate in coordination. The spread and the curtains and the ruffled pillow shams and the lampshade and the upholstery on the chair were all the same fabric. The colors were echoed exactly in the shag carpet and the tissue-box holder on the nightstand and the fluffy dress on the doll that sat in the middle of the bed. The colors were also picked up in the huge embroidered Lord's Prayer that hung on the wall.

Buddy walked in and looked around nervously. "Shouldn't we move that doll?" he said. All he had taken off was his boots.

Lucy moved the doll gingerly to the dresser and folded back the spread. She wasn't surprised to find matching sheets underneath.

"That's more like it," Buddy said. "Why don't you just crawl into bed there and turn out that light ... and I'll be back in a minute."

Buddy was nervous. The realization came as a surprise to her. She slipped between the cool, good-smelling sheets and thought about what a sweet man she'd married. A lot of men would have had nothing but sex on their minds, but not her Buddy. No, he loved her more than just sexually.

The sense of awe returned. She was a married woman in bed waiting for her husband. They could touch and kiss and explore each other's bodies all night long and it was perfectly legal. The sin had been wiped away forever with just a few sentences, and now sex was supposed to be beautiful instead of dirty.

She listened to the water running in the bathroom and considered her luck. And it was luck. There was no doubt in her mind about that. Buddy's proposal had been a gift that she would have to work hard to be worthy of. She would never take him for granted. Never forget how close she had come to losing him.

Buddy had gone back to college after the night they "went all the way" in his pickup. He'd answered Lucy's long letters with cute little postcards and he'd come home to see her nearly every weekend. Then football season started and Buddy was transformed into a star. His playing drew praise from the local sportswriters and he no longer had free weekends or time to send postcards.

Lucy had had a raise at the law firm, and the Clare trailer once again boasted a connected telephone. She sent Buddy the number and waited for him to call. When he finally did, it was to tell her— in a fumbling, roundabout way—that he didn't think they should be so serious anymore. Shortly thereafter Buddy brought a sorority girl home to meet his parents, and Lucy had to feign illness in order to avoid the pain of seeing him in church with his weekend date.

Then, in a stroke of pure chance that changed both of their lives, Buddy was tackled hard from the side during the last game of the season. The doctor said his knee could be repaired, but there would be no professional career for Buddy Skidmore. His playing days were over. His parents brought him home to Walea for the surgery and convalescence. The sorority girls did not come to visit. Lucy did. She tiptoed into the hospital with all his favorite things—Goo Goo Bars and Hostess Snow Balls and fresh cherry-limeades and *The Guinness Book of World Records*—and she never once mentioned the sorority girls or the months she'd spent in misery. When Buddy was released from the hospital he announced that he'd had enough of college and that he intended to stay put in Walea and get serious about life.

That news was fine with the Reverend and Mrs. Skidmore. They'd heartily approved of the football, but the college itself had been worrisome to them. It had not been one of Texas' Christian institutions and they'd been constantly nervous about the immorality and perversion Buddy could be exposed to there—both in and out of the classroom.

They encouraged Buddy in his decision and didn't even complain when Buddy began dating Lucy again. At least Buddy was "setting his sights near home and not chasing after a spoiled little heathen from Dallas or some other godforsaken place," as Charity put it when she accepted Lucy back into the picture.

Lucy spent as much time as possible with Buddy. She took on the responsibility of nagging him about doing his rehabilitation exercises. She helped him map out job plans. And she had Suki send birth-control pills from Dallas so they could continue their couplings in the confines of his pickup without fear.

She'd been prepared to carry on like that for years, supporting Buddy emotionally and supporting her family financially and using every ounce of energy she possessed to do a good job at both. Then one night Buddy sat up after he climaxed, massaged his knee, grimaced, and said, "I guess we oughtta get married now."

Lucy was remembering that proposal—thinking how charming and Buddy-like it had been—when her new husband came sprinting out of the bathroom and dived between the sheets. The yard light filtering through the curtains kept the room from being completely dark, and she had a brief glimpse of Buddy's white underwear and his ghostly pale skin before he burrowed into the bed.

Lucy propped herself on her elbow and started to giggle. "We're really married. Isn't that amazing?"

"Yeah," Buddy said with a twinkle in his eye. "No more sinnin'!"

He wiggled around till he had his underwear off and then dropped it out onto the floor. Lucy waited. She wanted it to be true. She wanted sex to be beautiful and romantic now. She didn't want to have that gray, unsettled feeling anymore.

His big hands found her under the covers and gently pushed her nightgown up around her armpits. "I'm gonna take good care a you, Lucy," he promised fervently.

"I know you are," she said.

Making love in a bed was much more comfortable than the

pickup arrangement had ever been. Lucy experienced a whole new host of sensations. But Buddy climaxed and collapsed before she could sort them out or learn what to do with them. And the gray feeling still spread through her when they were done.

He flopped over onto his back with a sigh. "Now you're really mine," he said.

The words thrilled Lucy and scared her at the same time. She tugged her nightgown down and tried to snuggle close to Buddy. But he was moving ... wiggling back into the underwear he'd somehow snared from off the floor. "What are you doing?" she asked as he sat up and threw the covers back.

He looked at her as though puzzled. "I'm getting up so you can change the sheets," he said.

Lucy sat up and stared at him. "Change the sheets?"

"You don't think we oughta sleep on these messy sheets, do ya?" he asked innocently.

"Oh ... no ... of course not," Lucy said quickly. She felt stupid for not having known that a wife was supposed to change the sheets after intercourse. She hurriedly climbed from the bed and stripped the linens.

"I'll just go on in and take my shower while you're doing that."

"Sure ... okay."

As soon as he shut the bathroom door, Lucy raced around in a panic. Where were the extra sheets? She opened drawers and looked under the bed. In doing so she realized that Charity had unpacked for her. The two boxes of possessions she'd sent home with Buddy the day before the wedding had all been neatly arranged in the drawers and closets.

She heard the water stop in the shower. Where were those damn sheets? Finally, behind a stack of towels in the hall closet, she saw the familiar flower pattern. Two sets of extra sheets. And of course they all matched.

She raced back into the bedroom and threw the sheets into place, finishing just as Buddy came out of the bathroom. He was dressed in white undershorts and a white short-sleeved undershirt.

"Guess I'll have another cool one," he said as he sat down on the bed and arranged the pillows behind his back.

Lucy stifled a yawn and sank down heavily on her own side of the bed.

"Aren't ya gonna get me a beer?" Buddy asked in a hurt, little-boy tone.

Without a word Lucy jumped up and ran to the kitchen. She

grabbed a beer from the refrigerator and a paper napkin from the cupboard so that Charity's nightstand wouldn't end up with a ring on it, and she hurried back down the hall to her husband.

Again she sat back down on her own side of the bed. "I'm really beat," she said. "Weddings are hard work."

Buddy reached over and patted her hand. "You do look tired, Luce. Why don't you run on in and take your shower now so we can get some sleep?"

"But I already took a shower," she said.

Buddy looked at her like a kindly teacher might look at a retarded student. "That was before we *did* it," he said patiently. "You wanna be all clean and nice to sleep, don'tcha?"

"Oh . . . sure," she said, thinking that there was a heck of a lot to learn and wondering if she'd ever get it all right.

18

The first two years of marriage sped by quickly for Lucy. She worked a full day at the law firm and then went home to cook and clean and launder. It took a lot of energy to live up to her husband's expectations, but Lucy didn't mind. If anything, Buddy's high standards were proof that he was indeed special, and she was determined to please him, thereby elevating herself and justifying his choice of her as a wife.

Throughout this time Lucy had Charity's constant help and advice. Her mother-in-law rooted around in their mobile home, making comments like: "It's time to turn the mattress and air the blankets" . . . or "That window in the bathroom may be frosted glass, but it still needs washing" . . . or "Lord in heaven, girl! you forgot to iron the tea towels!" Each time she came, Charity brought supplies. Lucy had not known about decorator air fresheners till Charity arrived with an assortment. She'd not been aware of toilet products that kept the water blue and sweet-smelling for hundreds of flushes, or fabric softeners that made her sheets and towels smell of perfume. She'd never seen a refrigerator deodorizer.

Charity's generous contributions were not aimed at just the house, either. She brought gifts to improve Lucy's personal habits as well. There were perfumed papers to line her drawers and sachet blocks to tuck in her clothes and odor absorbers to stuff into her shoes in the closet and disposable douches and freshening suppositories. Charity clucked over the half-empty bathroom shelves and filled them with tooth whiteners and giant bottles of mouthwash and stacks of scented toilet paper and baskets of flower-shaped soap. With Charity's guidance, Lucy was becoming the wife Buddy deserved.

Buddy had given Lucy the responsibility of keeping his beer

both hidden and cool, and Lucy lived in terror of his mother's discovering it. She ended up keeping the cooler in the bedroom closet, buried beneath a stack of folded clothing. Each day she would replenish the beer, dip out the water, and refill the chest with ice. And cross her fingers that Charity would never have a reason to look in that spot.

The plan worked for a while. Then one day Lucy came home from work to find that Buddy was gone and her mother-in-law had decided to clean out the bedroom closet. Charity was just finishing the chore as Lucy arrived.

"This box . . ." Charity said, indicating a grocery carton with the top taped neatly shut, "is for the church's next bazaar. It's full of things that my boy can't possibly wear anymore."

Lucy stood frozen in the bedroom doorway. She looked down at the box and nodded.

"And there on the bed . . ." Charity gave an exasperated sigh. "My word, darlin', those just aren't the sort of things a young wife oughta have in her wardrobe. Why don't you give them to that little sister of yours to run around in?"

Lucy turned her head to look toward the bed. There, in a stack, were her favorite faded jeans and her most comfortable T-shirts and her canvas sneakers.

"I know you can't afford to run out and buy more appropriate clothing right now . . . so I brought over some things of mine for you. Hung 'em right up nice and neat. They'll need some takin' in, but your mama can do that in no time. Come on over here and let me show 'em to ya."

Charity took several steps back toward the closet and Lucy bit the inside of her lip and moved on into the room. She held her breath and peeked inside the closet.

"Those are real nice," she said of the ruffled blouses and poly-ester knit pantsuits Charity was displaying, but her eyes strayed downward. Her folded clothes were in place. No sign of the cooler showed. Charity had somehow missed it! She allowed air back into her lungs and smiled weakly at the woman.

"I knew you'd like 'em," Charity said. She reached out to pat Lucy's hand.

"Let's go in the kitchen and have a glass of tea," Lucy suggested. She wanted to get her mother-in-law out of the bedroom as soon as possible. The hidden cooler throbbed inside the closet like the beating heart in a scary story she'd read once.

"Not now, sweetie." Charity patted her hand again. "The rev-erend's bringin' some important folks home tonight and I've got somethin' special cookin'." She lifted her chin and a dreamy look came into her eyes. "Beef Bore-gin-on," she said. "It's French. Called for wine in the recipe but I found this cookin'-wine stuff at the Piggly Wiggly . . . it's exactly the same as regular wine except there's not a drop a alcohol in it!"

As she talked, Charity moved out of the bedroom and down the hall. Lucy's knees were trembling from the close call with the closet. She couldn't believe her good fortune.

At the front door Charity stopped and turned back toward Lucy. Her mouth curved into a sugary smile but her eyes were granite chips. "There are all kinds of weaknesses, Lucy, and every man falls prey to one sometime during his life. It's up to his wife to steer him away from weakness. To keep him on the right path."

She smiled again. "We mustn't ever forget . . . women are the foundation. The Lord created bad women to tempt men and good women to keep men strong."

Charity opened the door and a blast of hot, heavy air fought its way into the air conditioning. "That little problem in the closet . . . that's your first challenge as a wife, Lucy. It's not my business and it's not the reverend's business. It's not even really Buddy's business. It's up to you and the Lord to straighten out. And you remember . . . I'm countin' on you. I've trusted my boy to you and I expect you to do right by him."

"Yes, ma'am," Lucy whispered.

She stood at the window and watched Charity walk up the path, past the Temple and through the trees to her sparkling all-electric house. Then she ran into the bedroom and dragged the cooler out of the closet.

Buddy came home hot and thirsty. "My boss is teachin' me ta golf," he announced as he flopped down onto the couch. "Them little holes is damn hard ta find," he said.

Lucy brought him a can of beer and sat down beside him. "We have to keep the cooler in the trunk again," she said after he'd polished off one can and started another.

"Ohhh . . ." Buddy made a face like a two-year-old. "I hate that. I can hear sloshin' every time I turn a corner. And the ice melts so fast out in that hot car."

"I know," Lucy sympathized, "but your mother cleaned out our closet today—"

"She didn't find . . . ?" Terror leapt onto his face and raised his voice several octaves.

"No," Lucy said. She hated lying to him, but Buddy was so afraid of his parents finding out about what he termed his "innocent little taste for beer" that she wanted to protect him from his mother's discovery.

"But she came close," Lucy warned. "It's just too risky leaving it in here."

Buddy carried the cooler to the car and showered while Lucy fixed supper.

He sat down to eat with a mournful look in his eye. "I wish my daddy and mama weren't so stubborn," he said. "Why, drinkin' a nice cold beer's the same as havin' a soda. It ain't like I was beltin' down whiskey or turnin' Catholic on 'em and hittin' the wine." He sighed heavily. "That beer's gonna be warm as piss all summer long," he said.

"We'll think of something," Lucy reassured him. "Maybe you could give me a car key and I could walk to your office every day on my lunch hour and buy a sack of ice and put it in."

"Yeah!" Buddy brightened and began shoveling ham and mashed potatoes into his mouth. "Yeah, Luce . . . that'd be great!"

Subjugation and lies. Marriage seemed to be made of an equal blend of the two. With her family background, the subjugation came easily, but she couldn't get comfortable with the lies. Dishonesty was contrary to her nature. Even exaggeration was foreign to her. Yet the care and nurturing of a marriage seemed to require constant deception. She found herself lying often—either to protect Buddy from his parents or to shield him from some unpleasantry. Deceit worked like sandpaper on all the rough spots of their life together. And wasn't that what a perfect wife was supposed to do—keep things smooth?

In their second year together, Buddy's insurance income reached a level that was high enough to support them.

"Now you can quit workin'," he announced proudly one night after Lucy had balanced their checking account and figured their budget for the upcoming months.

"Quit?"

The word struck her like a blunt object.

"Yeah. Quit." He smiled at her. "Stay home like a wife oughta . . . and throw away them birth-control pills." He winked and raised his eyebrows suggestively.

Lucy didn't dare do battle over this openly, but she attacked it in subtle ways. She planted suggestions about how many nice things they could afford if she kept working awhile. Things Buddy wanted, like a boat and a four-wheel-drive vehicle and a bigger color television. And she went on about how the law office depended on her and how hard it was to find a new girl and train her. And she showed him magazine articles about how modern wives often worked outside the home and how two-job marriages kept the relationship fresh.

But it wasn't just Buddy she had to contend with. The Skidmores were set against her working and pointed out that the only decent wives who worked for money when they didn't have to were the ones who had a true talent to offer, like interior decorating or fashion-show coordinating.

Day by day Lucy felt her grip on her life slipping away. The threat of losing her job made her realize how much she wanted to keep it. She loved going to the ordered world of the law office, where everything she did was right and her opinion was respected. She loved the people she worked with there. And the check she deposited twice monthly in the Mr. and Mrs. DuWayne Skidmore, Jr. bank account gave her a feeling of satisfaction that she knew would never make sense to Buddy or the Skidmores.

Mr. Tully was upset when she gave him her notice. He made her feel so bad that she went into the ladies' room and cried. Then, on her last day of work the office staff gave her a going-away party at lunchtime. They had all gone together on a gift for her—an expensive thirty-five-millimeter camera—chosen, they explained, because she obviously didn't need anything in the way of household goods, and the men in the office didn't want to be included in giving anything too personal. Chosen, she knew in her heart, by Mr. Tully, who she'd once told about the Rolleiflex camera she used to have.

Lucy blinked back tears when she opened the camera. The gift said so much to her. They thought she deserved something luxurious and expensive. And they thought she was smart enough to use a complicated piece of equipment. They believed in her. Just like her father had. Just like Ms. Conroy had.

That night Buddy took her out to dinner to "celebrate her freedom." His spirits were high as he talked about their future together. The children they'd have. The house they'd build. The place in Walea's social structure that was theirs to claim.

"You'n me are gonna make a great team, Luce. I'm glad we got married. You got real class, ya know? My mama says you got class enough that nobody's gonna remember where you really came from."

Lucy worked at keeping herself content. She spent every morning using the super-deluxe nine-attachment vacumn cleaner Buddy had given her for her twentieth birthday, making certain the tops of the door moldings and floors beneath beds and

couches were clean enough to eat from. She replaced the refrigerator deodorizer before the suggested date and the toilet-bowl
freshener before the Caribbean blue faded to acquamarine. She
fiddled with house plants, learning to take cuttings and propagate
so well that the trailer overflowed with greenery. She made home-
made catsup and jars of pickle relish and embroidered mono-
grams on all their towels. And she did everything she could to
make her mother's and sister's lives better.

Buddy's devotion to his in-laws had faded rapidly. He considered himself too busy for handyman chores or problems, whether
they arose at the Clare trailer or his own home. And he even
refused to visit there, saying that it didn't make sense to go to
such a cramped, hot (or cold), run-down, depressing place when
Wanda and Anita could come on over and visit in the comfort of
the double-wide.

There was logic to what he said, except Wanda seldom had
the luxury of visiting without working. She couldn't drive over to
Lucy's and sip iced tea because she always had another load of
laundry that needed to be switched from washer to dryer or dryer
to ironing board.

So Lucy visited Wanda on her own whenever she could get a
ride from Charity. She spent long afternoons wielding screw-
driver or wrench and folding clothes and listening to stories about
the past. All Wanda's stories seemed to revolve around the past.
Her mother talked about a young sober Lydell, and Suki's twirling days, and Anita's babyhood—and she made it sound as though
all of them were dead now.

Anita, who worked part-time at the new Taco Mike's, was seldom at home with Wanda anymore. Her sulkiness had grown
worse and she waved her resentment of Buddy round like a red
flag.

"Don't know what's got into her," Wanda would mutter. "She
used to be such a good baby."

"It's just a stage," Lucy would always assure her. "She'll be
fine."

But Lucy's assurances were empty. She too was worried about
Anita. Several times, when Anita was supposedly in school, Lucy
had seen her riding through town on the back of a motorcycle.
And all of Anita's boyfriends suddenly were the type that sported
tattoos and questionable backgrounds.

Lucy went by the Taco Mike's at closing time one night specifically to talk to her sister alone. Anita was wiping down the
counters. The engraved gold locket Lucy had given her winked
in the hollow of her throat.

"Hey!" Anita said when Lucy walked in. "You're too late . . . we already put everything away."

"That's okay. I didn't come to eat. I came to see you."

"No shit," Anita said, and continued to work.

Lucy was momentarily disconcerted. The easy vulgarity was something new. "I thought I'd take you somewhere for a Coke as soon as you're finished for the night."

"Oh, yeah? Where's ole Buddy-boy?"

"Lion's Club meeting," Lucy said. "He went with his father, so he left the car."

Anita smirked. "Lucky you. Does he know you're using it to see me?"

"Well, not exactly . . . but he wouldn't mind."

"Sure," Anita said sarcastically. "He always lets you go out alone at night, right? And he just loves for you to spend time with your sister."

"Anita!" Lucy was becoming exasperated. "Will you stop trying to make trouble? You don't understand what being married is like. You don't understand about living with a man."

"Bullshit. I understand plenty. He goes out. You stay home. He sees who he wants. You don't see nobody except Mama."

Lucy thought about that as Anita went into the back to change out of her uniform. Lately Buddy hadn't been home much in the evenings. He had joined every organization that his father and his boss belonged to, and the meetings seemed to occur back-to-back. He'd never actually ordered her to stay home. He just always needed the car, so it worked out that way.

Buddy and Charity had been encouraging Lucy to join organizations of her own. The pressure had been steadily mounting and Lucy knew that membership in something was inevitable. But the Ladies' Literary Club and the secret thing with the initials and the Friends of Moral Decency Auxiliary (which Charity herself had founded) were all intimidating or boring or both. She had stalled by saying that she hadn't assembled a proper wardrobe yet. And she stalled Buddy on buying the wardrobe with the excuse that she might become pregnant anytime now that she'd gone off the pill, and she didn't want to waste money on new clothes if maternity was on the horizon.

"You one a Nita's sisters?" a boy asked her as he swept the taco-littered floor.

Lucy nodded and smiled.

"You the baton champion or the artist?"

The question surprised her. "I must be the artist," she answered.

Anita came out of the back in tattered jeans and a knit top that made her lack of bra clear. She wore her hair long and straight and huge earrings dangled at her ears. Lucy had to look away. Her sister's appearance brought back visions of Ms. Conroy.

"We goin' or not?" Anita demanded, and the spell was broken.

Ms. Conroy had been warm and giving and full of love. Sixteen-year-old Anita did not fit that description.

"I told my ride to go on without me," Anita said as she slid into the passenger side of the car. "So you're stuck takin' me home too."

"That's fine," Lucy said. "I intended to."

Lucy pulled in beside the Girlie Pancake House's flashing sign. "THEY'RE STACKED BETTER" it said beneath a bosomy waitress bearing a platter of pancakes.

"I hate this place," Anita said as they walked in the door.

"It's open, though," Lucy countered dryly.

They settled into a booth and ordered soft drinks. Anita also asked for well-done french fries.

"Why did you tell your friends I was an artist?" Lucy asked gently.

Anita's cheeks flushed. "Well, you used to be. And you still could be if you wanted to. I mean . . . it's not something that goes away."

Lucy looked down at her hands. It had been years since they had held a paintbrush. Years since she had believed that the visions she had were worth capturing.

"I never was any good, Nita. I never was an artist. It was just a phase I went through when I was close to Ms. Conroy."

"Ms. Conroy thought you were good," Anita protested. "God, I used to wish you'd teach me to paint someday. Those pictures you used to do—"

"You were just a baby," Lucy said sharply. "What do you know about it?"

They sat in silence till their drinks came.

"So . . . what is this?" Anita asked sarcastically. "Lecture time?"

Lucy shook her head. "No. I just . . . I wanted to spend some time with you. I never see you anymore."

Anita's face softened. "Yeah," she said. "I kinda miss seein' you too."

The rest was easy. In less than an hour Lucy felt closer to Anita than she had since her marriage. And the ease with which she won her sister back filled her with remorse. Was this all Anita had needed? A little special attention . . . a little private time together? Had she herself been causing Anita's unhappiness by not trying hard enough with the girl?

"So, I'm thinkin' of going to visit Suki," Anita announced casually as they were driving toward the Trailer Village.

"Really? Did she invite you?"

Suki had never wanted anyone to visit her in Dallas. At first Lucy had thought her older sister might be concealing something from them. Suki's stories were all a little too grand and Lucy had believed that she discouraged the visits because she didn't want them to see the truth of how she lived. Gradually Lucy had realized that Suki's motives were different, though. She wasn't embarrassed by her living conditions at all. She was ashamed of her mother and sisters, and she didn't want her city friends to see what kind of family she'd come from.

"Are you sure she wants you to come?" Lucy asked carefully.

"Why wouldn't she? I mean . . . it's not like I was Mom or you. I'm not gonna care if she smokes dope or lives with a guy."

Lucy stared straight ahead at the road in an effort to conceal her shock. When had her little sister started talking and thinking like this?

Anita chuckled. "You fit right in with all the stiff-necked church people in this town, Lucy. I guess you were meant to be one of 'em, all along."

Lucy didn't respond.

The lights were out inside the trailer and Wanda was obviously asleep, so Lucy didn't get out of the car. "I was thinking . . ." she said hesitantly. "I can't teach you to paint anymore, but how about learning to make another kind of picture?"

Anita waited in guarded silence.

"The office gave me this wonderful camera for a going-away present. I haven't done anything with it yet, and I . . . well, I thought it might be fun for us to experiment and learn how to use it together."

"A camera?" Anita said skeptically. "You mean like a Kodak Instamatic?"

"No, I mean a *camera!* Like professionals use. With meters and settings and filters and a tripod and everything."

"Wow!" Anita's eyes widened. "Maybe we could become famous photographers and travel all over the world."

Lucy smiled. "When can you come?"

It was complicated working out a schedule. They wanted to

learn in daylight, but they had Anita's school and job to contend with. And the weekends were ruled by Buddy's plans. Eventually they hit upon a rotating series of afternoons that would work.

The sessions with the camera were fun. More fun than Lucy had anticipated. She'd initiated the activity as a way to be closer to Anita, but it quickly became more than just a social vehicle. The magic of the camera excited her in a way that she hadn't been excited for years. She immersed herself in F stops and lighting questions and film speed and she cut corners on the grocery budget so that she'd have money for developing.

"What's wrong with you?" Buddy finally demanded. "Supper's late half the time and it's always hamburger ... hamburger ... hamburger!" He shoved his plate of hamburger casserole away. "And Mama says that sister a yours has been hanging around here a lot while I'm at work."

The guilt that had suffused Lucy when he first began to speak dissolved in the face of indignation. "What's wrong with my sister being over here?"

Buddy shifted uncomfortably in his chair.

"What's wrong with Anita coming over here?"

"Aw, Lucy. Don't make me say it," Buddy pleaded.

"Say what?"

His eyes wandered around the room as though looking for help. "I don't like her around, ya know? And I don't like people seein' you with her."

"What?"

"Aw, fer Chri'sakes!" Buddy shoved his chair back from the table and went to the refrigerator for one of the beers he'd brought in from the trunk earlier. He slammed the refrigerator door, popped the top, and turned to glare at Lucy. "Your sister's nothin' but trash, Luce. She runs with trash and she acts like trash. Everybody in town knows it. It's kids like her who're ruinin' this town. Hell, my folks have even been talkin' about throwin' her outta the church."

He sat back down heavily in his chair. "There. Glad ya made me say it? Huh?"

Lucy went through the rest of the evening mechanically. She had never felt such consuming anger toward her husband. She didn't know what to do with it all. It was much too big for tears or cross words. Too big even for shouting.

When Buddy fumbled to lift her nightgown that night, she said no for the first time since they'd been married. Buddy got up and went back out for more beer. When she found him the next morning he was sprawled on the living-room couch surrounded by crushed cans.

The bad feelings stretched on and on, and there seemed to be no way around them. Buddy stood by his judgment of Anita, but he was meek about his stance at first, hanging his head and moping around the house while he consumed vast quantities of Budweiser.

"I can't believe you're actin' like this, Lucy." The catch in his voice and the hurt in his eyes made Lucy feel like an evil stepmother. "It's like you're a different person. It's like I don't even know you."

The next day he turned mean. Lucy could tell he'd talked the situation over with his parents and they'd pumped him full of righteous anger. That was the beginning of a full-scale war between them. And the bloodiest battlefield turned out to be their king-size bed.

"You're my wife, Lucy," Buddy said on the fourth night of their troubles. "You gotta stop all this and remember your place."

"I'm not just your wife. I'm also still a sister and a daughter, and I'm not going to throw those parts of my life away just because you and your parents say I should."

Lucy slipped into her side of the big bed. "Good night," she said, and turned away from him to hug the edge so that no accidental contact could occur.

But Buddy had just come from a pep talk with his parents and he was armed with Reverend Skidmore's wrath and a host of direct quotes. "You're goin' against the natural order, Lucy. You're goin' against God." He produced a piece of paper. " 'Wives, submit yourselves unto your own husbands, as unto the Lord. For the husband is the head of the wife, even as Christ is the head of the church.' " He slid beneath the sheets and punched her arm. "You awake? Huh?"

Lucy sat up. She rubbed her arm and glared at him. Buddy was so much like a child—whenever he couldn't make a strong enough point verbally, he resorted to a punch or a shove.

"I'm awake," she said. She glanced over at the paper and saw the reverend's strong slanted handwriting.

"What I read was straight from the Bible. And listen to this one." He cleared his throat. " 'Let the woman learn in silence with all subjection. But I suffer not a woman to teach, nor to usurp authority over the man, but to be in silence.' "

Buddy's voice lowered and assumed the timbre and quality of the reverend's as he read. Goose bumps rose on Lucy's arms and she had a moment of nameless dread. "Someone just stomped on your grave," Wanda would have said.

"Buddy ... all those Bible quotes are fine, but this isn't church—this is our home."

"And that's where you're goin' wrong!" Buddy shouted as though she'd just proved his point. "Our home is s'posed ta be an extension of the church. An *extension!*"

She could tell he'd been coached to use the word "extension."

"God is tired of all this fussin'. He wants me to put you back into line."

"Who said?"

"My father said."

"Then it's your father who's advising you ... not God."

"Are you sayin' God don't speak through my father!" Buddy screamed. His face turned crimson and his thick neck bulged with cords.

Lucy frowned. Was that what she was saying? She'd never thought about it in quite that way before. Most of the flamboyant preachers in Walea claimed God spoke through them. And the guy on television claimed that. And there were several radio preachers who billed themselves as the voice of God. She realized that she'd never believed any of that to be true. Especially when there were running feuds between a number of the men and big differences in their translations of God's wishes.

"Maybe I am saying that. Maybe I think God doesn't speak through any one person."

The slap stunned her. Her head snapped back against the headboard and she raised her hand to her stinging cheek and stared at him in disbelief. "You hit me." She tasted the sharp tang of blood in her mouth. The force of the blow had made her bite her tongue. "You actually hit me."

This was not one of Buddy's standard punches or pokes. This was serious.

"You deserved it," he said. There was an edge of awe to his voice, as though he was impressed by his own capacity for violence. "Since you're not actin' like a adult, I'm gonna have ta treat ya like a child. A bad child."

Tears stung Lucy's eyes. She threw back the sheets and lunged sideways, but Buddy caught her. His huge hand closed around her forearm and he dragged her roughly back across the bed.

"I've had enough a this shit!" His eyes glittered with excitement and menace. "You hear me?" His grip on her arm tightened painfully as he leaned out to switch off the bedside light with his free hand. "Now . . ." He jerked her nightgown up and rolled over so that the weight of his body pinned her to the bed.

"No! Please! I don't want to, Buddy! I don't want to!"

"Shut up. Just shut up! You been makin' a fool outta me in front of my parents." She felt his erection against her leg. "But no more! You're gonna learn your lesson now. Understand?"

He shoved his penis into her roughly. It hurt. But not nearly so much as her heart. Her heart was breaking.

The next morning she looked in the mirror to find that her cheek was discolored slightly. She had expected to see more. If not from the slap, then from the destruction she felt inside. She cooked Buddy's eggs and sausage and grits and served them in silence. Every time he moved, she jumped, fearful of what he might do next.

"Come mere," he said gently as he was ready to leave. He pulled her into a tender hug. "Everything's gonna be fine now," he said.

Lucy stood in stiff, watchful silence.

Buddy smiled benevolently and reached out to tweak her chin. "That's my girl," he said. "That's my good girl." He turned toward the door, hesitated, and then turned back. "Say, why don't you borrow my mama's car and run into town and treat yourself to somethin' nice?" He nodded as though approving his own kindness. "Yeah. I'll call her soon as I get to the office and tell her it's okay ta give ya the keys."

Lucy showered till the hot water ran out. Then she dressed and walked up to the Skidmores'. Charity's powder-blue Lincoln had been backed out of the garage and stood on the circular drive in front of the door.

Before Lucy could knock, Charity appeared from around the side of the house. She had on a ruffled pink gingham sundress and a big straw hat and gardening gloves. Her expression was falsely sweet and openly smug. "Begonias are such a bother," she said. "Don't know why I didn't just put in all marigolds."

Lucy hated her mother-in-law at that moment. It was one of the purest and most uncomplicated surges of emotion she'd ever experienced.

"We were so pleased at Buddy's phone call. We knew . . . with the Lord's help . . . that you two would get this all worked out."

How badly did she want the car? Lucy asked herself.

Badly.

If she didn't get out of that double-wide and away from Charity and the Temple, she thought she might go crazy.

"Can I have the keys now?" she asked quietly.

"They're in it, darlin'. I got it out of the garage and ready to go the minute I received that joyous phone call. My boy sounded so happy. The Lord's proud of you, Lucy."

Lucy turned and went straight for the car. She thought she might scream if she heard one more word. She drove to see her mother first. Wanda was ironing. Beads of sweat stood out on her forehead.

"Let me take you into town and buy you a nice lunch, Mama," Lucy pleaded.

Wanda looked at her daughter as though she'd suddenly spoken in a foreign tongue. "Since when do you spend your afternoons lollin' around in restaurants?"

"I don't. I just thought today we might . . ."

"You suddenly rich or somethin'?"

Wanda set down the iron and eyed her. "You got somethin' ta tell me?" Her face lit up. "Am I gonna be a grandma?"

"No, Mama." Lucy sighed. "I just wanted to talk a little."

"Fine," Wanda said, and resumed her ironing. "No harm in talkin'."

Lucy sat in silence for a while. Her tongue hurt when she moved it against her teeth, and there was a tiny throbbing in her cheek. She'd covered the discoloration with makeup.

"Did you and Daddy ever have fights?" she asked finally.

"Sure. Don't everybody?"

"I mean bad fights. Where Daddy got real ugly and mean."

Wanda eyed her again. She put the iron down and reached up to mop her brow with a white cotton handkerchief. It was one of Lydell's old handkerchiefs. One of the few things he'd left that was of use to anyone.

Wanda sighed heavily and went to the refrigerator for the pitcher of iced tea. "I reckon now's as good a time as any to take a break." She poured two glasses full and carried them over to the chipped Formica table.

Lucy sat down and stared at the glass. She drew circles in the beaded moisture with her fingertip.

"You've lasted longer'n most," Wanda said. "Pert near three years you been satisfied. That's somethin' to be thankful for."

Lucy swallowed hard against the lump in her throat. She knew she should reassure her mother, tell her not to worry . . . that nothing serious was going on. But she couldn't.

Wanda sighed again. This time it was a weary sound. An age-old sound.

"We all start with dreams. Guess that's the nature of bein' human. And I swear . . ." Wanda smiled nostalgically. "You been a bigger dreamer'n most. Just like your daddy . . ." Wanda ducked her head in a rare display of emotion. The weakness was brief. When she raised her eyes to meet Lucy's again, her expression was suffused with quiet strength. "You can't take those dreams with you into womanhood, Lucy. A grown woman's gotta take up her man's dreams and then her children's. That's what keeps the world goin'."

Wanda took a long drink of tea.

"You been lucky. No babies right off. And you an' Buddy been kinda feelin' your way together. But it may be Buddy's ready for you ta buckle down and finish growin' up."

"What about Buddy?" Lucy protested. "When does he have to grow up?"

"Thought you'd a learned the answer ta that from your own daddy." Wanda smiled ruefully. "Men don't never have ta grow up. Don't ask me why. I heard a old woman say once it was 'cause men don't never have ta give birth." She shrugged as though it wasn't worth giving too much thought to. "Don't matter why, though. Why ain't gonna change nothin'. All that matters is . . . that's the way things are. So you'd best be gettin' used to it and findin' your own way a livin' with it."

Lucy stood and paced around the trailer. She felt empty and frightened. But she couldn't say anything more to her mother. She couldn't increase her mother's burden with her own confusion. What did wanting to be treated decently have to do with dreams? What did immaturity have to do with wanting consideration and kindness and respect? Was it naive to think that her needs and her opinions should count for something?

"Listen ta me . . ." Wanda said self-consciously. "Givin' all this advice when Lord knows I ain't figgered my own life out too good. But I gotta tell ya, Lucy . . . there's something real important you gotta learn about men. Men are a whole different breed than us. And you gotta watch 'em every minute, 'cause they'll trample you right into the dust without realizin' that they're causin' any harm. Kinda like a dumb, blind-eyed, clumsy-footed horse, ya know?

"So you gotta learn ta feed 'em and care for 'em without gettin' too close. Know what I mean? You keep back so's you don't get accidentally hurt."

Lucy bent to give Wanda a one-armed hug. How could she ever have seen her mother as villain and her father as hero? How could she have seen herself as so different from her mother? How could she have escaped the realization that the world was divided into something much more dangerous than rich and poor, black and white, educated and uneducated—the world was divided into male and female.

She straightened and attempted a smile. "Thanks, Mama."

"I'm proud of you, Lucy. You're the only one a my girls who's amounted ta anything. The only one who's knowed what was right and stuck by it."

The lump in Lucy's throat rose up again and her eyes burned. She wanted to throw herself on the floor and bury her face in her mother's lap and sob. "I feel a lot better now," she said. "I'll see you later."

She drove into town and arrived at the law office just in time to join a group that was going out to lunch together. They treated her appearance as a big occasion and raised her spirits with their enthusiastic welcome.

But she had trouble concentrating on the light banter as they ate their longhorn-special burgers. She felt strange, calm and whole on the outside and fractured on the inside.

"How are you, Lucy?" Mr. Tully asked as they walked through the parking lot to their cars. The question was weighted and he was walking slowly enough that the rest of the group quickly pulled away.

"Why, I'm . . ." She could feel her face coloring. "I'm fine, Mr. Tully." She tried to smile and concentrate on the odd assortment of thoughts that were bouncing around in her head. Mr. Tully seemed younger to her than he used to. And Suki had been right—he was attractive.

"It's Preston," he insisted. "Preston." He smiled at her warmly. "You should come by the office more often," he said. "We all miss you."

She could feel herself losing control.

"What's wrong?" he asked, stopping completely and reaching out to hold her arm so she had to stop too.

"No . . . It's nothing . . ."

"Let me help, Lucy."

A humiliating stream of tears leaked from her eyes and she was suddenly very angry. Not just at Buddy for smashing whatever fragile notions she'd had about their marriage, but at every male who had ever hurt or disappointed her. That young construction worker named Billy who had destroyed her fantasies and taught her to fear. The principal who'd pulled up her dress and paddled her in front of the whole kindergarten and first grade. Reverend Luke, who'd stolen Ms. Conroy's heart and brought disaster down on all of them. Her lazy, self-pitying father. Her cruel, self-righteous father-in-law. Gary at the trailer factory, who'd taken his revenge by having her fired. The office manager who'd fired her.

The list was long. And it included Mr. Preston Tully, who had befriended her and walked her to the altar, and then sneaked so conspicuously out of her reception with Suki before the cake was even cut.

"You can trust me, Lucy," he said, sincerity beaming from his eyes.

And she knew that he had absolute faith in the truth of his statement. He really did believe that he could make everything right in her life if she would put herself in his hands. If she would only trust him.

She pulled her arm free of his grasp. "You're a man, Mr. Tully. I know you can't help that, but you see, I can't afford to ignore it."

His eyebrows knit in a perplexed frown as she spoke.

Before he could respond, she turned and ran for Charity's car. As she pulled out of the parking lot she glanced in the rearview mirror. Mr. Tully was still standing there, watching her exit with a baffled expression. And she wondered if men ever had to learn the lessons they taught women.

19

Juliana

Death can have a solidifying effect on a family, bringing together the disparate elements into a unified front. Such was not the case with the Van Lydens. The fabric of the family raveled beneath the stresses of grief and guilt and disgrace.

Juliana, in a state of shock, was shut in her room with Charlotte in attendance. Edward retreated to Mignon. Ellis was taken first to the police station and then, after a torturous period of time in which it was confirmed that Yvonne's death was indeed a suicide, he was spirited away under Grace's protection. And Aubrey escaped by helicopter to Elysia and put the security force there on double shifts. The details of the funeral and burial were left to Edward's longtime social secretary.

The tragedy was mercilessly exploited. International news was slow that week and there were no major sporting events, natural disasters, or political contests, so Yvonne Van Lyden's suicide provided the juiciest morsels available for the insatiable appetite of the ever-circling media. Despite heavy security, the private funeral service was infiltrated by a reporter posing as a church janitor and the brief graveside scene was covered by a half-dozen photographers with telephoto lenses perched on rooftops and utility poles.

The family arrived at the church in four separate limousines and took their places with little more than eye contact passing between them. They could have been strangers. The official church service provided little for the media mill other than detailed descriptions of the curious crowds outside and the dozens of security people required to keep that crowd at bay.

At the graveside, however, the photographers struck gold through their long-range lenses.

The funeral director had whisked the closed casket to the cem-

264

etery and arranged it artfully before the family's arrival. Dozens of magazines and newspapers ran photographs of the elaborate white marble coffin banked by cascades of flowers. So many flowers that the coffin appeared to float atop them.

Aubrey and Edward arrived within moments of each other. They walked up to take their places without a word passing between them. Ellis and Grace were next. The tabloids later reported that the "Jungle Boy" appeared to be heavily sedated. One creative publication recounted rumors that Ellis was so wild and distraught that he had to be hypnotized by an animal psychologist before he could be trusted to attend.

Juliana and Charlotte arrived last. Inside their car Juliana was clinging to Charlotte and begging not to have to go to the grave. Unfortunately for the media, the glass was dark and the limousine was soundproof.

"I don't want to see the dirt! I don't want to see the hole!" Juliana cried. She was sobbing so hard that she could barely breathe. "Please, Charlotte . . . please. They're going to throw dirt on her. They're going to bury her in the dirt so she can't ever get out! They're—"

"Stop it!" Charlotte shook the girl's shoulders hard then folded her into a tight hug. It was more a restraint than a giving of affection. "You have to go. It's your duty. Remember who you are."

Juliana walked stiffly beside her governess toward the white marble box that held her mother. Her legs worked mechanically. External sensations did not reach her.

Until she saw Ellis.

She hadn't been aware of him at the church. Everything there had been blurry and she hadn't noticed who came in after her or sat in the rows behind her. Now suddenly she saw him. For the first time since she'd caught him kneeling over her mother. She saw him standing there so clean in a new black suit. All traces of her mother's blood washed from his hands. All traces of his guilt hidden. Standing right there between her father and her grandfather. Like he belonged. Like the grief was his. Like Yvonne was his.

And she flew at him, screaming and clawing, knocking him to the ground and rolling with him. She was still screaming as they pulled her off. Thanks to an inventive young newshound, the gravesite had been "bugged" the night before and the audio portion of the scene was transmitted to the ecstatic occupants of a van outside the cemetery. This was quickly transcribed to provide an accompaniment to the dozens of photographs of the incident. The only facet of the scene that the media missed regurgitating for its audience was the scent of the hundreds of flowers that were crushed as the cousins rolled together on the ground.

The day after the funeral, Grace took Ellis to Europe. Edward closed Mignon and moved into Great House. Aubrey left for Ellesmere Island and the polar-bear project.

Juliana spent two months in her room. Charlotte stayed with her constantly. A doctor came periodically. Edward visited once a day. At the end of the two months Edward stepped in and announced that enough was enough. "You're a Van Lyden," he said. "You come from sturdy stock. It's time you came down out of that room and showed what you're made of."

The child who emerged was not the same child who'd skated through ballrooms or given tea parties for statues or worried about bothering her parents. This was a child who'd lost all illusion. Who'd lost the capacity for joy. And who'd lost that fine edge of control she'd sharpened for so long.

For the most part she did what she was supposed to. She ate, bathed, dressed, and followed orders. She replied to questions and made the proper moves at cribbage. But she was dead inside. There were no more exciting thoughts, no more wishes, no more sarcastic comments to keep to herself. There was nothing but bitterness and pain and hate. And sometimes that molten poison erupted, spewing out of her uncontrollably.

Her fits of temper kept the entire household on tiptoe around her, but she didn't perceive their treatment of her as cautious distance. Instead she felt unnoticed. Insignificant. Invisible. Obscured by a bleak gray cloud, a clinging, heavy fog. The outside world didn't see her. Her grandfather saw her only when he chose to. Sometimes even Charlotte's eyes skimmed over the air as if she didn't exist.

She was as invisible as her mother. As dead as her mother. And she wished she could dig down with her hands and open that marble box and crawl in safe beside her mother.

Whenever Charlotte was busy or out of the house on errands, she took out the extra housekeeping key and crept into the white womb of her mother's rooms. Except for occasional dusting, the suite had been untouched since her mother's death. It remained as constant and sacred as a shrine.

She spent hours in those rooms, fingering the everyday jewelry that Yvonne had strewn carelessly across her dressing table, drinking in the familiar smells of her mother's perfume and powder, staring at the rust-black stain on the pale carpet.

Sometimes she talked to her mother. Shared her emptiness and her grief. Sometimes she buried her face in the satin of a dressing gown as though Yvonne were cradling her. Sometimes she pressed her face to the stained carpet and wept.

Tutors came and went. Outings with her grandfather increased in frequency. Her father appeared and disappeared. It wasn't important to her. She nursed her anger, hating everything and everyone for going on without her mother.

She especially hated her father. His abrupt departure after the funeral and his rambling good-bye letter festered inside her. "I don't know why your mother took the coward's way out," he'd written, "but I can't let that stop my own life. If anything, this terrible tragedy has made me yearn even more strongly for freedom and grand purpose. I hope you can understand and forgive. I'm not leaving you so much as I am seeking myself."

She didn't understand. And she couldn't forgive. And she wanted to tear him apart for saying her mother was a coward.

Years passed. The sullen gloom of adolescence prolonged the darkness and hatred. Then, when she turned fifteen, the fog suddenly began to lift. She looked around and was surprised to find that life might be shiny and interesting again.

The darkness inside her retreated to a deeper level and she became aware of strange new truths about herself. Somehow, during those poisoned brooding years, she had become a young woman. And she had started to wish again . . . to want. It drifted inside her like a siren song . . . a mysterious amorphous wanting that fluttered in her belly and whispered in her blood: "I want . . . I want . . ." But she couldn't finish the sentence. It was impossible to pin down the hungry restlessness growing inside her.

Her mother's rooms still beckoned, but now there was a different tone to her visits. She tried on her mother's clothing and jewelry. She experimented with the makeup. "Mama," she whispered into her mother's huge oval mirror, "will I ever be pretty? Will anyone ever love me?"

She lay across her mother's bed and read novels stolen from the maids—stories about women who were swept away by pirates or ravished on balconies. In the poetry text her tutor gave her she found a poem about a woman in love with a mysterious masked highwayman and she imagined herself as that woman, leaning out of her window at Great House as he rode up in the moonlight.

She stared at her reflection in the mirror for hours at a time, analyzing her eyes as too narrow and her cheekbones too pointed and her hair too thick and her chest too flat. She clipped plastic-

surgery articles from magazines and badgered Charlotte to hire
the hair and cosmetic experts whose names appeared in print.

The restlessness expanded. she wanted something to happen.
She wanted to be different. She wanted to be swept away by something. Anything.

Shortly after her sixteenth birthday there was a message that
her father was returning home for a month. Her grandfather was
well aware of her bitterness toward Aubrey and he announced
the visit carefully, expecting a violent reaction. The news settled
into her, bumping into a number of emotions, but curiously, it
didn't upset her. With the passage of time and with the birth of
all the restless yearnings, her intense anger toward her father had
diminished. To her surprise, she realized that she might even
want to see him.

He stormed into the house with piles of equipment—cross-
country skis and mountain-climbing paraphernalia and high-tech
tents and rifles in padded cases. The sight of him, tanned and fit
and turned out in a custom safari jacket, tugged at something
deep inside her. This was the golden father of her infancy. The
brilliant sun father. A figure worthy of the hero's role in one of
her stolen novels.

"Hey, there, Jinxie! How's my girl?"

She approached him cautiously but did not resist when he
swept her into a hug.

"What a lady you are! My God, look at you! Have I been gone
that long?"

"A year," she said evenly.

"Then we have a lot to make up for, don't we?"

A little snort of sarcasm escaped her. He had a lot more than
a year's absence to make up for. A lot more.

Her coldness stopped him and he focused on her in a way he
never had before. He looked straight down into her and she didn't
flinch or weaken a bit. She stared back with reckless defiance.

He cocked his head slightly, his brows a perplexed line and
his eyes questioning and worried. "Maybe . . . after dinner . . . we
could shoot some pool together," he said. "Do you like pool?"

"No," she said, and left him standing there with his mountains
of equipment and flurrying servants.

He was solicitous at dinner, asking how she liked each dish
and carefully including her in his conversation with Edward. Afterward he asked if she'd care to join the men for their ritual
brandy in the lounge. Edward's brow furrowed and he blinked as
though Aubrey had thrown something at him.

"No, thank you," Juliana said, and went straight up to her room. A little thread of pleasure wound through her as she climbed the stairs.

The next morning Charlotte burst into her room. "Wake up! Wake up! Your first flowers!"

Two dozen yellow roses. Juliana rubbed her eyes and opened the card.

TO MY LOVELY DAUGHTER,
FROM THE FIRST OF YOUR FUTURE'S MANY ADMIRERS.
P.S. MAY I TAKE YOU TO LUNCH TODAY?

Juliana used a sheet of the notepaper she'd taken from her mother's room. "YES," she wrote. Her hand was shaking.

Never had she been so excited or so nervous. She drove Charlotte to distraction, choosing and discarding one piece of clothing after another, throwing shoes, twisting her hair up and then tearing the pins out.

"You look wonderful," her father said when she finally went down to meet him, making the excruciating process all worth it.

She was tall now, nearly as tall as he was in the heels Charlotte had let her wear. And she knew that there was a resemblance between them. Charlotte had commented on it just that morning ... how there was something about her carriage and facial expressions that was exactly her father. Pride suffused her as she stepped out the door with him. She had a sense of them looking good together and of the envy and interest her being with him would cause in others.

Somehow her father had managed to talk Edward into allowing her out in a restaurant without the security of a private room. How could she possibly complain when that coup had been achieved? It made her wonder, though: was her grandfather softening or had her father been capable of engineering this all along? She chose to think it was her grandfather.

La Caravelle. The name sang to her. An enormous thrill, a heady tingling blaze of satisfaction coursed through her as she walked in the door beside her father. Aubrey took her elbow lightly as he spoke French to the man seating them. Pride filled her. This elegant man was her father. She smiled at him as he slid into the plush crimson banquette with her, and he returned the smile, making her glow with the full incandescent power of his charm and attention.

This was not the sort of restaurant her father preferred. She knew that. His favorites were the ones that offered slabs of steak or poodle-size lobsters served in a haze of cigar smoke. She looked around at the soft Parisian murals and the tiny shaded lamps and the fresh flowers, and she knew that her father had chosen this place especially to please her.

Her last reserve of bitterness melted, and suddenly she was caught in a volcanic swell of complete adoration. Her love for her father nearly took her breath away.

Juliana sailed through their meal on a wave of euphoria. Laughter bubbled from inside her. She was captivated by every word her father said and she basked in his attention, feeling more witty and charming by the minute. When her father called for the check, she came down with a crash. The act of leaving was physically painful. She stopped on her way out and turned back to memorize the room.

"Will you take me out again?" she asked.

"As often as you like," her father said.

Of course that didn't turn out to be true. What she would have liked was for her father to take her out every day. And every night as well. What she would have liked was for him to show her every wonderful place on the whole island of Manhattan.

Her grandfather's new permissiveness didn't go that far, though. He vetoed most of Aubrey's plans for her, forbidding a parade and horseback riding in the park and an afternoon of baseball at Yankee Stadium. Each "No" infuriated her. She wasn't a baby anymore. And she wasn't her grandfather's property.

"You're just being evil!" she screamed at Edward. "You liked it when I hated Papa and now you're jealous that I have so much more fun with him than I ever have with you!"

"I'm thinking only of your welfare and your safety," her grandfather said, ignoring the vehemence of her outburst. His calm added fire to her anger.

"When he leaves, I'm going with him!" she cried. "You just wait . . . he'll take me this time. I'll run away with him and you'll never find us!"

Edward's eyes were sad as she stormed from the room.

And all too soon her father was packing.

"Don't go yet, Papa," she begged. "Please don't go."

"I have to, Jinx. I told you from the start when I'd be leaving. I've got plans, you know. Obligations."

She threw herself at him, clutching at him as a drowner clutches at a lifeguard.

"Take me with you! Please, please, take me with you. I can go everywhere you go . . . do everything you do. I can—"

"Jinxie, Jinxie, Jinxie . . ." He pried her hands free and hugged her gently. "You belong here, where I know you'll be safe and comfortable. I'm going straight to the mountains for a month of rough living. That's not for you."

"I could do it. I can be as tough as a boy."

"Even if I thought you could . . . what about the other men? They don't bring their wives or daughters. What do I tell them?"

She tried to stifle a sob.

"I know . . . I know . . ." He patted her back. "I'm going to miss you too. If I could stay a moment longer, I would. But the plans were made long ago. I can't let my buddies down, can I? Would you want me to be the kind of guy who lets his friends down?"

He released her and made a mock jab at her chin. "Hey, champ, lighten up. We've got the rest of the day. And I promise. I swear to you. The minute I leave those mountains, I'll come straight back to you. You're my girl now. I'll be counting the days till I can get back to New York and see you again."

He left that night and Juliana locked herself in her room to mourn.

Edward was especially nice to her after Aubrey's departure. A month went by, and then two. She wandered the house listlessly and waited for her father. Every ring of the telephone made her jump, every peal of the door chimes brought her running.

She ignored her grandfather's concerned looks and his elaborate efforts to distract her. But when he finally surprised her with the invitation to the races, she weakened.

"The horse races?"

"Opening day at Saratoga."

"In with the crowd? I mean . . . no private race or anything?"

"A box right in the middle of the festivities."

Even though she still wanted to punish her grandfather and keep the vigil for her father, she couldn't refuse.

On the drive to Saratoga, Juliana wondered what had come over her grandfather. The races? When had he ever been interested in the races? And how had he decided that it was okay for her to go there when it wasn't okay for her to go to a baseball game?

Opening day was a true spectacle. Juliana delighted in the beautiful clothing and the grand flourish of the affair. She looked over the horses beside her grandfather and then went with him to the box, trailed of course by the big men in cheap suits.

Her grandfather seemed restless once they were seated. His eyes kept darting from the track to a box on his left.

Curious, Juliana looked over at the box. It was full of beautiful people in white linen with old-fashioned hats, laughing and having a great time together. She watched them in wistful envy. The race was called, and the people took their seats and faced forward. Something inside her tightened. She stared harder. It couldn't be true. But it was.

One of the laughing men in the white panama hats was her father. The father who had had such pressing obligations. The father who had promised to come to her the minute he stepped out of the mountains.

She sat very still for a moment. Her grandfather cleared his throat and fumbled with his racing program.

She took a deep breath. "You knew he was back. You knew he'd be here. You knew I was a fool to believe in him."

Her grandfather didn't answer. After a while he said, "We don't have to stay."

She rose and led the way out. Behind her she thought she heard a voice call "Jinx," but she didn't stop.

Her grandfather eyed her for days, waiting for the explosion. But there was no rage this time. There wasn't even anger. Instead, something deep inside her hardened.

"Don't worry, Da Da," she finally said. "It doesn't matter anymore."

After that there was a subtle shifting in her relationship with her grandfather. His eyes no longer dismissed or patronized when she spoke. He began to study her, gauging and measuring her constantly, weighing her actions and words as though accumulating data.

Her relationship with her grandfather had never been complicated by the obsessive need she'd felt for her parents. There had never been desperate hunger or raw chasms of intense expectation to negotiate around. Now it reached an even stabler plateau.

He planned outings with her as though he welcomed her company, as though their time together was more than just duty. He discussed itineraries with her. He gave her choices. He asked her opinion. She felt enlarged in his gaze. She felt herself crystallizing, gaining importance and the first wispy stirrings of power.

And she responded by rising to a new level with him. She joined in his manic collecting, studying the American Aesthetic movement he so fervently wanted to capture and eagerly playing pupil to his years of experience. She became more companion than granddaughter, and their relationship developed the comfortable strength of a long-held partnership.

It was as Edward Van Lyden's junior partner that she agreed to attend the dull political function. She did it out of loyalty, because he needed her. Edward's co-sponsor, Hamilton Buchanan, had announced that his granddaughter would be hostessing for him, and Edward hated to be outdone.

Juliana's reservations went well beyond the anticipation of boredom. She did not want to meet Daphne Buchanan, the child terror, again. Charlotte tried to reassure her with talk about how much people change as they grow and how silly childhood fights are when viewed from a mature perspective, but still, the memory of that incident with Daphne was as ugly and sharp as ever.

The dreaded night arrived. She dressed in a new designer evening suit and new shoes and she wore her hair pulled severely up into a knot so that she'd appear older and more formidable.

She was pleased to find that the nineteen-year-old Daphne was only five-one or so, a good four inches shorter than herself. And though Daphne's dress was beautiful and she carried herself well in it, she had the suggestion of plumpness.

"She's certainly grown into a healthy girl, hasn't she?" Edward said under his breath, and Juliana chuckled with wicked delight.

Greetings were exchanged. The two old-line gentlemen reintroduced their granddaughters.

"If it isn't little Juliana," Daphne said. But she had to look up to say it.

Juliana had the urge to return with, "If it isn't short, chunky Daphne."

The two girls weren't required to have much contact. Each was supposed to decorate her grandfather's arm and be charming to the assembled politicians when called upon.

Juliana's mind drifted above the clouds of political double-talk and cigar smoke. She took in the details of the fabled Waldorf and studied the toes of her beaded shoes and considered Daphne.

What had she expected? Certainly someone more intimidating than this. She'd thought that *The* Daphne Buchanan—the terrible Daphne of her memories, and the social Daphne who was often mentioned in the gossip columns Charlotte loved to read aloud— *The* Daphne Buchanan would be more imposing . . . more threatening than the young woman stifling a yawn across the room.

This Daphne made her curious. Who was she? What was she like? Charlotte had nagged her endlessly to get acquainted with her "social equals." Maybe that wasn't such a bad idea after all. Maybe she was ready to try herself with Daphne and crowd. To show them all that she was someone to be reckoned with. But how? A party maybe? Of course! A party would create the fun and excitement she longed for. A successful party would make her special and important to everyone.

But how could she ever persuade her grandfather? Even assuming he'd agree to her mingling with other teenagers, Great House had not had one guest invited across its threshold since the terrible ending of the Van Lyden gala. Edward had sworn that no outsiders would be allowed in to gawk and speculate or to gloat over the shameful tragedy that had stained the family name.

An hour crept by. Her mind raced.

She leaned close to her grandfather's carefully barbered white hair. "How much longer will this last?" she whispered. She was sick of the nauseating performances these men were putting on for him, flattering and cajoling him with such transparency.

He lifted her hand and patted it indulgently. "I think my granddaughter's tiring of politics," he said to the assembled group. The men all made a show of chuckling as though she were a toddler who had done something cute. "She has reminded me, however, that the evening is passing rapidly, and I've yet to pay my respects to all of your colleagues. So, if you'll excuse us . . ."

The men bowed and scraped as Edward turned to go, and Juliana wondered how much he'd contributed to each of their campaigns. A lot, she supposed. She'd overheard one man joking that Edward owned a piece of every Republican in the state of New York.

"Here we are!" Edward announced expansively as they approached yet another group. "I trust you gentlemen are enjoying a pleasant evening?"

Juliana groaned inside as the huddle parted and began fawning, chorusing an assortment of complimentary replies.

"Good . . . good." Edward beamed. "That's what I've brought us together for. But before I neglect my manners," he said, "I'd like to present my granddaughter . . ."

Juliana jerked her eyes upward from trying to read the watch on one of the men's wrists and was met with the same aging arrogant confidence and practiced pleasantries she'd been meeting all night. She nodded briefly, forced a smile, and swept her eyes mechanically over the group.

One forgettable face blurred into another. Then suddenly she was confronted with blue eyes that were not so aging or arrogant. Or forgettable. And they were fixed directly on her. And they smiled—a smile tinged with amusement. Confusion seized her and she quickly looked away to focus on other faces in the group.

Luckily she wasn't required to say anything. The men were making a ceremony of being pleased to meet her and they were taking turns reciting their names for her. None of the names registered but his.

"Matthew Rhysdale," he said simply. No phony enthusiasm. No arrogance.

She risked meeting his eyes again, and the bottom dropped out of her stomach.

Matthew Rhysdale. She stared at the toes of her shoes and repeated the name to herself while the circle of men vied for her grandfather's attention. Matthew Rhysdale. Who was he? What was he doing here? Was he somebody's son?

She was afraid to look at him again. Afraid he might catch her.

Then he began to speak. She knew his voice immediately because it was so different from the others that filled the room. It was easy. Casual. Almost country. A voice that inspired confidence.

"You can fill a barrel with excuses," he was saying. "But the answer's plain. There's no base ... nothing solid to take hold of. Honesty and common sense have been thrown out the window."

He was concentrating on the other men as he spoke, so it was safe to study him. His manner changed from casual to intense and she realized he was older than she'd first thought. Not old like somebody's father, but definitely an adult. He had blond-brown hair that fell boyishly across his forehead. A tanned face. Straight white teeth. Incredibly blue eyes. He could have manned the deck of a sailboat for a television commercial. He could have smiled down from the back of a horse in a magazine ad.

His eyes challenged the other men. "Why, where I grew up," he said, "if you sold a man a dry cow to milk, you were a liar and a cheat—not a clever negotiator."

A portly man took his cigar from his mouth and chuckled. "Perhaps our young assemblyman should stay in the sticks where he belongs and not try to mix into city politics," he said.

"City or country ... what's right is right everywhere, Congressman," Matthew Rhysdale answered. "And it appears to me that most of my legislative fellows are ignoring that."

Juliana was stunned. He was an assemblyman—someone in the government. Someone important.

The congressman jabbed his cigar toward Rhysdale like a

weapon. "What's a hick-town, wet-behind-the ears, smart-assed assemblyman doing comin' in here and giving me speeches?"

"Take it easy, Carl," someone broke in. "He's got a sponsor. He was invited, same as you."

"And he's got some good lines," another chuckled. "Maybe you should be taking notes."

"Gentlemen . . . gentlemen . . ." her grandfather said. His voice lacked the deep heartiness that usually characterized it, and Juliana knew he was tired. "We're here to learn to work as a team. This great state needs a Republican machine that functions smoothly. Every cog and gear has to mesh."

The group obediently sat up and barked agreement. Only Matthew Rhysdale held back. Juliana imagined that Rhysdale might even have the courage to disagree with her grandfather right in the middle of Edward's smoothly meshing machine.

Edward excused himself to move on to the next group, and Juliana drifted away, pretending interest in the melting ice sculpture. She didn't see Rhysdale approach. He was suddenly just there.

"Hello," he said.

"Hello."

"Your name is Juliana?"

"Yes."

With her chin high and her arm just so, she offered her hand. "And you're Mr. . . . ?" she pretended not to remember his name.

"Rhysdale . . . Matthew. Call me Matt." He took her hand and the contact sizzled through every nerve in her body.

"I didn't expect such a lovely hostess," he said.

She wanted to say thank you but didn't trust herself. Instead she turned toward the ice sculpture and said, "This poor elephant is about to lose his trunk."

"And his ears." Rhysdale laughed.

"Was there something else you wanted to say to my grandfather?" she asked, assuming that was where his interest was leading.

"No. I wanted to talk to you."

He smiled just enough to crease the corners of his mouth. It was a vaguely challenging smile. Her entire body responded. He pinned her with his blue, blue eyes and the melting elephant and the noisy gathering receded, leaving her in a still, magnified center.

"Why?"

"I liked you the minute I saw you."

"The exact minute . . . or the minute you realized how few females were in the room?"

He grinned. "If we were alone . . ."

"What?"

The grin widened and his eyes teased. "Come out with me when this is over and we'll find out."

"No . . . I can't! I mean . . . I'm sorry, but I have other plans."

His eyes narrowed slightly and the grin faded. "Then I guess we'll never know the answer, will we?"

Juliana stiffened. She wanted to be angry, but she felt like crying.

"Guess I'll run along back to the boys," Rhysdale said. "Let you get back to your grandpa."

She watched him walk away. She stood alone, surveying the gathering and wondering what Rhysdale had thought of her. Had she sounded stupid or childish? Would he talk to her again? Should she approach him this time? Should she slip him a note with her unlisted number on it?

She picked him out of the crowd and willed him back to her, but before he could react to her mental powers, Daphne Buchanan sidled up to him. Daphne raised her glass in a toast and laughed, sparkling up at him as though they were sharing a private joke. Juliana dug her nails into her palms and stalked out to the haven of the ladies' room.

She washed her hands slowly, staring into her reflection above the sink. Did he think Daphne was prettier? Did he think Daphne was more interesting? Did he like that sparkly, laughing way Daphne had looked at him? Should she hate Daphne or should she try to learn from her?

She stepped through the bathroom door into the adjoining lounge area to find Daphne seated at the mirror touching up her makeup. Smoke drifted from a cigarette resting between her fingers.

"My my," Daphne said. "Don't tell me the princess comes out of her ivory tower to pee just like the rest of us."

"What?"

Daphne smirked and put her eye pencil down on the counter. "Sit down and have a smoke. There's nothing happening out there that you're going to miss."

Juliana sat down several feet away but declined the cigarette offered from the gold case. Daphne snapped the case shut and exhaled with amused superiority.

Juliana wished she'd taken the cigarette. She wondered if she could have fooled Daphne into thinking she knew how to smoke.

"I can't believe I'm here," Daphne said. "There's only one interesting guy in the whole room. The rest make me want to gag."

Juliana held a careful silence. She knew who the interesting guy was.

"Maybe this sort of thing doesn't bore you ... I mean, what do you get to do anyway? Everyone knows how your grandfather keeps his precious little fragile princess locked away from harm. Locked away all sweet and dull and nice."

"I'm not locked away, Daphne."

"Daffy," she said turning back toward the mirror to sweep her cheeks with a brush. "People under thirty call me Daffy."

"My grandfather worries a lot about keeping me safe, but he doesn't lock me up ... Daffy."

"Right. And that's why I've never seen you at a dance or a club. That's why no one even bothers inviting you to things."

"Maybe I don't care to do things like that," Juliana flared defensively. "Maybe I'm not interested!"

Daffy laughed and stubbed out her cigarette. "Well, princess, all I can say is I'm glad I never had to play at your house again. Sounds like the isolation might have had permanent effects."

Juliana watched the door swing shut; then she picked up the ashtray that held Daffy's smoldering cigarette butt and threw it against the wall. Damn! Damn! Damn! She had managed to behave stupidly with the two people she wanted to impress.

She returned to the gathering still seething with anger and frustration and was immediately accosted by her grandfather.

"What's bothering you?" Edward demanded. "And where have you been all this time?"

She sighed. And suddenly everything fell into place. She knew how to win the party from her grandfather. "I'm upset because Daphne Buchanan doesn't like me."

"What do you mean, doesn't like you?" Edward bristled. "Was she rude? What did she say?"

"It wasn't any one thing she said. She just treats me like I'm beneath her. Like I'm not good enough for her and her friends."

Edward's face darkened. "Why, I'll take care of that! I'll speak to Hamilton and have that stopped immediately!"

Juliana shook her head. "Thanks, Da Da, but that wouldn't help. That would only give her another reason to look down on me." She sighed for her grandfather's benefit. "What I need is a chance to win her over. To change her mind. To impress her."

Edward stroked his chin in puzzled thought. "A dinner perhaps? An invitation for Daphne and Hamilton to join us at a restaurant?"

Juliana shrugged. "I'm afraid it would be hard to have much girl talk with you two right there."

Edward paused in thought again.

"But you're right ..." she encouraged him. "A little get-together would be perfect ... something where I had control. Where I could invite Daphne and a few others and really get acquainted with them." She paused. "But I know I can't have company at Great House."

"Hmmm."

Juliana held her breath.

His face brightened. "Why not Elysia? Yes! Years ago we used to have what we called country weekends ..."

"Oh, yes, yes, Da Da!"

This was far better than she'd expected.

"Guests come Friday night or Saturday morning and stay through till Sunday. You could invite a few girls and—"

"A party at Elysia! You're brilliant, Da Da! You're brilliant!"

Her grandfather cleared his throat and frowned, but his eyes glowed with satisfaction.

"Except ..." This time her sigh was real. "What if no one will come?"

He tucked her hand firmly into the crook of his arm. "We'll take care of that," he said. He led her straight to Hamilton Buchanan and Daphne, who were engaged in a conversation now with Matthew Rhysdale.

"Say, there, Edward ... have you met Piedale yet?" Hamilton said.

"Rhysdale, Grandpa," Daphne corrected.

"The young fellow's got some interesting ideas, Edward. I think we ought to capture him sometime for a spirited bit of discussion." Buchanan slapped Rhysdale's back. "Bounce him off the ropes a little, huh?"

"Only if you swear he can't whip the two of us together," Edward said.

There was polite laughter. Rhysdale was clearly flattered by the attention.

"I've been thinking, Hamilton. It's time I put some life back into that country place of mine. Thought I'd have a few friends out for a weekend ... maybe have the young people get together at the same time."

Daffy's eyebrows went up. She nudged her grandfather with her elbow, but Hamilton Buchanan was too busy agreeing with Edward to notice.

"Your granddaughter will receive a proper invitation, of course," Edward said, "but while we were here I thought I'd mention it, get your acceptance in advance, so to speak."

"Right-o, right-o, Edward. Great idea. Haven't been on a country weekend in years. Looking forward to it, aren't we, Daphne?"

"I can't wait to go home and mark it on my calendar," Daphne said.

"Of course, one party will be separate from the other," Juliana explained quickly. "I mean, everyone will be at Elysia, but—"

"But you young people don't want the old grandpas slowing down your fun," Hamilton finished with a good-natured chuckle.

"Well, I don't see—" Edward began, but Juliana cut him off before he could ruin anything.

"You don't have to worry, Grandfather. I'll take care of the details. I'll make sure our activities don't bother you and your friends."

She glanced at Matthew Rhysdale's amused blue eyes and had a sudden flash of inspiration. "And I'll make certain you gentlemen have plenty to keep you occupied," she promised. "Maybe it would be the perfect opportunity for that spirited discussion you mentioned, Mr. Buchanan. Maybe Mr. Rhysdale would agree to come bounce off the ropes at Elysia with you that weekend?"

"Splendid idea," Hamilton declared.

Rhysdale's expression was surprised and pleased. "I'd be delighted," he said.

"It's all settled, then," she said, immensely proud of herself.

But when she met Daphne Buchanan's eyes she knew that only the first round had been won.

20

Ellis

Ellis opened his eyes. White-and-gold walls. Heavy velvet at the windows. Sunlight around the edges of the velvet. His head throbbed. His mouth tasted terrible. He turned in the bed and realized he wasn't alone. Immediately he recoiled.

Memories of the night before came in a rush. The party. The wine. The woman's long black hair. God . . . what was her name? Countess something. He couldn't remember.

He slipped from the tangled sheets as quietly as possible and gathered his scattered clothes. The bathroom he locked himself into was ornate and mirrored and filled with scented soaps and bath oils and a mysterious array of cosmetics. A woman's room. But not the right woman. It was never the right woman.

The face that stared back at him from the mirror made him wince. It looked closer to a hundred than to twenty-one. He did enough to feel human, using his finger to brush his teeth and his hands to wash his face. The shower was tempting but he wanted to escape as quickly as possible.

How had he let himself do this? He'd sworn after the last time that it would never happen again.

"So you are dressed and you leave," she said when he stepped out of the bathroom.

She was sitting up in bed with the sheets gathered to her slender shoulders, lighting a cigarette.

"Yes. I need to be off."

"No matter," she said. "But if you like café before you go, I can ring for it."

"No. Thank you."

She smiled and drew deeply on her cigarette.

Ellis was immediately stricken with guilt. "I suppose I do have time for a coffee."

She used an old-fashioned bellpull and a maid bearing a tray appeared and soundlessly disappeared.

Ellis sipped his espresso. On the table beside him were framed photographs. A wedding portrait. A college graduation. A young woman on the ski slopes. He looked for the countess in the pictures, but saw no likeness.

"My children," she said.

He nodded.

"Do not be so . . ." She struggled for an English word and he realized that he hadn't let her know he spoke Italian. "Do not be uncomfortable," she finished.

He wondered if he should switch to Italian now or if she would be angry that he hadn't told her sooner.

"I really do have to go," he said.

"Do you want a taxi?"

"No. I like to walk."

She put out her cigarette. Amusement played across her classic features. "If you wish for company, you may come back," she said. "The evening was . . ." She smiled. "Bellissima. Era bellissima."

"Well . . ." Ellis put down his coffee and stood. He crossed to the bed and leaned down to kiss her cheek.

Her laugh was graceful and musical. "You will go far," she said. "But you must learn to remember a woman's name. In passion a woman wants to hear her own name called. I am Gabriella . . . not Yvonne."

Ellis left through the courtyard feeling guilty and sick at heart. No, she wasn't Yvonne. Why had he ever let himself believe she could be?

The narrow streets and splashing fountains were usually a balm to his pain. But not today. Today he couldn't ignore the morning clatter of waiters setting out chairs at sidewalk cafés or the swarm of German tourists at the Spanish Steps or the takeout litter from the new McDonald's. Everything added to his anger. He was angry at the noise and clutter, and he was angry at himself.

He'd lived in Italy for three years. And he'd lived through hell. Nightmares and depression so deep that his own death had seemed the only relief for a time. Yvonne haunted him. Frank haunted him. He was tortured by sudden flashes of memory. Visions of Yvonne's sightless eyes. Visions of her ruined head. The sharp-sweet scent of her blood. Frank's waxen face disappearing beneath mounds of dirt.

Their blood was forever on his hands. The stains were indelible. But he'd conquered the depression and he'd learned to cover the stains with layer upon layer of the present. Parties. Expensive clothes. The university. A kaleidoscope of revolving acquaintances. Thick muffling layers that hid and protected him.

The survival lessons he'd had to learn had been every bit as hard and cruel as those lessons in the mountains, but he was a master now. He was strong and he knew the rules.

He zigzagged through the heart of the old city, taking the long way to allow himself more time. The streets of Rome were his sanctuary, charming him with idiosyncrasies and nurturing him with the anonymity he'd found there. His need for the scent of pine or the sharp sting of high country wind or the calm, ordered beauty of that other world had faded from a constant ache to an occasional yearning, and when he heard the song of the mountains it was faint and far away—muffled by his protective layers. This was home now. This timeless enigmatic passionate city was his home.

He paused at a coffee bar for another espresso, then turned down Vicolo dei Venti toward Piazza Farnese. As he crossed the piazza he paused by habit at one of the two fountains that marked it. They'd been built by the Farnese family in the 1620's—pleasant but comparatively undistinguished fountains with ornate central designs crowned by the Farneses' symbolic flower. But the water flowing from those flowers trickled down into great granite basins looted from the ruins of Caracalla, and it was this remnant of Caracalla that drew him.

Ellis had been to the site of the ancient Roman bath many times. It lay just beyond the Forum and the Circus Maximus, a pleasant walk from his home near the Farnese Palace. Caracalla's massive remains were fascinating. To think that such a place had existed nearly two thousand years ago—twenty-five acres of gymnasiums and therapeutic baths and saunas and gardens and libraries used regularly by the citizens of ancient Rome.

Now these stolen basins from Caracalla soothed him. Here were human-crafted objects from nearly two thousand years ago. Solid proof that man had been building and destroying and scavenging and rebuilding for aeons, yet the earth and her nonhuman inhabitants still survived. Life was a chain that men could not break.

Each time Ellis paused to consider the timeless granite, he was filled with both awe and hope. Maybe the earth would endure. Maybe there was a future for the planet. Maybe there was a future for him.

The sun hung in a cloudless crystalline sky, casting shadows down the cobbled streets between the ocher-hued buildings. He didn't want to go inside. He wanted to sit down by the fountains and watch the water. His mother would be waiting for him in their sprawling ten-room apartment. She was always waiting.

He climbed the stairs of the spacious old building past the second-story landing with its narrow window and view that would have included Pompey's Theater if that stone structure were not buried beneath the Rightetti Palace and the streets and piazzas of present-day Rome. There were times when the history of the place caught his imagination and he thought he might want nothing more out of life than to dig through the skeletons and hidden closets of the great city's past. He pictured himself covered in centuries of dirt, breaking through into the fabled lost room where Caesar's bones lay at the base of Pompey's statue.

Legend taught that the room had been walled up on the day Caesar fell bleeding from his wounds, saying "You too Brutus?", and Ellis was captivated by the possibilities. No doubt that room was still out there, beneath the junk shops and weekday markets of the Biscione area or the modern Satiri Theater or the forlorn chapel on the corner of Grottapinta ... waiting. Waiting to be discovered.

But when he was in a more practical frame of mind he realized that he had no true calling to archaeology. The mystery of the past would become just another layer to hide beneath. And eventually he would suffocate.

He opened the door to the apartment and was immediately greeted by his mother's voice. "My God! Is that you?" She descended on him from the living room with a flurry of hugs and nervous hand gestures. Her breath was sour with alcohol. "I've been so worried, Ellis! I canceled my afternoon hair appointment and I've called the police twice for news of accidents."

"I'm sorry." He rubbed his forehead wearily. "The party was boring. I drank too much and I ended up at a friend's."

"Why didn't you call? I would have come for you. I would have—"

"I didn't want to wake you at four in the morning," Ellis said, shrugging out of his jacket to avoid meeting her eyes.

She blinked and dabbed at her red-tinged eyes with a delicate embroidered handkerchief, though there were no visible tears and the redness was more or less permanent. "Who is this friend? Is it someone I know? Is it someone who can be trusted?"

"I'm a big boy, Mom."

Her face collapsed and real tears suddenly burst forth. "I knew it!" She made no move to use the handkerchief now that it was needed. Instead she let the tears flow unchecked and twisted the handkerchief helplessly around her fingers. "I knew they'd be after you soon. Trying to trap you and destroy everything we've built."

"What are you talking about?" Ellis studied her carefully, estimating how much she'd had to drink.

"What do you think I'm talking about!" Her voice had a hysterical edge. "I'm talking about girls who want to marry a Van Lyden. I'm talking about sex!"

"Calm down . . . please." Ellis took her arm and gently steered her into the living room. "Let's get you into a chair and get you some coffee. Have you had any food today?"

She ripped her arm from his grasp and whirled to face him. "Don't patronize me. I was worried sick about you and I was lonely . . . so I had a little something to steady my nerves. But that does not mean I'm drunk." She made a show of raising her chin and settling herself primly into a chair. "You don't understand the seriousness of this, Ellis. You're coming to an age when you're prime marriage material and every scheming little opportunist in the world is going to be waving her body at you."

Ellis couldn't help but smile.

"It's not funny!"

"I'm sorry . . . I just had this vision of waving bodies . . ."

She glared at him.

He crossed the room and threw open a window. "I've told you before, Mom . . . I don't like girls my age. They are silly and insubstantial. So I doubt that I'm susceptible to scheming little opportunists."

"Then who were you with?" she demanded.

"It wasn't a girl," he said, which was true, because Gabriella was most definitely a woman.

"It wasn't a girl?"

He nodded.

"You always tell me that. Anytime you've been out. It's always this boy or that. Or it's someone nameless. But it's never a girl. Are you . . . ?"

He laughed. "No, Mom. That's one worry you can put completely to rest." But he wondered if a part of her hadn't hoped he was gay. That grasping jealous part of her that wanted to bind him to her forever might have liked the idea that there would never be another woman in his life.

Grace sighed and sank back into her chair.

"I'll order us lunch," he said. "Then I'll take you out for gelato. And we could go to Saint Augustine's. That's where the Raphael fresco and the Caravaggio are that I told you about last week."

"No. No." She waved her hand. "I'm too tired. Fix me a drink and we can play cards. We'll take a picnic and go out all day tomorrow."

"I have plans tomorrow," he said, knowing she would react but determined not to feel guilty.

"Plans?"

"Yes. I'm going to Ostia Lido with friends."

"And am I invited to the beach with these friends, or are you leaving me to spend Sunday alone?"

He drew in a deep breath and closed his eyes. He knew the expression on her face by heart. The hurt, pouting, accusing, needy look.

"Why don't you make plans too?" he asked carefully. "You hardly see your friends anymore."

"I don't see my friends because I think it's important to spend time with my son." Her bottom lip quivered. "Because all those years of your life were stolen from me and now I want to make up for it."

"All right. All right. I won't go to the beach. I'll stay in town and we'll do whatever you'd like."

"No." Her tone was martyred now. "On second thought, I really shouldn't squander a whole day like that. I have so much to do. And I don't expect you to help. Males are never good at this sort of thing."

Reluctantly he took the bait and asked, "What sort of thing?"

"Well, I was saving it for a surprise . . ." Her face transformed from wounded to glowing and she smiled—the vulnerable expectant smile of a giver presenting a gift. "We're moving to Paris next month."

He was stunned.

"Aren't you thrilled? You said you wanted to see Paris. You said you wanted to travel."

"That was two years ago, Mother."

The corners of her mouth melted downward. "You aren't pleased?"

He lifted his hands helplessly and let them fall to his sides. "I've made friends here now. I like my classes. I'm fluent in Italian. I don't want to leave."

"You don't want to come with me?"

"I didn't say that." Again he gestured with his hands. Expressing any kind of emotion to her was usually unwise, so he had to be careful. "I'm finally at home here. I like Italy. The more I explore it, the more I find that I haven't seen before. I'd like to stay longer."

"Your new friends are more important than your mother."

"Stop it!" he shouted. It was the first time he'd ever raised his voice to her and he startled himself with the outburst.

Her eyes widened and her hand flew to her mouth. "Nothing I do is right," she cried. "I try so hard to be a good mother, but nothing I do can erase everything we've lost. You don't love me anymore. That monster father of yours destroyed all the love you ever felt for me."

"That's not true."

She bolted from her chair. "Yes! Yes, it is. There's nothing left for me in the world if you don't love me. Your father robbed me of everything. I ought to kill myself like Yvonne!"

All the safe cushioning layers were ripped from him and he was kneeling in blood again, staring down at those dead eyes. Yvonne . . . Yvonne . . . Yvonne. He buried his face in his hands. He had murdered her just as surely as he had murdered his father. He had killed her by loving her too much.

Was he now killing his mother by not loving her enough?

"Mom . . ." He pulled her into a clumsy hug and held her until her sobs faded. "I love you. That's never changed and it never will."

"You'll come to Paris?" she asked in a tiny hopeful voice.

"I'll come to Paris," he said.

The two and a half years in Paris were a replay of Rome. He worked at learning the language and becoming familiar with the city. He worked at his studies. He roamed the museums. He met people and fell into a social round of parties and activities. He cushioned himself from the past.

Through it all his mother drank and pleaded and berated and smothered, her anxiety increasing in direct proportion to his independence. She drank so much that it was common for Ellis to help her to bed when he got home.

Though he detested dishonesty, he found himself leading a secretive and often dishonest life—evading her questions, obscuring his activities, and above all concealing his contacts with the opposite sex. Parisian girls were no more interesting to him than Italian girls had been, so it was still true when he told her that he hadn't been with a girl. But women ... Paris was full of women. They teased and flirted. They sent champagne and passed perfumed notes in restaurants. And every so often one reminded him of Yvonne.

The horrible scenes with his mother escalated. He decided to move to his own place, but she again threatened to kill herself. Then a calm settled. She began talking about Manhattan. How homesick she was for Manhattan. How important it was for him to live in Manhattan and spend time with his relatives.

When she announced her plans to move back to New York, he came close, very close, to refusing. But in the end he told his friends and the city good-bye and packed.

21

Juliana

Juliana could barely sit still. The hum of the limousine's tires against the road matched the vibration in her stomach. It was Thursday afternoon. She and Edward and Charlotte were on their way to Elysia. The first guests were arriving tomorrow.

The party had consumed her in the weeks since Edward had agreed to it, expanding in her imagination, becoming the answer to everything. It was the guiding star to her future, shining just ahead as the ultimate promise.

The guest list had enlarged. The vision magnified. From the tiny seed of an intimate country weekend the plan had blossomed into an extravaganza. And it had already changed her life. Handling the arrangements had made her feel more competent and pleased with herself than ever before, and overseeing the myriad details had won her the right to go out regularly without her grandfather. The right to pick up the phone and call for the car and the security men on her own. All with Edward's permission, of course, but still ... sliding into that seat alone and pressing the intercom button and telling the driver where to take her was a heady sensation.

"I'm not looking forward to this," Edward said abruptly.

Neither Juliana nor Charlotte answered. They no longer had to waste energy on persuasion or argument. The party had a life of its own now.

"And I still don't see why we couldn't have made it a birthday party," Edward grumbled. "You used to beg for birthday parties."

"You promised you wouldn't mention my birthday," Juliana reminded him.

"Yes ... yes ... yes. But I still say seventeen is nothing to be ashamed of."

"It's not just that I'm younger than everyone else, Da Da. Didn't you understand what we were saying?"

"A birthday party is not considered a very sophisticated event by young people," Charlotte put in carefully.

"And remember you were the one who came up with the country-weekend idea. Why change it because it happened to fall so close to my birthday? A country-weekend party sounds beautiful."

Edward frowned but settled back in defeat.

Juliana flipped open her leatherbound notebook and scanned the guest list. The Buchanan, Chandler, Wildenburg, and Gravesend girls; the Ashton, Snelling, and Lorillard-Harris boys. That was the core group. No one else who was coming really mattered. At least that was what Charlotte said, and Charlotte was the expert on the New York social scene.

The names jumped out at her. Daphne Buchanan. Whitney Chandler. Peter Ashton IV. And she had a moment of pure panic. How could she possibly win them over? Especially after her grandfather had had to pull favors to ensure their presence? To calm herself she turned to the pages on Matthew Rhysdale.

"What is all that?" demanded Edward.

Juliana looked up from her notebook. "Things to remember for the party. Guests' preferences . . . that sort of thing."

Edward raised his eyebrows and set his lower lip in a thoughtful expression. "I must say, I never thought you'd take your hostessing duties so seriously."

"Oh, she's a natural," Charlotte assured him. "She was born to be a grand hostess."

Juliana smiled her most innocent smile. It was true. She was being a conscientious hostess and she did have guest preferences recorded. Charlotte had made discreet calls to household maids so that each guest's room could be stocked with personalized toilet articles and favorite perfumes, and she had all that in her book. And she had reminders and lists too. But what she was studying now were her notes on Matthew Rhysdale.

"Well," Edward said gruffly, "don't let me stop you. Keep it up."

She went back to her book. She'd used a clipping service her grandfather employed. They'd furnished her with three years' worth of newspaper articles mentioning Rhysdale. From those she'd gleaned the precious kernels of information that she kept in her book.

Matthew Rhysdale had been born in Willet, New York. He'd worked his way through a small upstate college by selling aluminum siding door to door. (She still wasn't sure what aluminum siding was.) His boyhood idol had been Davy Crockett. He liked western art. He had a small gun collection and a passion for guns. His goal was to be a United States senator.

Following the miniature biography were the notes on her research. She had facts on Remington and Russell taken from her grandfather's art books. Nothing too flashy, but enough that she could discuss western art intelligently with him. And she had page after page about guns.

Her intention had been to do a little quick reading and then amaze Matthew Rhysdale with a shared interest in guns. But it hadn't been as easy as she'd expected. In order to produce an adequate passion she realized she'd have to be involved with the celebrated gun collection at Elysia. She'd have to be able to show Rhysdale the collection knowledgeably, identifying and talking about individual weapons. Toward this end she'd been forced to put in hours of reading and memorization.

She skimmed over the pedigrees of the more interesting pieces in Elysia's collection, imagining herself and Matthew Rhysdale alone in the gun room. In less than two days it would happen. If not in the gun room, then somewhere else. She was determined to be alone with him.

That night Juliana could not sleep. Everything was ready for the weekend. Even the redwood hot tubs and the miniature-golf setup and the antique bubbling jukebox were in place. She'd ordered them in frenzy and she would have kept on ordering if Edward hadn't halted her credit line. She wanted a guarantee that the party would work. It had to be fabulous enough to make Daphne and Whitney and the rest like her. It had to be spectacular enough to dazzle Matthew Rhysdale.

She lay awake worrying about whether she'd done enough, or whether she'd forgotten something. Whether Matthew Rhysdale would still want to be alone with her. Whether her grandfather would keep his friends separate as he'd promised. And on and on in a repetitive cycle that always ended with worrying about not getting enough sleep and looking terrible the next day.

It was nearly noon before Charlotte awakened her.

"Why'd you let me sleep so late?"

"I thought you needed it."

"Damn!" Juliana scrubbed at her eyes and threw back the sheets.

"There's something you should know," Charlotte said, and her expression brought Juliana instantly alert. "Your grandfather received a cable from your Aunt Grace. She and Ellis will be arriving today or tomorrow."

"No ..." The word was barely a whisper. "No! No. He's not coming here. I won't let him come here!"

"You have no choice. It seems Grace planned their arrival to coincide with the party."

"That bitch!"

She wrapped her arms around her stomach and bent forward against the pain. Ellis in her house again. Ellis at her party. Ellis with his spooky eyes and his bloody hands and ...

It hit her in waves.

Ellis and her cat. Ellis slashing her with his knife. The stitches. The ugly scar on her ribs.

Ellis and her father. The afternoon rides. Aubrey's fawning and beaming and slapping Ellis on the back.

Ellis and her mother. Oh God! Ellis and his spooky eyes and his hands touching her mother and walking with her mother in the park and laughing with her mother on the dance floor and coming out of her mother's room like he belonged there ... and kneeling over her mother ... and the blood ... the dark red blood ... red on white ... red on his hands ... his bloody hands ...

"Stop it! Stop it!" Charlotte's fingers bit into her shoulders and Charlotte's voice cut through to her. "Are you going to let him destroy this for you, Juliana?" The fingers squeezed harder. "Think! You'll never be more than a pitiable child if you don't learn to think!"

Involuntary sobs ran through Juliana, but she was listening. She was hearing Charlotte.

"Think about it. Think about how much is at stake here. If this doesn't work, you may not get another chance with the right people. Think about how much grief he's already caused you. Are you going to let him ruin this too?"

The sobs lessened. Charlotte was right. She had to think. Remember how much he'd stolen from her. How much he'd won. If she let herself go to pieces and let the party fail, she would be handing him yet another victory. She would be allowing him to kill something else in her life.

She got out of her plush bed and stood up very tall and straight.

"Well, then, Juliana ... what have you decided?"

She whirled back toward Charlotte, unleashing the fierceness inside her. "Nothing is going to ruin this! Nothing!"

Charlotte expelled a satisfied breath. "That's my girl," she said proudly. "That's the Juliana Van Lyden I like to see!"

The arrivals began after lunch. Her grandfather's friends came first. Juliana greeted them and had the butler shuffle them quickly into Edward's care. She waited by a window overlooking the drive and tore at her cuticles with her teeth.

Denham DuPree was the first of her guests to arrive. She watched him get out of the car and stare nervously at the house before following his driver and suitcase to the door. He appeared to be as frightened as she was. She raced down the hall just as the butler was taking the suitcase.

Denny DuPree wore ill-fitting glasses, looked fourteen instead of eighteen, and acted twelve. It was impossible to be intimidated by him. Meeting him calmed her.

The next arrivals were a bit more difficult. As soon as she saw the burgundy limousine winding toward the house, she hurried to the door. J. Allen Hollingshead, who was called Jay, and Leland Snelling, who was called Lee, burst through the door singing a bawdy college song. Each had an arm around the other's shoulders and at the sight of Juliana they stopped the noise and bowed in unison.

"Your wish is our command," the taller one said, only Juliana couldn't remember whether he was Jay or Lee.

"And Van Lyden wishes are very commanding," said the other, whereupon both of them broke into a fit of private-joke giggling.

On the way upstairs to their rooms one of them offered Juliana a drink from a silver flask with a Harvard insignia and the other offered her a pill of some kind.

Before Juliana could finish with them, the front-door chimes sounded again. This time it was Kathryn Englehard, Caroline Brissot, and Alexandra Wildenburg. Missy, Cee Cee, and Willy. They stood unsmiling beside a mountain of Italian designer luggage.

"Hello," Juliana called to them as she entered the hall. "How was your trip?"

The three exchanged glances but didn't answer.

"I've brought my maid," Missy Englehard said. "I want her in a room near mine."

"Of course." Juliana motioned to the butler. "Kleiman will work it out."

Kleiman nodded and started up the stairs. The three girls and the maid followed the butler, dismissing Juliana as though she were a servant.

Juliana watched them ascend the stairs with a welcoming smile painted on her face—just in case any of them turned around. Then she turned to Charlotte and swallowed hard against the lump in her throat. "They all hate me, don't they?"

"What difference does that make?" Charlotte said sternly. "This is not about friendship, Juliana. Don't think for a minute that it is."

Juliana stared at her.

"Friendship is a rare treasure for a girl in your position. It's not found easily. And it's seldom found among others of your kind. Your mother learned that hard lesson"—she sighed— "among many others."

Still Juliana stared. She understood what Charlotte was saying but she didn't want it to be true.

Just as dinner was announced, Olivia Gravesend, who meekly introduced herself as Gabby, descended onto the back lawn in a private helicopter. Her arrival was easy. She smiled shyly, thanked Juliana for inviting her, and then trooped dutifully in to join the assemblage for dinner.

The guests attacked the enormous buffet to the tunes of a sixties rock band. Charlotte's suggestion had been a good one. The lighthearted buffet was a much better way to begin than a formal sit-down meal would have been. Lee and Jay's juvenile antics with the food stirred the three ice princesses into laughter, and Edward and his friends stayed as far away from the music as possible, thereby keeping their comments and disapproving looks at a safe distance.

Juliana couldn't relax or eat. The most frightening opponents still remained to be faced. Whitney Chandler, Daffy Buchanan, Perry Lorillard-Harris, and Peter Ashton IV. As young adults they'd become the social equivalent of the Mafia, controlling everything and everyone. And being forced to attend by their grandfathers had undoubtedly made them furious.

Juliana tried to formulate different strategies, but she felt powerless against them. What did she know about the dynamics of this social system? She had spent nearly all of her seventeen years behind Van Lyden walls and she'd never learned how to function in society.

Dessert was being cleared when Charlotte came to whisper, "They're here."

Juliana entered the front hall to find a uniformed driver standing at military attention. She glanced questioningly at Kleiman, and the butler gave her the tiniest shrug.

"Are you Miss Van Lyden?" the driver asked stiffly.

"Yes."

He held out four engraved calling cards.

"Announcing Miss Whitney Alton Chandler, Miss Daphne Lowe Buchanan, Mr. William Perry Lorillard-Harris, and Mr. Peter Ashton IV."

Juliana stood transfixed. She and Charlotte and the butler were the only audience, yet the driver's performance was worthy of a royal-ball entrance. The absurdity of it gave her courage. "Fine," she said. "So where are they?"

The driver frowned and turned toward the door. He waited until Kleiman had opened it for him, then marched out to a stretch silver limousine and grandly assisted the emergence of the four young people.

Juliana's heart sank. They were dressed in evening wear, long shimmering gowns and dinner jackets, and they stepped into the house as if entering a slum.

Daffy's eyes swept over Juliana's casual dress. "Sorry we couldn't dress down for the occasion," she said.

"We had to go out and have some fun before we came," added Whit with sarcastic sweetness, "and we simply didn't have time to change."

"She doesn't mind, do you?" asked Four as he took Juliana's hand and made a sarcastic bow over it.

"No," Daffy sighed. "I suppose she'll take us any way she can get us." She brushed past Juliana and started up the stairs. The others followed. "Well?" she said, pausing to turn and frown down at Kleiman. "I assume our rooms are in this direction, but I did expect some assistance."

Juliana kept her poise while she watched Kleiman hurry after them. The light in the empty hallway was suddenly too bright and she could feel Charlotte's probing gaze.

The chimes sounded. Mechanically she pulled open the door.

"Surprise!"

It was her Aunt Grace.

"We caught an earlier flight, so we just hired an airport car and . . . well, here we are."

Juliana was too stunned to speak.

Grace stepped past her into the hall and Juliana saw that Ellis was out on the drive lifting luggage out of the trunk with the car's overweight driver.

"I'm so glad we could make it for the party," Grace said. "It's such a nice way to come home."

Ellis backed in the door with an armload of luggage. He wasn't the gawky boy Juliana remembered. He wasn't a boy at all. He was a tall, broad-shouldered man with a stylish haircut and fashionable European clothes. The reality of him, the spooky demonic wildness, the treacherous menace of him, was completely hidden. But she knew it was there. She knew who he was beneath the polished facade.

"Now, dear . . ." Grace twisted her hands together and the familiarity of the gesture brought a little catch to Juliana's chest. Maybe she didn't really hate her Aunt Grace. Maybe nothing was Grace's fault. "I hope you don't think we're barging in. We just . . . well, we were planning the trip anyway, and when we heard about your party, we said, why not go early and join the fun?"

"Why not?" Juliana said flatly.

"Ellis . . . Ellis," Grace insisted. "Stop fussing with those bags and say hello to your cousin."

Ellis straightened to face her.

What was he, twenty-two or twenty-three? Not that much older than some of the boys she'd invited. Yet he seemed so . . . so absolutely adult. So separate and inaccessible.

He smiled tentatively. Was he afraid of her? Afraid she'd leap on him again and claw his eyes out? His uncertainty filled her with satisfaction and she returned his smile with her most evil upturn of lips and narrowing of eyes.

"Happy birthday, Jinx," he said. "Last week was your birthday, wasn't it?"

The greeting infuriated her. She was certain he was gloating over her age. Pointing out what a child she still was to him.

"You should have just sent a card," she said. "You came a long way to crash a party."

Grace laughed nervously. "What a thing to say! But then, you always did have an odd sense of humor."

"Just remember," Juliana said, zeroing in on Ellis and ignoring her aunt, "this is my party and you weren't invited, so keep out of the way."

The butler returned then and Grace pounced on him. "We'll want to see Mr. Edward right away, Kleiman."

"Yes, ma'am."

Juliana returned to the hunt room to find that her guests had disappeared and the band was packing up their instruments. "Who said you could stop playing?" she asked them.

"That lady with the kinda reddish hair . . . she told us to quit," said the leader. "We can keep playin' if you want."

"No. Go ahead. Everyone's gone now anyway."

She searched the downstairs. The boys were all involved in a raucous game of pool. She peeked in the door but went on without speaking. She went upstairs. There was a bar of light beneath the door to her grandfather's suite. She stared down at it. Imagining the three of them inside. Imagining Ellis twisting the truth of himself around ... trying to fool her grandfather with his smooth exterior ... trying to take over what was hers again.

Restlessly she wandered the shadowy hallways. Her feet made no sound on the thick carpets. Her passing did not register at all. She was hollow. She was dust. She was invisible. Maybe she was a ghost. Maybe she was a nightmare that someone else was trying to wake from.

Closed doors loomed to mock her as she passed. She knew the guest arrangements by heart, knew who was hidden from her behind each door. If only just one would open to her.

When she reached Daffy Buchanan's room she heard noises. She edged closer. A chorus of laughter sounded from within. Daffy had company. She leaned her forehead against the smooth wood, imagining the warmth and shared confidences that were closed to her by that door.

"Juliana? What's wrong? Are you ill?"

It was Charlotte, descending on her from out of nowhere like some kind of spying vulture.

"Leave me alone!" Juliana hissed, whirling to face the woman. "This is my party and my house and my life and that was my band you told to quit playing."

"Now, now," Charlotte soothed.

"Don't you treat me like that. Don't you ever treat me like that. You're not my mother and you're not my friend. You're just another servant."

Charlotte's face whitened and she drew back as though she'd been struck. Juliana turned and ran. She wanted to vanish. She wanted the pale haven of her mother's rooms at Great House. She wanted to die and be reborn as someone who was beautiful and heroic and beloved. She slammed the heavy door to her room and threw the bolt. Nothing in the whole world was right. Nothing would ever be right.

Lovingly she picked up the small Ott and Brewer pitcher that she'd placed on her dressing table when they arrived Thursday. She turned it over and studied the coveted "Belleek" imprint with its accompanying crown and sword marks. It was a treasure for her grandfather's collection—a surprise she'd bought to thank him for the party. But where was he now when she needed him? Where was he now when she wanted to give him his surprise?

With Ellis.

She dropped the pitcher into an empty wastebasket. There was an almost musical tone to the shattering of the delicate gilded porcelain. The sound went through her in a satisfying wave.

She turned out all but her small bedside lamp and crawled into her huge draperied bed. To hell with them all. She would show them. She would show everyone.

She burrowed into the softness of her bed and hugged her pillow. Everything would be better tomorrow. She would forget today, wipe it away like it never happened. Tomorrow would be bright and new. Tomorrow would be hers. And tomorrow would bring Matthew Rhysdale.

22

Next morning's poolside breakfast was a disaster. There was no way to save it. Juliana went upstairs afterward and threw up what little she'd eaten.

Her grandfather and his friends were being obnoxious and intrusive. Daffy Buchanan was telling everyone how she couldn't wait to go back to Manhattan. And Matthew Rhysdale hadn't arrived yet. The only plus of the morning was the absence of Ellis. Grace had joined them for breakfast, but Ellis went riding very early and spared Juliana the embarrassment of having to introduce her infamous cousin to her guests.

When she came back downstairs Juliana found Charlotte trying to organize a shuffleboard game amidst a chorus of groans and one of her grandfather's friends shouting about teenage morality to poor Gabby Gravesend and Denny DuPree. She stood at the edge of the terrace for several moments, a spectator watching a sinking ship.

Finally, out of desperation, she yelled, "Come on, everybody, let's get out of here!"

The group responded immediately, knocking over chairs and leaping the terrace's low stone wall to follow her.

"Where are you going?" her grandfather and his friends demanded in unison.

Their voices faded as she raced down the sloping back lawn toward the woods. She led her whooping guests straight into the cover of the trees and didn't stop until she reached a wildflower meadow that had been a favorite of hers as a child. Once there, she sank to the grass. The others dropped around her, laughing and breathless.

The sun was high enough to heat the meadow, and a hypnotic quiet settled over them as their breathing returned to normal.

The droning of the bees and the scent of ripe grasses and flowers mingled with the warm air. The poised and perfect Whitney Chandler pulled off her blouse and lay back, eyes closed, face tilted toward the sun. All the other girls except timid Gabby Gravesend followed suit.

Juliana willed herself not to show her surprise. No one was wearing a bra, and bare breasts poked up in the grass around her like exotic plant life. She glanced around at the boys. Perry and Four ignored the show and opened their own shirts. Jay and Lee eyed the display hungrily. Denny was staring at an industrious dung beetle.

Should she follow suit? Gabby hadn't, and that seemed to be all right with everyone. She fingered the top button on her cotton shirt and glanced at Jay and Lee again. Did she want boys to look at her like that? Did she want everyone to see that she had a bra on?

Tree branches rustled at the edge of the clearing. It was a horse and rider. Ellis.

He appeared startled at discovering them in the meadow.

The girls all sat up.

"Sorry," he said, and started back into the trees.

"Who is that?" Whitney demanded. "Call him over here."

Willy and Missy and Cee Cee jerked their tops back on as Juliana reluctantly summoned her cousin.

Ellis had on faded jeans and scuffed boots and a shirt with the sleeves rolled up. He was astride her father's favorite stallion. The animal glistened with a fine sheen, and the smell of sweat and leather and horse mingled with the other scents of the meadow.

Daffy turned on her side and casually propped herself on her elbow. "Who the fuck are you?" she asked.

"I'm Ellis . . . Jinx's cousin. Sorry about the disturbance . . . I didn't realize anyone was here." His voice was serious and polite but the crinkling at the corner of his eyes gave him away. He was laughing at them.

Whit was staring at Ellis with an intensity that would have unsettled most men. She tossed her hair, arched her back, and lazily raised an arm to shade her eyes from the sun. "Thank God you're only the cousin," she said. "For a minute I thought you were Heathcliff."

Ellis laughed. He didn't seem to be bothered by her naked breasts. It was so easy for Juliana to see that he was enjoying himself at their expense.

"What a glorious horse," Whit said. Her scrutiny of Ellis had not lessened and her voice was full of suggestive teasing.

"That's my father's horse," Juliana said. "Nobody is supposed to ride him but my father. Nobody."

"That's why he's picked up so many bad habits," Ellis said. "A horse has to be ridden or it forgets its manners."

The hatred wound and curled inside her, sticky tendrils finding new things to cling to. She hated the way he looked at her, like he had the right to feel close to her. And she hated him for ruining the closeness she'd felt with the group just moments before, and she hated him for the stupid way Whitney Chandler was suddenly behaving.

"You're right," Whitney said. "Horses have to be ridden to stay in shape." She rose and walked toward Ellis, holding the collar of her white blouse in her fingertips. It trailed after her in the grass like a bridal train.

The stallion snorted and rolled his eyes at her approach, but Ellis reined him in firmly.

"I'm too hot to walk all the way back to the house," Whit said. "Why don't you give me a ride?"

"Sorry." Ellis' grin was knowing and easy. The crescents that etched the corners of his mouth deepened. "He doesn't ride double. I wouldn't want to hurt you."

Silence fell as Ellis rode away. Everyone stared after him and then turned to fix on Whitney. She was watching the far-off spot in the trees where horse and rider had disappeared from view.

"Wow," Willy breathed. It was joined by a sigh from Cee Cee.

"Why didn't you just pull him off the horse and fuck him?" Four said.

Whitney sighed theatrically and shrugged into her blouse. "My dear . . . I was afraid if I pulled him from his horse that you would grab his cock before I could."

"How selfish and unkind of you to think that." Four clicked his tongue in a scold. "We're all such old friends here . . ." He paused and suddenly looked at Juliana.

Everyone looked at Juliana. She stood completely still, willing her shock and confusion into hiding.

"Don't worry about her." Daphne Buchanan moved closer to Juliana and touched her hair. "This is what she wants us for. Isn't it, sweetie? Being a good little girl is so dull, and the naughty people are so exciting."

Jay and Lee launched a grass fight then, saving her from further scrutiny. Did her inexperience show? Could they tell how startled she was by their language and attitudes?

"I'm ready for a swim," Four announced.

"The pool's—" Juliana began.

"Oh, God, not the pool," Daffy said. "Isn't there a pond or something out here where we can stay by ourselves?"

"Where we can swim *au naturel?*" Whit added.

"Well, yes . . . there's a spring-fed pond," Juliana said. "But it's an awful long walk."

"Then let's ride." Perry casually buttoned his shirt and tucked it in. "Let's go to the house for our boots and ride out to the pond."

There was unanimous agreement, but when they arrived back at the house the plan disintegrated. Ellis had finished riding and was doing laps in the pool, so Whitney and Four immediately raced for their suits. Jay disappeared in the direction of the game room, with Gabby following close behind him.

"That politician came while you were off gallivanting," Charlotte whispered. "I gave him your apologies and sent him to your grandfather. He hasn't even been taken to his room yet."

Juliana found Matthew Rhysdale in the formal garden, already arguing politics with Edward's contentious group. She tried to make her approach casual.

"There you are!" Edward said. "That was a rude bit of nonsense you pulled."

Juliana felt herself reddening, but held tightly to her poise. "Mr. Rhysdale," she said. "I'm so glad you could join us."

Matthew Rhysdale stood. He was wearing beltless slacks and a knit pullover shirt with a tiny animal embroidered on the chest. The clothes were wrong, but that didn't matter. His dark blond hair and his white teeth glistened in the sunlight. "The pleasure's all mine," he said.

He smiled, and the bottom fell out of her chest.

She cleared her throat and turned to include everyone. "Lunch will be served shortly in the hunt room, gentlemen. I trust you'll give Mr. Rhysdale a chance to refresh himself before the seating. I understand he hasn't even been up to his room yet."

Edward waved his hand in dismissal. "Go on, go on," he said. "Juliana can take you."

She could think of nothing to say as she led him up. All the lighthearted comments and flip remarks she'd imagined using with him seemed wrong.

"This is it," she said, swinging the door to his room open. "I hope you'll be comfortable. We didn't know . . ." But she let her words trail off because he wasn't listening. He had moved ahead of her and was examining the room, picking up objects, running his hand over upholstery. His face had a strange look, part awe, part hunger, part satisfaction.

"Is it . . . all right?" she asked timidly.

"Yes," he said, squaring his shoulders and turning to face her. "It's fine. Just fine." He spotted his luggage and crossed the room to it. Instead of opening the battered cloth bag or the cracked vinyl shaving kit, he planted himself in front of them, shielding them from her view, and she realized that he was embarrassed by their shoddiness. The action touched her. It gave him more depth and sensitivity.

"Just ring if you need anything." She smiled. "And if my grandfather will share you, maybe I'll show you the house later."

"I'd like that," he said.

She pulled the door to his room shut after her and closed her eyes and leaned against the wall for a moment. He had come. He had really come. And she knew that he hadn't come just because of her grandfather. She was filled with an incredible lightness as she went back down the stairs.

Lunch was an improvement over breakfast, if only because of the whispers and winks. The plan was back on. After lunch they were all going riding and swimming in the pond. Lee kept wiggling his eyebrows. Jay passed his flask around under the table so everyone could doctor their soft drinks.

Whitney had managed to seat herself at the end of the table beside Ellis. At his other side was Grace's conspicuously empty place, leaving him no one to turn to for relief from Whitney's attentions. The girl fawned over him, touching him at every opportunity and brushing her breasts against his arm in what Juliana considered a disgusting display.

What did Whitney Chandler see in her cousin? Whitney Chandler—crown princess of Manhattan! It didn't make sense. Whit and Daffy and Four and the rest—none of them were the people Juliana had believed them to be. Only Matthew Rhysdale had remained constant to her fantasies.

She let her eyes and her thoughts wander to him. He was at a separate table with her grandfather and his cronies. She could see him in profile. When she turned her attention back to her own group, she realized that Daffy Buchanan was watching Rhysdale too.

Lunch was ended as soon as Perry stood and announced that he was going up to put on his riding clothes. Chaos set in. The servants fluttered about uncertainly with coffee and tea that had not been poured, looking to her for a signal as to how to proceed. Cee Cee and Willy broke into hysterical giggling, and Whitney, who had been a nationally ranked junior-horse-show competitor, jumped up and begged Ellis to come teach her how to ride.

Edward frowned disapprovingly from across the room. Juliana shifted her gaze to avoid meeting his eyes, only to be confronted by Daphne Buchanan staring holes through her.

Juliana bolted from her seat. "Boots, everyone!" she called shrilly, and the milling crowd at the table turned into a stampede for the stairs.

They walked to the stables down a pleasant winding path through a grove of huge maples and sycamores. Juliana kept to the rear, avoiding both Daffy and Whit. Everyone was cheerful, and eager to tease Whit about her failure to capture Ellis as a riding instructor.

The ride to the spring took thirty minutes because of Lee's insistence that they all ride slowly enough to pass marijuana cigarettes back and forth. Juliana declined. "Not now," she said casually, hoping no one would guess she'd never had one.

They tied their horses in the trees and raced to the water's edge. Juliana hadn't been there for years, but the clear deep pond was as beautiful and inviting as she'd remembered.

"Boots?" Perry asked her, and she realized that he was offering to pull her boots off for her. The gesture filled her with warmth and gratitude.

Everyone ripped off their clothes and ran for the water. Whit was the only exception. She made a ceremony of removing each piece and slowly caressing herself.

Juliana was afraid, but it was exhilarating, the sort of fear that accompanies a first trip down the ski slope. She undressed awkwardly and found a chin-deep spot in the pond where she could feel secure and watch Whitney. She was fascinated by the girl's total self-absorption—the half-closed eyes, the long-fingered hand gliding across the smooth white skin of a shoulder or pausing to cup a breast.

"She's acting out her fantasies," Daffy whispered from behind her. "She's pretending she's undressing for your cousin." Daffy let herself float around to Juliana's side. "Don't you wish Matthew Rhysdale was here?"

Juliana splashed away from Daffy, dog-paddling so no portion of her naked body would rise to the surface of the water.

Jay floated by on his back. She glimpsed his penis.

Nothing was pretty. The boys' bodies didn't look anything like the marble statues at Great House; the girls' breasts were not perfectly symmetrical. They all had birthmarks and ridges around their ankles where their socks had pressed into their skin beneath their boots.

"Get your dick away from my leg," Perry snarled, and Four grinned and paddled lazily away.

Juliana edged to the side, where she could sit on a submerged boulder and still keep the water level up to her neck. Gabby smiled shyly at her. Juliana smiled back gratefully. At least there was one person here who understood how uncertain she felt. Gabby Gravesend had to be almost as inexperienced as Juliana was.

"Shit, fuck, damn," Jay muttered as he floundered toward the shore. "I am comin' down fast and I'm cold as hell."

"Hell is not cold," Missy and Cee Cee said in unison. They looked at each other and broke into a fit of giggles. Suddenly bodies were heaving themselves out of the water all around Juliana. Willy and Missy and Cee Cee emerged. Denny's white toothpick legs flashed on the opposite bank. If she didn't make her move soon, she would be left in the water with Whit—fair game for everyone to stare at as she exited.

Her face burned as she crawled from the water. She dressed quickly and climbed over a tumble of rock to sit with Gabby. "It's pretty out here, isn't it?" she said, trying to engage Gabby in conversation.

"Oh, yes," Gabby agreed. "It's so . . . so natural."

Juliana let her legs dangle over the rocks toward the pond. Whit floated below in a water-ballet routine, oblivious of the activity around her.

"Whit's very good at that," Juliana commented idly.

"Yes . . . very good." Gabby smiled shyly. Perry says you're a lot like Whit."

Juliana glanced sideways at Gabby to see if the girl was joking.

"Perry says Whit is like a sleeping princess . . . waiting for someone to wake her up."

"A sleeping princess?" Juliana chuckled wryly. "I'd hate to see what she's like when she wakes up."

"Perry is a real poet, you know."

"No." Juliana tried to match Gabby's serious tone so she wouldn't offend the girl. "I didn't know."

"Oh, yes. He wrote a whole poem for Whit about sleeping princesses. About how nothing hurts till you wake up."

Juliana opened her mouth and then shut it again. The line made her think of her mother. She stood and brushed off the damp seat of her pants.

Gabby smiled up at her. "Perry likes you."

Juliana wasn't sure how to respond.

Gabby cocked her head and blinked against the sunlight. "That means you're in."

"But what about Whit and Daffy? They don't—"

Gabby shook her head. "If Perry says so, that's it."

As Juliana led Gabby around the rock-strewn edge of the pond to join the others, she felt a curious mix of elation and disappointment. Was that all there was to it? She was in?

"This is it, boys and girls," Jay announced with a flourish. "Get comfy, 'cause Uncle Jay has something mellow for ya."

Willy and Missy and Cee Cee giggled, but otherwise there was no noise. Everyone settled quietly into a ragged circle, lounging against rocks or sprawling in patches of grass. Juliana took a spot and looked from face to face. These were her friends now. This was where she belonged.

When the joint came to her the first time, she choked and coughed violently. To her surprise, no one made fun of her. Willy pounded on her back and Lee showed her how to suck the smoke into her lungs and hold it. She was better on her second turn.

"C'mon, Jinx old girl," Jay coaxed, and several others picked up the chant.

It felt good to hear them use her old nickname—even if it had been Ellis they'd picked it up from. She grinned as she let the smoke out, and everyone except Whit and Perry grinned back. Whit had her eyes closed and Perry's might as well have been closed. He was watching her with an impenetrable, almost sad look that she resented. It reminded her of the way Ellis had looked at her earlier.

Jay kept busy rolling and lighting and passing, and she took her turns diligently, wondering why the stuff was such a big deal. Aside from watering eyes and raspy lungs, she felt nothing. She lay back on the ground. Beneath her she could feel each tiny blade of grass poking into her skin. Somewhere there was hysterical giggling. But it was far, far away. In Africa maybe.

Sometime later she sat up, completely disoriented, and tried to make sense of where she was. She pushed herself to her feet and walked uncertainly toward the trees. Peeing in the trees. She hadn't done that for years and years. The thought made her giggle. Or was that someone else giggling?

She stumbled along, looking for a good spot. The giggles became groans. Groans in the bushes. She giggled at the groaning bushes and pulled them apart to step through. Jay was sitting on a stone slab and leaning back against a tree with his mouth hanging open. His pants were puddled around his ankles and his knees were splayed open.

Juliana blinked hard and puzzled over the picture. Gabby was kneeling in front of Jay. She looked up at Juliana and grinned her shyest grin. Juliana grinned back so she wouldn't hurt anyone's feelings. So Jay wouldn't know how ugly his private parts were—monstrously ugly and swollen and slimy with Gabby's saliva.

Jay opened his eyes. "Join the party or beat it," he ordered in a slurred monotone.

"Excuse me," Juliana said, and stumbled off in another direction.

Time got lost somehow. Awareness of it came back gradually. Finally she looked around and realized it was late.

Her throat felt scratchy and she was incredibly thirsty.

"Don't drink that!" she yelled, catching sight of Lee bending down to the pond with cupped hands. He looked up at her and blinked vacantly. "All right, come on, everybody!" She poked Cee Cee and Willy with her toe to rouse them. "Come on. We have to get back before someone comes out after us."

Quietly Perry stood and began helping her move people toward the horses. By the time they rode to the stables and then walked back to the house, the group was alert and complaining.

"Your grandfather has ordered dinner seating in an hour and a half," Charlotte warned her, and immediately Juliana herded everyone up the stairs and told them to shower and dress.

It was strange, telling these people what to do. Perry was faintly amused. Daffy was sullen. But they listened to her and trooped off obediently.

She was the first dressed and down. Charlotte and her favorite maid had worked over her like demons so that she would be ready in time to pacify her grandfather.

The hunt room was set for dinner. The private-pattern china gleamed. The private-design crystal sparkled. The two-hundred-year-old sterling had been polished to a mirror brightness. She surveyed it with satisfaction.

"It looks lovely."

Juliana turned to find her Aunt Grace standing in the doorway.

"Your mother would have been proud," Grace said.

Juliana shrugged.

Grace moved further into the room and Juliana could see that her makeup had been applied haphazardly. Juliana glanced ner-

vously toward the door. Grace's eyes had a belligerent glitter and
her posture was odd. She walked toward the windows, faltering a
bit as if there were invisible bumps in the smooth oak floor. "Or
your mother might have been jealous."

"What do you mean?" Juliana followed Grace, certain now
that her aunt was drunk, but lured by talk of her mother.

Grace stared out at the aquamarine rectangle of the lighted
pool. "You should have filled it with flowers," she said absently.
"Or turned out the underwater lights and floated candles on the
surface. That's what I would have done at your age . . . floated
candles."

"But about my mother," Juliana prodded. "What do you mean,
she might have been jealous?"

Grace frowned as though perturbed by her niece's stupidity.
"Because her own parties were merely adequate."

Juliana shook her head. "No. That's not true. I can remember—"

Grace laughed. It was a brittle sound that broke apart in the
empty room.

"It's hard to have much perspective about one's mother, isn't
it? Almost as hard as with one's child." Her voice softened and
trailed into vagueness. "But they're the same as the rest of the
world . . . just the same. You can give them everything, but they
still leave you. One way or another . . . they always leave you."

"Mother!" Ellis strode into the room looking like a gentlemen's magazine cover in a white dinner jacket. "Mother, I've been
looking everywhere for you."

For once Juliana greeted her cousin's appearance with relief.
"I don't think your mother is feeling well, Ellis."

Ellis studied Grace, and a brief flicker of disappointment
showed in his eyes. "Do you feel well enough to join the party
for dinner, or would you like to have it sent to your room?" he
asked gently.

"Why?" Grace demanded. Her whole manner changed. "Has
Edward sent you? Am I forbidden to come down to dinner?"

"Mother . . ." Ellis was obviously trying hard to be patient. "No
one is forbidding you to do anything."

Grace sighed and looked out the dark glass as though she could
see far beyond the terrace. "There's no moon," she said. "It's
going to storm."

"The weatherman called for it to be clear," Juliana said. "We're
having fireworks after dinner."

"Did you hear that?" Ellis said as he took his mother's arm.

"There aren't any storms to worry about." Gently he led her out of the room.

Juliana stared out the same glass, riveted to Grace's vision. No moon. A storm. What did her aunt know about storms? And what did she know about Yvonne, either? She was turning into a crazy lady. Just like so many of the Van Lyden women before her.

Dinner was flawless. Juliana looked down the table. There was laughter and conversation. The candlelight glowed in the faces of all the beautiful well-dressed people and reflected on the windows. Hundreds of tiny dancing flames shining in the glass. A rumble sounded. People stopped talking and raised their heads to listen. Another rumble. Juliana saw Grace turn toward the windows and smile just as the first rain struck.

"Oh, no!" she heard someone cry. "What about the fireworks?" Other voices joined in and rose in a chorus of disappointment. "What'll we do?" and "What about tomorrow?"

"Tonight we'll dance," Juliana announced confidently. "And tomorrow we'll all take mud baths."

The group laughed. Her grandfather peered at her from the end of the table as though questioning whether he'd heard correctly. Suddenly she felt giddy. Impulsively she pushed back her chair and stood. "Mr. Rhysdale," she called down the table, "would you like to dance?"

Jay and Lee hooted their approval, and the rush to the dance floor began.

Juliana stood waiting. Thunder crashed outside and the band swung into a wild rock number that sent her grandfather and his friends scurrying from the room. Rhysdale stood but made no move toward her. She held out her hand. "Well?" she said lightly, but still he didn't respond.

She dropped her hand. From the corner of her eye she saw Daffy watching her. "Are you turning me down?"

"No," he said helplessly. "I'm stalling for a slower song."

Juliana took his hand. It was as warm and damp as her own. "I don't know how either," she admitted, laughing, "but I'm told that all you have to do is move."

Juliana stayed awake until two-thirty before she crept down the dark stairs and through the quiet house. Everyone was asleep. Just as she'd hoped.

She curled up in the corner window seat and watched the storm. The wind drove the rain against the glass in a lashing, rattling fury. She stared into the blackness, waiting for the next flash of lightning. She felt so different tonight. She would gladly have read the poetry assignments her tutor always forced on her.

Tonight everything had depth and significance. The woods held secrets. The storm was an omen. And she was more than herself. More than Juliana. More than Great House. More even than the generations of Van Lydens who'd forged her destiny. She was a woman. For the first time in her life she felt like a woman. And she felt no shame in it.

A woman waiting for a lover in the darkness.

Just thinking "lover" gave her a thrill, and she let her imagination take over, envisioning herself as every woman who had ever waited with her heart. She was Juliet and Sleeping Beauty and Bess, the black-eyed innkeeper's daughter from that poem about the highwayman.

She glanced at the glowing dial of her watch. It was 3:07. He was late. Was this nothing to him? Shouldn't he have rushed down early? Shouldn't he have been pacing in front of the fireplace?

She sighed and moved to stand by the window. The glass was cool beneath her fingertips.

What if he didn't come at all? What if he was laughing at her this very minute? Or what if . . . ? She checked her watch again. It was a sport watch that her father had sent her, suitable for diving to extreme depths and telling worldwide time. The glowing dial usually made her think of her father and wonder where he was. This time it didn't. She didn't care where he was.

. . . What if he'd died trying to come to her? He could have tripped down the stairs in the dark or been stabbed by a burglar or discovered by her grandfather and killed in a duel. She shivered.

"Juliana?"

She whirled toward the source of the whisper, and there he was, materializing magically in the darkness.

"I'm sorry . . . I got lost . . . this house is like a maze."

"Yes," she agreed quickly, "just like a maze," though Elysia had always seemed simple and straightforward to her.

There was a long silence. Juliana was acutely aware of the sound and rhythm of his breathing. It overpowered her own rhythms, then pulled her along to keep time so that they were perfectly matched.

He took a step toward her.

"Well," she said, briskly clicking on a flashlight, "this room is a good place to start. It's a gentlemen's smoking room or den."

She swept the beam of light over the polar-bear rugs and elephant-foot side tables.

"I like the fireplace," he said.

She trained the light on the fireplace, and the muted grains of color running through the carvings stood out with unnatural clarity. "I don't remember the exact story on that. It's some kind of petrified wood."

She pointed the flashlight toward the floor and led him out into the hall. "This house is supposed to have every kind of wood ever used in the world. My grandfather has it all documented . . . what wood's where and all that."

Matt whistled softly under his breath.

She swung open a heavy door. "Here's the trophy room." She played the light over the rows and rows of blank glass eyes. "Every generation of Van Lydens has added its own record kills to this room." She handed him the flashlight. "You can go around and read the plaques if you're interested."

Slowly he moved down the row of mounted heads, pausing at the white tiger and the silvertip grizzly and the rhinoceros. His face was lit with eerie lights and shadows as he leaned forward to read the plaques in the flashlight beam.

"I'd like to come back here tomorrow," he said finally. "Do you think anyone would mind?"

"No. My grandfather is delighted when people take an interest in family history."

Matt passed the flashlight back to her. "Do you have any trophies here?"

"No." She kept the flashlight away from her face as she casually dropped the first of her well-planned lines. "I love guns and shooting, but I haven't had the opportunity to go on a big hunt yet."

"You love guns?" His voice rose in almost childish excitement. "I love guns too! You might call 'em my worst vice."

She smiled, pretending surprise. "There's no question, then. We'll go to the gun room next."

"The gun room? My God! Is this where the Van Lyden gun collection is kept?"

"What we keep of the collection is housed here," she explained, warming to her position as authority. "The majority of it is on loan to museums."

She used the key she'd stolen from her grandfather's desk to unlock the metal door. "It's fireproof," she pointed out. "There are no windows, and the entire room is made like a vault."

Once she'd locked them inside, she switched on the banks of lights that were recessed in each of the glass-fronted showcases. She took out another key and activated the mechanism that un-locked all the showcase doors.

Matt stood in the center of the room as if dumbstruck.

"What would you like to see?" she asked.

"I . . ." He held up his hands helplessly. "Everything!"

Juliana felt very controlled and mature in the face of his won-der. She swung an oak-and-glass door open and reached inside. "This . . ." She pulled out a mildly interesting piece to begin with and handed it to him. ". . . is a Colt double-barreled shotgun from the 1880's."

Matt fondled the gun hungrily and raised it to his shoulder to test its presence. She waited, then pulled out another gun she was familiar with. "And this . . ." She handed him the second one and put the first back in its place. ". . . is a Winchester 44/40—known historically as the buffalo gun."

On down the line she went, pointing out only those guns whose pedigree and identity she'd studied, but keeping it casual, as if the entire collection were familiar to her. Finally she skipped to the star of her show. She grinned at him as she reached in to pick it up. "This beauty is a Heym sidelock side-by-side double from Germany. It was made as a gift for Teddy Roosevelt."

Matt took the Heym from her like it was made of spun glass. "My God, I think I've heard of this one."

"Possibly," she said. "The walnut for the stock came from a four-hundred-year-old tree near the Turkish-Russian border."

Matt stared down at the rifle in his hands, and the look in his eyes made her almost jealous. She wanted him to look at her that same way.

"The engraving and gold inlay took the artist over three thou-sand hours . . . that's more than ten months of constant work. And you can see . . ." Juliana pointed out several areas, brushing his hand as she did so. ". . . every metal surface is engraved. The artist used an intricate filigree on the trigger guard and English scroll-work to detail small areas, and then . . ." She leaned close and guided him in turning the gun slightly. ". . . he designed and hand-cut this little ornament on the rib as kind of a personal touch. Almost like his signature."

Matt caressed the rifle lovingly and then held it up to sight as though handling a religious object. His hands looked strong and capable holding the gun. Watching them sent a thrill through Juliana.

Reluctantly Matt returned the Heym to its cradle. "This is all so staggering. I've never seen anything like it."

She shrugged. "The really great pieces aren't even here."

Matt shook his head and whistled under his breath. "Someday . . . boy . . ." He shook his head again, then grinned at her. "Think if I was ever president somebody would send me a Heym like they did ole Teddy?"

"I'd send you one," she said.

He turned so he was looking straight into her eyes. "You would, would you?" The words were soft, like a caress.

"Yes," she whispered.

He searched her eyes for the longest time while she prayed for him to kiss her. Everything was perfect. Just like her fantasies.

Matt pulled back suddenly, cleared his throat self-consciously, and scanned the room. "Does your father ever shoot any of these?"

The spell was broken. She tried to hide her irritation.

"Some of them. But we have so many guns around . . . There's not much point in using these. And of course the virgin guns are kept that way."

The word "virgin" was out before she knew it. It was a term her father used in reference to the guns, and she'd spoken it without thinking. Now it seemed to swell and grow in the air around her. Virgin. What a detestable word.

She glanced at Matt but he seemed unaffected by the word. His attention was back on the guns.

"Do you think I might be able to talk my way in here tomorrow?" he asked.

She relocked the cabinets and switched off the lights. "Just tell Kleiman you'd like to see the gun room. He'll arrange it." She was angry now. Were guns all he could think about?

"You've already seen the hunt room," she said. "That's probably the best-known room in the house. The fireplace is made of stones from a medieval castle and it's big enough to hold eight-foot logs, either lying down or standing up. And then there's all the wood and the carving and the murals, but then, you can look at that anytime. The rest of the downstairs is pretty standard: ladies' parlor, family dining room, kitchen, and service areas—all that. And then there are the game rooms, which you've seen."

She trained the flashlight on the hall's Persian carpet and led him back toward the servants' staircase. "It's getting late. Since we have to go up anyway, I'll show you the family library as a finish."

He didn't protest. He didn't beg her to stay up and watch the sunrise with him or tell her that he couldn't bear to say good night. He just nodded. Her anger built.

She stepped into the library and shone the light around the intricately carved teak that formed the walls and ceiling. "It was lifted in pieces from an old maharajah's palace and reassembled here. Every single square inch is carved."

Matt chuckled in amazement. "How can you read in here?"

"What do you mean?"

"Sitting in the middle of all this . . ." He swept his hand in an arc. "How can you concentrate long enough to do any reading?"

Juliana shrugged. "I've grown up with it." She moved away from him. "These chairs probably have some long history too, but that doesn't stop me from sitting on them. And my bed . . . it's centuries old, with a top and draperies and all this weird carving. But I never think about that. It's just my bed."

"I'd like to see it," he said lightly. "It doesn't sound like just a bed."

The anger dissolved. Her fingertips buzzed and the lobes of her ears burned. She turned away from him.

"It's this way." She pressed the flashlight's off button and led him stealthily through the dark hallway. He followed her into her room and locked the door. She heard the bolt slide home.

Total darkness enveloped them. Outside, the wind whipped the branches of an ancient oak that grew close to her windows. She thought about how she used to climb out into that oak with Sparky and pretend it was the entrance to another world.

She crossed to her writing table and turned on the small stained-glass lamp. The jeweled colors in the shade bathed the room in a rich glow. She turned toward him, but he was preoccupied, wandering about, studying this and that. His fingers trailed over the sterling brush and comb on her dresser, lingered on the black pearls she'd worn to dinner, and then picked up a diamond earring, holding it out to dangle in the soft light.

"I heard someone mention that you just had a birthday," he said casually.

"Yes."

He put the earring down. "Which birthday was it?"

"My eighteenth," she lied.

His head jerked up in surprise. "Eighteen? I thought you were at least nineteen . . . hopefully twenty."

"Eighteen isn't so young!" she bristled. "I can vote!"

"Only if you vote for me." He laughed, then shook his head.

"No. You're right ... eighteen isn't so young." His gaze took in the room again. "Especially when you own the world." He turned his attention back to the dresser, picking up a crystal flacon of perfume. "I've never known a woman who had things like this." He pulled the stopper and held it briefly under his nose like a wine connoisseur appreciating a fine bouquet.

She held her breath. There was something sensual about watching him enjoy the perfume—the same perfume she wore, the same gardenia scent that had been created for her mother.

He moved toward her in slow motion, covering the space between them in dreamtime. Every cell in her body froze into waiting. He raised the crystal stopper and slowly traced a line of perfume along the side of her neck and down into the hollow of her throat. He closed his eyes and bent close to take in the scent. So close that his breath warmed her skin.

"Beautiful," he whispered.

His lips brushed her neck and then the line of her jaw. She closed her eyes and he kissed her eyelids.

The world spun away.

"I want you," he breathed. "Do you want me too?" His mouth was so close to her ear that she could feel the words as they came through his lips.

She nodded mutely. Want him? She wanted to lock him in one of her closets and never let him out.

He unfastened her belt, then slowly began undoing the tiny covered buttons on her dress. She had a momentary flash of panic. Would she be clumsy or stupid? Would he guess she was a virgin?

He slipped the dress off one shoulder and touched his lips to her collarbone. She felt dizzy and short of breath. A climber out of oxygen.

Her dress dropped to the floor perfectly, just like in the movies, and he gathered her into a long deep kiss that lasted all the way to the bed, where they fell together into the piles of ruffled pillows. It felt very sexy, falling like that. She wished she'd unpinned her hair.

Lying beside him was exciting, and she lifted her face for more kisses, but he turned away from her, onto his back, and said, "Undress me."

She fumbled with the buttons on his shirt and made a half-hearted try at his belt buckle. This was all wrong. She wanted to be swept up in a whirlwind the way it happened in her stolen romance books. There were no zippers or shoelaces in a whirlwind. And seeing a naked man wasn't part of the fantasy either.

"You'd better do it," she said, and closed her eyes until he was back beside her.

His hands trailed up and down her body, followed by his mouth, and he discarded the final layers of her clothing with such dexterity that she barely noticed. The melting started, the same way it did when she read the books and touched herself, only this time it was better. So much better. This time it felt like even her bones were melting.

He rolled them together so that she was on her back and he was staring down at her and she could see herself reflected. In his eyes she was beautiful and desirable. She was all that she had ever wished to be. The power of that reached down to all the empty places within her, filling her, nourishing her, suspending the darkness, and banishing all pain and rejection.

She forgot about books and whirlwinds. She needed him. She needed him more than she had ever needed anyone.

He entered her in one stabbing, searing motion. She gasped. But it hurt for only an instant. And even the hurt was good. The sacrifice was good, because now she truly had him.

He held her wrists, pinning them to the bed, and she wrapped her legs around him, wrapped the power and the heat of herself around him, drawing him straight into her heart.

"Oh, Matt . . . Matt . . ."

He released her wrists and she clung to him, digging her fingers into his back, faint and breathless and joyously out of control. She followed him up . . . up . . . toward something vast and bright . . . up . . . up . . .

Then he froze. His body stiffened and his head jerked forward and a rushing "Ahhhhhhhh" escaped his lips like air from a balloon. He collapsed on her chest.

She lay still for a moment, then tried moving beneath him. Nothing happened. The brightness faded and the melting congealed into frustration. Surely there was supposed to be more. "Is that it?" she asked.

Jake raised his head. "You didn't come?"

"I don't think so."

"Very funny," he said, pulling away from her to lie on his side.

"I'm sorry. I didn't mean . . ."

"That's okay." He grinned. "We'll try again soon."

She slid in close, pressing herself against him, moving lightly against him while she kissed his throat. "I think we should try again now," she whispered.

23

Lucy

Lucy Skidmore did not become pregnant as expected. At first she didn't worry about it. Her mind was occupied with other problems. She was still reeling from the ugliness with Buddy and the loss of her last marital illusions.

Then Anita appeared in the middle of a schoolday. Lucy was in the front room of her Expando home, pressing knife creases into Buddy's stiffly starched jeans, when Anita walked in.

"Hi." Lucy continued her attack on the stiff denim. She resisted the urge to ask immediately why her sister wasn't in school.

Anita stood awkwardly just inside the door. She had on tight faded jeans with ragged knees and a stained T-shirt beneath an oversize black leather jacket. Her skin had recently flared up and her hair hung in a tangle around her face. She looked out of place in the tidy perfection of the room.

Anita just stood there without speaking, so Lucy turned off the iron and busied herself with pouring iced tea and opening a package of the girl's favorite cookies.

"I didn't know you had a leather jacket."

"It's not mine."

"Oh, well, come on in and sit." Lucy arranged the tea and cookies on the kitchen table, pulled out a chair for Anita, and sat down across the table. "I'll swear . . . you look like something the cat dragged in. Is that the 'in' thing—looking like an orphan?"

Anita moved to the table and picked up the glass of tea, but she remained standing. She took a long drink, then shoved a handful of cookies into her jacket pocket.

"I guess manners aren't 'in' either," Lucy said.

"Bullshit!" Anita slammed the glass down onto the table. "It's all bullshit."

Lucy stared up at her sister in surprise. At the crooked teeth

317

that had been too expensive to straighten and the gold locket that was never taken off and the narrowed angry eyes, and she wanted to scream out her own rage: "You're young and you can still make your life into something. What are you always whining about? What's holding you back? You're not crippled. You're not dumb. You're not imprisoned. You're not . . ." She realized with a start that she'd been thinking "married"—"you're not married." As if being married were another handicap.

Lucy blocked out the thoughts quickly and kept her voice calm. "What's wrong?"

"As if you didn't know," Anita shot back sarcastically.

Lucy paused a moment and drew in a deep breath. "I *don't* know."

The girl eyed her suspiciously, then relaxed a fraction. "Maybe you don't. Maybe it was all just his idea. But sounds to me like you agree with him just the same. You can't help it, I guess. You can't live with the pigs and stay clean, as Mama would say."

Lucy ate a cookie and wondered how to deal with whatever was going on. Agree with what? Him who? Sometimes Anita's puzzles tried her patience to the limit.

"Anita, did Buddy say something mean to you? I wish you'd just go ahead and tell me."

"You gotta be kidding. Buddy never does his own dirty work. I got reamed out by the great reverend himself." Anita scowled and put clenched fists on her hips and looked around as though ready to do battle. "The bastard made me bawl like a baby."

Lucy rested an elbow on the table and cradled her forehead in her hand. "Damn! I am so sorry, Nita. I know how awful he can be."

"Ahhh . . . Fuck him and the horse he rode in on." She shrugged, brushing the whole thing off. "I gotta go. I got somebody waiting."

"Oh."

"Remember I said a while back that I was thinking of visiting Suki?"

"Yes."

"Well, it didn't work out. But I'm gonna try it again."

"Oh." Lucy started to ask if she'd called and gotten permission, but she held back. There would be time for a practical discussion later, when Anita was in a better mood.

"Can I have some of those prints where we used the timer?" Anita asked. "The ones of us together."

"Sure. You know where they are. Take as many as you like."

Anita went to the hall closet and rummaged in the box of

pictures for several minutes. When she came back she had an envelope in her hand.

"I hope you aren't planning on showing those to anyone," Lucy said. "We were acting pretty silly that day."

Anita smiled sadly, almost wistfully, and her tough wise fragile innocence grabbed Lucy's heart and squeezed. "Would you like to stay?" she offered. "Maybe get the camera out? I can call Buddy and make some excuse why he can't come home for lunch—"

"No." Anita backed toward the door. "Like I said"—she shrugged apologetically—"I got a friend waiting."

Lucy followed her to the door and watched her leave. There was a boy sitting on a large black motorcycle up near the road. The sight of him made Lucy suddenly afraid. "Be careful!" she called after her sister, wishing she'd kept Anita inside and wishing she'd had the serious talk with her that she'd been intending to have for a long time.

Be careful. Such a helpless thing to say. A mother's thing to say. A teacher's thing to say. "Be careful . . . this isn't a game." Ms. Conroy's last words seemed to apply with increasing frequency as Lucy grew older.

She watched Anita run up to the road. Anita, who never hurried, was running to please the waiting boy. Lucy could feel his impatience. How did men do that? she wondered. There must be an inborn system that allowed men to telegraph their displeasure to the receptive females in their lives. She thought about that as she watched Anita climb onto the bike and attach herself to his back. And she thought about Anita's hair looking so messy because it was windblown, and about how she ought to buy Anita a safety helmet if the girl was determined to go on clinging behind boys on motorcycles. She thought about a lot of things, but she never thought that she might not see her sister again.

Anita didn't come home that night or the next. She didn't report for work. Lucy called the police.

Wanda said she wasn't surprised—that she was used to being deserted. The police said that Anita would probably be back or call soon and that since she'd mentioned leaving to her coworkers at Taco Mike's and taken personal items, there was nothing terrible to worry about. "Terrible" translating into "abduction" or "murder" (or worse, Charity whispered). Buddy said she had probably run off to live with Suki and that having Anita around would damn sure teach Suki a lesson. The reverend said it was for the best and that maybe his little talk with her had made her want to put her shameful life behind her and make a new start.

Lucy alternated between frantic worry and seething anger.

How could Anita have done this? And how could Wanda react so callously? Her own child, her own baby had disappeared. And Buddy, instead of being sympathetic, was behaving like a gloating ass. And the reverend, the self-righteous hypocritical son of a bitch, was actually pleased that he'd driven a teenage girl from her home.

Only Charity had little to say through it all. She watched Lucy with careful, measuring eyes and she kept silent. The scrutiny lasted for weeks, as though Charity expected some disastrous outburst, some destructive explosion of emotion.

There was none. Conditioning and natural inclination kept Lucy's hostility inside, as always. Days stretched into weeks, and there was no word. Lucy's anger melted into despair. The girl did not go to Suki's. She simply vanished. And the jolting finality of it, the simple everyday randomness of it, haunted Lucy almost as much as the uncertainty and regret. A person had to be very careful indeed, not just sometimes, but all the time. Love was fragile. People slipped away. It wasn't a game.

Her own family circle took on new importance. She immersed herself in being the Lucy that everyone wanted. The glue that would hold them all together and keep them close. For the reverend she became official church photographer. For Charity she became a companion, tagging along after her to help conduct the Christian femininity seminars ("Day of Beauty for the Soul") that Charity was becoming regionally famous for. She filled the gap between Buddy and his parents, reassuring them and gilding their son with her own perfection.

Keeping Buddy happy was easy too. Hot meals. Cold beer. Clean sheets. Matched socks in his drawer. It was all so simple. She couldn't imagine why she'd had so much trouble before. Marriage consisted of jobs to be done, expectations to be met, and appropriate responses in bed at night. That was all there was to success. And she knew how to stay back now. How to keep from being "stomped on," as Wanda called it.

Engineering her mother's happiness proved to be the most strenuous task. Wanda changed after Anita's disappearance. She receded. Her voice shrank in texture and authority. Her body sagged inward. Her indomitable will faded into vagueness, and the stoic pragmatism that had seen her through her difficult life fermented into something small and bitter. And nothing Lucy did for her was quite enough. Being the perfect daughter was more difficult than being the perfect daughter-in-law. Or wife.

And she had started to think that maybe a positive pregnancy test was the answer to everything. But that simple goal was proving more impossible to achieve than any task she'd yet undertaken.

It was ironic to her, this lack of conception, after her previous worries about contraception. It was funny to think of all that spilled semen when they were young, all the pirated birth-control pills, all the sleepless nights when her period was a day overdue. They'd gone without birth control for some time, and still there was no pregnancy. She began to watch the calendar and say little fertility prayers.

Her twenty-second birthday and her fourth wedding anniversary passed. She could no longer appreciate the irony of her conceptionless coupling and she was irritated by the hopefulness of Charity and her mother. No, she wasn't feeling sick or weak or unusually warm. Yes, she'd had her period on time.

The sight of pregnant women depressed her. When she helped with the infants in the church nursery each Sunday, she was filled with longing. She wanted a child. A tiny little girl with soft hair and an infectious laugh and chubby clinging hands just like Anita had been as a baby. Her own little girl. To spoil and protect and teach. A little girl with arms to reach for stardust and eyes to see rainbows and hands to paint them both.

At night she would wake up and cry—softly, so she wouldn't bother Buddy. And she knew she was stupid to cry and she knew she had a lot to be thankful for and she knew childlessness wasn't the end of the world, though it certainly felt that way at times. What was marriage for if not to produce children? What was her life for if there was never a child to love?

Dr. Henry Howell, the family practitioner that Charity swore by, could find nothing wrong with her. He sent her to Dallas for tests. The whole procedure made Buddy nervous, so Charity made the arrangements and drove Lucy there.

She spent all morning undergoing procedures and then went to the hospital cafeteria, where she'd arranged to meet Suki for lunch.

It was thirty minutes past their agreed-upon time when Suki finally breezed in. She had on a leather skirt and spike heels and ten more pounds around her hips and thighs. The cute, softly rounded body that had knocked the boys dead as a teenager was now betraying her with matronliness.

"Where's the gingham witch?" Suki asked as soon as they'd hugged.

"Charity's shopping and meeting friends," Lucy said.

"Friends! That woman has friends?"

Lucy giggled. Suki's sarcastic irreverence was just what she needed.

They started through the food line together.

"Maybe she's secretly having an affair." Suki raised her eyebrows hopefully.

"No. These are Christian ladies. She's helping them plan some big campaign."

"Oh, God . . . don't tell me . . . they want bras to have alarms and panties to have locks."

"Close! They're worried about all the jiggling that's going on. Among other things, that is."

"Jiggling?"

"Yes, you know. Women's bodies. Jiggling destroys the moral fiber of men."

"Jeez . . ." Suki rolled her eyes. "Does she want us to wear body casts or what?"

"When we go to the bathroom later, I'll show you the new bra she gave me." The cashier peered at them, and Lucy leaned over close to whisper the rest. "Impossible to jiggle in it. Cleverly conceals protruding nipples too."

"God forbid anyone should know we all have nipples," Suki said, and they collapsed into a booth, laughing as though they were teenagers again. The food was funny. The hospital was funny. Life was funny.

"So . . . what's the problem with your plumbing?" Suki asked finally.

"The problem is that no one can find a problem. If they could find something wrong, they could try to fix it."

Suki took a bite of her macaroni salad. She had on peacock-blue eye shadow and dark coral lipstick and her hair was cut into a precise wedge. The extra weight had filled out her rounded face and made her cheeks look even more pinchable. Like cheeks in a baby-food commercial. She made a face, pushed the salad away, and used metallic gold fingernails to pull a cigarette from a package.

"Maybe it's Buddy," Suki suggested coolly. She arched an eyebrow and blew out a stream of smoke. "Maybe your Mr. Wonderful is shooting blanks."

Lucy straightened. The mood was ruined. Suki always managed to do that, one way or the other.

"It *is* possible," Suki insisted.

"I know. I talked to Dr. Howell about it."

"And?"

"Well, it's probably my fault. Some kind of female problem or other. And Charity's afraid it might really upset Buddy for him to be tested, because in order to get a semen sample, he'd have to . . . you know . . ."

"You mean jerk off?" Suki shaped her lips into a pouty O as she exhaled. "Big deal. He probably did it every night after bedtime prayers when he was a kid."

Lucy added mustard to her sandwich.

"Now, don't give me that look and clam up," Suki said. She squashed her half-smoked cigarette into her plate. "Besides, what has Charity got to say about it? It's none of her damn business. Who told her anyway?"

"Well, the doctor called to talk to Buddy about testing him, and Buddy told his mother, and then Charity called the doctor and . . ." Lucy sighed. "Dr. Howell is a very loyal member of the congregation, and when Charity—"

"Shit! I don't believe this! This is insane, Luce. You're not married to Buddy . . . you're married to his mother."

"Oh, it's not that bad."

"Sure."

Lucy finished her sandwich in silence. "Mama might live with us," she said finally. "I think I've about talked Buddy into it."

"You're kidding! Mama's moving out of the old trailer?"

"Well . . . she's still thinking about it," Lucy admitted.

"Thinking about it? If Buddy says yes, what's to think about?"

"Well, the whole plan is that she'll move into one of our extra rooms and she'll help me around the house and she'll get part of my household money, which I give to her now anyway, and of course she won't have any room-and-board expenses so she won't need to work anymore. She likes the idea of living with us, only she doesn't want to quit working."

"She wants to keep washing?"

"Yes. She's real stubborn about it. Says she doesn't want to let her ladies down. They depend on her, and nobody else knows how to wash for them."

Suki shook her head in disbelief and lit another cigarette.

"Buddy says he won't have a washerwoman living with him. It's pretty complicated, trying to work everything out. The main thing in my mind, though, is that Mama needs a rest. She deserves to relax."

Suki snorted air through her nose. "Glad they're not my problems," she said, balancing her cigarette on the edge of her plate.

She picked up the stainless knife from her tray and used the blade as a mirror to reapply her lipstick.

Lucy studied her. Something was different about Suki this time, and it had nothing to do with hairstyle or eye shadow or weight gain.

"You know, you ought to stay in Dallas for a day and get a decent haircut or go to a makeover salon. You're looking like a washed-out farm wife, Luce."

Before Lucy could respond, Suki reached over and poked her arm. "Look at that guy over there in the scrub suit! Wow. Suppose I could fake a faint and get him to run over and give me mouth-to-mouth?"

Lucy swiveled to glance at the man Suki had her eye on. "I thought you had a serious boyfriend."

"I did," Suki said wryly. "But I found out recently that he has a wife and kids he neglected to mention."

"Oh, Suki, I'm so—"

"Forget it. It's spilled milk." She inhaled on her cigarette and grinned sarcastically. "Mama and all her warnings about men being roosters . . . hah! She didn't know the half of it. There's a lot worse than roosters out there." She grinned evilly. "You ought to be glad I left Buddy for you."

Lucy made a show of scowling and reaching over to pinch her sister's arm. Any jealousy she'd felt over Suki's past association with Buddy was long dead, but this little routine played on and on. Suki seemed to need the reassurance of it.

Suki grinned and preened, basking in her own satisfaction. "So, to get back to Mama . . . you think you can get it all worked out between her and Buddy?"

Lucy began gathering their trash into a neat pile on her tray. "I hope so," she said. "I know she's lonely out there by herself." She wiped Suki's ashes off the table with a napkin. "I think she really misses Anita."

"Yeah. Miss Dramatics. You'd think she could have just left home like a normal person. . . . That's all that's bothering Mama. Not knowing where the little snot is. If Mama did know, then she'd relax and never give the brat a second thought."

Lucy straightened and clenched her hands together in her lap.

"There you go with that look again. Blaming me. Like I'm the bad guy! Like precious little Anita never did anything wrong. Well, I didn't screw up my life or get an abortion or run off and worry everybody to death."

Lucy stared at her sister wordlessly. Abortion? Had Suki said abortion?

"Whoops." Suki slapped a hand over her mouth. "That was supposed to be a secret."

"Anita had an abortion?"

"Yeah. Guess it can't hurt to spill the beans now. She wrote a big sob letter to me, so I helped her get it all set up. She came on the bus one morning. Wanted to stay over a few days, but I made her go right back home that night before anybody missed her."

Lucy sagged back against the hard plastic bench. "She never told me. She never . . ."

" 'Course she never told you! She wanted you to think she was Miss Perfect. She'd have told Mama and suffered hellfire and brimstone before she told you."

"And you just sent her home by herself on the bus?"

"Damn right. If she was big enough to screw around, she was big enough to get back home to her own bed, where she wouldn't be putting anybody out." Suki frowned. "Don't look at me like that. I took care of her problem, then I sent her home to teach her a lesson. There's nothing wrong with that."

"She was just a baby. How could you have sent her off alone like that?"

"That's exactly the reason I sent her off. To grow her up. It's too dangerous out there for babies."

They sat in silence for several minutes. Suki fumbled for another cigarette.

"I have to go," Lucy said finally. "Charity's meeting me for the next consultation."

"Yeah, well . . . it's been grand."

They slid out of the opposite sides of the booth and walked toward the door together.

"I hope this works out, Lucy. I hope you get pregnant."

Lucy shook her head, turned away from her sister, and then turned back to give Suki a hug. She couldn't afford to stay mad. She had to be very careful. Suki was the only sister she had left.

"You know . . ." Suki's mouth jerked into a failed attempt at a grin. "I've always been kind of jealous of you getting married and having that nice place to live and all, but now, if you can't have kids . . . well, I'm gonna feel terrible about being jealous."

Lucy laughed and pushed her away. "Get out of here. You are terrible! Just get! Before Charity shows up and forces you into one of her cast-iron bras."

Suki paused to fish for car keys, leaving her face naked for a fraction of an instant, and Lucy realized what it was that had changed. Her eyes were different. As long as Lucy could remember, her sister's eyes had held a raw excitement, a continuous charge of expectation. That was gone now.

"Well, tah tah as they say." Suki waved the keys and grinned. "Have a good ovary or whatever."

Later that evening, when Lucy was riding home in the plush front seat of Charity's newest Lincoln, she thought about the poking and prodding she'd undergone and about what Suki had said. Why should it be such a trauma for Buddy to provide a semen sample? It certainly couldn't be any worse than what she'd been forced to endure. And what else could they do now? The doctors all said there was no problem with her tubes and passages and processes. What was there left to do but check Buddy?

Charity was rambling on about the Dallas shopping mall she'd been to that morning, but Lucy couldn't even pretend to listen. Finally Charity stopped talking. She glanced sideways at Lucy as though reading her mood.

"Sometimes the Lord moves in strange ways," Charity said piously. "Could be he doesn't have the right baby for y'all yet."

"You don't believe that any more than I do," Lucy said.

"I most surely do! Everything is the Lord's will. If he wants you to bear fruit, he'll show you the way."

"I don't need him to show me the way. I know the way. And I'm going to make Buddy get tested so we can find out once and for all what we're up against."

Charity punched the off button on the tape player, and the gospel music stopped abruptly. The only sound to fill the void was the fine-tuned hum of the luxury automobile.

"You're too fine a woman to do that to your husband, Lucy. You're just sayin' this because you're overwrought. When you've had time to think—"

"That's ridiculous. I'm not going to *do* anything to Buddy. It's a very simple test, Charity. He doesn't even have to go to the doctor's office. I can take the sample in for him."

"Why?"

Lucy stared at her mother-in-law. Charity had taken to wearing her hair off her face in a stiffly sprayed two-tiered puff. It gave her a severity that contrasted with her ever-present ruffles and frills and made her look like a woman in a faded daguerreotype.

"Why what?"

"Why would you want to put Buddy through that?"

"I don't think taking a simple test is—"

"That simple test requires him to perform a perverted act on himself and risk damnation."

"I'm sure it's not perverted when it's for medical reasons," Lucy said.

"And then what?"

"I don't understand the question."

"What about after the test? After he's soiled and humiliated himself in God's eyes and my eyes and Dr. Hank's eyes, then what about the results? What do you think it would do to him to learn he couldn't father a child?"

Again Lucy stared at Charity.

"Do you want to crush him with the news that he's nothin' but a gelding?"

"We don't know that," Lucy said. "Until he takes the tests, we don't know anything."

"Come on, now. Don't play dumb with me." Charity's saccharine bubbliness went flat and her voice became cold and businesslike. "The problem has got to be Buddy's."

"But we don't—"

"Yes, we do. Hank thinks that Buddy's testicles got burned up when his friends put that hot liniment on him for his team initiation."

Lucy's mind reeled. "Are you saying that I went through all this for nothing? That you and Dr. Hank knew all along that Buddy was sterile?"

" 'Sterile' is such an ugly word, Lucy. And not precisely true. Hank thinks Buddy may still be capable of producin' some seed."

"And Hank never told Buddy a thing?"

"Of course not. I wouldn't let him. Men's egos are as fragile as their private parts."

"But you let me go through all that? You let them do all that to me?"

"We had to be sure there was nothin' else going wrong, didn't we? Nothin' else contributing to the problem."

Lucy sagged back into the seat and watched the headlights play ahead on the road.

"You had to go through some pain, Lucy, but you're a woman. You're strong and you can take pain. And if you'd found out your female organs weren't right, why, you'd just go on about your life and most likely adopt, whereas Buddy . . . why, learnin' he wasn't a whole man might just destroy him."

Charity waited, but Lucy didn't trust herself to speak.

"It's not hopeless," Charity offered. "Dr. Hank says there's probably still seeds bein' made—just not very many of 'em—so it could take a lot of trying. And if you try awhile and nothing works"—Charity glanced over at Lucy with narrowed, calculating eyes—"we'll explore some other alternatives—other ways of making you pregnant. Maybe artificial insemination like they do to the purebred cows. We could arrange that without anybody havin' to know a thing. Even Buddy. He'd never know the difference."

She glanced at Lucy again. "Remember, the Lord provides most to those who do for themselves."

Lucy thought about opening the car door and jumping out.

"In the meantime," Charity said, switching on her brightest, most guileless tone, "I have just the news to take your mind off all this nonsense. Your mama and I had a talk last Sunday after church."

Charity waited, dangling the information between them like a lure.

Something fearful and slimy was crawling around in Lucy's stomach, and she didn't know what to do. What was real here? What was right? Should she open her mouth and let Charity know just how twisted she thought the woman was, or should she keep her mouth safely shut and find out how Charity intended to use her mama?

"What did you talk to Mama about?" she asked wearily.

"Oh ..." Charity's tone was conspiratorial and smug. "She started tellin' me how she just couldn't make up her mind about whether to move in with y'all. Asked my opinion. You know how she values my opinion. Well, I was kinda rushed at the time and wasn't able to advise her. But maybe you'd like me to explain to her how this is her chance to become a fine lady. How all those washin' clients she values so highly are gonna think a darn sight more of her if she starts dressin' up and attending their club meetings than they ever did when she was scrubbing out their husbands' shorts."

Charity kept her eyes carefully on the road. "Would you like that? Would you like me to help you with your mama? I could speak to Buddy too. Tell him how bad it looks for him to be a success and leave his poor mother-in-law out in that trashy place by herself."

Lucy gripped her hands tightly together in her lap. Could she afford to refuse this deal and unleash her indignation and disgust? Could she afford to have this woman as an enemy? She turned her head to look at Charity, the mother of her husband, the epitome of Christian womanhood, and she saw a monster. She could confront that monster now, if she dared. But then the monster would destroy her. She didn't doubt that for a moment.

"Yes ..." Lucy's throat was so tight she had to force the words out. "I'd like you to help me."

"That's a girl." Charity smiled. "We'll get that mama of yours right where you want her. Leave it to me. And we ought to figure out some other things that would make your life happier. Try to get your mind off babies for a time. No reason to be down just 'cause God's not giving you a baby soon as you'd like."

Charity pushed the gospel tape back in and tapped her fingernails on the steering wheel in time to the music. "I know! We'll get you a car! I'm positive Buddy will agree. He's not gonna want to see you moping around, feeling bad because these tests showed that you might not be able to get pregnant right away.... He'll agree to a car the minute I explain it all to him." Charity beamed a smile in her direction. "How's that sound? Your very own car?"

"Fine," Lucy whispered. "Fine."

She felt numb for the rest of the ride, and when she got home she went straight to bed and curled into herself.

"What'd them tests say?" Buddy asked when he got home from work. "It ain't nothin' to do with me, is it?"

Lucy sat up. "Were you worried that it was you?"

"Naw ... not really. I had kinda the opposite problem when I first got to college, so I figured it was you."

"What do you mean, the opposite problem?"

Buddy tortured the carpet with the toe of his boot a moment, then sank down on the edge of the bed. "Don't never tell my mama I told you this, okay?"

She nodded.

"When I first got ta school, I wadn't too smart about protectin' myself, and I had this girlfriend who got me in big trouble. She threatened to tell my coach and my daddy and her folks that I got her pregnant."

"And what happened?"

"My mama came and took that girl away and I never saw her again. I heard later she'd transferred down to Austin and was a cheerleader, but I never ran into her."

"But what happened with the pregnancy? Did she have an abortion?"

"Oh ... hell, no. That's against God. You've heard my daddy preach about abortion—it's the same as murder."

"Then what happened? Do you have a child somewhere that I don't know about?"

"Calm down, Luce. Nothin' bad happened. My mama took that girl off for a few days to talk some serious religion into her, and the girl had a miscarriage while my mama was with her. Mama said that was God's way a gettin' rid of a sinful mistake. She said that girl was nothin' but a scheming Jezebel and I was to forget I ever knew her."

Lucy lay back down and curled away from him.

"You're feelin' bad about them tests, huh? What'd they say? You gonna have ta have an operation or somethin'?"

"Go ask your mama," she said.

Buddy sounded puzzled. "Okay. I'll do that." He started to leave the bedroom, then stopped and turned back toward her. "How long till dinner?"

"Ask your mama," Lucy repeated before shutting him out completely.

In just a matter of weeks Wanda was installed in the larger of their two extra bedrooms and there was a shiny new maroon Ford sitting in the driveway. Lucy found it difficult to enjoy either. She was heavy and sleepy and there was an ache around her eyes that made them feel as though she'd been crying. But she hadn't been crying because she didn't have the energy to cry, and why would she cry anyway when there was really nothing wrong?

She'd finally managed to include her mother in the fine, easy life she herself had been leading. She had a car and leisure time and a generous allowance and a husband with clean fingernails and a respected position in the community. Someday she would have a baby—she had no doubt that Charity would see to that. So what was there to cry about?

"What's the matter with you?" Wanda kept asking. "You ain't yourself these days."

"Cheer up," the reverend urged. "The Lord loves you whether you're barren or not."

"Come on, Luce," Buddy pleaded. "Where's my perky gal?"

"It's a phase," Charity whispered knowingly to them all, not caring if Lucy could hear. "It's just a phase."

A phase, Lucy repeated to herself.

But as she chugged through the endless days, she wondered: Had she entered a new phase in her life? Or was it that she was leaving an old phase behind?

24

Juliana

"Be careful," Charlotte kept telling her. "Take your freedom slowly. Don't push your grandfather too fast or he'll lock you back up and throw away the key."

But it was hard to go slowly. After years of starvation, everything was suddenly laid out before her on platters. She'd won freedom from her grandfather. And she was somebody now. Her success at Elysia had unlocked all the magic doors. The phone rang constantly, and each new week brought a different invitation in the mail. She was desirable. She was envied.

There'd even been a mention in the gossip columns: "Jinx Van Lyden entertained at the Van Lyden country estate last weekend. Among the guests were Perry Lorillard-Harris, Whitney Chandler, and Daphne Buchanan. Little birds say to look out for the dashing Aubrey's daughter!"

Juliana read the sentences over and over. She sent out for more papers and hoarded them like gold.

"Be careful," Charlotte warned her. "Be careful."

What a worrier Charlotte was.

Worry. Worry. Worry. Juliana was sick of it. God, she was seventeen years old! And she was still following most of her grandfather's rules. She never went anywhere without a driver and bodyguards, and she never left the house without checking with him first. Didn't Charlotte realize that she could take care of herself? There wasn't anything to worry about.

Except for Matthew Rhysdale. But then, Charlotte didn't know about Matt. No one did.

Charlotte was harping on her favorite theme again that morning. "In five months you'll be eighteen and you'll come into your first money. Don't jeopardize that. Don't underestimate your grandfather."

"Stop nagging me!" Juliana had said as she picked up the phone to call for a car. "I know what I'm doing."

But in the car she wondered what Charlotte had meant. Could Charlotte possibly know? Might Charlotte tell her grandfather?

The question stayed with her all the way to the hotel and made her more cautious than usual. She made doubly certain the bodyguards were still sitting in the lobby where she'd told them to wait before edging out of the restaurant and around the potted palms to sidestep into a waiting elevator.

She prided herself on these clandestine manuevers. They made her feel highly sophisticated and clever, and they intensified the excitement of meeting Matt. As the elevator rose, she closed her eyes and savored the drama of her secret affair.

Tap, tap, tap. Pause. Tap, tap. Pause. Tap. Their special knock. The door swung open.

Matt didn't speak. He just stood there looking at her. His tie was gone and his shirt collar was loosened and his sleeves were rolled up. The sight of him made her weak.

She tossed her bag aside and shrugged out of her fur, letting it fall to the floor. Beneath it she wore a lace camisole and matching lace panties, a garter belt and black silk stockings, and an opera-length strand of priceless gray pearls. And nothing else.

His eyes danced with startled pleasure.

"Surprise," she said, needing reassurance.

He kissed her long and hard. She was reassured. He pulled her tight against him, then lifted her up to sit facing him on the long wooden dresser. She closed her eyes and waited while he undressed. It was a slow process and she wondered if he did it because he was fussy about his clothes or because he liked to make her wait.

The first contact was his mouth. She threw back her head and gripped the dresser edge as his tongue explored her through the lace. Moans slipped out with her escalating breath. Just when she thought she couldn't hold on any longer, he stopped. Slowly he slid her high heels off. He pulled her forward so her bottom was barely balanced on the wooden edge. She kept her eyes tightly shut, waiting to find out what he would do with her next. The helpless uncertainty was exquisite.

He lifted her legs and thrust deep and hard. She gasped and let go of the dresser to wrap her legs around his waist and her arms around his neck and he held her standing until she came. Then he staggered to the bed and they fell on it together and he pulled away.

She knew what he wanted.

She knelt on the bed and wound the pearls around the base of his erection, binding him to her with the priceless heirloom. She licked and sucked feverishly, her head tilted so she could watch his face. Sometimes she regretted ever having let him in her mouth. Now that was all he wanted, and she was tired of it. She felt cheated when she had to snap out of her postclimax haze and labor so hard over him, and she missed the weight and heat of his body shuddering against hers when he came. But then, it was mostly her fault, because she'd always pretended pleasure, and she'd learned that her mouth gave her tremendous power over him. She could coax him out of bad moods, make him say yes instead of no, even make him beg if she wanted.

His body tensed and she knew he was close. She couldn't stand it. Not today. Today she'd take control. She stopped working and jerked the pearls free. His eyes flew open as she settled onto him. The look was questioning and faintly annoyed, but so caught in mounting frenzy that he was completely at her mercy. She was suddenly excited again. She leaned forward so her breasts hovered over his mouth.

"Suck me," she ordered, and when he obeyed, she came almost instantly.

They lay exhausted afterward and she felt the first wave of desolation. It was always this way. The anticipation and the physical intensity were followed by days of desperation.

"I want to stay together," she said, but he was already up and headed for the shower.

The ravenous look was gone from his eyes and she desperately wished she could call it forth again.

She showered after him and pulled on a knit dress she'd had folded in her bag. "We should have ordered room service. I'm starved."

"I did," Matt said. "They should be here any minute."

They settled together on the bed, pillows propped up and legs extended. They had forty-five minutes left.

"So how'd you get away today?" he asked.

She smiled. "Same old thing," she said nonchalantly. "I'm supposed to be having lunch in the dining room with friends."

Matt had no idea how many precedents she'd had to set in order to have her time free. He assumed that she'd always done exactly as she pleased. The privileged little princess with no rules but her own whims. He thought that every difficulty she'd had in seeing him stemmed from the need to keep their relationship secret.

She'd only recently told him the truth about her age, and he'd been furious. She couldn't bring herself to add that she was not only underage, she was also sheltered and inexperienced and far less sophisticated than he believed her to be. That he was her first boyfriend. That she'd been a virgin and unprotected from pregnancy when they made love that first time in her bedroom at Elysia.

"And did you tell your friends that you were supposed to be meeting them here?"

"Sort of. I told a few girls I needed a cover for this afternoon if anyone asked any questions."

"But you didn't say who you were meeting?"

"Matt! We've been through all this. I haven't told anyone about you. My friends think I'm stuck on some mystery man." She tickled his neck. "How does that make you feel? Should I get you a black cape?"

He didn't respond to her teasing.

"What are you so nervous about?"

He sighed heavily. "It's been a bad week."

"Tell me about it."

"Not yet."

"Okay . . ." She filled in with chatter. He always enjoyed news of her family and friends.

"Aunt Grace is hitting the bottle again. She's trying to keep it hidden from Grandfather, but I can tell. She's terrified that he's going to send her someplace to dry out."

"Would he do that?"

"Sure. He'll have her hauled off screaming if she pushes him hard enough."

Matt stared straight ahead, and she could tell something was bothering him.

"Anyway, I don't blame her for drinking. She has to get up every morning and face what her son is. I'm surprised all she needs is alcohol."

"That may not be why she drinks. Most parents never see the truth about their children."

"But how could you miss it with him! You talked to him that day at Elysia. How did you see him?"

Matt frowned in thought. "I remember thinking that he was . . . dangerous."

"See!" she said, pleased that Matt had so easily seen through the Armani clothes and the cultured manners.

"Men like that . . ." Matt shook his head. "It's a question of flexibility. It takes a lot of bending to get along in this world, and men like Ellis don't know how to bend. That's what makes them dangerous."

"Flexibility?"

He patted her hand—a gesture she despised. But she held in her irritation. He was on the edge of a bad mood and she didn't want to push him.

"You didn't ask me what the surprise was for," she said.

"What was it for?"

"Tomorrow is our six-month anniversary." She pulled a narrow box from her bag and dropped it in his lap. He opened it and stared down at the gold pen-and-pencil set.

"I found out the president has one just like it," she said.

"It's terrific," he said. "Thanks." He closed the box. "But I don't have anything for you."

"That's okay," she said lightly. She'd said that every month when she gave him an anniversary gift and he didn't have one for her. She'd said it at Thanksgiving and New Year's. But it wasn't really okay. He could have gotten her some little thing like he did at Christmas.

"You always think of such good presents," he said.

"Just wait till my birthday, when I get my trust and I'm not on an allowance anymore. I'm going to take you shopping for decent clothes and I'm going to get us an apartment and—"

"Stop it." His voice was flat. It frightened her. Terror stirred just beneath her heart.

"Why? What's wrong with a little daydreaming? As soon as I come of age and get that money, we're free. We can go for walks in Central Park and eat dinner in restaurants like ordinary people, and—"

"We are not ordinary people! We never will be. Your turning eighteen won't change that."

"Well ... there's still nothing wrong with planning for our future, is there?"

"We don't have a future! Not together." He swung his legs over the edge of the bed so his back was to her. "We have separate futures. You'll be the latest thing in crazy heiresses and I'll be the sincerest new face in Washington."

"Washington?" The word came out in her tiniest, most cowering little-girl voice. The voice she detested. The voice she'd never known she had until she met Matt. No future? Separate futures? What was he talking about?

He leapt to his feet and spun to face her. "What do you think

I've been working for all this time? Do you think I want to slog around in the local chickenshit forever?"

"I thought you liked New York."

"New York is fine. For a stepping-stone. But the power ..." He looked up and held his hands as though lifting something. "The raw power is Washington. Those men hold us all in their hands. They hold the world."

"I could go to Washington too," she offered uncertainly. "If we were married ..."

All at once everything about Matt sagged. His hands, his shoulders, his perfectly sculptured face. As though he were disintegrating before her eyes. He collapsed into a chair and buried his face in his hands.

"What is it?" she cried, but she was afraid to go to him.

He dropped his hands and looked at her. "I didn't know how to tell you ..." Moisture gathered in his eyes and his voice cracked with emotion.

She waited. Her heart waited. Her lungs waited. She was suspended by fine threads.

He stared at the floor and covered his mouth with his hand. Then he peeked up as though hoping she'd disappeared. "Something has happened ..." he began weakly. He cleared his throat. He took a deep breath and squared his chin. Once again he was clothed in the strength and humble sincerity that had brought him political success. He stood and began to pace.

"My life isn't my own, Juliana. Just as yours doesn't belong completely to you. We have commitments and responsibilities. You're a Van Lyden. I'm a servant of the people."

Lifting his chin, he paused and struck a pose. She thought how beautiful he'd look as a bronze statue in the Capitol. Heroic young crusader. Lancelot as politician.

"A long, long time ago, when I was a young boy working from dawn to dark in the heat and the dirt, I made a promise. I pledged myself to public service. I pledged my entire life ... every hour of every day ... and I swore to make whatever sacrifices were required."

The noble pose held for a moment and he seemed far away. Then he turned toward her, blue eyes unchangeably bright, sunlight from the window painting gold in his hair, and he said, so softly that she felt the words rather than heard them: "And the biggest sacrifice I'll ever have to make is you. I can't have you. I can't marry you. I can't show you off in public. I can't live with you and your servants and your history and your priceless antique toilet seats. It would ruin me. It would destroy me."

She shook her head, slowly at first, then faster. "No. No. I could help you. I could—"

"Kitten . . . believe me . . ." He looked at her. His eyes were gentle. "You can't help me. Not now."

She didn't move. She didn't speak.

"You don't make this easy," he said. He sighed and rubbed his forehead with his fingertips. A gesture he always managed without disturbing his hair. "There'll be a formal announcement tonight at the Young Republican dinner. I'm running for the state senate and I'm becoming engaged to Carole Wakefield, daughter of a former senator, granddaughter of an ambassador, and great-granddaughter of a vice-president. It's all been arranged."

"Engaged?"

He looked suddenly sad, as though he felt very sorry for himself.

"I wanted to tell you before you found out from someone else. It doesn't change how I feel about you."

Juliana closed her eyes. She felt dizzy. The room spun crazily around her and she thought she might throw up.

"You do see, don't you? I can't start a political campaign with an underage girlfriend hidden in the woodwork. Tell me you understand," he pleaded.

Replies flew around in her head. Scathing remarks sizzled. Pleas echoed and bounced. But all she could do was stare at him.

He took her silence as acceptance, and his face brightened. "This doesn't mean the end," he said. "We just have to stay apart till I'm elected. Let things settle and come together. Then we'll find ways to see each other."

Somehow she maneuvered off the bed and stood. Her body was a mechanical thing.

"Carole is an opportunity," he said. There was a frantic edge to his voice. "It's a partnership. She and her family get a prime candidate and I get their name and their support. It's for the cause . . . one more step toward Washington . . ."

She flew at him with such sudden ferocity that he had no defense. He fell backward and his head struck the corner of the wall and she fell with him, scratching and punching while he raised his hands in a dazed attempt to protect his pretty face.

"Get . . . off . . . stop . . ." He cuffed her, knocking her sideways, and she grabbed a huge lamp and launched it at him, but it was still plugged in, so the lamp sailed to the end of its cord and then smashed straight to the floor.

"You crazy bitch! You fucking spoiled bitch!" He eased back from her, snaring jacket and tie and overcoat as he moved. The mirror stopped him.

"Look what you've done to my face! I can't go to the dinner tonight!"

Juliana threw the ceramic ashtray at his head. He ducked and it crashed into the mirrored closet door behind him, shattering the silvered glass.

"You fucking lunatic!" he screamed as he slammed out the door.

She ran after him into the hall, but he was already out of sight. A wide-eyed maid stared from behind her service cart, but Juliana didn't give a damn. She returned to the room and sank down on the end of the bed and hugged herself.

"Matt . . . Matt . . ."

The pain bent her double.

She picked up her coat and bag. Shoes. Shoes. She needed her shoes. There was blood on her feet. She sat on the toilet to pull the slivers of glass out and wipe off the blood. Despair filled her.

"Oh, Matt . . . Matt . . ."

She rocked herself back and forth, her head striking the wall with increasing force. Then suddenly she straightened. She had to leave. She had to make it to the safety of Great House and the comfort of the white rooms before she fell through the shattered mirror. Before she fell too far into the darkness and was lost.

25

Ellis

Ellis Van Lyden looked at the two suitcases beside his closet. He'd had them packed for weeks, but they hadn't gone anywhere. He hadn't gone anywhere.

He glanced at his watch. Time to go down. Sunday brunch was a requirement at Great House these days, and Edward hated it if anyone was late. Sunday brunch. It was part of the luxurious fabric of his life now . . . the meaningless, irrelevant fabric of his life.

He walked past the suitcases. They were silent accusers, mutely leveling their charge of cowardice each additional day that they stood there. Reminding him that the only chains holding him at Great House were the links of his own weakness.

Why couldn't he break free of the webs his mother and grandfather spun so busily around him? Webs of guilt and flattery and need. Why couldn't he find the strength to leave? Was he so dulled by the comfort and familiarity? Or did he want to stay? Did he want to let go and fall completely under the spell of money, burying himself so deeply in it that he lost the texture and memory of reality? So deeply that he lost himself . . . and lost the past?

He stepped out into the hall and was greeted immediately by his mother, as if she'd been hovering outside his door.

" 'Morning, dear," she said.

Just two innocent words, but they grated against him and churned in his stomach. She sounded so fragile, so falsely bright, and so pathetically eager to please.

He stopped and closed his eyes momentarily, summoning strength and patience before turning to acknowledge her.

"Ellis . . . did you hear me?"

"Yes, Mom. Good morning."

She was beside him quickly, linking her arm in his. Her face was chalk-white beneath the uneven layer of makeup she'd applied.

"Did you sleep well?" She made the inquiry in the same tone parents usually reserved for small children.

"I have no complaints. And you, how was your night?" He regretted asking as soon as he'd spoken the words.

"Oh, you know me . . . I'm not one to complain." She smiled bravely. "I'm fine as soon as I see you each morning. That's all that matters."

Why? he wanted to shout at her. *Why is that all that matters?* But of course he didn't. He was afraid to put his anger into words. There was no telling what sort of self-destructive reaction she might have.

His mother ignored his silence. She carefully ignored any signs of discomfort or dissatisfaction from him, filling his silences with her own chatter. "It's a lovely day," she chirped. "I thought we'd go out to the Hamptons for a while. These may be our last good beach days."

"Grandfather hates the beach."

"Oh, I was thinking of just the two of us. We've had so little quality time together these past months."

Ellis gritted his teeth. Quality time? What did she want from him . . . blood?

"I don't know about the beach, Mother . . ."

"Oh," she scolded. "You love the beach. Why, you used to cry every time I made you come home from the beach."

"That was a long, long time ago." He tried to make a joke of it. "I only cry now when I skin my knees."

She looked at him blankly. Her eyes were darkly ringed beneath her makeup. It was hard to remember the vibrant woman she'd been before he was taken to the mountains. And of course that was the main source of his guilt, the realization that she'd been so damaged by his absence.

"But you still love to swim and body-surf and—"

"Yes. Yes. Yes. I still like going to the beach. That wasn't the point. I just don't know if I'm up for several days at the beach right now."

"You have plans, don't you?" Her voice had a wounded quaver in it. "Something you haven't told me about."

Ellis shook his head, but there was no stopping her.

"It's that Whitney Chandler, isn't it? You're seeing her again! I should have taken you away as soon as you were free of her the first time, so she couldn't get her hooks back into you."

"Stop it," Ellis said flatly. "You don't know what you're talking about."

"Yes, I do! Believe me, I do! It's you who don't know. You haven't led an ordinary life, Ellis. You have no idea what young women are all about or how treacherous they can be."

"Mother, I'm twenty-three years old. I don't need or appreciate this sort of counseling."

He could have reassured her more about Whitney. He could have told her that the girl had been a mistake. A diversion he quickly regretted.

Whitney had seemed so polished and wise and aloof when he met her at Elysia, not at all like other girls her age. And he'd given in to her tenacious pursuit because he hadn't made any other friends yet and because he assumed it to be a diversion for her as well. He'd never meant to hurt her.

"Do you love me?" she'd asked one night, lying naked and sated beside him.

Immediately he knew that he'd miscalculated her involvement. "Why do you ask me that all of a sudden?"

She was quiet a moment. Then she sat up and laughed. "Just checking. I mean . . . I wouldn't want you to fall in love with me or anything."

He'd broken off with her shortly thereafter because he saw then how vulnerable she was. And he'd tried to stay away from women since.

Before the door to the breakfast room, Grace stopped. Her hand was like a claw on his arm. "You'll understand someday when you're a parent. When you have your own baby . . ." The conviction in her voice didn't match the pleading in her eyes. "There are things I have to protect you from. It's my duty."

Abruptly Ellis opened the door. It was the only escape route. Exposing her to the family's view transformed her. She conjured up an instant smile, loosened her hold on his arm, and floated into the room beside him like a butterfly in her multicolored caftan.

"Good morning," Edward's voice boomed from the head of the table. He checked his pocket watch as he spoke the words, silently underlining the fact that they were five minutes late.

Grace slipped into her designated spot opposite Edward. Ellis sat across from Juliana.

"And how are you this morning, Ellis? Hungry, I hope." Edward beamed a benevolent smile in his grandson's direction. "I understand Cook has included some nice little fillets in the menu this morning."

"Fine." Ellis nodded politely and busied himself with unfolding his napkin and choosing fresh juice from a tray that the maid offered.

It was a relief to be in Edward's company. As long as his grandfather was present, he was shielded from the full range of his mother's behavior. The relief came with a stiff price, though. In order to share his grandfather's company peacefully, he had to constantly censor himself. He had to endure Edward's bigotry and lack of social conscience and feign indifference to the serious topics that most concerned him. To coexist with his grandfather, he didn't dare verbalize his views on nuclear waste or oil spills or the budget deficit or military aid.

"I hear that you were up rummaging around in the night, Grace. Were you ill?"

"Oh, no." Grace smiled sweetly. "Just restless."

"Perhaps I should hire you a companion."

"Why, whatever for?" Grace asked lightly, but the fear was evident in her eyes.

Edward had threatened to send her away if she couldn't stop drinking on her own, and any companion he hired would be instructed to keep a careful watch over her.

The maids finished serving and Edward turned back to Ellis. "Are you going to the auction?"

Across from him Jinx's hand tightened around her juice goblet and her entire body went very still.

"No. Not this time," Ellis answered.

"He's too busy breaking hearts," Juliana said.

Grace stiffened.

"Nonsense. Now, listen here, Ellis, even Juliana has developed an eye. You should take to it easily."

"I'm not interested, Grandfather."

Juliana's eyes were deadly. "Why don't you offer him something?" she said. "Maybe his interest has a price."

Edward's eyes narrowed but the corners of his mouth curved upward. "Is that right, son? Are you holding out for a reward?"

And suddenly it was so clear to Ellis. Edward knew exactly what he was doing. He was using Juliana's fierce antagonism and he was using Ellis' guilt. He was pitting them against each other.

"What could I possibly want, Grandfather?" Ellis tried to keep his sarcasm light. "You've given us everything, haven't you?"

Grace piped up then with some nervous chatter about a show she wanted to see, and the tension loosened a notch.

Ellis cut into his steak and studied Juliana. She'd bloomed after the weekend at Elysia, turning almost overnight into a striking, luminous young woman. But over the last weeks all that had changed. She'd lost too much weight and she'd turned from tawny to sallow. She let her newly short hair fall forward across her eyes and made no effort to brush it away. Instead she used the sullen curtain of hair to shut everyone out, like a wounded cougar crouched behind a rock.

He wanted to find out what was wrong and help. But he knew that was impossible. He still carried her mother's kiss in his heart. He still wore her mother's blood on his hands. And every time she looked at him, he was reminded of that.

"Isn't that right, Ellis?" Grace said with sugary insistence.

Ellis looked at her blankly.

"I was telling your grandfather that you and I thought we might breeze out to the Hamptons for a few days while the weather's still nice."

Edward cleared his throat. "Hmm, well, if you think you're up to it ..." He spoke to Ellis, asking with his eyes whether Ellis would assume responsibility for Grace's sobriety.

"The question is not whether I'm up to it—" Ellis began, but Edward cut him off.

"The beach might not be such a bad idea for all three of you. Juliana could use a little sunshine and fresh air, herself."

Across the table Juliana's head jerked up and she stared at her grandfather as though he'd just said something in Swahili. "I'm not going to the beach with them," she said.

"It would do you good," Edward said. "You look terrible." His pronouncement was very close to being an order.

"I'm not going," Juliana said.

"Take a girlfriend too," Edward suggested expansively.

"Well, if she doesn't want to go ..." Grace began sweetly.

"This discussion is pointless," Ellis said. "I'm not going to the beach either."

His mother's bright surface collapsed. "Who is it?" she demanded. "Who are you seeing now that's more important than your own family?"

"Don't start this, Mother."

A weight settled on Ellis and he felt incredibly tired. His grandfather was frowning at his mother, and across the table Juliana had perked up and was the picture of attention. He tried to catch his mother's eye. "Let's talk about it later," he said as calmly as he could.

"Oh, no!" The shrillness of her voice told him that she was unraveling. "You can't put me off like that. I'm your mother, and

I've a right to an answer! What girl has you panting after her now? What little slut is stealing you from the people you belong with?"

Ellis stood and threw his napkin down on the table. He looked at his mother, at the fire of righteous indignation that was melting into fear. He looked at his grandfather, whose unruly eyebrows were knit in a regal display of disapproval. And he looked at his cousin, whose appearance had gone from wraithlike to predatory alertness in the space of seconds.

"I'm leaving," he said simply.

Edward cleared his throat and muttered something that ended with an admonishment about leaving the table before a meal was over.

"I'm not just leaving the table. I'm leaving the house. I'm leaving the state. I might leave the country."

His mother gasped, Juliana's eyes widened, and his grandfather's face went red.

"Don't you think you're blowing this little disagreement all out of proportion?" Edward asked. His level tone was obviously a great effort.

"It's not because of this little disagreement," Ellis said. He looked at them. This was his family gathered around the table. Should he try to explain? Should he tell them that he had to break free before it was too late? Should he tell them that he had to confront his demons or succumb to them?

He looked at them—his family—and he was chilled. He saw that his explanations wouldn't matter. They would try to hold him at any cost. They would destroy him.

"I can't stay here anymore," he said.

"You're leaving me!" Grace cried. "After all the years of loving you and caring for you ... after all the sacrifices I've made to be a good mother ... after all those years that were stolen from me ..."

Edward stood. He brushed Grace's anguished cries away with an angry wave. "Ellis, you don't know what you're saying," he said. "Whatever it is that's bothering you can be solved right here where you belong. Running away never helped anything."

"I'm not going in order to leave you, Mother."

Ellis looked from face to face.

"And I'm not running away. I've finally stopped running away."

26

Lucy

Wanda Clare lasted five months in the comfort of her new color-coordinated, work-free existence. The up-to-date perfection of the Expando home intimidated her and she behaved as if she were a temporary guest, tidying up after herself so obsessively that there was never a visible trace of her inhabitance. She kept busy with baking and scrubbing, insisting that the tasks were relaxing for her, and she volunteered for every committee and cleanup crew at church, but she was not happy.

None of the ladies' clubs she had dreamed of joining would accept her as a member, and she had no hobbies or long-dormant interests to pursue. Shopping with Charity made her nervous, movie theaters made her claustrophobic, long car rides made her nauseous, and gardening hurt her back. She watched her favorite afternoon soap opera each day and drew diagonal lines across the pages of the television guide, marking the passage of time like a prisoner waiting for release.

Then, one morning, after making twenty dozen snickerdoodle cookies for an upcoming church function, Wanda collapsed onto the kitchen's sparkling vinyl floor and died. Dr. Howell said her heart had given out.

Charity took care of all the arrangements and staged a funeral that was grander than the sum of Wanda's entire life. Brother Dean Ed and Sister Dora Mae provided live music, including selections that Charity insisted had been Wanda's favorites. There were speeches and masses of flowers and a number of nice hams. Wanda, resplendent in a peach chiffon dress from Charity's closet, presided mutely over it all from a coffin that was the same shade of powder blue Charity favored in cars.

Lucy moved through the endless event in a fog. Suki, who had driven over that morning from Dallas, assumed control of Lucy, steering her this way and that, nudging her when responses were required, and even forcing her to eat after the service from the overflowing platters of food.

Lucy didn't break down once during the long day, but when Suki went back to Dallas that night she wept uncontrollably. Suddenly she felt abandoned and alone. The solid nucleus of her family was gone and she had no center, no point of reference to guide herself by.

Maybe Anita had been right. Maybe it had always been inevitable that she become a Skidmore. With her mama gone Lucy could feel them readying their forces, preparing to absorb her so completely that there would be no trace of Lucy Clare left in Mrs. Buddy Skidmore. Everything about her and her family that had given the Skidmores' cause for embarrassment or discomfort would be wiped away with Lucy's history. She would be cleansed and recreated. And lost to herself forever.

Lucy attempted to explain this to Suki over the phone, but her sister reacted with anger, declaring that Lucy was ungrateful and stupid and must be having a breakdown. Suki then compounded the betrayal by calling Charity to say that Lucy was "talking crazy."

Charity watched Lucy closely after that. She bustled in and out of the mobile home constantly, bearing casseroles and coffee cakes and tidying and straightening as though Lucy were an invalid. The reverend stopped by frequently to read passages from the Bible to her. And Buddy was more considerate than he'd ever been, never demanding meals or complaining about missing socks, not even asking her to read the television listings to him or look up numbers in the phone book.

Lucy settled into a reclusive haze. She spent most of her time in the room that had briefly been Wanda's, sleeping on the sheets that smelled of her mother's lilac talc and sorting and resorting her mother's boxes of possessions. There were pictures and pressed flowers and movie-ticket stubs and tiny locks of hair and yellowed baby clothes. There was a newspaper obituary column with the lines "Two-day-old unnamed infant boy. Survived by parents, Mr. and Mrs. Lydell Clare, of rural Walea. No funeral planned."

This evidence of sentiment was so unlike the mother Lucy had known. When had her mother ever been so impractical as to waste time pressing flowers? When had her mother seen a ticket stub as anything more than trash? For that matter, when had her mother ever gone to movies?

Lucy squinted hard at the old formally posed portraits, trying to guess which relatives were which and wondering why Wanda had never shown the pictures to her daughters. She examined the scant offering of snapshots and school photos that traced hers and her sister's childhoods, puzzling over that other time, that other existence. And she fingered the cellophane-wrapped baby curls and the delicately handmade little dresses and imagined that some of these cherished mementos belonged to her. That one of the lovingly preserved dresses had been made for her. That one of the bright red curls was brown enough to have come from her head.

And the newspaper clipping! What a surprise that was. The disintegrating newsprint was nearly unreadable in places, but marked lines were still clear. And so was the date at the top. Wanda had had a baby before Suki, and this secretly mourned dead baby had been the firstborn—not Suki. The knowledge gave Lucy a perverse satisfaction. How different would their lives have been if "unnamed baby boy" had lived? Would her father have been happier and longer-lived and her mother less fixated on Suki and . . . And. And. She could stretch it out into a dozen different scenarios, each more pleasant than the actual course their lives had taken, but always at the end she got around to asking herself the same question: Would she have ended up married to Buddy Skidmore?

Lucy's "delicate state," as Charity referred to it, lasted for nearly a month. During this period she wouldn't leave the mobile home, even, to the Skidmore's chagrin, to attend the reverend's Sunday services. Then one morning after Buddy had left for work and before Charity or the reverend had a chance to drop by, Lucy closed the door on the fading lilac of Wanda's room and put on her favorite going-to-town outfit and drove the maroon Ford into Walea. She circled aimlessly at first, then finally pulled into the law-office parking lot.

The women were already gone to a lunchtime baby shower for a new secretary Lucy didn't know. Mr. Tully was in, though, and he insisted that Lucy join him for lunch. The invitation gave her a nervous thrill that she refused to analyze.

They drove separately to the Hog Haven and then sat down together for barbecue and pinto beans and onion rings and coleslaw. Lucy was suddenly ravenous. Food had never tasted so good. She finished everything on her plate and downed two mason jars full of iced tea and ordered pecan pie and coffee for dessert. Mr. Tully tried making small talk, but Lucy was so busy eating that she barely participated. By dessert he had stopped all effort at conversation and was watching her with an amused expression.

"I can't remember the last time I've seen a woman enjoy a meal so much," he said as she finished the last bite of pie.

Lucy felt herself blushing and fumbled for an excuse.

"No!" He laughed. "There's certainly no grounds for an apology. It's a pleasure eating with someone who isn't picking at salads and moaning about her weight."

Lucy sipped the coffee. She didn't know why she'd ordered coffee. Buddy didn't like it and so she hadn't had any for years. It tasted almost foreign.

"I never did thank you for that lovely arrangement the office sent to Mama's funeral," she said. "That was really thoughtful."

"Yes, you did," he insisted. "We got a nice thank-you card in the mail."

"Those were from Charity. She signed my name to all of them, but they weren't from me."

"Oh. Well, that was kind of her to take that worry off your shoulders."

Lucy didn't respond.

"And how is your family? Buddy and Charity and Reverend Skidmore—how are they all doing?"

"Fine. But they're not my family."

"Uh-oh. What's all this about? You having problems at home?"

"Not really. It's just true, is all. They're not my family and they never will be."

He frowned and drummed his fingers on the table. Then he brightened and leaned forward, visibly excited by some new thought, and she felt a pang of nostalgia. Working for him had been more than satisfying. She'd been young and timid and unaware then, but looking back, she could see how important his intelligence and energy had been to her. The air in that office had been constantly charged with new ideas and possibilities and she'd been carried along with it, caught in the exhilarating forward rush.

Now her life had no forward motion.

"Come back to work!" he said. "Why not? Come back part-time and go to school part-time. Make a career for yourself. Be a paralegal or an office manager. Get wild and go to law school if you want . . . God knows you're smart enough."

She stared at him over the rim of her coffee cup. How had Mr. Tully ever developed so much faith in her? It was a complete mystery. And while it was enormously flattering, it was also a burden, because she had to worry about him finding out the truth. She wasn't smart enough. She wasn't talented enough or clever enough or fearless enough. And she wasn't careful enough. She wasn't nearly careful enough.

"I couldn't go back to work. Buddy would think it was some kind of statement about his failure as a breadwinner, and the Skidmores would be humiliated."

"What about school, then? What about taking some classes? You wouldn't have to say you were working toward anything. Why, hell, my partners' wives are always taking Styrofoam art or antique refinishing or something. Classes are an accepted outlet for ladies of leisure."

"I don't know . . ."

"You could start small. It's only a twenty-minute drive to that little college east of here. You could go a few afternoons a week . . . maybe take a literature course . . . maybe something in art or photography."

Lucy was touched by his concern and by the way he always seemed to remember every little thing she'd ever told him about herself. Buddy, who supposedly knew her as well as anyone, would never have thought to suggest art or photography classes.

She tried to keep a serious face, but his enthusiasm was contagious. "College? Do you think I could? I mean . . . do they let people like me in?"

He laughed heartily. "If they've got any sense they do."

"I wouldn't know where to start . . . how to apply or anything."

"I'll help."

College. The very word was magical. Could she actually do such a thing? She'd managed to complete high school through the evening adult-education program before she married Buddy, but she'd never dared think of college.

"I'll have to figure out what to say to the Skidmores," she said, feeling breathless with excitement and terror. "I can't let them find out until I've got a plan."

"It's our secret," he promised. He reached across the table to shake her hand in a formal sealing of the pact, and the contact with his flesh was unaccountably disturbing.

She pulled her hand back quickly and reached for her purse.

"I'll get this," he said.

"No," she responded a little too emphatically. "We go halves, like always."

"Right," he said with a gentle grin that made her more nervous than she already was.

They walked to the parking lot together and agreed to talk again in a week, at which time Mr. Tully hoped to have the admittance and class information for her.

Lucy drove home without seeing the streets. Her thoughts were flying joyously. College! She wished her mama and daddy were alive to hear this. Not that she really expected to make anything of it like Mr. Tully had suggested. The idea of her being able to get a college diploma was pretty farfetched, and aiming for something serious like law was about as realistic as wanting to be an astronaut, but taking a few classes ... Yes. She could imagine herself doing that. And imagining it made her life feel new and shiny and pregnant with possibility. By the time she'd reached home she was ready to launch her campaign to win the Skidmores' consent.

That night she surprised Buddy with his favorites: fried ham, mashed potatoes, and biscuits with red-eye gravy, and Seven-Up-lime-Jell-O salad with marshmallows, all recipes she'd been given by Charity. She invited the reverend and Charity and made a dessert the reverend favored. The three Skidmores kept exchanging glances during the meal as though they were all gauging her and checking each other's reactions. Lucy ignored them and poured herself into being a hostess. At last, during dessert, she took a deep breath and plunged.

"I want to thank all of you for being so patient with me these past months," she said. "I know it's been hard and I appreciate what y'all have done."

The Skidmores had never been strong on open communication, and the declaration was as big a surprise as the meal. The reverend cleared his throat repeatedly and Buddy hunched forward and flicked his eyes back and forth between Lucy and his mother.

Charity was immobile for a fraction of a second, wavering between reactions; then she broke into her widest, sweetest smile, clasped her hands together beneath her chin, and cried out, "Lord be praised! Our Lucy girl is back."

Dessert disappeared quickly, with Charity fussing and encouraging the reverend to "eat a little more, Daddy." Afterward Buddy and the reverend moved to the living room to sit in the matching plaid recliners and watch television. Lucy and Charity cleared the table and started the dishes.

"The Lord works in strange ways," Charity said as she pulled on a pair of yellow rubber gloves to protect her hands. "One day you're wastin' away from grief, and then he works one of his miracles and you're up and smilin' and cookin' like an angel."

Lucy tried to smile agreement. "I can't wait to get back to church now," she said, wondering if the words sounded as false to Charity as they did to her own ears. The truth was, she hated going to the reverend's church. His sermons had changed over the years, becoming more and more vicious, more rabidly frenzied. She hated listening to his fiery condemnations and his bigotry and his damning of people and places from the news. And she especially hated it when he singled out local people, people from right out of the congregation, for his finger-pointing, spittle-flecked diatribes.

Charity glanced sideways at Lucy and neatly soaped a dish. She handed the dish to Lucy to put in the dishwasher. It was a familiar routine. Charity didn't trust the dishwasher to get the dishes clean, so she insisted on washing them first.

"I'm sure the congregation will be tickled to death to see you back up and around," she said.

"Yeah ... I need to get myself busy and concentrate on more positive things," Lucy said, reminding herself that this was like checkers and she had to outmaneuver Charity or she was lost.

"Like being a better Christian and being a better wife?" Charity filled in.

Lucy nodded and quickly ducked her head down to peer inside the dishwasher.

"I'm so pleased to hear that, Lucy. Then I can tell Marvinia you'll teach Sunday school this next term?"

"Well ... sure. If she needs me, I'd be glad to. But, well, I've been thinking ... Maybe I spend too much time here around home and the church. Maybe that's why I'm so backward whenever I go out to a seminar with you or when I try to go to those clubs that Buddy wants me to be in. Maybe I ought to get out around people more and develop some interests ... you know, learn some things so I wouldn't seem so dull and hickish to people like the Burrights and Fimples and Newberrys."

Charity focused on washing dishes, but she was alert and waiting. Like a coyote poised at a rabbit's hole.

"Anyway, I was thinking I could do with a little self-improvement," Lucy offered hesitantly.

"Such as?" Charity asked.

Lucy shrugged. "A class maybe."

"A class?" Charity had stopped washing dishes and turned her head to give Lucy her full attention.

"You know ... furniture refinishing, Texas history, photography ... whatever. All the wives of the lawyers where I used to work took classes like that."

"Umm-humh," Charity said with her mouth closed so it sounded like she was starting a tune. "And is that what you had to talk to Mr. Tully about today?"

Lucy nearly dropped the glass she was holding.

Charity raised her eyebrows. "Surely you don't think a married woman can lunch out with a man other than her husband and go unnoticed, do you?"

"But it wasn't like that," Lucy said, knowing even as she said it that her face was red.

"Doesn't matter whether it was or wasn't. What matters is how it looks to other folks." Charity soaped the ham platter and handed it to Lucy. "A good Christian married woman goin' to that college by herself would have to be extra watchful about avoiding just those sorts of potentially embarrassing situations."

"You're right, you're right," Lucy agreed fervently. "But with your advice I'm sure I'd do fine."

Charity peeled off the gloves and rubbed lotion into her hands. Her actions were slow and deliberate, stretching the seconds into hours. Finally she looked at Lucy. Her eyes were shrewd and hard.

"You think I started out with soft hands and a closet full of clothes and a fancy name like Charity? Uh-uuh. I've earned everything I got by diggin' my fingernails into whatever came close and hangin' on. I'm what they call a self-made woman. And I've pulled the reverend right along with me. Made him a self-made man."

Lucy held her breath. It was clear that her amateurish attempt to play in Charity's league had been a miserable failure. She'd been a fool to try outmaneuvering her mother-in-law, but she couldn't tell if her clumsiness had lost her the game or not.

Charity smoothed some imagined stray hairs into place, straightened her dress, and started toward the living room. "Daddy," she called sweetly, "you'll never guess what Lucy and I just thought up for her to do!"

One month later Lucy began classes. She signed up for darkroom techniques and art history and a Bible-as-literature class to reassure the Skidmores, and three times a week she whizzed down the highway in her maroon Ford with the radio playing and the open air singing around her. The campus was beautiful and separate and different. The students possessed a careless sophistication. The teachers were infinitely wise and endlessly fascinating. She clutched her glossy hardbound books smelling of newness and promise and her thick binder with the colored dividers and her zip bag full of pens and pencils and highlighters and markers, and she gratefully entered the cushioned never-land of academe.

It was strange being around young people. At twenty-four she still regarded herself as young, but she quickly realized that she had crossed that invisible line separating the truly young from the young-only-by-comparison. She was lumped with the grand-mothers and the retirees and the other mature types. They were the older folk. The visitors from the outside. And they were in-visible to the full-time students, whose lives were centered within the campus.

Even this outsider status pleased Lucy. It freed her from all social concerns, enabling her to function on a purer level. She could slide into the back of a class with complete anonymity. When she crossed onto the college grounds, the layers of her identity peeled away; the reverend's daughter-in-law, Buddy's wife, the poor kid from the Trailer Village, the kindergarten sex-ual offender—all were shed and she was created anew.

Lucy did not dare communicate any of these feelings to Buddy. From the beginning he'd been uncertain about his wife going off to such a suspect environment. Even though it was just the small local campus and even though Lucy was there only three after-noons a week and even though his boss's wife was also enrolled there in an interior-design class, he remembered his own colle-giate days and worried. He called home constantly, monitoring her comings and goings and insisting that she not stay at the campus one minute longer than necessary. If she tried to do homework in his presence he kept her distracted with constant requests for beer and neck rubs. He told her long stories about insurance coups he'd made and asked her to look up phone num-bers and get prospective clients on the phone for him. When none of the above kept her from her assignment, he turned the television up as loud as he could and flipped the channels with the remote. In order to reassure him, she had to pretend that the homework and the whole experience of going to college were an annoyance for her.

Deception and evasion became the cornerstones of their re-lationship. There was little that Lucy could afford to be candid about. A mention of studying at the library sent him into a ti-rade—"You think I don't know about all the boys that go sniffin' around them places? You think I'm dumb?"—and an effort to share an exciting new idea with him led to a condemnation of "all those sorry assholes who got nothin' better to do than stand up in a classroom and talk crazy shit."

He railed at her for looking shabby, then accused her of trying to dress up for other men when she bought a new outfit. He yelled about the amount of gas she was using in the car and checked the mileage each night to see how far she'd driven.

When she found ways around his complaints, he ran to his mother.

This time Charity was on Lucy's side. "Stop bein' such a bear," she told him. "Lucy's tryin' to put a little polish on both a you." But Buddy's grouchiness continued.

Lucy looked forward to his going to work in the morning. Once he was out the door she could breathe a sigh of relief and relax. The evenings he spent at his boss's watching football on the large projection television began to seem like gifts, and the nights when he went toward the Arkansas border with friends for secret poker games were even better because he usually didn't get home till well after she was asleep.

For escape Lucy turned to her camera. She took long walks, photographing clouds and other natural phenomena for the darkroom experiments she'd been working on in class. The teacher had shown them how to transpose images, a technique that was used if clouds were needed in a cloudless sky, and Lucy had liked the effects so much that she was combining all manner of elements from different negatives. She'd printed a tornado funnel in a shopping-center parking lot and a jumbo jet in a swimming pool. The darkroom work was tedious and the effort wasn't always successful, but the creative process washed her clean and infused her with purpose.

Sometimes at night when Buddy was grunting and groaning over her she stared at the ceiling and wondered what life would be like if he didn't ever come home from one of his late-night poker trips. She felt trapped. Hooked. She saw so clearly how that expression had evolved. The struggling and flopping that marked the beginning of a relationship and the slow suffocation afterward. Just like a hooked fish.

She disobeyed Buddy constantly, ignoring his growing list of forbidden activities. She continued to use the college library and have snacks in the cafeteria, and she still went by the law office occasionally, and she filched money from the grocery budget for extra film and other things he hadn't given permission for. The tension between them grew.

The day the semester ended, Buddy surprised her by proposing dinner out at the Cozy Inn Steakhouse.

"I want a table with a candle," he told the hostess.

Lucy laughed, assuming he was kidding, but he didn't respond with one of his usual jokes, and after they were seated he looked around regretfully, puckered his lips, and blew out a loud sigh. "This ain't such a great place, huh?"

"It's fine. Really. I've always wanted to try it."

"Yeah? I thought it'd be more ... you know ..."

"The food is supposed to be very good." She reached across the table to open his Leatherette menu for him. "Besides, you hate candles. You've always said you like to get a good look at what you're eating."

He brightened a little and glanced at the menu. "I'm gonna have the rustler-size sirloin. How 'bout you?"

Lucy opened her mouth to answer, but it was unnecessary.

"Why don't you get that fillet. Sounds about right for you."

"It does sound good, but I thought I'd try the skewered beef. I've never had that."

"Why would you want to have it if you don't know what it tastes like?"

"Because I want to—"

The waitress appeared then, costumed in a red gingham dress and a white apron. "Y'all decided yet?" she asked brightly, poising her order pad and pen.

"Yeah," Buddy answered. "The rustler sirloin for me. Rare. And my wife will have the fillet. Medium-rare."

The waitress began scribbling. "Baked potato or rice?" she asked without looking up from her pad.

"Baked."

"Chicken velvet soup or green salad?"

"Soup."

"Drinks?"

"Iced tea."

"Okeydoke." The woman leaned over to pick up their menus. "I'll have that tea out in a sec," she said, and breezed off toward the kitchen.

"I wanted the skewered beef," Lucy said.

Buddy looked at her as though she were a child to be humored.

"And I wanted rice."

"That chink food?" Buddy said in a halfhearted attempt at a joke.

"And I wanted the salad, not the soup."

"What's the matter, Luce? Is it the wrong time of the month or what?"

"No. You've just always done that to me."

"Aw, Lucy, come on ... don't be cranky. Tonight's supposed to be sort of a celebration."

The waitress brought the tea in big glasses with slices of orange and lemon floating on top. Buddy fished out the fruit with his fingers and dropped it in the ashtray.

"We need ta bury the hatchet, Luce. We been at each other and at each other and ... well ... startin' tonight, everything's gonna be different." He leaned across the table, punched her forearm lightly, and grinned disarmingly. Suddenly he was the old Buddy—the irresistibly boyish, fumblingly charming Buddy.

"I gotcha a surprise." He produced a small wrapped package. "Go on. Open it," he said eagerly.

Lucy undid the wrappings and flipped up the lid of the velvet jeweler's box. Inside were tiny diamond studs. Pierced earrings.

"They're real," Buddy assured her. "Took me my whole lunch hour to decide between them and your birthstone, but I figured ya can't go wrong with diamonds. You like 'em?"

"Oh, yes. Thank you, Buddy. That was very sweet."

He ducked his head and shrugged, and his face radiated pleasure. "Why don'cha go ahead and put 'em on?" he urged.

"Not yet. I want to wait until I can put them on in front of a mirror."

The soup arrived. Lucy began eating, and wondered where she could go to get her ears pierced the next day.

"It's funny," Buddy said. "How you turned out prettier than Suki. My mama says she always knew you would. Says short, cute girls like Suki always grow into chunky women, whereas girls with a lotta bone take a while but they turn out better in the end."

Lucy didn't know what to say. The evening was full of surprises. A dinner invitation, a gift, and now this flattery. Could it be true that she was pretty? Prettier even than her sister? Over the years she'd gone from plain and skinny to acceptable, but pretty? Could she have crossed over into pretty, or was Buddy just using some of his sales psychology on her?

Buddy attacked his steak with gusto when it arrived, and launched into an optimistic monologue about his hopes for the future. He wanted to open his own insurance agency. He was tired of working for a boss and he was tired of putting in so many hours and he didn't see why he shouldn't be the boss and have his own "peasants" to order around. He wanted to be rich and he wanted to have a house that was bigger and fancier than his parents' and he wanted Lucy to be a hostess in the fancy house so he could throw the best parties in town. He wanted a swimming pool and a race horse. Maybe two or three race horses. He wanted his own projection-screen television and a satellite dish so he could pick up sports transmissions from everywhere.

Lucy listened and nodded and wondered where her own wants fit in. She wanted to enroll in school full-time and maybe even get her degree. She wanted to start a little photography business and have her own studio and equipment. She wanted to drive into Dallas or Fort Worth on weekends and go to art museums. She wanted to excommunicate herself from the Temple of Light and never set foot in it again.

"We're gonna do fine," he said after the table had been cleared and dessert ordered. "We got a great future together, Luce. We're gonna make our mark on this town."

Lucy rolled those words around in her mind a lot in the following days. "A great future together." The phrase left her vaguely depressed, and she reminded herself over and over that she was lucky to have a man like Buddy and lucky to have a life of comfort.

She hadn't found a way to tell him that she was going back to school, even though she'd already filled out the forms and paid the admission fees. He was so happy now. He beamed at her and fussed over her and behaved as if she were his date rather than his wife, and Lucy hated to spoil it by mentioning the upcoming school term. Instead she had her ears pierced and kept quiet.

When the flu struck, she had an added excuse not to tackle the problem. She burrowed into her bed and nibbled at the crackers and Jell-O that Charity brought over, waiting for the virus to burn itself out and refusing to think while she felt so horrible. The illness dragged on for a week and finally Charity drove her in to be poked and prodded by Dr. Howell.

It took an hour for the lab results to come back. Dr. Howell called both her and Charity into his office to hear the verdict. She was pregnant.

Lucy was stunned. She wanted to crawl back into bed and curl up and hide.

A baby? Now?

27

Ellis

Ellis looked down at the map and then out across the vast expanse before him. The map gave everything names. There were the great Northern Rocky Mountains and lesser ranges like the Bitterroot, and the Sawtooth and the Lemhi and the Salmon River and the Smoky and the Lost River. And there were tiny snaking lines labeled as rivers. The Salmon, the Payette, the Chamberlain, and the Big Lost. But nothing on the map could tell him where he and Frank had hunted or fished or struck winter camp. Nothing could tell him where he'd tangled with the grizzly or squatted beside Badger's fire or first made love with Thea. Nothing could tell him where he'd murdered his own father.

He pocketed the useless map. Words on paper didn't matter. He knew the location of the truck stop where he and Thea had come out. That was really all he needed to start in the general direction.

He drew in a deep lungful of the air. Mountain scent filled him, bringing with it a rush of bittersweet memories.

He'd outfitted himself well: two good knives and an almost weightless down sleeping bag and fishing line and hooks and packs of dried food and tablets for emergency purification of water. He had waxed matches in case he'd lost his touch with a flint, and he'd even found a passable bow and some commercial arrows that would do until he could make his own.

Fall came early to the mountains, and he could already taste it in the air. Funny how quickly his senses were sharpening. Or maybe they'd been sharp all along and he'd been denying them. Like the night at Jinx's party when his mother had predicted a storm. He'd smelled it in the air himself, but he hadn't been able to admit it because to do so would have made him feel like a freak.

He tried to discipline his scattering thoughts. There was no time for daydreaming or intellectualizing. He had to go in now or forget the idea until next spring. If he waited even a week to think it over, he might not reclaim his skills and get himself established before the first of killing winter hit. And he had not come here to die—he had come here for life. He had come here looking for the answers that would enable him to make sense of his life.

He drew in another deep breath. Somewhere down there were the lost pieces that would make him whole.

The mountains lay sprawled before him like a well-remembered lover. He turned his head and tried to see some vestige of civilization behind him. In the distance a curl of soot-black smoke rose. Everything else was obscured from his view by the terrain. He had lived in both worlds, and there was no question that the civilized one held more terror and anguish and uncertainty than the natural one. But what if he never came out again? What if he was destined to be wedded to the mountains like Badger?

Resolutely he shouldered his heavy pack and plunged into the green labyrinth of his past.

Reawakening. Rebirth. He felt both as he traveled. He polished his skills and built up the calluses that wilderness life required, and he rediscovered the splendid logic of it all. This world made sense. There was a forthright cause and effect at work here that he'd never found in a city. There was economy and fairness and dignity unknown to human society.

After three weeks of steady traveling he'd located the area where he'd nursed Thea through her sickness. Pure joy coursed through him, making him drop his pack and run whooping through the trees. Everything was still here for him to find. Every place. Every memory. And there were no longer any doubts in his mind. He could do it. He could find whatever it was that he really wanted to find.

He made camp that night and stared up at the same trees that had sheltered him with Thea so long ago. He remembered her cynicism and gentleness. He remembered the sweetness in her lovemaking lessons. He remembered her words. "That was real," she'd said. "But most of the time it's not real. Not for girls. Most of the time it's just part of the act." He understood those words now. What Thea had said was true for him as well. Sex was an act for him. A superficial physical act. A search for that one person who could reach down inside and touch his soul. A search for a woman like . . .

No. He couldn't think of Yvonne yet. He wasn't ready to think of Yvonne.

He forced his thoughts back to Thea. Where was she now? he wondered. Was she happy and healthy? Had she made peace with herself? He hoped that the money had helped her.

The money.

He closed his eyes. It was useless. . . .

Yvonne . . . Yvonne . . .

Just hours before dying, Yvonne had made all the arrangements. He hadn't even known about it until a year later, when a detective contacted him in Rome and told him that Thea had been located and the gift had been delivered in the guise of an inheritance.

Yvonne.

He could still picture her sitting beside him in the park with the wind stirring her hair and the autumn leaves painting colors around her. If only he'd been older. Maybe he could have saved her. Maybe . . .

He propped himself up in his sleeping bag and stared into the blue heart of the fire. Bare skin. Rounded breasts. Firelight turning the curve of a naked hip to gold. The taste and smell and warmth of her came back to him in an aching rush.

Why?

Did she die because he hadn't been experienced enough or strong enough or perceptive enough to save her from her pain? Or did she die because he'd caused the pain—because making love with him had destroyed her?

Would he ever know the answers?

He eased down into his bag and closed his eyes. Tomorrow he would go on. Toward the place where he'd buried his father. He had to sleep. He wanted to sleep.

But his sleep was fitful and he was grateful for the rosy softness of dawn and the need to put his muscles back to work. He pushed himself, looking for relief in exhaustion. Still, it took five days to find the hot spring where he'd washed off his father's blood.

He dropped his pack and knelt to peer down into the water. It looked as clear and clean as it had all those years ago. The taint of murder had not changed it. He turned and started up toward the spot where they'd camped. His feet were leaden and his throat went suddenly dry. But he couldn't turn away now. This was the birthplace of the darkness that crawled inside him—the center of his netherworld.

He threaded through the trees. The clearing opened up before him like a welcoming smile. It was as green and innocent as the first day he'd seen it. He was suddenly disoriented. Could this be it? The scene of his nightmares? Could this be the shadowy place where his father dragged a girl in from the night and threw her down to the cold ground—eyes glittering, tongue wetting his lips in greedy anticipation?

Could this be the place where he'd murdered his father? Nausea gripped him and he leaned weakly against a sturdy lodgepole pine. The sharp scent and the rough bark against his cheek were reviving.

He straightened and walked toward the grave at the far edge of the clearing. It was undisturbed. The rocks he'd piled on top had kept the animals from digging there. The pieces of the wooden cross he and Thea had fashioned remained, though some gnawing creature had eaten the rawhide that bound them together.

He stared down at the jumble of stones and encroaching grass. There was no sign that anything sinister had ever happened, yet he knew that his father's bones lay beneath the rocks and sod there.

He had the strangest urge to dig. As if some truth might be learned from looking at the remains. Or maybe just to prove to himself that the horror of that night had actually happened. That he had killed. And that his father, that looming immutable force, had been mortal.

Sunlight slanted gently into the clearing around him, dividing into beams where it was filtered through overhanging tree limbs. All around him the birds and tiny animals were resuming the activities that his appearance had interrupted. He sat on an outgrowth of rock and cradled his head in his hands. Racking sobs tore through him, pulling the grief and remorse that he'd harbored so long from their moorings deep inside him.

When it was over, the sun had changed position. Velvet shadows blanketed the clearing. The day was almost over.

He scrubbed at his face with his hands and looked around, as surprised and disoriented as a sleeper coming out of a deep dreamstate. The air had turned chill. Mechanically he headed back down to the spring. He would sink his line in that spot just above the spring, where the cold water pooled before mixing with the warm. He would catch enough fish for dinner. He would build a fire. He would eat.

Concentrating on these simple tasks pulled him through the

next few hours. Then it was night. He built his fire in the clearing, but the flames held neither warmth nor comfort. He slid into his bag and watched the fire die down to a pulsing red eye. Noisy and Frank and Yvonne made circles in his thoughts. They were drowning in blood. He dived in, fighting the sucking whirlpool, choking on the taste of their blood, but he couldn't save them.

He woke shaking and covered with sweat. The first pink fingers of light reached through the trees. Night was over and he had survived. He rose and walked barefoot down to the spring. The water reflected the sunrise. He stripped off his damp clothing and plunged in where the hot current mixed with the cold. There was no more horror, just a vast sadness.

Frank—or his ghost—had not come out of the dark to destroy him. His own guilt and remorse had not consumed him. Lightning had not struck. The mountains had not spewed rock to bury him.

His murderous act had been forgiven and forgotten here. The spring, the clearing, the remains buried in the grave—all had returned to being no more or less than parts of the whole. They were of the mountains, woven into the endless chain of life and death and rebirth, just as his own body would have been had he died while trying to escape from his father. Just as Frank would have been earlier had the she-bear reached farther back into the rocks. Just as the grizzly would have been if Ellis had had his father's killing instinct.

He stepped from the water feeling clean and whole. And after he'd eaten and repaired the cross and scattered the remains of his dead fire, he set off to find Badger.

The cabin stood in the eastern shadow of a very distinctive wall of rock. Ellis had always thought of it as Badger's wall because it was the landmark that led him to his friend from any point. Now he made a day's climb to a windswept ridge, spotted Badger's wall in the distance, and set off. The hours of sunlight shortened as he traveled. Small animals scurried around him in the undergrowth, frantically preparing for the long winter. The wind changed direction, singing down through the trees on cold, exuberant currents, and the air took on a new smell. The smell of snow. He had to make it to the cabin fast or stop and build himself a shelter from the coming storm.

Digging into a snug shelter would have been the most prudent course of action, but Ellis could not make himself stop. He had come so far, and now he was so close. Excitement pulled him and irrational fears pushed him. He had to see Badger. He couldn't afford the week or more that it might take to wait out a storm.

The animals quieted and the sky changed overhead. Clouds obscured the weak sunshine, and the light assumed an eerie, shadowed quality, as if it had been dreamed by some mad painter with no connection to reality. Still, he couldn't stop. Familiar landmarks were all around. In just hours he would be at Badger's door.

The first snow flurries began in midafternoon. He hadn't stopped for lunch. Instead he'd eaten dried food and continued moving. If he traveled through dinner as well, he figured he would reach the cabin by late evening.

Even though he was deep within the sheltering trees, the wind whipped around him. Bits of dirt and pine needles and tiny ice particles pelted his face, and the gusts tore at his clothing and pack. He wrapped his face in a scarf, leaving only a slit for his tearing eyes. His progress slowed. He had to stop frequently to check his bearings, squinting into the wind and the swiftly dying light.

He lost all track of time. He stumbled and fell, and found that he could not get up. He'd become separated from his body. Mental commands produced no results. Nothing moved. Nothing registered. There was no pain or cold or exhaustion. His mind was floating alone in the turbulent darkness, unattached to anything physical.

He closed his eyes. Sleep gnawed at his consciousness. He imagined he was inside Badger's cabin, secure beside a roaring fire, drifting off for a night's rest. Yvonne's face floated toward him, dark eyes full of mystery and passion. He reached out to her eagerly, but before he could touch her, she was gone. Replaced by Badger. Steady, imperturbable Badger. Only Badger was angry. He was shaking his fist and cursing Ellis for stupidity and weakness and disrespect.

Ellis opened his eyes to escape the disturbing tirade. Once more snow and wind bit at his vision through ice-encrusted lashes. He was dying. He was curled on the forest floor, meekly allowing himself to be frozen to death. No wonder Badger was so angry.

He summoned unknown reserves and forced his limbs to move. They responded like crude wooden stumps, but somehow he made it to a standing position again. He shrugged off the heavy pack. It fell into the snow with barely a sound. Forward, he ordered himself. One leaden foot at a time. Forward.

When the glowing rectangular eye appeared, he couldn't think what it was. He had to concentrate on moving. The eye was good. He moved toward it. The eye became a tiny window set into a log wall. Badger's cabin. He had made it. The wind howled around him and his stiff mouth cracked into a smile beneath the layers of wool.

He couldn't move anymore. The wall was in his way. He leaned against it, contented with its solidity. His eyelids felt so heavy. Rest. He just needed a little rest. He looked down. The drifts of snow gathering at the base of the wall looked as soft as a pile of feathers. He wanted to sink down into the softness, but caught himself and clung to the rough-hewn log wall instead. Somewhere there was a door. He inched forward, feeling his way, afraid to lose contact with the wall for even an instant. A corner. Another wall. Finally he reached the indentation that marked the doorway. He raised his hand to knock but hadn't the strength to make any sound. He fumbled clumsily with the latch. It was bolted from the inside.

Rest. He would just rest a little; then he could knock harder. He slid down the door to the soft snow. Rest. His chin fell forward on his chest and consciousness drifted away on the wind.

"Swallow!"

The command came from somewhere outside of him. He choked on hot liquid. "Swallow!" he heard again, and this time his throat worked.

Gradually he became aware of other sensations besides the heat in his throat. There was pain. Burning, throbbing pain. He tried to open his eyes, but they wouldn't respond.

"Swallow!"

He obeyed the order. The effort was exhausting. He was grateful when the grip on his neck loosened and his head fell back down. Now he could rest. He needed to rest so he could knock harder on the door.

When he awoke he was in a rawhide hammock inside a cabin. Badger's cabin. The light was dim. The fire was low. He was alone. He shook his head and tried to remember. Had he knocked finally? His head hurt with the movement and his eyes felt like they'd had an acid wash. He sat up slowly and swung his feet around toward the floor. They were encased in unfamiliar fur-lined moccasins. Beneath his swaddling of blankets he was naked.

The door opened. From the gray half-light, Badger walked in.

His arms were loaded with firewood. "The snow spirit has decided to live," he said flatly. His mouth was untouched but his eyes danced.

"Do you know me?" Ellis asked weakly. His lips split into painful cracks as he spoke.

Badger closed the door, stepped out of his snowshoes, and piled the wood beside the stone hearth. He turned toward Ellis and smiled his odd straight smile. "No. But I knew a boy who is a part of you."

There was a kettle simmering over the fire. Badger dipped into it and handed Ellis a steaming cup of soup. "You have much eating and sleeping to do before your body is your friend again."

Ellis accepted the cup. He looked down at his covered feet. "How are my toes?"

"There were no sacrifices. You were lucky."

Badger filled a cup for himself and sat down on the thickly furred bear hide. His long black hair was going gray, but otherwise he was just as Ellis remembered him.

The fire crackled. Ellis sipped at the hot broth and looked around the cabin. A thick layer of hides was secured over the window, and the only light was from the fire, but he could see well enough. The cabin had not changed much over the years either.

"You've covered the window."

"Yes. That is the wise thing to do in a storm."

"But last night . . . It was storming last night too, and I saw the light through it. That's how I found my way."

Badger drank from his cup. "I knew you were coming," he said. "So I left the window bare to guide you."

"You knew I was coming?"

"Yes." Badger's face was unreadable.

Ellis stared down at his cup a moment and tried to absorb this. "And you also knew that I was coming at night and would need the light?"

"No. But half of every day is darkness, and you always could travel by moon as well as by sun."

"You knew I was coming?"

"Yes."

Ellis finished his soup. His raw, aching eyelids grew heavy. "I feel tired again."

"Sleep." Badger took his empty cup, then turned away as if offering Ellis privacy.

Ellis was asleep immediately. Sometime later he woke. Badger was sitting cross-legged by the fire, sewing. Uneven balls of raw-hide lace and buckskin of all shapes and sizes surrounded him.

Again Ellis sat up. This time he felt stronger. He clutched the blanket around him and pulled himself into a standing position. His feet burned and tingled inside the soft moccasins.

"Let the blood find your head," Badger cautioned without looking up from the path of his needle.

Obediently Ellis waited, holding on to the wall for support until the light-headedness subsided. His feet did not improve correspondingly, but he ignored them and moved around the firelit room.

"There is stew." Badger still hadn't lifted his eyes.

Ellis ladled himself a healthy portion from the kettle hanging to the side of the fire. He ate standing. "How long have I slept?" he asked between bites.

"Long enough."

"How long have I been here?"

"Two nights. Two days."

Ellis swallowed a chunk of meat in surprise. "That long?" He moved to the window and pried at a corner of the hide covering to peek outside, wondering if it was now day or night. The hides were cut and fashioned specifically for this important function of sealing the window. Ellis remembered them as having been cared for faithfully and replaced when necessary, but these were old and slightly brittle, as though they'd been unused and neglected. "These are almost rotten," he remarked absently as he fingered the hides.

Badger didn't respond.

"Just how long have you kept this window uncovered to guide me?"

Badger's hand hesitated over his sewing for a fraction of an instant. "Five years. Maybe six. I am too old to keep track."

Ellis fought down the smile that tugged at the corners of his mouth. "I see."

Badger's needle stopped. When he looked up at Ellis, his eyes were full of mischief and amusement. "I knew you were coming, and you came."

"Yes," Ellis said. The laughter inside him suddenly broke into something else. If he had been laughing out loud, it would have turned to sobs. He was glad he had kept it in.

Clumsiness overtook him. His hands were too big to hold the stew bowl. His feet had no place in the confines of the cabin. His voice couldn't be trusted. Self-consciously he covered the small distance and sat down beside the fire. He was separated from Badger by the sewing clutter and the years.

Badger took his needle back up and worked in silence.

"What are you making?" Ellis finally asked.

"A shirt that will fit your shoulders. You have grown far beyond mine, so I have nothing to give you."

"You don't . . ." Ellis stopped himself. The words were reflex. You don't have to do that. Civilized words. Falsely polite words. Unnecessary words. They had no place in this cabin. Instead he reached out to finger the hides. As soon as he touched the buttery skins, he knew that they were the best Badger had tanned that fall.

"I can't wait to wear it," he said honestly. "Can I help?"

"No." Badger's fingers moved rhythmically. "It is my gift, and the labor is part of the gift."

Ellis settled back down to the sounds of the fire and the gusting wind outside. He felt a rush of contentment. Of belonging.

Later, when the stew was gone and the shirt was finished and the fire was blazing with newly added wood, Ellis leaned back to stare into the flames. The silence between them had been good, but he was ready to talk now.

"So much has happened since I saw you last."

Badger nodded solemnly. "Tell me the stories," he said.

The words brought back other nights and other fires, hours filled with Badger's own stories and those of his relatives and friends. Nothing was related simply or personally. Every particle of the past was a tale, a complexly woven segment that fitted in with other tales to form a greater story. And the greater stories spread out to mingle into one.

Now, in Badger's company, Ellis found himself relating his own facts in story form. He told it all. Even the parts Badger already knew. The boy becoming a man, the grizzly and her cubs, the father, the hawk—they were all characters in the narrative he wove. The hours stretched on. Thea. Rape. Murder. Soul-deep sickness and confusion and guilt. When he finished the part about the bloody hawk lying at the boy's feet, Ellis was shaking and covered with sweat.

Badger stood.

"There's more," Ellis warned him.

"Not tonight. Stories must have beginnings and endings so people can rest. We have come to an ending and it is time to sleep." He rolled himself in a rug beside the fire, signaling that Ellis was to sleep on the bunk.

Ellis lay down, certain that he wouldn't be able to sleep. He breathed in the smells of burning wood and tanned leather and cooked venison. The next thing he was aware of was the smell of breakfast cooking.

In the days that followed, he told the story of Yvonne. He told of his mother and his grandfather, of Aubrey and Juliana. The time in Europe became a set of small stories that he strung together. By the time he was finished, the storm outside had exhausted itself and so had he.

"These are rich stories," Badger said at the end. "They offer much to think about."

"Is that all you have to say?"

"For now, yes. Did you expect that I would be able to change the stories for you?"

"No. But I thought you could help me find answers . . . make me understand . . . help me find a way to accept."

"Here are some answers for you. The hawk would not have survived long after you released her. She did not know to fly south for the winter. She would have stayed here and died. Does that mean you should have sacrificed your years to stay in the mountains and care for her? I say no. Does that mean you should never have rescued her in the beginning? Again I say no.

"Those are some answers. But they are only my answers. Who but me can know if they are right?"

Badger's eyes held him.

"You want to understand. I can teach you the center of things: how to kill only for food and clothing; how to honor other living creatures; how the earth is mother of us all and the sun is the father; how death and birth are different ends of the same truth. I can teach you all this, but I can make you understand nothing."

Badger stood and took down two bows from a peg. "Today we hunt. We will accept with gratitude whatever the earth yields us. We will accept with reverence the animal life that is sacrificed for our benefit." He handed Ellis the longer bow. "That is all I know of acceptance. It has always been enough for me."

Ellis took the bow and turned away. The disappointment he felt was nearly overwhelming. He'd been so certain that Badger could ease the burdens that the psychiatrists and his family and lovers hadn't been able to touch. Now he saw that the man possessed no magic healing power. Badger was nothing more than a backward eccentric.

Dispirited, Ellis followed the bowlegged graying little man out into the brilliance of a sun-dazzled snow-covered world.

"Remember how easily snow blindness strikes," Badger cautioned. "And remember how too much thought can confuse the hands and heart."

Ellis nodded. He needed no lessons on hunting. The disappointment festering inside him made him resentful of the simple reminders. Later, after he had missed two rabbits and an antelope and was facing the walk back to the cabin empty-handed, he wondered about blindness and excessive thinking. Both seemed to have gained significance during the course of the morning. But this was not what he had walked through a snowstorm for. He hadn't come for hunting lessons or mystical references to nature. What he needed now was a way to cope with real life. The dangerous, senseless life of cities and people. He watched Badger skin a squirrel and thought of Badger's declaration of acceptance. What did that have to do with anything real?

"I'll be leaving in a few days," he announced.

"Yes," Badger said without looking up.

"Maybe even tomorrow."

"Yes." Badger dropped the dressed squirrel into a pot and carried it toward the cabin. "But we are hungry. That is what is important now."

And so the long mountain winter passed, day by day, week by week, and still Ellis shared Badger's fire. Thoughts of leaving occurred to him with less and less frequency, and finally a sort of peace descended over him. It was a peace born of emptiness, for his time with Badger had cleansed him of all emotion. He woke each morning feeling nothing—no guilt, no regret, no dissatisfaction, no restlessness, no yearning, no hope. He woke to each new day feeling nothing more complex than hunger.

He hunted with more skill than he had ever had before, linking with his prey in the act of death, consuming the animal's soul as he would consume its flesh. Humanity and civilization melted away. Once again he felt a part of the great cycle. Every rock and tree and drop of blood made sense. His own existence made sense. There was a pattern at work, more intricate and magnificent than the greatest art and science, more awesome and timeless than the greatest bridges and buildings.

"You are better now," Badger said one evening.

They were in the heart of winter, the long fire hours when darkness seemed to be gobbling the daylight faster than it could be replenished. Spring had not even begun to whisper yet.

"Better?"

"Yes. When you came to me in that storm you were suffering from more than the cold. Now you are better."

Ellis smiled—at himself, at his own stupidity, at the endless wonder of this man he was privileged to call friend.

"Yes. I am better."

Spring teased and flirted with the mountains, then finally opened herself in a rich flurry of wildflowers and birdsong. The firelit hours grew shorter and the days longer.

"You must leave soon," Badger said one night as they sat at an outdoor fire beneath millions of stars.

"No! I can't leave the mountains. This is all there is for me now. This is where I belong."

Badger smiled his curious straight-across smile. "There are many worlds. You cannot know where you belong until you see them all."

Ellis shook his head. "You're not making sense."

"Your ears do not want to hear sense."

"Stop it!"

"Stop what? Speaking the truth?" Badger's eyes penetrated from across the fire. "Much has happened to you. But you have not yet seen the world as a man."

Ellis laughed. It was a short, bitter laugh, ugly in the spring night. "I'll never see the world as a man. I'm not a man out there. I'm a Van Lyden. I live like an animal in a padded cage, hemmed in with money and tradition and my grandfather's obsessions. Don't you see, here I'm ... I'm real. I'm something more. If I go back, I'll be a Van Lyden again."

"It does not have to be so." Badger's voice came close to conveying emotion. "You broke away from your soft cage to come here. Break away from this soft cage you are making and go on to see what else you find."

"I don't want to lose the mountains again."

"The mountains will be here for you. You will carry their beauty with you always, and you can return if you ever need or want them. You can return if you find nothing else that captures your heart."

28

Juliana

Juliana went straight to the attorney's office the morning of her eighteenth birthday to take possession of the 2.8 million dollars her mother had left for her.

The attorney, Morris Rifkin, was not a Van Lyden man. Her previous contact with him had been by phone and letter, and seeing his modest offices in the faded downtown art-deco building and meeting Mr. Rifkin himself, Juliana understood why her grandfather referred to "Yvonne's adviser" with so much disdainful sarcasm. Rifkin's clothes had a slept-in appearance, his skin was coarse, and the tips of his fingers were stained yellow. He presented quite a different picture from the polished Van Lyden Ivy Leaguers she was accustomed to seeing.

"Call me Mo," he insisted.

Reluctantly she shook his hand and sat down stiffly on the edge of the chair in front of his desk. She wanted to get through the legal procedures as quickly as possible, get out of the shabby office, and turn her money over to the Van Lyden financial managers, where it belonged.

"I can see your mother in you," he said.

Juliana was annoyed. "I don't look at all like my mother."

"It's not that you look like her. It's ..." He settled into his chair and leaned back. "You've got the same kind of stuff going."

Juliana sighed in exasperation. "What are you talking about?"

Rifkin's eyes twinkled. "You got sex appeal, kid. I don't know how else to say it. You got that same natural kind of sexiness your mother had, and that's a fact."

"And you've got a lot of nerve!"

"Ahhh ..." He waved his hand at her. "Take the compliment and be happy. It won't cost you."

"Let's just get on with this." She checked her watch. "I'd like to be at my other attorney's by ten."

Amusement played on Rifkin's features as he laid out the papers in front of her, and she saw that he was handsome in a crude way. Had her mother found this man attractive? Was that why she'd put all her assets into his care? For the first time she wondered if her mother had had affairs. Had her mother been taken in by other men besides Ellis?

"Did you know my mother well?"

He hesitated a moment, rubbing his chin in a thoughtful expression as though deciding how to answer.

"I met your mother just after she came to New York," he said. "I was fresh out of law school and doing some sticky Native American work. She saw an article about it and gave me a call. Sent a healthy donation to help with the work, but asked that her identity remain anonymous. Then, later, she asked me to take on all her personal business. Said she wanted at least one person in the world she could trust."

"And she trusted you?"

"Yeah."

"Why?"

"Because I couldn't be bought by men like Edward Van Lyden."

"That's all? There wasn't . . . a more personal reason?"

She could see in his eyes that he knew exactly what she was asking.

"No," he said with an edge of regret. "I wasn't involved with her. Your mother was solid. She'd made a commitment and she took it seriously."

Juliana sank back into the chair. "I still don't understand why she couldn't trust the Van Lyden attorneys. She must have made my grandfather very angry."

Rifkin chuckled. "Van Lyden was furious. He tried to have me disbarred, and hired two guys to—" He stopped himself midsentence and affected a casual shrug. "No need to dig up old dirt on your grandpa, is there?"

Juliana studied him. "Was she afraid of my grandfather?"

His good-natured amusement sharpened instantly to a careful, shrewd expression.

"Isn't everyone?" he said, but it wasn't a question.

Juliana studied her folded hands in her lap. Was everyone afraid of her grandfather? And was it true that her mother had turned to Mo Rifkin because she didn't trust the family she'd married into?

"It took a lotta courage for your mother to keep me on. But

she was set on this. She said she wanted her daughter to have a cushion that wasn't stuffed with Van Lyden feathers. That's what she said . . . Van Lyden feathers. Said she wanted to be sure that your grandfather couldn't touch the trust, and the only way to do that was to keep it out of his attorney's hands."

"What would my grandfather want with two million dollars? A small amount like that is nothing to him."

"But it's something to you at age eighteen, isn't it? Your mother knew it would be. And she wanted to fix it so your grandpa couldn't withhold it or use it to control you."

"And how did you stand up to my grandfather?" Juliana asked, measuring the man and seeing someone quite different than she had when she first walked in. "How did you win?"

Rifkin fastened his eye on hers. She felt the ruthless street-wise danger of that look all the way down her spine.

"Why would a nice little girl like you want to ask a question like that?"

"Maybe because I could use some advice on winning against him myself now and then."

The attorney snorted softly through his nose and leaned his head back to stare at the ceiling. "I gotta tell ya. I'm having real déjà vu here. Your mother said almost the exact same thing."

"And what did you do?"

"I gave her advice on winning." One side of his mouth turned down, and he tugged absently at the loosened necktie that hung like a noose around his neck.

"And . . . ?"

"She had courage, but she wasn't tough enough to follow through. Sometimes you gotta have that killer instinct to win. She didn't have it."

Juliana took out a cigarette. Rifkin made no effort to light it in spite of the matches on his desk.

"I'd like to retain you as my adviser and financial manager," she said.

"I thought you and your grandpa had already made other arrangements."

"I've changed my mind. I need the same kind of advice you gave my mother."

He leaned forward and studied her skeptically over steepled hands.

"I was raised a Van Lyden," she assured him. "So I'm a lot tougher than my mother was."

"We'll see," he said.

She was a little irritated with him as they finished up the details and made an appointment for the following week. For someone who was as smart as he obviously thought he was, there should be no doubt. Of course she was tougher than her mother.

"Oh, and there's one thing I'd like you to start on immediately. I had a nurse who was discharged when I was ten. My grandfather never would tell me where she went. I want you to find her and give her something from me. Whatever she needs. Money ... a house ... whatever."

She wrote Gittie's full name on a piece of paper and handed it to him.

"No problem," he said.

She left his building in an adrenaline rush of excitement. Mo Rifkin was a prize. And he was her prize. She felt as if she'd undergone a rite of passage in his shabby office, an official crossing over to adulthood. She was eighteen and legal and financially independent. She was strong. She was tough. She'd survived all the losses and lessons of her childhood ... but now she was through being just a survivor. Through sitting back wishing and waiting. From now on she would meet life head-on and make her own destiny.

As a first step in her declaration of independence she was taking Edward and Grace and Charlotte out, collecting them in her brand-new custom limousine and buying them lunch with her own funds.

Everyone was ready when she arrived at Great House. Edward was dressed in one of his tailored English suits and had donned a boutonniere for the occasion. Grace, who was seen mostly in caftans at home, was quite presentable in a new crepe suit. And Charlotte looked almost festive in the bright turquoise dress Juliana had given her.

"This all seems a bit backwards," Edward grumbled on the way to the restaurant. "One shouldn't be the host on one's own birthday."

When the car pulled up in front of Lutèce, his mood improved. "At least you're not taking us to some hovel," he said grudgingly.

Juliana didn't let him bait her and she didn't lose her composure. She felt separate from her grandfather now. Unaffected by the barbs and disapproval and withholding he had used to rule her. She could feel the power growing inside her. She met each of their eyes as they made their birthday toasts and she reveled in what she saw. Grace eyed her with fear. Charlotte's look was full of awe and pride and vicarious ambition. And Edward, her fierce, feared-by-everyone grandfather, watched her over his glass as if she'd become a force to be reckoned with.

Something more heady than the champagne sizzled through her veins with those toasts. She coasted on the high, but she kept herself tight at the same time, suppressing the giddiness and silly overconfidence that usually spilled out in periods of elation. She wanted to hold on to this newfound strength. She wanted to savor the sweetness of it.

"Are you not having fun?" Grace asked nervously.

Charlotte noted her barely touched food. "Should I tell the waiter to send the chef out? Would you like something different?"

"No ... no ... I'm fine." And suddenly she was filled with a great magnanimous affection for them. These were her people. With Ellis gone and her independence established, she could relax and be charitable.

She smiled at the two women and they brightened as if she'd turned an electrical switch. Their instant response made her feel even stronger. She could make people happy or sad with a few words. There was nothing she couldn't control. She sat aloof, amused, as she listened to their petty concerns.

Edward vented his anger at the city of New York for suggesting that he donate his entire collection to the Metropolitan Museum instead of setting up his own facility. Charlotte related society gossip. And Grace finished glass after glass of champagne and turned maudlin, crying about the cruelty of life and the tragedy of her missing son, as if Ellis were a kidnapped child again.

"My detectives are doing all they can to find him," Edward told her irritably. "If you can't control yourself in public, you won't be allowed champagne."

Grace sniffed and pulled herself together.

Juliana wasn't angry with her aunt. She saw Grace as hopelessly weak and helplessly trapped into loving her son, but she no longer blamed the woman for anything. Grace was Ellis' victim as much as anyone else. She wouldn't be surprised if he managed to kill his own mother as he had killed hers.

"I'm sorry," Grace said to her. "I didn't mean to spoil your luncheon."

Juliana reached across to pat her aunt's hand.

"We should have brought your gifts with us," Grace said, recovering her brightness.

"It's so gauche to have gifts in public," Charlotte said.

"I intend to present mine, regardless," Edward announced.

"Juliana, in honor of this significant birthday, you may choose a piece of jewelry from the vault to keep, and you will receive a staff of your own. Bodyguard, driver, and maid. May you use them in good health."

"Oh, Da Da!" She flashed him her biggest smile. "What perfect gifts! I'll begin interviewing right away."

"That won't be necessary. I'll procure them through the usual channels."

Right, Juliana thought to herself. And they'll report to you and be nothing but spies.

"No. I'll take care of it. I owe you that, Grandfather. I'm going to work hard now and learn the practical side of being a Van Lyden so that you won't be burdened by me any longer."

"Hmmm ... well ... that's very commendable, but—"

"I knew you'd be pleased. And I can't tell you how important it is to know that you trust my judgment the way you do."

"I see." Edward leaned back in his chair and studied her. There was a trace of amusement in his stern gaze. "Can I also trust your judgment in friends?"

Juliana's heart registered the veiled threat. "Are you worried about the party tonight?"

"This party your friends have arranged is a small piece in a larger picture."

"Meaning?"

"I would think the meaning quite clear. You've been allowed increasing liberties over the past year. Now that you're eighteen, I take it that you expect the freedom accorded an adult."

Juliana nodded ever so slightly.

"Then as an adult you will be held accountable for your actions and your associates ... and your errors in judgment. Is that clear enough?"

Juliana nodded more firmly.

"I certainly hope so." Edward raised his glass. "I'm afraid you'll find, Juliana, that this adult world you're rushing into can exact a heavy toll for even small mistakes."

What was her grandfather up to? How much did he know? What did he mean? The questions nagged at her all the way home and throughout the process of dressing for her birthday celebration. But the worries melted away the moment she stepped into the heat and sound of the club. There was unlimited champagne and an open bar and a cornucopia of mood enhancers furnished by Lee. Daffy brought in a well-known rock group to perform all evening. Whitney arranged for the caterer and the enormous cake, which Jay fell into and then used as ammunition in a raging food fight. Willy, Gabby, Denny, and the rest contributed to the mayhem, and Four was the organizer and foreman.

Only Perry seemed to have made no contribution. He drifted around the smoky rooms like an observer rather than a participant, and Juliana was unsettled by the way she'd caught him watching her. After a number of drinks, Juliana confronted him.

"What's wrong, don't you like birthdays?"

He was leaning against a railing. The combined effects of the alcohol in her system and the colored strobes flashing overhead in the darkened room gave Perry an eerie cast. His dark brown hair was black, then blue, then black, then red, and his dark eyes were shadowy staring holes.

"You shouldn't drink any more," he said. "And stay away from Lee's trash."

"Hah! What're you, the housemother here?"

He started to walk away, making her angry, because Perry had always been so nice to her and she expected it from him. She grabbed his arm and yanked him back around, and suddenly he wasn't the Perry she knew at all. He shoved her roughly against the wall and held her face and kissed her so hard that it hurt.

She was stunned. When he pulled away, all she could do was stare at him.

"Let me take you home," he said.

But before she could make sense of the situation, Four yelled, "Surprise!" and two male strippers burst into the room wearing ribbons and gift tags.

She pretended to watch them gyrate for the hooting crowd but could feel Perry burning holes through her with his eyes.

"You are so weird tonight," she said, whipping around to face him.

He pushed her toward the strippers. "Go ahead. Four probably set it up so that he could have one and you could have the other. Go on and stake your claim before he gets first pick."

She turned away from him. The stripping progressed and the shouting and catcalls reached a deafening pitch. She threaded through the crowd toward the bar for another drink. Who were all these people anyway? She didn't know one-third of them, but they all acted as though they knew her. They called her Jinx and smiled and joked as if they were old friends.

Perry was dead wrong. More alcohol was exactly what she needed, because in the middle of all this celebrating she was suddenly feeling down.

"Say there!" Lee pounded on the bar with his hands, keeping time to the strip music. "If it ain't the birthday girl herself! I'm the purveyor of good cheer, so what'll ya have, birthday girl?"

Juliana leaned her elbows on the bar. "Ummm, I don't know. I'm sick of champagne. I hate the taste of whiskey. I don't want orange juice or tomato juice or coffee flavors or things with cream in them . . . and the last time I took one of your famous pills, it put me to sleep. So what do you recommend?"

"Ah . . ." He bent and came up with a hand mirror and a tiny bottle. "This calls for my birthday-girl special."

"What is it?" she asked, but as soon as he dumped the white powder out onto the glass, she knew.

He sniffed up a line through the drinking straw and held it out to her.

"I don't know . . ."

"Hey! It's a hell of a lot safer than my mother's fucking prescriptions!"

She giggled and wrinkled up her nose. "Is that where you get all those pills? From your mother?"

"Don't knock my mother. She's a true connoisseur." He pressed the straw into her hand. "C'mon, Jinx. This stuff is harmless as a puppy."

She took the straw and quickly sniffed up two of the lines. Her nostrils burned and the back of her throat numbed.

"One more," Lee urged. "You need more . . . even though this is fine stuff."

She took another. It hit her in a rush. A sweet hard exhilarating rush. She held on to the edge of the bar and lost herself in it. When she finally let go and turned, there was Perry staring at her again. His eyes were dark slits now. His mouth was set in a line.

"Oh, lighten up, Perry! Either lighten up or fuck off!"

"Yeah, you tell him, Jinxie," Lee cheered.

She stormed off toward the crowd, burning with restless energy and abandon. The people around her didn't seem so unappealing anymore. The blues had evaporated. She felt terrific as she pushed forward to see the strippers. They were down to itty-bitty bikinis and a chorus of voices was chanting "All the way! All the way!"

The noise level rose as a commotion broke out near the door. Juliana stood on tiptoe. Whitney Chandler moved up beside her. "Can you see what it is, Jinx? God, I hope it's not a fight . . ."

A wave rolled forward through the crush of people. The strippers stopped. The music stopped.

Two policemen broke through into the open near the strippers.

"Oh, no," Whitney moaned. "My grandfather will kill me."

All at once both uniformed officers raised their arms and whipped off their hats. Long hair tumbled out around their faces. They were policewomen, not men, and they were smiling.

There was a moment of collective perplexity. Then the music started up again and the two policewomen dropped their gunbelts and jerked their pelvises to the beat.

"That Four!" Whitney breathed. "I'm going to strangle him. He's sick if he thinks that was funny!"

Juliana laughed till her eyes teared and she had to hang on to Whitney's shoulder to remain upright. Everything was so funny. Everyone was so much fun. The music penetrated, stirring her arms and her hips and her feet, and she was dizzy with the dense perfume of jubilance that permeated the air.

The fake policewomen spun and threw off their shirts to reveal sequined bras with tassels. A roar of approval rose.

"C'mon, Whit . . ." Juliana clamped onto Whitney's arm and pulled her forward. "Let's dance."

"Oh, no. No. No. No."

Juliana managed to pull her out into the circle with the dancers, but then Whitney jerked free.

"Go, Jinx!" somebody yelled, and the cry was taken up by others.

She laughed and shook back her hair and imitated the other dancers' movements. Immediately the two bikini-clad males moved close and began to partner her like she was in a 1940s musical, holding her arms and twirling her and lifting her into the air.

The music pulsed through her body and the strong hands gripped her, freeing her of constraints and filling her with a child's recklessness. She flew, she dived, she spun wildly, trusting in hands to catch her before she fell. Up and down. Around and around. The faces and colors and sounds blurred.

"Jinxie . . . Jinxie . . . Jinxie . . ."

The flashing lights and the litany of her name became hypnotic. She was outside herself, lifted on a giant outpouring of love. Everyone loved her! She was the center of the universe.

"Take it off! . . . "Take it off!"

She was undoing her clothes when Perry stepped out of the crowd and snared her. He grabbed her around the waist and lifted her like a mannequin, and all she could do was blow kisses to the disappointed crowd as she was removed.

"I wouldn't really have stripped," she told him when he released her.

"Right," he said.

She twined her arms around his neck and smiled up at him. "Why is Perry mad at Jinx tonight?"

His dark, watchful eyes filled with confusion, and she realized in that instant that he was malleable. That she could shape and control him if she chose.

She pressed her body closer against him and his Adam's apple moved uncertainly in his throat. Perry Lorillard-Harris—the tortured poetic soul of the society set. Perry the adored and Perry the admired. Perry the aloof and untouchable.

She could have him if she wanted.

The knowledge gave her almost as big a rush as the cocaine had earlier.

"Come away with me," he said. "Now."

She cocked her head to the side and feigned innocence. "But my party's not over. Wouldn't that be rude?"

"No one will even notice."

She switched from innocence to coyness. "Where would we go?"

He smiled down at her. Not a conventional smile, but a lightening of his features that made her feel like he was smiling.

"There are a million places I'd like to take you," he said. His voice was just above a whisper. "We could go for Chinese if you're hungry. Or to a diner I know where all the chefs eat after their restaurants close. Or we could walk to the middle of the Brooklyn Bridge and watch the lights. Or ride back and forth on the ferry till the sun comes up."

Juliana dropped her arms and pulled back from him. "Are you crazy?"

"Yes," he said.

"Okay, let's go."

It was thrilling, ducking out on her grandfather's bodyguards and sneaking into Perry's low-slung sports car. She gave a note to the doorman to pass on to the bodyguards later. On it she'd written simply "Go home, riding with a friend."

It was the first time she'd ever ridden in anything but the back seat of a chauffeured limousine. Speeding along in Perry's antique roadster with the windows down and the wind whipping her hair was as delicious as forbidden fruit.

He parked on the street. She could see the lighted top of the Empire State Building to the north, and across the way was a half-darkened park with human forms stretched out on the benches. A man passed them on the sidewalk, wearing running clothes with night-reflective strips.

Suddenly she was gripped by an attack of such anxiety that she couldn't get out of the car. She had never in her life been out on the street without guards. Now here she was at two in the morning in a seedy part of town with no one but Perry Lorillard-Harris to keep her from harm.

"Are you okay?" Perry asked.

She nodded but didn't move. "Is it safe to be out like this?"

"Reasonably," he said. "But if you'd rather not . . ."

She willed herself out of the car and he took her hand and led her down sidewalks and across streets and onto a huge walk-way with traffic buzzing beneath them.

"Are we on the bridge?"

"Yes. But you can't stop or look around till I say so." He pulled her along so fast that she had to concentrate on her feet to keep from tripping. Finally he stopped.

"Where am I?" she laughed.

"You're halfway," he said.

She leaned her arms on the railing and looked out and down. To the north were the lights of Manhattan. To the south the lights of Brooklyn. Out in the upper bay she could see the Statue of Liberty. And she was suspended between them in the darkness, hanging over the rushing black water.

He kissed the back of her neck. She turned and he kissed her lips.

"Come home with me," he whispered.

She didn't say yes or no. Instead she took his hand and led him back toward Manhattan. She could feel his tension. When they reached the shadowy darkness of the massive arched Gothic tower where the bridge cables converged, she stopped. She reached up under her dress and pulled off her panties. Then she leaned back against the rough stone and slid her dress up around her hips.

"If you want me, you can have me," she said. "But it has to be here. It has to be now."

He stared at her, and she fed on the uncertainty and need in his eyes. This was the way to have a man. On her own terms.

Never again would she relinquish control. Never would she let someone hurt her like Matt had.

There was pain in Perry's surrender. She saw it as he fell toward her. She felt it in the first fevered crush of him against her.

His pain was intoxicating.

She met him in a consuming pyretic frenzy ... she met him with the aphrodisiac of victory surging through her veins.

29

"You have a call, Juliana."

"Hmmm . . ." Juliana stretched and burrowed deeper into her bed. "Tell him I don't want to talk to him." She had been seeing Perry for months but she didn't want him to think that he could just call her whenever he felt like it.

"All right," Charlotte said. "But it's not Perry."

"Who is it, then?"

"He won't give his name but he says it's urgent. Rifkin called earlier too. He said that he has some more candidates for you to interview."

Juliana dragged herself up out of her warm cocoon and took the receiver from Charlotte.

"Hello."

"Hello . . . Jinx?"

The voice was unfamiliar. "Who is this?"

"It's Sparky . . . Sparky McCann. Do you remember me?"

"Sparky? Of course I remember!"

"I'm kind of . . . I'm in Times Square and I only have two dollars left and . . ." There was a rustling as the phone was fumbled from ear to ear. "I don't have anyplace to go . . ." His voice broke into fractured sobbing.

"It's okay, Spark. Don't worry. I'll send someone right away. Tell me exactly where you are."

She called Rifkin with the problem. Who else could she call?

The attorney accepted the assignment without question. "And where do you want him taken?" he asked.

"I don't know."

"How 'bout a hotel?" Rifkin suggested. "The Marriott Marquis in Times Square . . . the big one with the restaurants and theater inside."

383

"Yes! Yes. That's perfect."

"All right. I'm sending one of the applicants. He's someone I trust, and I can get him right away because he's waiting around in town for the interview with you."

"Good. Tell him to stay with Sparky until he hears from me, okay? And tell him to get whatever Sparky needs . . . food or whatever . . ."

As Juliana rode toward the hotel with her grandfather's two men in the front of her car, she suddenly felt the need for extreme caution. Her childhood friend had been stolen from her once, and now he was back and in trouble and she didn't want her grandfather or anyone else to find out and interfere.

The hotel was ideal, huge and bustling with tourists and easy to navigate in without attracting attention. She ordered the men to stay with the car and hurried inside to Sparky.

A deep "Who's there?" came through the door when she knocked.

"It's Jinx," she whispered.

The door was opened by a very broad-shouldered, very tall, very black man. He had a gold earring and faint scars on his face and a gun peeking from beneath his jacket.

"Excuse me . . ." she said, taking a step backward, "I must have the wrong—"

"I'm Zeke," he said with a slight Southern drawl. "Your friend's in the bedroom."

Juliana edged past him and went to the open door he'd indicated. A television blared against the wall and an emaciated male form was stretched out on the bed watching it.

"Sparky?"

The figure on the bed leapt up. He was close to her own height and his hair was long and stringy and his eyes were red-rimmed and his skin had an unhealthy pallor. But beneath it all he was still Sparky.

"Jinx!" He rushed around the end of the bed, stumbling on trailing bedcovers, and threw his arms around her. "I knew it! I knew you'd come."

He backed away, wiped his eyes and nose, then motioned her into a chair as if he were hosting a polite visit. "Have you met my silent savior in the other room? Of course you have! You sent him, right?" He forced a laugh, then moved nervously to turn off the television and sit down on the edge of the bed opposite her.

"Actually, I did just meet him," she admitted in a hushed voice. "I'm supposed to be interviewing him for either a guard or driver position. I don't even know which."

"I think he's definitely your guard type," Sparky whispered. He used a tissue from the nightstand to wipe his nose again.

"I can't believe how grown-up you are! You're a woman! I mean ... I knew I grew up, but I still imagined you as ... you know ..." He laughed hoarsely. "Well, you're probably asking yourself where in the hell this guy dropped in from after all these years ... and what does he want from me. And I don't blame you for wanting answers and I'm going to—"

"Spark ..."

"I'm going to tell you. Just give me a minute here and—"

"Sparky, you don't have to explain anything to me."

"I don't?"

"No."

But he did anyway.

Zeke ordered sandwiches and beer from room service and Sparky ate and drank and talked for nearly two hours. His story was rambling and disjointed, skipping about in time as if his past eight years had been thrown together into a pile and he was sorting through them at random.

He talked about how his parents had disowned him and his sister pretended he was dead, but it was unclear whether this was a recent development or an old wound. He talked about how he'd run away shortly after that last summer at Elysia. How he'd found love and a home and how his parents had been sorry that he hadn't died on the street. He talked about being "in love." About having a lover who was everything to him and about devoting his life to the man and being devastated when he ended the relationship.

It took Juliana several moments to absorb what Sparky was telling her. "You were in love with...? Are you saying you're ...?"

He nodded.

"But all that time I knew you, I had no idea. No clue."

"I don't think I knew either," he said sadly. "It's so confusing. Even now I'm confused. I wonder sometimes ... was I born gay or did he make me that way?"

"You're talking about the man you were in love with? Saying that he forced you to be—"

"No, not forced me. Taught me. He took me in and taught me about love and pleasure and ..." Sparky's face crumpled. "I trusted him! I thought we'd have our whole lives together. I thought ..." He buried his face in his hands.

Juliana thought of herself and Matt and the pain that could still take her breath away in unguarded moments. The mutual heartbreak deepened her feelings of kinship toward Sparky.

"Do you ... do you ever look at girls? I mean ..."

"I know what you mean." He took a deep breath and shook his head. "No. Not that way. Not like some guys I know, who can be in love with a man one minute and then in love with a woman the next." He shook his head again. "I can't imagine sex with a woman."

Juliana burst out laughing, and he jumped from the bed with a wounded expression.

"Sit down. Sit down," she said, wiping her eyes. "I'm not laughing at you. I was remembering why we were separated. Why we weren't allowed to be friends anymore. Do you remember?"

He grinned. "I never knew exactly. Was it because ...?"

"Yes it was. You were nearing puberty and everyone was afraid something naughty might happen between us. If they'd only known!" She fell into laughter again, but stopped herself as soon as she realized that he wasn't going to join her. "Don't you think that's funny?" she asked.

"Yes," he said. "But it's also sad. Everything changed then. My whole life changed."

"Yes," she agreed. "Everything changed. But here you are, and we're going to change things back to the way we want them, right?"

He brightened hopefully. "Can we do that?"

"Yes. I have money now, Spark. My own money. I can make things happen." She stood up, full of purpose. Yes, she could make things happen. She could protect Sparky and take care of him and heal his broken heart and get some expensive doctors to restore his health. Everything was possible with money. Hadn't her grandfather always taught her that?

Her mind raced with plans. She would find him a place to live. An apartment! She would buy an apartment. There were places listed in the back of *The New York Times Magazine* every week. Cute little places with nice views of Central Park. Rifkin would know how to go about it. But first—first she had something very important to do.

"Just stay here for a little bit, Spark. I've got to take care of something, and I have to take Zeke with me."

"Mr. Silent?" Sparky laughed hoarsely. "Believe me, I won't miss him. He hasn't said two words."

She turned Sparky's television back on and pulled his door shut as she left him. Zeke was leaning back against a small wet bar, chewing on a drinking straw. "Tryin' to quit smoking," he said as he threw the shredded straw away.

"I understand you're interested in working for me," she said, assuming what she hoped was a businesslike demeanor.

He turned, picked another straw out of the container on the bar, and put it in the corner of his mouth.

"Maybe."

"Maybe? Mr. Rifkin said you'd been waiting to talk to me."

Everything about him had a slow and easy rhythm, but there was a disquieting tension underneath.

"I have been waitin' to talk to you," he said, "so's I could find out if I wanted the job or not."

Juliana didn't know what to say. She was completely taken aback. Her other interviews with prospective employees had not gone this way at all.

"Well, ah, why don't we postpone the interview for now, and since you're already working for me temporarily, you can continue to work for me . . . temporarily."

"Doin' what?"

"I need you to come downstairs and help me get rid of two guys, then take over until I have time to find someone permanent."

Zeke didn't answer one way or the other, he just pushed off from the bar, realigned the holster beneath his arm, and straightened his designer jacket.

"What kind of gun is that?" she asked.

"A handgun."

She stopped abruptly. "Don't get cute with me and don't patronize me. When I ask you a question, it means I want an answer."

He neither apologized nor became defensive. His expression betrayed no reaction at all. "It's a SIG-Sauer P230. Nine-millimeter."

"Eight rounds?"

"Seven."

She tried not to grin as she marched up to her grandfather's lackeys with Zeke beside her, but the sight of their faces was priceless.

"Calm down," she said. "This is my new man. You're no longer needed. You can run along home and cry to my grandfather about it."

They looked at each other and then back at her as though dumbfounded.

"We can't—" the bodyguard started to say, but Zeke stepped forward and quietly took over.

"The lady asked you to go," was all he said. He didn't say it in a voice that was particularly menacing, but the two men backed down immediately.

Juliana was delighted.

"This is my car." She gestured toward the gleaming white limousine that the men had been lounging against.

Zeke didn't react at all. She'd hoped he would be impressed.

"You can drive me to Mr. Rifkin's office now, and I'll see about a place for Sparky. Then you'll drive me back here and . . ."

She was reciting the plan as quickly as it formed in her head. It never occurred to her that Zeke might not do as she asked.

One side of his mouth curled in amusement, and the tiny gold cross dangling from his ear winked as he shook his head. "I don't drive," he said.

"You don't drive! What the hell do you do, then?"

He folded his thick arms and peered down at her. "I eliminate hassles. Keep life smooth. And safe."

"That's just great. Just great. Because smooth as our life might be right now, we have no way to go anywhere in this car. I don't know how to drive, you don't know how to drive, and I just got rid of the two who do know how."

He opened the door and climbed in behind the wheel.

"What are you doing?"

"Get in."

"You're not learning to drive in my car!"

"Didn't say I didn't know how, lady. Said I didn't drive for people."

"But . . ."

"I'm willin' to do you the favor of pilotin' this vehicle temporarily. So if you wanna go somewhere, get in."

She glanced around, hoping there were no witnesses to the scene; then she opened the door for herself and slid inside.

"Rifkin's?" he asked as he started the motor.

"Yes . . . please."

"Hold on to your hat. I never drove a monster like this."

Juliana groaned and sank down lower into the leather seats.

"When we get around to that interview," he said, "remember—I don't drive for people." He pushed the button that raised the partition between them, giving her the impression that it was more for his own privacy than for hers.

It doesn't matter, she kept telling herself. He's temporary. There would be other applicants, other, more suitable men to drive and protect her. For now she had to concentrate on getting Sparky settled. And putting off Perry, who she'd promised to see that night. And calming her grandfather, who would undoubtedly be disturbed over the way she'd sent his men home, and doubly disturbed over the tale they would tell him about her "dangerous new black man."

She sighed and ran her hand across the glove leather of her car. Eggshell, the salesman had called it. The same color as her mother's rooms. Except it was all her own. Her very own. She looked out the tinted glass and saw people on the street noticing as she passed by. And she felt very smug and secure behind her dark glass and her dark, gun-carrying driver. Life was good. Life was becoming very, very good.

The following weeks were a whirlwind of shopping and doctors and dentists. She wanted to give Sparky everything—the finest designer clothes and handmade shoes and all the little luxuries that caught his eye. Nothing was too good for him. And she took him to the best doctors and the same dentist who did all the television anchors in New York.

She told Perry the truth about what was happening but refused to accept his help or allow him to share any of her time with Sparky. This was all hers. Sparky was all hers. And she wanted to keep him that way.

Perry wasn't taking the situation very gracefully. His requests for more of her time evolved into demands, and Juliana punished him by ignoring him.

Zeke's temporary employment stretched from days to weeks, and Juliana forgot about interviewing other candidates. She realized that only Zeke would do. Zeke was different. She liked his shadowy CIA background and his fluent Spanish and his sleek Swiss gun. She liked the way he did his job without groveling or judging. And she liked the fact that even Rifkin couldn't fill in the gaps in Zeke's history.

"You can't be serious," her grandfather said, but she argued and she stood firm, winning out over all his misgivings.

She and Zeke went up to Rifkin's office to negotiate the working contract.

"Who'm I gonna have to ride with?" Zeke asked before they even sat down. "Who'd you hire to drive?"

Juliana gathered herself. She hadn't said anything to him yet.

She'd waited, wondering about the best strategy to use in persuading him. "There won't be anyone else. Your salary will be more than doubled and you'll be a combination bodyguard and driver."

"Oh, no." Zeke laughed a little and shook his head. "I'm not a fucking chauffeur. I'm not a driver. I told you that from the beginning."

"She's offering a lotta money, Zeke," Rifkin said.

Juliana was actually afraid she might lose now. "I can't find a driver I want. I've looked and looked. And what good is it to have you—to have a man I trust so completely—if I'm forced to put one of those all-American crew-cut Neanderthals behind the wheel? I've been around those types all my life and I can't stand it anymore. And I'd never be certain the jerk wasn't a spy planted by my grandfather."

Zeke looked at her for several long moments. His gaze was intense but his expression held no clues to his thoughts. Finally he blew out an exasperated breath and rolled his gaze to the ceiling. "No uniforms," he said. "And I don't answer to 'Driver' and I don't do auto maintenance."

"Fine," she agreed quickly. Any compromise was worth it. Zeke was the guardian of more than just her safety.

After that win she felt generous. She called Perry and told him she would go to his friend's yacht party that night after all.

They boarded the huge boat at twilight and circled Manhattan. It was a warm fall night, almost Indian summer, and there was dancing on the forward deck. The band slipped into a slow number and Perry held her close. "It's been too long," he whispered, nuzzling her neck.

"Has it?"

Instead of laughing, he looked at her and frowned. "Yes. It has."

"Oh, don't start," she said, pulling away from him. She walked from the dancing toward the back of the boat and leaned against the rail to watch the phosphorescent wake. She knew he would follow her.

"Move in with me," he said.

She stared at him, not able to believe what she'd heard.

"Well, then, go to Paris with me. Go somewhere with me! We've got to get free of all this."

"You're crazy."

"No. No, I'm getting saner and saner. That's the problem. I'm getting so goddamned sane that I can't stand how we live and I can't stand your little games and your endless tests."

"Then why do you stay with me?"

"I thought I could give you enough faith in me to stop the games. . . . I love you. I honestly love you."

"There is no such thing as honest love."

"Only because you won't let it be honest. You won't let yourself be honest."

"I don't know what you're talking about."

"Yes you do!" His fingers cut into her arms and his face was anguished for a moment. "Is this the start of a new test . . . a new game? 'See if I can get Perry to throw me into the river' or maybe 'See if I can get Perry to fuck me in a lifeboat.' What is it? What are you trying to prove with me tonight? What do you want now?"

"You're hurting my arms."

He dropped his hands and stared off at the lighted necklace of the Verrazano Bridge.

"You're jealous of Sparky, aren't you?" she asked.

"Yes! I am! How do you think it makes me feel when you go for days without returning my calls or seeing me, yet you drop everything and run if that wasted cokehead crooks his little finger."

"Sparky needs me."

"I need you too."

She turned away from him and looked out over the bay. She hated Perry when he was like this. She hated it when he tried to confuse her or trick her.

"Sparky is very fragile right now. He needs me to be with him. He needs me to take care of him."

"He needs you to buy him drugs."

She whirled back to face him. "Stop being so cruel. What do you know about friendship? What do you know about loyalty?"

"I've been trying to show you what I know."

"How? By bullying me and belittling Sparky and trying to get me to throw him back out on the streets so I can devote every second to what Perry wants and what Perry needs?"

The wound flickered in his eyes and she was dazzled by her own marksmanship.

"This thing with Sparky isn't normal, Juliana. You're obsessed with this neurotic dead-end relationship because it's a way to hide. A way to distance yourself from anything real or meaningful."

"Like what I have with you, you mean?" A part of her wanted very much to stop, but she couldn't. "You want honesty? Okay, I'll get real honest here. My neurotic obsession is a hell of a lot more real than anything between us. And as for meaningful . . . I could fuck anybody on this boat and it would have just as much meaning."

He stood very still for a moment. His dark eyes held a fleeting sadness before he closed himself to her. "Good-bye, Jinx," he said.

But even before he turned away, the Perry who'd loved her was gone.

30

Lucy

Pregnancy changed everything for Lucy. After the initial shock and disappointment subsided, she succumbed easily to the miraculous wonder of her condition and the influence of the hormones in her system. She dropped her plans for further classes and put aside her dream of a photography studio, absorbing herself in books about pregnancy and magazines about baby care. She learned to crochet and quilt so well that she produced stacks of tiny booties and baby blankets and miniature sweaters.

Buddy was delighted at first. He called her his little mama and made virility jokes to all who would listen and bought a complete peewee football uniform. He didn't complain about leaving for work each morning without his ration of bacon because the frying smell made her nausea worse, and he didn't complain about dinner being constantly late or about the fact that she was always falling asleep in his favorite recliner so he had to watch television from another spot. He didn't complain when his mother insisted he start carrying the trash out to the burn barrel for his wife, and he didn't complain when his mother made him pitch in on things that involved lifting or other heavy work.

Then the novelty wore off.

At first he whined about how he was losing weight and not getting fed right anymore. Then the whining escalated into general displeasure at not being able to relax in his own home and not being appreciated. He pouted over perceived slights—his mother asking how Lucy was feeling before she asked how he was, or Lucy falling asleep right in the middle of his recounting each of the prime insurance policies he'd sold in the last year.

Eventually the whining turned to hostility. He made comments about Lucy's appearance and about her shoddy homemaking skills, and he talked about the baby in constant negatives. "It bet-

ter not puke on me if it knows what's good for it." "I'm not gettin'
near it till it knows how to shit in a toilet." "Don't think you're
gonna stick me at home baby-sittin'."

And he pressured Lucy in bed at night, sometimes seeming to
be the most interested when she felt the worst. At first she submitted dutifully. Then, as her swelling belly earned her more
power, she began to say no.

The only real pleasure Lucy had ever had from married sex
was the pleasure of pleasing her husband. The pleasure of having
him look at her with need and the powerful surge of warmth and
giving and tenderness that she experienced when he shuddered
to a climax inside her. That pleasure had been killed the night
he hit her and forced himself on her. After that night sex became
a chore. It was something she did for Buddy in the same way that
she cooked and laundered and organized his tax records. She
began refusing him in bed partly because she felt awful, partly
because she was too tired to go through the ritual of changing
sheets and showering, and partly because she could get away with
saying no now and it felt good to say it.

Buddy tried to behave in front of his parents, but his attitude
was impossible to conceal. Finally, after receiving stern lectures
from both the reverend and Charity, Buddy changed his approach. He spent no time at home.

"The Vanishing Man," Charity nicknamed him, and indeed he
became an artist at it. He had endless places to go and reasons
to work late. He had clients who needed their hands held at odd
hours. He needed to view all sports on his boss's projection television. He could stretch a simple errand into all day. And sometimes he didn't stumble into bed until three or four in the
morning.

This suited Lucy just fine. She never questioned him. Without
Buddy, life was smooth and uncomplicated. Gone were the evenings of cringing beneath his silent disapproval, the tense Sat-
urdays of tiptoeing around him with a knot in her stomach, the
stressful Sunday dinners when she'd always felt obliged to be
cheerful for both of them. With Buddy gone so much, she could
relax and concentrate on the baby.

She spent increasing amounts of time in Charity's company.
Her mother-in-law fussed and clucked over her, and Lucy was
content to lie back and let herself be pampered. In her current
state of dreamy lethargy, she could forget everything bad about
her mother-in-law. All that mattered was the baby. And Charity
was connected to the baby too.

By the fifth month Lucy was feeling physically well and deliriously happy. The baby fluttered inside her like a magical secret, both stirring and soothing her with its primitive rhythms. Nature wasn't just a surrounding anymore. She was part of nature. She was rich and bursting. She was rain and earth. She was the ancient fertility goddess from her art-history book.

Her energy level returned and the fever of anticipation built. She had a whole new vocabulary of terms like "bonding" and "engorgement" and "transition," and she had a nursery that was finished and waiting. Charity had accomplished the nursery. After poring over wallpaper patterns and curtain fabrics together, Charity had surprised her by secretly ordering and arranging everything. The resulting room was magazine perfect with coordinating fabrics and wall decor and crib ensemble. Even the nightlight matched.

Lucy had been angry over the surprise at first, and accused Charity of stealing the fun from her, but later she realized that it wasn't worth fighting over. She didn't want anything to spoil the joy of her condition.

Charity brushed off Lucy's anger, saying that it was normal for an expectant woman to be high-strung, and they fell back into their baby-centered closeness. Lucy's opinion of Charity had ridden a roller coaster through the years. Loathing, admiration, fear, gratitude, simple hatred—she'd felt so many things toward the woman, but none of that seemed important anymore. Charity had become indispensable. There was a bond between them now that was more substantial than their connection through Buddy, more permanent than any animosity or friendship that the two women felt for each other. The growing child carried both their blood, held both their futures hostage.

Buddy and the reverend were incidental. The pregnancy belonged to the women. And when Buddy refused to consider the "natural-birth bullshit" that Lucy wanted, it was Charity who stepped in as childbirth coach, a position that made Lucy even more dependent on her. They were a couple. They were a team. And if the rest of the world fell away into a void, neither would miss it.

Still, whenever Lucy visited her mother's grave, she cried. This was an experience she should be sharing with Wanda, not her mother-in-law. She knelt in the grass beside the flowery headstone that Charity had ordered, and wept bitterly. Her mother would never know this baby inside her. Her mother would never hold the tiny hand or kiss the fuzzy head or beam proudly at Lucy for completing that eternal mother-to-daughter-to-grandchild circle.

Charity was understanding to a fault. She sensed when Lucy was blue and she sheltered Lucy from Buddy's increasingly cruel criticisms. She even participated in the surprise shower that the law office gave, taking extreme measures to keep the party secret from both the reverend and Buddy so that Buddy would not ruin it.

Lucy was in her seventh month when Suki's surprise call came.

"This is Sherry Kay Clare of Dallas, Texas, calling," Suki said with exaggerated formality, "to announce her wedding to Delmar P. Boone, also of Dallas, Texas."

"Oh, Suki! Are you kidding?" Lucy put her hand over the mouthpiece and whispered, "Suki's getting married!" to Charity, who was sitting at the kitchen table poking stuffing into a toy bear she'd made.

"When? Where? Tell me everything, Suki!"

"It's this Friday at city hall."

"So soon! Did this just happen?"

"Yes . . . and don't you dare talk to me about soon. I've been waiting my whole life for this!"

"Well . . . I . . . I don't know what to say."

"Just say you and Buddy'll come."

"I . . . I'm not very graceful at this point and . . . Let me call you right back, okay?"

Charity took off her sewing glasses. "What's wrong?"

"It's this Friday and she wants Buddy and me to come."

"And?"

"Well, I didn't know what to say. I'm not in great shape, and with Buddy's mood so bad these days . . . I'm afraid to ask him."

"You have to go," Charity said firmly. "She's your sister. That's very important." Charity drew in a deep breath. "I always regretted not having a sister. Or a daughter. If God saw fit to give me only one child, it shoulda been a girl."

"But you and the reverend are so proud of Buddy . . ."

"Oh, I'm not sayin' I wanna throw Buddy into the creek or anything. It's just that when you raise a girl you end up with a friend. When you raise a boy you end up with a gift for another woman."

Lucy was too surprised to reply.

"Anyway," Charity said, putting her glasses back on and picking up her work, "you call Suki back up and tell her of course you'n Buddy'll be there."

"But Buddy might not—"

Charity held up a hand. "You just leave Buddy to me."

Lucy made the call and immediately began worrying about a maternity dress suitable for a city-hall wedding and a gift suitable for her sister, but Charity took control and by Friday morning all was in order. Clothing had been assembled and there was a fat envelope of cash which Charity, after consulting several etiquette books, had determined to be the most appropriate gift. Buddy's car was in the shop, so Charity stocked Lucy's maroon Ford with pillows and snacks and cassette tapes and maps.

Buddy grumbled all the way to Dallas, reminding Lucy that he hated wearing a tie and he hated weddings and he considered Suki selfish for expecting them to drop everything and appear on such short notice.

Lucy pointed out that maybe her sister was trying to be considerate. Maybe Suki hadn't wanted to delay because she knew the trip would be harder for Lucy further on in the pregnancy. At which point Buddy smirked and said Suki didn't give a damn about anybody but herself.

The remainder of the trip was silent.

Delmar Boone turned out to be a thin man with a pompadour hairdo and a polyester western suit. He had the sort of attractiveness usually associated with hard living and prison movies, and with his slow smile and vocabulary of "Yup, nope, maybe, and pert near," he was exactly the kind of male Suki would have turned up her nose at once upon a time. Lucy was shocked. What had happened to all Suki's dreams of marrying a rising young executive? But Suki clearly adored the man, and he seemed pleasant enough, so Lucy pushed away all misgivings and concentrated on the spirit of the event.

Charity had sent packets of rice and a bottle of champagne and a good-luck penny for Suki's shoe. Lucy had brought a silly blue satin garter and a delicate lace handkerchief from Wanda's keepsake box for her sister to carry as something old.

Suki looked outrageous but wonderful. She'd lost some weight and was dressed in a white leather suit with a tight skirt and form-fitting jacket. Beneath the veil her eyes glowed.

Del and the friend who was acting as best man went inside, leaving Suki to last-minute primping. She slipped the penny into her shoe, slid the garter up her leg, and carelessly stuffed the handkerchief down the low-cut V of the suit jacket.

"All set," she announced. "How do I look?"

"Terrific," Lucy assured her. "But wait . . . you don't have anything borrowed!"

Suki rested her index finger on her bottom lip and looked

around. She zeroed in on Buddy and giggled. "How 'bout if I borrow your husband? He can walk me up the aisle."

"There is no aisle," Lucy said, ignoring the eager expression on Buddy's face

"But there's stairs. A bride shouldn't have to climb stairs without a big strong arm to lean on."

Lucy followed the two of them in. She watched Suki's spike-heeled, hip-swaying, helpless walk and noted the way her sister held Buddy's arm and leaned in toward him and the way Buddy's face flushed with pleasure, and she wondered why she wasn't even a tiny bit jealous. At one time she'd have been furious with Suki. Now she felt only amazement at Buddy's stupidity and a mild irritation at having to follow along alone in her ungainly state.

The ceremony was brief and businesslike. Lucy photographed the key moments and then posed the couple outside near some shrubbery for a wedding portrait. Buddy popped the champagne and they toasted with plastic glasses in the parking lot.

"We thought we'd all head over to our place awhile," Suki said, "then go out together for a celebration dinner."

Lucy glanced at Buddy, but he had warmed to the occasion and was already agreeing to the plan.

Del and Suki's place turned out to be a tiny rental house with an overgrown yard and a driveway paved in beer-bottle caps.

"The guy who rented it to us swore them caps go down more'n a foot," Del told Buddy proudly, and Lucy and Suki were left behind as all three men rushed into the house to open beers and add more caps to the collection.

Suki smiled indulgently after them and then turned to Lucy and sighed, mingling awe, happiness, and relief. "Guess I'm Mrs. Boone now," she said.

"Looks that way," Lucy agreed.

Suki unpinned the veil from her hair and hooked her arm through Lucy's. "We're both just old married ladies, Luce."

They started slowly up the uneven walk.

"Wish Mama was here," Lucy said.

"Yeah. Me too. I got me a man now and a real house, not some shitty trailer like she always had. And I live in the city, not wipe-ass Walea nowheresville. There's not a damn thing she could be naggin' me about now."

"Oh, Suki, that's not—"

The baby started to kick and Lucy stopped to put her hand on her belly and enjoy the movement.

Intense jealousy flashed across Suki's face, then faded into wistfulness. "Me'n Del would like a family right away, but he's afraid his ex-wife might get pissed and take away his visiting rights with his kids."

"He's been married before?"

"Yeah," Suki said mournfully. "He's had real bad luck with women before he met me."

"He's been married more than once?"

"Three times. One of 'em was crazy. One was a drunk, and the one with the kids is just a cast-iron bitch who was lookin' for a free ride."

Lucy cleared her throat and tried to keep her face blank. "What does Del do, anyway? I mean, for a living?"

"Oh, God! Didn't I tell you? He's a musician. A real artist! He's gonna be the next Porter Waggoner!"

"No, you didn't tell me."

"Yeah, that last bitch he was married to nearly ruined his career. Made him work a day job on top of singin', and expected him to mow the lawn and all that ordinary stuff, and it nearly squashed the music right out of him. Which was stupid on her part, because if she'd just helped him along in his career, she'd be rich and livin' in a mansion by now. She only hurt herself."

Suki's eyes danced. "If he'd met me years ago, he'd already be a star. I'm gonna help him. Manage his career and fight off all those damn chippies who flock around the stage. When we get enough money built up, we're gonna buy one of those fancy buses and I'll go everywhere with him. How's that for an exciting life, huh? Beats marryin' one of them stuffy business types I used to go for. And it damn sure beats anything Walea ever had to offer."

"I hope you'll be happy," Lucy said.

"Hell, why wouldn't I be? I got everything a woman could want now!"

Lucy followed Suki into the house. "Shabby" would have been a compliment. There were empty beer bottles and country-music magazines and overflowing ashtrays strewn about. The furniture consisted of a bedraggled wicker chair and a tattered floral couch covered by an old bedspread just like the couch they'd grown up with. Lucy had the urge to lift the fabric skirt and check for a brick propping up a corner.

"This is temporary," Suki said. "Artists have to sacrifice a little in the beginning, you know."

Fighting down a wave of sadness, Lucy sank into the couch and rested her hands on her belly. Memories haunted her. Wanda, Anita, Lydell. Suki sparkling in a twirling costume. The whispered confidences of sisters sharing a bed. Dreams. Wanda's red hands and Anita's hungry eyes and Lydell's drunken smile. It had seemed then that Suki was the one with the answers.

"Who's next for the can?" the best man called. His name was McArthur Peck, and though he'd introduced himself as Mac, both Suki and Del called him Pecker.

"Ain't he a hoot?" Buddy chuckled as he settled beside Lucy on the sagging couch. "He used to play college football too."

The beer flowed, the jokes grew raunchier, and Buddy began to ridicule her in small ways. The others encouraged him by laughing uproariously whenever he made fun of her.

"Is anyone still interested in dinner?" Lucy finally asked.

"I told ya!" Buddy waved his bottle of Lone Star for emphasis. "She's just like an old fat steer in a feedlot. All she's lookin' for is her next meal."

"I'm sorry," Lucy said to them all. "Since I'm pregnant, I get sick if I don't eat regularly."

"Yup," Del said, and stood. "My wife was the same way."

"Del," Suki whined, "I'm your wife now. You have ta call *her* something else."

They filed outside. The newlyweds climbed into Suki's little car, which Suki had decorated herself with "JUST MARRIED" signs and crepe-paper streamers. Buddy insisted that Mac-Pecker ride with him and that Lucy sit in the back. Lucy climbed into the back without complaint, consoling herself with the thought that the evening couldn't last too much longer. Buddy had promised his mother that they would be home early.

The restaurant was on the edge of town and looked like a big barn. Inside was a dance floor and a live band, surrounded by tables and several different antique-looking wooden bars. Toward the back Lucy could see a pool table and miniature bowling area, and upstairs there was a loftlike arrangement with more seating. The walls were covered with animal heads and horse harness and wanted posters and barbed wire and wolf traps and severed neckties from those patrons who hadn't read the "NO TIES ALLOWED" sign at the door. The noise was deafening.

"I can give y'all a table upstairs right away," the hostess shouted. "Otherwise it's a half-hour wait."

The others moaned their disappointment, but Lucy was silently grateful. The upstairs had to be quieter.

After they were seated, a waitress came and told them they had a choice between steak and chicken, both cooked over mesquite. She left with the food order, and the first round of beers arrived.

"We want to make a toast," Lucy said, raising her glass of club soda and nudging Buddy beneath the table with her toe.

"To the bride and groom," Buddy filled in, "and . . ." He fumbled inside the jacket he'd draped over the back of his chair and pulled out the envelope. "We didn't know what y'all needed, so we thought cash was the best gift."

The envelope contained five hundred dollars, an amount Charity had suggested as adequate for the purchase of dishes or monogrammed sheets and towels or various other possible needs.

"Holy shit," Suki breathed. "Five hundred bucks! I could pay off the car."

"Yup," Del said, "but then wha'cha got? A paid-off hunk of junk. Is that what life's about? No siree." He threw back his head and broke into a twangy tune. "Life's about smellin' the roses and punchin' some noses and sharin' watermelon with kin. Life's about findin' a gal and helpin' a pal and raisin' a brew with a friend." He lifted his beer for punctuation and took a long swallow.

Buddy applauded and Pecker whooped and hollered and Suki leaned over to whisper, "He just made that right up," into Lucy's ear.

The steaks were served hanging over the edges of the plates, and crocks of pinto beans and corn relish and mashed potatoes were put in the center of the table along with a basket of bread.

By the time dinner was over and the plates cleared, Lucy was having trouble pretending enjoyment. The others were in varying stages of drunkenness and Buddy was using her as the butt of his jokes again. Miss Priss, he kept calling her. "Miss Priss wouldn't say 'shit' if she had a mouth full of it. Miss Priss is still lookin' for the stork that brought that baby. Miss Priss is such a tight-ass she has to fart through her nose."

She escaped to the bathroom and spent a long time staring into the mirror stretching over the bank of sinks. The woman reflected there looked very much a grown-up. Maybe even a Miss Priss. What was the connection between the grown-up woman in the glass and the uncertain little Lucy inside her? What was the connection between the woman in the glass and the sister and husband outside? Everything felt very disjointed. The only reality was the fluttering life in her womb.

Lucy returned to the table to find that Del and Pecker had gone to play pool. She sat down wearily and glanced at her watch. It had been a long day and her back and feet were aching.

"We need to head home," she told Buddy. "They predicted rain, and the roads will be slow going if we get caught in it."

"Yeah, yeah, yeah," Buddy replied.

He was extra mean and belligerent whenever he drank past a certain point, and Lucy was dismayed to see that the point had been reached.

"Think I'm too dumb to figger that out for myself?" He stood, tipping his chair over, and grabbed Suki's arm. "Me'n the bride are gonna do a li'l steppin'. Right, bride?"

Suki was pouting because Del was paying more attention to his friend Pecker than to her. "Tha's right," she said, stumbling out of her chair to lean heavily against Buddy. "Who needs a groom?"

Lucy watched them go, angry because Buddy was drunk and because he was being such an ass and because in all their years together he'd never once consented to dance with her. Not that she wanted to dance at that moment. She was exhausted and her eyes stung from the heavy layer of smoke in the place, and the only thing that kept her going was the knowledge that she would be on the way home to her own bed soon.

When the waitress came around again, Lucy ordered coffee for the entire table and a king-size Styrofoam cup for Buddy to take with him.

Del and Pecker drifted back to the table first. Lucy tried to engage them in conversation about music, but they kept exchanging looks and laughing, so she stopped. Suki and Buddy finally returned from the dance floor, flushed and disheveled, and Lucy pushed the coffee toward them.

"Hell," Pecker said, drawing the word out into two syllables. "The night is just a weanling and y'all got five hundred ta spend and I happen ta know where there's a all-night blackjack game outside a Fort Worth."

"Woo-eee!" Del pounded on the table. "What say, Suki girl . . . wanna go out and do some livin' with your ole man?"

Suki, who had been strangely subdued since returning from dancing, shrugged and sipped at her coffee.

"How bout you, Buddy-balls? You game?"

Lucy stiffened and waited. His face was contorted with wanting to go.

"Aw . . ." he said, running his thick fingers through his hair.

She knew better than to say anything. If she pushed him at all, he would use it as an excuse to get mad and go with them.

"Come on, Bud. Ya only live once."

"Forget it," Suki said suddenly. "It's my weddin' night and

Buddy can just get on home. You too, Pecker. You're both tryin' to ruin it." At that she burst into tears.

"Reckon that's it, then," Del said casually.

"Yeah," Buddy agreed in a man-to-man tone. "Guess I gotta take my ball and chain home too."

The silence and fresh air of the parking lot revived Lucy. "Well," she said as she and Buddy threaded through lines of cars toward her Ford, "at least you weren't bored like you usually are at weddings."

Buddy grunted something unintelligible and glared at her. "You think you're too good for me, don'cha?" he demanded.

"What? What are you talking about? What did I say?"

He didn't answer.

When they reached the car she went to the driver's side, but he pushed her away.

"Please let me drive, Buddy. You've had a lot to drink."

"Just shut up and get in," he said.

As they pulled away from the restaurant Lucy handed him the huge cup of coffee. "Here, I got this for you."

He took a sip, grimaced, and threw it out the window. They drove in silence awhile. The forecast rain began to fall, and the silence was punctuated by the slap-slap of the windshield wiper. Lucy sorted through the tapes and put on a singer she knew Buddy liked.

"Is that the way you see yourself, Buddy?" she finally asked, knowing as she did that she shouldn't, but unable to keep the thoughts to herself. "Are Del and McArthur the kind of people you wish you could be?"

"What the hell's that supposed to mean?"

"I don't know. You live by your parents' rules and you work at a job your parents arranged for you, and I always get the feeling that you'd have chosen a different life if you could. Now, seeing you with those two made me wonder if that's who you'd like to be."

"You think you're so smart, don'cha? Well, I've had more college'n you. And I'm the one who knows how to make money and get along in the world. What the hell are you good at anyway, except naggin'?"

He was at his worst, the worst she'd seen him in months, and she knew that she should retreat and sit quietly, but the evening had left her in a reckless depression.

"What made you go off on that 'Miss Priss' tangent tonight?"

" 'Tangent.' One a your twenty-dollar college words, huh?"

"It's just an expression. It means—"

"Just shut up! Shut the fuck up!" His face contorted and his foot mashed down on the accelerator as he screamed, "I don't need you tellin' me what nothin' means! You and my mother—"

The car fishtailed on the slick road and Lucy grabbed the dash with one hand.

"Aw, Miss Priss is scared a the car goin' fast. Poor Missy Prissy." He hit the accelerator hard and jiggled the steering wheel back and forth. The car lunged this way and that, throwing her around and making the shoulder belt cut into her swollen stomach and breasts.

When he was driving straight again, Lucy unfastened her seat belt. "I'm going to lie down and rest my back," she said, turning to make the clumsy climb over the seat. She knew better than to ask him to stop so she could get out and then get into the back of the car in a more dignified fashion.

"Oh, ya are?" he asked, resuming the acceleration and jerking the wheel even harder than before.

She was halfway over the seat. The motion slammed her sideways.

"Buddy! That's not—"

But the car was spinning crazily and there was a sound coming from Buddy's throat like when they rode the roller coaster at the Texas state fair and she couldn't hold on to anything and she felt like a rag doll in a clothes dryer. And she screamed. And the spinning slid into sideways slow motion—jarring, crunching, twisting.

Then there was pain.

Then blackness.

31

"Lucy."

The voice sounded far away. She tried to make sense of it.

"Lucy. It's Dr. Howell. Can you answer me?"

There was a garbled sound. She wasn't conscious of making it, but she knew it came from her own throat because it hurt.

"Your throat is sore from the airway. Just try to whisper."

She had been seeing the room without connecting sight to thought. Suddenly she was aware. She was in a hospital room. She was in bed.

"We were in the car . . ." she whispered.

"You had an accident," Dr. Howell said. "You were brought here unconscious."

She stared hard at his face and tried to think.

"You had us all worried for a while."

"Where's Buddy?" she whispered.

"Buddy's fine. Just a little banged up. He's right outside with the reverend and his wife. Are you ready to see them?"

She nodded. The simple movement made her hurt in dozens of places.

Dr. Howell looked down at her a moment with a thoughtful frown. "We couldn't save the baby, Lucy. She was too early."

He moved away and she heard the door open and close. The words made no sense. What did he mean?

Tentatively she lifted a hand and found her belly. The mound was gone.

"We couldn't save the baby," he'd said.

She opened her eyes. Charity. The reverend holding an open Bible. Buddy's face loomed over her. There was a butterfly bandage on the bridge of his nose and his eyes brimmed with emotion.

"My baby," she cried hoarsely. "Where's my baby?"

Buddy bent so close she could smell his after-shave. His hand touched her cheek and he buried his face in her hair. "I said you were drivin'," he whispered. "You gotta back me up . . ."

She squeezed her eyes shut and the screaming inside her head filled the room.

"Go on! Get out! Leave her to me," Charity's voice commanded.

Then there were hands on her shoulders.

"Lucy. Lucy. Talk to me. It's Charity."

"The baby . . . Charity . . ." The rasping sobs burned in her throat and chest.

"She's gone," Charity said, and the word "she" added more pain. "You were in hard labor by the time the ambulance got you here. The surgeon worked on your chest and Doc Howell delivered your baby at the same time. They did everything tryin' to save her, but they couldn't. I watched 'em. They worked hard on her."

"You saw her?"

Charity nodded. "She had dark hair like yours. But she was too small and she couldn't breathe. I think she was glad when they stopped workin' on her and let God take her."

"Where is she? What did they do with her? I want to see her. I want to hold her."

"Nonsense. Don't be morbid. You gotta forget about the baby. We can't bring her back. We have to pick up the pieces and carry on."

"Buddy killed her! Buddy was—"

"Stop it! The baby's dead. Do you want to destroy your husband too?"

"But he was—"

"They did tests. They know he was full a alcohol. But as long as you were drivin', it don't matter to the police how much he had to drink."

"But—"

"You want him to get charged with drunk drivin' like a criminal? You want him to be drug into court and humiliated and destroyed and maybe sent to prison for something that can't be changed?"

Lucy didn't try to say anything more. She didn't have the energy. She didn't care. She wished she had died with the baby.

"There'll be other babies, darlin'. Doc says you're gonna be good as new." Charity paused. "Soon as you're well, you could start goin' to town more again. Maybe get friendly with that nice Mr. Tully. Maybe get another baby on the way a little faster this time."

Lucy was suddenly very cold. She closed her eyes to escape Charity's gaze.

There was the sound of the door and then Buddy's anxious voice asking, "How is she? What's she sayin'? Is she sayin' crazy stuff?"

"She's fine," Charity assured him. "She just needs rest." Charity smoothed the hair from Lucy's forehead and fussed with the pillows. "Just a little rest and she'll be back to our old Lucy again. Right back to our same old Lucy."

Days passed. Lucy floated between medicated reality and crashing despair. She had a cast on her left forearm and a tight wrap to support her broken ribs and a patchwork of stitches on the back of her head. Her most serious injuries had been a concussion and a collapsed lung, but her broken ribs had the most lasting impact. Every breath hurt and the slightest movement caused searing flashes of pain in her chest. She was trapped. Stuck in the hospital bed in the closetlike room with no escape from the Skidmores or her own misery.

Charity insisted on coming to the hospital each day at noon to help her manage lunch. Buddy came each evening after work to watch her struggle with dinner. She told them not to come. She told them to leave her alone. She pretended she was asleep or simply turned her face to the wall and refused to acknowledge their presence. Their visits grew briefer, but they wouldn't stay away. They came dutifully, as if they had to try to cheer her. Beneath their false smiles she saw guilt and anger and irritation.

Charity brought huge baskets of fruit and flowers from the Temple of Light congregation. Buddy proudly presented her with the title and keys to a new car. The Ford had been too badly damaged to repair.

"It's a Buick," he told her. "Real nice, with a light blue bottom and a white top. I parked it right out in the parking lot where you can look outta your window and see it when you feel good enough ta get up." The color told her that the car had been Charity's doing. When she didn't respond, he put the keys and paperwork in the drawer of her nightstand.

Mr. Tully and her friends from the law office sent a bouquet of balloons but didn't visit because Charity had spread the word that Lucy wanted to be alone. Charity had even had the nurses tape a "NO VISITORS EXCEPT FAMILY" sign to the outside of her door. Lucy wished it said "ALL VISITORS EXCEPT FAMILY." The only family she wanted to see was Suki, who had called several times but was vague about whether she could drive over or not.

Family. Every time the door was propped open she could see the sign, and that word jumped out at her. Family. The Skidmores were not her family. They never had been and they never would be. How could she have been so stupid as to believe otherwise?

She saw the three of them so clearly now. They were part of a whole. A three-headed monster out to devour or crush everyone in their path.

After a week the reverend came in and gave her a lecture about depression and grief and letting her family and the Lord support her in this time of trouble. He also told her that she ought to think of others, not just herself.

Lucy didn't argue. There was no point in arguing with him, just as there was no point in trying to communicate with Buddy or Charity. They existed in a separate dimension now. They couldn't touch her. They were all part of her past.

Lucy Skidmore was part of her past too—the Lucy who had been Mrs. DuWayne Skidmore's dutiful wife and Charity's and the reverend's perfect daughter-in-law. That Lucy had died in the same twisted metal that claimed her baby girl.

At night she lay awake in her dark room, taking strength from her ability to fight the pain with less medication than before, pulling herself up from the bottomless anguish that weighted her days, and she replayed her life. She searched for answers and understanding. She wrestled her fear of the future. And she unleashed her anger. An anger so pure and intense it felt like a newly found religion.

How had she ever thought she loved Buddy? How had she ever found him sweet or charming? How had she seen him as anything other than the cowardly, mean, and despicable man she now knew him to be?

And Charity. How had she ever let that woman slip into her mother's place? How had she come to trust and care about someone who was as principled and loving as a rattlesnake?

The anger scoured away years of accumulated mental sludge, awakening her senses and making her feel more alive and real than she had in years. It also made her feel very alone.

But she couldn't hang on to that anger because eventually she had to bow to the physical pain and ring for medication. And when she did, the pills robbed her of that cleansing sharpness. She drifted in the cloudy haze of drugs, and all her strength ebbed away. She foundered then, in that floating void before sleep, and sank back into the regret and guilt that occupied most of her daylight awareness.

Foremost was her guilt over the baby. The baby was dead because she hadn't been wearing her seat belt or because she hadn't forced Buddy to let her drive or she hadn't stopped Buddy from drinking so much or she hadn't placated and petted him out of the mean mood that had made him jerk the steering wheel.

The self-torture spread out to include the past too. Anita was gone because Lucy hadn't been stronger and more perceptive. Her father was gone because she hadn't been good enough or loving enough or lovable enough to make him want to stop drinking. Ms. Conroy was gone because she'd been stupid and childish and jealous.

And her mother . . .

Her mother had died of a broken heart because Lucy hadn't been able to give her the contented happiness she deserved and because Lucy hadn't been able to keep Suki or Anita from leaving and because Lucy had never been able to light up her eyes or lighten her burden by being the daughter who mattered.

Lucy had failed everyone. She'd never been smart enough or caring enough or resourceful enough or talented enough or pretty enough for anyone who loved her. She had failed them all.

Which brought her back to the baby's death. To her failure as a woman and a mother.

It was at these times that her whole body wept. Milk dripped from her swollen breasts and blood seeped from her cramping womb and tears leaked from the desert of her eyes. She had failed the baby she'd carried.

Her fluids were draining away. Soon she would be hollow. Empty. Soon she would crumble into powder and blow away.

The physical pain lessened by tiny increments each day, and Dr. Howell began to talk of her going home. He offered it as a gift, a goal she would reach quickly if she was a good girl and followed his instructions. But the "home" he referred to was the old Lucy's home, not hers, and the thought of sharing a bed or a meal or a moment of intimacy with Buddy Skidmore both repulsed and terrified her.

Late Monday afternoon Dr. Howell announced that she was progressing nicely and he expected to release her on Wednesday. Charity and Reverend Skidmore arrived soon after, apparently having been advised of the news before Lucy. Charity bustled in with a gift-wrapped package, which she unwrapped, supplying a stream of bright chatter as if Lucy were a child whose attention could be held with the pretense of excitement. The package yielded a shapeless ruffled dress. A going-home dress. Charity hung it on the outside of the closet door so Lucy could see it.

Charity went on and on about how she'd cleaned the mobile home from top to bottom in preparation for Lucy's homecoming. How she'd filled the freezer with casseroles and stocked the cupboards and changed the toilet deodorizers and the room fresheners and sorted through and organized every nook and cranny.

Buddy had moved into his parents' house while Lucy was hospitalized, so the mobile home had stayed pretty much as Lucy had left it. Obviously that had not been good enough for Charity.

The woman then explained how she and the reverend wouldn't be visiting the hospital the next day. They were going out of town to accomplish some pressing Christian business so that Charity would be free to spend all her time with Lucy after the release.

Lucy closed her eyes and feigned sleep, an act that usually sent the Skidmores tiptoeing from the room. Not today. Today the reverend, who had been little more than Charity's shadow on previous visits, declared that he had a prayer for Lucy. Charity could not conceal her surprise and anxiety over her husband's announcement.

"Lord Jesus," he called out in his ringing voice, "deliver this woman from the burning pit of sorrow you have cast her into. Guide her back to us just as you guided her behind the wheel of that car, just as you guided her into sacrificing her unborn child to atone for her own pitiful human frailty."

Lucy watched him the same way she would have watched a spitting cobra or a serial murderer.

He raised his arms and threw his head back. "Now, dear Lord, gather this poor unworthy creature to your breast and heal her spirit so that she might learn to serve you better. Teach her so that her child will not have perished in vain . . . so that her loved ones will not have suffered the shame of her sin in vain . . . so that—"

"Reverend, honey," Charity said, catching his elbow in a vise grip and forcibly breaking his concentration, "I'm sure Lucy appreciates your good words, but we hafta be runnin' along now. You can finish speaking to the Lord later."

Reverend Skidmore appeared annoyed but allowed himself to be pushed toward the door.

"We'll be here about eleven on Wednesday," Charity said, blowing a kiss at Lucy as she left.

Buddy came shortly after their departure. There were wet circles beneath the sleeves of his shirt as he pulled a chair up beside her bed and sat down. "Boy, it's gonna be good ta have you home," he said, forcing a lightness that was not reflected in his eyes.

Lucy stared at him. He had a bright red hairline scar from the accident. It detracted a little from the open boyishness that sold so much insurance.

She wanted to ask him who he was.

"Ya know, Luce"—he studied his big hands a moment—"I was put on this earth ta play football, and everything good was over for me when that sonuvabitch hit me from the side on the forty-yard line. When God took my knee, he just might as well a took everything. Guess that's one a the reasons I been flauntin' my sinnin' at him. Kinda wavin' a red flag, ya know ... darin' him ta come on down and get the rest."

Lucy could tell he was referring to more than just drinking and playing poker, and he was anxious to dump whatever mess squirmed inside him, expecting her to absolve and forgive and make him better again.

"Get out of here," she said.

He sighed and hung his head, wallowing in his own guilt. "It ain't fair that he punished you for what I done. I'm the one who's bad. I'm the one who ain't fit ta have people call him son or husband. And it ain't just the crash, it's—"

"Get out!" Lucy screamed.

He slouched to the door and paused. "I don't much blame ya," he said. "But I'm gonna make it up." He fidgeted self-consciously. "I was gonna save this for a surprise, but guess I just as well tell you now. ... Don't look for me to visit tomorrow 'cause I'm gonna do my outta-town calls all day and work late and get all caught up so I can take off Wednesday and help Mama bring ya home, and then I'm gonna take my vacation so's I can stay there with ya every minute for the whole first two weeks you're home."

He waited expectantly for a response. When there was none, he scratched his head and said, "Maybe I'll bring home Mc-Donald's or Kentucky Fried so nobody has to cook Wednesday night." He brightened at this idea. "Yeah! It'll be like a party."

After he was gone, Lucy raised her bed into a sitting position. Wednesday. One day away.

She eased herself off the bed and stood. The movement stoked the fire in her ribs and took her breath away. She waited, holding on to the bed rail until it settled; then she shuffled to the chair by the window and carefully lowered herself into it.

The day after tomorrow.

She wished her mother or father were alive to rescue her. She wished Suki would swoop in and carry her off to Dallas. She wished the earth would open up and swallow her, or better yet, swallow the Skidmores. She wished and fantasized and wished.

From her seat at the window she could see the powder-blue-and-white car that matched the keys and title in her bedside drawer. Dusk crept in, and the parking lot's lights snapped on, making the shiny new automobile gleam.

She couldn't go back to live in the mobile home. She couldn't. Because she knew if she did, Charity would twist things around and Buddy would do something to make her feel sympathetic and little by little she would lose sight of the fact that Buddy had killed her baby. And she would slip back into accepting life with him. And she would believe again that whatever faults their marriage had lay with her.

And the slow suffocation she'd been suffering before her pregnancy would begin again. And worst of all, she might get pregnant again. She might once again expose a helpless infant to Buddy's self-centered cruelty.

She sat in the chair until the nurse came in with her bedtime pills, pushing herself to see how much her body would tolerate. It was amazing to see how far she'd come since first waking in the pastel green room. She shrugged off the nurse and put herself to bed.

The pills were easy to palm and hide without the nurses knowing. She didn't take any that night. It was a test to see how badly she needed them. Sometime in the night she relented and broke off half of one from her stash, but that was only because she knew she had to have the sleep. By morning she was confident she could survive without them.

After Dr. Howell made his usual morning rounds, she got up and put on the shapeless dress hanging on the closet door. She gathered her things from the room, took the car keys from the drawer, and quietly slipped out of the hospital.

The humidity was high and the air was thick and still. After her long stay in the air-conditioned hospital environment, she wasn't prepared for the East Texas heat. It added to the heaviness of her breathing and the slowness of her movements.

She slid behind the wheel of the car. White upholstery. The brand-new smell of carpet and fabric and plastic. She concentrated on her motions. Turn the key. Shift into reverse. Back up. Drive slowly. Watch the road.

The drive-in window of her bank was her first stop. She asked for a balance in their joint savings account and withdrew half that amount. Seven thousand dollars in hundred-dollar bills.

She pulled into a Honk and Holler store and bought two bottles of extra-strength Tylenol at the drive-in window. Then she headed for the Expando double-wide she'd called home since her wedding day.

The cast on her left arm ended at mid-palm, so her driving was not impaired. Still, she felt like a beginner. Her heart raced and there were unremembered signs and lights and sudden dips in the street. She was drenched in sweat by the time she reached the gravel drive with its huge Temple of Light sign.

No one was in sight.

She eased the car down the drive, wincing at the noise, but no one popped from the bushes to challenge her. Getting out of the car made her ribs burn with pain, but that was predictable and therefore manageable.

A feral cat bolted from the undergrowth and raced up the drive toward Charity's. Lucy's heart jumped with it.

The air was stuffy inside. She could tell that the place had been closed up while she was gone, but she resisted the urge to open windows or turn on the air conditioner.

She began to gather what she wanted. There wasn't much. Her camera. Her stash of negatives and pictures. Her art and photography books. A few basic pieces of clothing. Ms. Conroy's antique shawl. And the shoe boxes full of Wanda's possessions.

Was there nothing else she wanted? Charity's coordinated household goods and Buddy's football memorabilia surrounded her and she realized that she'd removed everything that was really hers and yet the house still looked completely intact. There would be no sign that she'd left. No sign that anything vital was missing.

She had purposely stayed away from the baby's room, but now she had to see it before she walked out. She took several Tylenol and went down the hall to the closed nursery door with the same mixture of dread and need that had pulled her toward her mother's coffin.

The room was empty. The crib was gone. The handmade blankets were gone. The curtains and wallpaper had been replaced. Charity and Buddy had stripped away all evidence of the baby.

She turned from the sight so quickly that she was momentarily immobilized by pain. Tears leaked from her eyes as she walked away from the empty room and the empty home and the empty life. She told herself it was the pain that was making her cry.

As she drove away from it all she dry-swallowed two more

Tylenol. The town seemed small and tired and hostile to her. No facet of it held pleasant memories. She had never seen Walea the way others did, an oasis in an otherwise godforsaken and treacherous world. She'd always felt like an outsider, the girl from the Trailer Village.

She pulled onto the highway, onto pavement so smooth her tires sang. The roadway stretched out invitingly before her and the billboard proclaiming "YOU ARE LEAVING WALEA, TEXAS—THE BUCKLE OF THE BIBLE BELT" whizzed by her and everything felt right. She wasn't just leaving Buddy and the Skidmores, she was leaving Walea too. Her life was her own now. She finally understood.

32

Juliana

The moon was full and white. As white as the drift of cocaine spilled across Juliana's lap.

"Shit," somebody muttered, and there was a scrambling for position. All four boys fell to their knees on the floor of the dimly lit limo and buried their heads in her skirt. The girls laughed wildly at the pushing and snuffling. White powder floated in every direction.

Juliana didn't laugh. Nothing was funny at the moment. Sparky was behaving like an ass, and some damn photographer had taken the notion to follow them all evening, and she was down, really down.

She hit the button for the intercom. "Have you lost him yet, Zeke?"

"B'lieve I did."

"Then let's go to Bluejay's."

"You bet."

They all settled back into their seats. There were seven of them—Daphne Buchanan and Cee Cee Brissot and Willy Wildenburg and Jay Hollingshead and Denny DuPree and Four Ashton and Sparky—all that was left of her entourage since Lee had made the dreary decision to go back to college and Gabby Gravesend had dropped out of sight. Whitney Chandler had been gone a long time, of course, having gotten married and moved to Europe shortly after Ellis vanished. And Perry, damn him, was still in Paris playing the tragic poet.

"Fuckups," Daffy yelled at the boys. "You're all fuckups! Next time I'll pass out the coke."

Juliana leaned her head back against the soft leather upholstery. The spilled coke wouldn't show up in here. That was one benefit of having a white car.

415

But then, the only person who would have seen it was Zeke. And it wouldn't bother him. Nothing bothered Zeke. He'd been with her for two years now and she'd never seen so much as a raised eyebrow from him.

Zeke pulled up smoothly in front of Bluejay's. The club was one of the hundreds of corner dives that stayed open illegally after hours and it was the sort of place that the group considered great fun after spending the first leg of the evening at the latest trendy spot. There was no posturing or posing for photographers or cheek kissing here. Slumming, they called it. Slumming made them feel loose and decadent and jaded and incredibly chic, and they treated the seediness like a movie set, an atmosphere created as a backdrop for their entertainment.

Juliana found it all vaguely discomfiting, though. The smoky darkness, the decay, the hopelessness that seeped from the hooded eyes of the regulars—it wasn't what she wanted life to be.

Finding and maintaining these after-hours havens was an art. If a busybody photographer ever tracked them there or a gossip columnist mentioned the place, it was ruined. Destroyed by a stampede of the Manhattan curious and the suburban voyeurs from New Jersey. But Zeke was an artist and he could always find someplace new.

Zeke rushed them to the door of Bluejay's like a shepherd protecting his flock. The bouncer peeked through his little window and unlocked for them immediately. Zeke slipped folded bills into the man's heavily ringed hand.

"Do you want to come in, Zeke?" Juliana asked.

Zeke made a show of being disgusted. "If I left that white pile a junk sittin' by itself in this neighborhood, there'd be nothin' but souvenirs left when we came out."

Few people looked up as they entered the club. No fawning hostess rushed out to greet them. The barmaid didn't smile.

Juliana led them through the smoky haze to a dark corner table. She lit a cigarette while Jay and Sparky hustled another table and extra chairs. Finally the eight of them were settled. Drinks were delivered. Juliana had to nudge Sparky twice before he came out of his trance and remembered to pay. She eyed him bitterly as he counted out bills from the wad she'd given him earlier. His handling the money was part of their unspoken agreement. She hated fumbling with the stuff, so Sparky always dispensed the cash on their outings. Now he couldn't seem to manage even that simple task.

What had happened to all of Sparky's promises? "I'll never fall in love again," he'd sworn. "I know all about trouble and heart-break and I'll never do that to myself again. Hell, I know how to jerk myself off! So all I need is a friend—a real, solid, stand-behind-me friend. All I need is you, Jinxie."

Sure.

What a fool she'd been to believe him. To think that the two of them could be mirrors, reflections of a whole. Like twins. Always together. Each providing the salve of cynicism and compassion that the other required.

After her break with Perry she'd concentrated completely on settling Sparky in his new apartment. She'd let him pick out stereo and television equipment and outrageous Italian furniture. And she'd planned her days around him. She'd indulged him and pampered him and held his head when he was sick from drugs and drinking. She'd coaxed him through so many of his periodic breakdowns that she knew the four-A.M. litany of regrets by heart.

And after he'd told her how bored he was, after he'd begged to go out, she had let him go everywhere with her, insisting that her friends accept him unconditionally. She had nurtured and loved and trusted him. And now he was betraying her. He needed someone else. There was no mistaking the moony expression that fogged his eyes every time Peter Ashton IV was around. Sparky was so intent on Four that he barely seemed conscious of his surroundings.

Jay glanced around casually, then pulled out the last of the coke. "Get ready, boys and girls."

Juliana tugged at the fine chain around her neck, pulling the tiny gold spoon up from between her breasts. It was the only gift Sparky had ever given her. She fingered the spoon as she watched the vial pass from person to person.

Damn fuckups.

Daffy was right. That's exactly what they were. Every single male at the table. If they hadn't been fooling around like first-graders while Jay was trying to divide the coke, then each of them would have a nice full vial now.

Fuckups. Jerks. Arrogant, imbecilic fools.

It was beginning to seem that all men shared those same characteristics. Some were just better at hiding it than others. Even gayness didn't save them from the curse. Wasn't Sparky proving that?

She snorted her meager share of the powder and leaned back to stare at the ceiling and wait for the rush. The process was mechanical. It no longer thrilled or excited her.

"What's on madame's mind tonight?" Daffy prodded snidely.

"Men," Juliana answered. She straightened in her chair and smiled at the high she was feeling. "All men are basically worthless pricks. It must have something to do with that hormone ... what is it?"

"Testosterone," Denny supplied.

"Speaking of worthless men!" Willy lit up as though her circuits had suddenly been activated. "Did you hear that Gabby Gravesend's stepfather disappeared with company funds?"

"No!" they all chorused.

"I've got something better," Cee Cee countered triumphantly. "Did you know that Whitney's getting a divorce already?"

"No!" they cried gleefully together.

"Yes!" Cee Cee giggled. "My ex-stepmother is sleeping with Whitney's lawyer and she got the whole scoop."

"Tell us more, tell us more," Daffy urged.

Cee Cee drew in a deep breath and leaned forward conspiratorially. "That phony Greek is taking her for five million."

"No!"

Cee Cee nodded knowingly. "And she'd already given him a million and a house on some island for a wedding gift."

"Poor Whit," Four sighed. "She must be so embarrassed. Six mil and a house. . . . Even if they fucked every day, he was still an expensive lay."

"She should have married your cousin Ellis," Willy said. "That's who she was really in love with."

Juliana stiffened. "How many times do I have to tell you! I don't want to hear that name!" She wished her cousin had died instead of just disappeared. And she wished everyone would forget he'd ever existed.

Willy shrank down into her chair and the others stared at their hands.

"Whit should have married Perry," Jay offered with almost comic seriousness. "I mean, if she was determined to get married, there's no better guy in the world than Perry."

"Oh, God, not the sainted Perry again." Sparky's voice and expression were laden with sarcasm.

Juliana clenched her teeth to keep from saying anything. It was Four who was always mentioning Perry, and Sparky's jealousy was painfully obvious.

"If Perry's such a great guy and such a terrific friend, then why doesn't he ever show up?" Sparky demanded belligerent-ly.

Willy stretched out her arms and shook her hair back from her face dreamily. "He's writing poetry in Paris or somewhere. You know . . . like the guy who cut off his ear."

"What a lot of crap," Sparky muttered.

From the corner of her eye Juliana noticed that Daffy was watching her.

"Perry would never have married Whit, would he, Jinx?" Daffy asked with the cyanide sweetness she specialized in. " 'Cause Perry was too fucked up by you . . . right?"

Everyone's eyes swung from Daffy to Juliana like spectators at a tennis match.

"Daphne . . ." Juliana exhaled the smoke from the cigarette she'd just lit. "You are so dull."

"But isn't that right? Didn't he abandon us all because you deliberately broke his heart?"

Juliana wanted another drag on her cigarette but she was afraid to lift it to her lips. Her hands were shaking too much. "I can't imagine where you got that idea. Perry was just tired of being here. He wanted to live in Europe."

"Well, it was the funniest thing. This friend of mine who lives in Paris sent me a book. A cheap little thing. Underground po-etry. She sent it to me because she remembered I knew Perry and she thought I might be interested." She threw a battered, slender volume onto the table and all hands grabbed for it at once.

"Imagine my surprise when I opened to Perry's poems and all of them were about Jinxie and how she destroyed his life."

Jay had won possession of the book and began to read loudly. " 'To Juliana. Trembling, smiling pain. Lost maiden stirring fe-ver—' " Jay stopped in mid-line, looked up, and blinked. "What the hell does it mean?"

"It means our precious Jinx was fucking with Perry's mind in addition to his other parts." Daffy clucked her tongue. "When we all felt so sorry for her because we thought she was still broken-hearted over her mystery man . . ."

Juliana groped for something sarcastic to fight back with, but nothing came. Instead she wanted to flop forward on the table and cry into her folded arms. She swallowed hard and glanced around. Daffy's eyes glittered with the scent of the kill. The others were staring at her. They wouldn't step in to defend her. They were all cowards.

She stood and looked down at them. Down at Daffy's evil, gloating face. Down at the weakness and betrayal in Sparky's slumped shoulders. Down at the whole phony, greedy, cannibalistic circle. And she hated them.

Suddenly she had to get away. She bolted from the table, toppling her chair as she left, and ran for the stairs that led to the bathrooms. She stumbled in the half-darkness before reaching the door. The tiny room was empty. She locked herself inside.

She hated everyone. Everyone.

She hated her dead mother for not loving her enough to want to stay with her and she hated her father for conquering the world without her and she hated Matt for being too weak to stay with her. She hated her Aunt Grace for being a drunk and she hated her grandfather for trying to control her and she hated Perry for leaving her just the way she'd thought he would from the first. And she hated Ellis—oh, how she hated Ellis—the embodiment of every evil . . . every nightmare.

But most of all she hated herself. The girl in the cracked, fly-specked mirror.

"Jinxie!"

The door shuddered beneath a series of blows.

"Jinxie, are you all right in there?"

"Go away, Sparky!"

"Aw, come on. Open the door. Don't let that Buchanan bitch get to you."

"Leave me alone! Go back to your panting after Four. I don't want you anymore. I don't want any of you!"

Silence.

He was gone.

Pleased with herself, she drew in a satisfied breath and looked around the fetid cubicle. There was no toilet paper and the towel holder was rusted and empty. At the base of the cracked porcelain toilet, debris floated in a brackish scum. The world wasn't what she'd thought it was going to be. Everything was filth. Everything was ugly.

Suddenly the door exploded inward. It was Zeke. "You aren't spendin' the night in here, are ya?" he asked.

She looked at his broad scarred face and the dainty little gold cross dangling from his right ear and she started to laugh. It was all so stupid. Her whole life was melodramatic and stupid. Why did she ever let herself take any of it seriously?

"I'm sick of everything, Zeke."

"Hey," Zeke said softly. He studied her a moment, then extended his arm. "Hold on tight, baby, 'cause you'n me are leavin' this place in the dust."

She clutched his thick arm and let him pull her out into the smoky darkness. But he didn't stop. He propelled her directly toward the exit. Behind her she could hear the commotion as the others scurried after her.

"Ya'll got a problem with the door ta the ladies'," Zeke told the bouncer on their way out. He slipped another bill into the man's hand. "Best get it fixed soon."

The bouncer nodded and saluted as they left.

Zeke handed her inside the car and the others filed in sheepishly behind her. Even Daffy looked contrite.

Juliana had to laugh at their faces. It began as a chuckle, then built into full-fledged hysterical laughter. The others exchanged nervous glances, then one by one joined in until they were all laughing and hanging on each other helplessly.

When it had died down, Juliana put a cigarette to her lips. Sparky lunged over Jay to light it.

She leaned her head back against the soft leather and thought about how complicated everything was now. Before, when her grandfather kept her prisoner, she had looked through the iron fence of Great House and seen happiness just beyond the horizon. Seen a prince on his way toward her.

Now she was free of that fence. She'd been beyond the horizon and she'd been to bed with the prince.

"What a dull night," Daffy said.

All the faces looked to Juliana to see if she agreed.

She smoked her cigarette and stared out the window, ignoring them. Hating them. Punishing them.

"Maybe we should find some more coke," Jay said.

There was a general murmur of agreement.

"Zeke isn't going to like it," Sparky muttered to no one in particular.

"Oh, relax," Four said, tweaking Sparky's chin and causing him to blush.

Juliana looked out the window at the fading moon. She imagined telling Zeke to stop and ordering them all out of the car. Banishing them from her life. What would they do then? She pictured them all flopping on the sidewalk like beached fish. None of them had a car like hers or access to the amount of money she did. They were all waiting for deaths or trust funds. And they were unable to function without a group and unable to maintain the group without a leader. Even Daffy with her vindictive wit and Four with his gay-blade-about-town persona. They were all waiting to be led into fun or mischief or sorrow because they couldn't find their own way. Whitney and Perry had led them before. Now the position was Juliana's.

And the truth was that she did still want them. What would she do without them? What if there wasn't anything else?

33

Ellis

Ellis Fielding Van Lyden had adopted the name Ellis McLeod. He had crisscrossed the country, assuming and discarding identities but always using "McLeod." It was the name he had seen on the last highway sign before Frank took him into the mountains, and he had never forgotten it.

The five years since leaving Badger had been filled with an erratic odyssey. He had shared the extraordinary lives of countless ordinary people and grown to see the entire country as his home, but he could not find a balm for the restlessness and dissatisfaction he still felt. And he was haunted by the dawning realization that his travels had brought him no closer to whatever it was that he needed.

He was no longer hiding or running. He kept in touch with his mother and grandfather and let them know what he was doing.

"I understand your leaving," his grandfather had said over the phone. "A boy's got to sow his wild oats." But Ellis had not been a boy since the day he buried his father's body in the woods. The trouble was, he didn't feel he had reached true manhood either. At twenty-eight he was stranded in some limbo between the two.

For the past year and a half he had been living in Kansas City, Missouri, working in construction as a low-paid apprentice to first a frame carpenter and then a finish man, convinced that building would give him the satisfaction that continually eluded him. His skills had developed quickly and he had several good offers after the completion of his last job, but in the course of learning the trade he also learned that he had no interest in helping to raise yet another shopping mall or office building or car dealership. He was ready to move on to somewhere and something else, which he would have already done if he hadn't seen a

tiny article in the newspaper about a home for special-needs children that was being patched together in the same run-down area
of town as the room he rented.

He went by the address to offer them a few days of free labor.
That was a month ago and he had worked on the home every day
since. Up until yesterday, when he drove the last nail and packed
up his tools.

Tonight he was at a gathering to celebrate the completion of
the home, and he was wishing he hadn't agreed to attend. He was
thinking about getting out of Kansas City and the whole damn
carpentry business and wondering how soon he could escape the
party without anyone noticing.

He had been trapped into several idiotic conversations during
the course of the evening and now he spied two fashionably
dressed middle-aged women with big jewelry and tight facial skin
heading in his direction, so he quickly threaded through the
crowd and slipped into the next room. It was the largest room in
the house and would eventually function as the recreation/play
area. Tonight it held the doctors and lawyers and priests and
rabbis and society matrons who had contributed to the project.
He found a trashcan for the sweet wine punch forced on him
earlier and resumed his crowd study. The place was full of females but they were all little girls or staunch matrons or smug
women with flashy wedding rings—three categories that were
strictly off limits. But he was restless and impatient, so he kept
looking.

He didn't notice her at first. The awareness was gradual, like
that of a hunter surveying the shade-dappled woods and slowly
realizing that something was staring back at him.

She turned away as soon as he met her eyes.

He moved closer out of amused curiosity and was surprised
to see no wedding ring. Funny she hadn't caught his eye sooner,
but then, she wasn't the sort of woman whose looks screamed for
attention. Nothing brassy or loud about her. In fact she seemed
to have a sort of protective camouflage.

She was five-foot-eight or so and she appeared slim and long-
legged beneath a loosely fitted black jacket and pants that could
have been a man's suit in a former life. The jacket hung casually
over a plain white T-shirt and she had rolled the sleeves up and
pushed them to her elbows.

Her hair was dark and pulled back into a knot at the nape of
her neck. There was no fashion statement to it. No artifice.

How could he have missed her before? She was strikingly different from the other women in the room and now that he had finally seen her he couldn't imagine having overlooked her.

She was standing with two other people who were both talking to her at once in an animated duet. She appeared to be giving them her full attention now. Ellis watched. He didn't think she was really interested in those people at all.

She raised her hand, lightly touching her index finger to her chin in an attentive gesture, but as she did, she glanced sideways toward him. It was only a flicker but it was all the invitation he needed, and it filled him with confidence.

"There you are," he said, stepping up beside her as if their meeting had been planned in advance.

The couple with her exchanged knowing smiles, then faded off into the crowd.

He expected her to say something coy or feign naiveté or lapse into the giddy flirtatiousness that usually accompanied his first contact with a woman. Instead the corners of her mouth went up ever so slightly and she skewered him with a direct, measuring look that pushed him completely off-balance.

"I'm sorry." He started to back away. "I didn't mean to intrude."

"Yes, you did." Her voice was casual and low. "You meant exactly that. You were just betting I wouldn't mind."

He stared at her, absorbing the details of her appearance—no jewelry or makeup, flawless fair skin made even paler by contrast with her dark chestnut-brown hair and feathery eyebrows—and thinking that she was unique rather than beautiful. Thinking that she had wonderfully intelligent eyes and a sensual mouth and was far more interesting than the flashy, shallow women he usually met and thinking that it would be refreshing to be with someone who might challenge him. Someone who might have read de Beauvoir or Nietzsche or Yeats or Donne. Someone who knew that acid rain wasn't a rock group. But at the same time thinking that a woman like her would probably be uninterested in the simple man he was trying to be.

"I'm the carpenter," he said, feeling clumsy and wondering how to relate to a woman like this.

"I know who you are," she said. "Arlene told me."

"She did?"

She smiled ever so slightly and he knew that if he left now he'd spend the rest of his life remembering that enigmatic sloe-eyed smile.

"I don't suppose you're interested in carpentry," he said.

For the first time since his teens he was bumbling and inept, a novice at the game, and he realized that he was having an attack of sorts. Ennui ... homesickness ... loneliness ... infatuation? Whatever it was had invested this moment and this woman with an unsettling power.

"I'm interested in everything," she said.

He couldn't tell whether she was serious. Her gaze was kind and wise and amused and incredibly sexy.

"Are you interested in going out for coffee with me?" he asked, and held his breath.

The question hung between them.

He met her eyes and he could see the hesitation. The uncertainty. The moment stretched and sharpened inside him. And suddenly he knew that he was poised on the brink of something vast and mysterious. Something that would change him forever.

34

Lucy

Lucy's only contact with Walea was through Preston Tully, who handled the divorce for her. He admonished her for settling for so little of the assets from her marriage, but she wanted nothing more. All that was important to her was that she be free of the Skidmores and Walea.

In spite of Preston's efforts to lure her back, she managed to avoid returning until the day of the final proceedings. When it was over and she was Lucy Clare once more, Preston insisted on taking her to dinner.

As she got in her car to leave Walea that evening, he asked her to call when she got lonely. As though getting lonely was a given. As though she would weaken with time. She smiled but vowed right then never to call him.

Suki was full of questions about the lawyer and convinced that he was Lucy's salvation. "You'd best string him along some," Suki advised in one of their weekly phone visits. "He'll look mighty damn good after you spend too many Saturday nights watchin' television and learnin' just how awful single life is."

Lucy tried to explain that she'd spent Saturday nights watching television when she was married and that now she could go to a movie or curl up with a good book or eat popcorn in bed if she wanted. Now her Saturday nights were special. Suki was skeptical.

After she hung up with her sister it occurred to Lucy that she could have said more. She could have told Suki that she'd already learned about loneliness. And the lessons had come during her marriage.

Suki had no business giving advice anyway when she was such a mess herself. Lucy thought about the conversation she'd had with Del the day she drove to Dallas from Walea.

"Suki's nervous as a cat about seein' ya," he'd said.

"Why? Because she didn't visit me in the hospital?"

Del laughed. "Naw, for ballin' Buddy in the parking lot when they were supposed to be dancin'."

Lucy was stunned.

He snorted. "Shit. Figgered you knew. Thought that was why you left the bastard."

Time passed and she had no urge to call Preston Tully, no desperate yearnings for the companionship of the opposite sex. Each month of freedom clarified and strengthened her resolve. If something happened with a man, that was fine, but she wasn't going to spend her life searching for it. And she wasn't going to make compromises. She would never again trade pieces of herself for a man's company or be tricked into believing that she needed marriage to validate her life.

She got a job as a photographer's assistant and lasted for nearly a year in Oklahoma City, but she never was content there. From the start she was ready to move on. She felt like a wavering needle waiting for the magnetic pull, waiting for a direction. Sometimes she fantasized about San Francisco or New York, but of course they were only fantasies. How could she dare believe that Lucy Clare from Walea could make it in one of the great cities?

And just when it seemed that she would never fix on a destination, she heard about Kansas City, Missouri.

Suki was ecstatic. "Kansas City is nice," she said. "It's no Dallas but it's nice."

Suki had never been out of Texas, but she considered herself more of an expert than Lucy on worldly concerns. "I'll come up and help you move," she promised, but when the time came Lucy packed her old Volkswagen bug and chugged to her new home alone. It was another new start. And this time she was determined to follow her own agenda. No more dreary assistants' jobs or subjugating herself to other people's goals—this time she would forge her own path.

She found a room and a bath in a converted motel near the interstate, where she could pay by the month. She established credit with the best color developing lab in the city and she booked two hours of weekly darkroom time at a photo store for her black-and-white work. Then she screwed up her courage and placed a classified ad: "PROFESSIONAL PHOTOGRAPHER. Any-type work. Color or black & white. Fast, reliable, cheap."

She became friendly with Duff, the owner of the photo store

where she rented darkroom time, and eventually, at Duff's urging, she amended her ad to: "PERSONALITY PHOTO. Weddings, parties, natural pet portraiture. Fast, reliable, reasonable." To her surprise, the jobs trickled in.

Five years passed. She learned to juggle, to tackle all the survival jobs her classifieds drummed up, and still leave time for photography lectures and classes in art or history or whatever caught her interest. And she learned to set aside inviolate time for her special personal work—the blissful days roaming with her camera or following the spark of an idea or losing herself in the darkroom. She didn't believe herself very good or worthy of attention, but once in a while she sent a print to a local publication anyway or took a portfolio to a gallery. Nothing ever came of the efforts, and her ego was too fragile for very frequent attempts.

On the whole she was content. She'd managed to stretch her money and make her own rules. She had a life of purpose and freedom. She had friends like Duff and a few women she'd met in her classes. And through her work she'd gained a feeling of self-worth, a feeling that she mattered.

Nearly six years of contentment. Not bad. A better score than she'd achieved in her marriage. But lately she'd been having attitude problems. Her survival jobs had become tedious, pulling her down and suffocating her with their sameness. The hours spent posing poodles or capturing the requisite minute-by-minute record of veil and gown and flowers and ring and garter and kiss and dance-with-father were not amusing anymore, and she had urges to throw the camera at the insufferable mother of the bride or the obnoxious pet owner and never look through a viewfinder again. And she asked herself why she was using the thing she loved most—photography—to do work she hated, and why she was wasting so much of her allotted time on earth, and other questions that ultimately had no answers.

The depression and frustration lifted magically whenever she had a day with her personal projects. Her real work. When she could free the insistent images that crowded her thoughts, capturing them on film and shaping them beneath her fingers in the darkroom. Her real work cleansed and soothed her, and in its wake she could look at herself and see what fueled her discontent.

Her real work had become more than pleasure, more than dreams. It was a need. A consuming need. And she was intolerant of anything that kept her from feeding that need on demand.

Her work had become an addiction. A drug that spun her away with the ecstasy of visions so intense that she lost all sense of herself in the rush. And when she exhausted herself on a project and the rush cooled, she was infused with hope and high spirits and generosity for days ... until the next images sparked and caught her in the flames. She craved both states—the burning rush and the gentle warmth it left in its wake.

She was in one of these euphoric postproject moods when she met a woman in the checkout at the neighborhood grocery. She was wearing one of her cameras. By the time the express line chugged to her turn, she'd agreed to do some photography for a charity fund-raising scheme that the woman, Arlene, was working on.

She completed the charity work quickly and some months later received a thank-you letter and an invitation to the open house at the finished children's home that her photos had helped publicize. She accepted, expecting nothing more than free food and camera-free human contact, both of which were important occasionally. And she walked in and saw a man. Not just passed by or looked at, but *saw* in the same way she'd *seen* her first skyscraper or her first wild fox or her first view from a mountain.

He had a wonderful face, full of the planes and angles that were so interesting on film. When he smiled, a pattern of fine lines played at the corners of his mouth and eyes. When he wasn't smiling, which was most of the time, he radiated a gentle sadness ... or maybe a world-weariness ... she couldn't decide which.

His hair was careless and wavy, a medium brown but with subtle highlights that could have meant hours in the sun or hours in an expensive salon. He didn't look like the salon type, but who knew, these days?

She watched him and let her imagination fly. His face had a special quality—an intense sincerity verging on innocence. And he had a casual ease, an engagingly natural way of moving. She studied him without restraint, as she would a photographic subject. His interactions with people seemed polite enough, but there was a distant quality, a separateness to him.

She considered asking him to pose for her but decided against it. Men got the wrong impression so easily. It wouldn't be worth the headache that might be created.

She decided to ignore him and concentrate on conversations, but her eyes kept straying back to him. She wanted to stare at his hands and his mouth and his lean runner's body and his long legs and the wide set of his shoulders. She wanted to know if his hair was as soft as it looked and if his arms were as hard, and suddenly she was tangled in the most exquisitely primitive longings.

"Who is he?" she asked Arlene.

"He's the carpenter," Arlene told her. "Single and very talented, but a little unsettling at times. Would you like to meet him?"

"No. I don't think so."

Arlene shrugged. "Let me know if you change your mind."

"I won't," she said a little too quickly, making Arlene smile as she moved away.

She hadn't closed herself to men in the years since her divorce. She'd enjoyed male company occasionally. But no man had affected her like this. No man had reached down inside her and stirred the fragments of her long-dead fantasies. She had the urge to run. To hurry back to the secure solitude of her little room, where she could think about this and examine it in safety. Away from him. Away from nature's tricks and the temptation to say: "Yes . . . I do want to meet him."

A couple stepped up and introduced themselves, gushing about her photography. She forced herself to concentrate as they recounted every disaster they'd ever had with a long line of cameras they'd owned. She tried to keep their stories straight but her thoughts were elsewhere.

Was it really possible? Was it possible to be swept away by a man? To be immersed in temporary insanity . . . bold and frenzied and frankly, wildly, carelessly sexual? Was that possible? To fall helplessly into sensation? To be lost and burning and relieved of rational thought? To experience real sexual passion?

Which was a crazy, stupid thing to be speculating about, because all her romantic bubbles had burst long ago. She knew the limitations of real-life sex and she knew that the problem with fantasy was that it worked only inside your head. And the trouble with a man, any man, was that he was real and not a fantasy.

And the problem with this man was that he was not only real but had appeared as suddenly as a comet or a tornado, forcing her to decide immediately whether she was willing to collide with him or run for shelter.

Maybe this tall, intriguing man wouldn't be interested in her at all. Maybe he hated photographers or Texans or women with dark hair. No. She didn't really believe that, because at a certain level men were always interested. A woman could spit on the sidewalk and they'd still be interested if they thought it was leading to sex.

The carpenter.

Maybe he was macho and overbearing and semiliterate. Maybe

if she met him she would be instantly repelled and could laugh off the entire incident.

She studied him again.

Suddenly she realized that he was looking at her. He'd caught her staring. He moved in her direction and she knew that the time for running was past. She glanced sideways at him and he stepped right into the middle of her life as though it had all been preordained.

"There you are," he said, and she had a moment of complete disorientation.

The couple she'd been talking to smiled knowingly and excused themselves.

He was close enough to touch, and he was staring at her as if he expected something, but she couldn't think of one thing to say. All she could do was look at him with all the fear and amazement that she felt.

Slowly the confidence faded from his eyes and was replaced by uncertainty. "I'm sorry," he said, and started to back away. "I didn't mean to intrude."

Her composure returned. He was uncertain too. Maybe even as uncertain as she was. Nature or chemistry or the cosmos was playing a joke on them both.

"Yes, you did," she said lightly. "You meant exactly that. You were just betting that I wouldn't mind."

One side of his mouth curved upward and his eyes showed a mix of relief and amusement and intense interest.

"I'm the carpenter," he said, and she nearly laughed aloud.

"I know who you are. Arlene told me."

"I don't suppose you're interested in carpentry," he said.

She wanted to tell him that this part wasn't really necessary.

"I'm interested in everything."

The statement was meant to be teasing . . . to put him back at ease. His diffidence was sweet, but much more of it might make her nervous enough to flee.

"Are you interested in going out for coffee with me?" he asked.

She held her breath. A great yawning chasm opened at her feet. Did she want to jump in? Did she . . . ?

"Yes," she said.

There. It was done.

On the way to the coffee shop she settled quietly back in her seat and let the outside noises fill the space between them. Close up he was every bit as appealing as he'd been at a distance. The only surprise was how self-conscious he seemed. She would have guessed him to be smoother with women.

She found herself filled with hope. Idiotic as it was, she wanted the fantasy to be possible. She still wanted to believe passion could be real.

Please . . . she begged silently. Please don't let him have a dozen hangups or be a bigot or a chauvinist or a whiner. Don't let him yawn with his mouth full or race his engine at stoplights. Please . . . just this one time . . . and I'll never ask for it again as long as I live. Just this one fantasy. Just this once.

They exchanged no history over their coffee and pie. He avoided his own as carefully as she avoided hers. She asked about carpentry. He said that there was no dignity in carpentry anymore. He asked what she did. She told him about the frustrations of photographing weddings and pet funerals. They talked about Arlene and the children's home, clinging to the subject like a life raft.

Under his self-consciousness he had power. It shaded his eyes and ran beneath his smallest movement; restless, undirected, raw power. The intensity of it thrilled and frightened her. She wondered where it sprang from and where it was taking him, but she didn't dare ask any personal questions. Fantasies had neither past nor future, only the present.

He had good manners, seemed well-educated, and treated her with consideration and respect. He hadn't done anything wrong. Not one thing. Her stomach clenched into a nervous knot. The moment of truth was at hand.

"Can I take you home?" he asked.

"No," she answered quickly. She didn't want to give him a glimpse of anything personal. She didn't want him to know how she lived. She especially didn't want him to know where she lived.

He looked perplexed and disappointed.

She drew in a breath. "But maybe I could take you home?"

He laughed, and on the way to his car he put his hand on the back of her neck, making her feel dense and hot and centered. Her body told her she'd made the right decision.

His furnished rental was as plain as her own, but larger and better-equipped. She surveyed the place and wondered how he fitted in there. He poured two glasses of red wine and motioned her toward the sagging green couch.

The fantasy was still intact, but honest-to-God sex was on the horizon, and though she thought of herself as mature and progressive, the fact was that her sexual experience was very limited. She had no protection. Would he have condoms? What should she say? Could she really do this? Here she was in a strange man's apartment, behaving as if she knew exactly what she was doing, and she suddenly realized that her concept of herself as a sexually liberated woman was built on air.

"I can't do this," she said, standing in the center of the room and clutching her shoulder bag to her chest like a shield.

"Sit down," he said gently. "Drink your wine. You can leave anytime."

She sat gingerly on the edge of the couch nearest the door and scolded herself silently. Why had she thought this would work?

He sat across from her and toyed with his wineglass. His hands were not what she would have expected of a carpenter. They were capable hands, but slender and expressive, pianist's hands or sculptor's hands or maybe doctor's hands. Not hands that hammered and sawed.

She pictured a black-and-white photo study of just his hands. Crisp enough to capture the fine hairs sprinkled across their backs and the shadowy veins that crisscrossed just beneath the skin and the austere bluntness of the fingernails.

She put her untouched wine down on the spindly coffee table. "I really have to go," she said, standing abruptly and taking two steps toward the door.

He stood just as abruptly and blocked her way. She didn't want to meet his eyes and stared instead at his neck and the small V of flesh where his top shirt button was left undone. But there was his chest hair and the faint suggestion of a pulse at the base of his throat and suddenly she couldn't look that direction either, so she stared off to the side at the wall.

He cupped her face gently with his hands and turned her head so that she was forced to meet his gaze, and she saw that his eyes weren't the everyday blue she'd thought. They were more gray. Thunderstorm colors. Soft near the pupil and shading to a deep charcoal at the outer rim. And there was gray in his hair as well. A tiny sprinkling of silver at his temples.

"Will you have dinner with me tomorrow?" he asked.

Wings beat inside her midsection, and the ends of her fingers had a life of their own and she couldn't seem to swallow enough.

She heard an imitation of her voice say "Yes" before she even had a chance to think, and she knew then that this mysterious chemical imbalance was going to proceed to its inevitable conclusion just like a hurricane or a volcanic eruption, and she relaxed, resigning herself to it. Why not let it happen now so she wouldn't have to agonize over it till tomorrow night? Before she could talk herself out of anything, she leaned forward and kissed him full on the mouth.

His gray eyes were surprised, then pleased. He locked them onto hers, never wavering as he slid the shoulder bag out of her grasp and eased the oversize jacket off her shoulders, tossing them both toward the chair.

"I don't have any . . ." she said, clinging to that one practicality.

"I do," he said. "Don't worry."

He pulled her close, but not into the crushing embrace she'd expected. Their bodies skimmed each other, meeting at dozens of heated points.

"Do you want to dance?" he asked.

"There's no music," she said, her voice sounding unaccountably hoarse.

He laughed as if she'd made a joke, then lifted her palm and softly kissed the center where all the lines of past and future met.

35

Ellis

Ellis woke early the next morning and went out for a hard cross-country run. He didn't want to be home if Lucy popped in with armloads of groceries and the announcement that she intended to cook him a good meal.

Last night she'd insisted on leaving. Said she had a bed of her own and didn't intend to sleep in his. She'd seemed genuinely anxious to get away, which had struck him as almost funny because he was so used to the opposite behavior—women who clung like barnacles. Women who wanted to sleep in his bed and then get up and fuss in his kitchen. Women who wanted to drop by unexpectedly with hot meals and new curtains and homey little knickknacks.

He had wanted to take her home to her place specifically to avoid all that. He wanted to be able to walk out if he chose, without her knowing his address or phone number.

He was four miles into his run and soaring on his second burst of energy when it occurred to him that she had accomplished exactly what he always tried to do. She had kept the evening on her own terms and had escaped before the awkward breakfast scene and given him no clue as to where she lived.

The day was overcast and threatening rain and he told himself that was why he cut his run short and headed for home. He had a lot of things to do, loose ends to tie up and decisions to make so he could leave Kansas City and figure out where he wanted to go next. But thoughts of her kept creeping in to distract him.

She wasn't beautiful. Her looks were too quiet to be labeled beautiful. But she had a way about her. A presence. And she had those eyes. He wasn't even certain what color they were. Not brown. That's all he knew. They weren't brown. But the color wasn't important anyway. It was their expressiveness that held him. The whole universe was in one secretive, kind, questioning, wise, wounding, sarcastic, amused, seductive sideways glance from her.

He had wanted to please her. He'd wanted to see pleasure in those eyes, but it hadn't worked. The sex had been full of miscues and clumsiness. He didn't understand why, except that she was so surprisingly hesitant and shy and stiff and he couldn't seem to say or do anything right. He was certain she hadn't come, though by that point he'd been afraid to ask.

Afterward he'd felt like a failure. Not that she'd looked at him in any accusing way. No. She was too generous for that. And he'd been annoyed with her generosity and the care she took with his feelings when it was so obvious that he'd failed and that she wanted to leave and forget him as soon as possible.

What was wrong with her anyway? How could a woman who was so frank and direct and sexually suggestive be that reticent or ignorant about her body? Had she been playing some kind of game with him? Or did she have a closet full of hangups or maybe a martyr complex? Who knew? These days a guy could run across just about anything.

Before he realized it, he was just blocks away from the children's home, so he decided to go visit with Arlene and maybe find out what she knew about this Lucy . . . this woman who'd run from his bed but wouldn't leave his thoughts.

Lucy

Lucy cradled the phone receiver between her ear and shoulder so she could search through her notes and index cards with her hands. She had a list of ideas that she wanted to shoot film for, but Suki kept calling her and the morning was nearly over and she hadn't even managed to escape her room yet.

"He'll be back, Suki. Del's always come back before, hasn't he?"

"That was different. This time he went to Nashville with some bitch in a white Cadillac. He told everybody at the bar he was goin'."

Suki's sentences were slurred and punctuated with sobs. The pitch varied from loud and angry to wailing and whiny.

"If you keep drinking so much, you're going to end up like Daddy," Lucy warned.

"You think that matters to me? I wanna die! It'd serve the fucker right for leavin' me alone so much. You don't know, Lucy ... you just don' know how bad it feels. He's breakin' my heart."

"And you're letting him," Lucy said. "Sometimes I think you even encourage him."

"What're you talkin' about! All's I want is for him to love me and to stay home with me. All's I want is a little respect."

"I don't think that's all you want, but even if it were ... how can he respect you when you have so little respect for yourself?"

"Oh! I know what you're gettin' at! You're still mad at me about Buddy. You think I'm not respectable 'cause a what happened with Buddy."

Lucy shifted the phone to her other ear and sighed in exasperation. "I've told you, I'm not angry about that. I don't think about it at all. I could have wiped it completely out of my memory by now if you didn't keep bringing it up."

"You never even yelled at me about it. You just hate me, don't you?"

"Suki, stop it. I don't hate you."

"You're cold, just like Buddy said. That's why I did it, ya know, 'cause I felt so sorry for the poor guy. He said you were frigid and mean and never did anything to make him feel good. He said he shoulda married me instead a you."

"That's why you had sex with your sister's husband on your wedding night ... because you felt sorry for him?"

"There, see! I knew you were still mad. You pretend to like me, but you really don't."

"Suki—"

"And I didn't *have sex* with him either, I only gave him a blow-job."

Lucy couldn't help it, she leaned back in her chair and laughed.

"What's wrong with you, Luce? This is not funny. My heart is broken and the only family I have left hates me."

"Do you want me to come down to Dallas? I could reschedule some jobs and come stay with you awhile."

"No. Del might come back, and you know how he is about wantin' me to hisself. He doesn't even like me to talk to anybody on the phone when he's home."

Even though it bothered Lucy to see her sister making so many of the same mistakes she'd made in her own marriage, she ordi-

narily held back from giving Suki advice. Today she was impatient. She was irritated at the endless cycle of complaints and she
wanted to get off the phone and she couldn't resist saying exactly
what she thought.

"You should talk to him about his possessiveness, Suki. Tell
him you won't stand for it anymore. He's always got friends
around and he has no right to object to your doing the same."

"Oh, sure. I'll do that. I'll just tell him."

"I think you like it when he bosses you around and wants you
to himself. I think it makes you feel wanted."

Suki moaned. "I'm sick. Sick in love."

Lucy gritted her teeth. "Why don't you take a few days off
work and get on a bus and come up and see me? Let him come
home to an empty house for a change. Let him see what it's like
to do without you."

"Oh, Lucy. I couldn't do that. If I wasn't here to cook for him
and do his laundry and give him some lovin', he might just turn
around and walk out for good. And I'm no kid anymore. I'm over
thirty! Too old to start lookin' for somebody else. Besides, who
are you to be givin' advice? I don't see you with a man in your
bed."

"No. And you won't, either. I need a man in my life about as
much as I need a three-inch spike driven through my head."

"Shit . . . you just say that. You're so jealous of me you can't
stand it."

"Suki. Please. Neither one of us can afford this call, and nothing constructive is being accomplished. I think it's time to say
good-bye."

Suki was sobbing loudly into the phone again. "Don't hang
up. Don't leave me alone."

"Take a shower and get yourself together and go in to work.
You'll feel better if you do."

"No, I won't. Everybody will stare at me. I look terrible."

"I have to go now. I'll call you tonight, okay?"

Lucy hung up on Suki's sobs. She knew from experience that
her sister would not say good-bye and the misery would drag on
and on and once it was over she'd get a call from the operator
saying that Suki was reversing the charges. And much as she
wanted to help Suki, this was a workday and the morning was
already gone and she had to get busy or she'd lose the light before
she could finish her outdoor shots.

She tied the laces on her sneakers and began packing film and
filters and a lunch into her camera bag. There was a knock at the

door, which was odd, because she never had visitors. She looked through the peephole. It was Ellis.

"What are you doing here?" she asked as she opened the door.

He held out his hands helplessly as if to say that he didn't know what he was doing there and he smiled and her body succumbed to a whole series of sensations.

"I'm busy. I was just going out to shoot."

"That's okay. I just wanted to say hi."

"Great. Hi. Now, if you'll excuse me . . ."

"Are we still having dinner tonight?"

"Dinner? I—"

"Remember, last night I invited you to dinner and you accepted."

"Oh. Yes. Well, that was before—"

"I was just wondering where you wanted to go. Or whether you might like to stay in and try my cooking. I'm great at Italian."

"Ellis . . ."

She couldn't understand why he was there. They'd had no sparks or rockets go off last night. In fact she'd had the impression that their lovemaking was a big disappointment to him. The fantasy was over and it all seemed a bit ridiculous in the wash of gray daylight that bathed them now.

"If you don't like Italian, that's okay too, because I like everything."

He was dressed in sweat clothes and running shoes and his hair needed a comb. She was afraid to look directly into his eyes.

"Dinner is not necessary," she said.

"Yes," he said. "I think it's absolutely necessary."

She wanted to say no. She knew that she should say no.

"All right. But not till eight or so."

"Fine. Great. I'll pick you up."

She had a hard time concentrating the rest of the day. The images she was looking for were simple in themselves because the idea she was working on was a collage. She'd thought about the technique she'd learned to add clouds to blank skies and jets to empty parking lots and she'd thought that it would be exciting to take that further. To shoot fenceposts or faces or smashed rabbits in the road, and then patch them together with darkroom techniques. The idea had grown. Then she saw Wanda Wulz's work—an old silver gelatine print called *Cat and I*—and it was a revelation for her, a blending of female and feline faces that sent her imagination soaring.

The possibilities had been burning inside her, but now that

she had a whole day of interesting gray light to play with she couldn't seem to keep her mind on the images she was after.

What more did he want from her? Did his ego demand a sexual replay or was he hung up on proving something? Either way, she wasn't going to bed with him again.

She was still overwhelmingly attracted to him, but if she gave in to the weakness he spawned inside her, then she would end up feeling sad and empty and disappointed and used. No ... she would not give in to temptation again.

But then, maybe an evening out with him would be good for her. Maybe having dinner with him and getting to know him as a person rather than a fantasy would help her overcome her infatuation and recapture the strength and certainty that had been shaken by this man crashing into her life.

Ellis

Ellis was completely unsettled as he pulled into the parking space in front of her flaking orange door. Who was this woman? Why was she having such an effect on him?

She hadn't told him much of anything about herself—just that she was originally from Texas and she did free-lance photography and she'd once had a job taking a funeral portrait of a dead hamster in a karate ghi.

He glanced down at his watch. He was early, so he decided to wait in his car for a few minutes.

Question upon question rolled around in his mind. Where in Texas and why Kansas City and why photography and where was her family and did she like horror movies and was she interested in running and what had been wrong with his lovemaking last night?

Everything felt upside down. He was used to women who tried to cram their entire life history into the first conversation, and their feelings about love, death, parenting, friends, and religion into the next. They usually dropped it all on him like a load of cement, making him want to run like hell before the whole thing hardened and stuck him in place.

Now here he was wishing that this woman would open up and

talk about herself and hoping that she hadn't already tired of him and wondering why she wouldn't communicate.

At eight sharp he got out and knocked. She came to the door quickly, stepped outside, and shut it behind her. She had on a skirt, making him glad he'd worn slacks, and she looked different. Her hair was down, falling past her shoulders in voluminous dark waves but pulled back from her face by a slender band. It was both innocent and sexy.

"You never did say what you'd like to eat," he said.

"Something juicy," she said. "A hamburger or some chicken ... whatever. I don't have a kitchen in here so I live on cold sandwiches."

Something juicy. He had to smile. He'd had all manner of responses to the "What would you like to eat?" question, but he couldn't remember a woman ever answering with "Something juicy."

"How about steak, then?"

She slid into the car. Her legs were long and slender and she had on Chinese cloth shoes—blue velvet with little gold dragons embroidered on the vamps.

"I have to warn you," she said matter-of-factly. "You might want to buy me a hamburger instead of a steak, because I'm not going to sleep with you again."

The statement hit like a well-aimed brick. His worst fears were confirmed. He'd failed miserably with her in bed.

"That has nothing to do with how much I spend on your dinner," he said indignantly, but even as he said it he admitted guiltily to himself that there had been times when the lavishness of the entertainment had been directly related to his expectations for later.

"So," she said after they'd ridden in silence for some minutes, "what part of town are you working in?"

"I'm not working now. I haven't taken another job yet."

"Oh. I didn't realize there was so much freedom in carpentry."

Her effort at conversation cheered him a little.

"The carpentry I've been doing is similar to a free-lance situation. Similar to your photography." He glanced over at her. She seemed very poised and determined tonight. "Is that why you stick with the photography ... because of the freedom?"

She hesitated before answering, and he had the sense that she didn't like talking about herself.

"I suppose the freedom is a factor in the type of jobs I hire out for. But it's not why I stay in photography."

"Then why do you stay in it?"

"I like photography."

"Then why don't you get into the higher-paying work?"

"Like advertising, you mean?"

"Yes."

"Because there would be pressure and schedules and dead-lines and I'd be helping to sell dishonesty. I'd end up photograph-ing beautiful nineteen-year-olds and touching up what few imperfections they have so that some company could use the im-age to sell anti-aging cream to middle-aged women."

"That's a good point," he said, impressed, but still curious about her Spartan living. "Wouldn't you like to live in a better place, though, have more money to spend?" He'd never met a woman who lived frugally by choice.

"What's the matter?" she asked with a mischievous glint in her eye. "You don't like where I live?"

"Well . . ." He shrugged his shoulders.

"You think I ought to earn more so I could afford a place like yours?"

"Touché," he said, kicking himself for his clumsy attempt at drawing her out.

He took her to his favorite steakhouse, an old-fashioned place that hadn't changed since its opening at the turn of the century. The lighting was dim and the elderly waiters all had on black bow ties and starched white shirts and aprons that looked like table-cloths wrapped around their waists.

The menus were covered in polished burgundy leather and he could tell by the way she touched and held hers that she appre-ciated them and that she was a little nervous now.

"I hate to admit it, but I've eaten here several times and I still don't know what 'prime aged Angus beef' means," he said, trying to put her at ease. "Being from Texas, you probably know all that."

"No. I don't know the first thing about cattle." Her expression was tinged with amusement and self-directed sarcasm. "We had a yard full of weeds and a few scrawny chickens."

The waiter appeared and ceremoniously asked whether they were ready to order. Ellis hesitated. Should he order for her? He'd always thought that was vaguely demeaning to a woman, that it implied she was incapable of speaking for herself, but some women preferred the old tradition and were even insulted if he didn't go through the archaic ritual. Above all he wanted to please her.

She took the decision from him by smiling up at the waiter and saying, "I'll have the skewered steak please, medium-rare, and with blue-cheese dressing on my salad."

"Very good, madam. And which potato—baked or lyonnaise?

"Oh . . . ah . . . lyonnaise, please."

After the waiter finished taking their order and left, Ellis, in a purely conversational tone, said, "You're having the skewered steak?"

"Yes," she replied sharply. "I've never had it and that's what I want."

He was startled. "That's fine," he said carefully. "I wanted you to order what you want."

He settled back in his chair and wondered what he'd done to set her off. The small flame flickering in the frosted-glass chimney bathed her face in soft light but did not illuminate her eyes. He still didn't know what color they were.

Her face had a delicate purity tonight. But her eyes gave her away. They were ancient, mystical, knowing eyes. The eyes of another creature peering from behind a mask. He had to hold himself back from leaning across the table and staring.

"Those earrings are from the sixties, aren't they?"

She relaxed a little, nodded, and reached up to finger one of the silver peace signs fondly. "I found them in a junk shop," she said. "They remind me of a teacher I once had."

He waited, hoping for more, but there was none.

"Your hair looks different," he said, casting about blindly for a safe topic.

"Your hair looks different too," she said. "Maybe we're with the wrong people."

The waiter brought their shrimp cocktails and she sat quietly for a moment, watching while he squeezed the lemon and added a few drops of hot sauce. Then she picked up her lemon wedge and copied him exactly. He didn't know if it was accidental or intended. Maybe she was teasing him again and it was so subtle that he hadn't caught the point.

She had him totally off-balance. He'd lost track of what was funny and what was serious. All he knew was that he desperately wanted her to like him.

"I've been through Amarillo on the highway," he said. "Is that anywhere close to your hometown?"

"No. I'm from northeast of Dallas."

"Oh."

"Texas is a big state."

"I know that—"

"People always think that because I'm from Texas I should know what Houston and Austin and San Antonio are like, but I don't." She sounded defensive again.

"Well, I didn't mean . . . I mean . . . That's not unusual. I lived in San Francisco for a while but I don't automatically know what Los Angeles is like."

They navigated their salads in silence. When the main course arrived he made a fresh start. "Do you like horror movies? The old ones that they play on the television late shows?"

She thought for a moment. "I don't think I've seen one."

"Never?"

"I don't have a television. I read a lot, though. Are your horror movies anything like Poe's stories? Or Stephen King maybe?"

"No. I'm afraid neither of them has ever captured the thrills of giant women or spinning turtles or mutated alien spores."

She smiled. It felt like a reward. He wished he knew some way to make her smile over and over.

"Sounds like fun," she said.

"It is! Add a bowl of fresh popcorn and you have one of life's premier experiences."

Another smile.

"Maybe you could watch one with me sometime?"

The smile faded. "Maybe."

"Tonight even. I think there's one on at eleven."

"I don't—"

"No. Don't say anything. Just wait. Reserve judgment, okay?"

She didn't say anything.

He managed to keep it light after that, and by coffee and dessert they were laughing easily together. Her smiles warmed him and the glow in her eyes filled him with reckless abandon.

His natural reticence melted in the circle of her warmth and suddenly there were words spilling out . . . thoughts that he had never shared with others. Not the personal history locked deep inside him, but the passions that fueled his interest in the world. Music, politics, old movies, science, art, books . . . the future of civilization—he let it pour from him in joyful release.

". . . and if you think about it, selling off wild public lands to reduce the deficit is like trading the country's most irreplaceable assets for consumable goods. It's like selling off the future!"

"You sound very hostile to government. I'm sure there are good reasons for what they want to do. They always do studies and—"

"Hah! You're joking, right?"

"Well ... no ... I don't know the whole story, so I'm giving the government the benefit of the doubt. I mean ... this is a great country and—"

"Yes. It is a great country! But its greatness lies with the people, and the people's welfare and wishes should control the government. Instead we have a government that has become so huge and unmanageable that it sometimes ignores the public and functions to protect or benefit only itself."

"I don't know ..." she said uncertainly. "I don't think ..."

"Well, you should think. Because terrible things are happening. Like where I used to live. In the mountains, in Idaho. In this beautiful, unspoiled, unpolluted wilderness. Turns out nothing there was so unspoiled or unpolluted because the government secretly released radioactive iodine into the air for six years. And you know what the official justification was when the truth came out? That it was normal operating procedure for the plant involved and that they only did it on days when the wind was blowing certain directions. Can you believe that? Two hundred times the amount of Three Mile Island, and they have the nerve to try to justify it!"

"That's terr—" she started to say, but Ellis didn't let her finish her thought. He was too wound up.

"They also dumped radioactive-waste water down a secret well that went straight into the aquifer. Turns out they pulled that trick for thirty years! That's what happens when people trust their well-meaning government.

"Our government isn't made up of people anymore. It's this lumbering, patched-up behemoth of thousands of special-interest groups ... little fiefdoms with their own petty monarchs. And all they care about is implementing their own special programs ... following their agendas ... holding tight to the power structure. And the public be damned. The earth be damned. And if you—"

Suddenly she jerked her napkin off her lap and threw it down on the table. "I'm ready to go home," she said angrily.

The gesture stopped him cold.

"Why? What—?"

"I don't enjoy being lectured to with the implication that I'm blind and naive and unaware of current events and maybe even just plain stupid. And what's more, I've never had skewered steak or shrimp cocktail and I've never even heard of lyonnaise potatoes so I'm a restaurant illiterate too, if you'd like to attack from another direction."

"Wait. Wait a minute." He reached across the table to touch her arm.

She stared holes through him.

"I got carried away. I don't usually . . ." He was suddenly very self-conscious. "I've never had anyone that I wanted to talk to like this, and I . . . I don't know what got into me."

Her expression softened a fraction.

"Well, anyway, I am sorry . . . but don't you like spirited discussions once in a while?"

"Not when it's used to point out my ignorance."

"That's not what was happening."

"Oh? What was happening, then?"

He wondered what to tell her. That she'd reached him in a way he didn't think he could be reached? That she'd pulled him so completely out of himself that he'd lost his bearings?

"I was enjoying your company so much that I forgot myself and started to treat you like an intelligent, interesting human being rather than a very attractive, somewhat unnerving dinner date."

She sat very still for a moment. Her eyes turned him inside out and left him naked. "An interesting, intelligent human being?" she said, cocking her head slightly and allowing the corners of her mouth to curve into the barest suggestion of a smile.

"Yes. And for what it's worth, I'd never had chili until last year, and there's a million other things out there I've never tasted or seen or thought or heard about. But that's what keeps life interesting. It's nothing to be threatened by. . . . And you're entitled to rant and rave yourself whenever you'd like . . . or to tell me to shut up."

Her eyes searched his again, but this time there was an element of vulnerability in her faintly perplexed but clearly pleased expression. She tilted her head, exposing a slender length of neck, and gave him a look that sank through his chest and sizzled in his groin.

"A horror movie," she said with a questioning lift to the sentence.

He was afraid of saying the wrong thing, so he simply nodded.

"And fresh popcorn?"

"The freshest."

"I suppose an intelligent person wouldn't pass up an offer like that."

"Definitely not."

Lucy

By the time the giant ants from space had devastated half the globe and been destroyed by a scurrying band of Japanese scientists in lab coats, Lucy was feeling secure. She'd made the right choice. Being with Ellis was good.

"There's a sequel you have to see sometime," Ellis said. His tone was serious but his mouth and eyes were teasing. "You know how the queen dragged herself off into that cave just before the giant dry-ice machine arrived? Well, in the next movie—"

"No! Don't tell me," Lucy laughed. "You'll ruin the suspense." She let her head fall back against his couch, and her eyelids sank in contentment.

"You're tired," he said. "I should take you home."

"No." She turned her head a fraction and studied him with a lazy half-lidded gaze. In the light cast by the flickering television screen his face was a study in lines and shadows. A photographer's vision.

She felt a sudden warmth spread through her body. A fevered expectancy that heated her skin and made her long for him to touch her. He bent toward her and brushed his lips along the length of her exposed neck. The sensation was exquisite.

She stood and took his hand, pulling him up off the couch and toward the bedroom.

"You don't have to," he said. "There's plenty of time. There are other nights." He grinned. "Even if it was an expensive dinner."

"Don't you want me?" she asked.

He laughed a little and pulled her tight against him. The kiss was long and sweet. She could feel his erection.

Would this really be different? Would this real man and this real moment be as different as she wished them to be, or was she dreaming?

He kissed her until her knees were weak, and she led him in to the bed with the heat and the strange wonderful urgency building inside her. She fumbled to turn off the bedside light, but he caught her hand.

"I want to see how beautiful you are. I want to see your face while I'm inside you."

"I don't know . . ." she said.

But he ignored the feeble protest and began to undress her

with his hands and mouth. She alternated between complete abandon and paralyzing self-consciousness, one minute lost in his caress and the next worrying about how she appeared to him. She'd never felt so exposed. She closed her eyes. Worries swam with the sensations, but she couldn't think.

"Do you like this?" he asked. "Or this?"

How could he talk during sex? It made everything so . . . so . . . But the only word she could come up with was "intimate," and she realized what that said about her past experiences. Of course sex should be intimate. Why had she ever believed differently?

He shed the last of his clothes and she kept her eyes closed, afraid to watch, afraid of her own curiosity and afraid that maybe she shouldn't watch. She'd never seen a man naked in the light. Erections had always been abstracts . . . shapes felt through clothing or in the dark. But now her old sexual patterns and assumptions felt like outdated maps to another world.

His mouth lingered over her breasts, then trailed a line of fire down her belly and beyond. Suddenly she stiffened.

"What are you doing?"

"I'm making love to you," he said softly.

"But not . . . I can't . . . I mean I've never . . ."

He raised his head and fixed her with a gently incredulous, almost sad gaze. "Do you mean that a beautiful, warm, sexy woman like you has never had a man make love to you with his mouth?"

She shook her head.

He lowered his head and she gasped again and held her breath the same way she had on her first roller-coaster ride.

Later, much later, they came together, Ellis on top and deep inside her, all the hardness of his body melting into the softness of her own. He locked his eyes on hers and cried out her name.

"Lucy."

The intensity of the moment shook her more than the wondrous climax he brought her to. And she knew that she was changed forever.

36

Juliana

Juliana looked at the massive door to her grandfather's office and took a deep breath before knocking. She had been officially summoned here today, and that meant trouble.

"Who are you?" she asked when a stranger opened the door to her knock.

"I'm Mr. Van Lyden's new secretary, miss." He held out his hand. "My name is Harold Stegner."

"You can go, Stegner," her grandfather's voice ordered from the inner sanctum. "Come back in an hour."

"Yes, sir."

Juliana lifted her chin and marched in to face Edward.

He was leaned back comfortably in the enormous leather chair behind the enormous wooden desk. It was a historic desk, of course. Edward wouldn't settle for something ordinary.

He didn't invite her to sit down. She sat anyway, crossing her legs and leaning back to display an ease she didn't feel.

Edward smiled as though conceding her a point. "Twenty-two years old," he mused, steepling his fingers and gazing at her benignly. "It seems like only yesterday you were a child running through the house and playing make-believe. Now look at you. So grown-up and independent."

"Is this about Grandmother's trust?" Juliana asked bluntly.

"In part. Did you encounter any difficulties in your meeting with the executors?"

"No. And since your lawyers are handling it, I'm sure you'd be advised of any difficulties without having to ask me."

Edward sighed theatrically. "You might as well know that I have serious doubts about your receiving this money."

Juliana sat up straighter. "Why?"

He gazed off into the distance a moment. "Your grandmother

was not the most sensible of the three women I married. Perhaps that's why your father turned out as he did." Another, more genuine sigh. "Grace's mother was so much more pleasant and reasonable, and yet Grace . . ." His voice trailed off.

Juliana waited. What was he up to? What was behind his threat?

"But then I realized long ago that the Van Lyden future lay with my grandchildren, not my children. Thank God I have enjoyed a long enough life to see my grandchildren grown and nearly ready to assume responsibility."

His use of the plural made Juliana uneasy. She was *the* grandchild. She was the Van Lyden heir and the family's future. Ellis was nothing. She wished that he'd died instead of run away, so that her grandfather didn't have a plural to use.

Edward fixed her with the learned stare that usually preceded a lecture. "Maturity is a long process. It's not something that happens overnight, and it is not necessarily connected to a particular age." He shifted in his chair. "When your grandmother entrusted her family's money, she designated her direct grandchildren as beneficiaries and chose an age that seemed suitable. She made two assumptions: first, that Aubrey would have several children for the money to be divided among; and second, that twenty-two was an age at which these children would be settled into adulthood and able to manage the funds responsibly."

He paused, steepled his hands again, and fashioned his mouth into a brief, chilling smile. "Unfortunately, neither of these assumptions has proved to be true. There is only one beneficiary to this substantial estate, and the financial responsibility and maturity of the receiver are in serious question."

Juliana leaned forward and gripped the arms of her chair. "What are you getting at, Grandfather?"

"What am I getting at?" He pronounced the words as though they had a foreign flavor. "I'd have thought it would be quite obvious, Juliana. You are not ready to take control of this trust."

"Why?" She bolted from her chair and faced him across the broad surface of polished wood. "You had no objection four years ago when I came into my mother's trust." But as soon as she said it, she realized that he couldn't have objected. Her mother and Mo Rifkin had placed that trust out of his reach.

"The amount was considerably smaller and I thought it a good test of your abilities," Edward said.

"And what was I supposed to do to pass this test? Double my

money in the stock market? Sponsor a bench in Central Park? Fund my father's latest expedition?"

"You were supposed to do something other than adopting drug-addicted homosexual whores."

Juliana sank back down into her chair as if she'd been punched in the stomach. "What do you mean?" she asked weakly.

Edward's chuckle was dry and hollow. "Not a very adult response from someone who is playing the part of an independent, grown woman."

"All right." Juliana summoned enough anger to overcome her fear. "What do you mean by prying into my life?"

"That's better. That's the spirit I like to see." He pulled a thick folder from a drawer and leaned forward to place it on the desk within her reach. It was labeled "Keith McCann, alias Sparky." "You may have it. I have a copy."

Juliana's heart thudded dully in her chest. "What is this?"

"My detective's report."

"Detectives! My God . . . don't I have any privacy at all?"

"A young woman of your stature cannot afford to have private doings that unravel beneath public scrutiny."

Juliana stared at him. He was no longer her grandfather. He was a multitentacled monster and she was living in his lair.

"I blame myself partially for the McCann boy. I should have put a stop to that when you were four years old. And I put partial blame on your father. If it hadn't been for his insane stubbornness you'd have had a sibling and this compulsion to pick up strays would never have developed. Beyond that, the guilt rests solely on your shoulders."

He knit his brows and glared at her. She glared back sullenly. His control seemed to drop away bit by bit, like a waxen mask melting to reveal the horror beneath.

"What could you have been thinking!" He leapt from his chair and slapped the folders with an open hand.

Juliana winced.

"This . . . this faggot of yours has actually tried to seduce acquaintances of mine! He's been crashing clubs and parties . . . and offering favors for money! And it's your name . . . it's the Van Lyden name he uses to gain entry. The Van Lyden name!" Edward roared. "You and your indiscretions are smearing it with filth."

"I had no idea, Grandfather. I would never knowingly do anything to—"

"Oh, no!" Edward's face was deep red and the veins at his temples stood out. "You've been trying hard enough! Promiscuous homosexuals. Street filth. Greedy politicians. You're no better than your father! He tried to destroy me with his sordid messes and his half-breed wife."

A deadly calm settled over Juliana. She could hear the ticking of the mantel clock and the pounding of her grandfather's pulse. She could taste the decay in the room and smell her grandfather's raging anger.

"Politicians?" she asked.

The word hung between them.

Slowly Edward sank back down into his leather chair. He took out a monogrammed handkerchief and dabbed at his forehead.

"You were spying on me then too, weren't you?"

"I had to," he said quietly. "Don't you see what a mistake you could have made with that Rhysdale?"

"You knew all about Matt and me?" Juliana turned to face the fireplace. "You knew . . . everything?"

"One can never know everything. But I knew enough. I waited for some months, hoping you would learn your lessons and dispense with him on your own terms. When that didn't happen, I settled the matter."

"Settled the matter?" Juliana focused on the bronze firescreen that shielded the hearth.

She spun to face him. "What did you threaten him with? His career? His reputation? Maybe the use of his arms and legs?"

Edward made a scornful noise. "Nothing so dramatic, my dear. Mr. Rhysdale was quite the pragmatist."

"No! I know how much he loved me. I know how hard it must have been for you to destroy that. Doesn't love mean anything to you?"

"Romantic love is highly overrated and usually destructive. If your mother had seen that truth, she'd be alive today. I hope you learn more quickly and less painfully than she did."

"Don't bring my mother into this," she hissed. "Don't you dare bring my mother into this. And don't ever refer to her as a half-breed again."

Edward's demeanor softened momentarily.

"I want the file," she said.

"What?"

"The file on Matt and me. I'll bet it's at least as juicy as this one."

"Well . . . I certainly don't see—"

"I want it now."

Edward studied her a moment, then opened the wall safe and

spun the dial. "I can't see what possible good this can do," he said as he handed her a large manila envelope.

She took it, scooped up Sparky's file from the desk, and turned to leave.

"Get rid of that faggot whore!" he shouted as she turned to leave. "Do you hear me?"

She turned back to face him. "And if I don't?"

"I'll block your trust." There was a tremor in his voice, but she knew the threat was real.

"That doesn't matter. I already own one apartment, as I'm sure you're aware. I can move in there and live perfectly well on my existing trust."

He snorted derisively. "You have no concept of money at all. Do you have any idea how much I spend for your clothing and toiletries? Do you know what Zeke costs me? Or Charlotte?" Or the maid who cleans and launders for you or the cook who prepares your meals? The paltry amount you have left from your mother's money would be gone in a year."

She glared at him and waited.

"You've disappointed me enormously, Juliana. It's not the sowing of a few wild oats that I object to, or your stubborn persistence in retaining your mother's unsavory attorney. It's this compulsion of yours to make emotional attachments to unsuitable people. Your judgment is seriously flawed. I assumed you'd grown out of it after the Rhysdale debacle. I believed you were conducting your affairs respectably, then I'm confronted with this humiliating information about Sparky."

Juliana covered her face with her hands for a moment. She was beaten and she knew it. "I'm sorry, Grandfather. None of this was intended to hurt the family."

"Maybe not. But it does. And you are hurting yourself as well."

Juliana made it as far as the upstairs library before she had to sit down and open the envelope on Matt. Her hands trembled as she sifted through the stark black-and-white photographs and the pages of notes and transcribed conversations. What she saw sickened her.

Her most private moments were recorded there. The eyes and ears of strangers had intruded on her lovemaking with Matt and made it dirty.

She skimmed some of the entries. Her private telephone had been tapped. The hotel rooms where they met had been invaded with electronic surveillance. And there had been a source, someone who was feeding them all sorts of information.

Source reports Miss V.L. used three hundred dollars of clothing allowance to buy subject a gift.

Source reports Miss V.L. has birth-control prescription in drawer.

Source reports Miss V.L. bought books *How to Be Happily Married* and *Keeping Your Man Happy in Bed.*

Source reports . . .

And suddenly it dawned on her who the source had to be.

She went straight to her bedroom. Charlotte was waiting for her in the sitting area that connected their adjoining suites.

"What did he say?" Charlotte asked nervously as soon as Juliana stepped through the door.

"He knows about Sparky. He's had detectives watching him, and apparently Sparky's a mess."

"I was afraid of that."

"Were you? And why were you afraid of that?"

"Well . . . because . . . He's terribly concerned for you and he's bound to hear things . . ."

"Oh? And could he have heard things from you?" She threw the files down onto the table between them. "Could it be you who went through my drawers every night like a filthy spy?"

Charlotte's eyes widened with terror. "I only did it for you. I wanted to help you. To protect you."

Juliana's hand closed over a heavy crystal vase. She wanted to throw it. She wanted to smash Charlotte so badly. But she jerked her hand away from the vase and crossed the room to the ornate desk. Her hands were steady as she wrote the check. Fifty thousand dollars. Severance pay.

"Here," she said, handing it to Charlotte.

She was calm now. Deathly calm.

Charlotte clutched the check to her bosom. Tears sprang out of her eyes. "You can't fire me," she said. "I don't work for you."

"Fine. You go crying to my grandfather and maybe he'll move you to the servants' wing and let you stay as a maid. But if you do, that check will be voided." Juliana picked up the phone and called Zeke to take her to Sparky's apartment. "I'll be out all afternoon," she said. "Make your decision and move your things out of here by the time I get back."

As she went down the hall Juliana heard a terrible keening wail. But she had no remorse. Charlotte had betrayed her trust. Charlotte was dead to her now.

Zeke's glance when she slid into the car told her that he read her mood.

"Yes, there's something wrong," she said, knowing that he would never ask. "My grandfather knows all about Sparky. He had files ... really disgusting stuff. And it's not just Sparky. He had a file on a man I was involved with before I turned eighteen. He had everything, Zeke—pictures, phone conversations, everything! Am I being watched all the time? Is every word I say recorded?"

"Take it easy now," Zeke soothed. "Take it easy. There are things I can do—people and equipment I can get. We'll find out exactly what he's got working and then we can either disable it or use it ourselves."

"Use it how?"

"By controlling what they hear. By lettin' 'em think they got you sewed up when they don't. Don't worry. Just leave it to me. And you can relax in here, 'cause the car is clean. It's an old habit of mine, checkin' out my car and my phone." He started the engine and swung around toward the gates of Great House.

Juliana stared straight ahead. "I fired Charlotte. She was telling them things about me."

Zeke glanced in the rearview mirror at her.

"I don't feel bad. She deserved it. I guess I was stupid not to have suspected her of something before this." She settled back and closed her eyes. There was a whirring sound. Zeke was closing the partition. "No. Leave it open," she said. "I don't want to be alone."

She thought about Sparky. He'd been elusive for some time, missing the big coming-home party for Whitney Chandler, seldom joining the group for nights out, and full of excuses as to why he was so busy. Not that she blamed him. He'd been dumped long ago by Four and there wasn't much of anything else he was missing. It was the same crowd doing the same boring things and pretending that something wild or significant was going to happen any minute.

But now she knew what he'd been so busy doing. Now she knew why his calls to her had become so erratic and why he insisted that she not come up to the apartment anymore. Oh, Sparky ... Sparky. Falling in love with Four had been bad enough, but this ... He had pushed too far with this.

Sparky had to go. There was no question. She couldn't have him anymore. But then, she hadn't really had him for a long time. She'd already done her mourning and resolved the bitterness. Whatever happened today would be just a formality.

"Do you want me to come up with you?" Zeke asked.

"Yes. I might need you."

She tipped the doorman to keep from being announced and took Zeke up with her in the etched-brass elevator. As always, the delicate brasswork lifted her spirits. It was part of her building ... her apartment. Did her grandfather know what a good investment she'd made?

Zeke pressed the bell five times before the door finally swung open. Sparky stood there, dirty and pale and thin and wearing nothing but a surprised expression. "I thought it was somebody else," he mumbled vaguely.

Juliana turned her eyes away in disgust and Zeke pushed past Sparky into the apartment. He came back with a towel that he wrapped around Sparky sarong style.

Sparky grinned. "Oh, wow. I'm being dressed! My valet has arrived."

His grin revealed a newly broken front tooth. There was a crusting of blood around his nostrils and the whites of his eyes had a red glaze. Suddenly he launched himself at Juliana like a huge puppy, hugging her and babbling about how glad he was to see her and how she was his best friend. His only friend.

"Nobody ever comes to see me," he whined. "Even cats don't like it here. I bring them in and buy them gourmet food and they just vanish. Poof! I don't know where they go."

Juliana pushed him away, wrinkling her nose at the stale-sweat-and-vomit smell of him. She looked around the living room. There were pizza boxes and half-eaten deli sandwiches and cartons of rancid Chinese leftovers strewn everywhere. The furniture was covered with dark blotches. The large glass coffee table held a jumble of silver straws and single-edged razor blades and bottles of pills. Juliana recognized Percodan and Quaaludes and Valium. The rest were unfamiliar. A used plastic syringe lay on the floor beside the table.

"Oh, Sparky ... you're having fun, fun, fun, I see."

"It's not all mine," he said defensively, and hurried over to stand beside the table protectively. "Friends leave stuff behind sometimes. You know ..."

"But I thought you said you didn't have any friends."

"Well, these aren't like people I *know* friends. They're like new friends. You know. Guys I meet and say, 'Hey, mi casa es tu casa,' and whadda ya know, they're here."

She crossed the room to open a window, and Zeke carried a wooden dining-room chair into the living room for her to sit on. The stuffed furniture was unthinkable. As soon as she was seated,

Sparky began pacing restlessly, sniffing and absently wiping his nose with the back of his hand.

"Sparky."

She said his name several times before he stopped pacing and looked at her.

"I can't let you live like this. You know that, don't you?"

His face crumpled like a two-year-old's. "Ah, Jinxie . . . don't be so mad. I was short of cash so I let the maid go. But I'll clean it up."

"It's not just the mess, Spark."

He fidgeted and roamed around the room.

"Come on, Sparky," she coaxed. "Sit down and talk to me."

"Uh-uh." He shook his head and darted his eyes around the room. "There's bugs in here," he whispered.

"Roaches?"

"No." He waved his hands to shush her. "The IRA," he whispered. "They killed my family, you know."

Juliana drew in a deep breath and rolled her eyes to glance at Zeke.

"I'll fix it," Zeke said. He made a show of reaching into the light fixtures. "There. Got 'em. No more bugs."

Sparky sighed with relief and grinned. But the funny thing was that he could be right. Her grandfather's men probably had put listening devices in the apartment.

"My God, Sparky, you're a wreck!"

Still grinning, he perched on the arm of the couch. One of his knees was twitching as though being tested for reflexes. "You're not," he said brightly. "You look gorgeous, Jinx. How'd the boob job go?"

"Don't change the subject, Spark. What has happened to you?"

"I don't know." He shrugged. "I thought I had a chance at getting back with Four, and then somebody told him a lie about seeing me at Averno and—"

"What's Averno?" Juliana asked.

"It's . . . you know . . . one of those down-under clubs in the meat-packing district." He grimaced and shrugged again. "Damn, Jinxie . . . you know. One of those *places.* You show your card and shed your clothes and see what kind of hunk you can snare."

"But you don't go to those places, do you? You've been going to private parties and expensive clubs."

"Yeah. See. I wouldn't go to those disease palaces." A tear leaked out of the corner of his eye. "Four hates me, huh?"

"I haven't heard Four say one thing about you."

"See! See how sneaky people are?" He sniffled. "I'll never get Four back, and nobody's ever going to love me again."

"Who'd want to love you? Look at yourself. You're disgusting!"

"You're right." He stood and looked around the room frantically. "I have to get myself together. I'll have a little toot and maybe a Valium, then I'll go out and buy new clothes. That's what I need. Nothing like a little shopping to put a person back on track. Right, Jinxie?"

"What you need is detox, Sparky. Serious detox." As she said it she realized that it was the perfect solution. She'd send him to that same discreet upstate hospital where her grandfather had threatened to send Grace. Gabby Gravesend had been there awhile too. Gabby would have the particulars.

"Oh, Jinxie!" He threw himself on the floor at her feet and rested his head against her knees. "You're the only one in the world who cares about me. The only one. My parents tell everyone I'm dead. They say I was kidnapped and my body was run through a wood chipper. They'd rather have me dead than gay. They don't care whether it was my fault or not. They don't care that I was kidnapped."

Juliana had heard so many versions of Sparky's history over the years that she had no emotional reaction left. "You ran away, Sparky. Remember? Your father blamed you for his being fired from Elysia and he beat you, so you ran away."

"Only sort of. I was thinking of running away, but I probably wouldn't have made it. I probably would have ended up back home if *he* hadn't taken me with him."

"That doesn't exactly make you a kidnap victim."

At that Sparky burst into tears. "I loved him. I worshiped him. But he never loved me back. He never loved anybody." The sentences were punctuated by gasping sobs.

Juliana rubbed her forehead wearily. "You knew what Four was like," she said softly.

"Four! Huh? Fuck Four."

She realized then that he was talking about the man who had devastated him before he'd come back into her life.

He raised his head suddenly, a look of wild excitement in his eyes. "Why don't we be in love! Yeah!" He smiled up at her eagerly. "You're the best friend I've ever had, and who says I can't be in love with a woman, huh? Who says I can't fuck a woman?"

Juliana looked down at his filthy hair and his dripping nose and his whisker stubble. He was repulsive and contemptible and pathetic.

"Yeah! I'll be just like him. I'll have a wife and a big house and then I'll fuck everybody. Men, women, kids . . ."

Juliana sighed heavily.

"Then I'll go running off to be a hero in the arctic or Tibet or someplace where I can fuck the donkeys and the bears and the native boys." He dissolved into sobs again.

The room suddenly had no air and Juliana couldn't think . . . didn't want to think. She refused to think. And she refused to hear another word.

"Zeke! Get him dressed."

Zeke took the sobbing Sparky into the bedroom while she went into the kitchen to use the phone. It hit her then. There was no Charlotte to call. No Charlotte to handle the details. She would have to handle the arrangements herself.

She called Gabby Gravesend first, explaining that Sparky needed help. Gabby sounded grateful for the call. Since the big Gravesend financial debacle and her long stint upstate, Gabby hadn't been a regular member of their crowd.

"Sure," Gabby said. "I'll look it up for you." Then, hesitantly, "Do you want me to call Charlotte and give her the number and the directions?"

"Charlotte isn't with me anymore."

"Oh."

There was a pause.

"I could go ahead and make the arrangements, Jinx," Gabby suggested timidly. "I know what to do."

"That would be great, Gabby. You can call my car phone in about thirty minutes and give me the instructions." As she hung up the phone she thought she heard a noise from the walk-in pantry. She pulled the louvered doors open to look. A matted, emaciated cat lay on the floor inside. Its eyes were sunken and foam flecked its mouth. There were deep claw marks in the wood from the animal's futile attempts to get out.

"Zeke!"

The big man appeared quickly and looked over her shoulder into the pantry.

"Do something for it . . . please."

Zeke squatted down beside the animal. Very gently he lifted it and then, with no forewarning, snapped the cat's neck.

"You killed it!"

"Sometimes that's the kindest thing," he said. "Sometimes that's the only thing left."

37

Lucy

Lucy held up her wet print and turned on the darkroom lights. In the past six months with Ellis she had given less and less of herself to her work, yet had understood more clearly what it was that she wanted to do. She wanted to use her skills to reveal truth, to dig down beneath the surface into the darkness and light of people's lives. Exactly the opposite of her hired work.

When people paid money, they expected her to conceal and flatter and present images that were all surface. All lies. They wanted their lines and flaws retouched and their bodies posed to look ten pounds slimmer and they wanted photographs of what they wished their lives to be. Lying photographs. And she didn't know if she could shape those lies much longer without turning bitter and threatening the vision that drove her real work.

She'd reached a plateau, a high point after years of climbing. At last she had a clear view of the terrain she'd already crossed and a sense of her destination. She could see that there was safety in staying where she was—in not venturing any further. But she couldn't stop. She had to find out how far she could go.

And she felt an urgency, a fear that she might lose the images and the vision if she didn't bury herself in her work and capture them as swiftly as possible.

She looked at her finished print. It was eight-by-ten, not as large as she would have liked, but this was only a test of her idea. In the center of the photograph was an old woman tied into a wheelchair. Lucy had burned out an area around the figure to create a fuzzy outline. Then the remainder of the space was crammed with a montage suggesting the old woman's history. The montage was crude and pieced-looking, but she knew she could smooth it out and perfect the technique in time.

In time, she thought sarcastically. Given the small amounts of time she devoted to her work these days, it would be ages before she got this picture right. The fear rose up again. What if she lost the sense of this piece before she could get it right?

She hung the print on the overhead line and began cleaning up after herself. As soon as she switched on the lights, Duff poked his head in the door.

"I saw the signal light go out," he said. "You aren't knockin' off early again, are you?"

She nodded and continued cleaning.

"Damn, Lucy. You're wasting an awful lot of darkroom time these days. I've got to charge you even if you don't use it."

"I know that, Duff."

"What's wrong? Are you taking more jobs?"

"Duff, please . . . I'm in a hurry."

He craned his neck to look at her hanging print. "Wow! What is that for?"

Lucy pulled the print off the line and laid it face-down on the stainless counter. "You know I don't like you peeking."

He laughed. "Just checking to see if my place is being used for sex stuff."

The statement was offered as a joke, as something that was absolutely ridiculous, but it made Lucy's cheeks burn. Sex stuff. Duff would never know how close he was to her thoughts. She was quitting early because she wanted to be with Ellis. Because she wanted to feel his hand against her bare skin and absorb the heat from his body and see the image of herself that was reflected in his eyes.

She packed her things and said good-bye to Duff and set off in her little Volkswagen. Just like Ms. Conroy's car. Just like Ms. Conroy. So hungry for the touch of a man that nothing else mattered.

She understood it all now. How an educated, savvy woman like Ms. Conroy could feel the pull of a man so strongly that she ignored good judgment and even danger. Passion, lust, desire. All the overworked romantic words. They were real. As real as terror. As real as heroin. As real as death.

It had crept up on her slowly. With patience and persistence, Ellis had remade her as a woman. He'd coaxed her into making love by candlelight and shown her the beauty of their joining. He'd brought her to climax in every way possible and he'd taught her to receive and give and accept her body's signals. Intellect and logic had fallen away through his guidance, and she'd learned to trust him. To follow his lead with absolute and complete faith. She was reborn. Baptized in the wet heat of orgasm.

They had been seeing each other regularly for six months. In the course of that six months Lucy had slowly slipped backward. She was catering to Ellis just as she'd catered to Buddy. She was structuring her days around his schedule. And right now she was rushing to buy groceries so she could surprise him with a good dinner. That's what she was doing with her precious darkroom time—rushing to cook a good dinner for a man. A man who made her tremble and burn. A man she couldn't get enough of.

She juggled the sacks of groceries and opened his door with the key he'd given her. This wasn't her first surprise visit. She'd been there many times while he was at work, scrubbing his dingy kitchen floor and repotting his plants and using her meager supply of disposable cash to supply his rooms with air freshener and blue toilet-bowl water and rubber dishwashing gloves and refrigerator deodorizer and curtains. She hadn't felt the need for any of these things in her own place, but conditioning dictated that she provide them for him. She cared about him; therefore she had to take care of him. She'd relapsed into Charity's training as though the disease had been lurking in her system all along.

She mixed and chopped and stirred, then whisked around the apartment to set the table with the coordinated tablecloth and napkins she'd given him. His dishes were chipped and shabby, so she'd dipped into her savings to buy him two shiny plates from the open-stock china section at the department store. When she finished with the table, it looked as good as a magazine spread.

There was still time before he arrived home from the new job he'd taken, so she straightened and tidied, arranging his shaving equipment neatly in the medicine chest, folding his ironing board, and stacking all his magazines and books in organized piles. When she was finished the apartment looked a hundred percent neater than she ever kept her own place.

She heard his key in the lock and hurried to the bathroom mirror to check her appearance. Everything mattered now. Were there circles under her eyes? Was the hairline scar below her jaw suddenly bigger and uglier? Had her ears always looked so funny? Were her lips chapped? Should she have worn more of that new makeup she'd bought? Would he like her earrings?

"Lucy?" he called from the doorway.

She stepped out and gauged his reactions. At times like this she functioned only as a measuring device. How happy was he? How surprised? Did he like the way she looked? Was he excited about dinner? Had he noticed everything she'd done in the apartment?

"Lucy . . ." His eyes swept the room and he sniffed the cooking aromas from the open kitchen. "You shouldn't have done all this."

Pleasure spread through her. That was the trap he'd caught her in—he hadn't expected anything. He hadn't whined or cajoled or carried on. He hadn't asked her for anything. If he had, she would have been able to draw back from him and summon indignation and anger. She'd have informed him that biology did not predestine women to be servants of men and she would have made it clear that she didn't intend to be any man's mommy.

But he hadn't asked for anything. All he'd done was given. He'd taken her places and bought her things and cooked for her and opened up new worlds of sensuality and adventure. And what did she have to give in return except her ability to clean and nurture and coordinate?

"I wanted to," she said. "Don't you like it?"

He had a strange look on his face that she couldn't quite read. "I've told you, I don't expect you to do these things."

"I know."

She crossed the room to hug him. His body was lean and hard beneath his clothes, and he smelled like cut wood. "How was your day?" she asked.

"Boring, frustrating, irritating. And how about yours? Take any prize pictures of poodles in tutus?"

She winced at his disparaging remark about her work, but she knew that it was her own fault. She'd never been able to open up and tell him what she wanted or how she felt or what the photography meant to her. She'd encouraged his belief that photography was simply a way to get by, and she'd never shown him any of her real work. There was too much at stake to be honest, and she didn't want to threaten him with the truth or take the chance that he might belittle her aspirations.

She insisted that he shower while she put the food on the table, and then forced him to sit down while she hovered and fussed. He cooperated, but with reluctance, and during the meal he was pensive and unresponsive.

She watched him eat. After six months he was even more attractive to her than he'd been in the beginning, and now there were no abstracts, no what-ifs. She knew what those beautiful hands felt like against her skin. She knew how it felt to be swept away. But suddenly, sitting across the table from him, watching him eat the meal she'd donated her afternoon to, she was seized by resentment.

Yes, she wanted this man. But was having him worth the cost? How much of herself was she willing to give up? And for what? For sexual pleasure? How much longer could the passion last?

"Did you like the stew?" she asked.

"Yes. It was very good."

"But ..." she prodded him. "I hear a 'but' in there."

He drew in a deep breath. "I like the stew, okay?"

"Are you mad at me?"

"No," he said, "but don't you have something more important to do than play house at my apartment?"

The question made her angry. How dare he not appreciate the sacrifices she was making for him?

"Oh. Why? Have I disturbed something here in your beautiful home?"

He put his hand down against the table in a gesture of controlled frustration. "I don't understand this female compulsion to take over. To move in and change everything. Are you trying to mark your territory, or does fucking a man stir up some crazy homemaking hormone?"

Lucy stood abruptly and picked up the serving dishes.

"Forget those," he said.

"No. I can't stand a dirty kitchen," she said, mimicking an old statement of Charity's but adding a dose of sarcasm.

He followed her with the two new china plates in his hand. "I don't want things like this!" he shouted, holding the plates in the air. "I don't want to be bound up in possessions and tied down and owned by a lot of material junk."

He let the plates slip from his fingers and smash to the floor.

Lucy slammed open the cupboard door and pulled out the dish soap, but he grabbed the serving dishes from the sink and threw them on the floor too.

"There," he said. "That's the way I pack."

Immediately Lucy marched toward the door, picking up her purse and jacket as she went, but he rushed after her.

"Wait." He grabbed her arm. "Please ... wait. I'm sorry. Lucy ... I'm so sorry."

Her resolve evaporated instantly. Those were such irresistible, such seductive words coming from a man. *I'm sorry.* If men only knew what power they had with those words.

She put her purse and jacket back down.

He was still wildly agitated. "Is this us?" he said. "I mean, what are we doing here? Who are we trying to be?"

She refused to respond in any serious way. "Is that a riddle I'm supposed to answer?"

"We're both caught up in these meaningless lives. I pound nails every day and you take pictures of spoiled pets and we're both just marking time and hoping that something better comes along and drops on our heads."

"You must have had a really bad day," she said.

He sighed and turned away from her. "Is this all you want?" he said, sweeping the room with his arm.

Something drove her on, compelling her to push him and withhold herself. "Well . . . it could use some paint and some wall decor," she wisecracked. "But what if it *is* all I want? What do you want? Do you want to be rich and fat and useless? Is that it?"

He frowned as though she'd struck a nerve.

She peered into his face, looking for something familiar. She knew the planes and angles by heart, yet she didn't know him. "Who are you?" she wanted to ask. "And what are you doing in my life?"

He seemed defeated or resigned or maybe just sad, and he went to sit on the couch in silence. She followed him and sat down, though not as close as she would have before.

"I don't want to be rich," he said quietly. "My family is rich."

She thought about that for a moment and then broke into laughter. "Don't tell me," she said, "you're out here leading a humble life to atone for their money."

"Maybe," he said defensively. "What's wrong with that?"

"There's nothing wrong with it. It's just so completely illogical. You go on and on about social problems and how you can't seem to make a difference . . . how nothing you do changes anything. Well, donating time to the literacy project and smoke jumping and remodeling children's homes are all wonderful, and I've said before that I think you're wrong about not making a difference with them . . . but don't you realize how much more you could do with money? My God, with money you could go so far beyond saving a few trees and patching up a place for a small group of children. You could step in and change people's lives."

"What do you know about it?" he snapped. "Nothing. Absolutely nothing! Just because money is in my family doesn't mean it's accessible to me."

She shrugged and leaned back. So that was the reason for his secrecy—he wasn't a hardworking blue-collar guy at all. It was enough to make her burst into laughter again. He was living an illusion, just as she was.

He was pretending to be ordinary. She was pretending to be talented and independent. They were both fooling themselves.

She folded her hands in her lap and glanced sideways at him. "Since you've shared that bit of information with me, I'll play fair and tell you a little about myself. I am not rich. My father died from a broken heart that he pickled in alcohol. My mother worked herself to death doing other people's laundry. And I do not eat egg salad because I enjoy depriving myself."

"I knew you'd hate me for my family," he said.

She smiled bitterly and shook her head. "Is that why you don't want me messing with your household ... because I don't do it as well as the servants would?"

The blow struck home and she was instantly sorry. "I didn't mean that. You know I have a wicked tongue sometimes."

He leaned forward, resting his elbows on his knees and holding his head in his hands. "I can't stay here, Lucy. I was ready to leave when I met you, and I stayed because of you, but I can't do it anymore. I'm useless here. Carpentry isn't what I want. This city isn't what I want."

"Nothing ever will be, Ellis, because your ideals are too high. High ideals aren't practical anymore. Only fools hang on to them."

He raised his head to look at her. "Is that what you believe?"

She hesitated. "Yes ... no ... who knows? I don't know exactly what I believe."

They sat in silence for several minutes. She felt the pull of him as strongly as ever.

"What do you want me to say, Ellis?"

"Say you'll go with me," he said.

She felt like a pinned butterfly beneath his eyes. She could not trust herself to speak, so she swung her legs up to lie across the couch and rest her head in his lap.

He stroked the hair from her forehead and bent to kiss her and she lifted her face toward him and twined her fingers in his hair, drinking in the clean smell of his skin.

Her need was urgent and uncomplicated. Foreplay was unnecessary.

They made their way to the bedroom, progressing only a few feet at a time, stumbling, falling together, tangling in clothing as they discarded it. She wanted him in her mouth. She wanted him between her breasts. She wanted him inside her. She wanted everything at once. And she didn't ever want to come. She didn't ever want it to be over.

When they were both drenched with sweat and near exhaustion, he sat up on the edge of the bed and pulled her onto his lap. She slid down on him easily and wrapped her legs around his hips and put her arms around his neck.

"Look at me," he said. "Don't stop looking at me."

He put his hands on the curve of her hips and moved slowly inside her. But it was his eyes that held her, consumed her, carried her to the edge of the abyss . . . and pulled her gasping into oblivion.

Afterward she cried. He didn't ask why. Which was good, because she wouldn't have been able to say it yet.

She wasn't going with him. Couldn't go with him. Had to salvage herself while it could still be done.

Passion. Sexual obsession. Yes. They were real. But now she needed to put them behind her and go forward with the rest of her life.

38

Juliana

Juliana could not stop thinking about Matthew Rhysdale. She read the file over and over. The detectives had been brutally thorough. She was enraged at the violation her grandfather had ordered and stunned by the realization that she'd never had any secrets, but she was not shocked. She had always had a sense of what her grandfather was capable of, and when she settled down to analyze his actions, she saw that they were perfectly understandable. His only true crime was that he had been wrong. Matthew Rhysdale had not been bad for her.

She traced the familiar outline of Matt's face in the photographs and her veins sang with the warmth of wanting him. The kind of wanting that had nothing to do with the men she had been meeting in clubs—the empty prettyboys who were interested only in her last name and how much money she might spend on them.

Matt. Matt. Matt.

She could not stop thinking about him. He hadn't left her at all. He hadn't fallen under the spell of another woman. He hadn't walked away—he had been dragged from her by dark and powerful forces.

She dismissed the negative biography of Matt that she read in the file. It didn't matter to her that he wore blue contact lenses or that his teeth were capped or that the blond streaks in his hair were added by a hairdresser. Didn't all political figures enhance their appearances some way or other? It didn't matter that he hadn't quite been the farmboy he claimed, or that he'd had a cheating incident in college, or that he had a long history with women.

Everyone had secrets. Everyone had a hidden self. All she cared about was that Matt hadn't really left her. He had not deserted her. He had not betrayed her. And maybe . . . just maybe . . . he still loved her to this day.

Her preoccupation with Rhysdale deepened. She lost interest in clubs and parties. She canceled lunch dates and shopping dates and ignored dinner invitations. The only one of her friends she talked to was Gabby, who had moved into Charlotte's old room and was functioning as Juliana's secretary-assistant.

Even the sudden arrival of her father distracted her only momentarily. She wouldn't have bothered to attend the big welcoming scene if her grandfather hadn't insisted.

They were all standing in the entryway—her grandfather and her Aunt Grace and her father—reenacting the same meaningless homecoming scene that had been played out so many times in her life. Except this time a different man came home. A deflated man. Thin and subdued and dispirited. A resigned man claiming that he was home to stay.

Juliana watched and waited. This drastic change in Aubrey made her vaguely curious and sent a small wave of vengeful satisfaction through her. But it aroused no sympathy. He deserved whatever suffering caught up with him.

Her father's eyes slid over and made reluctant, almost embarrassed contact with her. "Hello, Jinxie," he said.

"Hi."

"Long time, huh?"

"Is it? I've stopped counting."

His battered canvas safari hat went slowly around in his hands. It was the first time she'd ever seen her father display such self-consciousness.

"Ummm." His lips signaled the barest suggestion of a smile. "And you've become a blond."

"It was the only thing left to be."

He laughed a little at that and reached out to pull her into an awkward, one-armed hug. She endured it without responding.

"You look hellish," Edward said. "Are you ill?"

"No," Aubrey said simply. There was no hearty laugh, no dazzling smile. The webbed belt on his cotton duck jacket was cinched tightly to take up the extra room at his waist. His eyes were shadowed with defeat.

"Well, then . . ." Edward cleared his throat gruffly. "You've made a wise decision. That nomadic life-style of yours was clearly detrimental."

"He's not sick," Grace gushed. "He's just worn out from all that trekking around and eating terrible food." She leaned forward to kiss her brother's cheek. "We'll have you fattened up and looking fit in no time."

"I'll open your old gym in the basement," Edward offered expansively. "Call in a trainer and have it refitted with the latest."

"You must be exhausted," Grace said, moving to ring the servants' bell.

"Your room has been prepared," Edward said.

"And I'm in my old room right across the hall!" Grace beamed. "Just like neither of us ever left."

Aubrey turned abruptly and followed his luggage up the stairs. His valet scurried after him.

In the days that followed, Edward treated his son with smug pleasure and Grace clucked and fussed as if Aubrey were her child instead of her brother. Only Juliana held back. She'd hardened herself to her father years ago and she placed little credence in his announcement of a permanent stay. Aubrey never stayed anywhere long. He grew restless in New York. He grew restless in the arctic or the Himalayas. And she wasn't going to let herself be taken in by this new fragility he'd developed.

Aubrey could not be counted on. He might be the perfect buddy for deep-sea fishing or grizzly-bear tagging, but he'd never come through for her as a father. She would never let down her guard and trust him again.

She ignored his presence in the household, dismissing it from her mind. Only Matt mattered now. All she could think about was Matt.

Did he still love her? If she could only make a new start with him . . .

With possession of her grandmother's trust, her adult status and her financial independence had become absolute. And Matthew Rhysdale was now a New York congressman with an office in Washington, D.C., a sterling reputation, and a favored position for the upcoming Senate spot. He was important and respected and adored by the media. Her grandfather wouldn't dare cause them trouble this time.

So Matt was married. There were no children, and everyone got at least one divorce these days. She imagined him turning away from his cold bitch wife at night and clinging to memories of their love. She imagined him calling out for her in his sleep.

Finally her emotional turmoil reached a point where she had to act or explode.

She called him.

"Good morning," a voice answered. "Representative Rhysdale's office."

She hung up in a panic and had to force herself to redial. "Juliana Van Lyden calling," she told the receptionist coolly. There were a few clicks and then suddenly she heard his voice.

"Hello. Hello, this is Matthew Rhysdale."

She froze. The voice sent cracks through what little composure she'd mustered for the call.

"Hello," he said again.

"Matt . . ." she managed, "it's me."

Silence. She could almost hear his uncertainty. Or was it fear?

"I'm surprised," he finally said. "I can't believe it."

"How have you been?" she asked lightly.

"Fine." It wasn't the answer she wanted to hear. She wanted him to say that he'd never been the same, that he'd been miserable without her.

He hesitated. "You didn't call me just to visit. I know you better than that."

"Yes. You do know me."

She closed her eyes and visualized him. His soft breathing came to her over the miles of lines and she could almost feel his skin. She'd meant the first conversation to be casual—a first step— but the contact with him stripped her of pretense.

"I want to see you," she said.

Another long pause. The silence engulfed her, leaving her sick and trembling.

When he spoke again his voice was brisk, decisive. "I've got business in Manhattan in two weeks. There's a place we can meet safely. Call me Wednesday night at the Waldorf and I'll have the details."

The line buzzed in her ear. That was it. He'd hung up.

She closed her eyes and imagined him—his touch, his eyes devouring her, his lips whispering close to her ear. Two weeks. It was an endless stretch of time.

She sat through breakfasts made unbearable by Grace's forced animation and Edward's continual nagging of Aubrey for more information, more stories, more clues to the mysterious change that had taken place in him. She sat through dinners that were replays of the breakfasts. And she wanted to scream and throw the dishes and tell them to shut up.

Aubrey made repeated attempts to get close to her. He tried to interest her in tennis or target shooting with him, but she refused even when she would have welcomed a distraction. She had long ago stopped trying to be good at his pursuits in order to please him, and she didn't want to give him the satisfaction of beating her at any competition.

Sometimes she caught Aubrey watching her and she wondered what he was thinking. Was he searching for the child she used to be? Was he sorry that child was gone? Juliana was beyond caring. Matt Rhysdale was the only reality. Nothing else mattered.

By the time she climbed the steps of the Brooklyn brownstone for their rendezvous, Juliana was convinced that her entire future waited just inside the door.

She rang the bell. There was static from an intercom set into the wall, then Matt's voice asked, "Who is it?"

She tried not to giggle. Matt had insisted on an elaborate ruse and an exact pass phrase for her to use.

"It's the decorating service to measure for drapes."

There was a buzz and the front door opened. She stepped into the foyer hesitantly.

"That's great," Matt said, looking her up and down in admiration. "I'd never know it was you."

She had confided in Zeke and he was responsible for the frothy auburn wig, huge sunglasses, and gaudy clothes. To complete the disguise she carried a shoulder-strap portfolio and an open toolkit containing measuring tapes and drapery-fabric swatches. Not exactly the wonderful first impression she'd have liked.

"Let me return myself to normal," she said. "I can't keep a straight face in this getup."

He showed her to a second-floor bathroom. She studied his back as he led the way. The perfectly barbered hairline against the tan neck. The perfectly tapered white-on-white shirt. The perfectly tailored slacks and the perfectly shined handmade shoes. Everything was perfect now—not just the eyes and teeth and hair color. He had reached a level of perfection that made a shadow of his former self.

"Can I get you something to drink?"

"Scotch and soda," she said.

The bathroom looked like a garish advertisement for a honeymoon resort. Gold-veined mirrors surrounded the huge glass shower and there was an oversize pink bathtub complete with built-in wine icer and sleek telephone. Quickly she stripped off the foreign clothing and hung it on a hook. The wig and glasses she tossed onto the bare Formica counter surrounding the sinks. As she smoothed her blond hair into place, she examined it critically. She'd switched to a more subtle tint and a more conservative style for the occasion, and now she was a little uncertain about it. As she changed into the sexy silk slip-dress she'd tucked into the portfolio, her stomach careened in a dozen directions. Moisture gathered in her armpits and on her forehead, and the heat in her face felt as though it might blister her skin.

There was a tap on the door. "Your drink's ready," Matt called.

She took a deep breath and opened the door. Without comment he handed her the glass and turned, leading the way into the long room.

He stopped at the overstuffed wraparound sofa, pausing to press a button that activated music on an unseen stereo system. She sat down near a corner of the gray velvet sectional and he sat on an adjoining piece so that they were cater-corner rather than side by side. Both of them leaned forward at the same time to put their drinks on the slab of metal that served as a coffee table, and their knees and arms brushed.

Juliana jerked back and settled as deeply as she could into the cushions.

Matt didn't seem to notice. "You look . . ." He shook his head as though speechless. "Wow. That's all I can say . . . wow!"

His face had developed new lines. They gave him more credibility, more character. She wanted to trace each line with her fingertips.

"What do you think?" he asked, raising his arms expansively. "How do I look?"

Gold flashed from the cufflinks at his wrists and the expensive pen in his monogrammed pocket and the wedding band on his left hand.

"You look successful," she said.

"And important?" He grinned like a mischievous boy.

"Yes. Important."

There was a silence filled by the music from the unseen speakers. Some orchestra was playing elevator country-and-western songs. She would have made fun of the decor and the music under other circumstances.

"How's Washington?" she asked.

The question ignited him. It blazed from his eyes and charged his voice with the intensity of its heat.

"Washington is everything I ever imagined . . . and more." He stared across the room, seeing nothing except his own destiny. "You grow up in New York and you think its the center of the world . . . you think the men in Albany and the money men like your grandfather have all the power imaginable. Then you get to

Washington ... and you see what real power is. You see how much more is possible ..."

He turned his head, focusing the blaze directly on her. "And you realize that there is no sacrifice or no price too great, and that whatever it cost you to get there—it was a bargain."

Juliana stared down at the coffee table. She wanted to scream that it wasn't a bargain. How could he say that? And she wanted to tell him to shut up about Washington. Washington felt like a rival whose eyes she wanted to claw out. She picked up her glass and sipped at the Scotch. It was awful.

"Your eyes match your drink," he said. "They're the same color as a good smooth Scotch."

Not so smooth a Scotch, she wanted to point out. For some reason the compliment—delivered with so much more finesse than the old Matt had possessed—was irritating rather than pleasing.

He picked up his own drink, raised it as though saluting her, and took a long swallow.

Everything felt wrong. She studied the hand that held the glass. His nails were professionally manicured, squared off and buffed to a healthy sheen. The wedding band glared at her again.

"How do you like married life?" she asked.

He set his drink back down. "That's not a very interesting subject."

"It is to me."

"All right." Beneath the feigned resignation was an undercurrent of irritation. "Anything special you want to know?"

"What's she like?" Juliana tried to sound casual.

"You've seen her picture." He shrugged. "That's exactly what she's like. Nice and proper, with a steel rod for a backbone and more political savvy than most of the men on Capitol Hill."

Juliana fought down the masochistic urge to ask more about her. It was already bad enough. He sounded as though he admired and respected her. He sounded as though he was glad to be married to her. And there wasn't one hint that he'd missed Juliana or regretted their parting.

"Come on, kitten." His voice and his eyes softened and he reached out to stroke her arm. "Let's not talk about her. She's my partner but she's not my lover ... not like you were. She could never take your place."

Tears sprang into Juliana's eyes. He took the drink from her hand, set it on the table, and kissed her gently on the lips. "Oh, Matt," she whispered.

With just a few words and a kiss he'd erased all the bad feelings, all the doubts. She was clean and new inside, ready to unfold for him like a ripe Georgia O'Keeffe flower.

"I've missed you so much. At first I thought I might die—"

"Shhh." He smiled gently. She took it as agreement.

Slowly he pushed her hair back and traced a line from her earlobe to her shoulder with his lips. Her entire body responded. She felt like a starving infant tasting a nipple, or a lost soul glimpsing God. It was so much greater than just sexual arousal.

He tore her dress off, breaking the thin straps and ruining the delicate silk. She clawed at his shirt. Buttons popped off. Cufflinks flew in different directions. He shed his slacks and underwear while she stripped off her hose; then they melted together into the soft cushions, skin on skin, sucking and tasting and touching one another in a breathless frenzy.

Only her bikini panties were left. She'd worn special ones. A wisp of silk fabric tied together at her hips with narrow ribbons. She straddled him, then sat up straight and pulled the ends of the ribbons. The bows came undone and the silk fell away.

He moaned and rolled her over with such force that they both ended up on the floor, kicking glasses off the table and pulling cushions from the sofa as they fell. The tang of spilled Scotch filled the air.

They came together almost immediately in a great shuddering burst. She bit his shoulder to keep from screaming.

Awareness returned gradually. The corny music, the hard press of the carpeted floor, the stickiness between her legs. But she didn't move. She didn't want to spoil what was left of their communion.

He sat up first. "Whew," he whistled soundlessly, then grinned. "Shower?"

"No, not yet." She sat up and stretched her arms, feeling lazy and decadent and contented. "Stay with me."

He stood and held his hand out to help her up. Then he led her back to the pink monstrosity of a bed.

She slid in between the synthetic satin sheets, watched while he arranged pillows to lean back against, and then rested her head against his shoulder. Everything was perfect. More perfect than it had ever been when they were together before. She considered the workings of fate. Maybe it was destiny that they were torn apart and had to rediscover their love.

"You should have taken off your ring," she teased lightly, touching the gold band with a fingertip.

"What?"

"You know ... like in the movies. The married man always takes off his ring when he's with the woman he loves."

"Oh. I never take it off," he replied. "Don't know if it even comes off."

She refused to be hurt. She refused to let the comment mean anything. She was still overflowing with the love he had poured into her.

"What kind of houses do they have in Washington?" she asked.

"Ummm. All kinds. Town houses. Condos. Mansions. And everything in between. We live in what I call a town house with pretensions. Others call it a mini-mansion."

She hated the word "we."

"Do people usually keep a place in Washington and a place at home?"

"Generally, yes."

She wanted to talk about where they would live together ... what their houses would be like, but her questions were not leading him in the right direction.

She let her eyes wander over the room. "I remember how particular you used to be about your clothes," she said, smiling with the tenderness of shared memories.

"I don't have to be particular anymore. Got a wife and a cleaning service and plenty of bucks to buy new ones."

"Do you? Have money, I mean. Does what you do pay well?"

"No." He laughed. "But I've got a rich wife and the biggest war chest on the Hill." He winked slyly. "Thanks to your grandfather."

"War chest?"

"Funds, kitten, funds. I can run the hottest Senate campaign the country's ever seen and still have plenty of eggs in my nest."

Juliana stared down at the shiny fuchsia sheet covering her legs, realized that she had lapsed into chewing on a fingernail, and angrily jerked her hand away from her mouth.

Funds ... thanks to her grandfather ...

"I don't know if I understand."

"Don't you worry about it, kitten." He stroked her leg. "The last thing I want to do with you is talk shop, so you don't have to understand much of anything."

"Matt, did my grandfather pay you to stop seeing me?"

"Hah! That wily old fart! Pay me? He set up my whole career. He sponsored me ... got all his friends interested in me ... billed me as the model young Republican, pulling myself up from farmboy shit-shoveler to top-of-the-heap shit-slinger. Compared me to the founding Van Lyden, who came over from some pissant old-country farm and scratched out a place in history with his dirty fingernails. By the time he was finished, I had contributions and support pouring in . . . not to mention a marriage proposal." He chuckled wryly.

Juliana slid out from under Matt's arm and sat up so she could face him. "Were you offered this package deal in exchange for dumping me, or did he start the ball rolling and wait for you to grab the hook?"

Matt chuckled again. "Oh . . . I'll tell you. That old guy is something. He slapped my back and dangled his goodies for months before I ever had a hint that he knew about the two of us. Even after his position was clear, the bastard was still subtle. Hardly mentioned your name. You talk about smooth—he's the one who should have gone into politics."

"So this was an ongoing thing between the two of you. He didn't suddenly confront you and make demands and threaten you."

"No. Not him. He led me right along like a catfish after a stink lure." Matt shook his head in wonder. "It's a shame you weren't born with balls, kitten. No telling what that old man could've made you into."

"You knew? You knew for months that you were going to marry that woman and dump me?"

"I never lied to you," Matt countered defensively. "I never made any promises. If you hadn't gone so wild, we could have cooled it and then maybe gotten back together after the heat was off."

"Never made any promises!" She dug her nails into her palms to keep from using them on him. "Every time you made love to me you were making promises! I thought you were the one person who'd never leave me. I thought we'd take Washington together. I even had fantasies about being the goddamned first lady someday."

"Kitten, kitten," he crooned. "That was kid stuff. You were just a baby then. Now you can see, can't you? The game doesn't work that way." He grinned and tweaked her breast. "You're built for the bedroom, not the boardroom."

She wanted to rip the grin off his face. She wanted to tear the lying tongue out of his mouth.

He reached down to adjust the expensive gold watch on his wrist. "Damn. Didn't realize how late it was gettin'. We're burning daylight here."

He was pulling back, lapsing into his country-boy-isms. Let him. He couldn't pull back far enough. He couldn't escape.

He slid off the bed and crossed the floor to make himself another drink. She saw him clearly now. The fish-belly skin of his thighs. The narrow weak shoulders. The fat pad around his middle.

"You can have the shower," he said. "I'll have to leave last anyway so I can lock up." He sprawled across the couch in arrogant satisfaction and winked at her over his drink. The wrinkled mass of his genitals hung limply beneath his belly flap. They looked as vulnerable as a half-formed creature, a mutant aborted before term.

Why had she ever been afraid of male genitals? Her thoughts flashed back to her father's oiled body and bulging crotch. Why had she ever thought maleness so powerful and intimidating?

"Come on, kitten . . . get your gorgeous ass in gear. I've got to make it back for an important meeting in two hours."

Juliana slid out of the bed, pulling the top sheet with her. She wrapped herself tightly in it.

"Don't look so blue," Matt teased. "We'll have lots of times like this. Maybe I can even get away for a couple of days soon— take you to some deserted island somewhere."

She smiled an Yvonne smile. A careful, closed-off smile.

"That's my girl."

He grinned and sat forward to swat her as she passed, but she sidestepped and locked herself in the bathroom. Slowly, methodically, she showered his touch and smell and essence from her body. With the water still running, she stepped out, wrapped herself in a towel, and picked up the phone. She called Zeke on the car phone with her plan, then dialed Information for the numbers of the most sensational New York City newspapers.

She turned off the shower and took her time reapplying her disguise and makeup.

Matt tapped on the door repeatedly, asking her to hurry. Relief was apparent on his face when she finally stepped out.

"Dammit, you took a solid hour!" He had a towel cover-up Velcro-ed around his middle. It was black with silver bunny heads, and he looked ridiculous in it.

She crossed to the street-side and opened the thin louvered blinds. Across the street and one house down she could see Zeke sitting in the driver's seat of an outrageous fluorescent-lime Cadillac. Directly in front of the house a cluster of men was standing on the sidewalk together. Several had cameras. They were staring up at the house.

"What are you doing?" Matt asked, moving to join her.

She grabbed his arm, pulling him into a passionate kiss and turning as she did, so they would be silhouetted in the window. He responded with precision accuracy to her tongue in his mouth. The unborn mass stirred beneath the bunny towel.

"That's to remember me by," she said, breaking the contact and pulling him away from the window before he could look out and see the excited audience. "Walk me down to the door?"

"I can't wait till next time," he said as he followed her down the stairs.

She unfastened the locks and chains and turned the knob, opening the heavy door a crack.

"Do I get a good-bye kiss?" she asked.

He smiled knowingly and pulled her tight against him for another crushing exchange of saliva. With her toe she edged the door all the way open.

"Congressman!" a voice called out. "Any comment?"

The rest was a blur of shouting and automatic cameras whirring. She ran out the door with her head down and one hand shielding her face. Then Zeke's huge arm was around her and she was being shoved into the lime Cadillac.

"Wait! Lady! give us a—"

Zeke left their pursuers in the dust.

Juliana crouched in the back of the car until Zeke told her it was safe to sit up.

"Where on earth did you find this car?" she asked.

Zeke glanced at her in the rearview mirror and shook his head. "Don't ask."

"Thank you, Zeke."

"My pleasure."

They rode in silence awhile.

Zeke cleared his throat. "People were tryin' ta reach ya on the limo's phone earlier." He kept his eyes on the road. "Sparky killed himself last night at the hospital." He waited several seconds. "And I thought I oughta warn ya . . . your cousin Ellis showed up this morning."

39

Ellis

Great House was no longer an albatross to Ellis, hanging in his thoughts as a reminder of his family's excesses and crimes of self-indulgence. It was a piece of history. A living museum. An aging artwork that belonged to the people. And if he had his way, it would soon be converted to the museum that it ought to be.

His family seemed different too. Edward had lost the power to intimidate him, and his mother had lost the power to snare him with guilt. The pain and accusation were gone from Juliana's eyes, leaving only hate, and hate could not twist him inside or tear him open. They had nothing left to control him with. He could share the orbit of their lives now without sacrificing pieces of himself.

In the beginning he hadn't examined the reasons why he was ready to go home. He had attributed it to the depression that set in after losing Lucy, the heavy grayness that took the joy from every city and every future possibility. But now, after being back for several months, he realized that he had returned because Lucy had been right: the Van Lyden name and the Van Lyden money could be used to make people's lives better.

There were so many issues to address—homelessness and toxic waste and illiteracy and environmental destruction. And if he didn't try to use his birthright to do something positive, then he was as big a criminal as the robber baron who had amassed the fortune in the first place and as conscienceless as the spoiled and squandering generations that followed.

He wasn't quite sure how to begin. He had a trust that he had never used, and of course he could finance everything from that for a time. But to make a real difference, to effect real change, he would have to gain his grandfather's support and have access to substantial funds. He would have to have full Van Lyden backing,

but he knew better than to approach his grandfather with candor.
To convince Edward, he would have to demonstrate the benefits
of his intended philanthropy first and prove that greater glory
could be attached to the Van Lyden name with such efforts.

Ellis felt more hopeful and energetic than he had in years. He
could make a difference. The Van Lyden money was not evil. It
was simply a tool. And now he knew how to build.

There were still times when the past haunted him. When he
had to escape. He turned to the green oasis of Central Park then.
He ran over the rolling terrain and through the tangled rambles
of the northern end of the park or he walked the same pictur-
esque paths he'd taken with Yvonne so long ago. The park soothed
and nourished him. It was a natural wonder in the midst of unnatural chaos.

Only it wasn't truly a natural wonder—not in the sense that it
could function by itself. The park required attention and maintenance to survive the onslaughts of the surrounding city. Each
time he went in, he became more aware of the problems, more
respectful of the crews that continually battled the litter and graffiti and the mindless vandalism, and more disgusted with the mul-
tiplying rat-poison signs.

It was not just the aesthetics of ugly poison warnings tacked
up along every meandering path, it was the use of the poison that
bothered him. The rats were undoubtedly building up immuni-
ties and requiring more and more poison for control, making the
park an increasingly hazardous place for pets and squirrels and
songbirds and human toddlers.

What had gone wrong? The park was large enough to function
as an ecosystem with a mix of prey and predator. Where were the
owls and the small hawks that should have kept the rodent pop-
ulation naturally in check? But then he realized that the answer
to that went back to the poison also. An owl or hawk existing on
a diet of rodents with poison in their systems would eventually
succumb or lose the ability to reproduce. The problem had obviously compounded itself. It was yet another case of human bun-
gling.

And that was when the idea struck. This was his beginning.
This was the hook to snare his grandfather's interest. Who could
object to benefiting Central Park? There were no touchy issues
involved, and it was a cause that could be seen as worthy even by
Edward Van Lyden.

The possibilities grew into exciting dimensions and he was
carried completely outside himself. He spent days without think-

ing about Lucy's smile or Lucy's sideways glance or the smell of her hair. Days without asking himself what he could have done or what he should have done or what had been so wrong with him that she would not even try to work things out.

He knew that he had hurt women along the way. And he sometimes wondered if the pain he felt over Lucy was payment for every moment of suffering he had ever inflicted. The sort of punishment a Solomon might decree. A just maiming of his heart so that he would never again be ignorant or unconcerned about the hearts of others.

When he was in the mood to be honest and ruthless with himself he could look back and see that they had been doomed from the start. Both of them had been too wary, too trustless, too afraid of vulnerability. And he wondered now if he had really even known her. Beyond the fact that he had loved the taste and smell and feel of her; the slow smiles and knowing eyes; the heady blend of gentleness and cynicism and kindness and sharp wit that made her a continual surprise; beyond that—who had she been? What did she dream at night?

Lucy. Lucy. Lucy. She had asked him not to call or write. He had ignored her and written anyway. The letter was returned. Her phone was disconnected. The message was unmistakably clear. She had shut him out completely. And now he had to learn to forget her.

But being with Lucy had melted something inside him. He wanted the softness and comfort of a real companion now, not just a parade of female flesh in his bed. He wanted someone of his own. Someone permanent. And he had begun to think about fatherhood. The idea of a child was taking hold in his imagination.

Children were everywhere. He supposed they had always been, but he hadn't noticed it till now. He liked to watch them play in the park, and sometimes, when he witnessed tenderness or anger or pride passing between a child and parent, he tried to imagine what sort of father he would be. Was he destined to follow the patterns set by his own parents or would he be able to break free and give his children something different? Something better?

He was ready to try. Just as he was ready to commit to a woman and believe in a future. If only he had known all this in the beginning with Lucy. Maybe he would have behaved differently. Maybe he would have avoided the same mistakes.

He was well into his park plans and ready to leave for a meeting about them when his private telephone in his room rang.

"Is this Ellis?"

"Yes."

The female voice was familiar, but he could not quite identify it.

"This is Whitney Chandler. I heard you were back and I thought you might call, but you didn't . . . so I just decided: what the fuck? Who cares if he doesn't want to hear from me?"

Suddenly he was filled with nostalgia, though he couldn't say why, because their brief relationship had been a relief to end and he hadn't missed her at all in the intervening years.

On impulse he invited her to meet him at the park after his meeting was over.

The playground he led her to was a new one. It had a curving slide of polished stone set into the side of a hillock and a wooden bridge and sprinklers that sprayed water on hot days. She sat down beside him on a bench. Her fine brown hair was still as soft and shiny as a child's but her eyes were those of an adult now. The easy confidence was gone. The brash devil-may-care attitude had been replaced by brittleness.

"So, I guess you heard I got divorced."

"Jinx told me. The guy sounded pretty awful."

"He was. But I asked for it, you know? I thought I was so smart . . . I didn't listen to anybody."

"All of us do that at one time or another." He watched a toddler squeal with delight at the spraying water.

"Want to find someplace quieter?" she asked.

"No. I like it here."

She peered very closely at him for a moment. "You've been in love, haven't you?" she asked.

"What is this, a new mind-reading game?"

"I'm serious," she said. "I can tell."

He didn't say anything, and there was a flicker of pain in her eyes. It made him feel guilty, made him regret that he hadn't loved her or saved her from the disastrous rebound marriage.

"What was it like—being out all over the country?"

He paused in thought. How could he answer that without going on for hours? How could he explain to her that there were whole other worlds out there and that Manhattan was not the USA.

"It was real," he said, then laughed. "You lose sight of things here, and when you travel, everything balances out."

" 'Course, I've been to Paris and London and the Seychelles and all those kinds of places," she assured him quickly. "It's not that I've never been anywhere."

"I've never seen the Seychelles," he said to reassure her.

"They're beautiful. Much nicer than all those overrated Caribbean Islands. A heavenly place for a honeymoon."

The sun glistened in her hair and there were tiny beads of sweat on her forehead, and the way she was squinting against the strong light made her appear to be frowning, and she was suddenly very appealing in her familiarity.

There was an awkward silence.

"It's wild about Gabby working for Jinx, isn't it?" she said, feigning enthusiasm. "Who would have ever imagined when we were kids . . ." She fidgeted with her bracelet. "Did you hear that Perry was back? I haven't seen him yet, but I hear he's pretty much the same."

He smiled in an effort to put her at ease.

"I have so many questions I'd like to ask you," she said.

"Then ask."

"Will you answer?"

He laughed. "Maybe."

"Okay," she said lightly. She leaned back. "Can you still tell time by looking at the sun?"

He laughed again. "Yes."

"Do you still get up so disgustingly early and run every day?"
"Yes."

"Do you still lose your reading glasses all the time?"

He grinned at her and nodded.

"Would you spend the night with me tonight?"

Everything stopped and he felt like he was poised at the top of a roller coaster.

"No one's ever made love to me like you did," she said softly. "I'm not asking for any kind of commitment. I just want a little sweetness in my life. A little warmth."

A vision of Lucy's face haunted him just before he took Whitney's hand.

40

Juliana

Rage simmered just beneath her heart. She couldn't eat, she couldn't sleep through the night, and it was a constant effort to be as calm and wary and watchful as she needed to be.

Ellis pretended that nothing was going on between them. He said polite good-mornings when they passed in the house, and then his eyes slid on as though he had no interest in her. But she knew better. Ellis was waging a war against her. A subtle, sneaky war full of well-planned maneuvers. He'd started the park thing first, stealing all the media attention and gossip-column space that was usually devoted to her—the important Van Lyden. The Van Lyden who mattered. Then he'd seduced Whitney Chandler, who'd been functioning as Juliana's primary companion and co-leader in the social group. He had Whitney behaving like a total fool. And now he was pushing her grandfather toward turning Great House into a museum. Great House. The house that had always been promised as part of her inheritance.

Her grandfather had really fallen for the Clean Up Central Park campaign that Ellis had launched. And everybody, even the goddamn mayor, was making a big fuss over Ellis bringing hawks and owls in.

She couldn't stand it! She wanted to smash television sets and tear up newspapers when she saw his name. People were such fools! Such blind fools!

She dreamed of exposing him, of showing everyone what he really was beneath that practiced facade. But so far Mo Rifkin's men hadn't been able to come up with anything she could use against her cousin. The files were thick, but Ellis had disguised himself well.

And there was nothing to distract her from this infuriating insidious war he had launched. There was nothing good happening in her life. Nothing to be excited about or to look forward to. Gabby woke her each morning with coffee and juice, and the day went down from there. Nightlife ... drugs ... drinking ... shopping. None of it was fun anymore.

And though she was surrounded by people, she was plagued by the most wrenching loneliness. It never went away. It swelled to engulf her right in the middle of dancing with friends or sitting down to Sunday brunch with her family. It followed her when she took a prettyboy to Sparky's old apartment, reminding her that Sparky would never be there again to laugh with her, and that the man she was with laughed only when he thought she wanted him to.

Perry was back in town, but she had not seen him. She knew that she ought to call him and be breezy to show him that his leaving hadn't mattered to her at all. To prove that she had been the one in control and that she had wanted him to leave. But she had been unable to make herself pick up the phone.

Who could cure the loneliness and distract her from the rage? Who did she have left?

She looked at the people around her, and surprisingly, it was her father who drew her interest. His health had returned, but not his ebullience. His dark silences and jaded sarcasm mirrored what she felt inside. Only he seemed beaten, and she most definitely was not.

She began making herself available to him. If he was in a room, she sat down there to flip through her magazine. If he was taking lunch by himself, she joined him. If he was shooting pool, she wandered in and picked up a cue.

"So. Are you ready to forgive me?" he asked one day after they had finished a round of eight ball.

She propped her cue on the edge of the table and studied him. "No," she finally answered. "I can never forgive you as a father. But I might want to be friends."

That was the beginning.

There were quiet matches in the billiard room and crime movies in the screening room and silent three-a.m. drinking bouts. They talked as little as possible, and when they laughed together it was never out of joy. But with her father she could hold the loneliness at bay.

"We're going out tonight," he announced one afternoon. "We're withering away in this damn bloodsucking house. We need to get out."

They dressed in evening clothes and Zeke drove them. As

usual, Zeke was formal in her father's presence. He opened doors for them and behaved as though he was a stranger hired to drive for the night. Zeke had never said a word against Aubrey, but Juliana knew he didn't care for her father.

Aubrey managed to get them a table at the fabled Rainbow Room, where reservations were required six weeks in advance. Juliana had never been there before, and the view through the wide expanses of glass raised her spirits. Manhattan shimmered below them like a fairyland.

"Do you know which buildings belong to Vanden Corporation?" she asked.

Aubrey's chuckle was fairly sarcastic. "What do you know about Vanden Corporation?"

"It's the family business. What else is there to know?"

One side of Aubrey's mouth curved up and he gave an elegant little shrug. "That's exactly what I used to say to your grandfather," he said. "I used to tell him that Vanden has a life of its own, so why should I learn all the niggling, dreary little details."

His mouth curved again. "I used to be able to make your grandfather very angry."

"But not anymore?" she asked.

"No. Your grandfather tired of my rebellion and disinterest a long, long time ago. That's what cast you as the great white hope, you know—his giving up on me."

Juliana thought about that for a moment. She had always assumed that her grandfather had never considered Aubrey for his successor. "You mean you were his hope before me?"

"Was I ever." Aubrey shook his head. "I was groomed for it from the moment of birth. I was the golden boy ... the future of the clan. I could do no wrong."

"And what happened?"

He laughed. "I finally did enough wrong to open his eyes."

"What about Grace? Did he ever think that she might ...?"

"You're not serious? Grace never had any strength. She had the audacity to want normal things—a plebian education, a commoner husband, a life as a wife and mother. He considered Grace flawed from the beginning, and then lost to him completely after she married Frank."

"And her child was lost too," Juliana filled in.

"Ellis? Yes. And doubly so after the kidnapping. Ellis might as well have been dead as far as Edward was concerned."

"So I was the choice by default."

"Yes."

"Unless you and Mother had had other children."

Aubrey hesitated. "That wasn't a possibility." He raised his eyebrows and grinned. "I had a vasectomy right after you were born."

Juliana didn't know what to say.

"It goes back quite a ways," he explained. "My own mother didn't leave me anything. Assuming me to be in line for the entire empire, she set up her trust to benefit my children. That was the trust you came into last year.

"I was college age when I finally crashed with Edward. He put me on a survival allowance and set up a trust that would be mine only if I gave him a legitimate heir. He also agreed to move out of Great House when I brought home the wife to produce this heir. It was all very businesslike."

"And my mother . . . did she know about this?"

"Not in the beginning. She found out eventually."

"And why the vasectomy?"

"Because my contract called for only one heir." He paused. "And because I knew how badly he wanted another grandchild."

"A grandson," she said flatly.

"Yes. A grandson." He chuckled ruefully.

Juliana turned her head toward the sparkling city. Everything looked so beautiful from far away. It was a shame that it ever had to be seen up close.

"But now he has a grandson," she said.

"What? Oh, you mean Ellis?"

"Yes. Ellis isn't dead or lost anymore. He's right here and he's sucking up to Grandfather with his grandstanding civic projects."

Aubrey studied her without responding.

"I won't let him take it away," she hissed fiercely. "I won't let him worm his way into what's mine with his do-gooder act."

"Jinx . . ." Aubrey's expression was compassionate. "I'm afraid it's too late. Your grandfather is already quite sold on Ellis."

The bottom dropped from Juliana's stomach. "What do you mean?"

"Your grandfather is very impressed with Ellis. Says that he's the first Van Lyden in generations who understands the meaning of work. He's become convinced that Ellis' philanthropic leanings will restore the family's image. And now, with the rumors of an engagement . . . I'm afraid there's no question of his favor shifting to Ellis."

"An engagement?"

"Henry Chandler told your grandfather that Whitney and Ellis are almost ready to make it official. That's all your grandfather needs . . ."

"I don't understand. He hasn't been anxious for me to marry."

"That's different. You're a woman. He wants to make sure you're tough enough to be a Van Lyden first and a wife second before you marry. Ellis is a man, so your grandfather just assumes that he will always be able to keep his feelings for a wife in perspective. With Ellis he sees marriage as a sign of the stability he's been lacking. And of course the fact that the bride is from a family nearly equal to our own and the granddaughter of one of Edward's oldest acquaintances is a powerful argument as well."

"But I . . . I'm the Van Lyden heir. I always have been. I'm the one who's done everything Grandfather wanted me to and . . ." Her voice developed a childish catch and she couldn't swallow away the lump in her throat.

"Oh, it's not so bad, Jinx." Aubrey reached across the table to pat her hand. "You've been too important to Edward. He's not going to write you out completely. My guess is that he'll split the works between the two of you." He chuckled softly. "Even half will make you one of the richest women in the world."

"But I won't be the heir. I won't be *the heir.*"

"But you'll be off the hook. Think about what a relief that will be. No more catering to that hard-nosed old bastard. You'll be free! You can flee that musty old prison and buy houses in England and Morocco and the Fiji Islands. Take lovers who don't even speak your language. Your life has been so insular. It's about time you started to see the world."

"But I don't want to go anywhere. I love Great House. Great House is supposed to be mine someday. Mine! I'm the heir! I'm the one who had to stay safe and had to be—"

"Jinx . . . Jinx . . ." Her father pried the wineglass from her fingers and stroked her hands until her clenched fists relaxed.

She took a deep breath and dropped her hands to her lap to hide the marks where her nails had dug into her palms. She had to stay calm. She had to think this out.

He filled in with meaningless chatter then, pointing out an overweight couple on the dance floor and discussing the merits of the band's Cuban sound.

She nodded absently as he spoke, and followed him across the dance floor after dinner, but she wasn't there anymore. All she could think about was Ellis. There was still time. She knew there was still time. She would stop Ellis and she would hold on to what was hers.

"Would you like dessert or a liqueur?" her father asked.

She nodded and found herself with a Grand Marnier to sip. The trickle of fire in her aching throat was good. The pain helped her focus.

Across the table was a man. Who was he? Never really a father. Not quite a friend. Suddenly she realized that he was her ally. Not as trustworthy as Zeke or as devoted as Gabby, but an ally nonetheless.

"Are you glad you came home?" she asked.

"Well," he said carefully, "I wanted to talk to you about that."

Juliana sipped at her drink.

"I ... Well, remember I told you that I received a settlement when you were born?"

She nodded.

"It's gone. I'm broke."

"That's why you came home?"

"Partly." He shook his head in resignation. "I was ready to come back, though. Not back under my father's wing, mind you ... but back."

"To be with me?" she said, testing his candor.

"Yes."

She waited, wondering how many other lies he would tell.

"When I came back, I was broke and disheartened and ill and I hadn't the strength to resist your grandfather. My companion was dead and I'd just been released from the hospital in Morocco, where I'd been suffering from a horrid bone virus."

Companion. What exactly did that mean? Had her father had a lover?

"Was she very important to you?"

"Who?"

"Your companion who died."

He gave her an odd little smile. "He, Jinx. He. Oh ... he seemed important, but I suppose that's only because we hadn't been together long."

She sat very still. Very, very still. This was her father. She couldn't pretend she hadn't heard. She couldn't turn away from the truth the way she'd turned away from Sparky's ramblings about the mystery man. Her expression must have given her away, because suddenly there was fear in his eyes.

"I just assumed you knew, Jinx. I was sure Sparky would have told you."

"No," she managed to say weakly. "Sparky never told me. There were hints, but ..."

Aubrey's face clouded with emotion. "This is all wrong," he said. "I never intended for ... I just assumed that Sparky had cried on your shoulder and told you every detail. I thought you knew everything there was to know about my private life."

"Did my mother know?"

"Yes."

"But I don't understand. I read an old letter you wrote to her. You loved her. How can you be gay and—"

"I'm not gay," Aubrey countered indignantly. "I'm not like Sparky and his weak little friends."

Juliana stared at him, trying to make sense out of what she was hearing.

"When I took Sparky in, he had a beautiful innocent strength. I thought I could help him develop that. But he failed me. He turned weak and frivolous. He lost the inner core that connects men to men. You see, that's what being gay is. It's when a man loses that glorious age-old male connection. It's not about sexual preference. Sex is a secondary issue. It's an effect ... not a cause."

He leaned toward her across the table. "Men have a courage and a purity you'll never know, Jinx. I tried to keep your mother happy, but how could I stay with her? How could I give up the man in me? How could I give up the bonds that form when you slip on a rock face and a strong pair of hands pulls you to safety, or when you sight rifles side by side and take down an animal in tandem, or when you step onto a playing field as teammates?"

He paused, but continued to hold her eyes. "Your mother was the most unique and desirable woman I've ever met, but no woman on earth can compete with those bonds. With the bravery and the beauty and the intensity possible between men."

Silence fell between them. Juliana felt drained of all energy and emotion. She saw her father for exactly what he was beneath that charismatic aura: twisted and disturbed and hypocritical, but curiously clinging to some better image of himself and his life. And curiously admirable.

"Do you hate me now?" he asked.

She hesitated before answering, but the truth was that she didn't hate him. She felt a complete absence of emotion. "This last companion didn't die of AIDS, did he?" she asked.

"No. That's an illness for the weak."

"Real men don't die of AIDS, huh?" she asked sarcastically.

"I get enough comments like that from my father."

"Grandfather? He discusses things like that with you?"

"In private, of course. He believes that he's finally gotten me under his thumb and that I'm forced to listen to whatever ignorance he chooses to display."

"How can you stand that?"

"That's precisely the problem. Now that my health is recovered, I *can't* stand it. I cannot live in the same house with him."

"So where will you go? What can you do? You said you had no money . . ."

The word hung in the air. Of course. That was what he wanted. That was the reason for the dinner and dancing and the shared confidences. He wanted money from her. Instead of hurting or angering her, the realization filled her with relief.

Money was something she had plenty of. As long as he needed her for money, she could own him. But she had to be careful. If she was too generous, he might get restless and take off.

"I'll buy you an apartment in Manhattan," she said. "And I'll set up a monthly allowance through my attorney—payable only as long as you keep your traveling to a minimum."

He expelled a deep breath. "Would you care to dance again?"

"No. Get my coat and call for Zeke. I'm ready to go home."

In the car Juliana settled silently back and watched as her father poured himself a drink from the recessed bar. His hands shook slightly.

Did she hate him? As a father, yes. And as her mother's husband, yes.

She closed her eyes for a moment.

"Why did she do it, Papa? Why?"

Aubrey stiffened. "I prefer not to talk about that."

"I don't care what you prefer. I want to talk about it."

His jaw tightened.

"Why did she leave us that way?"

He took a long swallow of his drink and his manner shifted into a defensiveness bordering on anger.

"Because life wasn't what she wanted it to be. Because she never learned to be flexible, to take things as they came and make her own happiness."

Flexible. Odd that he should have used that word. Matt had once said that Ellis was dangerous because he'd never learned to be flexible.

"I always wondered if it was partly my fault."

"No," he said. "If anything, you were the reason she didn't do it sooner."

"And Ellis. Don't tell me he isn't to blame."

"Why this 'blame' fixation? What does it matter now?"

"It matters. I know Ellis killed her."

"That's absurd."

"She loved him. I could see it when she looked at him."

"What of it? She loved you and she loved me as well. Does that make us killers?"

"I don't know," Juliana said. "Does it?"

Aubrey scowled. "I refuse to probe this wound of yours any further."

Fine, Juliana thought to herself. She would let him go this time, but only because she had other things on her mind.

Her father was hers now. She had won him absolutely, and the bittersweet taste of that victory made her better prepared to go against Ellis. If a war of wits was what Ellis wanted, then she was ready to give it to him.

She would reactivate her interest in her grandfather's collection and never-ending museum plans. That was something Ellis couldn't compete with. And she would develop an attraction to good causes. Two could play that game. Ellis might have a corner on the environmental issues, but New York was full of other opportunities. Something to do with the arts, maybe. Her grandfather was a sucker for that. Handicapped painters' art exhibitions or underprivileged children's dance programs or recognition for women in literature. She chuckled to herself with delight. The possibilities were endless.

But the first order of business was the impending Whitney Chandler–Ellis Van Lyden engagement. There had to be a way to break up that nonsense.

She tried to remember all the things Whit had spilled in their last heart-to-heart talk some months ago. What had Whit been moaning about? Something about a woman that Ellis was hung up on. A woman that he couldn't forget. That was an avenue worth exploring. She would have Mo Rifkin check the files to see what he could find out about it. Another woman might be just the antidote to a Van Lyden–Chandler alliance.

And then there was always Perry. She could impress her grandfather with a sensible interest in William Perry Lorillard-Harris, whose family was every bit as blue-blooded as Whitney Chandler's and whose grandfather was also one of Edward's longtime acquaintances.

Yes. There were solutions to everything. A person just had to be willing to do whatever was necessary.

Now she saw what Matt and her father meant when they talked about flexibility. About people needing flexibility or lacking flexibility. She had it. She knew when to bend.

41

Lucy

Lucy looked in the mirror at herself. It was her birthday. She was thirty-two years old.

Today she was taking herself out to lunch and balancing the treat with a dreaded round of taking her portfolio to galleries. She had stayed in Dallas after the funeral because she needed a change and because there were more opportunities than in Kansas City. More places to show her work. More places to invite criticism and rejection.

She wrinkled her nose at her reflection and began making herself presentable for the outside world. If she hadn't been forcing herself into such masochism, she would have stayed in her worn sweatsuit. It was all she wore lately. The only thing she didn't do in it was sweat. She hadn't felt like running for a while. Not since Suki's death.

It was still hard to believe that Suki was gone. She kept waiting for the phone to ring.

Suki had been calling her weekly in Kansas City to cry and moan and babble, and one day Lucy just couldn't take it. She had been hurting over Ellis and trying to put her work back on track and she didn't have the patience to sit through another whining session, so she had told Suki she didn't want to hear any more. She had told her sister to grow up and get the courage to do something about her life. Suki had been sobbing as she hung up.

Lucy could still hear that sound. It made her ache inside to think of it.

The next day Del called to say that Suki had consumed the wrong combination of pills and alcohol and was in a coma. Lucy dropped everything. She packed her possessions into the Volkswagen and headed for Dallas.

She had failed her sister. She had failed to be there when Suki needed her.

She sat beside the narrow hospital bed every day and held Suki's hand and stared at the tubes and wires and begged Suki to get well. Begged Suki to give her another chance. But Suki died anyway. There was no second chance. Suki had needed her and she had been too wrapped up in herself to respond.

Del didn't offer any help, so Lucy took all responsibility for the funeral. She arranged a private service, using up the small cash cushion she had left in her savings account; then she took Suki's body back to Walea to bury her next to Wanda and Lydell.

She was not surprised when Preston Tully showed up at the cemetery with his wife and twin boys. The Walea grapevine was still working and she was sure that others knew about the burial as well. She thanked Preston and fussed over his apple-cheeked, squirmy toddlers. But instead of cheering her, the presence of the babies only made the pain in her heart worse.

She was thirty-two years old. What did her life amount to? She had no one left to care about and she was nearly broke and her work was unanimously hated by everyone who saw it and she barely had the energy to get up in the morning.

She finished applying the small amount of makeup she used for public occasions and stared at her reflection. The woman in the mirror was a stranger. An over-thirty stranger. A grown-up.

She touched her cheek. Who had Ellis seen when he looked at her? Who had he wanted? And how many more years would it take for her to forget him?

Wearily she brushed her hair back off her face and gathered it into one thick braid in the back. When she was finished she pulled the braid around so it hung forward across her shoulder. She had the urge to cut it off the same way she'd done after leaving Buddy. To chop and hack at it with her nail scissors until she had a ragged stump to throw out. But she had to look decent for peddling her wares. She had to look like someone who took pretty pictures or they might not let her in the door. Except that she didn't make pretty pictures anymore. Her work had changed dramatically.

After Ellis she had buried herself in darkroom technique and come up with the effect she wanted. She had perfected the combining of images, sometimes incorporating sharp elements into one print and sometimes creating a mix of blurry and sharp elements. Some of her prints were random collections of images and some were calculated—items she arranged or live models she hired and posed exactly to her specifications. Some of her prints were a joining of the two.

After she achieved a combination that satisfied her, she added touches. Sometimes she glued things into the print—tiny black-and-white images onto a color print, or vice versa. Most often she painted the photographs. Small dashes of color usually, but every piece was a surprise because she never knew which techniques would feel best as she worked toward her desired effect.

After Ellis there was a new dimension to the visions in her mind's eye. Sex. Ellis had awakened a part of her that flowed over into her work, and a portion of her prints now had sexual undertones. A few were even overtly sexual. They weren't remotely pornographic, however. Or at least she hoped no one viewed them as such.

The print she'd devoted the most time to was the largest and most complex of her collection. She had hired three models. Three teenage girls. A round, dimpled redhead, a gangly girl with chestnut hair, and a slouchy lank-haired brunette. She had posed them in simple dresses and used huge rented fans to blow their clothes and hair wildly in all directions. She shot them in color.

Then, after much experimentation, she had captured a shot of a whirlpool in a large tub of water. Not quite a tornado, but as close as she could come. She enlarged it so that the tub was cropped out and the swirling water filled the print, giving the appearance of a dark liquid tornado that the viewer was looking down into. Still not satisfied, she worked with her tornado, experimenting with different blurring techniques so it looked more like a dense swirling air mass. To this swirling air she painstakingly added what appeared from a short distance to be bits of debris. Up close the tiny pictures could be identified as run-down trailer houses and beat-up pickup trucks and rusting refrigerators and shabby overstuffed furniture. All in black and white. Then, in the eye of the tornado she incorporated the color shot of the three windblown girls. Her title for it was *Texas Trash*.

She had had the final product framed and kept it propped up against the wall opposite her bed. It was inspiring or amusing or depressing, depending on her mood. She would have liked to have everything framed, but she couldn't afford it. Her cash nest egg had been gobbled up by camera equipment and models' fees and developing supplies. And Suki's burial.

She flipped the braid back out of the way and frowned at her reflection. "You are going to have a positive attitude today," she said. The woman in the mirror appeared skeptical.

She stopped to check her mailbox on the way out. Three envelopes at once. It was like hitting a jackpot. She glanced through them and opened the one from Duff in Kansas City first. It was a birthday card. A silly riddle card in which Duff had pasted a cut-out of Lucy's face over the face of the woman inside the card. On the back was a note:

Hope you're doing well and keeping your nose clean. Not much new around here. Thinking of selling the store and moving to California. Let me know if you're interested. Ha ha! (In either the store or in going to Calif!) There's been people trying to track you down. Bet you didn't know you were so popular. Been giving out your current address. Hope that's okay.

Miss you,
Duff

She felt a rush of tenderness. How sweet of him to remember her birthday. If only she'd been able to feel something for him. Good, dependable, trustworthy, loyal Duff. How nice it would have been if she'd slipped into a safe loving relationship with Duff instead of falling into Ellis' magnetic field.

Coasting on the good feelings, she ripped open the credit-card company's envelope. Rejection! Damn, damn, damn. She crumpled the form letter into a ball.

She started toward her car. Three little black girls were playing tea party in the weeds beside the walk and she squatted down beside them and asked if the white rabbit was there yet. They exchanged wide-eyed glances and told her they weren't allowed to talk to strangers.

"That's right," she told them, and quickly moved along. They confirmed what she'd thought upon seeing herself in the mirror that morning. She was a stranger.

Absently she tore open the remaining piece of mail. It was from some foundation or other in New York. Probably wanting money from her to free all laboratory rats or to support research into flying nuclear waste to the moon. She seemed to attract mail like that wherever she lived.

It appeared to be a letter rather than the customary illustrated brochure. She unfolded it.

Ms. Lucy Clare:
    You have been selected for inclusion in the Van Lyden Foundation's *New Women in Photography* show . . .

She read the letter through, looking for the gimmick or the catch. There had to be one. This couldn't be real. Twice she read it. Then three times. They were sending her an airline ticket. They were mailing her a check to cover shipping her work to the show. They were paying all expenses while she was in New York. At the bottom was a telephone number she could call collect if she had any questions or needed assistance in making her travel and shipping arrangements.

She read it through one more time, then raced for the telephone.

42

Juliana

"It worked, Zeke!"

Juliana slid into the back of her car.

"It worked! The woman called an hour ago. She's coming."

Zeke shook his head and flashed her a look of exasperated amusement. "Her comin' is no guarantee this thing's gonna work."

New Women in Photography was real enough. The show had been set up through the fledgling foundation Juliana had created for her philanthropic activities. So far she had a downtown office, a telephone line, and a secretary, and she had four different projects in the works. She'd come up with the idea after learning that Ellis' old flame was a hack photographer out in Middle America somewhere. And she'd hatched the plan to lure the woman to New York.

The war with Ellis had escalated, and Juliana couldn't afford any weakness. Her grandfather was wholeheartedly backing Ellis' expanding park and playground refurbishments now, and he'd begun to discuss making Great House into a museum as though it were an actual possibility. Great House. The house where her mother had died. Her house. The last of the great privately owned mansions in Manhattan, and it had always, always been promised to her.

Ellis was spouting tripe about the house being a work of art that should be shared, and he'd gotten her grandfather all excited because he'd given Edward the idea that both Mignon and Great House should be put into some kind of museum trusts, with Edward's collection on display at one and the Van Lyden historical art and guns on display at the other.

And everybody was talking about how wonderful Ellis was and how he was revitalizing the family. But she knew what was really happening. Ellis had tried to steal her mother from her and now he wanted her birthright.

500

She wouldn't let him have it. None of it. She would burn Great House to the ground before she let him steal it out from under her.

She had spent hours raging at Mo Rifkin, telling him to find some legal way to stop all this. A way to block any transfers of property or any revisions of Edward's will. A way to declare her grandfather incompetent, if need be. A way to keep Ellis from destroying everything. But Mo had not found a way.

All she could do publicly was be the dutiful granddaughter and recently inspired supporter of the arts. Privately she had started luring Perry. And secretly she was acting as fairy god-mother to a certain female photographer who just might be the answer to everything. Mo's detectives had put together a thorough file on the woman for Juliana, details not only on the woman's relationship with Ellis but also on her pre-Ellis history as well, and Juliana saw great potential there.

In the beginning her intention had been simply to wave the woman around and effect a breakup of Ellis and Whitney. Now she thought even more might be accomplished. If she could get Ellis and the woman back together, her grandfather would come to his senses fast. Wait till Edward got a load of Lucy Clare's background. It would make Yvonne look like a princess from an ivory tower. To that end she had concocted a plan for getting the woman into New York weeks before the show and keeping her there some time afterward.

Thinking of the possibilities filled her with delight as she dropped by Rifkin's office to sign the check for her father's new apartment, and she was in a euphoric mood when she arrived at Perry's downtown loft.

"I'll buzz you on the car phone if I'm staying over," she told Zeke. He nodded and waved her into the building. She hoped she did spend the night.

She walked into Perry's high-ceilinged cavernous space to find that Perry had cooked dinner for her. By himself. With no ser-vants or any help at all. She was too surprised to speak. The table was set with flowers and candles and the food was nicely arranged in bowls and platters. No one, male or female, had ever cooked for her unless paid to do it.

"What is it?" she asked.

"Baked ziti with three cheeses," he said. "And a salad of aru-gula and pine nuts. Followed by a dessert that cannot be divulged yet."

All through dinner he kept looking at her. Watching her with his dark poet's eyes. His appearance hadn't changed much in the years he'd been gone, but he was different. He was much tougher. And so far she hadn't been able to crack through the distant amusement or spark the tiniest flicker of vulnerability in those eyes.

She thought he wanted her. But she couldn't even be sure of that. He'd resisted all her advances.

She nodded and pretended interest in his "God as metaphor" discussion while she studied his eyes and hands. He had to want her. How would she ever get control of him and use him to impress her grandfather if he didn't want her sexually?

"This is such a strange place to live," she commented after he'd wound down on metaphors.

He laughed. She liked his laugh. The way his dark eyes narrowed down to slits and crescent-shaped lines appeared at the corners of his mouth and the faint dimple in his square chin deepened.

"This is an almost normal place to live," he teased. "That mausoleum you call home is a strange place to live."

She waited a heartbeat.

"Are you going to make love to me tonight?"

She was tired of subtlety.

"It depends," he said.

She'd expected to throw him off-center with the question, but nothing seemed to faze him anymore. "Depends on what?" she asked, trying to keep the annoyance out of her voice.

"On how badly you want it."

"Hah!" She stood up and threw her napkin down on the table. "You've got a lot of nerve!"

He stood to face her.

"When we were younger, I let you have things your way, Jinx, and you wrecked it. This time we're doing it my way."

He leaned toward her slightly, and the intensity of his gaze made her hold her breath.

"I don't want your power-trip sex or your imitation-of-a-climax sex. I don't want your games or your tests or your challenges. No, Juliana, we're not going to bed together until you want to fuck me so bad you can't stand it. Until you want to tear my skin open and suck on my heart. Until you want me inside you as much as I want to be there.

"I won't settle for less."

He reached across the table, picked up her napkin, and held it out to her.

"So sit down and behave while I get dessert."

43

Lucy

Lucy left the snug confines of the airplane and moved down the long canal of the jetway. Everything she owned was in her suitcases or in the crates she'd shipped. She'd left nothing behind her. But what was ahead?

She emerged into the bright clamor of La Guardia Airport and was momentarily disoriented. People brushed by her. The P.A. system blared. She felt suddenly small and uncertain. Then she saw the large black man with the sign: "LUCY CLARE FROM DALLAS."

"I'm Lucy Clare," she said.

He smiled a slightly off-kilter smile and the tiny gold cross in his ear winked. "I'm Zeke," he said. "Follow me."

He took her carry-on bag from her and led her to an open area where a woman was watching something inside a large Plexiglas box. It was a giant version of a fascinating toy—a whimsical perpetual-motion device with balls that dropped from buckets and roller-coastered down different channels and tripped switches to trigger bells and new movements before eventually returning to the beginning to start again. The effect was an endless cycle governed by random chance.

The woman was totally engrossed. She was Lucy's age or slightly younger, and she had unusual coloring. Skin tones of ripe apricot and eyes the color of clear whiskey. Her platinum hair didn't suit Lucy's artistic sense, but it did nothing to detract from the woman's beauty. She would make a fascinating portrait subject.

"This is Miss Van Lyden," Zeke said, and the woman smiled politely.

"Call me Juliana."

"You got your baggage tickets?" Zeke asked.

Lucy fished them out and handed them to Zeke, who promptly disappeared.

"Have you ever seen one of these?" Juliana asked.

Lucy shook her head, and the two of them stood transfixed for several minutes watching the travels of the metal balls. Lucy was grateful for the distraction. She hadn't expected to be met by Juliana Van Lyden herself, even though she had had two brief phone conversations with the woman. One to confirm that she was coming and then another just days ago offering an interesting free-lance job—photographing the details of the Van Lyden mansion and the individual items in an art collection.

Lucy had quickly accepted. But beyond the show and the job, she had no plans. She was afraid to consider the future. Her savings account had been mortally wounded by all the framing and packing, and though she'd been promised a premium for the Van Lyden work, she had no illusions about how far the money would take her if she stayed in New York.

She was living entirely in the present now. But what a present! New York City. She could remember talking about New York City with Ms. Conroy. The mecca of the art world, Ms. Conroy had called it. She had said anything was possible in New York. She had also said that New York was farther from Walea, Texas, than the moon.

Zeke gathered them into a long white limousine. Lucy had to suppress a laugh as she climbed in. A real limousine. The idea of Lucy Clare from Walea riding in a stretch limousine was hilarious.

"Would you like something to drink?" Juliana asked, revealing a compact refreshment bar.

"No. Thank you."

The woman was cool and composed, as only those with power over others can be. Lucy could feel the woman scrutinizing her.

"I guess you don't get many visitors from Texas," Lucy said.

The woman brushed over the comment without response, saying, "You're booked into a suite at the Sherry-Netherland this week. Your apartment sublet begins after that. Zeke will arrange a car and driver for you."

"Thank you . . . but it still seems like too much."

"I thought we'd already agreed upon the terms of your employment," Juliana said curtly.

"Yes, we have," Lucy said with a smile. "But I'm afraid I'm long past the days of thinking a client is always right. You'll probably have to put up with a lot of questions from me."

This is business, Lucy told herself. This is the way rich New York women conduct business. She would not take it personally. She turned her head to concentrate on the city passing outside the dark glass.

"What area is this?"

"Zeke, where are we?" Juliana called.

"This is Queens," Zeke said over his shoulder. "We're takin' the Triborough Bridge into the city."

Juliana continued to study her. Tension curled from her like invisible smoke. "Do you have any decent clothes?"

Lucy glanced down at the khaki skirt that had seemed just right for traveling. It was wrinkled and had a pattern of mysterious gray smudges. "I didn't bring my ball gowns, but I can do better than this," she said, hoping to lighten the mood.

Juliana did not smile. "Zeke," she said, "call Gabby and tell her to meet us at the hotel. She can go through Lucy's things and decide what's appropriate for the city. I suspect we'll have to do some filling in."

Lucy was incredulous. "Excuse me, but I don't need any help with my clothes."

"She's my assistant," Juliana said regally. "That's part of her function."

"That's fine, but my clothes are my own business."

"I am only trying to save you from embarrassment, Lucy. You do want to project a successful image, don't you?"

"Oh . . . I wouldn't want people to get us mixed up," Lucy said, trying again for something lighter.

It fell flat.

Juliana's eyes dissected her. Lucy could feel a strange blend of curiosity and disdain in the sidelong glances.

"Is there something you'd like to ask me?" Lucy finally said.

Juliana pulled back slightly. "Why?"

"The way you keep looking at me."

"You're not what I expected," Juliana said coolly. "You're not *nearly* what I expected."

"Oh?" Lucy smiled and met her eyes with a sideways glance of her own. "You're not what I expected either. I was so afraid that you'd be a bitch."

A charged silence fell in the car. Lucy imagined the loss of both show and job. The return trip to the airport. The "Don't ever come back to New York" orders as she was thrown onto a plane. But she still wasn't sorry. She'd come too far in life to put up with petty hostility and mind games.

Suddenly the tension evaporated. Amusement played in Juliana's eyes and tugged at the corners of her mouth. "I'll pick you up for dinner at eight," she said.

Zeke glanced up at them in the rearview mirror and Lucy saw that the dinner was a surprise to him.

"Oh, you don't have to . . . I didn't expect . . ."

"I insist. . . . Please."

"All right. Thank you."

Juliana

Juliana leaned back in her chair and watched Lucy cross the restaurant in search of the bathroom. She hadn't known where to take a dirt-poor Texan to dinner, but Zeke had suggested Tavern on the Green and it was a good choice. The diverse crowd and the visual distractions filled the holes in the conversation. Nevertheless she'd insisted that Zeke join them as a backup measure.

"What do you think, Zeke?" she asked without taking her eyes off the retreating figure.

Zeke turned his head to watch Lucy along with her. "I think you're not so sure a things anymore," he drawled.

"What do you mean?"

Zeke shrugged.

Juliana tried to read his eyes, but that was impossible, as usual. She gave up and pulled out her cigarette case. "I was so certain she'd be pathetic and shallow and backward. I mean, you read her file too . . . isn't that what you thought?"

"You got ta be careful with files," Zeke said. "They don't always give ya the real picture."

"Yes, well, I certainly had Lucy Clare wrong. God, I'd give anything to know what really went on between her and Ellis. I'll bet she saw through him from the beginning. I'll bet she hates him now."

"Maybe," Zeke said. "Maybe not. Love is strange."

"I know I'm right," Juliana insisted. "She's not like Whitney at all! She's not the kind of woman to fall for someone like Ellis." She lit a cigarette. "I need to rethink my plans. She's not as . . . as tractable as I thought she'd be. I'm afraid she might pack up and leave if I don't handle things carefully."

Juliana smoked and thought while she waited for Lucy to return. It had all seemed so clear before. Get the simple little Texan here, make her happy by throwing her the show and the job, and then shove her in front of Ellis. But Lucy hadn't turned out to be so simple.

"Maybe she should be settled into the job and the city before I let Ellis discover her. I want to make sure she's into everything enough that she won't want to leave town the minute she sees him."

"Show's in five weeks," Zeke said. "Chances are he'll hear her name then anyway."

"That might work out okay." She mashed her half-smoked French cigarette into the ashtray. "By then she'll be well into photographing the art collection and she'll be in her own apartment. She wouldn't walk out on all that."

Lucy appeared in the doorway and started back toward them. She had on a black straight skirt and a red silk T-shirt and a man's black-and-silver paisley smoking jacket from the thirties.

"Can you believe that she admitted buying that jacket at a secondhand store?" Juliana said, watching Lucy intently.

The woman had a quirky, pleasing grace and a calm dignity. She had an appealing sense of humor—dry and understated, but never cruel. And there was something else about her ... some elusive undercurrent in her eyes ... a gentle sadness, a weary acceptance ... something ... Something that reminded Juliana of her mother.

"What do you think, Zeke? Maybe I should send out for some secondhand clothing?"

A faint shadow of amusement played across Zeke's face. "What's the new plan?" he asked.

"I don't know. Maybe I should entertain her a little, make sure she enjoys it here. Maybe I should be friendly."

Lucy

Lucy awoke the next morning and wandered through her suite. The luxurious bedroom. The huge Queen Anne living room with the view of Central Park and Grand Army Plaza. The elegant, old-fashioned bathroom with its etched-glass shower and vintage bathtub and spigots in the shape of water sprites. She still couldn't believe it all.

She poured juice from the stocked refrigerator in the service kitchen and began to get ready. Juliana was to pick her up in less than an hour.

The woman was a complete puzzle to her. She'd been so cool and bitchy at first, and then almost too friendly by the end of dinner. Lucy had felt like a contestant in some game whose rules and whose object she didn't know. Only Juliana knew. And the woman was constantly measuring and analyzing, scoring Lucy's performance.

It was infuriating. But it was also intriguing. And Lucy was strangely drawn to her. There was an intensity about Juliana, and an exciting unpredictability, as if she were living on an inner edge. Lucy wanted to share that edge, even for just a moment, wanted to look beneath the shifting surfaces of the woman and discover the source of that intensity. And she wanted to capture it on film.

The white limousine arrived precisely on time. Lucy slid into the back. This morning Juliana wore her chin-length hair loose. It hung casually across one eye. She was dressed in tailored beige linen slacks, a striking ornate leather belt, and a billowy silk blouse.

"You promised casual dress," Lucy said.

Juliana glanced down at herself as though surprised by the comment.

"That's not casual," Lucy assured her. She held out her arms to display her own jeans and embroidered Mexican shirt. *"This* is casual."

"All right, then," Juliana said. "The first thing we'll do is go shopping." She leaned forward slightly. "Zeke, take us someplace interesting to shop. Not the designer boutiques or the big stores. Someplace different."

An hour later they were wandering through the streets of SoHo and Greenwich Village. Zeke followed them with the packages and bags that Juliana was accumulating. It was fun for a while. There were odd little places to poke through. There was a high-fashion clothing store, Rue des Rêves, that was full of roaming animals—dogs and cats and birds and fish. And of course there was the wonderful street life to savor. The corner musicians and the pushcart vendors and the artists who propped their work against walls. The wildly divergent dress and attitudes and ethnic mix of the people who spilled across the sidewalks and streets.

But the vitality and energy of the surroundings were quickly over-shadowed by Juliana's voracious appetite.

There was something ugly about the way she swept into a shop and bought piles of clothes without even trying them on. Finally Lucy could take no more.

"That's it," she said. "If we go in one more clothing store, I'll scream."

"I've had enough too," Juliana agreed. She'd forsaken her linen and silk for a pair of frayed, preworn jeans and a loose African batik shirt. "This is really fun. I don't know why I never thought of coming down here before."

Zeke went after the car and they wandered slowly, peering in the windows of small art galleries while they waited for him. At the corner a young man had spread out a sampling of his work. The paintings were complex and amusing.

"These are very good," Lucy said, pausing to look closer at one.

"You like them?" Juliana asked.

"Yes. They're wonderful." She smiled up at the bespectacled young artist and he beamed back at her. He had a fascinating face. A blend of Asian and black. And she wished she hadn't let Zeke talk her into leaving her camera in the car.

"We'll take them," Juliana announced. "We'll take them all."

The young man was stunned and then jubilant. "I didn't tell you the prices yet," he said.

"Whatever." Juliana waved her hand dismissively. "Just package them up quickly, please. This woman's from out of town and we have sightseeing to do." She turned and smiled at Lucy.

It was a guileless smile, full of the pleasure of life, and Lucy was torn between exasperation and amused wonder.

Juliana

Lucy had been in town a month and her presence had changed Juliana's life. Juliana's days were no longer empty. She didn't have to pacify the gnawing loneliness with trips to her father's new apartment. She didn't have to sit around Great House and listen to Ellis' latest exploits. She had Lucy.

Even now that Lucy had started to work on photographing the

art collection at Mignon, they were together most of the time. Juliana met her at Mignon early each morning and sipped cappuccino while she answered Lucy's questions about individual pieces and about the American Aesthetic Movement. She liked being the expert for Lucy. She liked the respectful way Lucy listened to her.

She perched on her chair, assuming what she hoped was an intellectual air. "Some say it's not quite real art because it encompasses the decorative and the functional—ceramics and wall hangings and silver and stained glass. It's the old 'painting-and-sculpting-are-everything mentality,' " she explained one day.

"That makes your grandfather a sort of hero," Lucy said. "For collecting and preserving all this beauty ... even back when it wasn't fashionable."

Juliana laughed. "Heroics had nothing to do with it. He chose the period because it was controversial and because no one had built a comprehensive collection on it yet. It was a good way to make a name for himself. And he'd dump everything right now if he found out he couldn't have a museum in his own name."

Lucy shook her head sadly. "It's a shame that the collection isn't yours. I can tell by the way you talk about each piece that you have a real appreciation for it."

Juliana sailed on the praise.

Even after Lucy went into her creative trance and stopped asking questions, Juliana always stayed. Juliana loved to watch her. Her absorption and attention to detail were fascinating. Juliana had never seen anyone so caught up in something, and she longed to join in, to be captivated by whatever it was that held Lucy when she stepped into that circle of lights and tripods and lenses.

"Will you teach me?" she asked.

"Sure," Lucy said.

"Great! I'll send out for cameras. What kind should I get?"

"No. No. No." Lucy shook her head emphatically, and for a moment Juliana was afraid she was angry. "You can learn on my equipment. Why buy anything till you find out whether or not you like it?"

Lucy talked off and on as she worked, softly explaining the lighting and the results she was after on each piece. Juliana tried to pay attention, but she wasn't really interested in the glare or the shadows or what Lucy called the essence of each object. What she wanted was the key to the mystery. To Lucy's mystery.

They'd fallen into a routine. Lucy worked till two, then they had a long lunch together and spent the afternoons wandering through museums and galleries. In the evening they had dinner out and saw a play or a concert, or they strolled and talked and watched the street life. One night Juliana invited Perry to join them, but otherwise she kept Lucy completely to herself.

"Seems like she's been here longer than four weeks, doesn't it?" Juliana said to Zeke on their way to meet Lucy at Mignon in the morning.

Zeke didn't reply to that. Instead he said, "What're ya gonna do next week when the show opens?"

"I don't know. Damn! I wish she wasn't in that stupid show. I need more time to figure things out. And she'll probably end up being humiliated anyway. I feel so bad now about putting her work up against all those New York photographers."

"Have you seen any of her stuff yet?"

"No. I know it arrived at the foundation but I've been afraid to go look. What if she's terrible? Oh, God . . ."

"Are you tryin' to talk yourself into jerkin' her outta that show so's there won't be a chance of Ellis findin' out she's here?"

Juliana was annoyed at Zeke for that comment, but she couldn't stop thinking about it. She watched Lucy work. She memorized the set of her hands and tilt of her head and the way she absently brushed the stray wisps of hair back out of her eyes and tucked them into her French braid. And she knew Zeke was right. She did want to pull Lucy from the show. She wanted to keep Lucy hidden from Ellis.

The morning dragged by and Juliana's anxiety mounted. There was no easy solution. Lucy wanted the show so badly. Wild, frantic ideas flew through Juliana's mind. Have the building burned. Have the building condemned. Have the show condemned. Have Lucy's work destroyed. Have all the work destroyed. But she had to be very careful. She knew that there were some things Lucy would never forgive.

She checked the clock for the hundredth time. She needed to relax over lunch and bask in Lucy's full attention. She needed to stop worrying and feel better.

"Aren't you done yet?"

Lucy whirled toward her. "Do you know how many times you've said that? If you're hungry, then go eat. But stop nagging me!"

Juliana felt herself shrinking. Back to the size when she had had to creep in quietly to sit on the floor beside her mother's chair. "I'm sorry. I'll be quiet now. I don't want to go to lunch without you."

Lucy put her hands on top of her head and stared up at the

ceiling a moment. Then she took a deep breath and looked at Juliana. "Why not? I'm not that hungry and I'm having some trouble getting this shot right. I'll get a sandwich later."

Juliana sat very still and studied her folded hands.

Lucy slammed her hand down hard on a table. "We can't be together all the time! Nobody can do that! You need to see Perry and your family. I need time to myself."

"I said I'd be quiet," Juliana whispered. "You'll never know I'm here."

"Can't you understand what I'm saying? It's not just now. It's not just this minute. You're taking over my life and I can't stand it!"

Juliana swallowed hard against the tightness in her throat and wrapped her arms around her stomach.

"Get out!" Lucy shouted. "Go on. I'm throwing you out."

The tears were flowing by the time Juliana reached the car.

"Take me to Fifty-seventh Street," she instructed Zeke.

She shopped quickly and then picked up takeout Chinese. Lucy was wild about Szechwan, so she bought cold sesame noodles and steamed dumplings and scallion pancakes and ginger chicken. She arrived back at Mignon in less than an hour, stashed the surprise behind a couch, and walked into the makeshift studio holding the food in front of her as a peace offering.

Lucy sighed, shook her head, and smiled. "All right," she said, holding up her hands in surrender. "It smells good and I *am* hungry now."

"That was our first fight," Juliana said as she tore open the bag and opened the containers.

"Yes. I suppose it was."

"Close your eyes. It's time to really make up."

Lucy eyed her with a suspicious half-grin but closed her eyes.

"Hold out your arms."

Lucy complied and Juliana laid the red-fox coat gently across her outstretched arms.

Lucy opened her eyes. She looked down at the coat and then up at Juliana in disbelief.

"What's wrong with you?" she shouted. She stalked around the couch and threw the coat into the open box that Juliana had left sprawled on the floor.

"You don't like it?" Juliana asked. "We can exchange it—"

"No! No! No!"

"But I wanted to show you how important you are to me. I wanted to . . . I . . ."

Lucy buried her face in her hands a moment, then raised her head to look straight into Juliana's eyes. "You're important to me too. My mother and my sisters are gone. The few close friends I've had in my life are gone. You're a little of everyone to me, and I feel like I've always known you ... but you can't swallow me. You can't suffocate me. And you sure as hell can't buy me. So don't ever try that again."

"I'll take it back. Right now." Juliana scooped up the fur and the box.

"Put it down," Lucy said, smiling and rolling her eyes and shaking her head in one motion. "Come eat your lunch first."

Juliana settled across the small table from her and played at eating. But she wasn't hungry. She couldn't think about food. "Are we made up?" she asked.

"Yes. We're made up. I won't strangle you this time, so eat."

And it came to Juliana, staring into Lucy's wise, compassionate, amused eyes: she didn't want to show Lucy to Ellis. She didn't want Ellis to have a chance with her at all. She couldn't risk that. Lucy was hers now ... and she would do whatever it took to keep her.

44

Lucy

Lucy reminded herself again not to appear nervous. There was still an hour before the doors were opened. Juliana would make it. Juliana would be there to support her. She wouldn't be alone.

The other photographers' work was fairly conventional except for one woman who was doing huge high-contrast studies of house mold and beeswax. No one had spoken to Lucy except the foundation secretary. It seemed that all the other women knew one another. She was the only outsider. The whole atmosphere felt wrong. How had she been chosen for this?

Her work had been hung when she arrived, so she'd had no say in its arrangement. At least it was thoughtfully presented, and one of her own favorites was first. It was a soft black-and-white study of a woman reclining on a chaise. The woman had straight fair hair that hung down and partially obscured her shadowed face. She wore a twisted snake earring that Lucy had combed the secondhand stores to find. Ms. Conroy's antique shawl was draped across her nude body. The arm and hand of a man extended into the photo from the right. The hand rested on the swell of the woman's partially exposed, very white breast. The hand was black. The only painting Lucy had done on the print was to dot a glittering red eye in the snake earring. The title was *Teacher and Friend.*

At ten-till the door was opened and the first wave of people poured inside. Lucy retreated to a corner. She considered leaving altogether. But that would upset Juliana and make her seem ungrateful.

It was hard to believe how quickly they'd grown close. Only with Ms. Conroy had Lucy formed such an intense connection to another woman. It was more than friendship. Their lives were intertwined somehow, as though the connection had been predestined. And it felt good. It felt right. Lucy had been overwhelmed by emptiness since Suki died. When she had boarded the plane for New York, it occurred to her that she could die in a crash and there would be no one in the world to notify. No one to mourn. Now she had a friend.

Only, where was she now ... this great friend who was supposed to be supplying the courage tonight?

Suddenly Lucy was seized from behind and squeezed into a hug. It was Juliana. Juliana with a new hair color. And she was gushing. That was the only way to describe it accurately. And her effusiveness held pride and awe and the unmistakable ring of relief.

"Your things are stunning, Lucy! That first one! It's sooo amazing! Have you been listening to what people are saying? I just heard a critic remark—now, wait, let me make certain I'm repeating it correctly—that you were Frida Kahlo with a camera ... or maybe it was Frida Kahlo's daughter with a camera. I don't know. And I don't know who Frida Kahlo is, but he liked it!"

Juliana took a break to breathe and Lucy held up her hand in warning. "Stop," she ordered. "You've got to calm down, because I'm relying on you to keep *me* calm."

Juliana transformed herself into cool poise instantly.

"Now," Lucy said. "Tell me about the hair."

"You always hated the blond, so I decided to surprise you in honor of your debut. My colorist says it's the closest he can come to my natural shade."

The honeyed brown completed the look that Juliana had been born to wear. Sexy and elegant with a touch of the exotic.

"The hair is just right," Lucy said. "And when this show nonsense is over next week, you're going to start posing for me."

Juliana raised her eyebrows and suppressed a grin.

The milling crowd grew, and Juliana eased Lucy through introduction after introduction. But beneath Juliana's poise Lucy detected an unnatural tension.

"I'm doing fine now," Lucy assured her. "Everyone's being very kind. You don't have to worry about me anymore."

Juliana smiled but didn't relax.

The evening was nearly over when Juliana glanced toward the door and stiffened.

"What's wrong?" Lucy asked.

"Family has arrived," Juliana said. "Remember my mentioning a cousin I don't get along with? Well, he's here."

Juliana's forced smile and her light sarcasm were both off-key.

"Don't let it bother you," Lucy said. "He won't be the first jerk I've ever met in my life."

Just then Zeke appeared. He came directly toward them through the crowd. "Seen the new arrivals?" he asked.

"Yes. No problem, Zeke. I've already explained to Lucy that she's stuck meeting the family pariah. At least he didn't bring his fiancée with him."

Then there was a surge of people around the white display partition, and Juliana said, "Lucy, this is my cousin, Ellis Van Lyden . . ."

And there was a voice—such a familiar voice—saying, "Lucy, Lucy." And there was no air. The room was too hot and too small and she was caught in some elaborate dream.

"Lucy?"

She said his name. "Ellis." And her voice was unreal to her ears.

"You two seem to know each other," Juliana said.

"What is going on here, Jinx?" Ellis demanded. "What are you doing with Lucy?"

"I don't know what you're talking about, Ellis."

"Right. The minute I saw her name listed in the paper tonight, I knew you had some twisted scheme cooking. You conned her into coming here!"

"You're crazy!" Juliana hissed. "You've always been crazy!"

"Shhh," Zeke cautioned. "Folks are starin'."

"I thought your last name was McLeod," Lucy said. "I thought . . ." But she was too stunned to put her confusion into words.

"I'm sorry, Lucy." Ellis' face was a storm of emotions. "I don't want to ruin the show for you. Can we talk afterward?"

Lucy nodded and watched as he moved away.

"I can't believe you know him," Juliana said weakly. "Isn't he awful? Where did you meet him? You'll have to—"

"I need some air," Lucy said abruptly, and started toward the door.

Juliana fell into step behind her.

"No. Please, Juliana . . . I need to be alone for a minute."

Lucy turned and walked back through the crowd, trying to maintain her composure. Trying not to think. There were people studying *Teacher and Friend.* There were people discussing *Texas Trash.* But that gave her no pleasure.

The street was pleasantly alive with strolling couples and animated groups and beautifully lit shop windows. But all she could see now was the litter and the dirt and the cracked pavement.

She leaned back against a rough wall and covered her face with her hands.

Ellis. Her worst nightmare. Her most treasured dream. Seeing Ellis again. Facing him. Reliving the pain of the choice she had made.

But it was more than that. What had he meant by "twisted schemes"? What was really going on here?

When she had composed herself enough to reenter the building, the show was over. A cleaning crew was at work. She stood uncertainly in the echoing exhibit space, listening to the laughter of the men and the whisper of their long brooms.

Ellis stood at her section, staring up at her work. He turned at her footfalls.

"Jinx is playing with you," he said.

"I don't know what you're talking about."

"You're not that big a fool. You think it's a coincidence that a woman I was so involved with is suddenly spirited to New York for Juliana's show?"

"I think there's got to be an answer. I'm going to wait till I hear her side."

"I'll tell you her side! All this is a hoax, a scam, a big setup so she can get to me some way through you. She's warped and she's dangerous, Lucy."

"Don't say any more against her, Ellis. I don't know exactly what's going on, but I'm grateful I was chosen and I'm proud of the reception my work got tonight. She hasn't hurt me . . . and I know her better than I ever knew you."

He turned away, focusing his anger on her work. "You're very talented," he said, studying the photographs. "Why did you keep that hidden from me?"

"Why did you tell me your name was McLeod and you were from Idaho?"

He spun to face her. His eyes were very dark gray and full of hooked barbs that sank into her heart. Suddenly she felt vulnerable and dangerously open to him. She knew not to trust herself.

"We didn't share much except our bodies, did we, Ellis?"

"That's not true."

"Isn't it? Think about it. We guarded ourselves from each other. We didn't share our pasts, or dreams for the future, or expectations. We weren't honest with each other."

"We had something important, though. You can't deny that, Lucy."

She wanted to laugh. She wanted to say something cruel. She wanted this to be over. "We had great sex. Earth-shaking sex. And

I don't deny or regret any of it. But that's all it was. Sex. Don't try to blow it out of proportion."

"That's not true! Don't you understand that the reason it was earth-shaking was that it went so much deeper than the physical act? It wasn't just sex, Lucy."

She wanted to run. Or to strike out at him before he could cut any deeper into her. "Why are you dredging up all this? We're nothing to each other now. It's been over a long time."

"It will never be over for me."

"Don't say that."

"It's true."

"You have a fiancée now, don't you?"

He winced. "She could never make me forget you. I've been honest with her. She knows everything. This whole engagement nonsense was her fantasy and my weakness. But she knew all along that you were the one I . . ." He reached for her and she backed away.

"Don't touch me, Ellis. I can't think when you touch me. And I need to think about this. I can't afford any more big mistakes."

He dropped his hands in a helpless gesture. "I didn't understand when we were together. But I do now."

"Don't do this, Ellis . . . please."

"I love you."

She hated him for saying it. "Love! You say that as if it's the magical cure-all . . . the solution to everything."

"Do you love me?"

"Don't you hear what I'm saying? Love isn't the answer. Sometimes it's not enough. Sometimes it's too much. But it's never a solution."

"Can you say you *don't* love me? If you can, I'll leave you alone."

"I don't need you in my life, Ellis. I don't want a lover. I don't want the uncertainty and the expectations and the small cruelties and the suffocation. I don't want to sacrifice everything I've worked so hard for."

"But you can't say you don't love me."

She closed her eyes. "No, I can't say that."

"That's all I need to hear, Lucy. We can work on the rest." He moved forward.

She fought the temptation to step into his arms.

"Please . . . don't touch me. Don't brush my arm, don't put your hand on my back when we're going through the door . . . nothing. Please."

He held up his hands. "I promise." He frowned and looked

away. Compassion or something close filled his eyes. "I have to go see Whitney now," he said. "Before she hears from someone else."

Lucy walked beside him out to the street to flag separate cabs. Don't touch her either, she felt like saying. Please don't touch her either.

45

Juliana

Juliana's feet were leaden. She'd been summoned to her grandfather's office. Something was wrong. Everything was wrong.

She'd gone to Lucy's apartment late last night and tried to talk to her. She'd concocted a story about Gabby giving her Lucy's name for the show, and tried to convince her that Gabby must have had ulterior motives. She knew Gabby would back her up.

But Lucy wasn't listening.

"I want the truth, Juliana, and I want it now," she'd said.

And Juliana had been so terrified that she'd told the truth . . . or a version of it. She'd sobbed and admitted bringing Lucy to New York to break up Ellis and Whitney. She said she'd done it to save poor Whitney. But when she met Lucy, everything changed and she'd never had a friend like her before and she was sorry . . . so very very sorry . . . but it had all worked out okay, hadn't it?

But Lucy would not bend, and Juliana had clutched at her, sobbing, and begged for forgiveness.

Lucy had made her leave then, and Juliana still didn't know if she was forgiven.

Then this morning she'd had two calls. The first had been from Mo Rifkin to tell her that her father had managed to bypass the safeguards, sell his apartment, and disappear with the cash.

The second call was from Perry. He wanted to see her, but she had tried to explain to him that this was a bad time.

He had lost his temper. "You're doing the same thing with Lucy Clare that you did with Sparky," he shouted. "You're hiding behind her and using her to push me away. You're afraid of a real relationship! You're afraid of committing to me!"

Then he had hung up on her and she couldn't call him back because it was time to go to her grandfather's office.

She held her stomach against the pulsating pain. Maybe she was having a nightmare. A long, long nightmare.

She reached the office door. Her face was alternately hot and cold and the door looked larger than normal. She stood there a long time before she remembered to knock.

"Juliana." Her grandfather opened the door himself. "Come in and sit down."

Her grandfather started to talk. It was very hard to concentrate on what he was saying. There was an odd buzzing in her head.

"So I'm sure you will be happy to know that the museum trusts are in place and the question over the fates of both houses is settled. Incidentally, I'm very pleased with that photographer you brought in. She's doing a splendid job of recording everything. Suitable for publishing, I should think."

Juliana tried to make her mouth smile.

Edward cleared his throat and poured himself a glass of water from a carafe. "Would you care for some?"

She shook her head.

"I want you to know how much I appreciate the effort you've put into my collection through the years." He smiled nostalgically. "I remember you bidding when you were so small that the auctioneer couldn't see your hand."

She waited. The hot and cold were back. And there was a waviness at the edges of her vision. Her eyes were trapped. If she tried to look sideways, the room went blurry.

"Are you all right?" Edward asked suddenly.

"Yes." Her voice sounded weak to her ears. "Fine."

Edward studied his hands a moment. "I suppose you know about your father."

"Yes," she said.

"Don't take it too hard. That's the way he's always been. It killed your mother, but I know you're made of stronger stuff than she was." He studied his hands again. "There's no good way to say this," he said. "I've got an appointment with my attorneys tomorrow. The will is being changed."

A voice started to laugh in her head. *There it is! I knew it!*

"Ellis will be the major beneficiary. It is clear he's the healthy choice for the family. You will of course still come into a sizable fortune, but you'll have no control over Vanden Corporation or any Van Lyden holdings. I'm sorry. But it's for the best."

She wasn't aware of rising from the chair, but she was standing and her grandfather was saying something and she looked at the elaborate antique paperweight on his desk. The voice said, *Do it! Pick it up and smash his head.*

"No," she whispered fiercely.

"Are you sure you're not ill?" her grandfather asked.

She nodded and left the room before the voice won.

"My grandfather isn't the problem," she explained to it as she walked down the hall.

Ellis was the problem. Ellis was the thief. The destroyer. The enemy. Ellis was dangerous. And dangerous things should be gotten rid of. Made to vanish. Poof! No more Ellis. No other choice for her grandfather or for Lucy. No one but her. Juliana. The real Van Lyden.

That was why everyone hated her now. Ellis had stolen her place and reduced her to nothing.

46

Lucy

Lucy sat forward in the leather seat and peered down the dark roadway. Zeke had left the highway behind and turned onto an eerie country road.

"You're going to love it. You're really going to love it," Juliana promised for the hundredth time. "Elysia is absolutely the most wonderful place. You'll want to take pictures of everything."

Lucy kept her eyes straight ahead. She wished she hadn't let herself be talked into the trip. But Juliana had been so insistent. And so desperate for proof of forgiveness. And Lucy had thought back to Suki and Anita and how she hadn't responded when they needed her. And she'd said yes. She would go with Juliana to Elysia. And when Juliana insisted that it had to be tonight, Lucy had wearily agreed to be ready.

She was excited about seeing the fabled Elysia. She'd brought her cameras and was planning to shoot all day tomorrow.

Her emotional state had evened out in the days since the photography show. She'd sorted through the turmoil of that evening and achieved what she thought of as a philosophical attitude. Her work was a success, so she was determined to forget all the humiliation and anger over the way her invitation had been fixed. And she had forgiven Juliana. But she was going to be more wary in the future.

After this night and this trip, which she thought she owed Juliana, she intended to put some distance between them. She would finish up the Van Lyden cataloging job and then she would find her own place to live. Make her own way. And she would not trust Juliana so easily again.

Ellis was the only question left in her mind. Did she want to try again? Did she want another chance? She had spent so much of her life regretting the lack of second chances. Now she had one. But did she want it?

523

She had seen him several times since the scene after the opening. He was anxious to open himself to her and had begun by
telling her the story of his father and Badger and the mountains.
A story that had been obviously painful for him to tell, but he
had insisted, sharing it with her like an offering. She had given
him nothing in return. She was too afraid.

He had made it clear what he wanted. He wanted to marry
her and have a child. And part of her longed for just that. But
there were so many terrible questions. Would she lose herself
again? Would loving him consume her, withering all the visions
and dreams as she bled herself to nourish him? Would she slip
into nothingness and live her life through Ellis?

And a child ... Oh, God, could she give her heart as hostage
again to the idea of a child? Knowing what she knew now, could
she open herself again to the potential for such loss?

She felt weary and irritable and disconnected. But then, Juliana was behaving strangely as well. One minute she was joking
and the next she was completely unfocused. Like a person slipping in and out of hallucinations. And she was twitchy and impatient and had an almost feverish gleam in her eye.

What drove the woman? Lucy wondered. What dreams did she
dream in her mansion at night?

She glanced over at Juliana, who was now smiling to herself
in the dim light. Poor Juliana. Poor fragile, grasping, greedy Juliana. So polished and fortunate, yet beneath it all she was as
hungry and disillusioned as Anita ... as insecure and self-
destructive as Suki.

They stopped at the gate and Zeke unlocked it with a key and
turned on the light at the closed-up cottage just inside.

"My friend used to live there," Juliana said as Zeke got back
into the car. "My friend Sparky. He got locked in a pantry and
Zeke broke his neck."

Zeke cast a darkly worried look in the rearview mirror.

They parked and Zeke opened the door and deactivated the
alarms.

"The staff's all gone," Juliana said. "There's only old Kleiman
left, and we don't want to wake him. We'll just wait and surprise
him in the morning."

"Are you all right?" Zeke asked carefully.

"Of course I'm all right. What would be wrong with me? You
can go back to the gatehouse now. I won't be needing you. Good
night."

Lucy watched Zeke's reluctant departure, then waited for Juliana to launch into a long description of the house or at least to begin a tour, but she showed no indication of it. She seemed very jumpy and her eyes darted sideways at the smallest sound.

"I need to check on some things," she said. "Make yourself comfortable."

Lucy looked around the softly lit room. Animal heads hung everywhere. Their eyes were eerie in the shadowed lighting.

There were sounds. Doors closing. Hurrying feet. Then Ellis walked in. "I came as fast as I could," he said.

Lucy was too surprised to speak.

Juliana returned from the other side of the room. "Oh, good!" she said. "We're all here now."

"What's going on?" Lucy asked quietly.

"I told Ellis to meet us here so we could all have a little party." Juliana was smiling happily. She carried champagne and glasses and had a leather pouch slung over her shoulder.

Ellis sank down on the couch with an exasperated sigh. "She called and said I had to meet you at Elysia right away," he said, looking at Lucy. "Then she hung up. I thought something was wrong."

"What would be wrong?" Juliana asked brightly. "Lucy is a big success. We need a toast to her future."

Lucy tried to decipher the undercurrents in the room. Ellis had said that Juliana harbored an old grudge against him, but that didn't explain the amount of tension in the air.

"Would you do the honors?" Juliana said, passing the unopened champagne to Ellis.

He uncorked the wine and Juliana carried it to the side table where she'd lined up the stemmed glasses. She gave a brimming glass to Lucy, then passed one to Ellis and poured one for herself.

Again and again she toasted Lucy's brilliant show, encouraging them to drink up with each toast. Lucy was nervous and drank more than she should.

The glasses were refilled and the toasts became sillier.

Suddenly Ellis blinked and looked around as though startled. "I don't feel well," he said.

"Maybe you've been working too hard," Juliana said sarcastically. "Stealing things can be very hard work."

Lucy set down her glass and shook her head to clear her thoughts. She wished she hadn't drunk so much.

"In just a minute you won't even be able to move," Juliana told Ellis gleefully.

He tried to get up, but fell and ended up sitting on the floor with his back against the couch. He could barely hold his head up.

"What have you done to him?" Lucy cried. She moved to his side unsteadily, banging her shin against the coffee table.

"It's just to keep him quiet," Juliana assured her. "To keep him from running away."

Ellis was still conscious but unable to move. Lucy smoothed the hair back off his forehead and whispered, "It'll be okay," in his ear before standing to face Juliana.

"What do you think you're doing?" Lucy demanded.

Juliana had moved back to the side table, where she'd left the leather pouch. She tipped it up and two guns spilled onto the marble tabletop.

Lucy's heart hammered wildly in her chest.

"Juliana. What is this?"

"I'm fixing everything." Juliana smiled hopefully. "You aren't mad at me, are you, Mama?"

Terror and adrenaline rushed through Lucy, but she forced herself to stay calm. "I'm not mad at you."

"Ellis is taking everything. He's bad, so we have to shoot him. Then we'll be blood sisters. We'll have blood between us and nothing can ever break us apart. We'll shoot him together."

"Juliana, I forbid this!" Lucy said in what she hoped was a stern motherly tone.

But Juliana wasn't listening. She was going over the guns, methodically checking to make certain they were loaded and ready. She hefted one, clicked off the safety, and aimed it directly at Ellis.

Lucy was dumbstruck. Time stopped. Reality stopped.

Lucy gathered herself. She willed strength into her legs and her arms. She lunged, slamming into Juliana's legs and grabbing for the gun at the same time. There was an explosion right next to her ear and there was pain and she felt herself falling. It was a distant feeling. Someone else was falling. The last thing she heard was Juliana sobbing: "I'm sorry, Mama. I never meant to kill you."

Ellis

Ellis came around in stages. First he heard voices. Then his head began to throb. He opened his eyes. He was outside somewhere, lying on a gurney. There was an ambulance nearby, with its red light revolving. Men and women in uniform swarmed around the house. Elysia. He was at Elysia.

He sat up. Everyone was too busy to notice. Suddenly he was assaulted by the most wrenching pain he'd felt since walking into Yvonne's bedroom at Great House all those years ago. Lucy was dead. He'd been propped up against the couch like a stupid sack of rags, trying to keep his eyes open . . . and he'd seen Juliana kill her.

He fumbled at the straps holding him to the narrow bed and rolled sideways off the gurney onto the grass. As soon as he moved, his stomach shed its contents. He stumbled and crawled toward the trees with a howling scream echoing through his brain.

47

Lucy

Lucy peeled off her hospital gown and gratefully pulled on the fresh clothes Edward had sent. She was alive. She was well. Juliana had swung the gun and struck her on the temple with it. The discharged bullet had gone into the wall, not her brain. And the miracle of it still made her tremble.

"You'll have some ringing in that ear for a while," the doctor had said, "and the headaches will continue for a time, but it's nothing to worry about."

She signed the release form and walked out into the hallway. Edward Van Lyden's secretary was sitting in a chair beside the door.

"Have they found Ellis yet?" she asked him.

"No." The man blinked rapidly. "Mr. Van Lyden requests that you please come to stay at Great House. He said he'd send a driver when you're ready."

"Tell him thank you, but no. I wouldn't be comfortable there. I'd like to stay in my sublet till the lease is up."

She wasn't strong enough to face Edward's grief. Juliana was dead. A suicide. She'd put a bullet in her own brain just like her mother before her. Ellis had vanished. Staying in Great House and seeing Edward every day would make those horrible truths impossible to forget. And she needed the peace of forgetfulness. She needed the dazed state to continue.

Her body was a mechanical wonder to her. Everything worked. She was alive and everything worked just fine. She walked out of the hospital into a hot June day. There was pleasure in the simplest thing. She fished for quarters in her purse and climbed on a bus. The ride was wonderful. She smiled at her fellow passengers.

The apartment was still and hot. She opened windows and

turned on fans and drew a tepid bath. The gauze dressing at her temple kept her from washing her hair, but otherwise she soaped every inch of herself, reveling in the touch of her own skin. Was this what people returning from war felt like? she wondered. So much more alive because of their brush with death?

She gathered every pillow in the apartment and made a nest for herself on the bed. In the hospital she hadn't been able to rest. Now all she could think of was sleep. She needed to escape from thought.

She woke twelve hours later. She called Great House for news of Ellis, but there was nothing. It was as big a puzzle to her as it had been to the police detective who talked to her. Why would Ellis have run away? And where would he have gone?

Ellis had been in a drugged sleep when the police arrived. After it was determined that he wasn't injured, he'd been strapped onto a gurney, carried out to the ambulance, and left while the crew rushed back inside to help the paramedics with Juliana and Lucy. No one knew what had happened to him next. Just as they didn't know who had rung the butler's bell for help. Had Juliana run for Kleiman just before she shot herself? And who had made the smeary partial footprint in the blood near Juliana's body? It hadn't been Kleiman's slippers, but who else had been up and walking around after that final shot but before the police arrived?

And beyond those questions, light-years beyond those questions, were the greater and more painful mysteries. Why had it happened? Could it have been prevented? Could Lucy have prevented it?

Thankfully she hadn't had to see Juliana's body. By the time she'd regained her senses she'd been en route to the hospital in an ambulance. But the moment of absolute terror when the gun fired so close to her own head—that was enough to fuel her nightmares forever.

The stitches came out and she was pronounced fit, but she felt as fragile as an invalid. She curled into her nest of pillows and covered her ears when the reporters pounded on her door and rang her phone. She didn't turn on the television for fear of hearing reference to the tragedy, and she refused Edward's many summonses to Great House. She was afraid to go out, even for Juliana's funeral. She couldn't take the ugly media circus or the stares or the pity of strangers.

Weeks passed and she grew stronger. The hiding turned into waiting. Waiting for Ellis. Where was he? When would he come to her?

Death and horror had stripped her down to the naked core, and she no longer had doubts. She wanted Ellis. She needed to see herself in his eyes. She needed the solid, immortal connection of love.

The reporters finally moved on to other bait, and she ventured back out into the sunshine. Where was Ellis? When was he coming?

But suddenly it hit her: Ellis might not be coming. And she realized then that she knew exactly where he was.

Ellis

Ellis stood and breathed deeply. Dawn was creeping over the tree line. He had spent another night without sleep. Sleep was the enemy. The monster. Sleep laid him open to the nightmares and the pain.

He planned to spend the day working on the cabin again. It had fallen into a state of disrepair since he'd last been there. He turned and read the message for the hundredth time, wondering how long Badger had been gone. "Hawkboy, Caben yors. Hope you don need it. I am going down. It's time. I ben here to long. Badger."

He must have used berries to paint it, because the letters were a dark purplish black. The words covered an entire wall and reminded Ellis of New York graffiti.

Ellis stretched and went outside to check on his hides. He had several in various stages of processing. He'd already made himself a shirt and moccasins, and soon he would be able to get rid of the jeans too. He wanted nothing manmade. He wanted nothing to do with human beings at all.

He sat down in front of a deer hide that was stretched to a sapling frame and started scraping at the hair. It was dull and tedious work. It was just what he needed.

Sometime later he was startled from his meditative state by a sound that didn't belong. It was not a forest sound or an animal sound. He heard it again. This time there was no question. People were coming.

He grabbed his bow and hid in the trees to listen. There were two people. One of them had heavy footsteps and one light. The lighter one moved carelessly.

He waited.

They stepped into the circle and he saw that it was a man and a woman. The woman had on a wide-brimmed hat and was very excited by the sight of the cabin. She dropped the small pack from her back and raced toward it.

"This is it!" he heard her cry. "He's here!"

It was Lucy. The woman was Lucy.

He stood and walked toward them. Was it some trick of the light? Was he dreaming?

"Lucy?" he whispered.

The forest was quiet and she heard the whisper and peered through the trees in his direction. He kept walking, and she saw him and her face lit up.

"Ellis!"

She ran toward him and he caught her and she was real. He buried his face in her hair and she was real.

"I thought you were dead . . . oh, God, I saw you die."

She held on to him tightly, clutching at his buckskin shirt and his neck. Her tears wet his cheek.

"No. I didn't die. I wasn't even shot."

"And . . . Jinx? Did they arrest her?"

Lucy pulled back slightly to look up at him. "She's dead, Ellis. Juliana shot herself."

"No . . . no . . . that's not possible. Why didn't Zeke stop her?"

Lucy studied him with a worried expression. "Zeke wasn't there, Ellis. Zeke was out at the gatehouse."

"But he *was* there. I saw him. It's very foggy, but he took the gun from Juliana and he was crying. That's all I remember. Did Zeke say he wasn't there?"

Something strange flickered in Lucy's eyes. "Zeke has been missing since that night. Everyone assumed he was so devastated by the news that he just left, but if he was there . . ."

Ellis stared down at the ground. "Maybe I was hallucinating. I was so drugged."

Silence hung between them for several moments until the man who'd walked in with Lucy cleared his throat loudly.

They had forgotten him.

"I'd be gettin' on back if I wadn't needed," the fellow said around a large wad of tobacco.

"Yes," Lucy said. "Go on back. I don't know how to thank you. You're a genius to have found this with the information I had."

He shrugged self-consciously as he turned to go.

"Wait." Ellis looked from Lucy to the man. "You can't just leave her here."

"She hired me to hep find you, son. My job's over."

"But you can't . . ." He looked at Lucy. "You can't stay. I don't know when I'll be able to bring you back down."

"I thought we'd go down together," she said quietly.

Ellis stared at the cabin. He couldn't look at her. "I'm not ready to go back down. Even with you alive. I don't know when I will be ready."

"I thought you might say that." She knelt and unzipped the duffel bag that the guide had been carrying for her. It was full of camera equipment. "I came prepared."

He shook his head. "Lucy, you have no idea how hard it is up here. It's not something you do on a lark."

She frowned up at him. "I know that. I've been walking for three weeks. I didn't come after you on a lark." She stood up.

He stared at her helplessly. He wanted her. He needed her more than he'd ever needed anything or anyone. He stared off into the trees, remembering Badger's long-ago words: "You have never found your place . . . your soul will never rest . . ."

"Ellis?"

He met her eyes, so full of questions, and he knew that it wouldn't be easy for either of them. But in that steady gaze he saw something as right and eternal as the mountains.

He saw where he belonged.

About the Author

This is Daranna Gidel's hardcover debut. A native of California, she now lives in New York.